Karen Rose was born in Ma[...] suspense and horror at the tender age of eight when she accidentally read Poe's *The Pit and the Pendulum*.

After marrying her childhood sweetheart, Karen worked as a chemical engineer (she holds two patents) and a teacher, before taking up a full-time writing career when the characters in her head refused to be silenced. Now Karen is more than happy to share space in her head with her characters and her writing has been rewarded with a series of bestsellers in the UK, the US and beyond.

Karen now lives in sunny Florida with her husband and their two children.

Praise for Karen Rose:

'Rose delivers the kind of high-wire suspense that keeps you riveted to the edge of your seat' Lisa Gardner

'A blend of hard-edged police procedural and romance ... more shockingly detailed than anything in Karin Slaughter or Patricia Cornwell's thrillers ... engaging' *Irish Independent*

'A pulse pounding tale that has it all' *Cosmopolitan*

'Rose juggles a large cast, a huge body count and a complex plot with terrifying ease' *Publishers Weekly*

'A high-octane thrill ride that kept me on the edge of my seat and up far too late at night!' Lisa Jackson

'Addictive' *Sun*

'Brilliant' *Essentials*

'Action and chills galore' Tess Gerritsen

# KAREN ROSE

# WATCH YOUR BACK

headline

First published in 2013 by
HEADLINE PUBLISHING GROUP

First published in paperback in 2014 by
HEADLINE PUBLISHING GROUP

1

Cataloguing in Publication Data is available from the British Library

ISBN 978 0 7553 8992 6 (B-format)
ISBN 978 0 7553 8993 3 (A-format)

Typeset in Palatino by Avon DataSet Ltd,
Bidford-on-Avon, Warwickshire

Printed and bound in Great Britain by Clays Ltd, St Ives plc

Headline's policy is to use papers that are natural, renewable and
recyclable products and made from wood grown in sustainable forests.
The logging and manufacturing processes are expected to conform to
the environmental regulations of the country of origin.

HEADLINE PUBLISHING GROUP
An Hachette UK Company
338 Euston Road
London NW1 3BH

www.headline.co.uk
www.hachette.co.uk

To my dear friend, Mandy, rescuer of horses.
And cats, dogs, goats, chickens, and cows. LOL.
Thank you for enriching my life.

And, as always, to Martin, my own hero. I love you.

# Acknowledgements

To Marc Conterato, for all things medical.

To Sonie Lasker, for answering all my mad texts in the middle of the night. Hooyah!

To Terri and Kay, for helping me through the rough spots.

As always, all mistakes are my own.

# Prologue

*Eight years earlier, Baltimore, Maryland,*
*Thursday, March 15, 5.45* P.M.

*I can't. I can't do this.*

The words thundered in John Hudson's mind, drowning out the beep of the cash register at the front of the convenience store. The customer at the counter paid for her purchases, then left, oblivious to the fact that the guy standing in front of the motor oil was a cold-blooded killer.

*But I'm* not *a killer. Not yet.*

*But you will be. In less than five minutes, you will be.* Desperation grabbed his throat, churned his gut. Made his heart beat too hard and too fast. *I can't. God help me, I cannot do this.*

*You have to.* The small print on the back of the bottle of motor oil he pretended to study blurred as his eyes filled with hot tears. He knew what he had to do.

John put the bottle back on the shelf, his hand trembling. He closed his eyes, felt the burn as the tears streaked down his wind-chapped cheeks. He swiped a knuckle under his eyes, the wool of his gloves scraping his skin. Blindly he chose another bottle, conscious of the seconds ticking by. Conscious of the risk, of the cost if he followed through. And if he did not.

1

The text had come that morning. There had been no words. None had been needed. The photo attached had been more than sufficient.

*Sam. My boy.*

His son was no longer a boy. John knew that. At twenty-two, his son was a man. But John also knew he'd lost the best years of his son's life because he couldn't recall much from that time. He'd spent them snorting and shooting up, filling his body with what he couldn't live without. Even now, standing here, he was high. Just enough to be borderline functional, but not enough to dull the horror of what he was about to do.

His addiction had nearly killed him too many times to count. It had pushed him to beat his wife in a frenzied rage, nearly killing her. Now it was killing Sam.

His son had pulled himself out of the neighborhood, kept himself clean. Straight. Sam had a future. Or he would, if John did what he was supposed to do.

*God. How can I?* His hand trembling, John flipped his phone open to the photo that had been texted to him that day – his son bound, unconscious, a thin line of blood trickling from his mouth. Tied to a chair, his head lolling to the side. A gloved hand holding a gun to his head.

*How can I? How can I not?*

The assignment had originally come via text yesterday morning from a number John had hoped he'd never see. He'd made a desperate deal with the devil and payment had come due. His target had been identified, the time and place specified.

The target came to this store every evening on his way home from work. John just had to show up. Do the job. Make it look unplanned. Wrong place, wrong time.

But he hadn't been able to do it yesterday. Hadn't been able to force himself to walk inside the store. Hadn't been able to force himself to pull the trigger.

So the ante had been upped, the second text sent, this time with the photo. And Sam was the pawn. *Son. I'm sorry. I'm so sorry.*

John heard the quiet beep of the door as it opened. *Please don't let it be him. Please don't let him stop here today. Please.*

*But if it's not him, you can't kill him. And then Sam will die.*

'Hey, Paul.' The greeting had come from the cashier, a fifty-something African-American woman who greeted several of her customers by name. 'What's shakin' in the hallowed halls?'

John's heart sank. *It's him. Make your move.*

'Same old, same old,' Paul replied, a weariness to his voice that somehow made John's task seem even worse. 'Cops put them in jail, we do our best to throw away the key. Most of the time they're back on the street so fast, the door doesn't even hit them in the ass.'

'Damn defense attorneys,' the cashier muttered. 'Same old, same old on the numbers, too?'

'My mother is a creature of habit,' Paul said, his chuckle now rueful.

'You're a good boy to pick up her lotto tickets every day, Paul.'

'It makes her happy,' he said simply. 'She doesn't ask for much.'

*Just do it! Before he makes you like him even more.*

He edged to the end of the aisle, closer to the cash register. Pretending to scratch his head, he reached up under his Orioles baseball cap to yank down the ski mask he'd hidden under it to cover his face. It could be worse. The three of them were the only ones in the store. If he had to dispose of a lot of witnesses . . . That would be much worse.

3

'That'll be ten bucks,' the cashier said. 'How's your wife, Paul? Pregnancy going okay?'

*His wife is pregnant. Don't do this. For the love of God, do not do this.*

Ignoring the screaming in his head, John wheeled around, drawing his gun.

'Everybody freeze,' John growled. 'Hands where I can see them.'

The cashier froze and John's target paled, his hands lifted, palms out. 'Give him what he wants, Lilah,' Paul said quietly. 'Nothing in this store is worth your life.'

'What do you want?' the cashier whispered.

*Not this. I don't want this.*

*Do it. Or Sam will die.* Of this John had no doubt. The photo he'd been sent flashed into his mind. The gloved hand holding the gun to his son's head had killed before. He would kill Sam.

*Do. It.*

Hand shaking, John pointed the gun at Paul's chest and pulled the trigger. Lilah screamed as the man went down. John caught a movement from the corner of his eye. Lilah had retrieved a gun from below the counter. Clenching his jaw, John pulled the trigger a second time and Lilah crumpled to the counter, blood pooling around the hole he had just put in her head.

*It's done.* Nausea churned in his gut. *Get out of here before you throw up.*

He took a step toward the door when he froze, stunned. Paul was struggling to his knees. There was no blood on the man's white shirt. Holes, but no blood. Understanding dawned. The man wore a vest.

*What the fucking hell?* John lifted his gun, aiming at the man's forehead.

4

The shrill beep of the door opening had him glancing to the left.

'Daddy!'

*Oh hell. A little boy.* The devil had never said anything about a kid.

*Fucking hell. Now what? What do I do now?*

What happened next, happened fast. Too fast. Paul lunged toward John, grabbing for the gun. They fought, and John tried to pry the man's hand away.

*I need a clear shot. Just one clear shot.* He'd aimed at his target's arm, just to shake him loose, when the little boy charged, fists balled, screaming, 'Daddy!'

John fired and Paul cried out in pain. And the child went silent.

Horrified, John and Paul looked to the boy who lay on the floor in a bloody heap. The bullet had gone through Paul's arm and into the boy. Into his chest. The child wasn't breathing.

*No. He'll die. I've killed a little boy. Oh my God. No. No.*

'No,' he gritted out.

Paul collapsed to the floor, shielding the boy with his own body. 'Get away from him,' he snarled. He checked the boy's pulse, tried to stop the bleeding, his hands shaking and desperate. 'Paulie,' he shouted. 'Paulie, it's Daddy. I'm here. I'm gonna take care of you. You're gonna be okay. Just . . . keep listening to me, son. Listen to my voice. You're gonna be okay.'

John had taken a step forward before he realized it. To help. To save the boy.

Grief and rage had Paul lunging to his knees once again, reaching to knock John's gun from his hand, still shielding his son with his body. 'You sonofabitch. Get away from my son.'

*Sam.* John had to finish it, or both of their sons would

5

die for nothing. Willing his hand to be steady, he lifted the gun, aimed at Paul's head. And pulled the trigger. The man dropped to the floor, covering his son's body with his own.

'I'm sorry. God, I'm sorry.' Staggering outside, John made it to his car, managed to get the key in the ignition. And tore out of the parking lot. As he did so, he could already hear sirens.

He needed to get away. Needed to report in, to get Sam back. Then . . . he didn't care. If the cops caught him . . . he didn't care. He just had to get Sam to safety. He pulled off the main road, took the back roads that he knew so well. He was on autopilot.

He was . . . numb. *I killed that woman. I killed that man. I killed that little boy.*

*I killed a child. I. Killed. A child.*

His throat closed. He couldn't breathe. He'd saved his own son. And killed someone else's. Sam would not approve. Sam would hate him more than ever. His son had strict notions of good and bad. Right and wrong. Sam would not have let his father kill to save his life.

*So he can never know. I'll never tell him.*

He reached the meeting place, where Sam was to be delivered to him. John got out of the car and fell to his hands and knees, retching. He hung there, drawing one breath after another. None felt clean. None felt right. None felt . . . enough. He was choking to death. He was breathing but his lungs couldn't get enough air.

*I killed a child. An innocent child. I need to pay for that. But first, get Sam back. Then . . .*

'I'll turn myself in,' he whispered hoarsely. But even as he said the words in his mind he knew he would not. He'd been to prison twice already. He couldn't go back there. He knew he would carry the shameful secret of what he'd just done to his grave.

He pushed himself to his feet, stumbled back to his car. Slid behind the wheel. With shaking hands, sent a text.

*It's done. I want my son back. Alive. Now. Or I'll blow the whistle on you so fast your head will spin.* He hit send, then pocketed his phone and leaned back, closing his eyes.

A few seconds later he heard the familiar buzz. A phone, receiving a text. But he hadn't felt anything in his pocket. He'd started to sit up straighter when he heard an even more familiar sound. The click of a trigger being pulled.

He looked up. Saw the face in the mirror. The devil himself. The man with whom he'd made a deal a year ago.

*I should have taken the drug conviction. I should have gone to jail.*

It would have been his third offense. Three strikes. He would have been separated from Sam for years. *Now it looks like I will be anyway. Forever.*

Because the devil himself held a gun to the base of John's skull. He was too tired to fight.

'I did what you said,' John whispered. 'I did all that you said.'

'I know. I appreciate it.'

'What about my son?'

'He'll be released. He won't remember anything about his ordeal.'

'Good.' *Thank you* was on the tip of his tongue, but he held it back. There were no thanks to be given. A woman, a man, and a child were dead. He never would have pulled the trigger if the devil hadn't pushed him.

*The devil made me do it.* He laughed out loud, the sound hysterical to his own ears. The last thing he saw was the devil in his rearview mirror, shaking his head.

# Chapter One

The knock on his office door had Todd Robinette glaring at the dark wood panels. He didn't ask who it was. He knew exactly who was there and why. When Robinette summoned, his staff came running. Fast. On any other day, for any other job, their dedication satisfied him. But not today. And certainly not on this job.

*Go away*, he wanted to snarl. *I need to do this myself.* Because if you wanted something done right . . . But he knew that wasn't the reason. His employees were the best. They'd go in, do the job, and get out. No mess. No fuss. No nasty clues for bitch cops to find. No worries.

*So don't lie, asshole. At least not to yourself.* He let out a slow breath. *Fine. I want to be doing this myself. I want some mess. I want some fuss. I want the bitch cop to beg me for mercy.*

That was the unvarnished truth. He wanted to see her dead, but that wasn't enough. For eight long years he'd wanted to see her suffer. Because what she'd cost him warranted a hell of a lot more than the simple ending of her life.

9

*I could do it. I deserve to do it. Nobody will know. Nobody will suspect.*

Except that one never knew when someone was watching – and all it took was just one overeager witness to send your world crashing around your ears, forcing a quick repair job. Quick repairs tended to be sloppy. Or, at least, very, very costly.

He'd learned that lesson eight years ago when he'd been on his own, just a guy with a job that hardly anyone paid attention to. It would be much truer now. He'd gained power, but with it had come visibility. Now he had board meetings and gave speeches to philanthropists. He couldn't just wander off and kill anyone he wanted to anymore. Which sucked, actually.

On the other hand, all that visibility made for an unshakeable alibi and, luckily for him, all that power necessitated a staff. He had a public relations director, a security manager, and a director of product development – all experts in their respective fields. More relevantly, he now had a cleanup crew who specialized in eliminating threats. A smart man would let them do what they were paid to do and Todd Robinette was a very smart man.

He glanced at the single photograph on his desk. *I'm a smart man who's sacrificed far too much to lose it all now.*

How many nights had he lain awake, worrying that his sacrifice hadn't been sufficient? More than he wanted to remember, especially during that first year.

How many times had he fantasized about silencing her permanently? More than he could count, especially during this past year. The past twelve months had been hell on his nerves. But he'd kept his cool, stayed his hand. Because none of those times had been the right time.

*But this is.* This was not just the right time, but the *perfect* time. He might not get a chance like this again. *It doesn't matter who does the honors, as long as she's dead.*

When the knock came again, Robinette ground out, 'Come in.'

Henderson, the most trusted member of his cleanup crew, closed the door and stood before his desk, eyes gleaming at the prospect of a new adventure. 'Robbie, whatcha got for me?'

Robinette took a breath. 'A new job.' He unlocked the cabinet behind his chair, pulled out a folder and slid it across his desk, which, with the exception of a sleekly modern laptop, the single photograph in the silver frame, and a well-worn Rubik's cube, was an empty, polished slab of black granite. 'Detective Stefania Nicolescu Mazzetti, Homicide. She goes by Stevie.'

Henderson studied Mazzetti's photo, clipped to the folder. 'May I ask why?'

*She humiliated me. Nearly destroyed me. She taunts me by breathing. And she can bury me.*

But he'd divulge none of those reasons. Nobody knew how close she'd come to taking him away in handcuffs. Nobody that was still alive, anyway.

Robinette turned the silver frame so that Henderson could see the face in the photograph and gave the one reason that was no secret. 'She killed my son.'

'Ah. So *she's* the one who killed Levi.' Eyes narrowing with undisguised malice, Henderson committed Mazzetti's personal profile to memory. 'Anything else I should know?'

'Yeah. She's on her guard. She's been physically threatened three times in the last week. The first was an attack with a knife, the second, a big guy with an excellent right cross. This afternoon someone shot at her. They missed.'

'*All* of them missed? Were the attackers ours?'

Robinette snorted. As if he'd allow such incompetence. 'Hell, no. This cop has more people mad at her than a gator

11

has teeth. They fall down fightin' and more pop up to take their place.'

'So our hit will be blamed on the other "gator teeth",' Henderson said dryly.

'Exactly.' Which was why now was the perfect time.

'Did any of the three attackers escape?'

'The third one did, the shooter.' Which was to Robinette's advantage. 'She disarmed the man with the knife, then pinned him till the cops came. She did the same with the second guy, the fighter. The shooter ducked into a white Camry and drove away.'

Henderson looked reluctantly impressed. 'She's only five-three. She must be very skilled.'

'Unfortunately, yes. Which is why I picked you to go after her. You have better skills.' Specifically an Army sharpshooter badge, amazing recall, a robotic ability to focus, and a cold-blooded tenacity that would put a dog with a bone to shame.

Back in the day, Henderson had been one of the few soldiers Robinette had trusted to watch his back. That hadn't changed. What *had* changed was the flag they fought under. Long ago and far away it had been red, white, and blue. Now, it was a hundred percent green. Benjamins, Lincolns, even Washingtons. Cold. Hard. Cash. It was the only thing that really mattered.

'I need Mazzetti taken care of,' he continued. 'And you're the best marksman I have.'

Henderson nodded once. 'True. Why is everyone else after her?'

'Her old partner was on the take, paid by rich parents who wanted the crimes committed by their misunderstood darlings to disappear. He'd plant evidence against innocent people and arrest them for the crimes. He was damn good at it – until he got caught. Now he's dead.'

'And she was in on it, too?'

'*I* think so,' he lied, 'but nobody else seems to.' His life would have been so much easier had she been. 'They're after her because she's trying to "right" all of Silas Dandridge's wrongs.'

Cold blue eyes flickered in recognition. 'Silas Dandridge? I remember that name. An article about him came through my newsfeed when I was in the Sudan, so that would have been March, last year. He worked for that lawyer who controlled a whole team of dirty cops.'

'And ex-cons. Stuart Lippman was an equal opportunity employer, now equally dead.'

Henderson frowned, pondering. 'The article said Lippman had it set up that if he died under "suspicious or violent circumstances", a record of all his operatives and the crimes they'd committed would be sent to the State's Attorney.'

*No, not all*, Robinette thought, but he nodded. 'That record was Lippman's life insurance. Kept his operatives from killing him and kept them watching each other, too. If one turned the boss in, all of them suffered.'

'Clever. So why does this one cop have so many enemies if she wasn't in on it?'

'Because she's been investigating the Lippman cases. She's closed four in the last month – three rapists and an armed robber who had innocent men sitting in six-by-eights, paying for their sins. Some folks aren't happy to see this particular beehive disturbed.'

'Guess not. Three rapists and an armed robber. Busy lady.'

Robinette shrugged. 'She's had some time on her hands.'

'She got fired, then. Guilty by association.'

*I wish.* 'No. There was an IA probe after Dandridge was exposed, but she passed.' With flying colors, none of which were cold-hard-cash green. She was a cop who couldn't be bought. 'She's on disability leave, shot by one of those crazy Millhouse KKK groupies outside the courthouse.'

'I saw *that* story on TV. It made international news when I was in Madrid, between assignments. That would have been in December, right before Christmas. Sixteen-year-old girl got pissed because her baby-daddy was found guilty of murder so she started shooting everyone on the courthouse steps. She shot a couple cops. Which one was Mazzetti?'

'The one that killed her.'

'*That* was Mazzetti? She nailed the kid right between the eyes, even though she was bleeding like a stuck—' Henderson abruptly halted. 'I'm sorry, Robbie. That was insensitive.'

Robinette shrugged. 'Just because it was insensitive doesn't make it less true. We'd already established that Mazzetti's got skills,' he added bitterly. After all, Mazzetti had nailed his son right between the eyes as well. 'Two of the three recent attacks were commissioned by rich folks, annoyed that she's making their offspring pay for their sins. The shooter wasn't caught, but I assume the same motive. The attacks will likely continue. Until she's put down for good.'

'Which is where I come in.'

'Yeah. You need to strike before the cops hide her away in some safe house. If that happens, we'll have lost our opportunity. I won't be happy.'

'Don't worry. You'll be happy.'

'Good. Now, to make your job a little easier, she'll be at the Harbor House Restaurant tomorrow afternoon at three.'

Henderson frowned. 'How do you know that?'

'Because tomorrow is March 15. For the past seven years

14

she's gone to that same restaurant at three o'clock on March 15.' Which he knew because he'd had her under surveillance all this time. 'She'll be meeting a psychologist visiting from Florida, Dr Emma Townsend.'

Henderson thumbed through the pages in the folder. 'There's no photo of Townsend here.'

'Google her. You'll find her photo on her Amazon page. She writes self-help books on dealing with grief. Try not to shoot her, too, but do what you have to do to get Mazzetti.'

Henderson looked up from the file, eyes gone flat and calculating. 'Mazzetti has a kid.'

'Cordelia,' Robinette said. 'She's seven years old. If Mazzetti is a no-show at the restaurant, you can get to her through the kid. She goes to ballet class on Saturday afternoons.'

'I see that here. Stanislaski's Studio. Okay, then. I'll call you when the job's done.'

'No, you won't. I'll take that folder back.' Henderson handed it over, and Robinette fed the contents through the shredder under his desk. 'I want no trail, paper or electronic. Nothing for the cops to find. When you're successful, I'll hear all about it on CNN. That'll be all.'

Dismissed, Henderson left, but Robinette's office door didn't close completely. Another head appeared in the gap. 'Got a minute, Robbie?'

'Sure.' Robinette waved his head chemist to enter. 'Not like I'm getting any work done.'

'When do you ever?' Fletcher's teasing grin abruptly faded at the sight of Levi's photograph out of place. 'So. You're finally gonna do it.'

'It' didn't need specification. Fletcher had been there for him at Levi's funeral, along with Henderson, Miller, and Westmoreland. His friends. His trusted team.

It had been an open casket funeral, because Stevie Mazzetti really was a damn fine shot. The hole her bullet had left in Levi's head was neat and clean, easily camouflaged by the funeral parlor's makeup artist and hairstylist.

Lying there . . . It had been the most at peace his son had looked in years.

Robinette returned the silver frame to its original position. 'Yeah. I'm finally going to do it. Henderson is, anyway.'

'It's about time,' Fletcher said roughly. 'We would have done it for you eight years ago, but I understand why you waited. You're more patient than we are.'

'No, not really.' *Just less willing to go to jail.* 'But, speaking of patience, how are the tests coming? You get any benefit from that obscenely expensive equipment you insisted we needed?'

Fletcher slid a single sheet of paper across the black granite. 'You be the judge.'

The plain white paper bore no company logo on its letterhead. There would be no connection of Fletcher's pet project to Filbert Pharmaceutical Labs. Or to its president. *Which would be me.* Or to the chairman of the board. *Which would be me, again.*

Because all of the company's other officers were dead. Robinette shot a quick, satisfied glance at the Rubik's cube. *May they all rest in peace.*

Robinette read the summary, handwritten in Fletcher's precise script. The news was good. Very good. He lowered the paper, gave Fletcher a hard nod. 'You're a fucking genius.'

'I know,' Fletcher said serenely, then grinned. 'It's not as good as we can eventually make it, but it's stable twice as long as anything else out there. Which is good enough for now.'

'Do they know?'

'Oh, yeah. I've received confirmation from three groups that took demo packages. When deployed, the payload was as potent as the day it was made, as promised. They were impressed.'

Robinette frowned. 'Who did they test it on?'

'Do we care? Nothing's made the news. I've been watching and listening.'

'Good. The last thing we need is an incident drawing attention.'

'I wouldn't worry. Our clients have always been discreet. Plus, they know if they get caught with it, we won't sell them any more.' Fletcher's brows lifted. 'And they want more. As much as I can make. As fast as I can make it.'

Robinette did a quick mental calculation as to what their profit would be and nodded, satisfied. 'How quickly can you have the first shipment ready to go?'

'Already boxed up. We're waiting on the next batch of vaccines to be ready to ship next Friday. Westmoreland and Henderson are on rotation next week, so they'll escort the shipment.'

Henderson should have completed Robinette's special project by then. 'That's good. We don't want our shipment to fall into the wrong hands.'

Fletcher's eyes lit up with greedy glee. 'The wrong hands being those not holding money.'

'You got that right.' Robinette fed the single sheet of paper into his shredder. 'Take the weekend off. You've earned it.'

'A few of us are going into town tomorrow night. A few beers, a little . . . companionship. You should come with us. It'll be like old times.'

'I can't. Brenda Lee says I can't drink in public anymore.

It's bad for PR, considering the work I do for teen drug and alcohol rehab.' Fletcher was a genius with the chemicals, but Brenda Lee Miller was a spin master. 'Plus she's still mad about that little beer-fueled "disagreement".'

Having spun Robinette from a murder suspect into a pillar of the damn community, she'd been none too pleased about having to make a bar brawl disappear last year. She'd been right – Robinette could have ruined eight years of hard work beating up that meathead. Luckily, Brenda Lee was also his attorney and she settled the matter quietly, discreetly, and confidentially.

Robinette had only wished his wife had been as quiet and discreet as Brenda Lee. Lisa had been irate and still brought it up from time to time.

Fletcher shrugged. 'So, don't drink. You can still find companionship. I know I need some. It'd be good for you, too, if you don't mind my saying so.'

'I think Lisa might mind you saying so,' Robinette said dryly. He expected Fletcher's eyes to roll and was not disappointed. 'She *is* my wife, Fletch.'

'Yeah, I remember. I was at the wedding. She's . . . I'm sure she's got some good points, like . . .' Fletcher feigned deep thought, then shrugged again. 'I got nothin'.'

Robinette snorted. 'She's rich, well-connected, and beautiful.' *And she makes everyone forget my unfortunate past.* 'Think of her as a business accessory. Like a power tie.'

'More like a damn noose.'

'Fletch.' Robinette murmured the warning. 'I allow you leeway because we're friends.'

'And because I'm the fucking genius that's making you richer than God.'

'That, too. But be careful. She is my wife, whether you like her or not. Besides, I couldn't go out with you anyway. Lisa and I have an event tomorrow night.'

Fletcher frowned. 'Another "Humanitarian of the Year" award? Didn't you just get one?'

'Brenda Lee's got them set up like dominoes. This one goes with the opening of another teen rehab center, which she scheduled to coincide with the anniversary of Levi's murder.'

His son had been high as he'd fled Mazzetti and her so-called investigation. After accusing Robinette of killing his second wife, she'd changed her mind, accusing Levi. Robinette's son had been terrified and disoriented and he'd run. Mazzetti had mowed his boy down like a dog.

'Well, have fun,' Fletcher said, still out of sorts over Lisa. 'I have to go.'

When Robinette was alone he leaned back in his chair. Closed his eyes. This time tomorrow his troubles would be over. Thanks to Henderson, Stevie Mazzetti would be dead. And then, thanks to Fletcher, Robinette's personal coffers would be running over for some time to come.

*Saturday, March 15, 1.59 P.M.*

Stairs. *Shit.* She hadn't remembered stairs.

Detective Stevie Mazzetti paused to stare, glare, and consider the four steps she'd need to climb to get into the front door of the Harbor House Restaurant. In all the years she'd come here, she'd never even noticed the stairs. Now, they seemed like a damn mountain.

She gripped the handle of her cane so hard her knuckles ached. *It's just four steps. You can do four tiny little steps.* But could she do them quickly?

She cast a look around her to ensure no knife-wielding assholes lurked about, waiting for her to display a moment of vulnerability. She could – and had – held her own

19

against an idiot with a knife and a thug with hams for fists. All in the last week. She could do it again.

Of course, if it was a gunman, she was a sitting duck. Yesterday she'd been lucky. The gunman hadn't had a clear shot and was foolish enough to chance a bad angle. So he'd missed.

But this downtown street offered a lot more places to hide, and a lot more good angles. Under most other circumstances, she would have avoided walking out in the open like this, at least until the ongoing investigations wound down. But today was March 15.

Eight years ago today, her life had been irrevocably changed, her heart had been broken into a billion little pieces.

Eight years ago today, her husband and her son had been ripped away from her, murdered in cold blood. Stevie had found her way out of the darkness and the depression with the help of the woman waiting for her inside the restaurant and the friendship they'd forged.

For the past eight years this lunch with her old friend, Emma, was a date Stevie never missed, no matter what was going on in her life.

No matter who might be lurking, waiting to catch her unaware. Stevie refused to hide, no matter how much her family and friends nagged at her to do so.

*This is my life. I'm not living it as a prisoner in my own home.*

Gratefully, she didn't see anyone lurking. What she did see was a sign pointing to the handicapped entrance, but at the speed she walked these days, getting there would take her ten times longer than just dealing with the damn stairs. She'd be exposed far longer that way.

*Plus, I'm late. Of course.* Everything took her so much longer since she'd been wounded on the courthouse steps, the day the jury had returned the verdict in a controversial murder trial. She'd expected guarding the prosecutor to be dangerous. She hadn't expected to wake up in ICU with a bullet hole in her leg. Three months later she was still struggling to find normality. *Whatever the hell that is.*

Tensing every muscle, she grabbed the rail and hoisted her body up the stairs as fast as she could. When she got to the landing, she used her momentum to keep moving forward. A few more awkward steps put her under the porch gable. She leaned against one of the supports, out of sight of the street. She needed the cover to . . . recover.

Because she was breathing like she'd run a marathon instead of having climbed four tiny stairs, goddammit. She was sweating, trembling. And then came the pain, shooting up her hip and down her leg. Gritting her teeth, she clenched one hand into an impotent fist and, with the other, held on to the cane for dear life, riding the excruciating wave until the worst of it passed. The fury that simmered at the back of her mind exploded, sparked by frustration and pain.

*Fuck you, Marina Craig.* Like it wasn't bad enough that the little bitch's bullet had almost killed her? Here she was, crawling up stairs like a . . . cripple.

*Cripple.* It wasn't the PC term and Stevie didn't care. It was *her* body. Her ruined leg. *I can use whatever goddamned word I want to use.*

*Stop it.* The voice of reason sliced through her silent, childish tirade. *You're better, and every day you do more. At least you're alive.* That last one always got her attention.

She'd lived. Others hadn't been so lucky. Including Marina Craig. Because after Marina's bullet had lodged in her leg, Stevie had returned fire. Marina was dead before she hit the courthouse steps. The girl had only been sixteen years old.

But she'd also been a stone-cold killer who'd have loved nothing better than to murder every last person gathered in front of the courthouse that day. Marina had been furious at the judicial system that had 'persecuted' her lover, an eighteen-year-old white supremacist convicted of a double homicide. She'd also been well armed, her modified Glock capable of creating mass casualties.

*I did the right thing. I saved lives, including my own. I'm alive.*

And she was grateful for that. Truly. But she was also tired of being . . . less than she'd been before. *Soon.* Just a little more time, a little more rehab. Soon she'd be back to normal.

'And everything will be fine,' she whispered aloud. 'It'll all be fine.'

It had to be true, because she'd never lied to her daughter.

'Everything will be fine' was what she'd whispered in Cordelia's ear twelve hours before as she'd held her, rocking them both until her daughter's shudders stilled. It was what she whispered every night that Cordelia woke from a nightmare. Which, thankfully, seemed to be happening less frequently. Those sessions with the child psychologist were finally bearing fruit.

Soon Cordy would be back to normal, too. *And everything will finally be fine again.*

Because everything sure as hell wasn't fine now. How long had it been since they'd been normal? How long had it been since her daughter had slept through the night?

The answer stung. It had been a year. An entire year. *The last time we were normal was when I stood here. On this very spot.*

It had been only a few weeks after her last annual lunch

with Emma that everything went to hell in a hand basket, courtesy of Silas Dandridge, retired homicide detective. Her old partner. Stevie had considered him her mentor, her friend. She'd trusted him to watch her back. She'd trusted him with her child.

Instead, he'd threatened Cordelia, shoved a gun into her ribs. He'd betrayed her trust. He'd betrayed them all. *So fuck you, too, Silas Dandridge. I hope you're finding hell to your liking.*

It was because of Silas that Stevie was hiding behind a damn post this very moment, worrying that one of his old clients – or even worse, one of his old accomplices – was out there, waiting to shut her up for good. Which pissed her off. *But at least I can take care of myself.*

Her daughter was a different story. Cordelia was only seven years old. Silas was her daughter's nightmare, a nightmare that was finally fading.

As had Stevie's trembling. But she was still on edge, the events of the week having a cumulative effect. She couldn't go into the restaurant a bundle of nerves. Emma would notice. Psychologists tended to be annoyingly observant about things like that.

Gathering herself together, she pushed the restaurant door open, determined not to waste this time with Emma, who'd seen her through Paul's death in a way no one else could have.

For seven years, Stevie had left this lunch feeling better. Renewed. She wasn't sure 'feeling better' was a reasonable expectation today. She'd settle for a little peace.

*Saturday, March 15, 2.02 P.M.*

*Well, shit.* Passing the restaurant, Henderson turned right at the end of the block, watching Stevie Mazzetti in the rearview mirror, seeing her just as she entered the building.

The only things Robinette had gotten right were the day and the restaurant. All of the boss's other information was dead wrong.

Mazzetti wasn't supposed to arrive until three, but there she was, a full hour early. Had she arrived at three, she would be dead. *Because I would have been set up on the roof of the building across the street, waiting to pick her off as she'd climbed the stairs.*

Had Mazzetti been on time, killing her would have been the easiest job ever assigned in the history of mankind. The cop had taken the better part of a minute to climb the stairs. She'd been a damn fish in a barrel.

But no. She was early. A fucking hour early.

Henderson still might have been on time to set up on the roof before her arrival, but double-checking the whereabouts of her daughter had taken longer than it should have, as well. Because little Cordelia wasn't at ballet class as Robinette had promised. She and her aunt had ended up at a destination a good twenty minutes farther away.

*So technically I'm still early, but I'm still too late.* Blaming failure on Robinette's bad information was an exercise in futility. Henderson had learned that lesson the hard way, the memory a sour one. *Dammit.* The car swerved a little. Henderson glanced at the steering wheel in surprise. *My hands are shaking.* This assignment had become more stressful than anticipated. A drink would settle the shakes.

*Not until you're finished. Celebrate when you're finished. Plan now. Celebrate later.*

Henderson parked the white rental Camry behind the building across from the restaurant. A morning scouting trip had identified this building as providing the best angle. *And should anyone see me, they'll tell the cops they saw a white Camry – the same make and model that yesterday's would-be assassin escaped in after taking a shot at Mazzetti.* Yesterday's assassin would be blamed, diverting any suspicion from Robinette. *Or from me, of course.*

Anticipation was a palpable presence in the air. It was time to get to work. Time to avenge the murder of Levi Robinette. It was time to give Robbie some long-overdue peace.

# Chapter Two

*Hunt Valley, Maryland, Saturday, March 15, 2.05 P.M.*

*D*affodils. The sight of them lining the drive up to the farm made Clay Maynard think of soldiers at attention. He didn't care much for flowers himself, but he had to appreciate the hardiness of the little yellow blooms. It was still so cold he could see his breath, but the daffodils didn't seem bothered.

His mother had always loved her daffodils. The memory of her tending her flowers was one of his favorites, one that he summoned when things got too dark. Today was one of those days.

March 15. The day Stevie Mazzetti's husband and son had been murdered. The day her life had been ripped apart by the event that, to this day, left her too damaged to love anyone.

*To love anyone? Or just you?*

He drew a quiet breath, pushing the thoughts from his mind. Pushing Stevie from his mind. Or at least to the corner. He'd tried to push her all the way out, many times. He'd given up. She didn't want him, but, damn his soul, he still wanted her. He had since he'd laid eyes on her the first time, a dedicated cop on the trail of a killer. A fierce mother protecting her little girl.

He'd seen her heartbroken and resolved. He'd seen her aroused . . . *by me* . . . and damn unhappy about it. He wanted her happy about it, wanted to be the man to make her forget the husband she'd lost. Wanted to be the man she started over with.

He wanted her to be the one he started over with.

*A man doesn't always get what he wants.* Clay had lost track of the number of times his father had uttered those words. As usual, his dad was right.

At least Clay had maintained his dignity after she'd kicked him to the curb in December. He hadn't driven by her house, not even once, not even to make sure she was all right. As far as the rest of the world knew, Clay had walked away and had moved on. Maybe, someday, he would.

All of a sudden there was a wide splash of yellow as the daffodils exploded from the orderly border along the road to a big field.

His mom would have loved the sight of so much yellow. He decided he'd break early this afternoon and lay some daffodils on her grave. She'd have liked that. And it would make his dad happy, too. God knew he hadn't given the old man much attention lately. Maybe he'd head out to the Eastern Shore tonight, take his dad out for dinner.

A whistle had Clay looking right to where Alec Vaughn, his IT tech, stared out the window, wide-eyed at the sight of two new barns and a dozen horses grazing in newly fenced pastures.

'Wow,' Alec breathed. 'When Daphne makes up her mind, she doesn't fool around.'

'No, she doesn't.'

The farm and its newest additions belonged to Assistant State's Attorney Daphne Montgomery, Clay's friend and client. Daphne had a personal fortune she enjoyed as a

27

result of her divorce from a very unhappy marriage. It had been a high price to pay, but now she could afford to do the work she loved and support the causes she believed in. Three months ago, Daphne had announced that she was adding to her ever-growing list of charities. This newest one was for kids who'd been victims of violent crime to interact with horses, teaching them to care for an animal, because giving them the opportunity to create a bond with another living creature seemed to help so many of them overcome their trauma. Clay didn't get the allure of the four-legged beasts, but apparently a lot of other people did.

'Daphne's been receiving applications from all over the country,' he told Alec. 'Child protective services, law enforcement, desperate parents. So she moved up the timeline. The new barns went up last week. The inspector blessed them on Wednesday and the horses arrived Thursday. She wants to start the first group as soon as we get the place secure.'

Thus, their presence at the farm. The private invest-igating side of Clay's business solved issues once they'd already occurred. The security side identified potential vulnerabilities and put systems in place to keep those issues from happening. Surveillance systems and private security forces were Clay's specialty.

Daphne's job with the prosecutor's office left her vulnerable enough. Her wealth simply served to make her a bigger target. Now she'd be bringing children onto the property. Kids who'd already been traumatized were magnets for predators. *Not going to happen on my watch.*

'I didn't know the application was available,' Alec said. 'It wasn't on the website when I was doing a security check on the server last night.'

'She hasn't developed a formal application, yet. She

only made the one announcement on the local news a few months back. The broadcast got uploaded to the station's website and emails have been flooding in to the TV station ever since. She let me read a few of them.'

'And?'

Clay blew out a breath. 'And, they . . .' *Broke my heart.* 'They indicate a huge, unmet need. Kids who've been through years of counseling and still can't . . . connect. Which, when I thought about it, really didn't surprise me.' Ten years in the Marine Corps and another ten in law enforcement had introduced him to countless children who'd been victims of violence.

Including the young man sitting in the passenger seat of his truck. Thankfully, Alec had moved past his own trauma years before, but the experience hadn't left him unaffected. Alec had developed a uniquely empathic insight into the pain and suffering of others. The kid saw emotions that people tried desperately to hide. *Including mine.*

But even as uncomfortable as it made him personally, Clay had come to depend on that insight. Alec's IT skills made acquiring information from online sources terrifyingly easy and his insight into particularly hard-to-read human sources had made the difference in a number of Clay's investigations.

The farm's drive ended in front of the main barn, where half a dozen vehicles already formed a line. Parking behind the Chevy Suburban that belonged to Daphne's son, Ford, Clay switched off the ignition. They had only a few hours of daylight left. It was time to get to work.

'Daphne calls the new program "equine therapy",' Clay added with a sigh. 'But what she calls "therapy", I'm calling a security nightmare.'

'"Nightmare" is a bit dramatic, isn't it? We're talking about little kids here, not al-Qaeda.'

'We're talking about kids, true. But we also have to clear the volunteers, the therapists, the horse trainers, and grooms. Even the parents and caregivers.'

Alec's nod was thoughtful. 'I guess we do. That's a lot of people.'

'Hell, yeah, that's a lot. Every person with a pulse has to be cleared – and watched.' There might be real trouble, or claimed trouble. Too many people saw Daphne as a deep pocket for a lawsuit settlement. It was Clay's job to protect her as well as every child under her care. 'We have to watch for any risk of violence against the kids and against Daphne. I wouldn't put it past the family members of some of the felons she's prosecuted to try to get one of the volunteer positions just so they can get close enough to Daphne to get their revenge.'

Daphne didn't give a rat's ass that she was in danger. Her fiancé got it, though. FBI Special Agent Joseph Carter had given Clay a very generous budget with which to keep her – and anyone she helped – safe.

Clay didn't have many true friends and Daphne was one of them. He would have taken this job for free. But he wasn't stupid. If Carter was willing to give him a blank check, he'd sure as hell take it. He could keep his staff gainfully employed for quite some time. Jobs like this one were the bread and butter of a security specialist's business. The PI side didn't pay that well and the cases he was willing to take were few and far between. His people had to pay their rent.

'I'll make sure you can watch everyone everywhere on the property,' Alec promised. 'I'll put a camera in every barn.'

'Not just one. I want a camera in every stall in every barn. Every corner of every pasture. If a squirrel crosses the property line, I want to know.'

'That's a lot of work,' Alec said doubtfully. 'A lot more than I planned on. I didn't order enough cameras. I'll have to increase our order if you want to install that many. I can do that, of course, but it'll take a few days to get them in. We can get started today with what we have.'

'That sounds good. I'm estimating that this job will take at least four days, maybe longer. You'll be working with DeMarco and Julliard.'

Alec frowned. 'I don't remember meeting them.'

'You haven't. We haven't done an installation of this magnitude since you joined the firm. They've done installation work for me before and I trust them. They'll dig the trenches, lay the cables. Your role is to ensure every camera is connected to the network and operational. I'll stay today to make sure everything gets started smoothly, then I'll stop by once a day. Questions?'

'None. I'll get to work.' Alec began unloading the cameras and storing them in the barn.

Leaving him to the task, Clay took a moment to visually inspect the property. DeMarco was walking the perimeter of the round training area that Daphne called 'the arena'. It always made Clay think of gladiators and lions, not children and horses, but whatever.

Daphne herself was inside the arena, wearing a neon pink suit and holding the lead line of a big gray horse. She waved to him, then turned and blew a kiss to the man leaning against the fence. That Joseph Carter was here was no surprise. It would have been more of a shock if he hadn't been. The Fed raised a hand in welcome and Clay headed his way.

Then stumbled, his head whipping to stare at the minivan parked between the Fed's Escalade and DeMarco's muddy truck. It was Stevie's minivan. *Goddammit*.

Clay gritted his teeth and forced his feet to move. If she

was here, he was leaving. But not until he'd gotten a glimpse of her. Just a glimpse. *Because I'm that pathetic.*

He stopped next to Joseph, having walked the fifty feet to the fence without craning his head to search for the woman who wanted nothing to do with him. 'Hey, Carter.'

'She's not here,' Joseph said quietly. 'It's just Izzy and Cordelia.'

Clay filled his lungs, felt the burn of the cold air, exhaled in a rush. Stevie's sister and daughter. Not Stevie. *This is good*, he told himself forcefully. 'What are they doing here?'

'Izzy's taking the photos for the brochures,' Joseph said. 'Daphne's got the fundraisers planned and hired Izzy to take the publicity photos and to cover the events themselves.'

'I didn't know Izzy was a professional photographer.'

'She wasn't. She lost her job with the department store in January. Photos are a hobby she's trying to turn into a business until something else opens up.'

'She any good?'

'She's *very* good.' The sassy voice came from behind them. Clay turned to find Izzy with an expensive camera hanging around her neck. Her mouth was bent in a saucy grin, but her dark eyes, so like her sister's, were grave as she studied his face. 'Clay. It's good to see you.'

'And you. How's Cordelia?' Stevie's little girl had stolen a piece of his heart long ago.

'In the barn, brushing a horse. She'd love to see you, if you have a moment.' She looked over at Joseph. 'I only need a few more minutes. I've already got most of what I need, but the sun's moved and the shadows will be different. Thanks,' she said as Joseph opened the gate for her. 'Cordy's in the second stall on the right,' she added pointedly to Clay.

32

Clay pushed away from the fence. 'I'll look in on Cordelia, then get to work.'

'Hey, Clay, wait a second.' Joseph shifted so that he could talk to Clay and keep his eye on Daphne at the same time. 'Daphne's planning a bridal shower for Paige.'

Clay winced. Paige Holden was his partner on the PI side of the business, engaged to marry Joseph's brother, Grayson. A third-degree black belt and weapons expert, Paige was an asset in the field, and an even better friend. Grayson was a lucky man and had the good sense to know it.

But a bridal shower . . . Daphne had teasingly invited him, but Clay's concept of friendship did not extend into such unfamiliar and potentially hostile territory. 'Yeah, I know. I plan to be far, far away that night.'

'Grayson and I do, too. We're going to charter a boat and do some deep-sea fishing. Grayson prefers that to a bachelor party. It would be Grayson, JD, and me. You're welcome to join in, if you're free.'

Warmth loosed some of the knots in Clay's chest, a welcome relief after the shock of thinking he'd see Stevie again. 'I'll make myself free. You got a charter lined up?'

'Not yet. Why?'

'My dad has a boat, moored at Wight's Landing, on the Bay. He takes small groups out from time to time. He knows all the best spots for rockfish. He'll give you a good rate.'

'Sounds great. Text me his info and I'll book it.'

'Will do. I'll see you later.' Clay headed off to the barn to visit with little Cordelia Mazzetti. And then he planned to dig trenches with DeMarco and Julliard. A little backbreaking effort might be just the thing he needed to kick Cordelia's mother out of his mind.

*Baltimore, Maryland, Saturday, March 15, 2.10 P.M.*

The sight of her friend had Stevie's heart settling. Her worry and her fury and her sadness were all still there, but muted. Bearable. 'Em.'

Emma's head turned at the sound of her name, her smile blooming as she rose and held out her arms. 'Stevie.'

Stevie hugged her hard. They were well matched from a size standpoint, she and Emma. Stevie was a firm five-three with her socks on. Emma Townsend Walker claimed to be five-two, but it was a lie. Her friend needed heels to even approach five-one.

In most other ways they were polar opposites. Emma was a girlie-girl who loved dresses, makeup and bangles, while Stevie was most comfortable in jeans and a T-shirt with a firearm holstered on her shoulder. Emma was an academic, an author even. Stevie couldn't sit still long enough to read a book.

Of notable exception was *Green Eggs and Ham*. It had been Cordelia's favorite when she was small. Stevie had so many fond memories of her little girl curled up in her lap, helping her turn the pages with chubby little hands, giggling at the pictures.

The other exception, perhaps even more notable, was Emma's book, *Bite Sized*, her work on how to cope with trauma. Stevie had read it over and over again until she could hear the words in her sleep. Until the words were louder than the lonely roaring in her head. *Bite Sized* had helped Stevie bear the unspeakable grief of March 15.

It was a day Stevie thought she'd never live through. Had it not been for the child growing in her womb, she might not have. Cordelia had given her a reason to live. Emma helped her figure out how to do so. One day at a time. One bite at a time. *You can eat an elephant, one bite at a time*, Emma was fond of saying.

'It's so good to see you,' Emma whispered fiercely. 'I saw the shooting on TV in December and I was so afraid we'd lost you forever. Are you all right? Really, truly all right?'

'Some days I'm more all right than others.' Stevie pulled back, leaning heavily on the cane for balance. 'But I'm still here and I'm damn grateful to be.'

'Sit, for heaven's sake,' Emma commanded. When they had, Emma took a long, measured look at Stevie's face. 'You look better than I expected. Your hair is longer. I like it.'

Stevie tugged at her hair self-consciously. It was the longest it had been in years. 'I've been too busy to get it cut.'

Emma's eyes narrowed slightly and for a moment Stevie thought she'd ask what had kept her too busy for a haircut. 'The style looks good on you,' was all she said, though. 'You should keep it longer when you go back to work.'

'When,' Stevie repeated resolutely. She'd get back to duty, to real duty, not some lame-assed desk job. She'd work the damn leg until it behaved. She would.

Emma's lips quirked into a sudden smile. 'I saw you walking up the sidewalk a few minutes ago. Your cane sparkled like a magic wand. Now I know why. Let me guess – Cordelia?'

'Who else? Cordelia decorated it with glitter and left it under the Christmas tree. I think she's been touching it up with more glitter every few days because we're still finding glitter everywhere – on our clothes, in our hair, in our shoes . . .'

'I wish I could see her,' Emma said wistfully. 'But I

promised Christopher I'd get to Vegas in time to see him give the keynote speech at the symposium he's attending. I have to be at the airport by four thirty. I hope I didn't mess anything up on your end with the time change.'

'No. Izzy's been taking her to ballet since the shooting, so my schedule's flexible.'

Emma leaned forward a little. 'How is Cordelia?'

*Becoming more brittle every day.* 'Too serious.' Her baby had been through so much.

'Is the counselor helping?'

'I think so. I take her every week, sometimes twice a week. Her nightmares are becoming less frequent. A little vacation might do her some good. Maybe she and I can come to Florida to see you and the boys soon. How are the boys? And Megan?'

'Megan's loving grad school. CJ got a chemistry set for Christmas. I haven't had to call the fire department once, which makes me happy. Liam got an NFL football from Will's dad.'

Will had been Emma's first husband. Just like Paul and Paulie, Will had been killed in a convenience store robbery gone wrong. Their shared experience was the reason Stevie and Emma had first decided to meet. But unlike Stevie, Emma had managed to go on, marrying her high school sweetheart, Christopher, and having two beautiful sons with him. She'd embraced Chris's daughter from his previous marriage as her own as well.

Stevie was fiercely happy for them even as she envied their happiness. Then she frowned as Emma's words sank in. 'Wait. *Will's* father gave him the ball? Not Christopher's father?'

'Will's dad bought that football the minute Will and I announced our engagement,' Emma said with a wistful smile. 'Will was an only child, but his parents always called me their daughter. They treat my kids with Christopher like their own grandkids. It's really lovely. Will's father had been holding on to it for all these years, just waiting for a grandchild – the right grandchild – to give it to. CJ wouldn't have appreciated it the way Liam does and Megan had lost interest in football by the time Chris and I got married.'

'Cordelia's not into sports. She loves ballet, but I suspect it's mainly for the shoes and the tutus.' Stevie swallowed hard. 'Paul's father still keeps the toys that he never got to give to Paulie. I've told him to donate them, but he's never gotten around to it.'

'Maybe—' Emma started, but the waitress interrupted to take their order, which they gave without even looking at the menu – a perk of meeting in the same restaurant every year.

'What I was about to say,' Emma said when the waitress was gone, 'was that maybe Paul's dad is holding on to them like Will's dad held on to Liam's football. You never know what's coming down the pike. You're only thirty-six. You could have more kids some day.' She switched to a twang. 'You've got ye a few good child-bearin' years yet and a decent pair of hips.' She grinned. 'That's what Christopher's dad said to me right before our wedding.'

'And you still speak to him?' Stevie asked dryly.

'Sure. He's great with the boys. This week is the boys' spring break and all four of the grandparents are taking them to Disney World.'

'Tag teaming so the boys don't wear them out?'

'You got that right. Meanwhile, Christopher and I get a Vegas vacation. Alone. No kids. He'll get his chemistry fix at the symposium during the day, and I'll get mine at night.' Her eyes went sly. 'You could come with me and I could set you up with one of Christopher's friends.'

Stevie's eyes narrowed. 'Don't start, Em. I mean it. I'm not interested in fix-ups.'

'Fine, fine.' Emma raised her hands in surrender. 'I just thought that you might be open to someone new since you broke up with the PI.'

Stevie blinked in surprise. *Clay Maynard*. Instantly Stevie's mind flooded with the memory of waking in the hospital to find him sitting beside her, his dark eyes so relieved that she'd finally regained consciousness, that she'd lived. But they'd filled with pain when she told him to go away, to find someone else to love.

She'd cried after he'd left. Wished she could take the words back. But she couldn't, shouldn't, and hadn't. She'd done what needed to be done. It was for the best. *For both of us.*

Just thinking about Clay today, of all days, made her feel guilty. No one could come close to taking Paul's place. To let Clay attempt to do so would be disastrous. *For both of us.* She'd never love him the way she'd loved Paul and eventually . . .

*He'd hate me.* She'd rather him hate her now than after she'd allowed herself to care about him. It would break her heart again. And more importantly, Cordelia's.

*All of which is no one's business but my own. Not even Emma's.*

'How did you know about the PI?' Stevie said, keeping her annoyance in careful control.

Emma winced. 'Your brother told me that you two broke up when you were in the hospital.'

*Sorin, I'm going to smack you.* Her twin was a worse gossip than any old woman. He was also terrified she'd end up old and alone and continued to nag her about taking Clay back.

'There was never anything to break up, whatever you

were told,' she said, and that was the truth. 'We never went out on a single date. He kissed me once, in the hospital. That's all. He was hanging around like a stray dog, hoping I'd take him in. So I cut him loose.' More harshly than she'd needed to. But she couldn't take the chance that he'd hold hope. It wasn't fair.

*To whom? To him? Or to you?*

Emma was watching her carefully and Stevie suspected that her facade wasn't as convincing as she'd hoped. 'Why did you cut him loose, Stevie? Was he unkind? Unattractive?'

Unattractive? *God, no.* Stevie's heart stuttered every time she thought about him. Tall, dark, massive. His face was . . . beautiful. His heart, filled with compassion and honor.

*He saved my life, risking his own.* Clay had run to her side while Marina was still shooting on the courthouse stairs, stopping the bleeding that the doctors agreed should have killed her. Anchoring her to life when she'd almost slipped away. *You will not die, dammit. You will not leave me. You will not leave Cordelia. Dammit, Stevie, we need you. I need you.*

Unkind? *No.* If anything, he was too kind. Too patient. He would have waited for her . . . forever. And that she couldn't allow. He deserved a life. More than she could give him.

'Emma . . .' She let out a quiet sigh. 'Please. I can't discuss this today, of all days.'

'Okay,' Emma said, but her eyes were still calculating. 'This is Cordelia's spring break week too, right? Why don't you buy two tickets to Orlando, leaving tonight? I'll go to Vegas, be with Christopher during his keynote speech, then I'll fly back to Florida and meet you tomorrow. We can join the boys and their grandparents for their vacation. Cordelia will love it.'

Stevie felt a mild flare of panic. 'No.'

'Why not? You said you'd bring her down to Florida sometime soon.'

'I said *soon*. I didn't mean *tomorrow*.'

'If it's a question of budget, don't worry. I've got it.'

'It's not the money.' Stevie lifted her chin, a defensive pose she recognized but couldn't stop. 'I'm not going to be able to walk well enough for a long time.'

'Rent a scooter.' There was no sympathy in Emma's eyes. 'You see them everywhere.'

Anger flickered in her gut. 'I'm not using one of those damn scooters.'

'Why not? We could glitter it up to match your cane.'

'I said *no*,' Stevie repeated, fighting not to grit her teeth. 'This –' she pointed to the glitter-covered cane '– is temporary.'

'The scooter would be too,' Emma said. 'You could have a good time with Cordelia instead of working on old cases when you're supposed to be recovering. You could be having breakfast in Cinderella's castle instead of fighting off thugs and their knives with your sparkly cane.'

Stevie's eyes narrowed. 'Not your business, Emma,' she warned coldly.

Emma's eyes flashed. 'The hell it's not. What if the next attacker is successful? What if the next assailant stabs you in the back before you can fight? You got lucky yesterday. What if the next bullet doesn't miss and your PI isn't there to save your life because you sent him away?'

With an effort, Stevie clamped her anger down. 'Sorin,' she uttered darkly, and wondered just how much her brother and Emma had planned what she'd say this afternoon. 'He had no right to tell you any of this. Not my health, my love life, or my job. *He had no right*.'

'No, he didn't. But that doesn't make what he said less

true. I'm not sure why you have this death wish, Stevie, but if you keep pushing these old cases, eventually your wish will become reality. Somebody's going to stab you or shoot you or blow your car straight to hell with you in it. And as you lay *dying*?' Emma's eyes filled with tears. 'You *might* wish you hadn't cut the PI loose. You'll *definitely* wish you'd had that Cinderella breakfast with your daughter. But it'll be too late because you'll finally get your wish. You'll be dead.'

Stevie bit back the torrent of words she'd never be able to take back. 'I need to use the restroom.' She needed to rein in her temper that seemed to grow more volatile every day. Lurching to her feet, she grabbed the damn glittery cane and wheeled around – only to smack face first into the waitress, whose tray was heavy with filled beverage glasses.

As she and the waitress went down in a clatter of metal and breaking glass, Stevie heard screams. And Emma's voice shouting her name. Stevie lifted up on all fours to see if the waitress was all right. The woman was on her back, staring up at the ceiling, broken glass all around her. She wasn't blinking.

The side of her head was gushing blood.

Which didn't make sense. It was just a few broken wineglasses. Stevie reared up to grab a napkin on the table to stem the blood flow and froze.

The window they'd been sitting next to was shattered and Emma was gone.

'*Emma!*' Stevie shouted.

'I'm here. Behind you.' Emma was kneeling beside the woman who'd been sitting at the table next to theirs. Now the woman lay on her back, just like the waitress. Emma had her fingers pressed to the woman's throat, taking her pulse.

41

The woman's companion was kneeling on the other side of her, pressing dinner napkins to the wound, trying to stop her bleeding, tears rolling down his terrified face.

'Elissa, stay with me,' he commanded, his voice shaking. 'Stay with me. Do not leave me.' His voice broke when she continued to stare at the ceiling. 'Please, baby. Don't leave me.'

Stevie heard Clay's voice in her mind, pleading with her as she lay bleeding on the courthouse steps. *Don't you dare leave me.* She snapped herself back to the present.

'Everybody get on the floor and stay there!' she ordered, then dialed 911 on her cell. 'This is Detective Mazzetti, Homicide. We have shots fired and GSW victims at the Harbor House Restaurant. One victim is a Caucasian woman, about fifty. GSW to the chest.'

Stevie felt for the waitress's pulse. There was none. 'The second victim is also a Caucasian woman, about twenty-five. GSW to the head.' On closer inspection, she could see the back of the waitress's head was gone. The woman was dead.

Crawling to the window, Stevie peeked over the sill edge, eyeballing the angle of entry. 'The shot may have been fired from the roof of the building across the street,' she told the operator. 'No sign of a gunman.'

'You said GSW victims,' the operator said, her voice calm. 'Are there any others?'

Stevie looked around, saw dozens of terrified people staring back. 'Anybody else hit?'

At first no one answered. Then a man pointed to Stevie. 'You are. Your arm.'

Stevie looked down at her biceps. Her sweater was soaked with blood, and . . . *Ouch.* Her arm burned like fire. But it wasn't bad. She'd had a lot worse in the past.

'Just me,' she told the operator. 'And it's a graze. I'm okay.'

'You've got help on the way, Detective,' the operator said. 'ETA less than two minutes. Stay on the line with me until they get there.'

'I will. Please request that Detective JD Fitzpatrick and Lieutenant Peter Hyatt come to the scene.' Stevie drew a deep breath. Her partner and her boss would help her make sense of this.

Except it did make sense. *Yesterday I was shot at. Again today.* Stevie desperately held on to her calm. *They were trying to kill me and killed two others instead. Nobody's safe around me.*

'Help will be here in a minute or two,' she said to Emma, who now pressed cloth napkins to the woman's chest while the man performed CPR.

Emma turned her head to meet Stevie's eyes, her own filled with horror. 'I think it's too late,' she said hollowly. 'I think she's dead.'

# Chapter Three

*Baltimore, Maryland, Saturday, March 15, 2.18 P.M.*

*Shit. Shit. Shit.* Henderson stowed the rifle in its case with quick, practiced movements. *I cannot fucking believe this.*

Shooting Mazzetti should have been like taking candy from a baby. Robinette would be displeased. He considered retreat to be a failure. But sometimes it was wiser to back away and try again from a different angle.

*So back away. Get moving!* Soon the entire area would be crawling with cops.

The shot through the window should have been perfect. Henderson's finger had been on the trigger, ready . . . squeezing . . .

And then Mazzetti abruptly jumped up, ran into a waitress and they both went down. There had only been enough time to pump off a single second shot.

*I think I nicked her. But I didn't kill her. Dammit.* Some might say the cop was charmed, but Henderson didn't believe in such nonsense. Mazzetti was simply lucky. Extremely lucky.

That the scope might have wobbled a millimeter because of trembling hands was too minute a possibility to even consider. *It wasn't my fault.*

Henderson slipped through the door that led to the street. No one was about. *No witnesses I have to kill. So I guess I'm lucky, too.*

It was time to move to plan B because the cop would be on double alert. Sneaking up on her wouldn't be so easy. Sneaking up on the child? A whole lot easier.

*Especially since I know where the child actually is right now.* Versus where Robinette had promised she'd be. Knowing Cordelia Mazzetti was not at ballet had nothing to do with luck, though. That was just smart thinking and advance planning.

The thing about luck was that, eventually, it ran out. Smart thinking was a permanent skill.

Henderson made it to the white Camry, put it in gear, and took a sip from the plastic water bottle in the cup holder. The clear contents burned as they went down and everything calmed.

*Thank God for vodka.* The best thing the Russians ever did.


*Hunt Valley, Maryland, Saturday, March 15, 2.20 P.M.*

Clay found Cordelia Mazzetti in the second stall to the right, just as Izzy had told him, busily brushing a dark horse with a white star on its forehead. Clay stood at the stall door for a long moment, hesitant to speak, not wanting to spook the big animal.

Not with a child the size of Cordelia in there alone, unprotected. She shouldn't be in there alone. Who was watching her? The barn was deserted. No adults anywhere to be seen and—

*Oh.* The stall opened into a fenced run. Sitting on a stool in the middle of the run, pretending to polish a saddle

45

while her eyes never left the child, was Maggie VanDorn, the farm's manager.

That Maggie was watching over little Cordelia came as no surprise. Cordelia Mazzetti had been through a lot in her almost eight years. Losing her dad before she'd even met him, being stalked by a mass murderer two years before. Last year, she'd been held at gunpoint by a man her mother had once trusted . . . Stevie's former partner. Her mentor. Her friend. A dirty cop.

Clay's gut burned with impotent fury. Part of him wished that Silas Dandridge hadn't been killed that day because he wanted to kill him himself. Silas had been willing to kill Cordelia while her mother watched. That Silas battled for the life of his own child was immaterial.

*You don't trade one life for another. Especially the life of a child.*

He winced, then looked down and realized he gripped the stall door with such force he'd driven a splinter into his thumb. Quietly he pulled it out and sucked on the wound, listening for Cordelia's voice, small but strong. And sweet. Like music. It wasn't until Clay focused that he realized the words she uttered in a sing-song tone were anything but cheerful.

'I didn't scream, at least,' she was confiding to the horse, 'so I didn't wake up my mom. But I couldn't go back to sleep. Then it was time to go to school and Aunt Izzy made me get up and I was so tired, so I fell asleep in reading class and the teacher yelled at me. She told Aunt Izzy I wasn't paying attention and then I got in trouble.' Her voice wobbled. 'It wasn't fair. But Mom says life isn't, so we have to deal.' A sniffle, then the clearing of a small throat. 'Do you dream? If you do, I hope it's about eating all the hay you want and running fast as you can.'

'Hi, Cordelia,' Clay said softly.

She peeked around the horse's powerful chest and her dark eyes widened, her cheeks pinking up prettily. 'Mr Maynard! I didn't know you were here.'

'That makes two of us. I didn't know you were here, either. Who's your friend?'

She pressed her cheek into the horse's neck. 'This is Gracie.'

Clay smiled. 'That's a nice name.'

'Daphne names all her horses after famous actresses. Gracie is named after Grace Kelly. She was famous a long time ago. Back when movies had *writing*,' she added firmly.

Clay's smile widened. 'Who said so? The part about writing?'

'My grandma. She says movies today are useless tripe. What's tripe, anyway?'

'Cow's stomach, I think.'

'*Gross.*' She hesitated, then sighed. 'You heard me talking to Gracie, didn't you?'

'Only if you wanted me to. Otherwise, I didn't hear a thing.'

Cordelia's mouth curved sadly, and Clay's heart broke a little. 'It doesn't matter,' she murmured. 'Little kids have bad dreams. They don't mean anything. I just have to learn to deal.'

Clay leaned forward, resting his forearms on the stall door. 'And who said *that*?'

'My mom.'

'Well, your mom's right about learning to deal with it.' He hesitated, loath to correct Stevie's parenting. 'I'm not so sure she's right about them not meaning anything, though. Or maybe she doesn't have the same kind of dreams I do. Because I dream, Cordelia. Often.'

She looked up, her gaze sharp. 'You do? About what?'

'Sometimes stupid stuff, like zombies stealing my cream cheese when I've just bought bagels or that I'm back in school and I didn't study for the final exam. Sometimes they're not really dreams, though. They're more like . . . memories that won't go away.' Her eyes narrowed and he knew he'd hit the right nerve. 'Like somebody videotaped my scariest moments and is playing them back, over and over. That's not "nothing". That's a big something.'

'What do you dream? When it's the videos?' she clarified. 'Not the zombies. Although zombies are scary, too.' She said it kindly, like she didn't want him to feel stupid. Another piece of his heart crumbled.

'Stuff that happened in the war,' he said honestly.

'You were in a war?'

He nodded. 'Somalia, which is in Africa. It was bad and I saw a lot of scary stuff. Then I was a cop and saw more scary stuff. I dream about that, too.'

'Now you're a PI.' Her forehead wrinkled as she thought hard. 'That means "private investigator". Your partner was killed. Not Miss Paige, but the other one.'

*Which one?* was on the tip of his tongue, but he bit it back. He'd lost two partners, both friends, both murdered. Three months ago he'd found Tuzak discarded like garbage in an alley, nearly decapitated. Two years ago he'd found Nicki gutted and left to rot. He still woke up screaming when his mind replayed the scenes. But another clip played an endless loop in his mind, sleeping and waking. He suspected a similar dream tormented Cordelia.

'What do you dream, Cordelia?'

A breath shuddered out of her. 'I see my mom getting hurt, almost every night. Even when I'm not asleep,' she added in a tortured whisper. 'I saw it happen on TV. On the news.'

*My God.* He hadn't realized that she'd actually seen

the TV coverage of her mother being shot. 'You saw your mother get shot?'

She nodded. 'Now Aunt Izzy won't let me watch anything but DVDs. But I still see her . . . I see her getting shot, over and over.'

'And?' he prompted gently.

'And she doesn't get up.' A tear rolled down her face. 'In my dream, she doesn't get up.'

'I know,' he murmured. 'That's the same dream I have, honey.'

She looked up at him, her eyes swimming. 'But you saved her. You're a hero.'

Her admiration had his chest swelling. 'Not so much a hero. I'm just a man who gets scared, too. I won't lie to you about that. I felt so helpless that day. I think that's what got stuck in my dreams. When I wake up, sometimes I'm shaking, it's so real.'

'Me, too,' she whispered.

'I would give a whole lot to have kept you from seeing your mom get hurt like that. But you did, and we can't unring that bell.'

'I know,' she said morosely, making him smile, but sadly.

'This is where your mom is right, though, sweetheart. You have to learn to deal with the memories. Eventually they'll fade, but you have to learn to deal. You're a growing girl who needs her sleep. You have to learn how to wrestle the dreams to the ground, so you can go back to sleep without worrying you'll have the dream again. Do you know how to do that?'

She wagged her head. 'No, sir.'

'Well, you make up a new ending. You have the power to do that. When you see your mom hurt in your dream and then you lie awake, afraid? You picture her standing up and brushing herself off. Maybe she even does a little happy dance. Can you do that?'

She seemed to think about it a minute. Then she said, 'I can try.'

'That's good. What else do you dream?'

'That I'm with Uncle . . .' She grimaced. '*Mr* Silas and he has a gun. It's . . .' She looked away, her chin quivering.

*It's shoved in to her side.* It took an effort, but Clay kept his voice calm. 'It's okay, Cordelia. You don't have to say any more.'

'And Mom doesn't get to me in time and he shoots me,' she blurted, as if he hadn't spoken.

For the millionth time, Clay wanted to murder Silas Dandridge. 'I think most people who've had a gun pointed at them have dreams like that.'

'Mama doesn't. She's brave.' She winced. 'Not that you're not brave. Because you are.'

He smiled down at her. 'I think you are, too.'

'No, I'm not. I just sat there. I didn't do anything.'

*Oh, honey.* Clay's eyes stung. She was just a baby. And to be thinking all those thoughts . . . He had to swallow before he spoke. 'Well. You know Miss Paige, right? My partner?'

She nodded solemnly. 'Of course. I go to her karate school, every week.' Her chin tipped up proudly. 'I have a yellow belt. Sensei Holden says I have an awesome kick.'

'Excellent,' he said approvingly. 'So, do you think Sensei Holden is brave?'

Cordelia's eyes widened. 'Of course!'

Her appalled response made him grin. Then he sobered, needing her to believe what he was about to say. 'Sensei Holden had a gun held on her once, before she moved to Baltimore.'

She searched his face, as if wondering if he told the truth. 'What happened?'

'She couldn't get away, and she got hurt. She's fine now, but I need you to think about this. She's a black belt and she couldn't do anything, either. So when that voice in your head says that you're not brave because you didn't fight Mr Silas? You tell that voice to shut up.'

Her eyes had gone round as saucers. 'I'm not allowed to say "shut up".'

He bit back a smile, keeping his expression serious. 'Then just tell it to go away. Tell yourself that you're brave. Say it out loud. Say it, right now.'

Again her chin came up. 'I'm *brave*.' Her voice rang out and he gave her a proud nod.

'Very good. Now, about the dreams with the gun. I've had them too, and they scared me.'

'How old were you then? When you were scared?'

He briefly considered a fib, but changed his mind. This child deserved his honesty. 'Forty-one,' he said and she blinked, clearly not expecting that answer.

'How old are you now?' she asked tentatively.

'Forty-one,' he said dryly, and her lips twitched. 'The thing that works for me? Play the scene again in your head, except make the gun shoot flowers instead of bullets. Or have it shoot out rainbows or Skittles or cute puppies or something that you really like. Turn it into something that's not scary. Something that makes you laugh, even.'

She frowned up at him. Then she nodded slowly. 'I could do that. I could try, anyway.'

'That's all anyone can do, Cordelia. Just try.'

She wrinkled her nose. 'That's what my psychologist says.'

'Have you told your psychologist about the dreams?'

'A little. But . . .' She shrugged. 'My mom is there, too.'

'In the room with you?' Clay asked, surprised.

'No, but after I talk to the psychologist, she talks to my mom.'

'She doesn't tell anyone what you tell her. It's like, a psychologist law.'

She shrugged again, clearly unconvinced. 'Do you ever talk to a psychologist?'

Clay was about to force himself to tell her the truth, but was saved by Izzy's frantic voice.

'Cordelia? Cordy?'

Clay waved to Izzy, who had just run into the barn. 'She's here, Izzy. What's wrong?'

'Nothing.' Izzy skidded to a stop next to Gracie's stall door. 'We just have to go home.'

'Why?' Cordelia cried, distressed. 'We haven't been here that long. I didn't get to ride.'

'I know and I'm sorry, but I have to get home now and change. I just got a call about a wedding. The photographer they hired has food poisoning, and she gave them my name as a backup.' She looked at Cordelia plaintively. 'I need the money, Cordy. I'm sorry.'

'I can take her home,' Clay said. 'It's no problem.'

Cordelia and Izzy locked gazes. 'I'll get my things,' the little girl whispered dejectedly.

Frowning, Clay turned to Izzy. 'What's wrong with me taking her home?'

Izzy shifted uncomfortably. 'It's not you. Well . . . Not like you're thinking anyway.'

'Then tell me how I should be thinking,' he demanded.

Izzy hesitated, then stepped to the other side of the aisle, motioning Clay to follow. 'Cordelia's not supposed to be here, okay? Stevie . . . Shit. Stevie thinks she's at ballet class.'

Clay's frown deepened. 'Why?'

'Because Stevie doesn't want her here, at the farm.' Izzy lifted her chin defiantly. 'Even though being with the horses is excellent therapy that *I* think Cordelia needs.'

Clay was losing his patience. 'Why doesn't Stevie want her here? Does she hate horses?'

'No.' She blew out a breath. 'It's . . . Well, it *is* you, Clay,' she said in a low voice. 'Stevie doesn't want Cordelia to hang out where she might be around you.'

Clay flinched, first stunned, then horrified. Then pissed off. *'Why?* I'd never hurt her. She really thinks I'd hurt her?'

'No. Stevie knows you'd never hurt Cordelia. She really does.'

'Goddammit, then why?' he thundered.

'Sshh. Because Cordelia worships you. Calls you a guardian angel. Stevie doesn't want her to get attached to you.'

*Guardian angel.* Clay immediately thought of the refrigerator in his kitchen. Fixed with magnets, front and center, was the picture Cordelia had drawn with crayons when her mother was in the hospital, fighting for her life. She'd drawn Stevie in the bed, blood dripping from her leg. Clay stood next to her, a halo above his head. He planned to keep the picture forever.

He rubbed his forehead, exhaling heavily. 'Dammit, Izzy. You can't keep this from Stevie. It's not right to put Cordelia in the middle like that. When do you bring her here?'

'Every Saturday afternoon. She's been coming for a few months. Ever since . . .'

'Since Stevie was shot. She told me she saw it on TV.'

'Stevie doesn't know that. It would kill her to know Cordy saw her get shot. I brought her with me when I started taking the photos for Daphne's brochures. Maggie took Cordy under her wing and I've seen her improve. She only screams in her sleep a few nights a week now instead of all seven,' she said bitterly. 'The nightmares are becoming less frequent.'

*No*, Clay thought, remembering what Cordelia had been murmuring to the horse. *She's just learning how to suppress her screams so she doesn't wake you up.* 'Does Stevie know they're becoming less frequent?'

'Yes. She's been taking her to a counselor for the past year and thinks it's finally working. But this equine therapy is the first thing that's really made a difference. She *needs* to be here.'

'I know she needs to be here.' Because he suspected she hadn't told the psychologist any of what she'd shared with Gracie the horse. She needed somewhere to share her thoughts that was truly private. 'Let me handle this. I'll take Cordelia home. And I'll make sure Stevie knows that in the future I'll stay away on Saturday afternoons. I'll clear the way.'

Izzy bit her lip. 'Stevie will know I deceived her. It was worth it, for Cordelia, but Stevie's going to be really mad at me.'

'You know the drill, Izzy. You do the crime, you do the time.' Clay patted her shoulder. 'She would have figured it out sooner or later, anyway. Your sister's not stupid.'

'Not too sure about that one. She let you go.' Izzy met his eyes, hers sad. 'She's just scared, Clay. Give her some time.'

'No. Not going there, Izzy.' His jaw clenched. 'She said no and that means no. I'm not the kind of man who forces a woman's hand. So let it go. Please.'

'Fine,' she said in a tone that said she was anything but. 'I have to go anyway. I have just enough time to change my clothes and get to that wedding.' She stood on her toes to give Clay an impulsive hug. 'Thank you. For everything.'

'You're welcome,' he muttered gruffly. When she was gone, he leaned over the stall door to see Cordelia putting away her brushes. 'Change of plans, kid. You get to stay.'

The little girl's eyes were cautious. 'For how long?'

'As long as you like. I'm taking you home. And I'll make sure your mom isn't angry with you.'

'Because she'll be angry with you instead,' Cordelia countered.

*So? What else is new?* 'I'm a big boy. I can take it. Now go . . . saddle up, or whatever it was you were about to do when I got here.'

Her smile reappeared. 'Thank you, Mr Maynard,' she said politely.

'You're welcome. In the future, tell your mom the truth, even if it's scary. She doesn't deserve to be kept in the dark that way.'

'Yes, sir,' she said as she ran out to find Maggie VanDorn and get her saddle.

For a long moment he watched her, thinking about what he'd say to Stevie. Wishing his heart hadn't started beating harder in anticipation of seeing her again. Even if it was only to hear her tell him to go away again.


*Baltimore, Maryland, Saturday, March 15, 2.42 P.M.*

The woman was going to die. Sitting on the floor, away from the shattered window, Emma watched the medics work on the injured woman as the husband stood by helplessly, tears running down his face. Emma hadn't been able to find the woman's pulse. The medics had found one,

KAREN ROSE

but it was weak. She'd lost so much blood. Too much. 'Dammit all to hell,' Emma whispered.

'I agree.'

She looked up, unsurprised to see a detective crouching beside her. She'd met Stevie's new partner long ago, long before they'd been teamed up in BPD's homicide division.

It had been over seven years before, at Cordelia's christening. JD Fitzpatrick was Cordy's godfather. Emma's path hadn't crossed his again until today. She wondered if he knew who she was, if Stevie told anyone outside her immediate family about their annual lunch.

Knowing Stevie, probably not. She was an intensely private woman. Which was part of her problem. Stevie was too private. And way too intense.

*And I certainly didn't help matters any. Way to go, Dr Walker.* She'd intended to confront Stevie with her self-destructive behaviors with a lot more subtlety. *But I got upset.* She sighed inside. *And then I upset her. I didn't mean to upset her.*

Fitzpatrick pulled a notepad from his pocket. 'I need to ask you a few questions, ma'am.'

'I'll do my best. I don't think I'll be much help, though. I didn't see the shooter.' Her voice stayed calm, but her body shuddered. Stevie could have been killed. *Like the waitress was. Like that poor woman I tried to help will soon be.*

'Just tell me what you can. My name is Detective Fitzpatrick.'

'I know. You're her partner.' She looked across the room to where Stevie was arguing with another pair of medics. 'She won't want to go to the hospital. Please make her go.'

'You were sitting with Detective Mazzetti?'

'Yes.'

He waited for her to explain and when she said nothing, he frowned. 'And you are?'

'Emma Walker. Dr Walker,' she clarified. 'You and I have met before, once. At Cordelia's christening. Stevie introduced me as Dr Townsend. I'm the grief counselor who helped Stevie start up the grief support groups at the police department.'

His eyes narrowed as he made the connection. 'Dr Emma Townsend. You wrote the book Stevie used in the grief groups she did with cops. I read it. It helped when I lost my first wife.'

'I'm glad,' she said quietly.

Fitzpatrick's expression had softened. 'You helped her through Paul's murder. And Paulie's,' he added gruffly, then briefly closed his eyes. 'Today's the anniversary. How could I have forgotten? I always take Cordelia out for ice cream on the anniversary. I forgot. Dammit.'

'You have an infant, right? Just three months old?'

'Jeremiah,' he confirmed.

Emma gave him an encouraging smile. 'Stevie told me about him. She was so thrilled when you asked her to be his godmother. I imagine you've had a lot of sleepless nights.'

'That's not an excuse. Cordy is *my* goddaughter. I should've remembered.'

'I think she'll understand, Detective. Cordelia's got a kind heart.'

'Apparently, so do you.' He gestured to her blouse that had been ivory but was now streaked red. 'None of that blood is yours, right? The medics said you were uninjured.'

'It's mostly Elissa's.' Emma didn't think she'd ever forget the way the husband had shouted his wife's name, trying to make her stay with him. 'The older victim. A little belongs to Stevie.'

'The manager said you tried to stop the victim's

bleeding, that you kept the husband relatively calm while Detective Mazzetti secured the scene.'

'Stevie was pretty amazing, taking charge like that. Never saw her in action before.' After calling 911, Stevie had slumped against the wall and Emma thought she was weak from blood loss. But her friend had been assessing the situation and within seconds was barking out orders, corralling the diners into a banquet room without windows. She'd tied a dinner napkin around her own wound, then had the staff close all the drapes in case the shooter was still out there.

'She's got a level head,' Fitzpatrick agreed. 'She's been trained on how to handle emergencies like this.'

'Unfortunately her level head doesn't extend to herself. She's telling the medics that it's "just a flesh wound", that she's had much worse. Which is true, but irrelevant. She thinks she can talk them out of a hospital visit.'

'Don't worry, she'll go. *He'll* make sure of it.' Fitzpatrick pointed to the door, where a tall, barrel-chested, bald man stood, fists on his hips and a scowl on his face. 'He's our boss.'

'Peter Hyatt,' she murmured. 'I met him at the christening, too.'

'So you and Stevie have remained friends all this time. I didn't know.'

'I didn't think she'd shared it. We have lunch together on the anniversary of her loss, every year. At first it was because she was finding her way, then because she'd started grief groups within the police department and I consulted with her. Now . . . we're friends. We get together in Florida from time to time. It's been a while, though. Sorry. I'm rambling, aren't I?'

'That's normal,' he said steadily. 'It doesn't bother me. Tell me what you saw.'

'Stevie and I were just sitting here. Arguing,' she said with a wince. 'Then out of nowhere . . . *Boom.* The window shattered and everyone started screaming. For a second I sat there, staring out the hole where the window had been. It was like I was . . .'

'In shock?' Fitzpatrick offered kindly.

'I guess so. Then my brain finally came back on line and I dove for the floor. I saw the woman next to me was hit, crawled over and started to help. Stevie yelled for me and I could see she was bleeding, too. But not as bad as the woman I was helping so I stayed where I was. Stevie called 911, then got everyone to safety. It wasn't till everyone was cleared out that I realized the waitress was dead.'

'What do you know about the couple who were sitting next to you?'

'Only what the husband told me while we were waiting for help to arrive. Elissa and Al Selmon. They were here for their wedding anniversary.' Her voice broke and she cleared her throat harshly as Fitzpatrick's eyes flickered in sympathy. 'It was their fortieth.'

'Did he give any indication that he suspected who'd shot his wife?'

She blinked at him. 'No. Not at all. I assumed . . . I thought Stevie was the target.'

'Why would you think that?' he asked.

She let her eyes close wearily. 'Because she's been attacked three times in the past week, which I'm sure you know. Because the last attacker, a shooter with thankfully really bad aim, got away. And because when the first shot missed today, this shooter tried again.' She lifted her heavy eyelids, stared Fitzpatrick down. 'Why would you think she *wasn't* the intended target?'

'Because the two of you were sitting in front of a window. If someone had wanted her dead, she was a

59

perfect target. Instead, she's barely got a graze on her shoulder. It could have been a random shooting. The target could even have been you, Dr Walker.'

Emma frowned, then rejected the notion, realizing he didn't believe it, either. 'Stevie's the one with all the enemies. It's far more likely that the shooter simply missed her. Stevie had just unexpectedly moved. We were arguing. I said some things that made her furious with me. She got up abruptly, turned around, collided with the waitress, and they both fell to the floor.'

'What did you argue about?'

She hesitated. 'I'm not her therapist. You know that. I'm her friend.'

'So nothing you tell me breaches confidentiality. I get it. What did you argue about?'

Emma sighed. 'Mostly the choices she'd been making lately. Not resting enough, investigating her old partner's cases, putting herself in harm's way.'

'I had the same argument with her. It didn't make her furious with me. Just pissed.'

'I brought up her love life. Or lack thereof. I'd really rather leave it at that.'

Fitzpatrick's brows lifted. 'You got on her for giving Clay Maynard the old heave-ho?'

She blinked at him again. 'You know about Mr Maynard?'

'Who doesn't? But I wasn't brave enough to confront her about it.'

'I hurt her feelings. I didn't mean to. Like I said, I'm not her therapist, I'm her friend. I got upset and handled it badly. Really, really badly.'

'She'll live. Figuratively and literally. If you hadn't argued, she'd have been sitting in the crosshairs when the bullet came through the window. So . . . this annual lunch of yours. Tell me about it, logistically. Where do you meet?'

'Always here, and always at three o'clock. Except this year.' Emma frowned. 'This year we met at two. I was supposed to be leaving for Las Vegas when lunch was over.'

'Why Vegas?'

'My husband's there, at a convention.'

'So your routine was disrupted. Who knows about your lunches?'

'My husband and kids, Izzy, Cordelia. Stevie's brother. My parents. Maybe hers, too.'

'Why are her parents a "maybe"?'

'They're lovely people and they love Stevie. They're just not big on talking about grief. Not everyone can. That's one of the reasons Stevie and I get together every year. To talk.'

'I understand. Who knew you'd moved the time?'

'My husband knew. The restaurant knew, because I called to change the reservation. On Stevie's side, I don't know. You'll have to ask her.'

'I will. Thank you, Dr Walker.' Fitzpatrick stood up. 'Can I take you anywhere?'

'To the hospital. I'm going with her.'


*Hunt Valley, Maryland, Saturday, March 15, 5.00 P.M.*

Clay checked his rearview mirror and frowned. The white Camry was still there.

Alec craned his neck around to look out of the back window. 'How long has it been following us?' he asked in a voice only slightly louder than a whisper.

The cab of Clay's truck was hushed, Cordelia having fallen asleep in the backseat.

'At least since we left the florist,' Clay murmured back. They'd stopped at a flower shop in downtown Hunt Valley after Cordelia had finished her riding lesson. Clay had picked up the daffodils for his mother's grave and Cordelia had asked if she could take some flowers to her mother, hoping to charm her into not being angry with her about the equine therapy.

The bunch of rosebuds she'd chosen for Stevie lay next to her on the backseat. Clay hoped they did the trick and that if Stevie got mad, she'd take it out on him and not her daughter.

'I thought we'd lost them at the ice cream shop,' he went on, 'but the driver was just playing with us.' Whoever followed them knew what he was doing, staying back just far enough to prevent them from seeing the license plate number.

'None of our current cases involve a white Camry,' Alec said. He held up his phone. 'I checked our database.'

'Thanks.' Clay checked the mirror again. The Camry was two cars back. 'Is Cordelia still buckled in?'

'Yes. Why?'

'Because I'm going to try to lose this asshole on the Parkway.' He merged onto the six-lane highway and waited for the Camry to follow. When it did, he waited until the next exit was in sight and at the last minute pulled onto the shoulder and stopped hard. The Camry shot by, unable to pull over in time to make the exit ramp. Clay peeled off the ramp, satisfied. 'I'll take us down back roads. It'll take us a bit longer to get Cordelia home, but it'll be safer. I don't want to lead him to Stevie's house, whoever the hell he is.'

Alec looked over his shoulder. 'She's still asleep. I can't believe she didn't wake up.'

Cordelia hadn't moved, still curled up in the corner of

the big backseat. 'She hasn't been sleeping well,' Clay said. 'I guess it just caught up to her.'

'Can't say I'm surprised,' Alec said quietly. 'Kid's been through the wringer.' His phone beeped and he checked it. 'It's a rental. The white Camry, I mean.'

Clay shot him a surprised glance. 'How do you know that?'

'I got the license when it passed us by. I ran a search.'

'On your phone. God, I am so old. Who did the renting?'

'This search engine doesn't give me the name. We'll have to check the rental agency.'

'The rental places at the airport will still be open on a Saturday night. We can head to BWI after we drop Cordelia off with her mother.'

It was a relief to have a task already waiting for him, because staying busy seemed to be the thing that kept him sane each time Stevie Mazzetti shoved him out of her life. That she would again tonight was a certainty. He was calmly driving into a tornado, knowing the cost.

And if that wasn't true insanity, he wasn't sure what would be.

# Chapter Four

'Hey, Mom?' Standing in his mother's kitchen, Officer Sam Hudson opened the door to the basement. 'Are you down there, Mom?'

'Yes, son.' Out of breath, she was struggling with a laundry basket.

*Oh, for God's sake.* 'Mom, stop that.' He took the stairs two at a time and lifted the basket from her hands. 'You're not supposed to carry heavy things. You just had heart surgery. Triple bypass. Remember?' Irritated, he started up the stairs without waiting for her reply.

*This* was why he stopped by on his way to his own apartment after every shift and on his days off, too. He half expected to find her at the bottom of the stairs, passed out under a pile of laundry. Of course it would be clean laundry. His mother would be too embarrassed to be found passed out under dirty laundry.

'Yes, son,' she repeated, climbing the stairs behind him. 'I remember. I was there, right there on the operating table. Just like I was there when you were born. Hmm. When would that have been? Let me think. Oh, right. Only thirty years ago. I'm sixty-two, last I checked. Which makes me both older and your mother. So stop telling me what to do. That's my job.'

He put the basket on the kitchen table. 'To tell me what to do or to tell yourself?'

'Both.' She nudged him out of the way to open the oven, allowing wonderful aromas to escape. 'And I have seniority so you're not getting my job.'

He took an appreciative sniff. 'You made pot roast. You are a queen among mothers.'

'I know,' she said regally, then laughed.

Sam smiled, finding contentment in the sound. He'd been so terrified he'd lose her during the surgery, that he'd never hear her laugh again. 'You're also a sneak, using the smell of pot roast to divert my attention from your bad behavior.'

'Whatever works,' she said cheerfully. 'If you want to help me, then set the table.'

Sam grabbed plates from the cupboard, pausing when the thick bubble-wrap envelope on the counter caught his eye. The envelope was propped up between the Washington Monument salt-and-pepper shakers he'd bought for his mother on a field trip to DC when he'd been eleven years old. They were only cheap souvenirs, but he'd bought them with money he'd earned himself because her birthday was coming up.

And because he knew his father would have forgotten because he was too high or out looking for his next fix. His mother had made a fuss over those cheap souvenirs like he'd bought her solid gold and had kept them on the counter ever since.

Sam picked up the envelope that read *Samuel J. Hudson*, cleanly typed on a mailing label. 'When did this come, Mom?'

She looked up from the potatoes she was mashing.

'Today. There's no return address. I thought it might be junk, but I wasn't sure. It's got something in it. Too heavy to be anthrax.'

He stifled his laugh because he knew she was serious. His mother watched entirely too much television. 'Come on, Mom, who would be sending me anthrax?'

She shrugged. 'You're a policeman. Maybe you made somebody mad at you.'

'It's not anthrax,' he muttered, opening the envelope.

'Isn't that what I said? So what is it?'

'Let's find out.' Carefully he emptied the contents on the table.

And heard her gasp. There was an old Orioles cap that Sam immediately recognized, and a dozen old, worn-out photos. And sitting on top of the photos was a plain gold wedding band.

She stood, pale as a ghost, her hand covering her mouth. Her eyes filling with tears. 'Oh my God,' she whispered. 'Sam. Oh dear God.'

Her hand trembling, she picked up the ring between her thumb and forefinger. 'It's his. It's your father's. It has his initials inside. I had it engraved the day before our wedding.'

Sam fanned the photos out on the table. They were either wallet-sized portraits or snapshots cut to be wallet-sized. His parents on their wedding day. A snapshot of Sam and his mom wearing leis, taken by his father on their one and only family vacation to Hawaii. The pictures of Sam were school portraits, all from elementary school.

When they were still a family. Before his father became a junkie who'd stolen from them, lied to them. Used his fists on them when he needed a fix.

The only recent photo was the one taken at the police academy, the day Sam had graduated. His father had shown up, shaved and sober. He'd behaved himself and Sam and his mother had once again hoped.

Six months later his father was using again. And then one day he'd simply disappeared without a trace. Without a word. There had been no contact of any kind . . . until today.

'Why?' his mother cried. 'What does this mean?'

'I don't know, Mom,' Sam said quietly, but that wasn't true. He knew exactly what it meant – and suspected she did, too. It meant that his father was dead and may have been for a long time. That someone either just found his stuff or just got around to sending it.

'He had his ring.' Her voice broke, her shoulders shaking with harsh, heaving sobs. 'He had his ring all along. I . . . Oh, God, Sam. I accused him of selling it. For his habit. He promised me he hadn't, but he wasn't wearing it the last time I saw him.'

Sam had never been able to stand seeing his mother cry, even though he had a lot of practice doing so, which was just one of the reasons he hated his father so much. Gently he drew her into his arms, patting her back. Wishing he knew what the hell to say.

How many times had they done this same thing? How many times had he patted her back helplessly as she sobbed her heart out? Not in eight years. Not since his old man had left without a backward look. That someone would put his mother through this now . . .

The wedding ring clenched into her fist, she pressed her face into Sam's shirt. 'It was the last straw, seeing his finger bare. Having him *lie* to me about not selling it. I told him to get out of my life. Never to come back. And he never did. God help me, he never did.' Her sobs became more desperate, each breath she drew harder than the last until Sam's helplessness became fear.

'Mom, please. You have to calm down. You'll have another heart attack.'

She shook her head. 'He didn't lie. He still had it. Why didn't he wear it?'

God only knew why his father had done any of the things he'd done. He'd probably pawned it for drug money or maybe even had taken it off because he was having an affair.

'I don't know, Mom. I don't know. But throwing him out was something you had to do. He was never going to get clean.'

Her sobs faded to little whimpers. 'But he might still be alive if I'd let him stay.'

'You don't know that,' Sam said gently. 'He was an addict. He wasn't going to change. That has nothing to do with you or what you said.'

Another heavy sigh. 'I suppose.'

'I *know*.' He tipped up her chin. 'Go wash your face. I'll finish mashing the potatoes and setting the table.'

Steeling her shoulders, she turned for the powder room, her step even less steady than it had been, and once again Sam cursed his father to burn in hell. Even dead, the old man managed to break his mother's heart.

He widened the mouth of the envelope to slide the hat and the pictures back in, but paused. Stuck in the bottom of the envelope, snagged by the bubble wrap, was a match-book. Carefully he worked it loose, pulled it out. Then froze. On the matchbook's face was a drawing of a woman wearing nothing but bunny ears, with 'The Rabbit Hole' printed beneath.

His heart was suddenly pounding so hard it was all he could hear. *The Rabbit Hole*. The powder room door was still closed. His mother hadn't seen. *Thank God*.

That the matchbook would be among his father's things

should have come as no surprise. It would have been the kind of sleazy place his father would have patronized, but it wasn't the kind of place Sam frequented. His mom had brought him up better than that. Sam had never been to the place.

Except that one time.

That one night. The night he'd made himself forget.

*Oh my God.* He thought about the timing of the arrival of the envelope in his hand and had to swallow back a wave of nausea.

*It's not possible. It's just not.*

The water stopped and he heard his mother's shuffling steps in the hall. Guiltily, Sam shoved the matchbook into his pants pocket.

Looking more worn than he'd seen her in weeks, his mother returned to the kitchen and lowered herself into a chair. She opened her clenched fist and stared at the ring on her palm. 'I just don't understand why today of all days,' she said wearily. 'Who could be so cruel? Who would even know?' She didn't look away from the ring. 'When was that envelope mailed?'

Sam's hand trembled as he turned the envelope over to check the postmark. 'Yesterday.' *Oh my God. This is not happening. Not possible.* But it was happening. 'From Baltimore.'

'Yesterday,' she repeated dully. 'The day I threw him out was eight years ago yesterday.'

Sam had to lock his knees to keep them from buckling. 'I didn't know that was the day you threw him out. I thought you threw him out months before.'

'I did. But he came back that night, not wearing his ring. So I threw him out and told him to never come back. And he didn't.'

*That night* . . . The night he'd gone to the Rabbit Hole had been eight years ago yesterday.

The night that had come before the morning he'd woken alone in a dirty hotel room on the wrong side of town, hung over and smelling like a brewery.

With a revolver on the floor beside him. A revolver that was not his Baltimore PD issued sidearm. A revolver that had been fired recently.

The morning he'd woken hadn't been the very next day. He'd woken just before dawn, *thirty hours later*. Not a moment of which he had any recollection of whatsoever.

He'd lost a day of his life. He'd lost *this* day of his life, eight years ago.

*Dad, what the fuck did you do?* Sam carefully exhaled. *And what the fuck did I do?*


*Saturday, March 15, 6.05 P.M.*

Two women were dead, their faces etched in Stevie's mind. The woman who'd done nothing more than show up for a wedding anniversary lunch with her husband had died in the ambulance on the way to the hospital. As had the waitress, who'd done nothing more than show up for work. *Because of bullets meant for me.*

Stevie paused at the bottom of her front porch steps, looking up at her house with weary determination. *Déjà vu.* She'd stood just like this a few hours ago, looking up at the stairs leading up to Harbor House's front door, cursing each step, her useless leg, and the crazy teenaged bitch who'd shot her three months ago.

Now she was cursing the steps, her useless leg, her arm that throbbed and burned like hellfire, the crazy teenaged bitch who'd shot her three months ago, and the gunman who'd shot her four hours ago. It hadn't been much more than a graze. But it still hurt.

*But you're alive. Unlike Elissa Selmon and Angie Thurman.* Tears stung her eyes and she blinked them back. *Goddammit.*

The house was dark. Quiet. The minivan was gone from the driveway. Cordelia and Izzy weren't home yet. Which would be perfect except that Stevie had no idea where they were because Izzy hadn't answered any of her texts, voicemails, or emails.

*Dammit, Izzy. Where are you? Where is my daughter? Please let her be all right. Please don't let her be hurt. Don't let her be—*

*Stop this. You'll be no good to anyone if you panic. Cordelia is all right.*

She *had* to be all right. Wherever she and Izzy were.

Which at least wasn't here. Stevie didn't want them around her. She didn't want anyone around her. *I have a price on my head.* And the collection agency didn't seem terribly worried about collateral damage.

'Um, Stevie?' Emma's calm voice came from just behind her, on her right. 'You're still a target, hon. Let's get you up the stairs and in the house.'

'Or I'll toss you over my shoulder and carry you up,' JD added grimly from her left.

Stevie clenched her teeth, but did as he said, propelling herself up her front steps. 'I don't need a bodyguard or a babysitter. If you touch me, JD, you'll be singing soprano for a week.'

'Yeah, whatever,' JD muttered. 'One last time, Stevie. Go to the goddamn safe house.'

'One last time, JD, *no.* I will not be driven from my home.' Stevie hissed a curse when her key missed the lock entirely. Her hand was trembling, dammit. Like an old woman's.

Or like a person who'd just watched two people die. *Because you wouldn't back off. You had to pursue Silas's old cases. You had to know. You won't leave well enough alone.*

71

The inner voice that taunted her morphed from her own to that of her twin. Sorin had been so upset when he'd called last night to beg her to stop the investigations that were bringing the slime out of the woodwork. Begged her to let the other cops review all of Silas's old cases.

She'd heard the love and fear in his voice . . . and then the furious disgust when she'd refused to back down, because BPD *was* investigating. They'd formed a special task force that had spent the last year reopening dozens of cases thrown by dirty cops working in secret for an even dirtier defense attorney. But there were so many cases and Silas hadn't been the only dirty cop.

*But he was my partner. My responsibility.* She couldn't, wouldn't walk away.

And now? Now that she knew that the dozens of cases BPD knew about might be only the tip of the iceberg? Now that she knew that more dirty cops still walked the street? Still wore a badge, just like Silas had done for all the years they'd been partners?

She couldn't walk away.

But none of this had she been able to share with her brother. Instead, she'd borne his rage in silence, which he'd interpreted as sullen stubbornness.

*If you don't care about your own life, have the decency to think about the lives of everyone around you. Our sister. Our parents. Your daughter. If the next bullet hits you, we'll mourn. If the next bullet misses you and hits one of them? What then?* His voice had broken, his next words choked with tears. *I love you, Stefania, and watching you destroy yourself is killing me.*

A sob was building in her chest. She forced it back down. He'd been right. He'd been so right. Two women were dead. *I'm sorry. I really am.* But it changed nothing.

Sorin didn't understand. Nobody understood. She couldn't stop investigating. There was this pressure in her mind, in her heart, pressing her forward. So many injustices. So many innocents paying for the crimes of others. And all under her very nose. For all those years . . .

She *had* to make it *right*.

Tears blurred her eyes and the key missed the lock again. 'Fuck,' she whispered.

Emma took the key from her hand and wordlessly opened her front door.

JD checked the first floor, then sprinted up the stairs to the second floor, his gun drawn. He was checking for monsters under the bed, true to his nature.

Emma locked the front door and began closing the blinds and drawing the drapes, plunging the living room into semi-darkness. 'Sit down,' she said quietly. 'You've got to hurt.'

Stevie obeyed, grimacing as she lowered herself to the sofa. *Elissa, Angie, I am so sorry.*

But nothing would bring the women back. All she could do to make it right was to catch the shooter and put him away forever. Which she couldn't do from a goddamn safe house.

With an eye on Emma, Stevie checked her cell phone for the two hundredth time in the last two hours. And scowled.

'No answer from your sister?' Emma asked.

'No. Cordy's ballet class finished hours ago. They should have been home already.' She took the cordless home phone from its cradle. No incoming calls from Izzy. 'She should have called me. She knows better. She knows I worry.'

'Stevie, listen. Today was a stressful day for you, even before all the craziness at the restaurant. But it's a stressful day for Cordelia, too.'

'She lost her father,' Stevie murmured. 'She never knew him.'

'Well, that, too. But I suspect her stress comes mostly from knowing how unhappy you are.'

'She doesn't know about that. I don't let her see it.'

Emma's brows lifted as if Stevie was the most foolish woman she'd ever known. 'You keep thinking that if it makes you feel better. Look, I bet Izzy's taken her somewhere to get her mind off things. Maybe they went to a movie. Izzy would have turned her phone off in the theater.'

Stevie closed her eyes, letting Emma's words wash over her. But the sense of foreboding was not abated. 'But what if something did happen to them? I'd never forgive myself.'

'The police have their descriptions, right? If something has happened, you would have heard by now. It's far more likely they're just having fun.'

Stevie drew a sharp, hard breath. 'You're right.' She focused on the next concern on her list – Emma. *Who shouldn't be here either.* 'You missed your plane.'

'It's okay. I called Christopher, told him what happened and that I'd need to stay with you for a few days.'

A few days? Under other circumstances Stevie would've enjoyed spending a few days with Emma. But not now. And she couldn't imagine Emma's husband being crazy about the idea of his wife sitting in the line of fire. 'And he was fine with that?'

Emma's slight hesitation was her answer. 'He's not fine, but he's not un-fine, either.'

'Uh-huh.'

'He was scared, of course. I just let him "what if" until he'd purged all the possible deadly scenarios from his mind. Then I assured him I was fine, that you were fine.'

She sighed. 'And then I didn't argue when he insisted on taking the red-eye to Baltimore tonight, as soon as he's given his speech. I'll pick him up from the airport in the morning.'

'I have a better idea. Have him fly back to Orlando. You take the next flight to Orlando. Then you can pick him up at the airport and have a wonderful vacation with your boys.'

Emma looked mildly amused, as if she'd expected as much. 'Nice try. Not goin' anywhere.'

'Dammit, Emma, you shouldn't be here. Not in Baltimore and really not *here*. In my house. You should be at your hotel. Where you'll be *safe*.'

Emma met her eyes, shrewdly. 'So you won't go to a safe house, but you'd put everyone you care about in one. Is that it?'

'Pretty much,' Stevie said, unapologetically. 'So when JD goes, he can take you with him.'

'Sorry, not gonna happen. I'm sticking.' Emma sat in a wingchair in the corner, far away, Stevie noted, from the window. Even with the drapes drawn, Emma was taking no chances.

'Emma. Be reasonable.'

Emma snorted. 'You've *got* to be kidding me. You want me to be reasonable? You want me in a safe house? Then you go with me. And before you threaten to push me out the door, just remember that I was there when the ER doctor examined you and I know all of the places you're bleeding and/or bruised. One good jab and you're down for the count.'

'I like her.' JD came down the stairs. 'She's smart.'

Stevie glared at them both. 'She's a stubborn pain in the ass.'

Emma shrugged. 'Hello, pot. Meet kettle. So, Detective

75

Fitzpatrick, do we need to worry about the Boogie Man jumping out of a closet when we go to sleep tonight?'

'Nope. I thought at first that someone had tossed Izzy's room, but I think it was Izzy. Clothes everywhere. Half of her closet's on her bed.'

Stevie frowned. 'Her room was neat when we left today.'

'Then either she's been home to change, or Goldilocks tried on her clothes, put on her makeup, and locked up her jewelry box before leaving.'

Stevie pushed herself to her feet. 'I'll check it out.'

'How do you know someone put on her makeup?' Emma asked.

'Her makeup brushes were still damp and there were lipstick-covered tissues all over the dresser.' JD lifted a shoulder. 'I have a wife who likes to wear makeup. I'm always shoving Lucy's brushes out of the way just so I can have a few inches of counter space to shave.'

'Poor baby,' Stevie muttered. She pushed past him and muscled her way up the stairs, with Emma behind her and JD bringing up the rear. Izzy's room was a mess, very uncharacteristic of her neat-as-a-pin sister. 'It looks like a tornado went through here.'

'Is anything missing?' JD asked.

Stevie stepped into Izzy's closet. 'Her glass slippers are gone.'

Emma stuck her head through the closet doorway. 'Izzy has glass slippers?'

'They're really acrylic or something, but Cordelia called them glass slippers when she was a toddler, and it stuck. Izzy wears them with her best dress.' Stevie sorted through the clothes. 'Which is missing, too.' She surveyed the shelves. Pointed to an obviously empty space. 'Her camera is missing. All her lenses and filters, too.'

'Maybe she took pictures of Cordelia at ballet?' Emma suggested.

'Maybe. But it was just a class. Cordy's recital isn't until next month.' *Or was it? Oh God, please don't let it have been today.* She'd already called the ballet teacher four times, but the teacher didn't usually return calls until all of her afternoon classes were over. Which should have been by now. Hurrying to Cordelia's room, Stevie dialed again.

Reva Stanislaski answered as Stevie threw open Cordelia's closet door. Her leotard and practice shoes were gone, but the pink tutu she wore to recitals was hanging there undisturbed.

'Mrs Stanislaski, hello. This is Stevie Mazzetti, Cordelia's mom.'

'Mrs Mazzetti. How good it is to hear from you. I hope Cordelia is well.'

Stevie frowned. 'What do you mean? You saw her a few hours ago. Wasn't she well then?' There was a pause during which Stevie's heart began to race. 'Wasn't she okay today?'

'I didn't see her today, Mrs Mazzetti. I haven't seen Cordelia in over two months.'

'I . . . I don't understand. She goes to class, every Saturday afternoon. My sister Izabela has been bringing her.'

'Izabela withdrew her from my class at the beginning of January, right after the new year. Cordelia seemed to be having some trouble.'

'What kind of trouble?' Stevie asked flatly.

'She seemed to get upset easily. The least little mistake and she'd burst into tears.'

Stevie's maternal defensiveness came to full alert. 'Perhaps it was the manner in which the correction was given.'

77

'I never corrected her,' Mrs Stanislaski said sadly. 'Cordelia was more than aware of her own mistakes. I tried to get her to relax. Have fun. But she grew more . . .'

'Brittle,' Stevie murmured.

'Yes, that is the word I was looking for. So your sister withdrew her from my class. She said that Cordelia was going to take a break for a while. I assumed you knew.'

'No. I didn't. Thank you, Mrs Stanislaski. I'll . . . Well, thank you.' Stevie hung up and slowly turned from Cordelia's closet to where JD and Emma waited, expressions troubled. 'Izzy hasn't been taking Cordy to ballet for months. But they've been gone every Saturday afternoon.'

'I'm sure Izzy has a good explanation,' JD said quietly.

Stevie bit the inside of her cheek, anger rising. 'If something was wrong with Cordelia, Izzy should have told me.' She heard the car engine outside at the same time JD did. Together they rushed to the window, each taking one side. 'Emma, wait in the hall.'

'Already there,' Emma said. 'I'm not stupid, Stevie.'

Emma had suspected Cordelia was having trouble and she hadn't seen her in a year. No, her friend was far from stupid. *Me, on the other hand . . .*

Stevie stiffened at the sight of a black truck pulling up to her house. There was something about the driver. Something familiar. He brought the truck to a stop and looked up, his eyes scanning the windows. Her heart skittered. *No way. No fucking way. It cannot be him.*

'Who is that?' JD asked, then exhaled a quiet 'Oh' when the driver emerged.

*Oh.* As in *Oh My God.*

Stevie's skittering heart simply stopped at the sight of the man standing in her driveway. It was him. Dark. Huge.

Massive shoulders. Layers of muscle. He was . . . He was too much.

'Who is it?' Emma called impatiently from the hall. 'Do I need to call 911?'

JD gave Stevie a few seconds to answer. When it was clear she wasn't going to, he called back, 'It's Clay Maynard. The PI.'

'Really? What's he doing here?' Emma inched into the room, stopping behind Stevie to cautiously peek around her shoulder. 'Oh my,' she murmured appreciatively. 'Oh my, oh my.'

*Oh my* was right. Clay appeared rough-hewn, like his face had been carved from solid rock. But Stevie knew that wasn't true. She knew that his lips were soft, his skin was warm and vital, and his eyes saw more than she wanted anyone to see. Ever again. And when he looked at her . . . She *felt* more than she ever wanted to feel again.

*Not today. Please. I can't do this today.* Clay walked around the truck to open the back passenger door and Cordelia hopped out, an adoring smile on her face.

Stevie stared, open-mouthed. Suddenly Izzy's ballet deception made perfect sense. Her sister had never approved of her sending Clay on his way. Izzy had begged her to 'see reason'.

Cordelia had been with Clay. All this time. *After I explicitly forbade it.*

Cordelia thought the man hung the moon. And why wouldn't she? She'd known Clay had saved her mother's life. It was natural for a seven-year-old girl to put him on a pedestal. *Which he deserves. Because he, like, saved your life.*

*And I'm grateful. I just don't want him in* my *life.*

Which Izzy hadn't respected, damn her to hell. *If she thinks that getting Cordelia attached to him will make me let him worm his way under my skin, she's got another think coming.*

79

This wasn't right. Wasn't fair. To Cordelia or to Clay. *Or to me.*

Stevie wasn't the cold stone everyone thought she was. She was lonely. She craved companionship. Male companionship. She craved Clay. What woman in her right mind wouldn't? But she knew that she'd never love him, not like she'd loved Paul. And Clay deserved better than that, even if he wouldn't accept it. If she let this go on, he'd be hurt. Cordelia would be hurt. *And so would I. I already am.*

*Because now I have to send him away, again.* And it was going to hurt even worse the second time around. *So do it. Just get it over with.*

Stevie's resolve kicked into gear, fury sending her pulse pounding. *Izzy, I am going to fucking murder you.* She took off for the stairs at a run, ignoring the searing pain in her leg along with Emma's startled shrieks and JD's panicked shouts.

*Saturday, March 15, 6.15 P.M.*

'I had a really nice time, Mr Maynard. Thank you.'

Clay looked down at Stevie's daughter, taking one last moment to hoard the smile on her face. It would be the last time he'd see it. Stevie wanted to protect her child from getting attached to a man who'd have no place in their lives. He understood her wish and he'd honor it. But it hurt. He was surprised at just how much it hurt.

He liked Cordelia Mazzetti. She was cute and funny and made him wish again and again that Stevie felt about him the way he felt about her. That Cordelia looked up at him with a combination of gratitude, affection, and awe . . . It made it even harder to walk away. He could be a father to this child. He could.

But he wasn't going to be. Swallowing hard, he returned her smile. 'You're welcome. Let me get that,' he added when Cordelia reached for the pink Tinkerbell bag that held her ballet gear. She'd wanted to change into her leotard and slippers as she did every Saturday afternoon before coming home, but he wouldn't allow it. Cordelia needed to come clean with her mother about the horse therapy, so she still wore the scuffed boots Izzy had bought used off eBay with money she didn't have to spare. Because she loved her niece.

Izzy's heart was in the right place. But Stevie didn't deserve to be lied to.

*Stevie. She's there. In the house.* Clay's need to see her again bordered on desperation. But he dreaded it at the same time. Dreaded the pain of looking at her face. Of seeing what he'd wanted for so long standing right in front of him. And not being able to touch. To have.

He dreaded how much it would hurt when he drove away. Again.

*This isn't about you,* he reminded himself. This was about what was best for Cordelia. *But when does it get to be about me?* Right about now, it was looking like never. He cleared his throat harshly. 'Don't forget your flowers,' he said to Cordelia.

'I've got 'em.' She held up the bouquet of rosebuds she'd chosen. 'She likes flowers. I hope it helps her be not so mad with me.'

Clay shouldered the pink bag covered with fairies and steeled his spine. 'I think she'll be angrier with me. I'll try to smooth things over.'

They'd taken two steps when the front door flew open. Stevie stumbled down the front steps, clutching the railing with one hand and a glitter-covered cane in the other. She righted herself when her feet hit the ground, stalking toward them, undeterred by her uneven stride.

She was furious. Beautiful and furious. Just like the first time he'd seen her. Clay's mouth watered and he had to grit his teeth and clench his fists to keep from reaching out and grabbing her. Because she'd hate that. Because once he held her, he'd . . . *God*. He'd kiss her until she couldn't breathe. Until neither of them could breathe.

She'd like it. She'd liked his kiss before. That one time he'd touched his lips to hers. But she'd hated that she'd liked it. Hated that she'd wanted it. That she'd wanted him.

Part of him didn't care that she hadn't wanted to want him. That part wanted to make her *see*, make her *know*. *Make her beg*.

But he couldn't. Wouldn't. Whatever her reasons, Stevie had told him no. So he'd back away. No matter how much it hurt. *This . . . this was going to hurt like a goddamn bitch.*

Stevie came to a stop midway between his truck and her house. Her chest was rising and falling with the breaths she took, a combination of exertion and anger.

Cordelia slowly approached, coming around the front of his truck, the bouquet of rosebuds clutched behind her back. Her little hand trembled and Clay's heart cracked.

'Stevie, it's not her fault—' he began, but she cut him off, her hand slicing the air.

'Go to your room, Cordelia. Apparently I have to explain things to Mr Maynard. Again.'

Clay flinched. This was going to hurt even worse than he'd anticipated.

Cordelia paled. Nodded. Then brought the flowers from behind her back. 'They're for you,' she whispered. 'I'm sorry, Mama. I shouldn't have lied to you. I just wanted to see the horses.'

Stevie looked at the flowers as if she'd never seen any before. Like she was having trouble figuring out what they were. She started to reach for the bouquet, but wrapped her arms around Cordelia in a hard hug instead, the flowers crushed between them.

Clay looked away, the sight making his chest ache. As he let out a long breath, he saw the car approach. A normal car. A red Chevy Impala, about five years old. Going about twenty-five on a residential street. Nothing special. But the car slowed and the hairs on the back of Clay's neck lifted. The seconds began to tick in his mind, each louder than the one before.

*Tick.* The driver was wearing a ski cap.

*Tick.* And was sliding an arm out of the window to lie flat against the car door.

*Tick.* The arm raised, a gloved hand holding a pistol.

Clay lunged, going airborne before tackling Stevie and her daughter, knocking them to the ground. With his left arm he pulled them to his body, hoping to take the brunt of the fall on his shoulder while his right hand whipped his gun from its holster.

He heard the cracking of wood. A shrill scream from the front porch. A terrified cry beneath him. *Cordelia.*

*Don't be afraid, baby. I've got you.*

But before he could push the words from his throat, the air was slammed from his lungs, his body propelled forward. Two strikes in rapid succession. Two shots.

Clay hunched his back as the Kevlar he never left home without absorbed the force of the bullets. Raising his arm, he centered the driver of the red Chevy in his sights and fired a single shot. He thought he saw the driver's arm flinch, but he ducked his head again at the sound of bullets pinging off metal and glass shattering.

The guy was shooting at his truck. *Alec's in there.* Praying that Alec had the time to hide, Clay curled into a ball, protecting the two beneath him first.

Curses came from the front porch, then large feet ran past his head, toward the street. The car engine revved. Tires squealed. The shooter was escaping. *Goddammit.*

Clay stayed where he was, counting the heartbeats pounding in his head. He could hear Cordelia breathing in uneven, hitching gulps. Stevie had gone very still against him. Her arms still banded around her daughter's body, but he couldn't hear her breathing. He could feel it though, shallow little pants against his throat.

A warm body knelt beside him. 'They're gone,' a man said. 'Anybody hit?'

Clay pushed himself to his hands and knees, hanging over Stevie and the child she clutched to her chest. Her dark eyes were wide as they met his. Wide, but sharp. And curiously unsurprised. 'Are you all right?' he rasped. His lungs had yet to refill.

'I think so.' Stevie glanced up to the man beside them. 'Clay was hit. Twice.'

Clay looked up to see JD Fitzpatrick evaluating them all through narrowed eyes. 'Can you stand?' JD asked, already reaching to pull him to his feet.

'Yes.' Rising, Clay saw the mess the fucker had made of his truck. Every window was shattered and holes riddled the doors. Alec was nowhere to be seen. '*Alec!*'

'I'm okay.' Alec's voice came back shaky. But alive. He crawled around the front of the truck and Clay had to lock his knees to keep them from buckling. *God.* 'I was right behind you,' Alec said. 'I dropped when you jumped.'

*If he'd been in the truck he'd have been killed.* Clay shook the thought out of his head. Alec hadn't been in the truck. He was okay. Everyone was okay. 'Get in the house. Don't stop to check on me.' Clay crouched down, took Cordelia into his arms, keeping his gun in his hand. *Just in case the shooter comes back.* 'Get Stevie in the house,' he said to JD, then beelined for the front door, looking over his shoulder to make sure JD and Stevie were following. Just turning to glance behind him hurt like a bitch.

Kevlar might have saved his life a time or two or three, but the shots still hurt. He'd be bruised and sore for days. He looked down at the little girl in his arms. She stared up at him, her eyes unseeing, her teeth chattering.

The flowers were crushed into her jacket.

Undiluted rage boiled up inside him, but he kept it far enough away from his eyes that he didn't frighten her further. JD was supporting Stevie's weight as she hobbled, but as Clay carried Cordelia through the door, JD picked Stevie up and slung her over his shoulder in a fireman's carry and ran the rest of the way in, slamming the door behind them.

Alec sat with his back to the wall, knees to his chest. Alert. Unhurt.

A small, blonde woman Clay had never seen before sat next to Alec, clutching a phone to her ear. She was talking to the 911 operator. Her voice was calm but her face was paper white and she pressed the heel of her other hand to her breastbone. Her shirt was bloody.

'Are you hit?' Clay demanded and she shook her head.

'It's from earlier,' JD said wearily. 'This is Stevie's second shooting today. Her third since yesterday.'

'Her third—' Clay nearly stumbled, but he kept himself upright. Kept Cordelia safe in his arms. 'What the hell, JD?'

'You'll have to ask Stevie. She knows better than everyone else.' JD said the words bitterly as he laid Stevie on the sofa.

She immediately sat up and reached for her daughter.

Pain flashed in her dark eyes and she hunched her left shoulder, but her arm stayed outstretched, waiting.

It was then that Clay saw the blood seeping through the sleeve of her Baltimore PD T-shirt. A white bandage peeked out from below the sleeve. Three shots in two days. She'd been hit.

'Give her to me. Please,' she added hoarsely.

Clay settled Cordelia in her arms and stepped back. 'Blankets?'

'Upstairs,' Stevie whispered. 'Hall closet.'

JD grabbed Clay's arm. 'I'll get them. You sit down. You look like shit.'

'Cops'll be here in less than three minutes,' the blonde said.

Holstering his gun, Clay sat down on the other end of the sofa. His lungs were beginning to function again. He drew a deep breath, testing his limits, then winced. Lungs worked, ribs didn't. He drew a few shallower breaths, then turned his eyes on Stevie.

Her eyes clenched shut, she rocked her daughter in small movements he wasn't sure she was aware of. Her lips moved soundlessly, all the color leached from her face. He'd seen her paler – the day she'd nearly bled out in his arms on the courthouse steps. But not much paler.

He focused on her mouth, on the words her lips formed. *I'm sorry*, she was saying. Over and over as she rocked.

One shooting yesterday. Two more today. Today, the anniversary of her husband's murder.

It seemed like too much coincidence. Clay had never believed in coincidence.

'Stevie,' he said softly, not wanting to distress Cordelia who now mewled pitifully, her face pressed against her mother's shoulder.

Stevie met his eyes over Cordelia's head. She no longer looked terrified. She looked haunted. Guilty.

'What the *hell* is going on here?'

# Chapter Five

Stevie opened her mouth, but no words came out. Clay was staring at her angrily, his eyes hard, his jaw clenched. He breathed shallowly. But at least he breathed.

He'd taken two bullets. *For me.* She pulled Cordelia closer to her body. *For us.*

'I . . . I c-ca—' She choked on the words, shaking her head. Rocking her daughter.

Clay's expression softened, anger becoming worry. Keeping his head away from the window, he slid off the sofa to kneel in front of her. 'Are you all right?' he murmured.

She managed a nod.

He hesitated, then ran his finger under the sleeve of her shirt, lifting it to expose the bandage the ER doctor had applied, what seemed like a lifetime ago. 'You're bleeding. How bad was it?'

'She had five stitches,' Emma said from against the wall. 'The ER doctor wanted to keep her overnight for observation, but she refused.'

Clay nodded, keeping eye contact with Stevie. 'A five-stitch wound isn't bad at all.' He brushed gentle fingers across Cordelia's hair. 'Did you hear that, Cordelia? Five stitches is practically nothing. Your mom is okay. Give me a little nod if you hear me.'

Cordelia kept her face pressed into Stevie's shoulder, but she nodded once.

'Good, honey,' Clay said, his voice soothing. 'That's good. Are you hurt anywhere, Cordelia? I know I'm heavy. I need to know if I squashed you.'

Cordelia shook her head and the constriction in Stevie's throat loosened.

'Good. I'm glad.' He stroked Cordelia's hair again. 'Squashing you would have been bad.'

Cordelia turned her face a fraction. 'My flowers,' she whispered. 'They got squashed.'

'We'll get more,' Clay murmured. 'Your mom knows you got them for her and that's the important thing.' He lifted his eyes to Stevie's once again. 'Are you hurt anywhere else?'

She hurt all over, but didn't know if any of the aches were new or not. 'I don't think so.'

'All right.' He looked over his shoulder, wincing with the movement. 'I don't think we've met,' he said to Emma. 'I'm Clay Maynard. That's my assistant, Alec Vaughn.'

'I'm Emma, a friend of Stevie's. You look like you hurt your shoulder. I'll get you ice.'

Alec came to his feet. 'No, I'll do it. I'll check the lock on the back door while I'm at it. No good in hunkering down here if anyone can just waltz in.' He went to the kitchen as JD came down the stairs, a stack of blankets in his arms.

'I watched the street for a minute,' JD said. 'I didn't see the red Chevy, but I did call in the description of the car, the driver as much as I could see, and the gu—'

Clay coughed loudly. 'Skittles,' he said firmly. 'Rainbows and flowers.'

89

Stevie frowned, but Cordelia seemed to know exactly what he was talking about.

'And puppies,' her daughter whispered, still hiding her face. 'I like puppies.'

'Well, who doesn't?' Clay asked pragmatically.

Cordelia pivoted her forehead on Stevie's shoulder to look at Clay. 'Mom says they drool.'

Stevie winced at the not-so-skillfully veiled criticism, but Clay just smiled. 'Naw,' he said. 'Puppies don't drool. Puppies chew. They'll destroy all of your shoes, but only one of each pair. They are diabolical. Now, big dogs drool. Big slobbery strings of drool that mess up your clothes. And let's not even talk about their sneezes.' He brushed the hair off Cordelia's cheek, serious again. 'You think of puppies, Cordelia. Cute little shoe-chewing puppies. Promise me.'

'I promise,' she whispered fiercely.

'Good girl.' He took one of the blankets from JD's stack and tucked it around the two of them, then sat back on his heels. 'When will the police be here?'

'They are here,' Emma said, hanging up the phone. 'The 911 operator said so.'

Alec appeared around the corner with several bags of frozen peas. 'I saw them driving up.'

'They're checking out the front yard and putting up roadblocks for the red car,' JD said. 'I told them we had things more or less under control in here. They'll be knocking in a few minutes to take statements. When they give the all clear, the EMTs will check you out, Clay.'

'I'm okay. But apparently hungry for peas,' he added with a frown.

'I didn't see any bags for ice,' Alec said, 'but frozen peas work just as well. Let's get your coat off.' He put the frozen vegetables on the floor and helped Clay remove his leather jacket, revealing a lavender oxford shirt.

On a lot of men a lavender shirt might have looked less than masculine. On Clay . . . Stevie wasn't sure the man could look anything other than completely masculine. He'd managed it even while holding her little girl's pink Tinkerbell ballet bag, which he'd been doing when she'd flown out of the house.

*Like an idiot.* She closed her eyes. *I couldn't have made myself a more accessible target if I'd painted SHOOT ME on my back.* And because of that Clay had been the one shot in the back. *He must have been wearing Kevlar and thank God for that. No more blood on my hands, please.*

'I'm not sure you can salvage the jacket, Clay,' Alec said.

She opened her eyes to see Alec poking two fingers through bullet holes in the leather.

'Sure I can.' Clay unbuttoned his shirt slowly, his movements stiff. 'That jacket's been patched ten times since I got it in '95.' He grimaced when he tried shrugging out of the shirt.

'Good God. Don't *any* of you know how to ask for help?' Emma demanded. She took over the task of removing Clay's shirt and . . .

*Hell.* The sight of her friend's small hands removing Clay's shirt made Stevie's stomach churn. Which was ludicrous on every level. Emma was happily married. And Clay . . . *Isn't mine. He might have been, but I sent him away.* For his own good. *I did it for his own good.*

Her thoughts splintered when his face contorted in pain. Alec and Emma were peeling the Kevlar off Clay's back. Alec's wince told her it was bad.

Cordelia shifted and Stevie knew she was watching. Clay must have noticed too, because he gave Cordelia a brisk nod.

'This is temporary,' he said. 'It's just a bad bruise. I'm not even bleeding, right, Alec?'

'That's true.' Alec lifted the Kevlar vest, so the inside was visible. 'See, Cordy? Not even a pinprick of blood.' He handed the vest to JD and grabbed a bag of frozen peas in each hand. 'Ice for twenty, then off. Ready?' He didn't wait for an affirmative answer before setting a bag on each of Clay's shoulders.

Clay flinched, his heavy pecs flexing. 'Yeah,' he said dryly. 'I'm ready.'

'The peas conform to the injured area,' Alec said. 'Better contact than with an ice bag.'

'He's right,' Emma said. 'I keep a few bags in my freezer for post-crying-jag face repair.'

Clay gave her a what-the-hell look. 'You cry a lot?'

'Oh no, not me. My daughter was, until recently, a teenager. Dramatic breakups, a zit on prom night, a back-stabbing friend? A bag of peas will shrink puffy eyes to normal in a snap.'

'I am *so* glad we had a boy,' JD muttered. He checked his phone screen. 'Text from Hyatt. He wants to take our statements. Can we do that in the kitchen, Stevie?'

'Of course.' Stevie shifted, intending to stand, but Cordelia wrapped her arms around her neck and held on. She was trembling again. 'Cordy, baby, I need to talk to my boss. I won't leave the house. Okay?' She tried to pry her daughter's arms from her neck, but Cordelia held on, whimpering. Stevie almost asked Clay to help, then remembered why she couldn't.

The man was here, in her house. And after not even fifteen minutes, it was as if he belonged. *But he doesn't. He can't. He doesn't belong here.*

'Emma?' Stevie said softly. 'I could use a hand.'

Emma sat on the sofa. 'Come sit with me, Cordelia.

We'll sit right here, so you can see your mom at the kitchen table.' Cordelia made herself limp as Stevie transferred her to Emma's lap. 'I have something for you, from my boys. When we're by ourselves, I'll give it to you.'

Cordelia's brows lifted. 'Why by ourselves?'

Emma kissed the top of her head. 'Because if your mom sees it, she'll eat every last bit.'

'I'm so glad you're here,' Stevie murmured and Emma smiled.

'Do what you need to do, Stevie. Cordy and I will be fine.'

The doorbell rang as JD pulled Stevie to her feet. Alec opened the door as Stevie held JD's arm to steady herself, feeling Clay's eyes on her all the while. 'Where's my cane?' she asked.

'Right here.' Hyatt came into the room, her sparkly cane in his hand. 'You dropped it on the ground outside.' He gave Clay a brief visual inspection, narrowing his eyes at the bags of peas. With a shake of his head, he turned to JD and Stevie. 'I've posted officers at the front and back while we process the crime scene. You need to tell me what in the hell happened here.'

*Saturday, March 15, 6.25 P.M.*

*Son of a bitch.* Henderson drove madly through the sedate little neighborhood, one hand on the steering wheel. The other hand was numb. *My whole arm is numb. Sonofabitch got me.*

Blood seeped from the shoulder wound and for an instant, the road blurred. *Just hold on.*

Ordered neighborhoods became open fields, then finally woods. Henderson heaved a sigh of relief when the turnoff for the side road came into view. Parked among the trees was the white rental Camry. *Exactly where I left it.*

Pulling off the road, Henderson stumbled out of the stolen red Chevy, its theft having been made so much easier by the rural owner hanging the keys from a peg just inside an unlocked kitchen door. *Gotta love the countryside. Nobody locks their doors.*

Tying a tourniquet around the wound was no small chore, but was finally accomplished, leaving Henderson breathing hard. But stable. *And not bleeding all over everything.*

The next question was, what to do with the red Chevy? Blood had seeped into the vinyl seat. *My blood.* But it could be worse.

Robinette had ensured that his team filed the paperwork to have their DNA wiped from the military's database when they were discharged and the cops had nothing in theirs, either.

*Because I've been careful. Never left blood or hair behind on a job before. Never got close enough to the victim for the cops to find anything even if I did.* Distance was a sniper's best friend. But apparently not today. *Get rid of the blood.* Just because the cops couldn't match it to anything in their precious databases was no reason to give them evidence to use later.

Teeth gritted against the pain, Henderson cut the seat away from its frame and tossed it into the trunk of the Camry, doused the grass around the Chevy with gasoline and tossed a match.

By the time the Camry was on the main road, the flames reached higher than the trees. Nothing would be left of the Chevy. But it had been close. Way too close.

Finally a safe distance away, Henderson's temper flared. Who the *fuck* had that guy been back there? That the guy had managed to wriggle free on the Parkway had been bad enough, but throwing himself over Mazzetti and the kid? Much worse. And shooting like a motherfucking Army Ranger? *He shot better than I did.* It was humiliating.

Unless Henderson had been extraordinarily lucky, Detective Stevie Mazzetti still breathed. *Goddamn that woman.* She had more lives than a frickin' cat. Robinette would be unhappy.

A glance at the bottle in the cup holder revealed it to be empty, all the vodka gone. Henderson curled trembling fingers around the steering wheel and held on tight. *Just get yourself home. You can relax when you get home.*


*Saturday, March 15, 6.30 P.M.*

Stevie took a last look over her shoulder toward the living room before sitting at the kitchen table with the others. Cordelia was curled up on Emma's lap, head on her friend's shoulder.

'Stevie?' Hyatt rumbled. 'I need you with me. Now. You can see to your daughter later.'

'I know.' Stevie carefully sat at the head of the table between her boss and her partner, every muscle in her body screaming for a hot tub.

Clay sat across from her, elbows on the table, head down, hunched over, still balancing the bags of peas on his shoulders. Alec sat at his side, casting worried looks at his back.

'Mr Maynard,' Hyatt began, 'you seem to have a habit of appearing at Detective Mazzetti's side at uniquely tense moments.'

Clay spared him a short glance. 'Ain't that the goddamn truth.'

KAREN ROSE

Hyatt's lips twitched, just a hair. 'So, tell me how you came to be in Detective Mazzetti's front yard this evening. With a gun.'

Stevie leaned forward. 'I'd like to know that, too. Not that I'm not grateful, of course. I'd also like to know where my sister is. I've been trying to contact her all afternoon.'

Clay's face had become expressionless, once again reminding her of hewn rock. He looked at Hyatt. 'Izzy got a last minute wedding job. I told her I'd bring Cordelia home.'

A beat of silence passed. 'From?' Stevie prompted, hoping he wouldn't say 'ballet'. To her knowledge, Clay Maynard had never lied to her. *Please don't start now. Please.*

'From the ice cream shop.' He shifted his gaze to JD. 'She said you always took her out for ice cream on the day her dad died, but that you'd probably forgotten.'

JD winced. 'She's right. I always take her to get ice cream. And I did forget.'

Stevie patted JD's hand. 'She understands about the baby.'

'She does,' Clay confirmed. 'She said you weren't getting any sleep and that she'd remind you in a few weeks. And maybe you'd feel so bad you'd get her a sundae instead of just a cone.'

'Wow, she's wised up young,' JD murmured.

'Yeah, she did,' Clay said in a sad way that indicated he spoke of more than ice cream. 'Before the ice cream shop we stopped at a florist. I was buying flowers and she asked if she could get some for her mother. So that she wouldn't be so mad at her.'

Stevie frowned, remembering the last few seconds before Clay had tackled them to the ground. Before the bullets started flying. *I'm sorry, Mama. I just wanted to see the*

96

*horses*. Stevie spun in her chair, squinting to see Cordelia's feet. 'She's wearing boots. Why?'

'Because Izzy's been taking her to Daphne's to ride the horses,' Clay said quietly.

'Equine therapy,' Alec added. 'Izzy thinks it's better for Cordelia than a counselor.'

'I see.' Stevie told herself that Izzy likely meant well. Izzy always meant well. 'Do you know how long this has been going on?'

'For a few months.' Clay addressed that answer and those that followed to Hyatt. 'I went to the farm to work on an upgrade for Daphne's security system. Cordelia and Izzy were there.'

'Why does Daphne need a security system on the farm?' Hyatt asked.

'For her new equine therapy program,' Clay told him. 'In a month she'll have kids, therapists, horse trainers, and God knows who else on that farm. I keep it safe.'

And it was a responsibility he clearly took very seriously, Stevie thought. 'So Izzy got called to a wedding job and you volunteered to bring Cordelia home?'

Clay's response was a brief nod, again to Hyatt. *Not to me.*

'How did you know to shield them from the shooter?' Hyatt asked.

'Instinct, I guess,' Clay said. 'I saw the red car, saw the driver was wearing a ski mask and it's not that cold today. I'd started moving, I think, before I saw the gun.'

*Skittles, rainbows, flowers, and shoe-chewing puppies,* Stevie thought. He and Cordelia had obviously had some kind of conversation about Cordelia's fear of guns and it seemed to have struck a chord with her daughter.

'Damn good instincts,' JD said gruffly. 'Good shooting, too.'

'JD said you fired once on the red car.' Hyatt frowned. 'Do you think you hit the shooter?'

Clay lifted a shoulder in a shrug that sent a bag of peas sliding from his shoulder to the table. 'I don't know. I thought I saw him flinch, but it happened too fast.'

'Exactly,' Hyatt said, still frowning. 'You seemed remarkably prepared. Like you expected trouble. Why?'

Alec opened his mouth to protest, but Clay waved him silent. 'It's fair, Alec. I fired a weapon. I expected the question.' He met Hyatt's eyes. 'I was already pretty hyped up and aware, so it made me more likely to notice the car and to take appropriate action.'

'Hyped up and aware of what?' Hyatt asked.

'We had a tail on our way here. We lost the car and took a longer route. It happens when you're in security. Potential clients want to see how good you really are and put you to the test. Or sometimes you just piss people off. Depending on who they are I might confront them, but we had the child in the truck so we got the license plate and figured we'd check it out later.'

'It wasn't the red car?' JD asked.

'No, it was white.'

Stevie jerked back as if she'd been shocked by a live wire. 'White what?'

Clay looked at her now, through narrowed eyes. 'A white Camry. Why?'

*Breathe.* She had to force the air from her lungs. 'Oh God.'

JD had gone still. 'You say you got the license?'

Clay nodded, then glanced at Alec. 'Give it to them.'

'It was a rental,' Alec said and rattled off the license plate number.

JD pushed to his feet, dialing his cell as he stepped away from the table.

'What's going on here?' Clay demanded. 'And don't tell

me it's none of my business. The holes in my best jacket say otherwise.'

Hyatt leaned in, lowering his voice because JD was relaying the plate number to dispatch. 'The driver of a white Camry shot at Detective Mazzetti yesterday and fled the scene.'

Clay's eyes shot to Stevie's face, but he said nothing.

JD returned to the table. 'Thanks, Alec. We hadn't gotten a plate. Yesterday or today.'

Stevie shook her head hard. 'Today? Wait. Was the car there, today? At Harbor House?'

JD nodded. 'We pulled the city's camera feed. Saw a white Camry on the street around the time you entered the restaurant. Traffic was bumper-to-bumper at two o'clock when you met Emma, and the Camry's plate was hidden by the car behind it. None of the cameras were angled to get a clear shot of the plate before the shooting. After, none of the cameras picked it up at all.'

Clay pulled the other bag of peas from his shoulder and tossed it to the table, rolling his shoulder. 'So you're saying the same guy has tried to kill Detective Mazzetti three times?' he asked, looking from JD to Hyatt, his voice very quiet.

'Yes,' JD said grimly.

For a moment there was silence around the table.

'But the white Camry wasn't tailing Detective Mazzetti during the last few hours,' Clay said, his voice dropping to a harsh whisper. 'It was tailing Cordelia, knowing eventually the two of them would be together.'

Stevie felt the blood drain from her face all over again as the events in the front yard spun through her mind. 'He would have killed her, too.' Then the significance of his words began to sink in. 'How did he know Cordelia was with you?'

He finally looked at her, really looked at her, and she saw the fear in his eyes. *Fear for my child. And for me.* But when he spoke, it was with a calm control that steadied her in turn.

'He obviously already knew where you lived. He did not follow me here. I'd lost him on the Parkway. Assuming this guy is the same one who's been after you, he must have ditched the Camry and changed to the red Chevy and come straight here. He could have been here earlier today and followed Izzy out to the farm.'

Stevie made herself think so that the terror didn't paralyze her. 'Where is Daphne's farm?'

'Hunt Valley,' Clay said.

Stevie nodded. 'The timing could work. Izzy and Cordelia left before I did. There would have been time to get to Hunt Valley, then into the city by two o'clock. After the shooting, there were so many emergency vehicles, then we were in the ER . . . It would make sense for the shooter to hang back, knowing I'd be with Cordelia at some point. But why not come straight here after the restaurant if he knew where I lived? Why follow you?'

Clay closed his eyes, his face grown pale under his winter tan. 'You would have been alert to any danger to yourself by that point. But if you came out to meet Cordelia when she arrived home, you'd be vulnerable.'

'But I ran outside because you were with her,' Stevie said, not caring that JD and Hyatt looked on. Clay looked absolutely ill and she needed to understand what he was thinking. 'How could he have known I'd do that?'

Clay opened his eyes, held hers. She couldn't have looked away if she'd wanted to. 'He didn't have to know, Stevie. Not if he intended to force you to run outside.'

And then she understood. *Oh my God. Oh my God.* A shaky breath rattled from her lungs as she tried to breathe.

Tried to keep from passing out. 'He would have shot her in the yard and I would have run to her. He was going to use my baby as bait.'

*Saturday, March 15, 6.50 P.M.*

*She finally understands.* Still, Clay wished he hadn't put that look of terror on her face.

*You didn't terrify her. The bastard who tried to kill her and her daughter did.* But logic was worth less than shit when the woman he'd never stopped wanting looked like she'd been slapped.

But her eyes never left his. Not even when her lieutenant covered her hand with his own.

'We won't let anything happen to Cordelia,' Hyatt said. 'But you have to promise to stop investigating. You're on disability. You're supposed to be recovering. Do I have your word?'

She nodded dully, her gaze still pinned to Clay's face. 'Yes. Of course.'

On the other side of her, JD sighed wearily. 'You'll go to the safe house now?'

Her nod was robotic. 'Yes, of course. I'll just pack a few of our things.'

'You sit here. I'll have one of the female uniforms do it for you.' Hyatt rose to give the order, then paused in the doorway. 'Thank you, Mr Maynard. I'm glad you always seem to be around at uniquely stressful times. Have you considered returning to the police department?'

Clay glanced at him, mostly out of respect, before returning his gaze to Stevie. 'You're welcome, Lieutenant. And no, sir. Not even once.'

Hyatt's smile was rueful. 'Didn't think so. JD, you'll

accompany Stevie to the safe house?'

'Yes, sir,' JD said. When Hyatt was gone, JD leaned closer. 'Where are you going, really?'

'To a safe place. But not a safe house,' she murmured, so softly that Clay barely heard her.

'Why?' JD whispered.

'Because I haven't found them all,' she said in that same soundless tone.

Clay took the chair Hyatt had vacated. With a tilt of his head he sent Alec to stand watch over Cordelia, who'd curled around Emma like a vine. 'Find all of what?' Clay asked.

'Silas's victims. I've been investigating his old cases and found four new instances where he framed innocent men for crimes they didn't commit. Four arrests were made this week.'

Clay frowned. 'Why are you investigating his old cases? I thought you all had a list, left by that lawyer he was working for. Lippman. I thought BPD knew all the cases Lippman fixed and all the cops involved.'

'No, not all. The list wasn't complete. When I started to dig into Silas's old cases, I found inconsistencies. Cases that Lippman paid him to fix, but that he couldn't have fixed alone because he was with me at the time. On some of them he could have been assisted by known dirty cops, but not all. I think there are a few dirty cops who didn't make Lippman's list.'

She looked away and Clay realized she'd answered all his questions but one – why the hell she was re-investigating her old partner's cases to begin with. He'd find out. Later.

JD looked worn out. 'Did you tell IA?'

'Yes, I did. I told Hyatt as soon as I'd figured out what I was seeing. That was on Monday and he and I went to see

IA yesterday morning. The attacks started on Tuesday. It's not hard to connect the dots. There's a leak somewhere in the department. JD, I know I can trust you. Hyatt, too. But I'm not sure I trust the cops you two would have to trust to keep a safe house safe.'

'So, one more time,' JD said, 'where are you going?'

'I don't know. But I'm not hiding in your house, JD.' She looked at her partner resolutely. 'I'm not putting Lucy and the baby in danger, too. And don't tell me you weren't just worrying about that. Whoever wants me –' she looked over her shoulder at Cordelia in the living room, then mouthed the next word '– *dead*, obviously isn't concerned with the safety of bystanders.' She pressed her fingertips to lips that suddenly trembled. 'Those two women in the restaurant died today and Cordelia might have, too. I don't want anyone else's blood on my hands.'

Clay remembered the blood on Emma's blouse. 'What happened at the restaurant?'

JD's brows went up. 'You haven't heard it on the news?'

'No. I kept the radio off in the truck. Cordelia was asleep in the backseat. What happened?'

'Sniper,' JD said. 'Positioned on the roof of the building across the street. He shot through the window wounding Stevie and killing a woman. He shot again, killing a second woman.'

Clay's heart began to pound again, not so fast this time, but hard. So hard it hurt. She'd come so close to dying today. How many bullets had she dodged? He'd held her back in December, watched her blood spill on the pavement. He couldn't handle it a second time.

He'd come so close to losing her, again. *Except she's not yours to lose.*

The realization hit him like a bat upside the head. *The hell she's not.* He'd been put in her path too many times at 'uniquely tense moments'. Call it Fate, the universe, elves . . . Maybe even God? Although it didn't really matter who or why. Or even how.

*Because she is mine and I will fight to keep her.* But how he'd keep her was the real question. Definitely he'd keep her alive. As for keeping her by his side? *Yeah. That, too.*

'Their blood isn't on your hands, Stevie,' JD was saying soberly. 'You didn't kill them.'

'I know. But now that I know he's out there and how determined he is, the blame for anyone he hurts because of their proximity to me – emotional or physical – will be on me. Don't worry, JD. I'll find a place to go that doesn't put anyone I care about in danger. That includes you.'

JD opened his mouth to argue and she held up her hand to stop him. 'Do you think I'd let Lucy go through what I went through eight years ago?' she demanded quietly. 'Your son will have a father. You . . .' Her voice broke and she swallowed hard. 'You will have a son.'

'You can't just disappear,' JD murmured. 'I need to know you're safe. If I don't know where you are, I at least need to know who you're with so I can contact you if I need to.'

The pounding Clay had heard in his head most of this day suddenly quieted. 'With me,' he said. 'She's coming with me. I can keep her and Cordelia safe while we find out who's shooting at them.'

Eyes wide, JD looked at Clay, then at Stevie, whose eyes were even wider. The cop pushed away from the table. 'I think that's my cue to leave. You got a gym bag in your truck, Clay? I can get you a change of clothes. If not, I've got a spare T-shirt you can borrow.'

'Yeah, I have a gym bag with some clothes in the backseat. Thanks, JD.'

And then he and Stevie were alone. He waited for her to speak. He didn't have to wait long.

'I appreciate the offer, Clay, but I can't accept.'

'Why?'

She closed her eyes. 'I can't do this today.'

'You don't have a choice,' he said sharply, making her eyes jerk up to meet his. 'You and your daughter almost died today. You say you don't want to endanger anyone you care about, so where would you go? To your parents? To Grayson and Paige? Would you put them in danger?'

Her lips thinned mutinously. 'Grayson's house has an alarm system. And a big dog.'

Clay nearly smiled. Stevie hated dogs, but she wasn't above using Paige's Rottweiler to win a point. Except this wasn't a game. 'So you plan to keep your daughter a prisoner in Grayson's house until you catch this guy? What's to stop him from targeting anyone coming into and out of Grayson's place to draw you out? It's been done before today.'

She flinched and he knew he'd struck an exposed nerve. 'That was a low blow, Clay.'

Because it had been her old partner Silas who had done that very thing the year before when Grayson and Paige had been his targets. Silas had shot JD in Grayson's front yard in order to draw Grayson outside. Stevie had chased the shooter – and come face to face with Silas.

She'd figured out earlier that same morning that the man she'd trusted had been dirty, but Clay didn't think she'd believed it until Silas pointed a gun at her as he made his getaway.

Clay had followed Stevie that day, to cover her back, arriving as Silas drove away. He'd watched as she called in the description and license plate on the car Silas had been driving, her voice steady and clear even though tears ran down her face.

It had broken Clay's heart to see. He'd almost taken her into his arms. He'd had the feeling she wouldn't have minded. Then. But later she would have cut him off. Just as she had from her hospital bed three months ago.

He'd accepted her rejection. He'd been the nice guy. Which didn't seem to have worked all that well for him. So dealing her a low blow? He hated doing it, but . . . hell. *Whatever it takes.*

'That it's a low blow doesn't make it less relevant. It's a well-worn tactic because it works.'

She crossed her arms over her chest, desperation in the gesture. 'I can take care of my daughter.'

'I know you can.' *But who will take care of you?* he wanted to ask. Wisely he refrained. 'But what about when you go out to investigate? Who will watch your daughter then? And don't even consider telling me you're backing away from this just because your boss asked you to. You may not like me, Stevie, but please don't insult my intelligence.'

Her eyes flickered wildly for a few seconds. 'I'd never do that,' she whispered.

'At least you give me that much,' he muttered. 'You don't want to endanger anyone you care about, right? Then I should be the perfect choice. I have no kids to protect, no wife, no one.'

Her eyes closed, sending a tear sliding down her cheek. It was all he could do not to wipe it away, to take her in his arms and tell her everything would be all right.

'Why?' she whispered hoarsely. 'Why are you so damned determined to save me?'

He bit back the answer that burned his tongue. He'd told her once. He didn't plan to tell her again until he was sure her response would be the one he wanted to hear. *I'm a patient man*, he told himself. *I can wait.*

'Because your daughter dreams at night,' he said instead. 'She's terrified to sleep.'

'She dreams of Silas,' Stevie said, her eyes still closed. 'He held her at gunpoint.'

'And for that alone I'd kill him if he weren't already dead. But that's not what she's been dreaming about lately. She dreams about you, Stevie. Getting shot on the courthouse steps. She saw it. On TV. She saw you fall down. In her dreams you never get back up.'

Her eyes flew open, filled with new horror. And tears. 'She *saw* that? Oh my God. I didn't know. I thought we'd kept her from it.'

'Hard to do. It was all over the TV. Cordelia said that since Izzy found out she'd seen it, she's only let her watch DVDs.' He let her cry for a minute that seemed like a lifetime. 'Stevie, listen to me. Today, your daughter's nightmares almost came true again. I don't intend to let that happen. I know you don't want her to get attached to me. Izzy told me so. She told me that's why you didn't want her out at Daphne's. That's why I brought Cordelia home.'

'To tell me how wrong I was?' she asked bitterly. 'Because it looks like I've pretty much fucked up everything and nearly got my daughter killed in the process.'

'No, I was going to tell you that Cordelia needs Daphne's program. That she's hurting but doesn't want to hurt you, so she won't let you see it. I was going to tell you that I respect your desire to keep her from getting attached to me, that I'd stay away from Daphne's on Saturdays.'

'I just heard a lot of "was going to". What about now?'

'I can't stand idly by and let her be hurt. If she gets attached to me in the process, so be it.'

'So *be* it? You'd let her get attached and then just walk away? You could *do* that?'

He couldn't control his flinch. 'I won't "just walk away". But if you decide that I can't see her afterward, then I won't have a choice. You're her mother. I'm just . . .' He shrugged, made himself say the words that he didn't want to believe. 'I'm little more than a stranger. I wouldn't want to let her get attached, only to have me disappear. I know how that feels. But I'd rather see her alive to hate me later, so my answer is yes. I could do that if it meant keeping her safe.'

Stevie looked away. Was quiet a long, long moment. Finally she exhaled, her shoulders slumping. 'Where would we go?'

*Yes.* 'I have a few ideas. Let's talk about it on the way.'

She still didn't look at him. 'This doesn't change what I said before. When I was in the hospital. I need you to know that. And to believe it.'

He nodded soberly. 'I understand.' And he did.

She met his eyes and he knew she'd seen right through him. 'I'm doing this for Cordelia.'

'So am I.' He started to rise, but she put her hand on his arm, so briefly he might have thought he imagined it but for the way his skin burned at the contact. And for the way she jerked her hand back, cradling it with her other hand as if she'd felt it, too.

'Wait,' she said. 'I want a promise from you.'

His brows lifted meaningfully. 'You want me to promise not to try to change your mind?'

Her cheeks flamed. 'No. I mean, yes, I want that, too, but . . .' She blew out a breath that sent her bangs dancing on her forehead. 'I want you to help me find out who's doing this.'

'I'd already planned on that.'

'I don't know which cops I can trust. Helping me could mean doing things that aren't entirely . . . aboveboard.'

He grinned. 'That's supposed to scare me away?'

Her lips twitched minutely. 'Somehow I thought that's what you'd say.'

He sobered. 'If we don't catch whoever's after you, you'll be hiding forever.'

Her eyes became sad. 'And if I walk away and take Cordelia with me when it's over?'

He found he had to swallow hard before he spoke. 'I'll survive. Until then, I've got your back.' He started to stand again and this time she didn't stop him. 'I'll go make the arrangements with JD.' He nudged a bag of peas, no longer frozen but still cold. 'You should put those on your face if you don't want Cordelia to know you've been crying.'

# Chapter Six

*Baltimore, Maryland, Saturday, March 15, 7.00 P.M.*

'He's got it bad for her,' Alec said softly.

Emma glanced away from her study of Clay and Stevie at the kitchen table to the young man sitting next to her on the sofa. 'I can see that.' She adjusted her hold on Cordelia, now asleep. 'You worry about him.'

'She broke his heart. And there he is, lining up to get it broken again.'

'He's an adult, Alec. I'm not sure there is much you'd be able to do to change his mind.'

'He does have a pretty hard head.'

'Then this should be interesting, because Stevie's head is made of solid cast iron.'

Alec's lips curved. 'You've known her a long time, then.'

'Eight years.'

He nodded. 'Since her husband died. Do you normally befriend your readers?'

She blinked at him. 'How did you know . . . ?'

'I Googled you. Your husband died in a robbery, just like Stevie's.'

'It's true. Her brother, Sorin, had emailed me about her,

asking if I'd meet her. You know how you meet someone and feel like you've known them for years? It was like that for Stevie and me. She's hardheaded, but she's also one of the most genuine people I've ever known.'

In the kitchen, Clay stood up, his face an expressionless mask. But it hadn't been. Throughout his and Stevie's conversation, a whole range of emotions had flashed across his face, from grief to anger. Intense yearning to sad resignation.

Emma looked up at Clay when he stopped in front of her. 'What's the plan?' she asked.

'Where are the cops?'

'Outside, processing the crime scene,' Alec answered. 'We've got uniforms at the front and back doors. One policewoman upstairs, packing bags for Stevie and Cordelia.'

Crouching, Clay looked up at them. 'They're coming with me,' he said quietly.

'Where?' Emma asked in the same conspiratorial tone.

'Don't want to say until we're gone.'

'Well then, make sure your vehicle's big enough for one more, because I'm going.'

He shook his head. 'You should be home, with your own kids.'

'My own kids are frolicking with their grandparents at the "Happiest Place on Earth". I'd just be in the way of their annual spoilage. I'm sticking, for a few days at least.'

Clay frowned at the sleeping Cordelia. 'I need to talk to you, out of her earshot.'

'She's asleep.'

'Maybe,' he said, scooping Cordelia into his arms with a gentleness that tugged at Emma's heart. There was something about a rugged, shirtless man holding a sleeping child to make a woman all fluttery. Why had Stevie sent this man away when she so clearly felt something for him? It had been all over her face at the restaurant in the moments before the window shattered.

Shattering lives with it. *So move, Emma. There are important things to be done.*

She stepped away from the sofa so that Clay could settle Cordelia in. He did, making sure the blanket was tucked securely around her. 'Don't leave her side,' he told Alec.

Cordelia opened her eyes, narrowing them. 'I want to know what's happening,' she said.

Clay's lips twitched. 'I thought you were faking it. When it's safe, I'll tell you what I can.'

'That's what grownups always say,' she grumbled.

'I know. But I'm not most grownups. When I can, I will. I promise. I can tell you right now that we're getting you and your mother away from this house.'

The relief in her eyes was unmistakable. 'Because the man with the gun will come back?'

'Maybe. I'm not taking any chances with your safety. Or your mother's.' He smoothed her hair away from her face. 'If there's anything you want to take, anything you can't sleep without, tell Alec. He'll make sure it's packed.'

With that he rose and motioned Emma to follow him. *Into the bathroom?* Indeed, that was where he was gesturing she should go. He shut the door behind them and motioned her to the toilet.

'This is the only room with a door on this level and there's a cop upstairs. You should sit.'

She obeyed, studying him as he studied her right back. 'What do you need to tell me?'

'The red car, the one that shot at us? The driver had

been following Alec and Cordelia and me, but in a different car. I lost him, but he changed cars and came here. He was at the restaurant, too. Since he missed Stevie then, I think he planned to shoot Cordelia, so that Stevie would come outside. He lucked out when she ran out to yell at us. She was exposed and too angry to care. Emma, I need you to listen. He was willing to hurt a child to get to Stevie.'

'I'm glad you told me to sit.' And then his implication became clear and her heart began to race, new terror crashing over her. 'You think he might go after my kids, too?'

'I think he's ruthless. Either he hates Stevie or he's paid by someone who does. If you or your kids were hurt it would kill her. Don't put any of us in that position. Please go home.'

Emma rubbed her forehead, her thoughts all a jumble. 'This has been a really shitty day.'

'Tell me about it.'

She made herself think logically. 'My kids are at Disney World with my parents and my in-laws. None of them go by "Townsend", my pen name, so it would be difficult to find them at their hotel. I'm private about my family. No photos of my kids online. They'd have to dig to find them. I think they're safer if I don't go leading crazy assassins to them, don't you agree?'

Clay seemed to consider that. 'Possibly. But do you want to take that risk? You were with Stevie this afternoon, and again tonight. He's seen you twice. You're clearly important to her.'

She narrowed her eyes. 'You are good. Now I see how you convinced her to go with you.'

His shrug was modest, but his eyes were sharp. He was much more than eye-candy, for sure.

'My first inclination is to run home as fast as my legs will carry me,' she said honestly. 'Or, a plane works, too.' That earned her a begrudging smile from the stern-faced man. 'My second, perhaps wiser, inclination is to hire private security for my family. Hopefully this will be over soon and all the kids will remember is making their grandfathers puke in the spinning teacups. Sometimes I get crazy stalkers, so I already have a security service.'

She met his gaze head-on. 'You need someone to stay with Cordelia when you're out investigating. Someone she trusts. This isn't the time to be bringing in strangers to watch her and you don't want to waste your best talent babysitting. I can do that. I can also handle a gun. I never leave my house unarmed when I'm at home.'

She lifted her brows, on a roll. 'Since your state doesn't recognize my concealed carry permit, I'm unarmed. If you don't count this.' She pulled a switchblade from her pocket, flicked it open. Watched his eyes widen. 'I've been threatened before, so I went to self-defense classes. I'm not a black belt like your partner, Paige, but I'm not afraid to fight dirty.'

He eyed her knife carefully. 'How do you know about my partner?'

'I Googled you. You're not that hard to find online. You guys haven't been low profile.'

After a moment he nodded. 'Have your security firm contact me. I'll brief them.'

'That I can do. I appreciate the help.'

'I won't keep you from your family too long, but I'm grateful to have you with Cordelia and Stevie tonight. Thank you, Emma. I mean it.'

'Um, let's just keep my going with you between us for now, okay? Stevie'll have a cow and blow our cover.' She winked at him. 'See, I learn fast.'

'I can see that.' He opened the door, then motioned her to go ahead. 'After you.'

She had a thought as she passed under his arm. 'What about Izzy?'

He grimaced. 'I forgot about her. She's photographing a wedding. She texted me that the reception would go on past midnight and they asked her to stay, but that was before all this happened. I'll let Stevie decide what to tell her.'

'It's not gonna be pretty, seeing as how Izzy lied to her. But Izzy did the crime,' she said with a shrug. 'She'll have to do the time.'

'That's exactly what I told her. I think we're going to get along fine, Dr Walker.'

She smiled up at him sweetly. 'Hurt my friend and we won't.' She turned for the stairs, his chuckle making her grin. Then her grin faded when she considered how she was going to break the news to Christopher. He'd be terrified, which was understandable. *Because so am I.*

*Saturday, March 15, 7.00 P.M.*

Robinette scowled at his reflection in the mirror on his bedroom wall. *Stevie Mazzetti is still breathing.* Henderson had failed. Not just once, but twice. Robinette couldn't remember that having happened before which made him wonder if Henderson was drinking again.

That *had* happened before, the soldier ending up in very serious trouble. Court-martial-sized trouble. Trouble Robinette had made disappear. Like magic. Or like hiding a body in the desert in the middle of the night, putting Henderson forever in his debt.

Up until today, the debt had been repaid with interest.

But today . . . Henderson's failure had made the situation far worse than it had been before. Before there'd only been the chance that Mazzetti's incessant digging would turn up a connection to Robinette. But now more people were dead. Two bodies had been removed from that restaurant this afternoon.

Robinette didn't know their names. He didn't care. But the cops would be looking for the shooter. The mayor would lean on the police commissioner until BPD turned up a reasonable suspect. It wasn't good for tourism to have innocent people shot while consuming lunch, especially in pricey restaurants on the historic registry.

The Baltimore police would leave 'no stone unturned'. So the commissioner had proclaimed to two dozen reporters at his press conference that afternoon. Pompous peacock.

Luckily a few of the commissioner's army of cops had lifestyles more extravagant than their pitiful city salaries could support. Robinette's salary supplements ensured he got information in a timely way. And that any and all trouble was swiftly contained.

*If I'd had the money eight years ago that I have now, I wouldn't be in this mess to begin with.* He would have had Mazzetti neutralized quietly. But he'd been poor and desperate.

He'd never be either of those things again.

Unfortunately, Henderson's failures had stirred a hornets' nest. Mazzetti should have been hit after she'd left the restaurant, should have been lured to some isolated place where the bullet could be retrieved from her body.

There would have been no need for the drive-by in the woman's front yard. There would be no bullet slugs on their way to the forensic lab right this minute. Two bullets in the restaurant. God only knew how many were left in the grass in Mazzetti's front yard, lodged in the frame of her house. At least two had hit the guy who'd protected her. Whoever he was.

So far, no one was saying. None of his sources knew the man's name. He wasn't a cop, of that much they were sure. All they knew was that he'd worn body armor. *Who goes around town wearing goddamn body armor?*

All those bullets were now – thanks to Henderson – evidence in a series of high-profile shootings. It would cost Robinette a tidy sum to make it disappear. If he could manage it at all.

It was time to make a staff change. He quickly made the necessary calls – first, to the gatehouse to bar Henderson's future entry. Second, to Fletcher and Brenda Lee, informing them to have nothing to do with their former colleague. The final call was to Westmoreland, ordering him to destroy anything that would tie Henderson to them. Including Henderson.

'Todd, darling, you'll be late for your own awards dinner.' Robinette's wife stood in the bedroom doorway, begowned and bejeweled. 'What's taking you so long?'

Dropping his phone into his pocket, he lifted his hands helplessly. 'I can't tie my tie.'

Lisa smiled, gliding across carpet that had cost more than his old man had made in his best year on that godforsaken farm they'd called home. More like hell on earth. He'd come a long way, baby. Big house. Beautiful, clueless, society wife. Successful business.

Respect. Todd Robinette had earned the respect of this city.

'Let me help you with that,' she said, capably managing the tie. She straightened it with a teasing tug. 'Do you have the speech I prepared?'

'I have the speech.' He patted the pocket of his tux. It wasn't the one that Lisa had prepared, but was instead the short, sweet, and to-the-point speech that his PR manager had written for him. Able to spin a way out of any disaster, Brenda Lee was worth her weight in gold. It had been her idea to begin donating vaccines to poor countries from the beginning, then setting up a series of rehab clinics in the city to help teen addicts get clean as a tribute to his lost son. Slowly but surely they'd transformed him from a man who'd been investigated for the murder of his second wife to a much-beloved philanthropist, honored by civic leaders.

Brenda Lee was a fucking genius. Lisa was smart, but she had a long way to go to best Brenda Lee. She'd be unhappy he hadn't used her speech, but he'd smooth that over later.

'Then we should go.' Lisa gave him a seductive smile. 'So we can come home again.'

He took her arm, cognizant of the picture they made together. They were called a 'handsome couple'. The men he met tonight would envy him. The women would want him.

Tonight would be a good night. Except the thought of Stevie Mazzetti alive, free to poke her nose where it didn't belong was enough to leave a sour taste on his tongue.

Lisa pulled back a little, frowning. 'What's wrong, Todd?'

He realized he'd let his anger show. 'Just a business snag. Nothing that can't be fixed.'

*Henderson is out, Westmoreland in. And if Wes can't manage it, I'll do it myself.* Robinette found the notion extremely appealing. Probably because it was what he'd wanted all along.

He curved her hand over his arm. 'Let's go. I'll knock 'em dead.'

*Saturday, March 15, 8.45 P.M.*

They'd left Stevie's house in two vehicles. She and Cordelia were with JD. Paige had picked up Clay, Alec, and Emma in her old pickup truck as Clay's truck – now riddled with bullet holes – had been towed away.

They'd parted ways, Clay and Paige taking Emma to her hotel and Stevie and JD supposedly headed toward the safe house Hyatt had arranged, she and Cordelia in the backseat. Her daughter was buckled in, but Stevie wasn't. Gun in hand, she sat as close to Cordelia as she could without sitting on top of her.

Cordelia clutched her favorite stuffed bunny, a gift Paul had bought her before he'd been killed. Her daughter couldn't sleep without it. Stevie hadn't thought to bring it with them, but Clay had made sure her daughter had packed whatever she needed to sleep.

After he left her sitting at her kitchen table, he'd been on the phone non-stop, planning. The only thing she'd had to do was to tell her family not to worry. And not to try to find them.

Wherever it was that they were going. Clay hadn't told her, which was infuriating. But logical. He hadn't said it out loud, so no one would know except him.

*What the fucking hell am I doing?* How had he talked her into this? Into trusting him? He'd given her those sad dark eyes of his, flexed his pecs to distract her, pushed the mommy guilt button . . . *Whoa. Stop right there.*

He hadn't done any of those things. His eyes had been sad, because *he'd* been sad. The flexing of the pecs was something Stevie had noticed because he'd been sitting at her table without a shirt the whole time and what woman with a pulse wouldn't notice?

And he'd never pushed the mommy guilt button. Not once.

He'd told her the truth. As much as it hurt, he'd told her the honest truth. And used logic.

Normally she liked logic. Respected it. But not when it was being used to bend her will. And not when she was in the wrong. As she had been.

She pressed a kiss to Cordelia's head. Her daughter had been in pain and Stevie hadn't understood. Hadn't seen what her own child needed. 'I love you, baby,' she whispered.

'I love you, too, Mommy. Don't be afraid. It'll all be fine.'

'I know, honey. It will be.'

'I asked Mr Maynard to get you a black cane,' Cordelia said. 'I think the sparkly one is pretty, but not safe. Somebody could see you coming from far away.'

Stevie found she could still smile. 'You are a smart girl, you know that?'

Cordelia's sweet smile was a balm to her heart. 'When this is over, can I see the horses?'

Stevie laughed softly. Canny kid. 'You are your daddy's daughter. He could charm the song out of a bird. But then he'd give it right back, because he'd feel bad for the bird.'

Cordelia fingered the locket around her throat. 'Uncle JD, I have the locket you gave me.' JD's gift for Cordelia's graduation from kindergarten, the locket held a photo of her dad's face. 'Mr Maynard said I should take anything I couldn't sleep without.'

Stevie thought of the backpack next to her feet. Clay

had said the same thing to her and she'd had less than five minutes to consider what those things would be. Practical things. Precious things. Irreplaceable things. Her computer. Paul's favorite sweatshirt that she'd never washed and still bore the faintest hint of his scent. Her son's stuffed bear. She'd stood in the bedroom she'd shared with Paul, nearly frozen for three of those five minutes, trying to decide what to take. The final two minutes she'd spent searching for the things she'd ended up packing.

It had taken Cordelia less than thirty seconds. She'd grabbed the stuffed bunny and the locket Emma had needed to fasten around her neck. Stevie's hands had been shaking too badly to manage the clasp.

JD looked at them in the rearview mirror. 'That's good, honey. You have your dad in the locket, right there with you.'

'And you, too. I took my picture out of the other side and put yours in there. I can see me anytime. So . . . where are we going?'

'Somewhere safe, Cordy. That's all I know,' he said soberly, but his voice held suppressed laughter. Cordelia was very good at worming information out of people.

'I don't know,' Stevie said before Cordelia could turn the question on her. 'Truly. No idea.'

Cordelia's frustrated sigh echoed Stevie's feelings exactly.

JD's car was silent after that, the drone of the engine nearly putting Stevie to sleep. After driving in circles for the better part of an hour, he'd turned off onto a particularly lonely road, close to the airport, but far from the main highway.

Headlights behind them had Stevie tensing. She tightened her grip on her gun, her heart taking off at a gallop when a red SUV pulled from a side road in front of them.

They were hemmed in.

'Relax, Stevie,' JD said softly. 'All part of the plan.'

The red SUV up ahead slowed and more headlights appeared behind them. The vehicles had come out of that same side road. Two black Escalades overtook them, one on either side of JD's vehicle. Stevie relaxed then. She recognized the Escalades.

One belonged to Grayson Smith, who worked for the State's Attorney's office. He'd been her friend for years. The other belonged to Joseph Carter, Grayson's brother and a special agent with the FBI. She trusted both men implicitly.

Of course, she'd trusted Silas, too. *So how good are your instincts, really?*

*No. Not goin' there.* She forced the self-doubt from her mind. Cordelia needed her alert and aware. Not second-guessing herself. When JD came to a stop, she looked behind them, unsurprised to see Paige's old pickup truck, Paige behind the wheel and Clay riding shotgun. They were protected on all sides.

The driver got out of the red SUV in front of them and Stevie blinked. In the headlights the man looked . . . different. Like he'd stepped out of an action movie. He had white hair and wore a black leather trenchcoat that flapped in the wind. 'Who is *that*?'

JD chuckled. 'Special Agent Deacon Novak. He works for Joseph. I worked with him back in December when you were in the hospital. He's a character.' A redheaded woman got out on the passenger side. Both wore tactical body armor and carried automatic rifles. 'That's Special Agent Kate Coppola,' JD added. 'Joseph trusts them both. So do I.'

'They mean business,' Stevie murmured, touched and comforted. And feeling safer.

Joseph got out of the SUV to their left and opened his back passenger door before opening Cordelia's door. 'Hey there, Cordy,' he said. 'I hear you've had an exciting day.'

'*Tell* me about it,' she said dramatically, making him smile. 'Are you going with us?'

'Nope. But you're going in my Escalade. It's got bullet-resistant glass,' he added to Stevie, 'as does Grayson's. Not bullet-proof, but as close as you're going to get unless you live at 1600 Pennsylvania Avenue.'

'Then that's pretty good,' Stevie said, glad her voice didn't wobble. 'Thank you, Joseph.'

'You know better than to thank me,' he said roughly. 'You've saved enough lives, Stevie. It's our turn to help you.'

Stevie knew he spoke of the bullet she'd put in Marina Craig's head in December. Marina's next bullet had his fiancée Daphne's name on it.

He opened his arms to Cordelia. 'Come on, squirt. Let's get this party movin'.'

She wrapped her arms around his neck. 'Is Tasha in there?'

He snorted. 'Yeah, right. Your mom would hurt me.'

'Who's Tasha?' Stevie asked.

'Daphne's dog,' Cordelia said with a tiny whine. 'She saves lives, too,' she added brightly. 'She saved Ford's life once. Ask Joseph. He was there.'

'It's true,' Joseph said, giving Cordelia a wink. 'Dogs are excellent companions for girls.'

'God, you are *so* your father's daughter,' Stevie muttered as she slid out of JD's back seat. She paused when he rolled down his window. 'So you did it this way so you could honestly tell Hyatt that I had myself hijacked and you have no idea where I went? Clever. Give Jeremiah

123

a kiss from his godmother. I'll be by soon to do it in person.'

'You'd better,' JD said fiercely.

'Gotta go. I'll find a way to contact you when we're settled.'

The other Escalade lowered its window, revealing Grayson behind the wheel. 'We're going to be working on this night and day,' he said. 'Don't worry. We got you.'

'I can see that. I'm . . .' She swallowed hard. *Overcome*. 'Thanks.'

Paige got out of her truck, helped Emma from the backseat, and escorted her to Joseph's SUV, making Stevie frown. '*Emma*. You're not supposed to be here.'

'Safer this way,' Emma said. She climbed up into the front seat, her expression grim. 'My hotel room was broken into. Everything's a mess.'

Stevie sucked in a breath. 'When did this happen?'

'Sometime this afternoon after two. That's when housekeeping made up the room.'

All of the worst possible scenarios blew through Stevie's mind. 'You could have walked in on them. They would have killed you.'

'No, I couldn't, because I didn't go into the room. Paige did. I'd given her my key because she was going to pack a few of my things.'

Stevie looked at Paige, who nodded. 'It was a mess,' she confirmed. 'Somebody really tossed the place. I called hotel security and Clay called Hyatt to let him know. He's on it.'

'But what were they . . .' The rest of the question stuck in Stevie's throat because she knew what they'd been looking for. Who they'd been looking for. 'You, Emma. They wanted you, because you could lead them to me. You were with me in the restaurant and now you're a target, too. You have to get out of here. You have to go home.'

Emma was trembling, but the glint in her eyes indicated it was from anger along with the fear. 'I'm safer here, for now.'

Clay hadn't pushed the mommy-guilt button on her, but Stevie was more than comfortable pushing it on Emma. 'Then what about your kids? Are *they* safer?'

'Yes, they are. If someone searched my room, they might be watching me at the airports, expecting me to go home. If I do, I'll lead them straight to my kids. Nobody knows where they are right now except their grandparents and Christopher. My parents' Disney hotel reservations and Christopher's travel plans were on my laptop, but the thieves didn't get it because I didn't bring it with me. I promised Christopher a no-work vacation when I got to Vegas, so I left it at home. I've notified the police in our neighborhood in Florida. Our house was untouched. I had a friend go in and get my laptop from there.'

'She's also hired a private security firm to guard her family,' Paige said. 'But her kids are pretty untraceable. Your friend is a smart cookie, Stevie.'

And stubborn to the core, Stevie knew. 'Emma, I am so sorry all this happened.'

Emma twisted in the seat to pin her with a glare. 'This is *not* your fault. Do not make me say it again, or I'll hurt you.'

Stevie took one look at her tiny friend and rolled her eyes. 'As if.'

'Don't dis the doc,' Paige said. 'Girl's got some skills. I'll see that you get some clothes, Emma. And I'll pick up your husband from the airport tomorrow. Don't worry.' She caught Cordelia's eye and bowed. 'I'll be expecting you back in class next week. Okay?'

'Yes, Sensei Holden,' Cordelia said respectfully.

Paige leaned into the Escalade. 'VCET found the red Chevy,' she said in a low murmur.

Stevie frowned again. VCET was the Violent Crimes Enforcement Team, an FBI/BPD joint task force, led by Joseph Carter. 'When did they take the case?'

'Probably while you were in the ER.' Paige frowned back. 'Which is when you should have called us. We would have been there for you.'

'I'm sorry,' Stevie said, dropping her eyes. 'I should have. I wasn't thinking.'

'I know. You get attacked and your brain fritzes. I thought Hyatt told you about VCET.'

'He should have, but he didn't. Nobody's told me anything. Which is not okay.'

Paige shrugged. 'They're trying to take care of you, trying to make sure they don't upset you further. It's making them stingy with the information. I disagree with their tactics.'

'So do I.' And she'd confront Clay about it whenever they got to wherever the hell it was they were going. 'Where did they find the red Chevy?'

'About twenty miles from your house, along a side road.' Paige winced a little. 'Burned.'

'Shit.' Any forensic evidence went up in smoke.

'I know.' Paige looked over her shoulder. 'Clay's coming. You can yell at him about keeping secrets from you later.'

'I will. Thanks, Paige. I appreciate it.'

Clay got behind the wheel of Joseph's Escalade and their little convoy began to move, all the vehicles turning around, jockeying for position so that their SUV was again in the center. 'What's the plan, Clay?' Stevie asked firmly.

'We drive until we get there. We catch the bad guys. We stay alive. The end.'

'Funny. You need to stop keeping information from me for my own good. Please.'

'Fine. We're going east. I've got a safe place for us to hide Cordelia and plan our next steps. It's located in a little town on the Eastern Shore you've probably never heard of. The property is accessible by land via one gravel road and by sea via a single dock.'

'Defendable,' she murmured.

'That's the idea.'

'Who owns it?' she asked.

He hesitated. 'My father.'

Stevie blinked, surprised. She'd never heard Clay speak of his family. 'And your mother?'

'She died,' he said quietly. 'A few years ago.'

'She liked yellow flowers,' Cordelia whispered. 'Mr Maynard bought some to put on her grave. But he didn't get to.'

*Because somebody shot at us in my front yard*, Stevie thought, the flowers Cordelia had held now making a lot more sense. 'I'm sorry,' she said and he shrugged.

'Happens.' He cleared his throat. 'As for the rest of the plan, most immediately, when we get to the main road, we separate. Paige will return to Emma's hotel. She'll stay in the room in case whoever tossed it comes back, hoping to find you there.'

'She's *bait*?' Stevie asked, horrified.

'She's *trained* bait,' Clay replied. 'If any person can take care of his or herself, it's Paige.'

'Grayson knows about this?'

'It was his idea.'

'Actually, Paige made him think it was his idea,' Emma corrected.

Clay shrugged. 'Whatever. The result is the same.'

'What about Alec?' Stevie asked.

'We dropped him off at my office,' Clay said. 'We may need him to run searches for us once we start digging deeper into this situation.'

'Doesn't he have a laptop?'

'Of course, but he can run searches faster from the computer in the office.'

'I'm worried about him. He was there when the shooter drove by, just like Emma was. What if they target him?'

'Alec's tougher than he looks,' Clay said mildly. 'Grayson and Joseph will go to your parents' house. Hyatt gave them a protection detail, but we're taking no chances. JD's driving to the safe house Hyatt arranged to let him know you aren't coming.'

'Hyatt's gonna be pissed,' Stevie said, biting her lip. 'I don't like deceiving him. But I don't know who he's brought into the loop on this.'

'JD's prepared to take whatever Hyatt dishes out.'

'I know, but . . .'

Emma sighed loudly. 'You'd do the same for JD, Stevie, and you know it. So hush.'

Yeah, she'd do the same for JD, but he wouldn't like it any more than she did right now. Which was not at all. 'What about the red SUV, the one with Joseph's people?'

'They follow us all the way and stand guard,' Clay said.

'For how long?'

'For the weekend, at least. They volunteered for the job.'

'But . . .' She frowned. 'They've never even met me.'

'They didn't need to,' Clay said quietly. 'They have Joseph's back, and Joseph has yours. These two will take the night shift. Two more will take days. They don't know you, either. You've got a lot of friends, Stevie. You don't have to do this alone.'

Her throat closed, emotion overwhelming her. 'Oh,' was all she could manage.

'Any more questions?' Clay asked. Kindly, she thought.

'No. Not at the moment.'

# Chapter Seven

*Baltimore, Maryland, Saturday, March 15, 9.45 P.M.*

Sam Hudson had finally been able to get his mother to sleep. Her chest rose and fell evenly, but her cheeks were streaked from the tears she'd shed as she'd cried herself to sleep.

How many times had he lain in his own bed as a kid, hearing the sobs she tried to muffle? Far too many. He'd covered his ears when he was younger. Then later, he'd forced himself to listen, forced himself to picture the bruises on her face. And he'd fantasized about all the ways he could kill his father and make it really hurt.

Staring at the ring his mother had laid so carefully on her nightstand, Sam remembered every single one of those fantasies. When he'd been younger, they'd brought a kind of hollow satisfaction. Tonight, though, they filled him with panic. He'd desperately wanted his father dead. Based on the contents of the package he'd been sent, it looked like his wish had come true.

But how had his father died? Drug overdose? Murder? Who'd done it?

The panic shot through him again along with the vivid memory of waking alone in a dirty hotel room next to a recently fired gun. His father had disappeared at the same time. Eight years as a cop had taught Sam the unlikelihood of coincidences.

*Me? Could it have been* me?

*No, I couldn't have.* His mother had loved the bastard, for reasons Sam had never been able to understand. Sam wouldn't have taken his father away from her. But something . . . *someone?* . . . had. Uncertainty rattled him. *God help me*, could *it have been me?*

*Stop panicking. Stay calm and think like a goddamn cop.*

He pulled his mother's door closed and crept down the stairs to her living room. His hand trembling, he drew the matchbook from his pocket, placed it on the coffee table, then sank to the sofa, staring into space.

The Rabbit Hole. The matchbook brought back the memory of that evening in stunning detail – the first hour of it, anyway. He'd only gone to the bar because an old buddy was having his bachelor party there. But when he'd arrived, he hadn't found the party. No one was there.

Well, lots of people were there, but no one he knew. No one he wanted to know.

He'd figured the party hadn't yet arrived, so he ordered a beer. If his friends hadn't shown up by the time he finished his beer, he was leaving. He kept his eyes to himself, not wanting to look at any of the other patrons whose eyes were glued to the strippers on the small stage.

He'd looked up only once. A waitress had served him his beer, then asked him if he wanted to buy a dance. When he'd looked at her face, he'd felt a confusing mixture of lust, pity, and revulsion. She was maybe eighteen years old and already she had the look of a used-up old whore. He'd given her a twenty and told her to go away.

The next thing Sam knew it was thirty hours later and he was waking up, freezing cold, and reeking of sour booze.

Just like his old man. It had been his first thought. *I'm just like my old man.*

Then his gaze had lighted on the gun on the floor next to him and his self-disgust had changed abruptly to fear. *Oh my God. What have I done?*

The delivery of that matchbook was a message, one that felt distinctly like a threat. *To me.*

What *had* he done? Sam drew a deep breath and came to his feet. It was time he found out.

He made his way down the basement stairs, past his mother's laundry room, his steps unerring even in the pitch black. He'd walked this path enough times in his life to know the way by heart. He stopped at the old crawl space his family used for storage. Somewhere, in all the boxes, were memories of better times. Photographs of Sam as a baby, as a toddler, as a kindergartner. All taken before his father had become an addict.

The boxes in the crawl space were empty of anything valuable. His dad had scavenged the boxes for years, hocking the family's belongings to buy drugs.

Sam hadn't been exempt. His baseball card collection had disappeared from one of these boxes, along with the pocket watch he'd inherited from his maternal grandfather. His father had even stolen the jar of cash he'd earned mowing lawns. Bitter, Sam had become inventive.

He moved between the boxes in a crouch, feeling his way along the bricks that formed the back wall of the crawl space. Tugging at the fourteenth brick, he pulled it out from the wall and carefully set it on the floor. Four bricks joined the first, revealing the small hole he'd dug in the dirt at age thirteen, determined his father would steal from him no more.

His father had never found this hiding place. Neither had anyone else.

The metal box was cold to his fingertips as Sam drew it out. It was heavy, filling him with both dread and relief. Taking out his cell phone, Sam shone its light on the box's lid as he carefully lifted it and looked inside. Wrapped in newspaper was a revolver, its six chambers empty. The four bullets he'd found loaded were in a small baggie, also in the box.

A rookie cop at the time, he'd checked the daily police reports avidly for weeks after waking in that hotel room for any incidences of gunshot wounds in which the weapon hadn't been found, but nothing had come up. He'd finally concluded that the gun hadn't shot anyone.

But now, with the timing of this delivery . . . He had to wonder if he'd concluded correctly.

He'd hated his father so much back then. His secret fear had always been that he'd killed the sonofabitch in a drunken rage. *And if you did? Will you tell your mother? Will you tell anyone?*

Sam let out a breath. *Yes. No. Hell, I don't know.*

He didn't know the answer to any of those questions. Right now he needed one specific answer – what, if any, crimes had been perpetrated by this specific firearm.

He made his way up the stairs and outside to his car, storing the metal box in his trunk. Tomorrow he'd start the wheels in motion. He prayed the outcome wouldn't ruin his life.

*Saturday, March 15, 11.30 P.M.*

Teeth gritted, Henderson focused on the dull painting of a landscape on the hotel room wall and managed not to scream. 'Dammit. That needle hurts.'

Fletcher looked up with a grimace that was both harried and angry. 'You want painless, go to a hospital. You called me to stitch you up, remember?'

Because Henderson hadn't known who else to call. 'I'm surprised you showed up at all.'

Fletcher was focused on Henderson's shoulder, and if the expression on Robinette's lead chemist's face was any indication of prognosis, it didn't look good. 'I guess once a doctor, always a chump,' Fletch muttered. 'You put me in a shitty spot by calling me.'

'I couldn't get Robinette to answer my calls. I was getting desperate. I tried to get to my apartment, but there was a fire nearby. Too many emergency vehicles to risk getting closer.'

'Robbie went to an awards dinner. It ran late.'

'Oh. I forgot about that. Anyway, I figured you still knew how to sew a straight seam. You stitched us all up more than once.' Being confined to the medical tent was one of Henderson's better memories of the war. The pain had been horrific, but the tent had offered . . . sanctuary. A little peace, some time to regroup before picking up their weapons and going back out again.

'And look where it got me,' came Fletcher's icy reply.

Fletcher was one of the casualties of the war – but the kind the brass liked to sweep under the rug. After putting too many torn bodies back together, Fletch had suffered a mental breakdown. A bad one. The kind that came with a medical discharge for 'mental disorder', keeping Fletch from practicing medicine as a civilian for years, maybe forever.

'I didn't think the boss would appreciate me skipping into a hospital,' Henderson said, changing the subject when Fletcher began to stitch again. 'They'd have to report the bullet hole.'

Fletcher's chin came up, their eyes met. And Henderson's gut twisted in a knot.

'What?' Henderson demanded. 'What aren't you telling me?'

Fletcher's gaze dropped, again intent on the stitching. 'Robinette was very angry with your . . . execution of his orders.'

'How angry?'

'You're . . . you're out.'

'Out. Like . . . out of rotation? That sucks.'

Fletcher didn't look up. 'No, *out*. Fired. He assigned Westmoreland to Mazzetti.'

Henderson jerked and Fletch's needle poked a nerve, sending pain radiating everywhere. 'What the hell? He *fired* me?' Nobody had been fired from the organization before. Nobody. 'I clean up Robinette's messes every goddamn day and I make one mistake and he *fires me*?'

'You didn't make one mistake, Henderson. You made two really big ones. Both made the news. Both made enemies out of the cops. And both left behind evidence.'

'Those bullets aren't traceable and you know it.'

Fletcher's shoulders lifted in a noncommittal shrug. 'Anything's traceable if you're smart enough. What about this wound? You had to have left a trail of blood all the way in here.'

'I didn't. I dressed it myself, then I disposed of the car. Nobody will find a drop of blood they can use against me. He can't fire me.'

'He told the guard shack that you'd never been an employee. He wiped your clearance to the facility. If you try to initiate contact, he'll give you up as a vet he once knew, but who now is mentally imbalanced. Any and all shots you took today are your full responsibility. And . . . the fire near your apartment? That *was* your apartment. He gave the order to have it burned down.'

Henderson's jaw dropped in shock. 'Who set the fire?'

'Probably Westmoreland. You've always known the price of failure,' Fletcher added gently. 'None of this should come as any surprise.'

'I did what he told me to do.'

'You fired on a crowded restaurant.'

'He told me to go there.'

'To wait for her. To follow her to someplace secluded and kill her there. Not to follow her to her front yard and shoot her in front of four witnesses. Five, if you include her kid.'

'He wasn't specific. He wanted her dead. Lots of people were shooting at her. I thought a public display would fit with the other attempted hits.'

'They might have, except that the cops know you were hit. They have a BOLO out on you at all area hospitals and clinics.'

'On me, specifically?' Fletcher's hand was cool against Henderson's forehead. 'Or a general Be-On-the-Lookout?'

'A general one for any suspicious GSWs. They don't know your name.' Fletch frowned. 'You're burning up. This wound is infected. I don't have any medicine to treat it.'

It was true. Henderson's shoulder was on fire. 'Can you get me something?'

'Only the vodka I brought you from my own liquor cabinet. I'm not even supposed to be here.' Fletcher looked up, frustrated. 'Robinette forbade anyone to help you. You're out.'

Out of a job. Out of the only family Henderson had ever known. 'Then why are you here?'

Fletcher tied off the final suture, then bandaged the wound. 'Because I'm bat-shit crazy?'

'Only in the most medical of terms,' Henderson said wryly and Fletcher laughed.

'I'll miss you, Henderson.' The ex-doc made fast work of packing up the used supplies.

'I'm serious. Why did you risk coming to help me?'

Fletcher looked away. 'Because he was wrong to cut you loose. Robinette forgot the cardinal rule – we don't leave anyone behind. I wonder if he's starting to believe his own—'

'His own what?'

A shake of the head punctuated the next words. 'No. I'm not going there.'

'His own press? That maybe Brenda Lee did too good of a PR job, rehabilitating his image? That maybe he's starting to believe he really is a good guy? Is *that* what you were going to say?'

'Leave it, Henderson.'

'I can't. It's not like I can get a job anywhere else, you know. Or antibiotics, for that matter. This isn't right, Fletch, and we both know it.'

'I'm leaving now.'

Henderson turned to watch Fletcher heading for the hotel room's door. 'And Lisa? Did she enter into your decision at all?'

Fletcher turned, eyes cold and narrowed. 'Excuse me?'

'Come on. A fool could see how you feel about Robinette. And Lisa.'

'He is my boss. Lisa is his *wife*.'

*Wife* was said with enough bitterness to confirm Henderson's suspicions. If Fletcher became angry enough,

Henderson might be able to make the former doctor an ally on the inside. 'He went to that black-tie dinner to honor his "philanthropy" tonight with Lisa clinging to his arm, draped in her daddy's jewels. She's rich, accomplished, gets him running in all the right circles. He's proud to wear *her* on his arm. And I hear she's a tiger in the sack, too.'

Fletcher flinched, growing pale. 'You ungrateful piece of shit. I took a big risk in coming here, and this is how you repay me?'

*Shit*. Too late Henderson realized the mistake in pushing Fletcher's buttons. 'I'm sorry, Fletch. I'm upset and I lashed out.'

A cool nod. 'I'll attribute your remarks to the fever that's unfortunately not likely to kill you. But I can still hope it's painful as hell.'

'That's fair. And so you know, it *is* painful as hell. Are you going to tell anyone I'm here?'

'No. Because you're right. Robinette will never take our relationship public. He's not that kind of a man. If I stay with him, it's with full knowledge of that fact.' Fletcher's brows lifted. 'And because I'm about to make him a shitload of money, twenty percent of which is mine. I'm not giving up the money, no matter whose ass I have to kiss. Keep those sutures dry. If you can get your hands on penicillin, take it. If you can't, keep the wound clean and use peroxide when you change your bandages.'

Henderson blew out a breath when the hotel door quietly closed. Fletch was in love with Robinette. Henderson wondered if the boss knew.

Ex-boss. *Because I've been tossed aside*. Henderson bitterly wondered if a clean hit on Mazzetti might fix things with Robinette. *But would I go back?*

Shamefully the answer was yes. Partly because

Henderson wasn't sure if anyone else was hiring personal assassins and if so, where to apply. Partly because Robinette had been the boss so long that Henderson couldn't yet think about working for anyone else. Partly because the debt Henderson owed Robinette went far deeper than simple gratitude. *He saved my life once. Saved me from a court-martial.*

But mostly for the cash. Fletcher was getting twenty percent of whatever the lab had been developing for the past year. Henderson had risked life and limb delivering Robinette's extremely illegal and dangerous goods into the dirtiest, most God-forsaken corners of the earth for the last seven years. *I was never offered twenty percent. I just got straight pay.*

*If I went back, it would be as a partner.* Which would require an act of God. Or really good blackmail. Not for the first time, Henderson wondered at the scandal that had plagued Robinette eight years before.

*Can I use it against him? Can I make him cut me in for a percentage? Can I ever trust him again?* That last one was a big fat no. But going back with eyes wide open offered some appeal. The least of which was revenge.

*Cut me out of a job, my ass. Wipe me from the records like I never watched his back through two hell-on-earth tours of duty? I'll see him dead before I let him toss me aside like this.*

But the thought of Robinette dead . . . *No. I can't do that. As much as I hate him, I can't kill him in cold blood.* Which was odd, Henderson had to admit. As the head of Robinette's cleanup crew, Henderson had murdered in cold blood in the past. But that didn't include Robinette.

*If he pointed a gun at me, maybe I could kill him. But otherwise? No. I can't do that.*

Lying down on the bed, Henderson pushed all the questions, the fury, and the confusion aside. Drowned all that roiling emotion in the high-quality vodka Fletcher had left behind.

There would be time to plan tomorrow. Tonight was for sleep.

*Wight's Landing, Maryland, Saturday, March 15, 11.45 P.M.*

The two-story beach house looked like many of the others they'd passed. Except for the six-foot wrought iron fence surrounding it. None of the other houses had a fence like this one.

Secure, Clay had promised. He'd certainly delivered. Stevie's feeling of well-being ratcheted up another notch. Along with her admiration of the man at the wheel. She hadn't wanted to be so impressed with him. So grateful to him. *But I am, on both counts.*

The driveway was blocked by a massive gate, which swung open when Clay activated a remote control. He pulled inside the compound and waited for the gate to close before raising the garage door, revealing a large, empty space occupied by a single late model sedan.

The red SUV that had followed them all the way from Baltimore came to a stop outside the gate, parking diagonally, blocking the driveway. Stevie turned around in her seat to see the two special agents who worked for Joseph emerge, rifles in hand, to begin sweeping the property.

Then the garage door came down and Clay switched off the ignition.

In the quiet, Cordelia sighed. 'Are we finally here?'

'We are,' Clay answered. 'Just in time for a little girl's bedtime. Come on in. My father should have everything ready for you.'

'He's got a bathroom, right?' Cordelia asked. 'Because I gotta go, real bad.'

'He's got three bathrooms,' Clay said, helping her from the vehicle.

Stevie gathered her backpack and her cane, prepared to open her door, but Clay beat her to it, opening Emma's door first, then her own.

Emma slid from the front seat with a wince. 'I hope one of those bathrooms has a tub. I'd sell my soul for a hot bath.' She hurried into the house, leaving the two of them alone.

Stevie looked at the hand he held out, debating the wisdom of touching him.

'It's a hand down,' he said, impatience sharpening his tone. 'Not a marriage proposal.'

She braced herself and took his hand, managing to stifle her indrawn breath, but not the shiver that raced down her spine. His hand was warm. Suddenly, so was she. She was unsurprised by her response to him. It happened every time she touched him.

As soon as her feet were steady on the concrete floor, he released her, stepping back. 'I'll show you where you'll sleep.' He turned for the door, taking his warmth with him.

She shivered again, this time from the chill – both from the temperature in the garage and the cold shoulder he'd presented. 'I'd like to stay with Cordelia,' she said to his back. 'Please.'

'I figured you would. It's arranged.' He held the door to the house open for her. 'Can you manage these stairs by yourself?'

There were two steps going up into the house and no railing for her to hold on to. She blew out a frustrated breath. 'Not tonight,' she admitted. 'I'm too tired.'

Before she could blink, he'd wound his arm around her

waist, effortlessly lifted her up the two stairs, and released her. Again he stepped back, gesturing for her to proceed. 'After you.'

She'd taken a few clumsy steps when she heard the sound of multiple dead bolts. But when she looked over her shoulder, he was flipping the only bolt on the door. The curved handle was the only other piece of hardware visible. 'What did you do?'

'Security door,' he said succinctly, demonstrating. 'Yank the handle up and bars extend vertically from the top and bottom of the door. They lock into the jamb, which is four inches of steel. The bolt extends bars horizontally. Breaking through this door requires a jackhammer.'

*Wow.* 'Are all the doors like this?'

'Yes.'

'And the windows?'

'Bullet-resistant, up to and including high velocity rifle fire. Nobody's coming in this house. You can sleep tonight, Stevie. I promised you and Cordelia would be safe. Here, you will be.'

Her shoulders sagged. 'Thank you.' Then her heart lifted at the sound of Cordelia's laughter. It had been a long time since she'd heard that sound. *Too long.*

She hurried through a large kitchen as fast as her leg would allow, pausing only long enough to sniff the aroma coming from the bubbling pot on the stove. 'God, that smells good.'

'Beef stew,' Clay said. 'Dad figured you'd be hungry.'

'He figured right.' She pushed open the swinging door and found herself in a great room with soaring ceilings and a giant plate glass window that looked out on the Chesapeake Bay. She imagined the views would be incredible when the sun came up.

She wondered how much bullet-resistant glass had cost

on a window that size. And why Clay Maynard's father's beach house had bullet-resistant glass and was fitted out like Fort Knox. But at the moment, she didn't really care why. She was just grateful it was.

And then she saw the reason for Cordelia's laughter. Her daughter knelt in the corner of the great room where four puppies frolicked. The one she'd picked up was busily licking her face.

'Of course he'd have dogs,' Stevie murmured with a sigh. But then Cordelia squealed, giggling wildly, and Stevie found herself grateful for the dogs, too.

Cordelia looked over her shoulder with a delighted grin. 'Mama, he's got puppies!'

Stevie was helpless not to smile back. 'I know, baby. I can see them.'

And she could feel Clay. He stood behind her, just close enough so that the heat from his body sent another shiver over her skin.

'Excuse me,' he said and eased around her, taking care not to touch.

He knelt beside Cordelia and picked up one of the other puppies, holding it against his broad chest. 'They've gotten big. Last time I was here they were half this size.'

'How old are they?' Cordelia asked. 'Are they boys or girls? What kind of dogs are they? What are their names? Who do they belong to? Where's their mama and papa?'

Clay chuckled. 'About eight weeks. Two of each. They're Chesapeake Bay Retrievers. You've got Mannix. That's Rockford and Pepper. I've got Beckett.' He frowned. 'What else did you ask? Oh. They belong to my dad. And their parents are around here somewhere.'

The back door opened, letting in a blast of cold, salty air, as well as a man wearing an Orioles ball cap, and two large brown dogs whose curly coats were beaded with drops of water. The dogs started to run toward Clay, but the man barked, 'Lacey, Columbo, sit,' and the dogs instantly obeyed. The man dried them with a towel, then released them.

'Okay,' he said and the dogs bounded over to Clay and Cordelia.

*This would be Clay's father*, Stevie thought and felt a shaft of panic. Had Clay told him about her? Did he know she'd told his son to go away? She had her answer a moment later after he'd shrugged out of his windbreaker and hung his cap on a peg by the door.

He crossed to where she stood, studying her with a level scrutiny that made her want to hide. He was of medium height and build. Fair-skinned and mostly gray-haired, he had a few threads of red still running through his military style buzz cut. His eyes were clear and blue, his mouth unsmiling. There was no resemblance between father and son whatsoever.

'So you're the detective,' he said quietly.

'I'm Stevie Mazzetti,' she said, just as quietly. 'Thank you for taking us in, Mr Maynard. I'm in your debt.'

'You're welcome and no, you're not. You're in his.' He indicated Clay with a sideways tilt of his head. 'And I'm not Mr Maynard. My name is Tanner.'

Stevie glanced down at her feet, then up again. 'Then thank you, Mr Tanner.'

'Not mister. Just Tanner.'

Clay came to his feet. 'This is my dad, Tanner St James. Dad, this is Cordelia Mazzetti.'

Tanner turned to give her daughter a nod. 'I'm glad you're here,' he said, and sounded like he meant it. 'I thought there was one more. Another lady?'

'She's in the bathroom,' Cordelia said in a loud whisper. 'She had too much coffee.'

Tanner's lips twitched. 'That'll do it. Are you hungry, little girl?'

Cordelia glanced at Stevie for approval before nodding. 'Yes, sir.'

'Then come on. I'll fix you some stew so you can sleep with your belly full. Leave the puppies there and wash your hands.' He turned his back on Stevie and pushed the swinging door open for Cordelia, then let it swing shut in Stevie's face.

*Yep. He knows about me, all right.*

'I'm sorry,' Clay said. 'He's my dad. He was, um, annoyed at you. On my behalf.'

'It's fair. I probably would have been, too.'

The kitchen door swung open and Tanner reappeared holding a large paper sack which he wordlessly handed to Clay before returning to the kitchen.

Clay held up the bag. 'Our dinner. We're going to eat while we talk.' He walked to the back door through which his father had come in with the dogs, then frowned when he saw she hadn't moved. 'I need to know exactly what I'm dealing with here. So please, come with me.'

Feeling a little like she was walking the plank, Stevie obeyed.

*Sunday, March 16, 12.05 A.M.*

Clay took a quick survey of the beach before closing and locking the gate behind them. It was empty as far as the eye could see. He didn't see any boats on the horizon, but the night was windy. Few would venture out on a night like this without a good reason.

Or an unfinished murder to commit.

'Stay close,' he said, drawing his gun from his shoulder

145

holster. She'd drawn hers as well, but limped slowly, her cane digging deep into the soft sand. He frowned as the glitter on her cane reflected the moonlight. 'You need a black cane. You might as well be carrying a damn flare.'

'Cordelia said she asked you about it. We'll worry about it later. Where are we going?'

'To the boathouse, there on the dock.'

Her chin jerked up as she stared at the small structure at the end of the two-hundred-foot long dock, her dismay apparent. 'Why?'

'You're not afraid of water, are you?' he said, surprised.

Her brows lowered. 'Of course not. It's just . . . Why don't we just stay in the house?'

'Because I'm going to ask questions that I doubt you want Cordelia hearing the answers to.'

'It's a two-story house, Clay,' she said, with exaggerated patience. 'Let's just go upstairs.'

A picture immediately formed in his mind – her, in his bed. Smiling at him, sated and happy. The image was a familiar one, only because it mocked him in his dreams with consistent regularity. It mocked him now, but his body still responded. Just like it always did.

He lifted his brows, releasing some of his frustration in sarcasm. 'All the rooms upstairs are bedrooms. We can if you want to, though.' He watched her eyes go wide with outrage, then narrow to slits as her cheeks grew pink. She opened her mouth to say something he also doubted she would've wanted Cordelia to hear, but he cut her off. 'I have equipment to check out there in the boathouse. I need to show you how it operates, in case you're here alone.'

'You could have just said so,' she muttered, shaking her head in disgust. With a determined set of her shoulders, she set off across the sand at a pace so slow that it was painful to watch.

*She's tired*, he thought. He considered picking her up and carrying her, but the brief contact they'd had when he'd helped her up the garage stairs had been far too much. But only because it wasn't nearly enough and unless she changed her mind, it never would be.

Still . . . 'Do you want me to help you?' he asked quietly.

Her chin shot up again, her eyes wary. 'How?'

'Tomorrow I'll lay plywood across the sand, to make it easier for you to walk. Now . . .' He held his breath while she stared at the arm he extended like it might sprout poison spikes.

After a few seconds she grabbed on, digging her fingers into his skin. She wasn't just tired. She was in pain. *Hell*.

'Hold this,' he said, handing her the dinner bag. 'And don't yell at me.' He scooped her up into his arms and carried her the remaining distance, across the sand and down the dock to the boathouse door. When he put her down, she was trembling. How much was exhaustion he didn't know. He suspected most of it was rage, though.

'Don't you dare do that,' she hissed as he unlocked the door. 'Ever. Again.'

'Get inside,' was all he said. All he could say. He needed a moment to gather his control, to keep himself from reaching again. Because she'd fit up against him just like he'd always known she would. Perfectly.

He pointed to a folding chair. 'Sit. This'll take a while.' He dragged a small table to her side and unpacked the stew. 'Should be a thermos of coffee in there, too.'

Her expression was still mutinous. 'How did your dad have the bag already prepared?'

'I asked him to get it ready when I told him you were coming. He knew I'd need to talk to you. Privately.'

'Oh.' She dug into the stew, saying nothing more while he cleared away the life preservers and tarps camouflaging his equipment cabinet. He unlocked it and spread the doors open wide. He, too, said nothing as he flipped switches and turned on computer monitors, figuring it would be only a matter of minutes before her curiosity overcame her ire.

It was actually more like thirty seconds.

'What the fuck is this place?' she whispered.

'More security. If you want to come over here, I'll show you how to make sure nobody sneaks up on you and Cordelia from the water.'

She crossed the small space, dragging her folding chair with her. When she'd sat, he began.

'These monitors display feed from six underwater cameras, fixed to pilings placed in a pyramidal formation. This monitor is the thermal imaging cameras. And this monitor—'

'Stop. Just . . . stop. You have a fence, a gate. Bullet-proof windows and bank vault doors.'

'Bullet-resistant windows,' he corrected.

'Whatever. And now this place? I feel like I just walked into a James Bond flick. Who is your father, that he needs this kind of protection? I'm not plugged into politics, but I think even I would remember if your father used to be the President of the United States. Which he was not. Is he a celebrity that I've just never heard of? Maybe an exiled king? This is a beach house, for God's sake, not frickin' Fort Knox. So what the hell is all this?'

Clay straddled the other folding chair. 'The fence and the motion detectors were for my mother, mostly. The rest is business. My business.'

She frowned. 'So you're not going to tell me?'

'No, I mean it's my business. What I do for a living.'

'You're a PI.'

'I'm also a security specialist. My first partner and I got

the PI license to do background checks on our clients' employees.'

'Your first partner? Nicki?'

Hearing Nicki's name still hurt, after all this time. Stevie had never known her, but she and JD Fitzpatrick had caught the sonofabitch who'd gutted Nicki in her own bed and left her to rot.

'No. My first partner was Ethan Buchanan. He lives in Chicago now with his wife and kids. He and I were in the Corps together, back in the nineties. In Somalia. I left after two tours, came home to DCPD. He stayed on, planning to be a career Marine. But he got hurt in Afghanistan. He came home about the time that I resigned from DCPD, so we went into business together. I trained personal security forces for businesses and private individuals.'

'Rich folk.'

'Most of them, yeah. Ethan had some contacts that got us started. We were pretty successful. Ethan did the computer end of security. He's a "white hat".'

'A good hacker.'

'Yes. His specialty is hacking into "secure" servers and showing businesses how vulnerable they are to attack. The businesses always hire him to fix the holes in their networks. We never did any real investigative work until . . .' He frowned. 'Until Alec was kidnapped.'

Her eyes widened in shock. 'What? When? Who kidnapped him?'

'Sue Conway, one of the most vicious women I've ever had the misfortune to meet. It was six years ago now. See, Ethan is Alec's godfather. When he found out Alec was gone, he started searching. I helped. It happened here. This house, in fact.'

Her eyes narrowed. 'Which your father now owns?'

His smile had an edge. 'One of life's little twists of fate.

149

That's the main reason Alec didn't come with us. I do need him in the office, but he still has issues with this house.'

'Understandable, I suppose,' she murmured.

Clay wondered if she realized how similar Cordelia's situation was to Alec's. Stevie's daughter hated their house. Which was completely understandable given the violence that had occurred there.

'How did your dad end up living here?' she asked. 'And why all the James Bond toys?'

'Well, like I said, the fence and alarm system was for my mother. She and Dad bought this place a few years after the kidnapping. My mother fell in love with the view and Dad agreed because the price was right, but that was because the house had been sitting on the market for two years. The realtor didn't tell them about the crimes that happened here. They wouldn't have bought it either. Dad was a cop for twenty-five years. He had no wish to live in a house that had been the scene of an abduction and a murder.'

Again her eyes widened. 'Who got murdered?'

'The fiancée of Alec's speech therapist was murdered here, in the boathouse, but not the one we're in now. The old boathouse was on the beach. And it was really a boathouse.'

'Not Seal Team Six Command Central,' she said dryly. 'I haven't forgotten my original question, which was why your parents bought this specific place? Are you from this town?'

'No. I was born in upstate New York, but grew up just outside of DC. My dad married my mother when I was five and moved us into his house. He was a DC cop, so we had to live close to the city.' He hesitated, then shrugged. 'My ex-fiancée lives here, in Wight's Landing. My parents bought the beach house when they thought I'd be moving here, too.'

Stevie's eyes widened, then narrowed. 'You had a fiancée?'

She sounded a tad pissed off and Clay liked that. 'I did. We ended it four years ago.'

'Why?'

'Because we were better friends than spouses and were lucky enough to figure that out before we ruined our friendship.'

'Does she still live around here?'

'Yep. Lou Moore is the sheriff. You've met her sister, Alyssa. My admin assistant.'

She still frowned. 'I remember Alyssa. Whatever happened to her?'

'She still works for me, but she's on vacation. Her boyfriend is a college student and this is his spring break. They went camping.' He shrugged. 'With tents.'

'You don't like camping?' she asked.

'Got my fill of tents and sleeping on the ground in the Corps.'

'Okay, so your parents bought the house as a surprise, but you canceled the wedding.'

Technically Lou had, but Clay didn't think that fact would add to the conversation. 'And then they couldn't sell it because buyers always would hear the story from a local. If my parents hadn't wanted to keep it such a big secret to surprise us, somebody would have told them, too. They couldn't move because all of their retirement savings were tied up in the house.'

'That stinks.' She pointed to the computer monitors, which, for the moment at least, were completely static. 'And the James Bond toys?'

He sighed. 'The woman who abducted Alec murdered

151

more than a dozen people before she was done with her killing spree. Alec was almost one of them. So was Ethan's wife, Dana.'

'Where is the killer now?'

'Sue Conway's serving life in an Illinois state prison, where she's developed quite a cult following. We get a lot of crazies here, wanting to see the place where Sue "started her quest for revenge". At first it was just annoying. Then one day one of the crazies came into the house and fell asleep in one of the beds. My mom was really rattled. The next day I installed security.'

'The fences and the alarms.'

'And the cameras on the outside of the house as well as the motion detectors on the beach. Made her feel safer. Then I realized I was selling a lot more of those same security features to my clients than I had before. I could say, "This is what I put on my own mother's house and I know it works". Over time I asked Mom and Dad if I could install more security features, just to try them out. Mom liked the idea. Dad wanted a tank so he could mow down the crazies.' He smiled at the memory. 'Mom put her foot down on that.'

Her lips curved in a small smile. 'I bet she did.'

'Sometimes a wealthy client wants something special that I have no experience with. I'll get a test version for myself, sell a helluva lot of them later. That's how I got all this "Team Six" stuff, as you call it. A celebrity client had a beachfront compound and wanted to keep the paparazzi away. When the photographers started diving off boats and swimming in, my client got pissed. Now he's got all this, only more of it and more expensive models. His family is safe.'

'And so is my daughter. When you see that client again, thank him for me.'

'I will.'

Her gaze skittered away, then swung back, meeting his eyes determinedly. 'Your father was right. I am in your debt, Clay. Thank you. This . . . This is more than I expected.'

*Someday . . . someday you'll say that to me. That I'm more than you expected.* His chest physically hurt, but he ignored it. 'You're welcome. Now I have questions for you.'

'I know. Ask what you need to. I'll do my best to answer.'

'Why is somebody shooting at you?'

She laughed, surprising him. 'I guess that's cutting right to the heart of it.' She sobered, blew out a breath. 'I told you and JD that I paid a visit to IA yesterday. I think we have more cops out there who might have been involved with Silas Dandridge's crimes.'

'You did, but I'm confused. I thought all the dirty cops were called out in that defense lawyer's post-mortem tattle report. Stuart Lippman, right? But earlier, when we were in your kitchen, you said you hadn't gotten them all.'

'Lippman didn't just tattle on dirty cops. He had ex-cons working for him, too. And other lawyers. We thought he'd named all the names, but I discovered there were others.'

'How?'

'Silas had a safe in the floor of his bedroom. In it were some throwaway guns and a ledger that listed the deposits he'd made to an off-shore account.'

'Payments from Lippman for services rendered?' Clay asked.

'Exactly. Silas listed amounts and dates, but not any details about which job was which. When Lippman was killed and his "tattle report", as you call it, was released, IA worked from that. The ledger was handed over to forensic accounting to track down the cash.'

'I'm guessing somebody eventually realized the deposits didn't match up with Lippman's tell-all,' Clay said and she nodded.

'I did. Accounting finished with the ledger – they never did find his stash – and returned it to the evidence room. They sent me a copy on a CD. I didn't look at it until after I'd been discharged from the hospital in December. I just did a quick count of the deposits and realized there were twice as many payments than there were actual jobs Silas had done, according to Lippman's report. I told IA and they got to work on it – but there were so many cases on the report to start with. They weren't getting through them very fast.'

'So you started looking yourself. Why? Why not let IA do their job?'

'Because they weren't getting through them very fast,' she said again, impatiently this time. 'I was home, recuperating, and all I could think about was all the innocent people sitting in prison because of Silas and Stuart Lippman. And all the guilty people walking around grinning because they got away with it. I got mad. So I got busy. I found three rapes and an armed robbery that looked off because they were. I gave IA the details with the suspects that should have been at the top of the list. Four innocent people have been in prison for years.'

'But you've rectified that situation. Those innocent people will get out of jail and the real perpetrators will get what's coming to them.'

'Yes. But then I looked at the timeline for one of the rapes. Silas couldn't have planted the evidence because he and I were on a stakeout that weekend. I was with him the whole time. I tried to figure out which of the cops on Lippman's list actually planted the evidence in my four new cases, but on two of them I couldn't find any of the known dirty cops that weren't somewhere else at that specific time.'

'So you think other cops are involved,' Clay murmured.

'I don't want to think that. But a few hours after I left IA, someone shot at me. Today, same thing, only twice and with more finesse.'

'I sure don't like the coincidence of it, but it could be someone else that knows you're digging. Maybe a perp from a case you haven't even gotten to yet.'

'That's possible, too. Or it could be both.' She cast her gaze up at the ceiling, then peeked at him from the corner of her eye. 'The attacks started before I went to IA, but we caught both of those guys.'

'*Both?* You've been attacked on five separate occasions? In one week?'

'It sounds really awful when you put it that way.'

He looked exasperated. 'Hell, Stevie. So, what's with the first two?'

'One guy had a knife. The other just had hard fists. Both are in custody.'

'You got away and called for backup?'

Her chin came up. '*I* cuffed 'em. The cane comes in handy for more than walking.'

He grinned at her. 'You hit them with your cane?'

'I did. Both attackers were related to cases that weren't on Lippman's list. Neither wanted me to continue my investigation.'

'Did Hyatt know about your visit to IA yesterday?' Clay asked.

'Yes. I realized there might be more dirty cops on Monday and took the information straight to him that day. He went with me to IA yesterday. That's why I was surprised he insisted on a safe house. He knew why I

155

wouldn't trust going to one. I hope he doesn't take it out on JD. Any other questions?'

'Where are your files?'

'Most of them are in the suitcase you moved from the trunk of JD's car into the SUV. Anything I downloaded is on my laptop, which is in my backpack. I left it in your dad's house.'

'Do you have any idea which cop – or cops – are involved in these new cases?'

'No. IA wouldn't say. Neither would Hyatt. Anything else?'

He met her eyes directly. Let himself stare until finally she looked away. *Yes. Why don't you want me? And what do I have to do to change your mind?*

But of course he didn't ask either of those questions. He stood, folded his chair, and stacked it against the wall. 'No,' he lied brusquely. 'Let's go back now. Hopefully Cordelia has had her fill of the puppies. I'm sure you're all tired. You need to get to bed.'

*As I will*, he thought, opening the door. *Alone. I am so damn tired of being alone.*

'Clay, wait.'

He didn't look at her. 'You don't need to keep thanking me, Stevie.'

'I wasn't, although I should. I was going to say you were wrong about something.'

'What was that?'

He could hear her slow exhale. 'When you were trying to convince me to come here, you said you knew I didn't like you. That's not true. I don't feel about you the way you want me to, but I never disliked you. You're a good man. I need you to know that I believe that.'

She'd let him down more easily this time. Still . . . breathing actually hurt. 'You forgot to say "You'll make some lucky woman a wonderful husband".' He said the words bitterly.

'You will. And she will be lucky.'

'She's just not you.'

'No. It can't be me.'

She said the words so sadly that he turned to face her, his back to the cold night air. She still sat in the chair, her shoulders sagging, her expression so dejected that he felt a spark of hope.

'Can't or won't?'

'Does it matter?'

'Yeah, it does. It matters to me.'

She stood up, leaning heavily on the cane. 'It's late. I need to get Cordelia to sleep.'

Hope gave way to frustrated anger and he took a step forward, blocking her exit. 'No.' He moved closer, crowding her space so that she had to look up at him. 'You can't keep saying that to me without a reason. I want to know why, Stevie. At least you owe me that much.'

She glared, but the pulse at the hollow of her throat fluttered. 'I don't *owe* you anything.'

'Yes, you do,' he said silkily. 'You said so yourself, not ten minutes ago. "I am in your debt, Clay" were your exact words. This is how I want to be repaid. I want the reason you believe it can't be you. And I want it now.'

# Chapter Eight

*Wight's Landing, Maryland, Sunday, March 16,*
*12.25 P.M.*

Stevie couldn't breathe. Clay was big, so big she could see nothing but him. Big in a way Paul had never been. *Maybe it was because Paul never loomed over you, looking so fierce.*

Paul had managed her with charm, never like this. Clay stood toe-to-toe, leaning so that he towered. *Forcing me to look up. Or away.* But she found she couldn't look away. His dark eyes held hers, demanding an answer, and she knew he wouldn't budge until she gave him what he wanted. There was a small part of her that was challenged. Excited.

A little bit turned on. *Which is so wrong of me.*

*You owe me that much*, he'd said. And even though she'd denied it, she knew he was right.

'I never wanted to hurt you, but I know I did. I'm sorry.'

He didn't move a muscle. 'That's not an answer.'

'I know.' She gave in to the urge to retreat, shuffling back a step. It didn't help. *Still can't breathe.* 'Can you give me some room? You're making this worse.'

He straightened a fraction. 'Stop stalling, Stevie.'

'I loved my husband.'

'I know you did. I'm sure you still do. And?'

She blinked, thrown off balance. 'And? And that doesn't bother you?'

'If you hadn't loved him, you shouldn't have married him. Wouldn't have grieved him.' He hesitated. Lifted a shoulder in a gesture that was anything but careless. 'You don't just stop loving someone because they're gone. Or because they don't want you to.'

She closed her eyes, his meaning clear. 'I won't love anyone the same way as I loved Paul.'

'Of course you won't.'

She looked up at him, frustrated. 'Stop that. Stop agreeing with me.'

One brow lifted maddeningly. 'Really?'

She gritted her teeth. 'You're making me crazy.'

'Join the club,' he said wryly. 'So you love him still. He's not here, Stevie. He's gone. He's not coming back. Do you think he'd want you to be alone for the rest of your life?'

'That's not the point.'

'I'm still waiting for the point.'

'The point is that I could never feel about you the way I felt about Paul. You'd be second best. Always. And eventually you'd come to hate me.'

Something flickered in his eyes and she wasn't sure if it was anger or hurt. 'You're not being rational.'

She sighed. 'You just don't like my answer. I've met your demand, now please let me go.'

But he stood firm. 'I want you to think about something. Seriously consider it. You didn't just lose your husband that day. You also lost your son.'

She sucked in a shocked breath, flinching. 'And?'

'You have Cordelia. Do you love her less? Is she second best to you?'

Stevie's mouth fell open, words failing her as she stared numbly. 'You sonofabitch,' she whispered. 'How *dare* you?' Then fury blasted through the numbness. She shoved him, but he didn't budge so she gripped her cane like a bat. 'Let me go or I will hurt you and mean it.'

He finally stepped aside. 'Just consider it,' he repeated. 'Please.'

She wished she could stalk out with her head high, but her leg ached and she could only hobble. She paused at the door, not looking back. 'I appreciate the use of this facility tonight,' she said stiffly. 'I'll find another place to hide with Cordelia tomorrow.'

'As you wish,' he said quietly.

She stared down the dock, hearing him lock the door to the boathouse behind them, aware of him following her. *Watching my back, still.* She wanted to yell at him, tell him to get the fuck away. But the truth was, she needed his coverage at the moment. It was either that, or let him pick her up again and carry her.

It had felt too good before. Too safe. *Not gonna happen again.* Besides, with all that James Bond equipment in there, there was no way anyone was close enough to take another shot at her.

She got to the end of the dock and stopped, dread filling her. The stretch of sand was only about a hundred feet, but it looked like a hundred miles. Lifting her chin, she took the first step.

And her leg buckled right out from under her, pitching her face-first into the sand.

Stunned, she lay there for a moment, turning only her head so that she could breathe as a sob began to build deep within her chest. She clenched her jaw, holding it in. *You will not cry.*

She could hear him behind her, feel him. But he said nothing.

She pushed herself to her knees and brushed the sand off her face, her chest growing tighter as she fought not to cry. Strong hands grasped her shoulders and she found herself lifted to her feet. His hands disappeared, but she could feel his warmth at her back. Still he said nothing.

*You lost your son. Is Cordelia second best?*

Suddenly it was simply too much. The day. The gunshots. The two dead women. Her throbbing arm. Her damn leg that shook pitifully beneath her weight.

She sank to her knees, the sob barreling out. Wrapping her arms around herself, she hunched her shoulders, rocking back and forth, wishing he weren't there to see her this way.

Glad he was.

A moment later she was in his arms again and he was carrying her across the sand. She turned her face into his chest, muffling the pathetic sounds she could no longer hold inside.

He let them in through the gate, but instead of going into the house, he carried her to a porch swing and lowered them into it, cradling her on his lap. Rocking them gently, he let her cry.

Finally the tears were spent and she felt hollowed out. He should be angry. He should hate her. Yet he held her tenderly and Stevie hated herself. 'Goddamn you,' she whispered.

'I know,' he whispered back.

'Why can't you hate me?'

His chuckle rumbled in his chest, tickling her cheek. 'I've tried. I've really tried.'

She shuddered out a sigh. 'I don't want Cordelia to see me like this.'

161

'Sitting in my lap?'

Stevie felt her cheeks burn. *That, too.* 'I meant I didn't want her to know I've been crying.'

He tipped up her chin. Winced a little. 'I think she's gonna know. I might have some frozen peas in the freezer, though.'

She smiled at him sadly. 'I wish you were a mean man.'

'If wishes were horses,' he murmured. 'You ready to go in?'

'Yeah. It's been a long day.' But she didn't move. For a moment she just let him hold her and soaked in the feeling. Because it felt good. Far too good. *You're going to hurt him again.*

Either way this went, she knew it would be true. If she pushed him away once and for all right now, he'd hurt. If she allowed him to wear her down, if they had a relationship, she was certain he'd be disappointed. Eventually, anyway. He'd leave and they'd all be hurt.

Especially Cordelia. *Who is not second best in my heart, dammit.* She forced her body to shift off his lap, testing her leg before taking a step.

'You okay?' he asked.

*No. Not even close.* 'Yes, thanks.'

'Then I'll show you where you'll sleep. I'll take you wherever you want to go tomorrow.'


*Baltimore, Maryland, Sunday, March 16, 2.30 A.M.*

The small beep woke him up. Robinette rolled over, reaching for his cell phone.

'Who is it?' Lisa asked sleepily.

He ran a teasing finger along her spine, pressed a kiss to

her temple. 'A text from Jimmy Chan in Hong Kong. I need to call him.'

'What time is it?'

'Only two-thirty in the morning. It's the afternoon for Chan. Go back to sleep.'

He slid from the bed, pulled on his pants, and headed down to his office. He dialed quickly, except it was not Mr Chan of the Hong Kong Stock Exchange whom he called. The text had come from his source within BPD. 'What is it?' Robinette asked.

'An address for Mazzetti's safe house.'

Robinette smiled. 'Good to know. ETA for arrival?'

'She's there now with her kid.'

'Solo?'

'Yeah. She made that a condition of going – that no one was to disturb her privacy.'

That sounded like the detective who'd made his life a living hell. Cocky and bossy. Her way or the damn highway.

'Text the address to 301-555-1592.' Westmoreland's cell phone. Robinette had every confidence that Westmoreland was smart enough to learn from Henderson's mistakes. Mazzetti would be dead within the hour.

'Will do.'

Robinette hung up the phone, satisfied. Now life could get back to normal. *And I can get back to Lisa*. He found those benefit dinners to be hellishly boring, but his wife thrived on the gowns and the jewels and the stares of every envious woman and lust-filled man in the place. If he played his cards right – and tonight he had – her excitement spilled over into their bed. She was still young and adventurous with a body made for sin, when she was in the mood.

And when Lisa took to her bed with a headache? There

was always Fletcher to scratch his itch. They'd always been good in bed, he and Fletcher. And while Fletch didn't like Lisa, his chemist was smart enough to never cross the line and demand anything more from their mutually beneficial, yet clandestine, relationship. He and Fletcher could have their cake and eat it, too.

They could have a hell of a lot of cake, in fact. Fletcher's improved formula was about to make Fletcher rich and Robinette even richer.

And with money like that, Robinette didn't worry about the state of his marriage. If he grew tired of Lisa, he'd just get another wife who was prettier, more socially acceptable, and importantly, more biddable.

He paused mid-way up the stairs, the thought having come as a surprise. He hadn't realized he was growing bored with Lisa until that moment. He wondered how to make a divorce work.

His first two wives had died, after all. A third wife's death would renew public scrutiny, arousing suspicions, something he'd avoid at all costs. But he had time to worry about that later. Lisa was in his bed, warm and willing. Fletcher was in the lab, working, making him money.

And Stevie Mazzetti would soon be dying. All in all, a good night.

*Wight's Landing, Maryland, Sunday, March 16, 3.40 A.M.*

It was a small sound. A shuffling sound. Clay lifted his head from the pillow, instantly alert and a half-second later on his feet, gun in his hand. Everyone was in one of the bedrooms, except his father who was standing guard downstairs.

Quietly Clay slipped through the bedroom door and let out a silent sigh.

Cordelia sat in the hall on the floor outside his room, her back against the wall. She'd drawn her knees to her body and had her face buried in her nightgown. Her shoulders shook with sobs.

Looked like he'd be comforting another weeping Mazzetti female. He was glad this one was Cordelia. She, he could help. Seeing Stevie cry simply tore him up inside.

Beside her, a canine head lifted watchfully. Columbo, his father's Chesapeake Bay Retriever, had slept in her room, at the foot of the bed she'd shared with her mother. Stevie hadn't argued the presence of the dog after Cordelia told her the dog always slept there.

'We're sleeping in his bed, Mom,' she'd said plaintively.

Technically, they were sleeping in Clay's bed, but he hadn't told them that. It was the most comfortable of all the beds in the house and he wanted Stevie to get a decent night's sleep.

Looked like Cordelia had wanted the same thing. Her head lifted when he sat down next to her, her little finger pressed to her lips. 'Sshh. My mom's asleep,' she whispered through her tears. Then she lowered her face to her knees again.

'We won't wake her,' Clay promised. He stretched his legs out, reaching out a tentative hand to stroke Cordelia's hair. She shuddered and leaned into him, so he put his arm around her shoulders, kissed the top of her head. 'Bad dream, honey?'

She nodded. 'I'm sorry I woke you up,' she whispered, stretching out her legs as he had. Her feet, which only reached his knees, were small compared with the boots he wore. 'But I hoped you'd be the one to come out. Aunt Emma's nice, but . . . you understand.'

Warmth unfurled in his chest. 'You want to tell me what the dream was about?'

She rested her head against him, closing her eyes with a tiny sigh. 'Mr Silas.'

'In the kitchen at your house?'

Again, a nod. 'I hate that kitchen,' she confessed.

Clay saw his father peeking around the head of the stairs, brows raised in question. With a tilt of his head, Clay gestured for his dad to go back down. 'We're okay,' he mouthed.

His father's graying head disappeared, his steps on the stairs nearly silent.

'I'd hate that kitchen, too, if I were you,' Clay murmured.

'That's where...' Cordelia stopped to breathe, her chest hitching. 'It's where he put the gun against my side. Mr Silas, I mean.'

'I know.' Clay kept his voice calm. Inside, fury churned.

She twisted to look up at him, curiosity in her eyes. 'How do you know?'

'Paige was there, remember? She told me later.' Somehow they'd managed to keep Cordelia's involvement from the newspapers, so she'd never had to worry about who else knew. 'Did you think of flowers or puppies coming out of the gun after the dream?'

'Yes.' She settled against him again. 'It didn't work. I'm still scared.' But she yawned.

'Which did you think of? Puppies or flowers?'

'Both.' She yawned again. 'Maybe next time I'll try Skittles. Or M&Ms.'

'M&Ms should work really well. They were my mom's favorite.'

'You didn't get to put the yellow flowers on your mama's grave. I'm sorry.'

'It's okay.' He ruffled her hair affectionately. 'I think my mom would have understood.'

'We don't put flowers on my dad's grave.' She paused. 'Or my brother's. I think my mom visits, but she never takes me with her.'

'She probably thinks it would upset you.'

'Because it upsets her?'

*I still love my husband, she'd said. You'd be second best.* Clay had to swallow hard. 'Maybe. She doesn't like for you to see her cry.'

'I would make her feel better. I can do that.' Her little fist clenched. 'I *have* to do that.'

She'd said it so determinedly. 'Why? Why do you have to do that?'

'Because I'm all she has left,' Cordelia whispered.

'Sweetheart . . . You're not. Your mother has a big family. Your grandparents, Aunt Izzy, Uncle Sorin. She has lots of friends who love her. You're not all she has left.'

Cordelia's eyes were wise and sad. 'But it's not the same. Sometimes she goes into my brother's room and she cries. She doesn't know that I know. But later, I make her feel better.'

Clay sighed. Tried again. 'You're not responsible for your mom's happiness. She's a grownup. She's responsible for you.'

She shook her head. 'I'm all she has left,' she insisted.

He'd been wrong. He would rather have comforted Stevie, even though it tore him up inside. This child carried a burden that broke his heart. Because this, too, he understood.

'I thought that way, too, a long time ago,' he said softly. 'My mom was a single mother, just like yours. Except that my dad didn't die. He just didn't care and he left.'

'I'm sorry.'

'It's all right, really. It turned out even better, because she met Tanner St James. She didn't think she'd ever meet a man who wanted a woman with a little kid already, but he did. And he . . . he is the best dad I could ever have. But before Tanner, I used to feel like you do. Like I had to take care of my mom. Like I had to keep her happy.' He hesitated. 'I sometimes even wondered if she really wanted me. If her life would be easier if I weren't there.'

Cordelia looked up at him suddenly, wide-eyed. Then her gaze skittered away, telling him all he needed to know. 'It wasn't true for my mom,' he said urgently. 'It's not true for yours either. She loves you with all her heart, Cordelia.'

She nodded, pressing her face against his side. 'I know.' Then, so softly he almost didn't hear her, she added, 'Because I'm all she has left.'

*Oh, Lord.* His eyes stung and he had no idea of how to respond. So he just sat there, eyes closed as he held her to his side, listening to her breathe. Within minutes her breathing evened out, her little body finally relaxing into sleep.

The creak of a floorboard had his eyes flying open. His heart sank. Stevie stood in the open doorway of her bedroom, pale. Stricken.

He glanced down at Cordelia, making sure she slept and wasn't faking it again. She seemed to be truly sleeping this time. 'How much did you hear?' he asked quietly.

Stevie crossed her arms over her chest, hugging herself tightly. 'All of it. Except for that last thing. What did she say to you?'

Clay sighed again. 'Let's get her back to bed and we'll go downstairs to talk.'

*Sunday, March 16, 4.10 A.M.*

Stevie sat at the kitchen table clutching her cell phone in her fist, watching Clay stirring a pot at the stove. Hot chocolate. The man was making her hot chocolate. From scratch.

'A mix would have been fine,' she murmured dully. There was a numbness in her chest . . . She was breathing, but that was all she could feel. *I'm all she has left.*

She could hear her daughter's fierce words, echoing in her mind. Then that look Cordelia had given him when he'd said he'd wondered if his mother's life would have been easier were he not there . . . *Oh my God. My baby thinks that. How could she think that?*

And what had she said at the very end to make Clay look like he'd been hit by a two-by-four? *Your mother loves you with all her heart.* What had Cordelia replied?

'Dad doesn't believe in mixes,' Clay said, quiet affection in his tone. 'He always says that anything worth doing is worth doing right.'

'You love your father. Your stepfather, I mean.'

He looked at her over his shoulder. 'Tanner St James *is* my father in every way that matters.' He turned back to the stove, whisking the mixture in the pot, then moving fluidly, as he always did, to grab a pair of mugs from a high shelf.

'Then why is your last name still Maynard?'

'He wanted to adopt me, to change my name, but my biological father went to court to stop it. Clayton Maynard, Senior, didn't want me or my mother, but he was selfish enough to want his family name to go on. In those days, that was enough for a judge. But it's okay.' He flashed her a grin. 'Clay St James sounds like a porn star.'

She snorted a surprised laugh. 'It really does.'

169

He slid the mug in front of her and took his seat. Too close. He was entirely too close. But he was warm. And Stevie was so tempted to lean into him.

Instead she sipped at the chocolate, finding it delicious, which came as no great shock. Everything he did seemed to be right. *And everything I do lately seems to turn out wrong.*

'What did she say, Clay? When you said I loved her with all my heart, what did she say?'

'She said, "I know. Because I'm all she has left."'

Stevie flinched. 'What? Oh my God.' Pushing the mug away, she covered her mouth with a hand that shook. Pain and denial and horror mixed together, surging up her throat, threatening to expel the chocolate she'd drunk. 'She thinks I only love her because she's . . .' *All I have left.*

Her eyes met Clay's, saw his sorrow. 'I've never said that to her,' Stevie said, her voice trembling. 'Not once. *Not ever.*'

'I know. You wouldn't.'

'I guess I didn't have to. She *is* all I have left. Of Paul, anyway. But that's not . . . That doesn't have anything to do with my loving her. She's my child.'

'I know,' he said gently.

'But that doesn't matter as long as Cordelia thinks it,' she said and he lifted a shoulder in agreement. 'What can I do to convince her that's not true?'

'I don't know. I don't have any experience with these things.'

'You seemed to be doing well enough with her,' Stevie muttered, then sighed. 'I'm sorry. I didn't mean it that way. I'm glad she talked to you. She won't talk to her counselor.'

'Because she thinks her counselor will tell you everything, because you're friends.'

Stevie huffed a bitter laugh. 'She's too smart for her own good. She thinks too much.' She glanced at him, saw what he was thinking but was too polite to say. 'Just like her mama.'

He lifted his shoulder again in agreement. But said nothing, just sat, sipping his chocolate.

'I'll talk to her, once I figure out what to say.' She stared at her phone. 'My cell woke me up.' Not the fact that her daughter had had a vicious nightmare and had left the bedroom to be comforted by someone else. 'I panicked until I saw she was with you. I knew she was safe.'

'Thank you,' he murmured.

'Thank you for being there for her. And for me.' She put her phone on the table. 'It was a text from JD. He wants us to call him on a secure line. I figured you'd have one of those.'

He was already halfway to the kitchen door. 'Wait here. I'll be right back.'

She was left alone with her thoughts and a mug of hot chocolate. As so often happened when she was troubled about Cordelia, Paul's face came to mind.

'I've really screwed things up,' she whispered to him. 'Turned our kid into . . .' *What?* Cordy was a great kid, thoughtful and kind. *And terrified to go to sleep, convinced her own mother only loved her because she had no one else.*

Paul would not have approved.

*But you're not here, are you?* she thought angrily. *I'm winging this solo, buddy. Because you are not here.* And Clay was right. Paul was never coming back.

Wearily she rested her head on the table, her cheek against the cool wood. 'Shit,' she said aloud just as the kitchen door swung open and Tanner St James came in with an old-fashioned corded phone. He gave her a sympathetic look, far different from his previous glare.

'You okay?' he asked as he plugged the phone cord into the wall.

'Yeah, thanks.' She didn't want to know what he knew. 'What's with the antique?'

'Clay said you need a secure line. The cordless isn't secure.'

Clay returned, a speaker in his hand. 'I've got sensors on the phone lines to ensure we're not being bugged.' He sat next to her and rigged the speaker to the old phone. 'Call him.'

JD picked up on the first ring. 'What took you so long?' he snapped.

'Sorry,' Stevie said. 'I just gave Clay the message. What's up?'

'A dead cop, that's what.'

She and Clay exchanged a worried glance. 'Who?'

JD blew out a frustrated breath. 'Her name was Justine Cleary. She was an undercover policewoman, five foot, two inches tall with shoulder-length dark brown hair.'

Stevie tugged at her own shoulder-length dark brown hair uncertainly. 'Where was she killed? When? And by whom?'

'In a hotel room in Silver Spring.' Which was forty-five minutes from Baltimore, in the opposite direction from Clay's beach house. 'An hour and a half ago. By another cop, who we now have in custody. He's in the hospital, in critical condition, with multiple gun shot wounds.'

'Were you there?' Stevie asked quietly, some of the pieces falling together.

'Yes.' JD's voice was flat. 'I shot him. After he killed Cleary in cold blood.'

Stevie exhaled carefully. 'That's why Hyatt wanted me to go to a safe house and didn't question when I agreed so readily. He set up a decoy. Did you know, JD?'

'Not until I got there. I thought Hyatt would be pissed off, but he had it all set up.'

Clay looked grim. 'How did the cop know the safe house was at that hotel?'

'Don't know yet. Hyatt thought we might have a leak, so he set it up this way so he could trace the flow of information. Justine had a marksmanship patch. She was a damn fine shot who should have been able to take care of herself. But the cop who came in knew the password. She opened the door for him and was dead before I could say a word.'

'Are you all right, JD?' Stevie asked quietly.

'I'm not hit,' he replied harshly. 'But I had to tell Justine's husband that she's not coming home. So, no. I'm not all right at all.'

'I'm sorry,' Stevie whispered. 'Truly sorry.'

'This isn't your fault,' Clay said firmly.

'He's right,' JD said, his voice softening. 'You can be sorry for her loss, but you played no part in her death, Stevie. That was all on the cop who shot her and anyone who fed him intel.'

'I know. I am sorry for her loss, though. And that you had to inform her family alone.'

'I wasn't alone. Hyatt went with me.'

Hyatt wasn't bad at informing families. This she knew from experience, professional and personal. It was eight years ago that she'd looked up from her desk to see Hyatt standing in front of her, his eyes filled with the pain of having to tell her that Paul and Paulie were gone.

'Who was the dirty cop?' she asked unsteadily.

'Tony Rossi. He's a detective in the robbery division.'

Stevie shook her head. 'I don't know him. I've never heard his name.'

'Well, he wanted to shut you up permanently,' JD said. 'And there's more.'

Dread rose, bile burning her throat. 'What?'

173

'He shot Justine twice, then kept shooting – at the bed. We'd put a large doll under the covers, so it would look like a child sleeping. If it had been Cordelia . . .'

Stevie's heart stopped. 'She'd be dead.' Trying to stay calm, she met Clay's furious stare. 'We need to get her someplace even safer than this. I want her far away. Like the goddamn moon.' She was on the verge of hyper-ventilating. 'Oh, God.'

Clay patted her hand, then shifted away. 'JD, what does Hyatt want to do next?'

Stevie sat back in her chair, eyes squeezed shut, hand pressed to her mouth, trying hard not to cry. Still a few hot tears seeped from beneath her eyelids. A warm hand closed over her shoulder, and her eyes flew open to find Tanner silently offering her a tissue.

'Thank you,' she whispered.

A final gentle squeeze of her shoulder was his only reply.

Clay was tapping the phone because JD hadn't responded to the last question. 'JD?'

'Sorry,' JD said. 'I had to find a quiet room. A couple of Feds just arrived, on loan to Joseph's task force. They're going on shifts to man the phones. We set up a hotline for info on the sniper this afternoon and the phones have been ringing off the hook.'

'Any leads?' Stevie managed, her voice more level.

'Not yet, just the usual crazies coming out of the woodwork. Okay.' They heard the creaking of a chair and the rifling of papers in the background. 'You asked about our next steps. The priorities are to trace the leak, ferret out all the bad apples in Hyatt's department, and keep Stevie and Cordelia safe, not necessarily in that order.'

*But all connected*, Stevie thought. 'He's assuming there are more dirty cops?'

'Safer to assume they're out there than to deny their existence,' JD said. 'Somebody leaked the safe house details. Worst case, we have a network of cops covering each other. Best case, that person did it unknowingly, but they still need to be identified. Rossi was not in a position to know where Stevie would have been tonight. He's in the burglary division.'

'Was Rossi the shooter at the restaurant?' Clay asked and Stevie gave him a second look. She had automatically assumed the shots were fired by a single gunman. Clay was right to assume they weren't.

'Not enough evidence to say definitively, although I'm pretty certain he wasn't the one who shot up Stevie's front yard.'

'Why?' Clay asked.

'Not the right body type, for one. I saw the gunman's arm when he shot from the red Chevy. Rossi's arm is short and thick. The gunman driving the red car would be leaner. But of course we'll check Rossi's prints against the white Toyota that followed you, Alec, and Cordelia, and the red Chevy that did the drive-by in Stevie's yard. What's left of it, anyway. The Chevy was abandoned about twenty miles from your house, lit on fire and left to burn.'

'I know,' Stevie said. 'Paige told me. Has forensics gotten anything from it?'

'Not yet, but they're going over every square inch of it. There was one good thing, though.'

'What's that?' Stevie asked.

'The driver's seat of the Chevy was missing. The frame remained, but the seat cover and all the stuffing had been removed.'

Clay's eyes glinted. 'Then I got him.'

'I'd say you did,' JD said, satisfied.

'Because the only reason he'd remove the seat was if he

left evidence behind on it,' Stevie said thoughtfully. 'Like blood. Did we check the street a few houses up from mine? His arm was hanging out the window. Maybe he dripped some as he sped away.'

'More likely I hit his shoulder and most of his blood spilled in the car,' Clay said. 'But it's worth a try. I take it that no GSWs have checked into area hospitals.'

'Only the one I just sent. Rossi was bullet-free when he arrived at the safe house. Hyatt and IA are at the hospital, waiting for him to come out of surgery. As soon as he's conscious, they'll grill him for details.'

Stevie frowned. 'But didn't Rossi expect me to have backup at the safe house?'

'No. Hyatt let it drop to a few people that you'd be alone because you were "too damn stubborn" to let them guard you. Anybody who knows you didn't doubt him.'

Stevie wanted to be offended, but couldn't. 'It's a fair cop, I guess.'

'He was dropping bread crumbs and wanted them to be believable. Now he has some leads on the leak.'

'How is he?' Stevie asked quietly. She'd worked for Peter Hyatt for a long time. He was gruff and sometimes a pain in the ass, but deep down he cared. That he'd put an officer in a situation that had gotten her killed would weigh him down.

'Angry as hell. He'd hoped you were wrong, you know. That there weren't any more cops involved. Now he knows there are and one of the good guys is dead.'

For a long moment no one said anything.

'That makes three today,' Stevie said, breaking the silence. 'Three dead and we still have at least one gunman out there, walking free. Until we catch him, I'm a target and I've made Cordelia one, too. And Emma.' Her voice trembled and she cleared her throat harshly. 'It could be anyone.'

'Not just anyone,' JD said. 'Someone who's connected to Stuart Lippman and Silas. Or to one of the crimes they perpetrated. I do see one benefit in all this, though.'

Stevie desperately needed a bright side. 'What's that?'

'The murder of a cop in a safe house by another cop blows this whole thing wide open. Whoever targeted you to keep you from investigating the crimes that didn't make it to Lippman's list now knows it's not just you looking. They can't silence all of us.'

Stevie's heart stuttered in her chest. All she could see in her mind was more bloodshed. 'That's not a bright side, JD,' she said hoarsely.

'It takes the spotlight off of you,' he said, his voice rough. 'Hyatt and IA should have made this public right away. The damn veil of secrecy put you in danger.'

'You're right,' she said, pushing away the dread. 'Now we – all of us together – have to rout this rot out of the department before anyone else gets hurt.' She thought of Justine Cleary, the undercover policewoman who'd died in her place. 'Or worse.'

'The answer is somewhere in those files you brought with you,' Clay said to Stevie. 'My bet is that we're looking for a case you hadn't uncovered yet. If it was one of the cases on Lippman's list, IA would have eventually gotten to it, so it would have made more sense to kill one of them. It's got to be one of the cases that didn't make it to the list.'

'You were hunting off the list,' JD agreed. 'It was only a matter of time before you exposed them.'

'So let's expose them now.' Clay caught Stevie's eye, his gaze sharp. 'How long ago did Silas start working for Lippman?'

'Nine years ago,' she said.

'And the other cops you know were dirty? How far back does that activity go?'

'The tell-all file that Lippman left behind recorded the first frame-job eleven years ago. He started with two cops on his payroll – homicide detectives Riddick and Payne. They were partners at the time. Riddick retired about five years ago, but died soon after. Payne's been in custody for the last six months. He was one of the first arrested.'

'And after that?' Clay asked. 'Who did Lippman recruit after that?'

'That would have been Elizabeth Morton, also Homicide. Lippman had one of his people hit her little boy with a car ten years ago. Ensured her cooperation by threatening to make it more painful for the boy "the next time". He wasn't even three years old then.'

'Sonofabitch,' Tanner muttered from behind her. 'Who does that? Who cripples toddlers? Who shoots at beds, hoping to kill little girls? My God. I was a cop for twenty-five years and I thought nothing could surprise me, but . . . Hell. Makes me sick that these guys wore a badge. The mother of the boy I might be able to understand, but still.'

'Don't waste too much understanding on her,' Stevie said. 'Elizabeth made it worse for herself. She killed Silas to keep him from giving Lippman's identity to us. In my living room, no less.' She still remembered the way her old partner dropped after Elizabeth Morton shot him.

'Why?' Tanner asked, confused.

'Because,' she said, 'Lippman made sure all of his operatives knew that if he was captured or killed, they'd all be exposed. We had Silas surrounded and he had excellent incentive to give Lippman up – Lippman had made good on his long-standing threat and abducted Silas's child.'

'That was the case where Paige met Grayson,' Clay said to his father. 'Remember, she told you about it the time she brought Grayson out here to meet you. Paige and Grayson had gotten too close to Lippman and the bastard had ordered Silas to kill them. Kidnapping Silas's child was Lippman's leverage, but then Paige's dog took Silas down and he found himself staring at a bunch of guns. He knew then that he was going to jail and that Stevie, Grayson, and Paige were his only hope of getting his little girl back.'

Tanner nodded. 'I remember now. Paige mentioned that another cop killed Silas.'

Stevie frowned a little, the thought of Grayson and Paige visiting with Clay's father mildly unsettling. Grayson had been Stevie's friend for years, yet he'd never mentioned this relationship. *Maybe because it involved Clay and Grayson knew I'd turned him away?*

Or . . . *Maybe because I've cut myself off from my friends.* She thought about that moment that they'd all rallied around her, there on the road. Supporting her. She'd been stunned, but she shouldn't have been. They'd always been there. *When did I shut them out?*

Her friends . . . Cordelia's pain . . . *What else have I been missing?*

'Elizabeth knew if Silas gave Lippman up, she'd go to jail,' she said to Tanner, 'and she didn't want that. She did earn a few brownie points, at the end. She killed Lippman to save other lives. She'll spend the rest of her life in prison, but the State's Attorney arranged for her to serve her time locally so her son can visit.'

'I remember Elizabeth Morton clearly,' Clay said. He and Joseph Carter had been responsible for her capture. 'Being in prison gives her a damn good alibi, though. She's obviously not the drive-by shooter. Nor did she leak the safe house location. So we're back to Rossi. JD, can you get your hands on Rossi's personnel file? Go back at least eleven years, back to the start of Lippman's crimes. We'll see if Rossi connects to any of Silas's cases that

Stevie's been reviewing. It has to be one of those cases, otherwise there'd be no reason to try to kill her.'

'I requested Rossi's file on my way back from the scene,' JD said. 'I should have it in an hour, tops.'

There was a moment of quiet, then. Stevie was mentally processing, making lists, trying to think of what else to ask. She figured JD was, too. But Clay was frowning, drumming his fingers on the table broodingly. 'What?' she asked him softly.

Clay's chest rose and fell with the deep breath he drew. 'Fine. I'm going to say what we haven't yet said, but what I'm sure we're all thinking because none of us are stupid. You told Hyatt about your suspicions of more dirty cops and you get attacked. Twice. You tell IA a few days later and the shooting starts. Hyatt arranges for a safe house and now a cop is dead. For sure there is an internal BPD leak. But how do we know Hyatt's trustworthy? How do we know that IA's not dirty, too?'

Stevie met Clay's eyes straight on. 'I don't. That's why I've been searching myself.'

JD's heavy sigh came through the speaker. 'IA I can buy. But Hyatt, too?'

'I don't want to think it,' Stevie said quietly. 'I didn't want to believe Silas was guilty either. But to save my child? Yeah, I'll entertain the notion that Hyatt's involved. I'll at least be careful of what I tell him.' She looked at the speaker. 'I trust you, JD. With my life. With Cordelia's life.' He'd put his life on the line for her more than once, something Silas had never done. Something Hyatt had never done.

But something Clay had also done. Once again she met his eyes. He deserved to hear her say the words aloud. 'And you, Clay. With my life and with the life of my child.'

His expression hardened, his eyes gone dark. For a

moment he didn't seem to breathe at all. 'Thank you,' he said, his voice nearly inaudible.

Stevie gave him a hard nod as JD sighed again, drawing them back to the matter at hand. 'Stevie, who knew the scope of your personal investigation? Other than IA?'

'Hyatt, of course. The records department, because I requested copies of the reports. The evidence room. The guy in the copy room. A lot of people,' she realized. 'Damn.'

'That's what I was afraid of,' JD said grimly. 'We'll figure this out, Stevie. Until we do, I need you to keep your head low and stay alive.'

'You can count on that,' Stevie promised. 'Thanks, JD.'

Clay disconnected, then shot her a wry look. 'Which thing can he count on? That you'll keep your head low or that you'll stay alive?'

'The second one. Until this is settled, my child is in danger. I'm not going to sit by, chewing my fingernails as I wait. But I won't take stupid chances. That I promise.'

He nodded. 'All right then. Let's get to work.'

'You're going to need something stronger than cocoa,' Tanner said from behind them and there was something different in his voice. All his previous censure was gone.

Stevie looked over her shoulder. 'Bourbon?'

He shook his head. 'Coffee. Extra strong.'

Clay pushed away from the table. 'I'll go get the suitcase with your files. Dad, you'd better make an extra large pot. This is going to take a while.'

*Baltimore, Maryland, Sunday, March 16, 4.15 A.M.*

Robinette was awoken once again by the soft beep of his cell phone. This time Lisa didn't stir. He'd worn her out and maybe even left a few bruises. He rolled over and checked the text. Then stared at Westmoreland's message in disbelief. *SNAFU. 411. ASAP.*

Westmoreland had failed, too? Jesus God, was the Mazzetti woman a goddamn cat?

He went down to his office to make the call, a concession Westmoreland had demanded, reasoning that if Henderson had been allowed to check in after the first failure, the second might not have happened. *Whatever.*

'What the fuck, Wes?' Robinette hissed.

'It was a trap. She wasn't in the safe house. The cops set up a decoy – a lady cop who looked like her along with Mazzetti's partner, Fitzpatrick. A cop named Tony Rossi took the bait. Now the lady cop's dead. Fitzpatrick shot Rossi, who's now in ICU. The cops knew they had a mole and were cleaning house.'

'How the hell did Rossi know where to find her?' Robinette demanded. Tony Rossi was *not* his BPD source.

'You said yourself that a lot of people wanted her dead. I guess Rossi's source knew before yours did. Rossi must be a dirty cop who wanted to shut her up.'

Robinette drew a breath, forced himself to think. 'What tipped you off that it was a trap?'

'Nothing. I would have been the one caught, but Rossi beat me to it. I got there a minute after he did and when the bullets started flying, I ran. The area was fuckin' crawlin' with cops.'

'Shit.'

'Yeah, that's what I thought when the bullets started flying. Is it possible that your source also tipped off Rossi? He gets paid by you and another cop?'

'Double dipping? Or double-crossing,' Robinette added darkly. 'It's possible. Once a cop goes bad, you can never really trust him. If he did double dip, and if Rossi lives to tell, then my source will be a suspect. The cops must have given out the false info, hoping to trap him.'

'Can your source be traced to you?'

'Not directly, but if they get any evidence from Henderson's botched attempts they may get enough for a circumstantial case. I don't want to risk it. Take care of him. I'll send you his contact info.'

'Okay. What about her?'

'I still want you to take care of her, too.'

A slight hesitation. 'Fine by me. Do you have any idea where Mazzetti's hiding?'

'No, but it's likely she's with friends. SA Grayson Smith has a place in Fell's Point. His family has a compound outside of the city. If she's there, you won't get her until she comes out.'

'Good security?'

'Top of the line. Designed by a Fed with a knack for systems. Special Agent Carter is shacked up with ASA Daphne Montgomery. Both are friends of Mazzetti. Both are richer than God. If Mazzetti needed a place to hide or money to run, she'd go to them.'

'I'll check them out.'

'Good. According to my source, the shooting at her house was witnessed by four people. One was Dr Townsend, the shrink she meets every March 15. One was Mazzetti's partner, Fitzpatrick. The other two were males, not ID'd. Find out who they were. It's likely she's with one of the other friends here locally, but those two might have an angle. Townsend lives in Florida. There's a chance Mazzetti may be hiding with her.'

'If she has rich friends, one of whom is FBI, she could be out of the country by now. If she's outside our borders, do you want me to follow her?'

'Not until we know her long-term plans. If she runs,

she'll run someplace civilized. Just keep tabs on her. Especially on the kid. If we get the kid, Mazzetti will come to us.'

# Chapter Nine

'Is she okay?' Tanner murmured.

Standing in the kitchen doorway, Clay looked over his shoulder to where Stevie huddled under a blanket on the living room sofa. 'She's asleep.' He tapped the kitchen table where Emma had dozed off, a stack of folders her pillow. 'Emma, wake up.'

Emma's chin jerked up, her eyes wide and groggy. She blinked hard, then pushed her hair away from her face and sat up, her expression disgusted. 'Hell. I fell asleep.' She'd come down two hours before, lured by the smell of fresh coffee. Taking one look at the table covered with police reports, she'd rolled up her sleeves and pitched in – until her eyes had grown too heavy to hold open. 'I only got through five reports before I conked out on you.'

'It's okay,' Tanner said, pointing toward the living room. 'Stevie didn't last much longer.'

'Poor Stevie. She must have been completely worn out to actually let herself sleep.'

Clay pulled the folders Stevie had been reviewing to his

side of the table and sat down. 'She didn't "let" herself sleep. She just collapsed face forward.' He'd tried to rouse her enough to get her back to bed, but she'd been unresponsive. 'For a minute I thought she was unconscious.'

'Well, if she could wake up enough to walk to the sofa,' Emma said, 'I'm sure she's okay.'

'She didn't walk to the sofa,' Tanner told her in a stage whisper. 'Clay carried her.'

Clay shot his father a warning look. Tanner returned a clueless blink, making Emma smile. Clay wasn't smiling, though, his chest still so tight he could barely breathe. He'd started to carry Stevie upstairs, but she'd cuddled into him in her sleep, making him want so much more than to hold her. Putting her in an actual bed? He couldn't do it. So he'd settled for the sofa, trembling as he'd laid her down. He'd still be trembling if he hadn't locked down every one of his muscles.

'That was so sweet of you, Clay,' Emma said, then frowned. 'Wait. How do you know she wasn't unconscious if she didn't wake up?'

'She opened her eyes long enough to look up at me when I covered her with a blanket, mumbled something about resting "for just a sec", then rolled over and started snoring.'

But before she'd rolled over, he'd seen something in her gaze. A moment of unguarded acceptance. A flicker of heat. It was enough for now. Enough to let him know that when he managed to break down her barriers, he'd find her willing. Please God, maybe even eager.

'All right,' Emma said with a yawn. 'How many more reports do we need to summarize?'

'Stevie did most of them over the past few weeks,' Clay said. 'We got through several more before she fell asleep and probably have another five hours ahead of us. So far, no mention of Rossi. We need to search all of the notes from the cases for links. The link may be secondary, but Rossi *is* implicated somewhere. He'd have no reason to attack the safe house otherwise.'

Emma bit her lip. 'You're assuming Rossi worked one of these cases in an official capacity. He may not be called out by name in any of these reports. He might be protecting someone else.'

Clay considered it. 'Possibly. Then that person would be a secondary connection.'

'Like what?' Emma pressed.

'How are any two people connected? Work, family, friends, hobbies, geography. Maybe he and Silas had a past partner in common. Maybe they played for the same ball team or lived in the same neighborhood. Lippman got to these guys through their families. He threatened Silas's kid and Elizabeth Morton's, too. Maybe Rossi has a kid. Maybe their kids played on the same soccer team. Hell, I don't know. But Tony Rossi's in one of these files, somewhere. Whatever he did, it's got to be big. Like major felony big. Attacking the safe house was a huge risk.'

'You're right,' Emma said thoughtfully. 'He had to know that he'd be up on murder charges if he got caught. Attempted murder at the very least if he'd tried and hadn't managed to kill Stevie. As it is, he'll be charged with the murder of the undercover policewoman.'

'And now that he's caught, it's a matter of time before someone connects him to his crime,' Tanner said. 'Whether it's through IA's efforts or yours, he aimed the spotlight on himself by attacking the safe house.'

'He believed the benefits outweighed the risk,' Emma said.

Tanner shook his head. 'It's more likely that he believed he wouldn't get caught.'

'Which puts IA under even more suspicion,' Clay said wearily. 'When they were doing the investigating, nobody was getting attacked. When Stevie discovered the Lippman list was not inclusive, the attacks began. Rossi didn't think he'd get caught when IA was holding the reins.' He grimaced. 'I want to believe IA was just incompetent and not corrupt, but we can't afford to.'

'I agree.' Emma's sigh was frustrated. 'We could read reports till the cows come home if we don't know what we're looking for. It's too bad all this stuff isn't in a computer somewhere.'

Tanner lifted a page from one of the reports. 'It is. It got printed out of the BPD computer.'

'Well, yes,' she said, 'but that's not what I meant. We can print out the reports, but it would be nice to ask the computer to find the connection for us.'

Clay felt like smacking his own head. He'd overlooked the obvious solution. 'We can. This is the kind of thing that Alec does best.' He dialed Alec's cell from the secure line, unsurprised when the boy immediately answered, despite the early hour. 'I need your help.' He told Alec about the reports and what they were looking for. 'We may be looking for a case that neither Stevie nor Silas worked on, one that Lippman contracted, but never added to his list. Can you work your computer voodoo?'

Alec chuckled. 'No voodoo, but I can input all the names and keywords you found in the reports into a simple database. Add whatever I can get from their service records, Google as much about their personal lives as I can find and cross-reference. It wouldn't take long, especially since you've got the reports summarized. Fax me the notes you have, keep summarizing, then send me the rest when you're done. I'll be in touch. Bye for now.'

Tanner gathered the notes. 'I'll fax them from my office.'

He went into what had been Clay's mother's dining room, now the office where he conducted his charter fishing business.

'This should save us time in the long run,' Clay said when he'd disconnected the call. He pulled the stack of reports they hadn't yet read to the end of the table where he sat.

One folder stood out from the rest, its bright green color a contrast to all the manila.

'Stevie kept starting to read that set of reports,' Clay said, 'but kept changing her mind.'

'What's in the folder, Clay?' Emma asked.

Clay opened the folder and let out a breath when he saw the dates on the reports. 'The first one was completed two weeks after her husband and son's murder, the last about a year later. These were the cases Silas investigated while she was on bereavement and maternity leave.'

Emma's shoulders sagged. 'Is the report on the murders of Paul and Paulie in there?'

'No.'

'Good. At least she didn't have to read it.'

Clay looked at her. 'You really think she hasn't?'

Emma sighed. 'You're right. I'm sure she has. But at least she doesn't have to again. Give me the folder. I'll go through them.'

Clay shook his head. 'We can do it together.'

They split the green folder, each taking a half, working in silence until Tanner returned to the table. 'Fax is sent,' he said. 'Pass me some of those reports.'

Clay did so with one hand, picking up the ringing phone with the other. It was Alec.

'I got the fax,' he said. 'I should be able to turn this around in a few hours.'

'Good,' Clay said. 'Because I have something else I

want you to do when you're finished. How much of that camera installation did you get done up at Daphne's yesterday?'

'About half, why?'

Clay thought about Rossi shooting at the bed in the safe house, believing he was shooting a seven-year-old child. His very attempt might be enough to dissuade any further attacks on Stevie. As JD had said, all of BPD now knew there were more dirty cops – and a department leak. That might be enough to ensure her safety.

But Clay couldn't afford to count on that. And if the attacks on Stevie continued, it would be safer for Cordelia to not be in Stevie's proximity. Stevie might not agree, but he wanted to have a place ready in case she did. He'd promised he'd keep them safe and he didn't break his promises.

'I want you to go back to the farm and finish it today. Once the cameras are installed, the farm will be secure enough for Cordelia, and she can continue her therapy with the horses.'

'Will Stevie come with her?' Alec asked.

'I don't know yet. Get the farm ready for Cordelia, and we'll figure it out from there.'

'Okay. Will I be up at the farm on my own, or will I have help? If I have to do it on my own, it'll take me more than another full day.'

'You'll have help.' DeMarco and Julliard would welcome the overtime pay.

Clay's father gave him a sharp look when he hung up. 'You're letting Stevie go?'

*Hell, no.* Clay kept his face as expressionless as he could, ignoring Emma's shrewd stare. 'I can't hold her here. She's free to go wherever she wants.'

'That's not what I meant,' Tanner said. 'And you know it.'

'I know what you meant. And I meant what I said. She's not a prisoner. Now let's get back to work, please.'

Clay dropped his eyes to the report in front of him, but his mind had already begun working the logistics for moving Cordelia to an alternate location. By land or by water? He had to be realistic. Once whoever was after Stevie learned she hadn't been in the safe house, they'd start looking for her elsewhere. That he'd been with her in her front yard would filter into the BPD grapevine sooner versus later. And though this place was secure, there were ways to connect this place to Clay through his parents, were someone determined enough.

Four shooting attempts in two days? And one in a safe house?

They were determined enough. It was only a matter of time before she was tracked here. The property itself was secure, but anyone that determined could be patient enough to wait on the road to waylay a car carrying Cordelia. And Stevie, if she decided to leave as well.

The road wasn't safe. Going by water would probably be safer.

Now he knew exactly what he'd do and exactly who he'd call to put his plan in place. That settled, he blinked hard and forced his eyes to focus on the page before him.

*Baltimore, Maryland, Sunday, March 16, 6.58 A.M.*

Sam Hudson pushed away from the wall he'd been holding up for the better part of an hour, waiting for the morning shift to arrive. 'Hey, Dee.'

Dina Andrews looked over her shoulder, a smile lighting her face. 'Sammy. What brings you to the tomb so early in the morning?'

They'd dated once, five years ago. Dina was one of the rarities in Sam's experience – an honest woman on the dating scene. She'd been upfront that she was looking for long-term. Sam had liked her, but not that way. So they'd stayed friends and few were more loyal than Dina.

'I come bearing gifts.' He held out a bag and a cup from the Starbucks on the corner. 'My mom's homemade pumpkin bread and a cup of decaf tea.'

She accepted the gifts with a suspicious narrowing of her eyes. 'Why?'

'Because I need a favor.' He followed her back to her cubicle, then held out the evidence bag with the revolver inside. 'Can you run a check on this?'

She took the bag, brows lifted. 'Is there a report to go along with it?'

'Not yet. It was left for me. Not too far from where I was sleeping.'

Not a lie. Technically. The revolver had been left for him, three feet from where he'd slept away thirty hours like the dead – eight years ago.

'Someone in the neighborhood maybe?'

'Who knows?' he replied. 'Maybe a guilty conscience or an innocent bystander.'

She studied him squarely and he knew that she guessed he was keeping secrets. 'Okay. I'll call you when I have something.'

'Thanks, Dee. You're the best.'

Sam walked away, dread pooling in his gut. She'd find something. He knew it. He should have checked eight years ago, but he'd been so afraid of what he'd find. So he'd said nothing.

*Please God*, he whispered in his mind. *Please don't let it be anything I can't fix. Please.*

*Wight's Landing, Maryland, Sunday, March 16, 8.15 A.M.*

'Mr Maynard?'

Cordelia's little whisper came from above his head, from the middle of the staircase. Clay looked up, relieved he'd locked Stevie's files in the closet under the stairs. There were crimes in those folders that adults should never have had to see, much less a child Cordelia's age.

Already dressed, with her hair brushed, she sat on the step that came even with his head, her face pressed between the spindles. 'Where's my mo— Oh. There she is.'

He looked over his shoulder, following her gaze to the sofa where Stevie slept soundly. 'She got up to work last night and fell asleep at the kitchen table.'

'She does that sometimes,' Cordelia said, aggrieved. 'She'll say, "I'm just resting my eyes", then the next thing Aunt Izzy and I know, she's snoring, really loud. She says she doesn't snore, but she does.' The last word was punctuated with a hard nod that made Clay grin. 'Did you have to put away all her reports so I wouldn't see them?'

His grin faded. 'Yes,' he said, wondering why he continued to be surprised at this child's solid grasp on the reality around her. 'Do you ever peek?'

'No. Mom says those papers will mess up my head. I think I'm already messed up enough. Puppies and Skittles,' she added with a dramatic sigh that tried to hide so much pain and fear.

'And flowers and rainbows. I'm sorry, honey.'

She shrugged. 'It's okay. Where is everybody?'

'Miss Emma went back upstairs to sleep.' Emma had lasted another hour before her eyes drooped shut once again. 'She tried to work but kept falling asleep on the reports.'

'Where's Mr Tanner? And the dogs?'

'Out for a walk and a swim. Dad walks, the dogs swim.'

'The water's too cold. They'll get sick.'

'Nah. They're bred to swim in cold water. They'll be fine.'

'Where are the puppies?' Cordelia asked.

'In their bed by the furnace.' He thumbed over his shoulder and she strained to fit her face between the spindles, trying to get a glimpse. 'Your head's gonna get stuck,' he cautioned mildly, making her giggle. The sound lifted his heart. *Too late, Stevie. Way too late for me not to get attached to your baby girl.*

Being around Stevie's child made him happy and wistful, all at once. *I should have had this. Should have had a daughter.* But the daughter of his blood was lost to him. He'd never seen her smile, never heard her giggle. He hadn't realized until that moment how much he'd hoped at a second chance at fatherhood with Cordelia Mazzetti.

*And with a child Stevie and I might have made together.* But Stevie had been very clear on that point. He might never stop hoping, but realistically he had to accept that the family he'd always wanted might never be.

He wanted to be angry with Stevie, but he couldn't. She was protecting her child and herself the best way she knew how. He had to figure out how to stop her from doing it.

'You look so sad,' Cordelia said quietly. 'Why?'

*You promised you wouldn't lie to her.* He couldn't discuss his issues with Stevie, so he gave her the only other honest answer he could. 'I miss my own little girl.'

Her eyes widened. 'You have a little girl?' she whispered.

He nodded. 'Not so little anymore. She'll be twenty-two this summer.'

Cordelia studied him through the spindles. 'What's her name?'

'Sienna.' It hurt to say it out loud.

'Why do you miss her? Why don't you see her?'

'It's complicated. She . . . doesn't like me.' Understatement of the damn century.

'Why not? I think you're nice.'

That made him smile. 'You're pretty nice, too. Like I said, it's complicated. Her mother kept her from me. I wasn't allowed to see her when she was growing up.'

'Why?' She sounded so distressed on his behalf that his own heart was eased.

'I could never get her mother to tell me. I didn't even know about Sienna until she was much older.'

'But now she's a grownup, right? You don't need her mama's permission, do you?'

'No, I guess not. Her mama's not living anymore, anyway. I've tried to contact Sienna, but every time I show up to see her, she's somewhere else. She lives out west now, in California.' At least that was the last known address he had for her. A rented mailbox in a UPS store.

Cordelia extended her small hand and patted his cheek gently. 'I'm sorry.'

'Thank you.' He swallowed hard. 'I'm going to make waffles. You want to help me?'

'*You* can make waffles?' she asked skeptically.

'You just watch me. Come on.' He held out his hand and she skipped down the stairs, taking his hand with an unexpectedly firm grip. He looked down at her fierce little face and saw Stevie in her eyes. 'What is it, honey?' he asked.

'Where am I going today?'

'Don't know yet. I'm waiting to talk to your mom when she wakes up. For the next hour, you can stick with me and I'll show you my mother's waffle recipe. I used to help her cook when I was your age.' He sniffed. 'Dad must be back from his walk. I smell fresh coffee.'

'Mom really likes coffee. Do you have chocolate chips?'

'For the coffee? Yuck.'

She giggled again. 'No, silly. For the waffles.'

'Chocolate in waffles?' He looked down again, relieved to see her fierceness replaced with a simple smile. 'Really?'

'Oh my gosh, yes.'

Stevie waited until the kitchen door swung shut before sitting up on the sofa. *I'm learning a helluva lot, listening in on my daughter's conversations.*

Clay had a daughter. That gave Stevie something to think about. But the words that stuck in her head were the ones she'd heard coming from Cordelia.

*I'm all she has left,* she'd said last night. And just now? *I'm messed up enough.*

*Dear God. What have I done?* She'd put her baby in harm's way repeatedly, that's what she'd done. In her head Stevie knew she'd been doing her job, an important job at that. She hadn't been negligent. Hadn't deliberately left her child unprotected.

But her heart shouted the truth. *I failed to keep my own child safe.*

She started to follow them into the kitchen, but held back, not ready to face Clay yet. She looked at the sofa, remembering exactly how she'd gotten there. She'd fallen asleep at the table, a stack of folders her pillow. And then she was being carried in strong arms, deposited on the sofa with a tenderness that had cut her deep, even in the fog of half-waking. He'd tucked her in as carefully as if she'd been a child herself. Brushed the hair from her face.

She'd opened her eyes to find him standing next to the

sofa, staring down at her with a yearning that stole her breath. But he hadn't said a word. Hadn't made a move. Just turned around and went back to the kitchen. And she'd fallen back to sleep, feeling safe.

A piece of her rebelled at the notion. She didn't need anyone to keep her safe. *I can take care of myself.* Grabbing her cane, she pushed herself to her feet and rolled her shoulder, the bullet wound from the day before still fresh enough to burn like fire.

*You can take care of yourself? Really? So how's that been working for you?*

*Shut up.*

Feeling foolish, she turned and lifted her eyes to the window . . . and froze. Before her was the most beautiful day she'd seen in a long time. The sun reflected off the Chesapeake Bay in countless sparkles of light that glittered like diamonds. The sky was a cloudless blue, broken only by the lazy flight of seabirds.

Something within her settled. *Quiet,* she realized. Here was quiet. On another day, under different circumstances, she might have even found peace.

'Oh,' she breathed. 'I knew it would be magnificent.'

'The view?' Tanner asked. She looked over her shoulder to see him approaching, a mug of steaming coffee gripped in each fist.

'It's amazing,' she told him. 'You can see forever. The water, the waves. The birds. You're lucky to be able to see it every day. Thank you,' she added when he gave her one of the mugs.

'Peace offering. I was impolite last night when you arrived. My wife would not have approved of my behavior.'

'It's all right. I understand about protecting your child.'

'Clay's no child and I was wrong to treat you harshly.

197

You'd had a hell of a day and I didn't make it any better. I hope you'll stay as long as you need to.'

'That's very nice of you. But I think Cordelia needs to be . . .' She drew a bolstering breath. 'Away from me. Bad guys want me out of the picture. I don't want her getting hurt because I'm too stubborn to admit someone else can protect her better than I can at the moment.'

'Not because you want her away from Clay?' Tanner asked carefully and her gaze shot up, locking with the older man's.

'No. That might have been true twenty-four hours ago, but it's not true now. Your son has helped my daughter more in a day . . .' Another bolstering breath. 'Than I have in the past year.'

'I don't know about that. But he does seem to put her at ease. He was always like that as a boy. Always trying to put everyone at ease.'

'Except himself?'

'Yep,' he said brusquely.

She had so many questions, but his expression said he'd tell no tales. 'He makes my baby laugh. I haven't heard her laugh in months. I guess I haven't given her much to laugh about.'

'You like to beat yourself up, don't you?'

The question startled her. 'Yep,' she said, echoing his tone, making him chuckle.

'You ought not do that.' He took a sip of the coffee, staring out at the Bay. 'I used to beat myself up, when I was your age.'

'What made you stop?'

'Something I learned a long time ago. Children watch and they emulate. You beat yourself up for everything that happens around you, to you, and that little girl will do the same.'

'She already does,' Stevie whispered. 'I have to make some serious changes. For her.'

'No. For you. You have to do it for *you*. You do it for her and you'll grow to resent the changes and her for forcing you to make them. Do what's right because it helps you be a better person and, in turn, a better parent. She'll see and she'll know it's real.'

Stevie had to swallow hard. 'Thank you. For the coffee and the wisdom.'

'Not my wisdom,' he said gruffly. 'My wife spent the best years of her life drumming that into my head. But I was a cop, too. I saw things on the job . . . so many things I couldn't fix, so many things I wished I could change. I brought the pressure home, even though I didn't mean to. Then I saw Clay doing what I did, beating himself up. By then it was too late. I'd taught him to be the man he is – a damn good man. There isn't a better one on God's green earth.'

His tone dared her to disagree. 'I know he's a good man, Tanner. I told him so last night. My wanting him away from Cordelia wasn't because of him, of the man he is. It was to protect Cordelia's heart. She gets attached to people. I don't want her hurt.'

He sighed. 'My wife said as much to me long ago.'

Stevie heard the echoes of pain in his voice. She'd heard those echoes before in her own voice when she spoke of Paul. After eight years she still did and this man's loss was even more recent. 'Clay told me she was a single mom. He also said that you were his father, in every way that mattered,' she added softly and immediately saw it had been the right thing to say.

'Thank you.' He cleared his throat. 'I knew my Nancy had a son before I asked her out, but it took more than a month of dating before she let me meet Clay, and even then it was only because I'd manipulated her into it.' His lips twitched at the memory. 'We were supposed to go to the movies, but she cancelled because her sitter got sick. I showed up at her door with three tickets to that night's Orioles game. When Clay saw those tickets, his eyes lit up like it was Christmas. Nancy was so angry with me, but she agreed to go because she couldn't disappoint Clay. They didn't have anything back then. She was waiting tables, barely making ends meet. But she was proud. Never accepted help. Unless it was for her boy.'

'How old was Clay?'

'Five. And what a mind that boy had. He knew every player on both teams, their stats, all of it. We had the best evening ever. But when I took them home and she'd put Clay to bed, oh boy, did the sparks fly. She told me that until she knew I was husband material she didn't want her son to get to know me. She didn't want him to get attached, only to have me walk away.' He glanced at her pointedly. 'Like his father had done.'

Stevie bristled. 'My husband didn't *walk away*. He was murdered.'

'I know. Clay told me. But the end is the same, right? He's gone, leaving a hole where a parent should be. You want to protect Cordelia, just like Nancy protected Clay.'

She didn't think it was the same at all, but saw what he was trying to say and appreciated the attempt. 'So you understand why I told Clay I didn't want him to have contact with Cordelia. My wishes had nothing to do with Clay himself. He is a good man. I've always known that.'

'Good. Now, because he is my son and I'll protect him to my dying breath, I need you to know one more thing. You're not the only one with a tragic past. Clay's got scars too, mostly inside where he doesn't let anyone see. Nancy and I waited for years for him to find someone to heal him, to unlock that heart we knew was there. For whatever reason, it was you.'

She sucked in a breath, not knowing what to say.

Tanner stared her down. 'I don't understand your reasons for not wanting him, because any woman should be proud to have him. You hurt him when you turned him away. Cut him deep.'

She felt a pain in her heart. Guilt. Remorse. Regret. 'I'm sorry,' she said softly.

'I'm sure you are. Yet here you are.'

Anger sparked. 'For Cordelia. To keep her safe.' Something Tanner had said clicked in her brain and she narrowed her eyes. 'Clay used my daughter's fear of losing me to manipulate me into agreeing to accept his help. Now I know where he learned the fine art of manipulation.'

Tanner's eyes flashed, his mouth tightening. Then, unexpectedly, his lips quirked. 'I can see Clay doing that and I can't deny that he learned it from me. Please, just be careful with him. When you walk away, try not to hurt him again.' He took another sip of coffee, then turned on his heel. 'I believe I smell waffles. Let's eat before they're all gone.'


*Baltimore, Maryland, Sunday, March 16, 8.30 A.M.*

'You're sure?' Robinette asked, keeping his voice icy calm. Inside, his fury roiled. Of all his people, Fletcher was the last person he'd expected to betray him. 'There's no doubt?'

'None,' Westmoreland said. 'I got a positive ID on both Henderson and Fletcher from the hotel clerk. I can email you a clip from the hotel's security video if you want proof.'

'No, don't email it.' Robinette didn't want any connections the cops could trace back to him. Cell phone conversations were dangerous enough. Even the 'disposable' cells they used could be traced if a cop was smart. And Stevie Mazzetti was too damn smart for her own good. *And mine.* 'Put it on a flash drive and bring it to me. Where is Henderson now?'

'Gone,' Westmoreland said disgustedly. 'The coffee in the cup next to the bed was still hot. The desk clerk admitted to being paid to look out for me and had called the room.'

'Where's the clerk?'

'Dead. I made him open the safe and the register first, so it'll look like a robbery. Surveillance system was closed loop, nothing uploaded to a server. I took the recorder with me.'

'What about Henderson's car?'

'The clerk admitted that Henderson arrived in a white Camry, so I sliced its tires on my way to Henderson's room. When I found it empty, I checked the security footage of the parking lot. Henderson stole a rusted old Dodge. Had it hotwired in five seconds flat.'

'Yay,' Robinette deadpanned sarcastically. 'Henderson still has some skills.'

'I found the Dodge abandoned a mile away. Lots of cops surrounding it. I got nervous that they'd ID'd Henderson, but they were there because a delivery guy reported his van stolen. The owner was holding the magnetic sign he kept on the door, so Henderson's out there in an unmarked white van. I'll keep looking. I do have good news, though – a lead on Mazzetti.'

'Do tell,' Robinette bit out.

'Right before I dealt with your BPD source, he ID'd the two men who were with Mazzetti when Henderson did the drive-by. They were Clay Maynard and Alec Vaughn.'

'Maynard?' Frowning, Robinette tapped a few keys on his laptop, then stared at a still taken on the courthouse steps the day Mazzetti was shot by the psycho teenager. In the photo, Mazzetti lay bleeding while a shirtless man crouched over her. Clay Maynard. 'He was there when she got shot back in December, too. Sonofabitch saved her life.'

'Well, he was her guardian angel last night, too,' Westmoreland said. 'Or her bodyguard.'

'Possible. He runs a security service. That's why he was at the courthouse that day. One of his employees had been killed the night before while guarding ASA Montgomery's son, who'd been kidnapped. Maynard was there to inform her. So, Stevie hired a bodyguard. Smart.'

'She got her money's worth. Maynard took two of Henderson's bullets in the back for her last night. Saved her life again, and the little girl's, too. I've checked all the other friends you named and she doesn't appear to be with any of them. Chances are good that Maynard's got her holed up somewhere.'

'What about the other man? Vaughn?'

'He's just a kid. Maynard's the main player. I'll go to his home and check it out.'

'You won't find Maynard's address easily,' Robinette said. 'He bought his house through a corporation, hidden in a tangle of other corporations. The guy's no beginner.' He looked up Maynard's home address in his old-fashioned pen-and-paper address book. There wasn't a hacker in the world who could break into his contact list. 'Write this down,' he said, and read out Maynard's address.

'How did you get it?' Westmoreland asked.

'I have my ways.' Actually, he'd waited outside Maynard's office one night and followed him home. Guy nearly lost him three times. 'Be careful. He'll have top-notch security and he's well-armed. Take backup.' Westmoreland maintained a security team who guarded the plant round the clock. Allowing Fletcher's special formulas to leave the plant in the wrong hands could get them arrested. Or worse.

'I can't right now. I've got my team looking for Henderson, who's running around loose right now in a pissed off mood. That worries me.'

The censure in Wes's voice scraped at Robinette's patience. 'You think I made a mistake.'

'Well . . . it might have been a hasty decision. I wasn't there, so I don't know what went down, but according to what little I could find about Maynard, he's a pro. His clientele are some of the richest businessmen on the East Coast – and they trust Maynard with their security. Knowing he's Mazzetti's bodyguard changes the game. If Henderson didn't have that intel . . .'

'You're saying I judged Henderson too harshly.'

Another hesitation. 'Hell, Robbie. I don't know that *I* would have expected anyone to leap in front of a stream of bullets. But now we have to deal with a pissed off Henderson. My team is watching airports and hospitals. From the bandage I found in that hotel room, Henderson's still bleeding pretty bad.'

'Fine. Just keep me informed.'

'Robbie, wait. What about Fletcher?'

'I'll take care of Fletcher.'

Westmoreland sighed. 'Hell. Just when things were gettin' good. We could've been rich.'

It was true. Without Fletcher, they'd have no product. Without product, no business, and no money. 'I didn't say I would kill Fletch. I'll just make sure this doesn't happen again.'

Westmoreland sighed again, this time in relief. 'Good to know. I always liked Fletch. But just as a friend,' he added quickly and Robinette found his lips twitching.

'Keep me informed.' Robinette hung up and immediately dialed the guard shack. 'Is Dr Fletcher in the lab?' It was Sunday, but Fletch often worked weekends.

'No, Dr Fletcher hasn't arrived yet. Should I take a message?'

'Yes, please. Tell Dr Fletcher to report to my office as soon as possible.'

# Chapter Ten

*Baltimore, Maryland, Sunday, March 16, 9.00 A.M.*

Henderson was pissed off. *He fired me. He burned down my apartment.* Now Robinette had ordered a hit. *Does he think I'm gonna go to the cops? He thinks I'm that petty? That stupid?*

And to top it all off, Robinette had sent *Westmoreland* to do the job. That was just plain insulting. Westmoreland couldn't shoot his way out of a church full of Quakers.

*I'd like to see him take a shot at Detective Stevie Mazzetti,* Henderson thought with a sneer. *Mazzetti.* The woman's very name tasted foul.

Or perhaps that would be the odor of the dirty diapers in the back of the delivery van. *Trust me to hijack a diaper delivery van. Goddamn, I wish I'd never heard of Stevie Mazzetti.*

Mazzetti, however, was at the bottom of the priority list at the moment. First was finding a place to hide. Second was finding medical attention. Food would also be good.

*I have to get outta town.* Canada wouldn't be bad. Australia would be better. *I have friends that don't work for Todd Robinette. I'll start over somewhere new.* For now, being any place other than Baltimore seemed smart. Cops hated cop-killers and hunted them down like dogs.

That Henderson hadn't been successful wouldn't buy much compassion, especially since Mazzetti was such a media darling. Who'd apparently hired a fucking body-guard.

*I should have Googled her* before *the restaurant hit. Should have gathered my own fucking intel.* Because an Internet search the night before yielded dozens of Stevie Mazzetti news stories and photos, most about the day in December when she got shot. And with her on the courthouse steps? The man who stopped two bullets for her yesterday – a guy who provided bodyguards.

*Shit. If I'd had that little piece of information I'd have set up the hit a lot differently.* To be fair, the guy hadn't been at the restaurant. *So that miss was on me.* He'd been guarding the little girl. Mazzetti must've thought she could take care of herself.

But Robinette had to have known about the bodyguard. *And he didn't tell me, that sonofabitch. And then had the nerve to send Westmoreland to . . .*

*Wait.* Henderson frowned. *How did Westmoreland know where to find me?*

*Fletcher.* But Henderson had known the chemist for a long time. Had never been aware of a single lie, a single betrayal. Eyes narrowed, Henderson dialed Fletcher's cell.

'I told you not to call me anymore,' Fletcher hissed. 'You want to get me fired, too?'

'Did you drive one of Robinette's cars last night?' Henderson asked.

'What? Of course not. All those cars have tracking devices.'

'Then did you tell Robinette where I was?'

'No. I said I wouldn't. I haven't even seen him since yesterday. He had that . . . thing last night, that black tie event. With Lisa.'

'Well, somehow he knew. I just escaped Westmoreland by the skin of my damn teeth. And he didn't come to bring me flowers.'

A beat of silence. 'He sicced Westmoreland on you? To kill you? Really?'

'I'm driving a diaper delivery van, Fletch. I had to get creative to stay alive. Yes, really.'

'Shit. That's . . . Well, I didn't tell. You can believe me or not.'

'I do believe you, actually. You helped me last night when you didn't have to. So here's a tip – if Westmoreland knew I was there and you didn't tell anyone, then either Robbie's following you or he has a tracker on your personal vehicle. Which means he knows you helped me. I wouldn't go into the office today if I were you.'

Fletcher sucked in a breath. 'Too late. I just signed in at the gate. Well, that explains why he wants me to come to his office, ASAP.'

'What are you going to do?'

'Fess up, play dumb, and pray. And if none of those work, I'll tell him I have my lab books locked away somewhere safe. If he wants his product, he'll keep me alive. Thanks, Henderson.'

'Like I said, you helped me. Speaking of, do you have any idea where I can go for more bandages and some antibiotics? Someplace that won't ask questions? *Please*, Fletch.'

Fletcher hesitated. 'Dammit. Yeah. There's a clinic in Largo, on Church Road, about two miles from the cemetery. Ask for Sean. Tell him I sent you. He'll fix you up.'

'Why didn't you tell me this last night?'

'Because last night I didn't know that Robinette had a tracker on my car. And you didn't have to call and warn me. But this is it, Henderson. No more calls.'

'No more, I promise. Thanks, Fletch. Be careful, okay?'

'I'll do my best. You, too.'

Henderson hung up. Largo wasn't too far away. *Just have to stay alert a little longer.*

'Goddamn that Mazzetti,' Henderson muttered. 'If she'd just died like she was supposed to, none of this would be happening. I'd still have a cushy job with good insurance. Dental, even. That woman is not worth all the trouble she's put me through. Robinette can kill her himself.'

Robinette probably would. Mazzetti had killed Levi, Robinette's only son. He really wanted that woman dead. She was worth something to him.

'How much is she worth to you, Robbie?' Henderson murmured. 'A plane ticket to Australia? Releasing Westmoreland from his assignment? My freedom? Maybe even Fletcher's twenty percent of the profits from the new formula?'

Robinette would balk. He wouldn't want to pay. *And then what would I do?* Kill her anyway? Auction her to the highest bidder? *No. Because either way she's dead and he gets what he wants.* No, the threat would have to be big. Like telling Mazzetti all of Robinette's secrets and setting the cop free. *That would make me a fugitive, but I am now anyway.*

Henderson would rather be chased by the cops than by Robinette, because Robbie knew all of his employees' secrets. He knew where they lived, where their families lived, and who they called friends. None of his employees – past or current – were truly safe if Robinette wanted them dead.

*Would I do that? Reveal all his secrets to Stevie Mazzetti?*

'Hell, yeah.' Henderson laughed thinly. 'I guess I *am* that petty after all.'

It would mean kidnapping Mazzetti. Taking – and keeping – her alive. A dead Mazzetti held no barter value at all.

If Westmoreland found Mazzetti first, there would be no way to escape a death sentence. Unless, of course, the executioner ceased to exist. The judge would have to go, too, before he assigned someone else. If Mazzetti was no longer a player, Westmoreland and Robinette would have to go.

*But could you? Really? Could you kill Robinette?*

Last night, the answer had been no. Now . . . Henderson wasn't so sure. *He'd kill you in a heartbeat. He's already tried.* So now the answer was yes. Probably.

But not definitely. On every other job Henderson saw a target, not a face. Not a person. But with Robinette there was history. Until last night, all of it good. How could he do this?

*How could he do this to me?*

*Maybe he's sick.* It was a hopeful thought. *Or crazy. Maybe he has a brain tumor.*

Or maybe this was who Robinette had been all along. *Maybe if I'd fucked up years ago, he would have tried to kill me then.*

*Picture yourself pulling the trigger. Do it.* But the only image that came to Henderson's mind was a dark room, a dead body and a lot of blood. *None of it mine.* And looming over the scene was Robinette, calm and composed, saying it would be all right. That he'd take care of everything. That the body of the man that Henderson had murdered would not be found.

That there would be no punishment. No prison. *That my life would continue to be my own.*

*If I have to kill him to survive, I will. But if I can avoid it . . .* Mazzetti was the key to freedom. *Barter the detective's life for your own. And do it fast before the choice is taken from you. Get yourself patched up so you can get to work.*

*Wight's Landing, Maryland, Sunday, March 16, 9.45 A.M.*

'I might have found Rossi,' Clay said.

The girlish chatter around Tanner's kitchen table abruptly stilled. Stevie glanced up at Clay who stood with his back to the counter, frowning at his phone. He'd been largely silent through the meal, speaking when spoken to, but mostly he'd watched her.

She'd avoided his gaze all the way through breakfast. *Coward. I'm a coward.*

Tanner had disappeared after gulping down a waffle to lay a plywood path for her over the sand, yet still she heard the older man's words circling around in her mind. *Try not to hurt him.*

But Stevie knew this would end in one of them being hurt. *Him or me. Probably both of us. I'll try not to let it be him. I'll try really hard.*

She kissed Cordelia's forehead. 'Why don't you and Aunt Emma check on the puppies.'

Cordelia looked from her to Clay. 'I want to know what's happening. Who is Rossi?'

Stevie glanced at Clay. 'The truth?' she murmured and he nodded, saying nothing. 'Rossi is a cop,' she told her daughter. 'A dirty cop who wanted to see me hurt. But JD caught him. He's in jail now.'

Cordelia looked down, then up again resolutely. 'You mean he wanted to kill you, Mama.'

A cold chill raced down Stevie's spine. 'He did. But he can't now. He was shot.'

'By who? By Uncle JD?'

'That you don't need to know,' Stevie said.

'But—'

Clay cleared his throat and Cordelia's gaze swung to his face. He gave her a stern look accompanied by a small shake of his head.

Cordelia looked down again. 'I'm not sorry I asked,' she said stubbornly.

Stevie's lips curved. 'I'd be disappointed if you were.'

Cordelia's chin came up, her eyes wide. 'What?'

'You're your father's daughter, but you're also mine.' She cupped Cordelia's cheek, her touch gentle, but her tone fierce. 'Always ask questions and *keep asking* until you're satisfied that you have all the information you need. Unless I tell you otherwise. Sometimes you're going to have to trust me.'

Cordelia's lips firmed. 'Okay. Then I want to ask a different question.'

Stevie smiled. 'Okay.'

'If Rossi is in jail, why did Mr Maynard just say he found him?'

'That's a darn good question, kid,' Emma said, sounding impressed. 'I had the same one.'

Clay sat in the chair across from them. 'We don't think he was working alone, Cordelia. Your mom doesn't know him, so we looked through her files last night to find something that would explain why he was so anxious to keep her quiet. And who has his back.'

Cordelia's eyes narrowed thoughtfully. 'You want his accomplice.'

Clay tried to hide his smile and failed. 'That's a big word for an almost-eight-year-old.'

Her chin came up defiantly. 'I'm not some dumb little girl, Mr Maynard.'

'Did I ever say you were? Did I ever give you a reason to believe I even thought it? Ever?'

Cordelia seemed to consider his question. 'No. Never. All right, Mom. I'll go play with the puppies, but that won't take very long.' Her expression went sly. 'If you want me out of your hair even longer, there's a computer in the room where I was sleeping. It's hooked up to the Internet. I know other words, too. Like "retail therapy".'

Emma snorted back a laugh. 'God, I love you, Cordelia Mazzetti.'

Stevie chuckled. 'So do I. You can pick out one outfit.' She held up an index finger. 'One.'

'With shoes?' Cordelia challenged.

'You have to stop spending so much time watching *Project Runway* with your Aunt Izzy. Fine. Shoes, too, but that's all. I mean it. Aunt Emma knows where I put my credit card.'

Emma put her arm around Cordelia's shoulders. 'Count me in for a purse. It can be an early birthday present.'

The two left, leaving Stevie and Clay alone in the kitchen. It quickly grew very quiet.

'That was exactly the right thing to say,' Clay murmured. 'That she was your daughter. That made her very proud.'

'Thanks.' Cheeks warm from his praise, Stevie stared down at her plate. 'So. You found Rossi in my files?'

'Indirectly. JD finally sent Rossi's personnel file a few minutes ago. Said there was some issue getting his hands on it. Rossi's PBA rep lodged an official objection.'

'I used to hate the idea of the union reps, but mine was useful.' She looked around the kitchen, anywhere but at him. But he was watching her. She could feel his gaze, heat shimmering across her skin. 'IA investigated me after we found out about Silas and all his crimes. My rep made sure they respected my rights. A lot of people couldn't believe I was so clueless as to not know what my own partner was up to all those years. A lot of people still don't believe me.'

'You trusted him,' Clay said evenly. 'And he was smart.'

'Yeah. My parents said that anyone who really knew me would know that I wasn't involved. That I couldn't have been. But we all thought we knew Silas and we were very wrong.'

'Which is why you've pushed so hard on these investigations. To prove yourself.'

'One of the reasons.' She absently scraped at a chip in the table's veneer. 'But mostly because they haunt me. All those innocent people victimized because Silas was a damn coward who allowed Lippman to bully him into sacrificing his integrity for the safety of his family.'

'But in trying to set things right, you've put your own family in the line of fire and you're wondering if it's worth it.'

She looked up then, met his eyes. Dark, intense, and focused on her face. And so full of understanding that her own eyes stung. 'Yes,' she whispered. 'Hell of an irony, ain't it?'

'Yes. But you couldn't live with yourself if you looked the other way. You're not wired that way.' He leaned forward, his hand covering hers. 'It's what makes you "you". And we will find out who's targeting you, no matter how many there are or how long it takes.'

'You make me believe it'll happen,' she said quietly. 'I'd started to doubt myself.'

'I know. Everybody's allowed to wallow a little in the

pity-pool.' He squeezed her hand hard before releasing it to retreat back in his chair. 'Time to get out of the pool.'

'You're right.' Squaring her shoulders, she cleared her throat. 'Rossi's personnel file?'

'From 2007 to 2009 Rossi was partnered with a detective named Danny Kersey in the robbery division. Kersey was senior, Rossi was newly promoted out of a squad car.'

'I don't know Kersey either.'

'Silas did. Kersey appears in one of the reports.'

She frowned. 'Which one?'

'One of the reports in the green folder.'

She felt her cheeks heat, this time in shame. 'I should've looked at them first.' But she hadn't because the dates in the folder made her uncomfortable.

'We always wish we'd checked the last place first,' he said kindly and she knew he knew why she hadn't looked at them. 'Kersey and Rossi were investigating what appeared to be an ordinary home invasion and robbery. Then the daughter of the homeowner was found raped and murdered the following day. They handed the case over to Silas who was working solo.'

'Because I was out on bereavement leave. What else?'

'Silas arrested a homeless man for the burglary, rape, and murder. That's all Silas had in his file. There was a short reference to Kersey's burglary investigation. A sentence or two, if that. Rossi was never mentioned, even though he was Kersey's partner.'

She gave him a sharp look. 'You remember Kersey's name out of all those reports?'

'No. I wish my memory was that good. I took notes on the reports in that green folder while you were asleep. Alec wrote a database to compare all the names from the notes you've been taking all along, mine from last night, and what he calls "extraneous" documentation. Things like

Rossi's personnel file, class lists from the Academy, stuff like that.'

'Wow. What a useful assistant.'

'Sometimes.' Clay smiled. 'Sometimes he's just a pain in the ass.'

She found herself smiling back, comfortable with him now that they were talking shop and not . . . feelings. 'So where is the report with Kersey's name in it?'

'Locked in the closet under the stairs. I didn't want to risk having your daughter see them.'

'Thank you. I appreciate that. Is there a place we can sort through the box of files? Where she won't overhear? She agreed to go upstairs far too easily and I know from experience that she has ears like a bat. The boathouse is small, but she won't hear us there.'

'The boathouse doesn't have a table where we can spread the files out, but the boat does.'

'The boat? Wait. Clay, wait.' But he was out of his chair and out of the room before she could blink. Stevie had no choice but to grab her cane and follow him.

*Baltimore, Maryland, Sunday, March 16, 9.45 A.M.*

'And on Tuesday you cut the ribbon at the groundbreaking for a youth rehab center in Reston. Wear your black Armani, with a blue tie. You wore the gray Huntsman with a red tie to the ribbon cutting last week and we want each event to appear different. For the Facebook posts, dontchaknow. Here's your speech. I've marked all the places you need to get choked up.'

Robinette saw Brenda Lee slide the typed page across his desk, but his main focus was on his laptop which displayed the feed from the camera aimed at the door to

Fletcher's office. Fletch had arrived forty-five minutes ago and still hadn't reported in, as ordered.

That his summons had been delivered was not in doubt. The guard shack had reported in, seconds after Fletcher's car passed through the gates.

He now regretted not putting a camera in Fletcher's office itself. He hadn't done so because Fletcher's office was one of the places they met for sex and Robinette sure as hell didn't intend to give his security guards a show. But that was then.

Now was a totally different story. He'd have a camera installed by the end of the day.

'Then on Wednesday,' Brenda Lee continued, 'you have a ten A.M. coffee at the Capitol in DC with the junior congressman from Louisiana to discuss your donation to the public school system in your old parish. I suggest you go nude, with your ass painted red like a baboon's.'

Robinette's eyes shot to Brenda Lee whose strawberry blonde brows were lifted in annoyance. 'I was listening,' he grunted, returning his attention to the screen. 'Monday, city planner for a dinner meeting at six. Tuesday, ribbon cutting, black Armani, be sure to cry. Have the guy with the red ass-paint in my dressing area by six A.M. on Wednesday.'

Brenda Lee laughed. 'You make me crazy, you know that?'

'I get the job done, don't I?' *Come on, Fletch. Open the damn door. I don't have all day.*

'I have to say you do. Last night you were at the top of your game. Nice speech. Excellent delivery. Even I believed you were humble.'

'No, you didn't.'

'No, I didn't. I know you far too well.' She hesitated.

217

'Robbie, are you okay? You've seemed a little . . . off for the last few days.'

'Yeah, just fine.' *Except for the fact that Henderson's running amok, Fletcher stabbed me in the back, and Stevie Mazzetti is still alive.* He flicked a glance at Brenda Lee. 'Really.'

'Okay, whatever you say. I have the rest of your schedule here. You can review it at your leisure.' She placed a folder on the edge of the desk. 'Call me with questions. Or about anything else. I know this isn't an easy week for you, no matter how you choose to play it in front of the team. Losing a child is never easy. And your circumstances were harder than most. You lost your wife, too – and at the hand of your son.'

Well, no, actually he hadn't lost Julie at Levi's hand. *I lost my wife at my very own hand.* Because she was too damn smart for her own good. *And mine, too.* She'd put two and two together and realized she'd lost her first husband – also at Robinette's hand. Her mistake had been in confronting him about Rene's murder.

Lesson number one: Never confront a killer. He'd been so startled at her accusation that he'd killed her before he'd given it any thought. Lesson number two: Lock your office door when killing your wife. Because her lead chemist had popped his head in just then.

So of course Robinette had had to kill him, too. And that was when his nightmare with Mazzetti had begun. The bitch had known. Somehow she'd known from the first moment.

Lesson number three: Don't put off 'til tomorrow what you should do today. *I should have killed Mazzetti eight years ago.* Should have found a way to make it look like an accident. Or even a suicide. She'd been so depressed after her husband and son were killed, no one would have doubted it.

But he'd been waiting for the 'right time'. There never was a right time. He should have been smart and made the right time. But Mazzetti had rattled him. She'd known he'd killed Julie and she would not give up trying to prove it. He'd panicked. The bitch had made him panic. He thought he hated Mazzetti for that most of all.

Because in his panic, he'd sacrificed his son. Pointing the cops in Levi's direction hadn't been hard. The kid had been a junkie and when Julie had died, the boy had lost it, staying high all the time. He'd figured Levi might do a little time. Maybe get sentenced to rehab.

He hadn't meant for Levi to die. Hadn't anticipated the bitch cop would murder his son. But she had. And when he was done with her, she'd be damn sorry she had.

'Don't worry about me, Brenda Lee,' Robinette muttered, conscious of her worried stare. 'I've moved on. I don't think about Julie anymore. I have Lisa now.'

'I wish I believed that,' she said sadly. 'But I don't.'

*Ah. Finally.* The lab door opened and Fletcher appeared, turning toward the elevator to Robinette's office. *Took you long enough, Fletch.* His chemist would be here in minutes.

Robinette gave his full attention to Brenda Lee, who looked alarmingly tired. 'What about you, BL? Are *you* all right?'

Her smile was tight. 'No complaints, boss.'

'You never do complain.' He knew she was in constant pain and had been since the day he'd pulled her out of a wrecked Humvee on the side of an Iraqi road, seconds before it went up in flames, having been targeted by an insurgent's rocket launcher.

She shrugged. 'Doesn't help. Now if you'll excuse me, I've got a kite to fly with my son.' Her motorized wheelchair whirred as she put it into reverse and did a quick K-turn.

'Excuse me? Did you say a kite?'

'I did indeed. Dax and I joined a kite club. Gives us mother/son bonding time. Why don't you come with us, Robbie? It's fun, and that's something you haven't gotten a lot of lately.'

He smiled. Brenda Lee was one of the few people he could just be with. 'Would you believe me if I said I was tempted?'

'Yeah, I think I would. But don't wait too long. March is halfway over already and April's lousy weather for kiting. Can you hit the buzzer?'

Robinette pushed the button attached discreetly beneath his desk, signaling the receptionist on duty outside his door. Immediately the door was opened and Brenda Lee wheeled herself out.

He heard her exchange greetings with Fletcher out in the hall and fought the urge to drum his fingers on the granite of his desk. *Stay calm.* He didn't want Fletch suspecting that he knew about Henderson. He wanted to see the look on Fletch's face when he sprung his accusation.

Because, he supposed, a piece of him didn't want to believe Fletcher was capable of such complete and flagrant disregard of a direct order. He didn't want to believe that his oldest living friend would go behind his back like this.

Henderson's carelessness had opened the rest of them up to potential scrutiny that could land them all in jail. Or worse. They needed to distance themselves from any police attention. Henderson had known that as well as any of them and now needed to be contained.

Fletcher closed the door. Gave Robinette a distracted nod. 'Robbie, I need to talk to you.'

Robinette watched Fletcher pace the length of his office. 'I sent for you,' he said calmly.

'I know. But let me go first.' Fletcher turned to face him. 'I saw Henderson last night.'

Robinette managed not to blink although it was hard. He hadn't expected Fletch to come right out with it that way. 'Why?'

'I got a call around ten. Henderson had tried to call you first, but you were at that event.'

'I told you to sever contact with Henderson. Why didn't you?'

'Because I'm a doctor. Even if I can't practice anymore, I'm still a doctor and I took an oath. If someone begs me to help them, I'm not going to say no. I couldn't live with myself if I'd let Henderson suffer, knowing I could have done something. If you're angry with me, so be it.'

'I'll be honest. I am angry. I gave that order to protect us. I didn't respond to Henderson's calls last night for the same reason. If Henderson is caught and tells the authorities the order to deal with Mazzetti came from me, we could have claimed ignorance, that the accusations were those of a disgruntled and perhaps mentally ill former fellow soldier. Because you answered the call, you've put us in a bad position.'

'I'm sorry. But I'll be honest. Given the same situation, I'd probably do it again. And it's not that bad anyway. If anyone asks, I'll just say I was responding to an old Army buddy in need. That I'm not a doctor anymore works in my favor. I don't have to report bullet wounds.'

'But that you had contact at all forges a link the cops can follow straight to us.' Robinette sighed, a mixture of relief and frustration. There had been no betrayal. Just Fletch being Fletch. Still, it was a problem. 'What am I going to do with you?'

'Do you really need an answer to that question?'

Robinette's groin twitched. He ignored it. Mostly. 'Where did you meet Henderson?'

'At the Key Hotel.'

It was the same hotel Westmoreland reported. There was no lie here. No duplicity. Therefore, no need to install cameras in Fletcher's office after all. Still, he needed to be certain.

He motioned for Fletcher to come around his desk, hitting another discreetly placed button to lock his office door. Fletcher obeyed, dropping to kneel between Robinette's thighs.

'I hated knowing you were with Lisa last night,' Fletch whispered.

Robinette watched those capable hands ease his zipper down, all the while studying his chemist's eyes. He saw discomfort and regret and guilt. Understandable and all in total sync with Fletcher's character.

'I know. But Lisa's temporary, a means to an end. You and I will go on long after she's just a memory.' Then he closed his eyes and let Fletcher . . . attend to his needs.

When they'd finished, he gripped Fletcher's chin between his fingers. 'Have you heard from Henderson since you left the hotel last night?'

Fletcher's eyes flickered, so minutely Robinette almost missed it. 'No. I didn't have any antibiotics in my kit, but I left a few painkillers from my last dental surgery. I'd be surprised if Henderson is awake enough to call anyone.'

'All right. If you're contacted again—'

'I know. I'll tell you immediately.' Fletcher rose. 'I'll be down in the lab if you need me.'

Robinette released the lock, his eyes focused on the door after Fletcher left. *Fletcher had lied.* He'd seen it in that tiny flicker. There had been additional contact between the two. And if a person lied about one thing, it was extremely likely they'd lied about others.

He picked up the phone, dialed his IT guy and ordered a camera to be installed in Dr Fletcher's office before this day became night. Then he called Westmoreland.

'Where are you?' Robinette demanded.

'About fifteen minutes from Maynard's house.'

'I want updates every hour.' Starting now, he'd be keeping a tighter leash on his operatives.

'Okay,' Westmoreland said uncertainly. 'Why?'

'Just do it.' Robinette hung up and stared straight ahead. At nothing at all.

*Wight's Landing, Maryland, Sunday, March 16, 10.05 A.M.*

This, Clay thought, was going far better than he had anticipated. He'd been watching Stevie eat breakfast with her daughter, not able to stop thinking about the look of unguarded desire in her eyes as she'd looked up at him in that moment before sleep had claimed her.

He'd been wondering how he'd get her alone so he could try to achieve that same look now that she was awake. *Unless she wasn't thinking about me.*

*Second best. You'd always be second best.*

Clay shoved the doubt away before it could take root. He'd stick to the plan. Protect her until the scum that would harm her were culled. Until she was herself again. Until the loss of her husband was no longer the first thing she thought of when she thought about them together. And she did think about them together. He'd stake his life on it.

For now, he had her totally alone.

'This space is surprisingly large,' Stevie said, turning a

three-sixty in the middle of the boat's cabin. 'And surprisingly steady.'

Clay rolled the suitcase filled with reports to the small table next to the galley. 'The bay's calm today. Yesterday would have been rougher.'

'Then I'm glad it's not yesterday. For a lot of reasons. Whose boat is this?'

'Dad and I own the *Fiji* together. He got it after Mom passed. He needed something to do and he'd always loved to fish. He has fun with his clients, supplements his pension, and I know he's socially engaged and not sitting out here alone, pining for her. At first I was afraid I'd lose him, too. He was such a wreck without her. You always hear about spouses that just check out after the other one—' *Hell. Way to go, Mr Chatty.* He could have sliced off his own tongue.

She looked over her shoulder, no smile on her face. 'After the other one dies?'

'I'm sorry. I didn't think.'

'That's okay. I know my family and friends worried that I might do exactly that. I might have if I hadn't had Cordelia.' She looked around again, her eyes everywhere but on him. 'This is good of you, Clay. To care so much about keeping your dad happy. Izzy, Sorin, and I should figure out some activities for my dad. He retired recently and just makes my mom crazy.'

'I like your parents. They were very kind to me when I visited you in December.'

'They like you too,' she said ruefully. 'If it makes you feel any better, I got a ration of shit from my family over what I said to you in the hospital that day.'

'It does make me feel better actually,' he said and she laughed. Just a little laugh, but it made him feel ten feet tall and bullet-proof.

'Glad to oblige.' She slid onto the bench seat and took out her laptop. 'Can you get me Silas's report that mentions Kersey? I want to find Kersey's report on that burglary in the department's database. He would have had to close his case, even just to say he'd passed it on to Homicide. Also, do you have a landline on this boat?'

It had been a nice few minutes there, talking to her. Intimate, almost. But she'd shifted gears and it was clearly time to work. Clay put the report and the telephone on the table, then slid onto the bench across from her. 'The phone line runs from the house. Who do you want to call?'

'JD. I want to know if Rossi's conscious and if he's talking. He might give up his source and none of this would be necessary.'

'I talked to JD right before you woke up. Rossi was still unconscious. He'll call when Rossi wakes up. Although he didn't seem too optimistic about Rossi giving up anything. His last words to JD before losing consciousness last night were, "Burn in hell, motherfucker."'

'Rossi killed a cop,' Stevie said flatly, pushing the phone aside. 'I don't think he'll find a jury going easy on him. He'll talk eventually. I'd like to be around to hear him, though. If he waits too long, I'll have to come out of hiding. Sooner or later one of them will get lucky.'

Clay's skin tightened on his bones. 'Don't even think that.'

She kept her eyes on the report. 'You're right. I'm sorry. I just keep imagining Rossi shooting up that hotel bed, believing Cordelia was in it.'

He gripped her wrist, waiting until she looked at him before releasing his hold. 'We have her, Stevie. She's safe. If you lose it, so will she.'

'I know.' She blew out a breath, ran her finger down the typed page. 'Okay. On November 12, seven years ago,

225

the Gardners' home was broken into. The thieves got jewelry and a gun collection. No evidence of forced entry. Tracy, their daughter, had forgotten to lock the door when she went to class at the university. She found the mess when she returned home.

'Silas says Kersey "and partner" canvassed the neighbors but got no leads. Then the next day, Mrs Gardner came home from work to find the back door open and Tracy's body on the kitchen floor. She'd been stabbed with a butcher knife. One was missing from the drawer.'

She sighed. 'The autopsy showed she'd been raped, asphyxiated, then stabbed. Silas questioned the neighbors again, then got a lead from some kids playing basketball a block away. They'd seen a "homeless-looking guy" lurking. Silas tracked him down, found the knife and one of the stolen pistols in the man's backpack. He was diagnosed with schizophrenia.'

'Did Silas get a confession?'

'Of sorts. "At first the suspect denied the charges, but once court-ordered medication had taken effect, he was horrified to learn of his actions and confessed,"' she read.

'What happened to the man? Can you check the court records?'

Stevie typed in the search. 'Richard Steel was sentenced to a medium-security prison where he's forced to take his meds. This case isn't on Lippman's list. Neither are Kersey or Rossi.'

'Why do you think Lippman included some of his operatives but not others?' he asked.

'I don't know. Maybe Lippman was lazy and didn't bother to add everyone he hired. Maybe just the threat of the list was enough to keep his employees in line. Maybe he liked some of the cops better than others. Maybe Rossi knows why.' She put Silas's report aside and typed some more. 'I want to see what Kersey put in his own report.' A few minutes later she sat back, met Clay's gaze. 'Kersey notes that Tracy Gardner had claimed to go to class the day of the burglary, but he touched the hood of her car as he left and it was ice cold.'

'Interesting thing to have done, touching the daughter's car. Sounds like he didn't believe her story from the get-go.'

'I agree. Maybe because none of her stuff was stolen. There's no follow-up noted except that Tracy's body was found the next day and the case was handed off to Homicide.'

Clay's phone buzzed and he checked the incoming text. 'Kersey's most likely not Hyatt's leak. He retired five years ago. Lives in Scottsdale, Arizona.'

Her brows bunched. 'How do you know that?'

He held his phone so that she could see the screen. 'Alec texted me. And don't ask how he knows. You probably don't want to know.'

'Your assistant's a hacker, too?'

He shrugged. 'I wouldn't say hacker. But he's damn clever.'

Her lips twitched. 'This is the kid whose godfather is your best friend from the Marine Corps? Your first PI partner, right? The one who's a "white hat", AKA "hacker"?'

That she remembered pleased him more than it probably should have. 'Alec may have picked up a trick or two from Ethan. But "hacker" is such a harsh word, don't you think?' he asked mildly and she grinned, lighting up her face and stealing his breath.

'I won't tell,' she said, but then her grin faded. 'We can cross Kersey off the dirty cop list. The active list anyway.

No telling if he had any involvement in framing Richard Steel for this murder seven years ago, assuming that's what Silas and Rossi did. I need to pass this one off to IA and keep looking for anyone Rossi might have partnered with in the past, who could have leaked the safe house information to him yesterday. Cordelia and I are being targeted now.'

But he could see the notion didn't sit right with her. If IA was somehow tainted, this case might not ever be resolved, assuming this was one of Silas's frame jobs. At a minimum, with the rate IA was investigating, this case would fall to the end of a very long line. It could be months or even years before justice was done.

'It'll only take a few minutes to call Kersey,' Clay said softly. 'Maybe you can right a wrong. At least you'll know. Then we can get back to our search.'

She went still. 'Everybody else keeps telling me to let it go. To stop investigating. To leave it alone, but I can't. You get it.' She hesitated, then added in a reluctant whisper, 'You get me.'

'I like to think so.' He made himself smile lightly even though his heart was pounding in his chest. 'That's what I keep trying to tell you.'

'I'll look up Kersey's—' She halted when he showed her Alec's next text. 'You already have the contact info. Of course you do.' She picked up the phone and dialed, engaging the speaker so that he could hear, too. 'Hello, can I speak with Detective Kersey?'

'He's not taking calls at this time,' a female voice said firmly.

'Oh. Are you Mrs Kersey? Can you give him a message?'

'I am and I can.'

'This is Detective Mazzetti, Baltimore Homicide. I wanted to ask him about an old—'

'Wait. He wants to know if you can Skype him. He wants to see who he's talking to.'

Stevie looked taken aback. 'Sure. I think. I have to figure out how.'

'I can show you,' Clay said and had the pleasure of seeing her smile again, this time ruefully.

'Of course you can,' she murmured. 'Mrs Kersey, we'll call right back.'

'He'll be waiting.'

# Chapter Eleven

*Wight's Landing, Maryland, Sunday, March 16, 10.30 A.M.*

'You just click the Skype icon here,' Clay said, reaching over her shoulder to tap her laptop's track pad. He'd moved, now standing behind her, so close she could feel his warmth.

She hadn't realized how cold she'd been.

Or how good he smelled. *Which shouldn't matter.* But it did. Because as much as she wanted to do the right thing and not hurt him, she wanted so much to lean into him. To press her cheek into the hard strength of his arm.

How long had it been since she'd felt a man's arms around her? Since she'd simply been held? The answer was like a thunderbolt in her mind. *Last night.* Clay had held her last night, letting her cry. Demanding nothing in return. Suddenly she wished he would.

*If only to balance the scales.* Yeah. That was it. It wasn't because he smelled good or made her want things she had no business wanting. It was because she didn't like being beholden to anyone and Clay was racking up the IOUs at an alarming rate.

*You keep telling yourself that if it makes you feel better, honey*. The thing was, it didn't.

*Oh, God. This is not going to end well*.

She chanced her voice, grateful when it came out even. 'I never took you for a geek.'

'That's because I'm not. Computers give me hives.'

He hovered over her, close enough to touch, but far enough away that it couldn't be accidental. *Wily bastard*. She had to hand it to him, though. His approach was working.

'After seeing your setup in the boathouse, I find that hard to believe,' she said wryly.

'The security equipment I can handle because it makes sense, but stuff like Facebook and Skype?' He sounded mildly horrified, making her smile.

'Not your thing, huh?'

'No. Alyssa set my computer up and taught me how to use my cell phone. She and Alec are trying to drag me into the twenty-first century,' he added with a self-deprecating chuckle. 'Okay. Now you're connecting. You'll see Detective Kersey as soon as he answers. He'll see your face, but nothing below here.' He tapped her chest, several inches above her breasts. Still, her skin tingled at the brief contact. 'I'll get out of the picture.'

He moved, but still stood what would have been far too close mere hours before.

*He knows exactly what he's doing*. But she couldn't make herself mind. She wasn't even sure she could focus on the call, but when the picture connected she was stunned into attention.

Kersey sat in a wheelchair with a head support. He was emaciated, his facial bones jutting from his skin. But his eyes were crystal clear and sharp. His wife stood at his elbow, adjusting a microphone close to his mouth.

'Detective Kersey,' Stevie said. 'I'm Detective Stevie Mazzetti. Thank you for your time.'

'You're welcome,' he said, his voice raspy. 'You've had some excitement, Detective.'

'We heard about Tony Rossi,' Mrs Kersey said. 'We keep up with Danny's old squad. Word travels fast. We're sorry about the police officer who was killed, but glad you're all right.'

Her husband nodded after she was finished and Stevie realized his wife had become accustomed to helping him communicate. 'Thank you. Did you expect me to call?'

'No,' Kersey whispered into the mike. 'But I'm not surprised. I was Rossi's partner.'

'I know. I wanted to talk to you about a case. Tracy Gardner. Do you remember her?'

Kersey's eyes closed slowly. 'Yes.'

'The day you and Rossi responded to her 911 about the break-in at her family's house, did you believe her story? She'd said she'd been at a college class, that she'd arrived home to find the burglary. But you touched her car and said it was ice cold. Why did you do that?'

'I didn't believe her. She couldn't meet my eyes.' Kersey went still, but held up his index finger. 'I sometimes lose my breath. It's ALS, dammit. Gehrig's, you know.'

'I'm sorry,' Stevie murmured. She didn't know much about Lou Gehrig's disease, except that it was a deterioration of the nerves and was always fatal. Now she could see how mercilessly it ravaged a person's body. Behind her, Clay squeezed her shoulder.

'Me, too,' Kersey whispered. 'Tracy Gardner said she went to class, came home, and called 911 right away. Two uniforms showed up before we got there. Rossi and I got there an hour later.' He stopped again, his breathing labored.

'Should I call back later?' Stevie asked, worried that he'd pass out.

'No. Need to do this today. Need to make it right.'

His wife touched his face. 'You didn't do anything wrong, Danny.'

Kersey smiled weakly. 'But I can still make it right. I use the Skype to see my grandkids. I drink in the sight of them. Lifts my spirits.'

'I'm glad,' Stevie said simply, wondering if his mind had wandered.

'I talk to my friends from the force on the phone. I don't want them to see me like this. But you . . . I wanted to see your face. Needed to see if it was true.'

'What was true, sir?' Stevie asked.

'That you've been investigating your old partner's cases because you feel guilty. Because you looked the other way or were sloppy.'

Stevie stiffened, felt Clay tense behind her. She'd heard the cops' whispers and rumors, tried not to let them hurt. But they did. 'Is it true?' she asked.

'I don't think so. I know you can work next to someone and not know they're dirty. And when I said I needed to make it right, you understood.'

'I saw the victims,' she said. 'And their families. They didn't get justice. And innocent men and women are sitting in prison. I can't let that continue without trying to make it right.'

'I still see that girl's face. Tracy Gardner. And her mother's face. She found her, you know.'

'I know. Who do you think killed her?'

'The boyfriend. I'll get to him in a minute. Tracy's car was cold, so I knew she hadn't driven it, but she could have caught a ride. I didn't ask because I didn't want her to know I didn't believe her. I went to Tracy's college the next morning. Talked to her professor. She wasn't in class the day before or that day either. He said she skipped class often, but a lot of the kids did.'

'So she lied to you. You think she was home during the burglary?'

'I thought she might have been. I knew she wasn't where she'd said she was. But I never got a chance to pursue it because she was killed later that day. Now, about the boyfriend. Edward Ginsberg, went by Eddie.'

'Berg with an "e" or a "u"?' Stevie asked.

'"E",' Kersey said with a frown. 'It's in the report.'

It was Stevie's turn to frown. 'No, it's not. Your report is very short, less than a page.'

Kersey's eyes flashed. 'Sonofabitch.' Then he started gasping for breath.

His wife stepped in. 'Tone it down or I'll end the call and you can write her an email. I'm serious.' She glanced at the webcam. 'I'm sorry, Detective Mazzetti. His health comes first.'

'Of course,' Stevie said.

'I'm calm,' Kersey rasped. 'Dammit, woman. Don't treat me like a child.' He took a few moments to catch his breath. 'My report was longer than a page. At some point it must have been altered if that's all you found. I don't need to be a detective to figure out who did it.'

'Rossi,' Stevie said. 'I found discrepancies in some of Silas's reports, too. I'm glad I kept my notebooks. Tell me about Eddie Ginsberg.'

'Tracy's father suspected Eddie, but Tracy defended him. Eddie's family had money, she said. Eddie had no reason to steal. Truth was that Eddie was a rich punk with too much time on his hands. Rossi and I went to his house after we left the school. He was playing video games, even though he should have been in class. I told him that

Tracy's father suspected him. He said Tracy could "handle her daddy". I didn't confirm or deny and Eddie got pissed. Then he laughed it off, saying it didn't matter what the bitch said, that he had three guys who'd swear he was with them, hanging out watching TV. We got the names, then Rossi and I went to lunch.' Kersey looked pained. 'I wish I hadn't gone to lunch.'

'What happened?'

'We went to her house after lunch to confront her. Knocked on the door. Nobody was home. Went back to the precinct to start calling pawn shops, trying to track the stolen goods.' Another pause while Kersey caught his breath. 'We went back to the Gardner house at about four o'clock, thinking to catch the mother. The mother was there. So was the ME.'

'Tracy was dead by then,' Stevie said. 'Raped, asphyxiated, then stabbed. Crime of rage?'

'I thought so. My first thought was, "Eddie did this. I goaded him and he killed her." But Silas found the home-less guy and I was relieved. I hadn't pushed Eddie to murder.' His face crumpled, his thin shoulders sagging. 'Now . . . God.'

'If Eddie killed Tracy, then it's on him,' Stevie said. 'Not you.'

'We all say that because it makes us feel better. But thanks for trying.' He looked away for a second, regaining his composure. 'Then Homicide showed up. Silas Dandridge.'

'Did you tell Silas about Edward Ginsberg and the fact Tracy lied about class?'

'Yes. And that I thought that Eddie was guilty of the crime. But Silas found the homeless guy, Richard Steel, with the murder weapon. He had a slam –' a gasp for breath '– dunk.'

'Did you think Richard Steel was guilty of Tracy Gardner's murder?' Stevie asked.

'He had the bloody knife and Silas said that Eddie had an alibi, but it worried me. However, Silas was Homicide's hotshot. Which I'm sure you know since you were his partner for so long.'

'The Finder,' Stevie remembered grimly. 'We used to call him that because he had a knack for finding what would become key pieces of evidence. Now we know how he managed it. It's easy to find the eggs if you're the Easter bunny. Did you ever suspect Rossi?'

'Not at first. At the end, yes. Nothing tangible.' He stopped to breathe again.

'He's getting tired,' Mrs Kersey said. 'You have to hurry up.'

'We think Rossi may have been working with someone,' Stevie said. 'Do you have any idea of who that might have been?'

'He was friendly with Scott Culp. I didn't trust Culp, either.'

*Holy hell*, Stevie thought, blinking in stunned surprise. *Scott Culp?* That name was very familiar. 'Why didn't you trust Scott Culp?'

'They hung out together on their off days, were more than friends. I thought they were gay, which was Rossi's biz, so I left it be. But there was always something about Culp. Smug bastard. Wore snazzy shoes. Italian suits. Liked to play the ponies. Rossi did, too. A few times I saw Rossi flash wads of cash, size of my fist. Said he'd won it at the track. Hell.' Kersey closed his eyes, clearly fatigued. 'You'll see that Tracy Gardner and Richard Steel get justice.'

It wasn't a request. 'I will. I promise.'

'Good.' He sank back into his wheelchair, away from the microphone.

'I'm sorry I took so much of your time,' Stevie said. 'And your energy.'

Mrs Kersey shook her head. 'This is all the talking he'll do today, but I know he considers it well worth it. He didn't expect your call, Detective Mazzetti, but he's worried that he'd hear from IA ever since Silas Dandridge was exposed. I remember the Gardner girl's case, Danny lying in bed, staring at the ceiling, worrying about what to do. But like he said, Silas had a slam dunk.'

'All of Silas's frame-ups were slam dunks,' Stevie said bitterly. 'I've spent my share of hours staring at the ceiling, worrying. I'll contact you when I have news. Take care.'

'You too, Detective,' Mrs Kersey said. 'Goodbye.'

Stevie hung up, turned to find Clay texting on his phone. 'What are you doing?'

'Getting info on Scott Culp,' he said.

'You don't have to. Him, I know.'

Clay leaned his hip against the table, once again encroaching into her space. 'Who is he?'

'He was in the robbery division. Did a short stint in Vice. Now he's IA.'

Clay's eyes widened. 'You've *got* to be kidding.'

'I wish. And Kersey's right – Culp *is* a smug bastard. He was there on Friday when I told IA I thought more cops were involved than were on Lippman's list. I told them that I'd been attacked twice already that week. Later that afternoon somebody – maybe Rossi – shot at me. Twice yesterday, more shots. Then last night Rossi did shoot, thinking it was me.'

Color rose on his cheeks. 'Culp is Hyatt's leak. An IA guy told Rossi where to find you.'

'Chances are damn good. I need to tell Hyatt.' She started to lift the phone's handset, then thought better of it and hung it back up. 'If someone in IA leaked the safe house location, Hyatt has the obligation to tell them. But IA could inadvertently give Culp the heads up. He'll bolt.'

'Chances are damn good,' Clay said, grimly echoing her words.

'I want to check him out myself. But I don't want to leave Cordelia.' Stevie gritted her teeth. 'It's a vicious circle. And even if Culp did tell Rossi where to find the safe house, we still don't know who did the drive-by yesterday. Or the restaurant.' She dropped her head into her hands. 'This is a nightmare and I'm trapped here because they know I won't leave my daughter.'

'Stevie, listen to me.' Clay's voice held a steel edge, demanding her attention, and cautiously she lifted her head. 'We have two Federal agents standing watch out front and my father inside the house, armed with a pretty impressive arsenal.'

Clay leaned forward until his face was inches away. 'Cordelia is safe here, even if you leave for a few hours. She'll be safe tomorrow.' He came closer still, until his face was all she could see. 'We will keep her safe until the threat is eliminated. And I have your back, no matter what we have to do to make that happen.'

Her fear retreated as his words took root. This was not a careless man. He planned for contingencies. He covered all the bases. He'd proven himself over and over again.

She trusted him to help her. And then, if she chose to walk away, he'd let her.

*I'd miss him.* The thought seemed to come from nowhere. But she knew better. She had been missing him since December. She'd missed knowing there was someone she could depend on, someone who was there when she needed him. And she'd missed the tight feeling in her stomach she'd get whenever she knew she was going to see him again. She'd missed his face.

That face that she'd always thought looked hewn out of solid rock. Unmoving. Unbreakable.

But he was breakable. *I broke him*. No, she'd hurt him. He was not broken. Far from it. He was made of stronger stuff than that. *Just like me*.

Stevie was breathing in short, shallow breaths because there didn't seem to be any air. His eyes heated, but he didn't move a muscle. He held her gaze with steady focus and waited.

Just like he'd waited during the months since December. And long before that.

Because all she could see was his face, she indulged, looking her fill. He was too rugged to be classically handsome, but there was beauty in every rough plane of his face. Her fingertips tingled to touch, her hand seeming to lift of its own volition.

She skimmed her fingertips across his cheek, his skin warm and resilient. *Alive*. He flinched slightly, but still didn't move. Like he was gentling a feral creature, allowing her to become used to him. She felt like that sometimes. Feral. Trapped and alone.

*You don't have to be alone. He's yours for the taking*. It was a heady notion. Too heady to consider at the moment, when all she could manage were those shallow breaths. She touched his jaw, already dark with stubble. He remained motionless. Holding her gaze. Holding his breath.

Until she cupped his jaw in her palm. He shuddered, the air pushing from his lungs in a pained gust that left his shoulders sagging. Bracing his hand on the table, he closed his eyes and dropped his head a fraction, sinking into her caress.

Like he was starving for touch. *My touch*. She didn't know a heart could feel sorrow and exhilaration at the same time, but as she lifted her other hand to his face, that

239

was exactly what she felt. Keeping the first hand where it was, she traced his brow, the line of his nose. His lips. *So soft.* His lips were so soft.

Through it all he didn't make another move. Kept one hand on the table, still clutching his phone. The other hand lay fisted at his side. Leaving it all up to her. *It's to be my decision then.*

Again, a heady thought that left her needy and aching, yet feeling powerful. Exhilarating.

But the sorrow remained. *I did this. I kept this from him. I kept him from this.* The touch, the closeness he hadn't had with anyone else. *Because he waited. For me.*

'I don't want to hurt you again,' she whispered. 'But I'm afraid I will.'

His eyes opened and she was hit full force with the sheer magnitude of his hunger. 'I'll risk it,' came his hoarse reply. And then his mouth was on hers, hard and fast. And good. *So good.* The hand he'd kept by his side was suddenly in her hair, pulling her even closer.

His phone clattered to the table, his other hand suddenly brushing the side of her breast on its way to her back and she was lifted to her feet, the kiss unbroken. His mouth . . . God, the man could kiss. Like he was starving, she thought again, more dimly this time.

*So am I. God, so am I.* She wrapped her arms around his neck and hung on, throwing herself into the heat of him, kissing him back. Making him growl, deep in his throat. Sending a vibration through his chest that she felt against her breasts.

More than a tickle, far less than a stroke, the brief sensation made her nipples hard, and she wanted more. She pressed closer and his hands slid down her back, closing over her butt, lifting her higher against him with ease. But not high enough. Not even close.

He ripped his mouth away long enough to let them both fill their lungs, staring at her, his mouth wet from hers. 'More?' he asked, the word barely intelligible.

She licked her lips, tasting him. More? *Hell yeah.* But he was waiting for her to answer. To use an actual word. 'Ye—'

He didn't let her finish, diving in again, giving her more. *More.* It was a pulsing in her head, overriding any other thought, spreading to her breasts, between her legs. He pivoted, lifting her to sit on the edge of the table, blindly pushing her laptop out of the way. He ran hands that trembled down her legs, pulling them wider so that he could move closer, all while he ate at her mouth with kisses that set every nerve in her body to buzzing.

*Buzzing.* Something was buzzing. It broke through the sexual haze and she groped around the table, searching for the source. *Cell phone.*

She pulled away far enough to whisper, 'It's yours.'

He was breathing hard. 'Let 'em call back,' he said. Then groaned. 'No. Give it to me.'

She handed it to him, gripping his shoulder with her other hand to keep her balance when her body threatened to weave. 'Talk fast,' she whispered.

'I will.' With an expression of supreme irritation he checked his phone's screen. Then went abruptly still, sexual frustration becoming lethal calm in the blink of an eye.

Stevie straightened her spine, a jolt of adrenaline clearing her mind. 'What is it?' she asked, but he was already running up the stairs to the deck, his gun in his hand.

'The underwater thermal cameras,' he called over his shoulder. 'Someone's coming. Stay here until I give the all clear.'

She opened her mouth to tell him what he could do with his 'Stay here', but years of training overruled.

241

'Think,' she muttered to herself because Clay was long gone. But rational thought was difficult with every maternal instinct she possessed clawing at her to *move*. To protect her child.

*Cordelia's in the house*. The house with bullet-resistant windows and security doors. *She's safe as long as she stays in the house*.

Clay's command still rankled, scraping at her pride, but down deep it made sense. The sniper at the restaurant was likely still out there. And the triggering of the underwater alarms coming so quickly after her call to Kersey sent up a red flag in her mind. Kersey could have been playing her, feeding her info to prod her into making a move into the open.

But that was ridiculous. There was no way he could have traced her call, either on the phone or through Skype. Clay's lines of communication were secure.

Plus, she'd believed every word he'd said. *Because he's dying?* No, that wasn't it. It was because she recognized herself in his eyes, his tone.

Besides, whoever was coming would have started out long before she'd called Kersey. Divers had to come from boats and that took a little time.

Stevie looked around for her cane, found it leaning against the stove in the galley. She wasn't stupid. She wouldn't make herself a target again. She'd stay out of sight until she knew what was what. And the stairs would take time to navigate. Better to be waiting at the top if all hell broke loose than to be stuck at the bottom.

The cop in her – and the woman as well – had no intention of letting Clay Maynard take any more bullets for her. Moving as fast as she could, she followed him up.

*Baltimore, Maryland, Sunday, March 16, 10.55 A.M.*

It had been an hour and five minutes and Westmoreland hadn't called. Robinette was not happy. He paced the length of his office, running through the list of his staff in his mind. Determining who was suspect and who could be trusted. Most of them he didn't trust simply because he didn't know them well enough. But those staff didn't have access to any confidential – and/or damaging – information.

Of his inner circle, those he'd served with in the desert? He still trusted Brenda Lee. He no longer trusted Henderson or Fletcher. Robinette was on the fence concerning Westmoreland at the moment. He'd specified one hour for updates. It shouldn't have been that difficult for Wes to send him a text or an email.

Unless he was in trouble. Or he had his hands full with Mazzetti. Or if he hadn't gone to the bodyguard's house at all.

Wes hadn't approved of Robinette's handling of Henderson or Fletch.

Maybe Westmoreland was taking matters into his own hands. His team had been riding him lately about the fancy tuxedos and formal events. That if he wasn't careful, the bow ties would cut off circulation to his brain. That he'd go soft.

Robinette had chalked it up to good-natured ribbing at the time.

What if they'd been serious? What if they'd been talking behind his back?

What if they thought they could do better? *What if they tried to take over?* Between them, they knew everything about his business. All the formulas – legal and otherwise, the customers, the pricing . . . everything. His inner circle was as capable of burying him as Stevie Mazzetti.

Where was Westmoreland right now? Robinette sat at his desk and pulled up the website he used to track the movements of the vehicles in his corporate fleet. Westmoreland was driving one of those vehicles – a black Toyota Sequoia. Robinette selected it and waited for the satellite to connect with the tracker. *Vehicle not found*.

Robinette blinked hard. It was like a little rubber band had just snapped in his mind.

*Before you get all mad, make sure the damn site is working correctly*. A search for all of the other vehicles in the fleet returned results. Most were parked here, on the property. A few were out making pick-ups and deliveries, preparing for the start of a new workweek.

He put in a special password and found Lisa's car. She had Sunday brunch with her family every week. And . . . Yes. Her Jag was parked in front of her parents' ugly mausoleum-like mansion, exactly where it was supposed to be.

Once more he looked for the Sequoia. *Vehicle not found*.

Westmoreland had disabled the Sequoia's tracking device. That didn't bode well.

*I have not gone soft*. And if his team needed to be reminded of that fact, Robinette would happily oblige. He opened his wall safe and removed the shoebox-sized gun safe, then pressed his thumb to the print reader to spring the latch. Removed the guns that had only been fired at his private target range. They were untraceable.

Not that he planned to use them. Even with a silencer, there were far less noisy ways to deal with human obstacles. But it never hurt to be prepared.

He also slipped his little address book into his pocket. In the book were important names and addresses. Like the family and friends of Stevie Mazzetti, including Mr

Maynard. And the family and friends of his inner circle. Just in case a little leverage was required.

Finally, he withdrew a set of car keys. He kept one vehicle that had no tracking devices and had been manufactured before the advent of automobile GPS. He loved gadgets and technology as much as the next guy, but sometimes old school was the way to go.

# Chapter Twelve

*Wight's Landing, Maryland, Sunday, March 16, 10.55 A.M.*

Clay took the stairs to the deck in two leaps, cursing himself. He'd promised she'd be safe, but he'd nearly ignored the very alarm that would keep her that way. *You're an idiot, Maynard.*

Except . . . he'd finally had her in his arms. And it had been even better than he'd hoped. It was like he'd flipped a switch, waking her up. Turning her on. She'd definitely been turned on. She'd definitely wanted it. *Wanted me. Thank you, God.*

He shook his head hard to clear it. *Pay attention or she won't be alive to want you.* He hit the deck running, only to skid to a stop. His father stood on the dock, looking at his wristwatch.

Tanner looked up, mildly disapproving. 'Took you long enough.' His eyes narrowed. 'Although, I guess I should be congratulating you on your response time. You might want to comb your hair. Or jump in the water. It should be cold enough to deflate . . . things.'

*What the fuck?* Yeah, he was still harder than a rock, but . . . *What the fuck?*

'Dad, get back to the house. We have an incoming diver.'

'I know. You can put your gun away. It's just Lou.'

For a moment Clay could only stare. Then he got it. 'You mean this is a damn *drill*?'

'Yes. Which, if you'll stow your hormones, you'll remember you specifically requested. If it had been real, you would have been cutting it very close, son.'

Clay holstered his gun and shoved his temper down. He *had* suggested a drill, to make sure the system functioned properly. He hadn't expected his ex-fiancée to be the tester.

He thought of Stevie, below deck. Knew there was no way she was staying down there. It wasn't in her nature. He was shocked she hadn't appeared already. *Probably only because it's taking her a minute to climb the damn stairs.*

It appeared he'd be introducing her to his ex sooner than he'd planned. He stepped up to the dock and looked down into the water, hoping to prep Lou before Stevie appeared. He and Lou were no longer a couple, but they were still friends and Lou was overprotective in the extreme. Unfortunately, she also knew what had happened in December.

Because Alec had been waiting for him outside the hospital when Stevie threw him out. The kid had taken one look at Clay's face, instantly knowing what had gone down even though Clay hadn't said a word about it. Alec and Alyssa were thick as thieves, so his admin assistant knew shortly thereafter. And whatever Alyssa knew, her sister knew in no time whatsoever. To say that Stevie wasn't Lou's favorite person was putting it mildly.

The water bubbled and two hooded divers bobbed to the surface. Both wore neoprene dry suits designed for

247

cold-water dives, full masks covering their faces.

'Who's her dive buddy?' Clay asked grimly. Lou knew that he was hiding Stevie and Cordelia because only hours before he'd asked for her assistance with Cordelia's transportation to the farm. But he'd expected Lou to clear any guests with him.

'Nell Pearson, the new deputy,' his father said. 'Nell's okay. I checked her out myself.'

'Fine,' Clay bit out. 'But next time, don't surprise me. I could have shot them.'

'That's why I'm standing here, son.' His father's tone dared further rebuke, crossing the line from fatherly into patronizing, and Clay felt ten years old again.

Rolling his eyes, Clay waited until the two divers had climbed most of the way up the ladder before extending his hand to pull them up to the dock.

Lou pulled the mask from her face. 'Holy shit, that water's cold. Did your alarm go off?'

'It did,' his father said. 'At the first camera. All the others triggered after that.'

She tugged her hood down. 'An advanced diver might swim a bit faster than we did, but you should have a solid three minutes to prepare before an uninvited guest surfaces.' Lou looked up at Clay. 'Why don't you look happy, hon? Your system works like a charm.'

'You should have told me you were coming,' Clay said quietly.

Lou smiled innocently, lightly tapping his cheek with her flat palm. 'Then it wouldn't have been a real test.' She looked over his shoulder. 'Plus, I wanted to meet Detective Mazzetti.'

Clay turned around to see Stevie standing on the deck, leaning heavily on her cane. Looking none too pleased. 'What's going on?' Stevie asked.

He helped her to the dock, holding her elbow until she had her footing. 'It was a drill.'

'A drill,' she repeated flatly.

'I didn't know. I swear I wouldn't have frightened you that way.'

'It's okay.' Stevie eyed Lou, who was kicking off her flippers. 'And this is?'

Lou stepped forward, her expression coolly distant. 'I'm Sheriff Moore. This is Deputy Pearson.' Nell Pearson, a blonde who looked to be in her mid-forties, stood off to the side, saying nothing. There was no move to shake hands on the part of any of the women.

Clay wanted to hit something but settled for rolling his eyes again instead. 'Lou, you and your deputy need to get into warm clothes. Change in the boathouse. Just don't touch anything.'

Lou's eyes narrowed. 'Fine. We have dry clothes in our pack.'

His father handed Lou a thermos. 'I made you some coffee to take off the edge.'

Lou leaned up to kiss his cheek. 'Thanks, Tanner. Can you give Guthrie a call? Tell him we made it and to bring the boat in to pick us up.'

'Who's Guthrie?' Stevie asked. She was studying Lou, her expression deceptively mild.

'Her other deputy,' Clay said.

Stevie maintained her mild facade, her voice remaining level. Cordial, even. But the flash of anger in her eyes gave her away. 'Hell of a lot of people know about our secret hideout, Clay.'

Lou stopped in her tracks. When she turned, her expression mirrored Stevie's. When she spoke, her tone was equally mild. Had this situation been happening to someone else, Clay might have laughed. But it was happening to him and all he wanted was to make it stop.

'Detective Mazzetti, I've been asked to provide assistance and backup. My deputies will be part of that assistance in any way I deem fit. But for the record, Deputy Guthrie doesn't know you and your daughter exist, let alone are being hidden here. I certainly didn't expect you to be standing out in the open, especially after yesterday's events.'

Stevie straightened her spine and Clay closed his eyes. 'Lou,' he murmured, 'don't.'

'Don't *what*?' Lou asked acidly. 'Don't make *sense*? Two people *died* yesterday when a sniper fired on you, Detective. Your daughter was nearly gunned down in your own front yard. A cop died while taking your place in a safe house last night. How do you know you're not being targeted at this very moment? How do you know you're not putting all of us at risk?'

Twin flags of scarlet stained Stevie's cheeks, her body so rigid it was a miracle she didn't shatter into pieces. 'I suppose I don't. I apologize, Sheriff Moore.'

'I don't think I'm the one you should apologize to. But thank you anyway. You have a few more minutes before Deputy Guthrie arrives, if you'd like to take cover. Seems like locking the barn door after the horse is stolen, but if it makes you feel better, you just go right ahead.'

Clay exhaled wearily. Lou hadn't just infuriated Stevie, she'd embarrassed her, too. And that last crack was just plain snide. 'Lou, back off. I assured Detective Mazzetti that she and her daughter were safe here. Nobody's getting close enough to target anybody. The test of the underwater surveillance was a success, so we're done. Let's all retreat to our respective corners.'

He expected Stevie to make her exit, but she didn't

move. She also didn't say a word, and that worried him. 'You okay?' he murmured.

She nodded silently and it was then he noticed that she was standing upright, her cane tucked behind her, and he understood. Any direction she chose to retreat presented obstacles, and she didn't want Lou and her deputy to see her stumble. But Lou didn't realize it and wouldn't, if he had anything to say about it.

'Lou, we can talk when you're not shivering. Go change into dry clothes.'

Lou gave him a pitying look, like he was the stupidest man alive. But she changed her tone, sounding professional. Finally. 'I'll bring the boat tomorrow morning at five A.M. You have the child ready and I'll assume responsibility for transport.'

Clay winced. He'd intended to share his plans with Stevie when they were on his dad's boat, but then she touched him and . . . Who could blame him for forgetting? He'd nearly forgotten his own name. He glanced at Stevie, who stared up at him, stunned. And even angrier than before.

Obviously she could, and did, blame him for forgetting. '*The child?*' she hissed through clenched teeth. 'Which child? *My* child? What the hell?'

Lou actually looked repentant. 'I didn't know she didn't know. I'll go change now.'

'Yeah, you go do that,' Clay muttered. 'Hell.'

'I'm waiting, Clay,' Stevie said quietly when the boathouse door closed behind Lou.

He inclined his head toward her, not surprised when she leaned back, away from him. 'Let's talk about this privately. I'll explain.'

A throat was cleared delicately. Deputy Pearson had been standing off to the side, looking very uncomfortable.

'I don't mean to intrude,' she said. 'Detective Mazzetti, I won't reveal your presence here to anyone. I have a child of my own and I can only imagine what you've been through in the last twenty-four hours. You can depend on my discretion.'

'Thank you,' Stevie said. 'I appreciate it.'

Pearson looked at Clay. 'My vote was to tell you about the drill, but your father and the sheriff overruled me. Lou didn't know you hadn't had time to brief the detective on your plans.' She smiled at him ruefully. 'It's good to finally meet you, although I wish the circumstances had been different. Your dad has told me so much about you, I feel like I know you already. Now, if you'll both excuse me, I'm going to get out of this suit because I can't feel my toes anymore.'

The moment the boathouse door closed behind Pearson, Stevie pivoted on the heel of her good leg and started walking down the dock toward the house.

'If you want to yell at me,' Clay said, 'it's better to do it on the boat. Cordelia won't hear.'

She slowly turned, fire snapping from her eyes. 'Don't you dare use my daughter to manipulate me into going where you want me to go.'

He held up his hands in surrender. 'Fine. You're right. Will you please go to the boat so we can figure this out? Besides, Deputy Guthrie will be here in about a minute. Unless you want me to carry you, you can't make it to the house that fast.'

She glared at him, outraged. 'That's just cruel.'

'Cruel, but accurate. You need to choose.'

Her glare sharpened as she passed him on the way to the boat. 'Don't touch me,' she snapped, smacking his hand away when he tried to help her down to the deck. 'I'd rather fall.'

She didn't fall, although she came close when the tip of her cane hit a puddle on the deck. She managed to keep her balance and went down to the cabin without looking back.

'She's got a temper,' his father commented casually.

Clay turned, aiming the same glare at his dad that Stevie had given him. 'What the hell were you thinking, having Lou come here?'

'I didn't think Lou would be so openly hostile. I'm sorry, Clay.'

'Yeah, well it might not matter that you're sorry. Your timing really sucks, Dad.'

'I'm sorry about that, too. But if you could have seen the look on your face . . .' He took a look at Clay's face and backed up a step. 'Right. I'll just go and check on the child.'

'Yeah, you do that. Run like the coward you are,' Clay muttered, his father already halfway down the dock. Clay waited, watching the boathouse, arms crossed tight over his chest.

Lou emerged, dressed in soft sweats and looking very subdued. 'I'm sorry. Really.'

'Why did you do it, Lou?' he asked. 'Why poke at her that way? She's had a hell of a twenty-four and you rubbed it in. There was no need.'

'I know,' Lou sighed miserably. 'I'm a terrible person.'

'At the moment I'd be forced to agree.'

She frowned, his easy agreement clearly surprising her. 'She has a lot of nerve to come waltzing in here like she owns the place. She's using you.'

He thought of those moments in the boat's cabin. Being used by Stevie Mazzetti had been one of the best experiences of his life. She could use him until he was nothing more than a dried up stub. 'I invited her here.'

'She had other places she could go. Other people to depend on. Why you?'

'Because I manipulated her into it,' he said honestly. 'It's my business, Lou. Not yours.'

'But . . .' She sighed again, frustrated. 'She broke your heart.'

Clay had to laugh. 'So did you. You broke up with me six weeks before our wedding and married someone else, but you don't see me hassling your husband.'

She had the good sense to be embarrassed. 'Yes, I did break up with you, but I didn't break your heart. I couldn't break your heart.'

His smile disappeared. 'Why? Because it's made of stone?'

'No. That's ridiculous.' She thumped his chest with her fist. 'You might be rock on the outside, but you're nothing but a big old marshmallow on the inside.'

'Don't tell anybody,' he whispered.

'I won't,' she said with a smile, then sobered. 'I couldn't break your heart because you were never in love with me. Not like you are with her.'

Clay looked over at the boat. Just knowing Stevie was there, waiting for him, even as mad as she was . . . it made him content. 'I think I knew the moment I saw her.'

'Please don't tell me it was love at first sight. You're nauseating me.'

'Fine. It wasn't at first sight. More like third.' He smiled at the memory. 'She was leaning over my office chair, getting in my face, tearing me a new one. Which I totally deserved.'

'What did you do?'

'I put her daughter in danger because I was an idiot. Remember the man that killed Nicki?'

'How could I forget? Poor Nicki. She made terrible choices, but nobody deserves that.'

'No, no one does. I knew who'd killed Nicki and I wanted to catch him myself. I didn't report him to the cops like I should have. He was stalking Cordelia as well.'

Lou sucked in a harsh breath. 'I would have done more than tear you a new one, Clay.'

'I know. But once I knew what else he'd done, I made it right. I gave them the killer's ID and Cordelia was unharmed. Stevie was like a mother bear . . . she'll do anything to protect her child. And so will I. They're important to me, Stevie and Cordelia. Don't swipe at Stevie like that again. Ever.'

Lou grasped a fistful of his shirt. 'I just don't want you to get hurt.'

'And I appreciate you caring, but it's not your business. It's mine. And I'll take the risk.'

She shook her head. 'Just promise me one thing. Don't let her shortchange you. You deserve a lifetime, not just a tumble or two in the cabin of your boat.'

He blinked at her. 'What makes you think I had a tumble?'

'Well, *tumblus interruptus* anyway,' Lou said with a wicked grin. 'Your hair was a mess when I got here. I lived with you for a year and never saw a single hair out of place. And you were . . .' Her eyes skirted down, then back up. 'Yeah. I remember that part very clearly.'

Clay quailed. 'Do not ever say that in front of her. Please.'

'I won't, I won't. Geeze. But promise me you'll make sure she loves you back and isn't just out to top off her tank. Or worse, just because she's grateful for your help.'

Clay winced. 'Are you finished now?'

'I guess. You're a big boy now. I've got to let you go. Try not to let the big kids steal your lunch money.' Lou patted his cheek. 'Tell her I'm sorry.'

'I will.' He pointed to Guthrie who'd begun his approach to the dock. 'Your ride's here.'

'Okay. I'll see you tomorrow when I come for Cordelia. Good luck with Stevie.'

'Thanks. I'm gonna need it.'

*Baltimore, Maryland, Sunday, March 16, 11.35 A.M.*

Technology was extremely useful, Robinette thought as he parked his car a quarter-mile from his final destination. He especially appreciated the benefits of tracking technology. He could keep tabs on his entire workforce with the push of a button. The trouble was, that same technology could be used by someone to track him, too. Which was not acceptable.

He jogged down the street to the storage unit he'd had ever since he'd come home a former soldier, discharged honorably, but with no skills that would make him his fortune. With his MP credentials, he could have been a cop, true. But unless they were dirty, cops didn't make jack shit. He'd found another way to make money, and now he owned a few dirty cops of his own.

He liked the irony of that.

He found his storage unit and unlocked the door, revealing a 1999 Chevy Tahoe. It was no sports car, but it also had no GPS. None of his team knew he owned it. It had belonged to his first wife. Levi's mother. She'd left it to rust in her alcoholic father's garage.

Robinette had driven it back from Louisiana after burying Levi next to the boy's mother, who'd OD'd when

Levi was nine years old. It had happened while Robinette had been deployed and his friends had been there for him then, mourning with him. He hadn't cared a single iota about the bitch who'd borne his son, but he hadn't let his team know that.

He hadn't expected them to come to Levi's funeral and had been touched that Brenda Lee had assembled the old gang to stand beside him at the gravesite. They'd made plans after the funeral, plans that were finally coming to fruition today. But back then he'd needed some time to think. Telling them he planned to rent a car and drive home, he stole the Tahoe right out from under his first father-in-law's nose and brought it here.

He used the vehicle when he went places he'd rather keep secret. Hookers, usually. His tastes probably wouldn't meet the approval of his current father-in-law. But he also used the Tahoe when he spied on his own people. Like today.

*Wight's Landing, Maryland, Sunday, March 16, 11.35 A.M.*

Clay took the stairs down to the cabin one at a time, giving Stevie fair warning so that she could prepare her lungs for the tirade he deserved. When he got to the cabin, he found her standing as far away from the stairs as she could. Which wasn't all that far, considering it was the cabin of a small boat. Two more steps and he'd be standing behind her, close enough to kiss the nape of her neck – exposed only because her head hung down dejectedly.

'Stevie, I'm sorry. I was going to tell you, I swear it. It's just that you touched me and—'

Her free hand cut through the air, stopping his words. 'I know you were going to *tell* me.'

257

Relieved that she believed him, he took one of the two steps he needed to be close to her. Then frowned when her words sank in. *Tell?* 'I don't under—'

Again the hand, again cutting him off. 'I guess the question is when would you have *told* me? As you were bundling her into a boat, allowing people I don't know to take my child?'

*Oh.* His mama didn't raise a fool. Now he understood. 'No. I would have explained your options long before then. Before we'd even left this boat.'

She laughed bitterly. 'Oh, no. No wriggling out of this, Mr Maynard. Explaining my options, my ass. I have no options. I haven't since you saved my life yesterday, have I?'

He opened his mouth, then closed it. This was a no-win situation.

Her head jerked up, sending her dark hair swinging to cover the nape he'd wanted to kiss. 'Well?' she demanded.

'I don't know how to answer that,' he said cautiously. 'If you're expecting an apology for saving your life, you'll be waiting a long time.'

She pivoted, jabbing her cane into the cabin floor with enough force that he felt the vibration under his feet. Her lips were pressed tight, her eyes narrowed. And red. She'd been crying. 'Don't you *dare* play word games with me, Clay.'

'Okay. Yes, you have options. No, you don't have many. You specifically said last night that we needed to find Cordelia a safer place to hide. "Even safer than this."' He hooked his fingers in the air. 'I did what you asked.'

'Without consulting me.'

'For that I apologize. I thought you needed to sleep. I was trying to be considerate.'

'Of course you were!' she gritted out between her teeth. 'That's all you've *been* is considerate. I'm so goddamn tired of *considerate* that I could scream.'

Annoyance sprang free and he drove his fists into his hips. 'You want me to take you and Cordelia to the nearest bus station and drop you off with a sandwich and bus fare? Maybe hang signs around your necks that say "Kill me now"? Would that make me less considerate?'

Abruptly she stepped forward, lips trembling, her dark eyes suddenly shiny. Leaning up on the toes of her good foot, she bored her index finger into his chest. 'Do not patronize me.'

Clay drew a breath, let it out. Did his damnedest to ignore her tears. 'Then stop behaving like a child, throwing tantrums,' he snapped. 'I'm serious about protecting you and your daughter. When you are too, feel free to join the party.'

She flinched as if he'd struck her, then turned so quickly that she stumbled. Grabbing the edge of the table, she regained her balance. She'd lost her grip on the cane, now holding it in the middle instead of at the top. She stood with her back to him.

'Don't you think I *know* I'm acting like an idiot?' she demanded in a whisper. 'Don't you think I wish I could make myself *stop*? For almost eight years it's been just me and Cordelia. And I have taken care of her. All by myself. No husband. No one to ask advice.' She faltered. 'Except for Izzy. Who in many ways turns out to be a better mother than I am. Who knew?'

'That's not true,' he murmured, but she swiped at the air with the cane and he stepped back.

'My point is, I was doing a damn fine job. We were fine. Now, nothing is fine. Everything I touch goes wrong. Every time I turn around someone is targeting my child to get at me. Do you think I want to need protection? Do you think I want to live in a place that has bullet-proof glass?' She extended her arm, still gripping the cane, reminding him of Moses parting the Red Sea. 'And if you say "bullet-resistant", I will brain you with this motherfucking thing.'

'I wouldn't dream of it,' he said quietly, because her voice was thick with tears.

'Thank you.' She held her breath, but a sob escaped. 'God, I sound so pathetic. Feeling sorry for myself at a time like this. I should be saying, "Thank you, Clay," and falling down on the floor to kiss your feet. Why am I being like this?'

'Maybe because your world hasn't stopped spinning out of control for the past year?'

She laughed, but it was a tormented sound. 'Yeah.' She was quiet for a moment, gathering her composure. 'So. This plan of yours. I'd like specifics. Please.'

'All right. You know about Daphne's equine therapy program. She'll be offering it to kids who've been victimized by violence. I'm doing her security. Last week we finished the electric fence that surrounds her property. It's ten feet high, topped with barbed wire, and positioned through the trees, so it's not obvious to passersby.'

'To keep the kids in?'

'No. To keep predators out. We put in a heavy gate as well, the kind you see at military installations. Daphne picked one with pretty curlicues so that it didn't look oppressive.'

'She'd think of that.' It was said gently, with a note of rueful affection. 'Is it pink?'

He smiled, relieved. 'No. I had to draw the line somewhere. Today Alec will finish putting in the cameras and we'll establish a security center. Tomorrow we'll add motion detectors and refit Maggie's house with security doors. No bullet-proof glass, I'm afraid. It's on order, but it won't be in for a few weeks. With the other precautions, hopefully we won't need it.'

'It sounds very safe. Who will man this security center?'

'For now, Paige and Alec. If we need more support, my best friend, Ethan Buchanan, is on standby. He'll be on the first flight out of Chicago if I call him.'

'Just like that? You call, he comes?'

'I've done the same for him. Would do the same for him again in a heartbeat.'

She nodded. 'Okay. No offense meant, but Silas Dandridge was one of my best friends. How do I know your best friend Ethan is reliable and trustworthy?'

'I can give you references. A social worker, a family attorney, a professor, a psychiatrist, an arson investigator, a firefighter, and a half-dozen cops. You can call them and ask yourself.'

'And if I'm not comfortable with Mr Buchanan watching my child?'

'Then we don't do it,' he said simply. 'Or you go with her. Or she stays here with my dad and Emma. Or any of the above with your parents or Izzy added in.'

'Why did you plan this? I know I said I wanted a safer place for her, but that was fear talking. Why risk moving her at all?'

'Because eventually someone will connect you to me and me to this house. It's in Dad's name and while he isn't the father listed on my birth certificate, he's easy enough to trace to me if a person is looking.'

'Maybe nobody else will be looking. Maybe they'll realize there's nothing more to be gained by killing me. That too many people know about the dirty cops now.'

'Do you really believe that?'

Stevie's shoulders sagged. 'No. When do I have to decide if I want to move Cordelia?'

'Not at this moment. Joseph's people outside are watching the front. They'll tell us if they see anyone suspicious on the road leading up to the house. She can stay here indefinitely if this place isn't compromised.'

'But if it is, it will be too late to get her out.'

'Not if we get her out by boat, which is why Lou was coming with her boat tomorrow. But, Stevie, if you don't want Cordelia to move, she can stay here. The farm can be our Plan B.'

'I'd like that,' she said. 'The farm is a good Plan B. The horses would be good for her. Especially with all this tension going on. What about transport?'

'When she's ready, Paige will drive Grayson's Escalade to Lou's house, which also has a dock. Grayson's Escalade is equipped with the same window glass as Joseph's.'

'Which, according to Joseph, is about as bullet-resistant as you'll get if your address isn't 1600 Pennsylvania Avenue,' Stevie said dryly. 'Got it.'

'Cordelia knows Paige, so she won't be scared. Paige will meet Lou at four thirty in the morning, whatever morning you choose, so that they'll have the cover of darkness. Lou will bring her boat here, pick up Cordelia, go back to her place so that the transfer is made before first light. Cordy arrives at the farm in time for breakfast, and Maggie's waffles are almost as good as mine.'

Her shoulders had stiffened at his mention of Lou, but when she spoke, her voice was exceedingly reasonable. 'It sounds like a good plan, Clay. Thank you.'

'I'm sorry I didn't tell you before Lou did. She's . . . well, subtlety isn't her strong suit.' He chanced putting his hands on her rigid shoulders and released a breath when she didn't shake him off. 'I should have realized that this situation would be even harder for you.'

She went still. 'Why even harder?'

'Because you're used to—' *Being on top*, was what he almost said, but that put all kinds of pictures in his head. 'Calling the shots,' he said instead.

Her self-denigrating laugh made him wince. 'In other words, I'm a bossy bitch.'

'I didn't say that.'

'It's okay. It's true. I suppose subtlety's not my "strong suit" either. Well, at least you're consistent in the type of women you're attracted to.' She squeezed the bridge of her nose. 'God, now listen to me. That was just plain bitchy of me to say. And unfair. I'm sorry, Clay.'

He lifted his brows. 'Do I detect a little jealousy?' It pleased him more than it should.

'Wasn't I supposed to feel jealous?' she countered and he had to give her points for that.

'That could have been Dad's intent. You know, look what you passed up.'

'She was your fiancée.'

He heard the question even though she hadn't technically asked one. 'She dumped me six weeks before the wedding because she realized she didn't love me the way she should have for that kind of commitment. She ended up marrying a doctor and they're very happy. I kept thinking at the time that I should be more upset, but realized I was more relieved because I knew she was right. She just figured it out before I did. And had the courage to verbalize it.'

She said nothing, but when he leaned right to see her profile, she was biting her lip. He wanted to take over that particular job for her. Instead, he gently kneaded her shoulders.

263

'What's bothering you, Stevie?'

'I don't know. I want to think I had the urge to claw her face off because she was bitchy to me. Because she *was* bitchy.'

He leaned in close so that she could feel his breath against her neck. Her shiver did a whole helluva lot for his ego. 'Agreed. But?'

'No "buts". None that I have a right to, anyway,' she added under her breath.

He wanted to thrust his fist to the sky, yelling in victory at the top of his lungs, but kept his voice husky as he grazed his lips against her skin. 'Go ahead. Say what you want to say.' He kissed the curve of her neck. 'It's just you and me here.'

'That's what I'm afraid of,' she muttered. But she let her head fall to the side, baring her neck for more, exhaling slowly when he complied. As if she'd been waiting. It was like a whip to his body, driving him to rush. To take. To feast. But he kept himself on a tight leash and was rewarded when she relaxed, her head rolling back to rest on his chest.

'Humor me,' he murmured, sliding his hands down her sides to cover her stomach as he continued to press soft kisses up her neck to her jaw. 'You wanted to claw her face off. Why?'

'I didn't really want to claw,' she said, her words thickening. 'Maybe just a hard slap.'

'Because we were engaged?'

She lifted a shoulder. 'It's the intimacy. Shared moments. Things you don't want to imagine two people sharing when you . . . I mean, she knows what you look like . . .' She turned her head abruptly, removing her cheek from his seeking mouth. 'I'm stopping this. Right now.'

But she didn't move. He would have instantly released

her if she had. 'We lived together for over a year, Stevie. We were intimate. I can't go back and change that. I wouldn't if I could. She's part of my past.'

'And your present.'

He sensed his progress slipping away. 'True. I see her from time to time – on both business and personal occasions. If that bothers you, I'm sorry.'

She twisted abruptly, turning so that she faced him. Looking up, she met his eyes. 'You shouldn't have to be sorry. Whatever I feel is my problem, not yours. And I have no right.'

'What do you feel, Stevie?'

Looking away, she closed her eyes, color infusing her cheeks. 'Dammit, Clay. I bring a past with me, too. A husband. A lover. Someone with whom I've shared those same intimacies. This is what I meant. This is how I'll hurt you. I'll want from you what I can't give you myself.'

'What do you feel?' he repeated.

'Let me go. Please.'

Immediately he stepped back, dropping his arms to his sides, and watched her limp away, leaning on that ridiculous glittery cane. 'Stevie, stop.' It was the voice he rarely used, one he'd perfected way back in the Corps. 'Please,' he added stiffly. Stevie stopped, but she was still poised to bolt. 'What do you feel?'

She laughed quietly. Self-deprecatingly. 'That I'm the worst mother on the planet. Before you came back, I wasn't thinking about Cordelia going somewhere presumably safer than here. I was thinking about how much I hated Sheriff Moore. Because she was bitchy. Because she cut me down a few pegs. Because she was right.' A long, long pause. Then the faintest of whispers, as if she wanted him to know, but hoped he wouldn't hear. 'But mostly because she'd had you.'

She took a step toward the stairs, but he was on her before she'd put her foot down. 'Stevie.' He grabbed her uninjured arm, his voice cracking loud and harsh. '*What do you feel?*'

Her gaze whipped up to his, full of fire. Defiance. Lust. What he'd only glimpsed before now hit him like a brick. 'I want you, okay?' She all but snarled it at him. 'I wanted you the first time I saw you. Are you satisfied n—'

He kissed her, hard. No gentleness. No finesse. Just raw, brutal need. *Are you satisfied now? Hell no. But I'm sure as hell gonna be.*

He'd known it. Known she'd wanted him. Wanted *this*. But hearing the words torn from her lips unleashed the beast that had clawed at him so relentlessly for so long. He'd wanted her for so damn long.

*Slow down.* The small voice buzzed in his head like a fly. He ignored it. Or tried to.

*Do not do this. Not like this. Not with her. Never with her. She'll hate you.* He started to pull away, hanging on to control by a single thread. A very thin, very frayed thread.

But then her cane clattered to the floor as she grabbed the edge of his jacket to yank him down, kissing him back, her need every bit as savage as his own.

The thread broke. Clamping his hands over her butt, he lifted her against him, blindly shoved her hard against the door at the base of the cabin stairs. He hooked her good leg over his hip and began to thrust against her, hard and fast. Relentless.

She coiled her arm around his neck, holding on tight. Digging her heel into the back of his thigh for leverage, she met him thrust for thrust. This was no slow build, no rocking, no sexy undulation. Later. They'd do that later. This was immediate, animal gratification.

But it wasn't nearly enough. 'God, Stevie. The things . . .'

– hoarse, harsh words, staccato fragments of sentences ground out between frantic kisses that skated the line between pleasure and pain – '. . . I want to do . . . to you. Inside you. I need to be inside you. *Now.*' Winding her hair around his fingers, he pulled back enough to see her eyes. As far gone as he was, he knew he had to be sure she was with him. 'Tell me yes,' he demanded.

She was breathing hard, eyes narrowed, considering. Then she nodded grimly. 'Yes.'

# Chapter Thirteen

*Wight's Landing, Maryland, Sunday, March 16, 11.50 A.M.*

*Yes. Stevie had finally said yes.* Clay reclaimed her mouth and, grabbing her butt again, supported her weight with one hand as he locked the door with the other. His blood burned and he could feel the start of an orgasm twitching at the base of his spine. *Goddammit, not yet.*

*Bed.* He needed her in a bed. Luckily he had one, just a few steps away. Going down on one knee, her lowered her to the mattress, shoving her T-shirt up and wrestling with the front clasp on her bra as he wedged himself between her thighs. She pushed his hands away, released the clasp, and pulled the bra and T-shirt over her head, tossing them to the bed beside them. Then she surprised him by taking off his shirt as well, dropping it on top of hers.

For long seconds he hung there, staring down. Looking his fill after only imagining for so long. She was delicately made. Perfectly made.

He dropped his head, drawing one dusky nipple into his mouth and he sucked long and deep. She cried out, her hips coming off the mattress to press into his chest, making him groan in his throat. *It's been years for her. Too many years. Go slow. Slow the goddamn fuck down.*

But he was too hungry. He'd waited so long. Had all but given up hope. He sucked her other nipple and she shoved her fingers through his hair, pulling him even closer, whispering impatient pleas as her hips continued to roll and pitch beneath him.

He leaned to one side slightly so that he could reach the buttons on her jeans while he sucked and licked her breast. 'Pretty,' he said with his mouth full of her. 'So damn pretty. Lift up.' She obeyed, lifting her hips as he pushed the jeans down her legs. He'd worked the denim to her knees when he stopped, drew a deep appreciative breath, and groaned again. Resisting her efforts to pull him back, he released her breast so that he could look at her face.

Her eyes were closed, her head thrown back. Her lips, swollen from his kisses, parted as she panted, her pulse a visible flutter at the hollow of her throat. 'I can smell you,' he whispered. She shuddered, licking her lips. But said nothing. 'Are you wet?' he murmured.

She hesitated, then jerked a nod.

He wasn't letting her off so easily. 'How wet are you, Stevie?' He ran his tongue up the curve of her arched throat, chuckling darkly when her hips lifted again, seeking contact with his hand. He was about three seconds away from indulging her, but he wanted her with him. Needed to know she was with him. 'Tell me, baby. How wet are you?'

Her eyes opened to glare, making him grin. 'Very,' she said, tone laced first with warning, then desperate plea. 'Don't tease. Please.'

He ran fingers that actually trembled across the lace edge of her otherwise utilitarian black panties. Panties with a telltale dark patch where her arousal had soaked through. *God*. 'If I touch you, will you come for me?'

Her swallow was audible. 'Yes.'

He slipped his fingers under the lace, his own swallow audible when he touched curls. He dipped his forefinger into her slit, swearing under his breath at her slickness. She was ready for him. Right now. *I could slam into her with one stroke and not hurt her.*

*Slow the fuck down.* 'I want to see you,' he whispered. 'Take them off.'

Without another word she toed off her shoes, shimmied the panties down to her knees, then pulled her good leg free. Eyes narrowing in determination, she pulled the knee of her injured leg to her chest, stripped her other leg free, and tossed the clothes to the floor.

And then she was naked. *Finally.* His heart was beating so hard he felt light-headed. *I finally have her naked in my bed.* She was beautiful. Hot. Sexier than his most potent fantasies. Holding his breath, he slid one finger into her. Deep. *So wet.*

He nearly came right then and there.

A whimper escaped her throat and she moved her hips impatiently. 'Stop teasing me.'

He watched her face as he worked his finger in and out. Harder, faster. Her eyes were closed, clenched tight. So were her fists, digging into the mattress. Her teeth sank into her lower lip as she fell into his rhythm, meeting each thrust. Taking his breath away.

'More. Please.'

He added a second finger and she moaned, making him glad he hadn't taken off his own jeans yet, even though his erection was throbbing painfully. The second he got naked, he'd be inside her. He didn't know how long he'd manage to last after that. And he needed this to last.

'Faster,' she whispered. 'Please. It's been so long. Please.'

*Good. God.* Certain his cock had the permanent imprint of a zipper, he complied, adding his thumb to the motion, pressing hard against her, gritting his teeth when her body arched off the bed. On a low, strangled moan she came, his two fingers feeling each and every contraction. He closed his eyes, imagining those contractions squeezing his cock. *Soon. Another minute.*

She collapsed to her back, her chest pumping as she fought to catch her breath. Slowly her body relaxed, hands lying limply at her sides. 'Oh my God,' she rasped on an exhale. 'Thank you. I'd forgotten how damn good it feels.' And then she was touching him, finally, one hand sliding up his chest to splay across his shoulder, the other darting down to cup his erection through his jeans, making him hiss through his teeth. Which made her lips curve wickedly. 'Why are you still wearing clothes?'

Hands shaking, he yanked at the button on his jeans, carefully pulling down the zipper before shoving the jeans off and kicking them away. Then he was on her again, his hands in her hair, his mouth eating at hers, his cock nudging at her entrance.

*Mine. Stefania.* Her given name she never used, the one he'd called her only once before. To her face anyway. In his fantasies he murmured it over and over as he moved inside her. As he told her that he loved her. Because in his fantasies, she'd said the words, too.

Now . . . this was no fantasy. She was real. She was here. She was his. *Mine.* He shifted, positioning himself to come home. Home. *Mine.*

She tore her mouth away, her eyes wide, blinking. 'Clay, wait.'

He jerked back as if he'd been electrocuted. 'What?'

'Do you have protection?' she asked fiercely. Desperately.

'Shit. I've been tested,' he said, hearing his own desperation.

271

'And I've been celibate for eight years,' she shot back. 'But I'm not on the Pill.'

Part of him thrilled at the idea of Stevie pregnant. *With my child.* But he was getting too far ahead of himself.

*Just need to get inside her. Now.* He cursed again, hoping like hell he'd left a few condoms in the drawer from the last time he'd had a woman in this bed too many years ago, his shoulders sagging in relief when his fingers encountered several slippery foil packets. A glance at the fine print set his heart back to beating. 'Not expired. We're good.'

'Thank God. I thought we were going to have to stop before I was all caught up.'

Clay dealt with the condom, then returned his attention to her mouth, licking the imprints her teeth had left in her lower lip, making her shiver. 'Not a chance.' He reached between them, making sure she was ready. 'I've waited too long for you. I'm not stopping anytime soon.'

'Good to know.' She hummed low in her throat when he touched her, found her wet as before. 'It's been such a long time. It might take a while to refill the tank. Oh my God.' Her nails dug into his shoulders when he ground his cock against her, giving her a moment to get used to the feel of him before he plunged deep inside. 'But I'm sure you're up to the task.'

It took a second for her words to filter through his sex-fogged brain, but when they did, he froze. 'What? What did you say?'

She blinked. 'Why did you stop?'

'*What did you say?*'

Stevie opened her mouth, closed it. 'I don't know. I don't remember. That it had been a long time? You knew that. You knew I hadn't been with anyone since Paul.'

Confusion had filled her eyes and Clay felt like a heel.

But he had to know. 'Not that. You said something about a tank.' But it was Lou's voice in his mind, as loud and inescapable as a church bell. *You deserve a lifetime. Not someone out to top off her tank.*

Confusion gave way to apprehension. 'I think I said that it would take a while to refill my tank. That wasn't supposed to make you so mad. What's wrong with you?'

He pushed up on his arms, flexing his shoulders to dislodge her nails. Hurt flickered through her eyes, but he had to know. 'Why are you here, Stevie? With me, right now?'

Her apprehension became annoyance mixed with a healthy dose of sarcasm. 'Well, hell, Clay, let's just analyze this situation. We're in bed. I'm naked. You're naked and on top of me, wearing a condom. By Jove, Sherlock, I think this means I'm here to have sex with you. What the *fuck* is wrong with you?'

*You deserve a lifetime.* As obnoxious as Lou had been, she'd been right. 'And after that?'

'After the sex? I don't know. We go back to your father's house and pretend we weren't in his boat fucking like teenaged weasels? What do you want me to say?'

*That you love me.* But she wouldn't. Too late he considered the way she'd agreed to all this to begin with. She'd been grim. Like he was making her walk the plank or something. Clay closed his eyes. 'This is a mistake.'

He pushed himself off the bed. Off her. She didn't move, just lay there staring up at him, legs still spread, her mouth slightly open in shock. When he started to walk away, she snapped into action, rearing up to grab his arm, her fury suddenly blazing.

'Oh, no. You don't get to walk away from this, pal. You pushed me. Bullied me. Made me fucking *cry*.' Contempt dripped from the word and he understood she was angry

273

that he'd made her lose control, not that he'd hurt her feelings.

*God forbid that she'd feel anything*, he thought bitterly.

'"What do you feel, Stevie? What do you *feel*?"' she was mimicking in a low voice. 'Until you finally manipulated me into admitting that I want you. Then you drag me off to bed like you're on fire, give me a very nice orgasm, thank you very much, and then you . . . what? Go bat-shit crazy on me? Are you some kind of *lunatic*?'

'No,' he said quietly. 'Just a very foolish man who wanted something so much that he convinced himself he'd heard what he wanted to hear. You were right from the beginning. This can never work.'

She sucked in her cheeks. Dropped her gaze deliberately. 'Then I think you need to have a firm conversation with Mr Happy. Because he still thinks he wants me.'

Clay's face heated. He didn't have to look down to know his cock still stood at attention. 'A cold shower should remedy that. If you'll wait for me, I'll help you back to the house.'

Without waiting for a reply, he carefully pried her fingers from his arm and went into the small head, locking the door behind him.

*Sunday, March 16, 12.20 P.M.*

*Lunatic. The man is a freaking lunatic. Certifiably insane.*

Stevie launched herself from the boat's deck to the dock backward, ending up on her butt. It wasn't graceful, but safer than trusting her legs. Either of them. They were both trembling.

She was trembling all over. For a few minutes there . . . God. She'd felt so . . . normal. Alive. She hadn't even

274

known what she was saying, but he'd obviously been in enough control to listen. And confabulate whatever delusion he'd come up with. The man was a lunatic.

*And you're a fool, Stevie. A goddamn fool.*

Gripping her cane, she slung her backpack over her shoulder and struggled to her feet. Checked her phone. She'd been out here for over two hours total. And now she couldn't even remember what she'd been about to do.

*You were about to have sex.*

Before that, she thought sourly. Before she'd been stupid enough to touch his face in the first place. She started to walk, her eyes on the end of the dock. Every step toward the house was a step farther away from the crazy man. Who'd made her feel so damn good.

*Think, Mazzetti.* Tony Rossi, scumbag, shot by JD after he'd killed a cop and kept shooting, thinking he was killing Cordelia. *Okay.* That was the bucket of cold water she'd needed.

*Protect your child. Then hate Clay Maynard.*

Phone call with Danny Kersey. Framing of Richard Steel for the murder of that girl . . . Tracy Gardner. Best suspect, her boyfriend. She frowned. Eddie Ginsberg. *Now it was coming back.*

Scott Culp. Her eyes narrowed. Rossi's partner in crime. Now a member of IA. He leaked the location of her safe house to Rossi. She was sure of it. Now she just needed to prove it.

She paused at the end of the dock. The plywood path Tanner had laid that morning was now covered with a thin layer of slippery sand. Concentrating, she took careful steps as she crossed the beach. Falling now would deal her pride a killing blow.

She let herself through the gate and found herself staring

at the swing on the back porch. Clay had held her there last night. Let her cry.

*I'm done crying.* She forced herself to sit in the swing. *It's time to be a cop again, Stevie.*

She dialed JD, relieved when he picked up on the first ring.

'Are you all right?' he asked.

*Hell, no. I'm nowhere close to all right.* 'I'm okay. I've got something for you.'

She told him about the phone call to Kersey. When she got to Culp, JD whistled.

'Culp's IA,' he said. 'He reports straight to the top guy.'

'Yeah, I know. Kersey said Culp and Rossi had something going on years ago. Something that allowed Rossi to carry a wad of cash around.'

'If we pick Culp up, he'll just deny it.'

'I know. Can you do me a favor?'

'Name it.'

'Can you track Culp down, make sure he doesn't skip town?' If he already hadn't. *If he skipped while I was wasting time with Clay, I'll . . .* She exhaled, reining her temper in. She'd cross that bridge when she came to it. 'I want to talk to him. I want to see his reaction when he sees me. I'm coming back into town. Just let me know where to meet you.'

'What about Hyatt?' JD asked hesitantly. 'Do we tell him or not? Your call.'

Stevie bit her lip. 'How about calling Hyatt, but after you get to Culp's house? If Culp tries to escape after you've called Hyatt, then we'll know we've got more trouble than we thought.'

'That makes sense. I can do that. What about Cordelia?'

'I'll leave her here with Tanner and Emma. She's safe here for now and we have a plan to move her to another secure location if this one is compromised.' She didn't plan to toss the baby out with the bath water. She was angry with Clay Maynard, but his plan seemed solid. 'I'll drive myself back to the city and meet you at Culp's.'

'What about Clay?' JD asked quietly.

'He's a big boy,' she snapped. 'He can find his own way home.'

A beat of silence. 'Okay. Call me when you're close to the city. Do *me* a favor?'

'Name it.' Unless he asked about Clay.

'Take Joseph's Escalade. I don't want any more bullets hitting you.'

'That makes two of us.' Stevie hung up, then looked over her shoulder when the door to the house opened. Emma came out, looking elegant in wool slacks, a silk blouse, and a soft scarf artfully draped around her neck. 'I'm glad to see you, Em.'

'Yes, you are. You have no idea how much.' Emma unwound the scarf from her neck and rewound it around Stevie's. She gave it an upward tug. 'There. That'll do.'

'It doesn't go with my Hanes *ensemb*,' Stevie dead-panned. 'Clashes with my tee.'

'Yeah. But it covers the hickey on your neck long enough for you to get past your seven-year-old who's on the other side of this wall.'

Stevie's eyes widened, her hand slapping against her neck. 'You've got to be kidding me.'

Emma gave her an exasperated look. 'Like you didn't know? Were you asleep at the time?'

She gritted her teeth. 'God*damn* that man. How did you know?'

'I saw it,' Emma hedged. 'When you were on the dock.'

Stevie scowled. 'Unless you were spying on me with binoculars, you are kidding me now.'

277

'I had binoculars, but I was looking at birds!' she added defensively when Stevie swore.

'Does Tanner know?' Stevie asked darkly.

'Who do you think gave me the binoculars? But Cordelia doesn't know. He distracted her with the puppies.'

'At least there's that. Please, God, let me have packed a turtleneck.'

'You can borrow one of mine if you didn't. Where are you going?' she asked when Stevie got up from the swing.

'To change my clothes, then back to Baltimore. I have a lead.'


*Sunday, March 16, 12.20 P.M.*

The cold shower hadn't helped. And it had been *cold*. Clay stared down at his erection with contempt. What was it about him that was determined to chase women who didn't want him?

Stevie wasn't the first. Lou hadn't even been the first, although he wasn't sure she deserved to be lumped in with the other two. The first had been the worst, or so he'd always believed. No other way to go but up. Or so he'd always believed.

His ex-wife had been a spoiled, pampered daddy's girl who Clay had truly believed would grow up eventually. He'd been wrong on so many levels. And lives had been ruined.

There had been women in between. Not a horde, but he'd had his share. Nice, pretty, smart women. Women who'd wanted him. He'd tried not to lead any of them on. Had tried not to break their hearts. He remembered all of their names. All of their faces.

He gave the wastebasket sitting outside the shower a perplexed look. He didn't have any idea which of them had left the condoms in the drawer, though. He couldn't think of a single former lover who'd carried chocolate-flavored condoms, but that's what he'd peeled off himself.

Maybe he hadn't been as considerate a partner as he'd thought, because that seemed like something he should remember. He only hoped he'd ended all of the relationships with the consideration they deserved. He prayed that none of the women he'd brought to his bed in the past had left feeling like he did right now.

*All I ever wanted was a goddamn family*, he thought wearily. People married, raised families every day, all over the world. Why was it so hard for him?

When he'd met Stevie, he'd . . . known she was the one he'd waited for. No lightning bolts, no bells. Just a sense of rightness that had sustained him for two long years. She'd been the first one he'd ever truly wanted. God help him, he'd prayed so hard that she'd want him back.

Didn't look like God was on his side in this one.

*Shoulda taken her when you had the chance*. He'd been so close. And she'd been willing. No, not willing. More like furiously resigned. *Are you satisfied now?*

No, and it didn't look like he would be. *You should have just done it*. And when he'd finished inside her? Knowing all it had meant to her was the scratching of an itch, a rain shower to end a 'dry spell', when for him it had been something far more? He would have felt cheated.

Dirty, even. *Yeah, but at least you wouldn't be in pain because your damn balls are blue.*

He glared at his palm, knowing he was going to have to finish himself off before he went anywhere. Partly because he didn't want his dad or anyone else making smart remarks about the steel rod in his pants. But mostly because he needed to concentrate. Needed to eliminate the threats in her life so that she could be free from danger.

*And free from me.* The further away from her that he got, the faster his life would get back to normal. Whatever the hell 'normal' was.

Grimacing, he gripped his cock and pumped. Until his fingers cramped and his flesh felt raw. Nothing. Nada. No relief. Frustrated, he dragged his hands down his face and—

He stopped mid-drag. He could smell her on his hands. *Goddammit.* Feeling like a perverted fool, he slipped his fingers into his mouth. And tasted her. Instantly his mind filled with the image of her coming, body arched, firm breasts flushed, lip trapped between her teeth.

The back of his head slammed into the shower wall, his body going taut as a strung bow as the orgasm shattered him. When he was finally spent, he picked up the bar of soap and lathered himself, rinsing his body with mechanical efficiency. Watched as the suds carried the evidence of his obsession down the drain.

He shut off the water, hollow inside. And more alone than he'd ever been in his life.

He carefully combed his wet hair, staring at his face in the mirror. The man who stared back was a stranger with eyes so bleak that Clay felt tired just looking at him.

He had to get Stevie Mazzetti out of his system somehow. Or she'd end up killing him.


*Baltimore, Maryland, Sunday, March 16, 12.20 P.M.*

Robinette was not impressed. He'd come all prepared to flex his B&E muscles only to find the side door into

Maynard's garage unlocked. As was the door into the laundry.

*I sure wouldn't hire him to do my security.* It just proved what he'd always known – the biggest weaknesses in the security of any organization were the humans who lived and worked in it. The fanciest alarm system on the planet could be neutralized if one employee blocked open a back door to make taking his smoking breaks easier. Or simply forgot to lock the door.

Keeping his head down, Robinette slid the baseball cap from his head, hiding his features with the brim as he tugged the ski mask to cover his face, all in one motion. No use in taking chances. Even if Maynard had forgotten to lock his door, he might have cameras.

*Get in fast, get out faster.* Robinette entered the living room from the laundry and turned in a slow circle, taking in the floor plan, the shelves, the china cabinet on the far wall. If Mazzetti was nothing more than a client, the file listing the location in which Maynard had hidden her would probably have been kept in the man's office. But Robinette had watched the film of that December shooting more than once. He'd watched the desperation on Maynard's face while performing first aid on the detective.

Maynard was in love with her, which made him choose to start here versus his office. Maynard wouldn't chance hiding Mazzetti just anywhere. It would be special. Extra-safe.

Robinette's glance into Maynard's kitchen confirmed his conclusion. On the fridge was a crayon drawing, torn in half, but fixed with magnets so that the halves came together. The signature scrawled in a childish hand was Cordelia Mazzetti's. Maynard displayed the child's artwork on his fridge. A man didn't get much more besotted than that.

The place Maynard had chosen to hide mother and daughter would be personal, just like the relationship. After giving the walls a quick check for a built-in safe, Robinette searched the closets and the cabinets for a strong box, a stack of file folders, any pile of papers that might hold property deeds or rental agreements.

And found nothing. Except that someone had already been here looking. The cushions of the sofa in the living room had been slashed, stuffing everywhere. The contents of the desk in Maynard's bedroom had been dumped on the carpet, the contents of every closet strewn. Books had been tumbled off shelves, clothing tossed from the drawers, the mattress pulled from the bed and slashed. Foam littered the floor. The box springs had been slashed as well. Pictures had been pulled from the walls, glass broken, photos pulled out and left where they'd fallen.

The chaos was orderly, methodical. Robinette recognized the technique.

Westmoreland had already been here. And had chosen not to inform him. There was no rage. No more feelings of betrayal. In that moment, Robinette mentally discharged one more member of his 'inner circle'. Westmoreland, Henderson, Fletcher . . . They were of no more importance to him now than a stranger on the street.

That was the way Todd Robinette rolled. *Fool me once, shame on me. Fool me twice . . . not gonna happen*. Anyone he trusted got one opportunity to screw him. If they tried, he cut them out of his life, quickly and irrevocably, as if they'd never been. And then he dealt with the betrayal.

No one was spared. Not his friends. Not even his wife, as Julie had learned the hard way. His second wife's accusations and betrayals had made it easy to kill her eight years ago.

But Julie's first husband, Rene . . . he'd been the worst.

This mess Robinette now found himself in? It all started with Rene. The man had once been his oldest friend. He'd allowed Rene to raise Levi while he'd been at war. Rene had given him a job when he'd come home.

But it had been a shit job. *Everyone starts at the bottom, Todd. You gotta learn the business from the bottom up, Todd.* Rene had started him in the goddamn *warehouse* reporting to high school dropouts. And when Robinette had found a way to make it work for him? Rene had accused him of stealing company property. Had threatened to report him to the cops.

That was it. Friendship over. Robinette had killed Rene without planning to do so. When Julie had figured it all out and accused him, threatened to turn him in . . .

Killing her had been even easier. *Nobody threatens Todd Robinette and gets away with it.*

Stevie Mazzetti was about to find that out. Yesterday he'd wished he could personally deal with the bitch cop who'd killed his son. *Looks like I'll get my wish. Once I find her.*

And he would. There had to be something in Maynard's house to point to where the PI had taken her, or at least to point to someone else Maynard loved. Someone who might be used as leverage to make Maynard talk.

Robinette squatted, picking up photos from the floor, taking care to only handle the edges. He didn't trust forensic scientists. They could lift fingerprints from fruit now. A print made through his gloves would be child's play.

He shuffled through the photos until one caught his eye. Maynard with an older man, standing on the deck of a boat. It looked recent. Robinette lifted his eyes, saw that the model boat Maynard had displayed on his bookshelf had been smashed to smithereens. From what was left of the wreckage, he could see the model boat looked much like the boat in the photo.

Robinette had stowed the photos in his backpack when he saw another frame amidst the trash. This one made him frown. They were military medals for valor and courage – a Purple Heart and a Silver Star. They'd been awarded to Maynard. They didn't belong on the floor.

Robinette might not serve the Stars and Stripes any longer, but he still had respect for those who had, especially anyone who'd been injured in whatever god awful place he'd served. What had Westmoreland been thinking?

Robinette shook the broken glass from the frame and leaned it against the dresser, then made his way back to the kitchen and checked the trashcan. It was filled with flour and sugar, salt and loose tea. Westmoreland had dumped all the canisters into the garbage rather than dumping all the powdery items on the floor and risking leaving a footprint. *I taught him well.*

Robinette had found nothing definitive upstairs to indicate where Maynard had hidden Mazzetti, but there was still a basement to check. *Wait.* He froze, lifting his head to listen. *The slam of a car door. Low voices.* Someone was coming.

He headed to the living room, stepping to the side of the sliding glass door so that he was hidden by the gathered curtain. And just in time. The door slid open and in walked a cop. *I must have triggered a silent alarm.* Good thing he'd hidden his face. It appeared that Clay Maynard had halfway decent security after all.

Robinette made sure his holster was unencumbered. He wouldn't use the gun unless he had to, but if he did have to, he wanted fast access.

He waited for the cop to walk past the door, reached out, grabbed the cop's head and . . . *Twist*. Robinette gave a good jerk, the sound of the cop's neck breaking filling him with intense satisfaction. He dropped the cop to the floor with a thud and listened.

The laundry room door creaked open slowly. The partners had separated, each taking a different door. Robinette crossed the room as the partner entered, grabbed his head and . . .

*Twist.* Another one bit the dust. It was his specialty, honed over years in the desert. Henderson had been their marksman. Westmoreland's weapon of choice had always been a dagger. Fletcher, poison. Robinette's most lethal weapons were his own bare hands. But, like Westmoreland, he liked knives, too. Guns were the weapon of last resort.

He slit their throats to make sure they were dead. Taking their radios, he grabbed his backpack, pulled the sliding door closed, then exited through the garage, the same way he'd come in. Anyone who saw him now would see only a workman. He pushed the ski mask up under the cap, keeping his head down. Then he got in his Tahoe and drove away.

His former team might believe he'd gotten soft. Robinette suspected the two dead cops in Maynard's living room would disagree.

*Wight's Landing, Maryland, Sunday, March 16, 12.25 P.M.*

Clay wrapped a towel around his hips as he'd left his clothes in the cabin with Stevie. Bracing himself for another confrontation, he stepped out of the boat's small head into the cabin.

It was unoccupied.

The bed had been made, military-grade creases in the spread. The files on which they'd worked had been packed into the rolling suitcase, which sat at the base of the stairs. His clothes were neatly draped over a chair, right down to his socks. His shoes had been precisely aligned. On the table where they'd worked was his cell phone, also precisely aligned.

Stevie, her laptop, and her cane were gone. With the exception of the large suitcase, no one would have known she'd ever been there.

Clay sniffed his fingers, relieved when the dominant scent was that of the soap. But she was still there, underneath the Old Spice. *Get her out of your mind. Now.*

He dressed quickly, then checked his phone. Snarled. Five missed calls, eight missed texts, most in the last five minutes. He couldn't even take a damn cold shower without someone bothering him. Then he frowned. The calls were all from Paige as were half the texts – and his business partner was not the hysterical type.

As soon as he looked at the other texts, he knew exactly what had happened. On any other day he would have been stunned. Shocked into immobility. But this wasn't any other day.

Someone had broken into his house, the alarm system sending the texts to his phone.

'Shit.' He grabbed the suitcase and muscled it up the stairs. Once on the dock, he broke into a run, dragging it behind him as he speed-dialled Paige.

'Where have you been?' she demanded.

'Busy,' he bit out. 'I need details and I need them now.'

*Sunday, March 16, 12.30 P.M.*

Stevie went into the house and directly up the stairs, hoping Emma would take the hint and leave her and her damn hickey alone. No such luck.

'What leads did you find?' Emma asked, sticking behind her all the way up the stairs.

'The leak's IA.' Stevie tried to close the bedroom door but Emma pushed her way in.

'Slow down a second,' Emma said, sitting on the bed. 'Let's talk details.'

Stevie slanted her a warning look as she searched for a turtleneck, throwing clothes from her bag every which way. 'Must we?'

'Yes, we must. You said you found the leak,' she said. 'Who?'

Stevie told her about Scott Culp. 'Which explains a lot about the lack of urgency in IA's investigations over the last year. Dammit. No turtlenecks.' Too bad she hadn't packed for sex. Which she technically had not had. *At least there's that.* 'Do you have anything in your suitcase that won't cost me a month's salary to replace?'

'No, but you can borrow it anyway.' Emma took the scarf off Stevie's neck and shook her head. 'How could you not know Clay did that to you?'

'I was busy.' Orgasming. 'Just . . . fix it, okay? And stop grinning at me.'

'Sorry. I'm glad you had fun.' But when Stevie didn't reply, Emma stopped rummaging through her bag and turned with a frown. 'You didn't have fun. Did he . . . Are you all right?'

'I'm fine. He just . . .' Stevie sighed. 'He's got issues. Can you let me leave it at that?'

287

'For now,' Emma said softly. 'As long as you don't shut me out forever.'

'I don't shut people out.'

Emma laughed bitterly. 'Oh right. And I'm a basketball star.' She tossed a sweater on the bed. 'Take off your shirt.'

Stevie scowled. 'I can dress myself, Mom.'

'You're bleeding, Stevie. Let me fix you. I don't want you bleeding all over my sweater,' she added lightly, but Stevie heard the underlying concern.

Silently, Stevie pulled the shirt over her head, not letting herself think about doing so in front of Clay. She was *so* not thinking about it. Hell. Now that's all she could think about.

Emma made a distressed noise. 'You pulled out two stitches. Are you sure you're okay?'

'Emma,' she murmured wearily. 'Please.'

Emma muttered something about Stevie not having the sense to come in out of the rain. 'Stay here. I have to get the peroxide.' She was back in less than a minute and proceeded to change Stevie's bandage with capable hands, all humor gone.

'You're sure you're not a medical doctor?' Stevie asked, trying to lighten the mood.

'I've got two boys that love to wrestle. I know all about bandages.' She grabbed the Kevlar vest that Hyatt had given Stevie the night before and guided Stevie's injured arm into one sleeve, waiting while Stevie shoved her good arm in the other, then fastening the vest's Velcro ties.

'What if I bleed on your sweater?'

'Goddamn you, Stevie,' Emma said, her teeth clenched. 'You're an idiot.'

'Excuse me?'

'You're going out there where people are trying to kill

you while you're not thinking clearly. You're upset by Clay, which has left you off-balance. You've already accepted that you'll bleed again. *Damn you*. You are not bullet-proof and I don't want to bury you.'

Emma was crying and Stevie blew out a breath, stared at the cashmere sweater in her hands, then frowned, her focus shifting. 'You didn't have that suitcase last night.'

Emma blinked at her through her tears, her expression incredulous. 'You ignored everything I just said.'

Yes, she had. Because something wasn't right. 'Where did the suitcase come from, Emma?'

Emma shook her head. 'If you're so desperate not to face your own mortality, fine. We'll talk about stupid suitcases. Joseph's agents brought it this morning when they changed shifts. Paige sent it with them. She stayed in my hotel room last night and repacked my things.'

Stevie's brain started to click. 'Hold on. Paige was in your room last night before you met me on the road. She discovered the mess in your hotel room, not you. Where were you?'

Emma's eyes snapped with fury. 'Clay and I went straight from your house to the gun range. Clay wanted me to prove I could handle a firearm so that I could guard your child. Which I did prove, thank you very much. Paige dropped us off there, then dropped Alec at their office, then went to my hotel to pack my things. She found my room had been broken into.'

'When? When did you do all of this?'

'While JD was driving you around, ensuring you lost any tails and giving all of your friends time to get together in one place.'

Stevie heard the rage in Emma's voice and ignored it. 'You planned to come with me all along, even though I told you to go the hell *home*. And Clay knew. He manipulated me. Again.'

'Uh-huh, he did.' Emma's chin came up, her eyes narrowed. 'He's also responsible for the adoration of Justin Bieber. He's a freaking mind control expert.'

Stevie clenched her cane, pushed herself to her feet. 'I'm serious.'

'You're also *wrong*.' Emma got in her face until they were nose to nose. 'Nobody manipulates you into doing anything. You do exactly what you want to do. Did we obey your orders? No. Did we try to support you? Help you? Guilty as charged, so beat me senseless. But we did not manipulate you. Anything you've done for as long as I've known you, you've wanted to do, and if anyone tries to help you, you push them away.'

Stevie was trembling again, which made her even angrier. She pulled the cashmere sweater over the Kevlar vest, adjusting the collar so that it covered the hickey. 'I'm sorry I upset you,' she said rigidly. 'I'll be back later this evening and we can discuss it then.'

Not waiting for a reply, she shouldered her backpack and made it down the stairs where she found the Escalade's keys on the kitchen counter where Clay had left them the night before.

'Cordelia?' she called. 'Where are you?'

Cordelia ran in from the laundry room, her smile big. 'Right here, Mom. Playing with the puppies.' Her smile abruptly disappeared. 'Where are you going?'

'To meet with Uncle JD. It's not dangerous and I'll be back before you know it.' She pulled Cordelia close. 'I have to make things safe for us again. So we can go home.'

Cordelia launched herself at Stevie, holding on hard. 'Mama, I don't want to go home.'

Stevie closed her eyes. She didn't have time for this. But

how could she *not* have time for this? 'I know you like it here, and I know you like Mr Maynard, but we can't stay here forever.'

'I know. But I don't want to go home. Can we get a new home?'

'A different house?' Stevie asked, surprised.

'Yes. Can we?'

*I hate that kitchen.* In her mind Stevie could hear Cordelia's whispered confession to Clay the night before and his murmured response. *I'd hate that kitchen, too, if I were you.*

Stevie felt the panic grip her chest. She and Paul had chosen that house together, scrimping and saving for the down payment. They'd worked hard to renovate, repair. He was all over that house. She couldn't lose it. It would be like losing him, all over again.

But her baby was shaking. 'Yes, we can. We can get a different house.'

Cordelia drew back, stunned disbelief in her eyes. *She'd thought I'd say no. That I'd choose the house over her.* 'Really?'

'Really. You are more important than any old house. It has a lot of memories, good and bad. We'll find a new house and make new memories. You and me. When I get back from the city, we'll go online and look at houses, okay?'

Cordelia beamed. 'Can Aunt Izzy come, too?'

'Of course.'

Cordelia's brows lifted. 'Can we get a dog?'

Stevie laughed, stunned that she still could. 'Now you're pushin' it. Give me a kiss.'

Cordelia smacked a loud one on her cheek. 'That should hold me for a while. Get Mr Tanner to lock the door behind me. Tell him I had to go into the city, but I'll be back soon. I love you.'

'Love you, too, Mama.'

'Stevie.' Tanner thundered down the stairs. *'Wait.* Do *not* leave this house.'

Stevie glared at the ceiling. *Emma, you damn tattletale.* 'Can't wait,' she called. 'Gotta go.'

Hurrying into the garage, Stevie climbed into the Escalade, adjusted the seat, fully aware she'd been holding her breath. *Get it over with.* When she inhaled, she smelled Clay, like she'd known she would. The scent of his aftershave had lingered.

*I can smell you.* She clenched her thighs when the warmth between them began to throb. She could see his face, intent in its passion, then . . . Nothing. His expression had gone blank. Like he'd been zapped with the freeze-frame button on a remote. *Why are you here?*

Why had she been? Had she been manipulated? Or had she been in complete control of her actions the entire time? 'I don't push people away,' she said to the quiet interior of the SUV.

But she sounded unconvinced, even to herself. With a tired sigh, she pushed the button to activate the garage door. *Time to go to work.* So why did it seem like she was running away?

When the door had fully opened, she started the engine and began to pull out of the garage. Only to have the door come back down. Bracing for an argument with Clay's father, she turned in her seat . . . and froze.

Not the father, but the son. Clay opened the passenger door, got in and slammed the door hard enough to shake the SUV. His expression was furious, his face as hard as stone. He hit the garage door control button and stared straight ahead as the door went up again.

'Drive, Detective. As fast as you can.'

# Chapter Fourteen

*Baltimore, Maryland, Sunday, March 16, 12.30 P.M.*

Sam Hudson stared at his cell phone as it vibrated its way across the dining room table in his apartment. After dropping the gun off at Ballistics, he'd gone to check on his mother. Then he'd come home, knowing if he stayed at his mother's house long enough, she'd sense his disquiet and nag him until he told her what was bothering him.

He couldn't say the words out loud to anyone, least of all to his mother. *I may have killed your worthless junkie husband, Mom.*

No, he couldn't be around his mother today.

Instead he'd sat in his apartment watching the phone that now buzzed with an incoming call. From within the police department. Probably from Ballistics.

Paralyzed, Sam watched his phone skitter across the table until the call went to voicemail. He picked the phone up, connected with his voicemail and listened, holding his breath.

'Sam, it's Dina. I got a hit on that gun. Call me or stop by. I'm here 'til four.'

Damn. Until now, he'd been able to compartmentalize

the gun as being simply 'recently fired'. Now, it was 'used in the commission of a crime'.

*Be a man, Sam. Get off your ass and go to Dina's office.* Find out who or from what they'd pulled the bullet that matched . . . that gun. And if the crime committed was a homicide?

*I'll deal with that when I come to it.*

*Wight's Landing, Maryland, Sunday, March 16, 12.40 P.M.*

*Drive, Detective. As fast as you can.*

Stevie considered making Clay explain, but a glance at his profile made her nix the idea. He was tense, little white lines bracketing his mouth, and somehow she knew this wasn't about them.

She pulled around the FBI agents' vehicle and headed for the main road. 'I'll drive as fast as I can, but I can't legally use the flashers, Clay. I'm on disability. I don't even have my badge. If we get stopped, we'll be screwed.'

'We'll have a police escort. Just get to the highway.'

*What the . . . ?* 'Okay. Figure out which of these switches works the dash flashers. Then check the glove box and see if Joseph has a portable.'

Ten seconds later, he'd activated the emergency flashing lights built into Joseph's dash. A minute later, he'd smacked a portable flashing blue light on the roof.

The side roads were deserted, so Stevie increased their speed, way over the legal limit. 'Who's our escort and where will they meet us?'

'Lou Moore. She's on her way toward Queen Anne Highway. She'll lead us from there.'

Of course it would be Sheriff Moore. *Let it go, Mazzetti. Just let it go.* 'Lead us where?'

'Across the Bay Bridge, back to Baltimore. Once we get over the bridge, we'll get another escort. I don't know who yet,' he added brusquely, before she could ask.

'Okay. Tell me what's happened.'

'Somebody broke into my place.'

She flicked him a surprised glance. 'Home or your office?'

'My house. I have a silent alarm that goes to my cell. If I don't respond, it alerts my backup. That's Paige. She's called the cops and is on her way to my place right now.'

'First Emma's hotel room, now your house. They're looking for me.'

'Yeah.'

*I'm sorry*, she wanted to say, but didn't. He'd find some way of bending an apology to his advantage. 'Given the James Bond setup here, I'm surprised anyone got into your house.'

'Me, too.'

*Okay*. It appeared she'd have to work for any information. 'How was the alarm tripped?'

'One or more of three ways.'

She blew out a frustrated breath. 'Which are what?'

'A cell phone signal that isn't mine, body heat, or a simple breaking of the contacts on the door or windows.'

'Do you have one of those fancy security doors?'

'I do.'

She started to snap at him, but knew that wouldn't help. 'If it was their cell phone, can your system access its drive? Get a name, provider, contacts? Anything that might help us ID him?'

She felt him shift, turn to look at her. She kept her eyes on the road.

'Maybe,' he said, finally. He sounded grudgingly impressed.

'Do they have to make a call to trigger the alarm, or is it just the signal itself?'

'Just the signal.' He turned back to the window, silent again.

Stevie drove like a demon for another ten minutes, but had to slow when they approached the city limits of Wight's Landing. Traffic parted when drivers saw the Escalade's flashers, but being a beautiful Sunday afternoon, it seemed all the town's residents had gathered on Main Street. Finally they cleared the town and saw the sheriff's car waiting.

Sheriff Moore took the lead and they were off again.

He made a quick move, answering his cell phone. 'Paige,' he said. 'I'm in the car with Stevie. I'm going to put you on speaker.'

'I'm at your place,' Paige said, slamming a car door. 'Peabody, with me. And no comments about me taking my drooling dog into your house.'

'I wasn't going to,' Clay said evenly. 'If somebody's broken in, I want you to have all the protection you can get.'

'Now I'm at your front door and . . . I don't hear a thing. No cops, no nothing.'

'I thought you called the cops a half-hour ago.'

'I did,' Paige said. 'There's a cruiser parked on the curb.' A beat of silence, a jangle of keys, then a tight exhale. 'Oh, no,' she whispered.

*Oh God*, Stevie thought. *Now what?*

'What is it, Paige?' Clay demanded when his partner said no more.

Paige cleared her throat. 'The officers appear to be dead. Two of them.'

Clay paled. 'Get out of the house, Paige,' he said, teeth clenched.

'I never went in. I'm headed back to my truck. I'll lock myself in and I have a gun. I have to call 911 now. I'll call you back as soon as I can.'

Paige disconnected, leaving Stevie and Clay in utter, stunned silence.

Then Stevie leaned on the accelerator. 'Call Sheriff Moore. Tell her we need to go faster.'

*Baltimore, Maryland, Sunday, March 16, 1.18 P.M.*

Paige was waiting in front of Clay's house. 'Both cops are confirmed dead. CSU's in there now, along with Joseph, Hyatt, and the ME. A few of Joseph's people are around back.'

'How did they die?' Clay asked, after making sure that Stevie was on the front porch where she was sheltered on three sides by the house. His body blocked her from the street so that she was completely protected. That this had been a ruse to lure him home – with Stevie in tow – had occurred to him right away.

'I saw slit throats,' Paige said. 'I don't know anything else. Hyatt took my statement and said I was free to leave.' She regarded Clay with a concerned eye. 'Are you okay?'

His partner knew him too well. 'I'm fine. Just tired. I didn't sleep much last night.'

'Well, you're not gonna sleep here tonight. I imagine they'll have this place tied up as a crime scene for several days. Are you going back tonight to wherever you were last night?'

He nodded. 'Yes. I'll keep the Mazzettis safe until this is over.'

'Well, if you need a place to stay later on, our house is always open. You know that.' Paige looked at Stevie.

'You, too. Grayson and I are worried about you guys.'

'We're okay,' Stevie said quietly. 'But thanks.'

She wasn't okay, Clay was certain of that. When he'd climbed into the Escalade back at his dad's house, she'd been furious, but instantly became a professional when she realized what was needed. More of a professional than Clay had been. He'd been sullen, uncommunicative.

*Because it hurt.* Being in the same vehicle with her for those forty minutes had sent acid churning through his gut and started a dull throbbing behind his eyes. But he had bigger problems than his gut, his head, or even his heart.

Two men were dead. Added to the three women from yesterday . . .

'You shouldn't go into the office until we know it's safe,' he said. 'If they broke in here, they may have tried to break into the office, too.'

Paige shook her head. 'They haven't yet. I asked Hyatt to send a cruiser to check the office. It hasn't been touched. I imagine the uniforms will stay there for a while, in case whoever did this does try to break in. With Alyssa out of town and Alec up at Daphne's place, none of us need to go into the office right now. I texted them both, though, and told them to stay away. Just covering the bases.'

'Good. Thanks.' At least his people were safe. For now. 'I want everyone checking in, every hour. No exceptions. Where are you going from here?'

'To the airport. Emma's husband's here. I was supposed to have picked him up already. I'll keep in contact, but I want you to do the same. Come on, Peabody.'

Clay watched to make sure she got into her truck safely, then turned when his front door was opened by Lieutenant Hyatt.

'Come in,' Hyatt said, motioning Clay and Stevie inside. Joseph Carter and Agent Brodie from VCET's forensic lab crouched next to one of the bodies, talking to Neil Quartermaine, the medical examiner.

The slain officers lay on Clay's living room carpet, near the sliding glass door that led to his deck. *They'd been so young*, he thought. *What a waste*.

'Neither of them over thirty,' Hyatt said and Clay realized he'd voiced his thoughts aloud.

'What happened?' Clay asked.

Joseph looked up. 'We think the attacker was standing against that wall. He hit one, then the other, before either of them could make a distress call.'

The two cops lay on their stomachs, heads turned at an unnatural angle. Throats slit ear to ear. 'No blood spatter,' Clay said. 'They were dead when he cut them.'

Agent Brodie looked up. 'Yes,' she said simply.

'He broke their necks first,' Quartermaine said. Still fairly new to the Baltimore ME's office, he'd taken over JD's wife's position when Lucy went on maternity leave last December. His first day on the job had been that fateful day, in fact. The day Stevie had been shot.

Now Stevie stood off to the side, her eyes sharp as she took in the bodies, the room. *My things*. He'd dreamed of the day he'd bring her to his home, sharing what he'd accumulated over the years. Sharing himself. He never pictured her standing over two dead bodies.

'And these guys had muscular necks,' Quartermaine was saying. 'They were in good physical condition. Probably lifted weights regularly. Your killer is strong, likely experienced in hand-to-hand. We could be looking at a professional fighter or someone with a military background.' He shook his head. 'Although *I* sure didn't learn that in the military.'

'I did,' Joseph said quietly.

'So did I,' Hyatt added.

Clay shrugged. 'Because I have an unshakeable alibi, I'll add my "So did I".'

'I almost feel left out,' Quartermaine muttered, making Joseph smile grimly.

'Have you ever actually done it?' Hyatt asked Clay and Joseph, more than idle curiosity in the question. 'Broken a neck?'

Joseph got real busy checking out the dead cops' slit throats. The Fed had paled slightly at the question, eyes flickering like he'd gone somewhere else for a second. Clay didn't know what the guy was remembering, but it wasn't a happy place. Quartermaine was giving Joseph a curious look. Brodie's was more knowingly sympathetic.

Clay decided to take one for the team, to get the attention off Joseph. 'Yes, I have. Why?'

'Because I personally have not,' Hyatt said evenly. 'I need to understand what is required to break the necks of two strong officers, two in succession. When did you do so?'

'In Somalia, when I was in the Corps.' Clay wasn't sure he believed the lieutenant's reason for asking, but the guy could get the details of Clay's story easily enough if he so desired. 'But I didn't do it to maintain stealth, like this probably was. We were under attack and I was fighting to stay alive. I used the only weapon I had at the moment – my hands. It wasn't pleasant, I'll tell you that. And I don't know that I could have hit two guys in quick succession like this.'

'Why not?' Hyatt asked, his curiosity genuine.

'There's an emotional component that goes with it,' Clay said slowly, aware of everyone in the room watching him and uncomfortable with the notion. 'It's still hard to admit, even after all these years, but when it was over, I staggered off and threw up. The sound of cracking wood still makes me cringe. There was certainly no joy in it. I might have been able to break two necks in a row, given the adrenaline pumping like it was, but I'm glad I never had to find out for sure.'

Joseph's jaw clenched and Clay somehow knew that whoever the Fed had disposed of in his past, he *had* taken joy in the action. Or if not joy, then at least satisfaction. Which meant that whoever Joseph had killed had to have been a monster, because Joseph Carter was one of the good guys. One of the few men Clay trusted as much as he trusted his old friend Ethan Buchanan.

'If you only broke one of their necks, how did you dispose of the other seven?' Hyatt asked.

Clay narrowed his eyes, his suspicion confirmed. Hyatt had known to ask the question. 'How did you know there were others?'

'I read up on you two years ago, Maynard. We weren't sure what kind of man you were and what, if anything, should be done about you back then. You'd obstructed justice, by your own account unknowingly, but there were those who thought you should have been charged with it.'

'I probably should've been,' Clay said bluntly. He'd known the identity of the man who'd killed his former partner, Nicki Fields, and he'd wanted to make the man pay. Personally.

'You're fortunate that I didn't happen to agree,' Hyatt said.

*Only because you don't know the whole story.* Clay returned his gaze to the bodies. 'What are their names?'

'Hollinsworth and Locklear,' Hyatt said. 'Both had exemplary records.'

'What time did they arrive?' Stevie asked.

'They reported their arrival to Dispatch at twelve twenty-four,' Hyatt said, then added grimly, 'and at twelve twenty-eight Dispatch received a report that it had been a false alarm and they were breaking for lunch.'

Surprised, Clay did a quick visual scan for the officers' radios. They were gone. Whoever killed them had bought himself a few more minutes by filing a false report. 'That narrows down the time of death considerably,' he murmured. He looked up at his sliding glass window, specifically at the hole in the glass where the lock had been. 'That was hurricane glass,' he said. 'Whoever came through there would have needed a Sawz-all with a diamond bit blade to get through it. They came prepared. Have the neighbors been canvassed?'

'I have Novak and Coppola doing that now,' Joseph said. 'Since this is related to the attempts on Stevie's life, it's linked to the restaurant attack, the drive-by shooting, and the safe house attack last night – all under the umbrella of VCET jurisdiction. You've got camera surveillance, I assume.'

'Of course. Can I have some gloves? Thanks,' Clay said to Brodie when she handed him a pair. He opened his coat closet, dropped to his knees and removed a sports equipment box from the shelf that sat eight inches off the floor and ran the width of the closet. Below the shelf were several pairs of shoes. Tossing them into the box, he tugged the shelf back from the wall enough to run his finger through the gap, unlatching a panel that served as the closet's back wall.

'Do you have backup batteries?' Joseph asked. 'Because they cut your power and your secondary power. They also cut both alarm sirens – both inside and outside.'

'The alarm runs on a different backup system. Once the alarm is tripped or the primary power is cut, it sends me an alert. The backup power they cut from outside is used when there's a legit outage, like from a storm. The cameras, thermal and cellular alarms have their own backup power sources. One's behind this wall and the other is in the basement.'

Clay cleared away the coats hanging from the closet pole, then gingerly gripped the panel and pulled it free, revealing his security system.

Joseph whistled. 'Do you have a Bat Cave, too? With a fire pole? Please?'

'Just a normal basement,' Clay said dryly. 'The cameras cover the entire interior of the house and run twenty-four/seven.' He popped the DVD from the recorder. 'I can run it on my laptop or you can run it on yours.'

'Mine's set up right here,' Brodie said, reaching for the DVD.

'Start it at noon.'

'Paige didn't call 911 to get a cruiser out here until twelve twenty,' Hyatt told him.

'But the first alert hit my cell at twelve ten. Because I didn't acknowledge it, the next alert went out at twelve thirteen, to both my cell and Paige's. She called me several times and when I didn't answer, she called 911 and started driving here herself.'

'She called me right after she called 911,' Hyatt said, 'but then I got the all-clear from Dispatch so I didn't come out. Now we know that all-clear was fake.'

'I've got the video cued up,' Brodie said and everyone crowded around her laptop.

'Wait a sec.' Clay carried her laptop to his fifty-two-inch TV and connected the two. 'Hit play. Camera three will give you his approach from the backyard to the slider. Camera five—'

Brodie motioned him to her laptop. 'Take the wheel, Clay.'

'Okay.' He chose the camera that focused on the slider

from the outside, fast-forwarded until a man came into the picture, dressed in coveralls and carrying a toolbox. He wore a baseball cap low over his face, hiding his features except for his ears.

'He's big enough to break two necks,' Hyatt commented.

'He's a wrestler,' Clay said. 'Or was. He has cauliflower ears.' He changed to the camera pointing toward the street and skipped back to a minute before the man had shown up around the back. The curb was empty until the man drove up in a nondescript Toyota Sequoia, its front plates obscured by mud. 'Shit. Can't make out the plates.'

He switched back to the camera focused on the slider and watched as the intruder boldly climbed the stairs to the deck, and using his toolbox as a stepstool, reached up to snip the siren wires. 'That's the first alert I got at twelve ten.'

'Why didn't you see the alerts?' Joseph asked.

*Because I was almost having sex with Stevie.* Clay avoided looking at her, lest he give them away. 'I was working out.' Not entirely untrue. He'd been sweaty and out of breath. 'Got in the shower and didn't get out until twelve twenty-five. That's when I saw all the texts and calls from Paige.' He pointed to the TV screen. 'Sawz-all.' The intruder was working at the glass with the handheld electric saw, cutting through in less than a minute. 'That's got to be one hell of a blade.'

Joseph shook his head. 'He came prepared, just like you said.'

'He's even wearing eye protection,' Quartermaine added bitterly. 'Gotta love the safety-conscious killer.'

The man unsheathed a knife as he entered the house. His next move was to locate the siren inside the house and snip its wires as well. Then he began slicing the sofa cushions, methodically searching. The goggles he wore covered half his face, the lens distorting the view of his eyes. A scarf covered the lower half of his face, rendering him unidentifiable.

'Safety-conscious and cocky as hell,' Hyatt murmured as the man looked straight up into the camera and gave two gloved thumbs up. 'Sonofabitch.'

'He didn't even try to turn the alarms off. He just wanted the sirens silenced.' Clay changed cameras, following the man through his house, gritting his teeth at the path of destruction he left in his wake. He dumped desk drawers and closet contents, knifed up mattresses, yanked pictures off the walls, breaking the glass and leaving photos strewn. In his bedroom closet, the man easily found Clay's firebox. He tucked it under his arm and kept searching. 'Shit,' Clay hissed.

'What was in it?' Joseph asked.

'Nothing to tell him where Stevie and Cordelia are hiding.' Clay blew out a breath, tamping his temper. 'It's my baseball card collection from when I was a kid. Which is wrong to get angry about, considering he's about to kill two cops.' He hissed another breath when the guy approached the model boat he'd built with his grandfather St James eons ago. 'Don't do it. Don't—' The guy reduced the model to a pile of splintered balsa. 'Goddammit.'

Joseph briefly squeezed his shoulder.

Clay's fists clenched at his sides when the man picked up a ceramic vase on his nightstand. He wanted to close his eyes, dreading what was probably coming. He flinched when the vase hit the floor and broke into dozens of pieces. *Dammit.*

A warm body moved close to Clay and he didn't have to look to know who it was. He'd know her scent anywhere. 'I'm sorry,' Stevie whispered. 'Who made the vase?'

'My mom. Right before she died.'

Stevie exhaled. 'I'm so sorry.'

He wondered what she was sorry for, but didn't ask. Didn't trust his voice. The bastard was crouching next to the broken pottery, flicking the pieces with his finger. He picked a few items from the rubble and held them up to the light coming through the window.

Impotent rage rushed through Clay as he watched the man toss his mother's watch and ring into his toolbox without care.

'You didn't have them in your safe?' Brodie asked, sadly.

'It was a twenty-dollar Timex. The ring I gave her when I was a boy. They're worth nothing, really.' And yet, everything. Goddamn that cocksucker. *If I ever get my hands on you . . .*

The intruder checked his watch and peeked out Clay's bedroom window at the street. Shrugging, the guy left the bedroom and went to the kitchen where he proceeded to empty every canister in the garbage. He rifled through cookbooks, leaving them on the floor. Then he snatched the picture Cordelia had drawn with crayon from Clay's refrigerator door.

*Don't do it. Don't you even touch it.* But the guy was, turning the paper over, examining it closely. His shoulders moved as if he laughed. Carefully he ripped the paper, then reaffixed it to the fridge with more magnets.

'What is it?' Hyatt asked.

Brodie patted Clay's arm. 'I'll get it.' She came back a few seconds later, as the man was rifling through Clay's coat closet, the very one that held his surveillance equipment. He crouched, checking for a panel, coming perilously close to finding it.

'It's a threat,' Brodie said.

'To who?' Stevie asked.

Clay looked at the two halves of the drawing Brodie held. 'To you, Stevie.'

Stevie gasped. 'That's . . . me. And . . .' She bent closer. 'And you?'

Cordelia had drawn her mother in a hospital bed and Clay standing next to the bed, a halo over his head. One knew the participating players because Cordelia had been considerate enough to write their names with bold arrows pointing to the people who were basically stick figures.

'Cordelia made it for me when you were in the hospital,' Clay said gruffly. At least it was salvageable, once he got it back from BPD's evidence room. If he ever did.

Mr Cocksucker had torn the page, neatly severing Stevie's head from her shoulders.

Clay forced his mind back to the cameras. The man was in the basement but there was nothing for him to destroy down there. Within a minute, he was back upstairs and leaving – this time through the garage. The front facing exterior camera showed him tossing Clay's firebox on the passenger seat, getting in, and driving away.

His whole 'visit' had lasted no more than seven minutes.

'Okay,' Joseph said slowly. 'He just left? I mean, just like that?'

'He's gotta come back,' Stevie said. 'Hollinsworth and Locklear didn't kill themselves.'

Clay fast-forwarded the video, slowing when a sand-colored Chevy Tahoe stopped on the curb. A different man got out, also dressed in workman's coveralls. This one had a backpack slung over one shoulder. He, too, wore a ball cap pulled low over his face.

Mr Backpack walked up to Clay's house, knocked on the front door. When there was no answer, he jogged around to the side, where he opened the door the first guy had left unlocked.

'What the hell?' Clay muttered.

Mr Backpack waltzed in through the laundry room, taking a moment to do a turn, taking the place in. He pulled the brim of the ball cap down to cover his face while he reached under the cap to tug a ski mask over his face, the movement fluid. Like he'd done it many times before.

Beside him, Stevie flinched.

'What?' Clay asked and she shrugged fitfully.

'It's just . . . There's something about that guy creeps me out.'

Mr Backpack followed the same path Cocksucker had, checking through the debris. In Clay's bedroom, the man sifted through the photos that Cocksucker had left on the floor, brushed off the glass, and put them in his pack.

'Sonofabitch,' Clay bit out.

'He took your photos,' Brodie said. 'Why?'

'I don't know. Other than the pictures of my mother, I don't even really remember all the ones I had out. They become kind of background noise.'

'I'm sorry,' Stevie murmured again. 'They're irreplaceable.'

'Not really. I've got the photos scanned to a flashdrive which is stored in my safe deposit box, along with anything else that he might have actually been interested in.'

'Well, what do you know about that?' Hyatt murmured. 'Look.'

The man had paused, pulling a shadowbox-style frame from the debris. 'My medals,' Clay said. 'My mother had them framed for me, years ago.'

Then the guy stunned him by carefully setting the frame against the dresser. 'We found them there,' Brodie said. 'I wouldn't have even considered that one of these guys would do that.'

'Most definitely former military,' Clay said. 'The way he

was careful with the medals? This guy saw combat. He may have even been wounded.'

'Why?' Stevie asked, leaning closer to the TV, trying to see the medals up close.

'One's a Purple Heart,' Hyatt said. 'The other's a Silver Star.'

'Purple Heart is for wounded in the line of duty,' Stevie said. 'The Silver Star for valor.'

'Yeah,' Clay said, suddenly uncomfortable.

Mr Backpack was jogging down the hall, checking the kitchen. Then he stopped. Cocked his head as if listening for something.

'It's twelve twenty-four,' Hyatt said, dread in his voice.

On the video, Mr Backpack stood at the side of the sliding glass door, waiting for the cop who came in through the slider. *Twist*.

A few seconds later the second cop came in through the garage. *Twist*.

Everyone gathered around the TV cringed, silently watching.

Backpack unsheathed a knife, slit the two cops' throats, took their radios, then waltzed back out through the garage. Clay switched the camera to street view and they watched him get in the Chevy Tahoe and drive away.

'Pause it,' Joseph commanded. 'Can you catch his back plate?'

Clay had already frozen the frame, and, heart suddenly racing, tapped Brodie's keyboard to zoom in. 'How's that?' he asked with satisfaction. Unlike the front plate, the number on the back was as clear as day.

'Perfect,' Joseph said grimly. He stepped away from the group to call it in.

Clay hit 'play' again, watching as the Tahoe drove away. And then something unexpected happened. 'Joseph.' Clay motioned him back over to the TV. 'Look at this.'

Joseph frowned. 'What the hell?'

The black Toyota Sequoia was back in the picture – literally. The SUV had come from the opposite direction, almost as if it had been waiting. Mr Cocksucker ran around Clay's house, up the stairs to the deck. He skidded to a halt outside the sliding glass doors, upset, but still enough in control that he kept his head down, his face hidden.

'He was waiting for something, but not for this,' Stevie said.

Clay frowned. 'He was waiting for you, Stevie. That's why he didn't even try to bypass the alarm. He knew the alarm would draw the cops, me, and by extension, you. He probably planned to take a shot at you when you walked from the curb to the front door.'

'God,' Stevie whispered. Then her chin came up, her jaw squared. 'But he's not waiting for me any more now. I wonder where he went.'

Mr Cocksucker had hightailed it to the black Sequoia, which he drove away quickly.

Clay forced himself to step away from her, turning his attention to Brodie and Hyatt. 'Do you need me to do a walk-through? Figure out what's missing?'

Hyatt nodded. 'Go with Agent Brodie. I need to talk to Detective Mazzetti alone.'

*Sunday, March 16, 1.25 P.M.*

Robinette had pulled the Tahoe into a parking lot a half block away from Maynard's office. There was a cruiser parked in front of the office, a small building that had the look of a bank. It would make sense that a PI would lease an old bank for his place of business. If the building had once been a bank, it would likely have walls of reinforced steel and a vault where the records were kept. No way he was breaking into there.

Maynard did indeed lease it. Robinette had found that much in the property records when he'd first become aware of Maynard's existence – back in December when the guy had saved Mazzetti's life on the courtroom steps.

He started his engine, then froze. A black Toyota Sequoia was driving by, Westmoreland at the wheel. The SUV pulled into a business a half block from Maynard's in the other direction.

Robinette slid down in his seat, hoping Westmoreland hadn't seen him through the window. His cell phone rang and he contorted himself to get it out of his pocket. It was Westmoreland. *How nice of him to call. Finally.*

'You were supposed to call me hours ago. Or was I not clear on my expectations when I said I wanted a report every hour?'

'I'm sorry, Robbie. I got tied up, getting into Maynard's house. It took me longer than I expected. He had layers of alarms.'

'How did you bypass them?'

'I didn't. I figured I had a few minutes to get in and out. I checked every room looking for deeds, a safe deposit box key, a computer, hell, even an old-fashioned address book. The only thing I took away was an old firebox that a three-year-old could've broken into.'

Robinette thought of his own 'old-fashioned' address book. Technology was good, but sometimes it was nice to know you had the only copy of something. That it couldn't be downloaded, hacked, or copied.

'What did you find inside the fire box?'

'His baseball card collection. He's got a Cal Ripkin, Jr,

rookie card, which, while very impressive, tells us nothing about where he might be hiding Mazzetti.'

'Where are you?' Robinette asked him, because not asking would have seemed suspicious.

'Sitting in a parking lot about three hundred yards from Maynard's office. There's a cruiser parked in front. I imagine the alarm at the house made Maynard send the cops out here to check. I've gotta be honest with you, Robbie. Maynard's office looks pretty damn well-protected.'

'How so?'

'It looks like it might have been a bank, back in the day. I could break in, but it would take a while. I don't want to attempt it with cops sitting out front.'

'Recommendations?' He couldn't wait to hear what Westmoreland had to say.

'We hack into his server and check his emails, documents, maybe the bills he's paid. If he's paying the electric bill on a place other than his house, that could be where Mazzetti is hiding.'

That actually made sense, making Robinette feel slightly paranoid for lumping Westmoreland in with Fletcher and Henderson. 'Can you do that? Hack into his server?'

'Given enough time, yes. And if I can't get through, he's got three employees who'll know access information. There's Paige Holden, Alec Vaughn – he's the kid who was with him yesterday, and Alyssa Moore. Alyssa is the secretary. She'd know more about the office finances and computer access passwords than the other two. I'd start with her, make her talk.'

'Sounds like a plan. Will you come back here to the office?'

'I can. Or I can work from home or even a coffee shop. Might be better for me not to work from the office. If

Maynard's got any traps set on his server, he might be able to track my IP address back to my location. I don't want to lead him back to you.'

'That would suck,' Robinette agreed. 'Fine. Try to hack in. In the meantime, I want a trace on Mazzetti's credit cards. If she leaves town, I want to know about it.'

'Done. I'll keep you up to speed.'

'One more thing.' Robinette ensured his voice sounded only mildly curious, holding none of his residual concern about Westmoreland's loyalty. 'I had to ask you where you were because the vehicle you took from the fleet no longer shows up on my tracking software.'

A short, pregnant pause. 'You're checking up on me, too, Robbie?'

'Of course. A, I check up on everyone. B, you didn't call when you were supposed to. Henderson's still out there and – as *you* brought up – presents a potential danger to all of us. I needed to be certain you were unharmed.' *And uncompromised.*

'Okay,' Westmoreland said grudgingly. 'I can accept that, because that's why I disabled the tracker. Henderson has the passwords to the system, too. I didn't want to be sneaked up on, especially while I was breaking into Maynard's house. Think about what would have happened had Henderson found me there and popped me off. The cops would have found my body and where would that have led them back to?'

'Me,' Robinette said grimly. 'I should have changed those passwords already. You should have reminded me.'

'Sorry. I didn't think about it until this afternoon.'

'I'll change the passwords now. Call me when you get into Maynard's server.'

Robinette waited until Westmoreland had pulled out of his lot and driven away before sitting up straight. Of all

313

of his team, Wes was the best with computers. Hacking into Maynard's office server seemed like a long shot, but if any of them could do it, Wes could.

Although Westmoreland's idea made sense, Robinette had been surprised that he hadn't suggested lying in wait at Maynard's house and office until he showed up. The cops were bound to call Maynard, especially now that there were two dead bodies on the PI's living room carpet.

But Wes hadn't known about the bodies. *Let him fool with the computers. You wait for Maynard.* Eventually he'd return to Mazzetti and when he did, Robinette would follow him.

Law enforcement would probably have swarmed by now. That 'going to lunch' report he'd made to Dispatch using the dead cop's radio had only bought him enough time to get away.

Maynard's neighborhood was sparsely populated – lots of acreage to each house. It meant that no one had likely seen him before, but also meant that he'd stick out like a sore thumb if he drove up to the house. It would be safer to wait at the end of Maynard's street. He'd see everyone coming and going and he might just get lucky.

# Chapter Fifteen

*Baltimore, Maryland, Sunday, March 16, 1.45 P.M.*

Stevie kept her eyes on the two dead cops. *Because of me.* They were dead. The female officer who'd stood in for her last night was also dead. Two innocents in the restaurant, dead.

Clay's home destroyed.

'I'm sorry,' she murmured, but Hyatt shook his head.

'This is not your fault. The undercover officer killed last night was not your fault. She knew the risk she was taking. Do you understand me? Believe me? Stevie, do you even hear me?'

She nodded, clinging to his words as her gaze clung to Clay's wide back. 'I hear you. I understand you. I . . .' She couldn't say she believed him. 'I needed to hear that.'

He frowned, following the direction of her stare. 'Maynard's telling you differently?'

She laughed hollowly. 'No. But he's not exactly unbiased when it comes to me.' At least he hadn't been. He hadn't looked at her once since they'd walked into his house.

*And can you blame him? You broke his heart – and now all this?* That stricken look he'd worn when that bastard broke his mother's vase . . . And that drawing from

Cordelia. She'd heard about it from Izzy, knew Cordelia had made it for him. Knew her daughter considered the man a cross between a guardian angel and Captain America, but . . .

He'd kept it. On his refrigerator. And he'd growled low in his throat when the bastard had touched it. She didn't think he was even aware he'd made the sound.

He was a truly good man. *And you've thrown him away how many times now?* Somehow she'd known he'd come back all the other times. But no more. She'd seen the resignation in his eyes when he'd pushed himself off her and left her in that bed alone.

*I'm just a foolish man who wanted something so much that he heard what he wanted to hear.*

*God.* She wanted to scream. To yank out her hair and cry.

'JD called me,' Hyatt said quietly, 'to tell me that Scott Culp from IA might have leaked the safe house location to Rossi.'

She saw the question in his eyes and didn't blink. 'You want to know why I didn't call you. I'm not sorry, sir. I can't be sure of who might be listening to your calls.'

Her boss held her gaze for a long moment and Stevie knew he'd guessed that she didn't trust him anymore. Guilt nagged, but she held firm. After another moment he looked away.

'JD's no longer watching Culp's house,' he said. 'Bashears is.'

Stevie's brows shot up. Bashears was one of the other homicide detectives under Hyatt's command. 'Why?'

'Is there something wrong with my sending Bashears?'

She understood what he was asking. *Don't you trust Bashears, either?* No, she didn't. Which was hypocritical on its face. Bashears had been partners with Elizabeth

316

Morton, one of Stuart Lippman's dirty cops. A tiny part of her wanted to yell, *Didn't you suspect a thing?*

She knew a lot of cops still said that about her with respect to Silas Dandridge. Bashears had been thoroughly investigated by IA, just as Stevie had been. Of course, IA's integrity was far from a given at this point, so their stamp of approval on Bashears meant little.

'Bashears is fine,' she finally said. 'It's just that I thought JD was going to stand watch.'

'JD had been. But then Rossi woke up and JD went to the hospital to question him.'

Stevie's eyes widened. 'Rossi's awake? Has he said anything?'

'Not yet. JD is probably just getting to the hospital.' Hyatt glanced left when Quartermaine approached. 'You're taking them?'

Stevie had heard about Quartermaine – the female population at the precinct was all a-twitter with gossip about the new ME. The women who'd gushed that he gave Brad Pitt a run for his money in the looks department certainly hadn't been wrong.

Tall, lean, and golden, he reminded her a little of Paul. She would have expected that to hurt, but it didn't. She would have expected it to send a shiver of anticipation, sadness, *anything* over her skin. But it appeared her physical responses were only triggered when she was around Clay.

*I can smell you. God.* Or, it seemed, when she as much as thought of him.

Quartermaine nodded. 'I've got my best techs on their way to retrieve the bodies. I'll get on these autopsies ASAP, so that they can be released to their families.'

Hyatt closed his eyes briefly. 'Thank you. I'll be doing the notifications when I leave here.'

'You can tell the families that the men felt no pain,' Quartermaine said gently.

'That'll help,' Hyatt said. 'Thank you.'

Quartermaine turned his attention to Stevie, extending his hand. 'Detective Mazzetti, I've heard so much about you. I wish we were meeting under different circumstances.' He made a wry face. 'But then again, we probably would have met over a body regardless, wouldn't we?'

'No doubt.' Stevie shook his hand, the pain in her upper arm confusing her for a second. *Oh yeah, the bullet from yesterday.* Seemed like a year ago. And she'd torn out two stitches, rolling around on that bed with Clay. Which seemed like a second ago. She forced herself to look at the bodies of Hollinsworth and Locklear. 'Thank you for taking care of our guys.'

'Always.' Quartermaine looked at Hyatt, his eyes sad. 'I don't envy you your task and I can't make this better, but hopefully I can hasten the process so they can begin to heal.'

*Heal.* The word smacked Stevie hard as he walked away. 'I used to do that,' she murmured.

'What?' Hyatt asked.

'Help people heal. Or I thought I was.'

'You were. The grief groups you did with cops were one of the most talked about "secrets" in the department. I've had a number of inquiries from cops, wives, families, house shrinks – all wanting to know when the groups will start meeting again.'

'I don't even remember when I stopped doing them.'

'Right after Silas,' Hyatt said quietly.

*Oh. Right.* 'I guess I was a bit of a mess after that.'

'You think?' he asked dryly and she managed a quick grin that instantly morphed to tears.

Embarrassed, she gave herself a little shake. 'Perhaps I should reconvene the groups?'

'Perhaps you should secure the oxygen mask on yourself before trying to help the passengers around you,' Hyatt returned, gently, but firmly, making her watery gaze shoot up to his. 'Not an order, Stevie. Just a suggestion.'

Her jaw clenched. 'You're saying I should see a therapist.'

He gave her an exasperated look. 'No. I'm saying you should see a podiatrist. Goddamn, Stevie, for a smart cop . . .' He rolled his eyes. 'Even if that leg of yours were a hundred percent, you won't come back to duty until the house shrink says so.'

'I can deal with the shrinks,' she insisted, her chin lifting on its own.

'Because so many of them are your friends, because so many of them respect your grief work, you think that they'll float you? *Bzz*.' He imitated a game show buzzer. 'Wrong answer.'

Her cheeks heated because that was precisely what she'd been thinking. 'Whatever. Back to Scott Culp leaking intel to Rossi. What're you going to do about him? Did you tell Culp's boss?'

Hyatt exhaled. 'You're one of the most stubborn cops I've ever "commanded", and I use that term loosely. Fine, we'll table the head shrink for now. I didn't go to IA. I went to Yates.'

She blinked, surprised. Then it made sense. Assistant State's Attorney Yates was Grayson Smith's boss. 'He'd be the one to handle an investigation outside the police department.'

'Especially if IA is compromised. Which, sadly enough, has happened before. Yates is opening a formal, but sealed, investigation. All hush-hush.' He lifted a shoulder with a carelessness that was a total sham. 'And I poked a little. Went to Carla Culp's Facebook page. She's Scott's ex-wife. Seems she just got back from a photo safari in Africa. And she drives a nice shiny Mercedes and has a rock on her finger big enough to put your eye out. Real estate records show she recently changed her address to one of the better zip codes in Potomac.'

Stevie whistled softly, impressed both by the information and by the fact that Hyatt knew how to get onto Facebook. He wasn't the most technically savvy guy. 'She remarry rich?'

'She didn't remarry at all. Culp's still paying her alimony.'

'Oh.' Stevie tilted her head, thinking. 'When did she buy the fancy house?'

He smiled. 'Now there's the cop I remember. She closed on the house about a month after Silas went down and Lippman's list came out.'

'Culp wasn't on Lippman's list. But maybe his ex-wife could prove he should have been?'

'My thoughts exactly. Yates is drafting subpoenas for the ex-wife and her shopping buddies in case they don't cooperate.'

'I'd like to be there when she's questioned. I want her to put a face with the crimes her husband's done and that she's enabled by not coming forward. I also want to be there when we question Scott himself.'

'I'd like you to be there, too. I want to see if there's any regret at all in Culp's eyes when we tell him that Rossi used his intel with the intent to murder a seven-year-old.'

Stevie's stomach turned over. 'If you'll excuse me, I'd like to take a look at the scene in the back bedroom before we head over to Culp's house.'

She'd gotten ten feet away when Hyatt's voice came

rumbling at her back. 'Remember what I said about putting the oxygen mask on yourself first, Stevie.'

She jerked a nod. 'I will.'


*Sunday, March 16, 2.05 P.M.*

Sam Hudson approached Dina Andrews's desk in the ballistics department with heavy feet and a sense of impending doom.

She looked up when his shadow fell over her keyboard. 'You got my message?' she asked.

'Yeah. The gun I gave you this morning turned up a match.'

'It's a cold case. The rifling matched a bullet taken from an unidentified Caucasian male found floating in the Severn River in May, just under eight years ago.'

*I couldn't have done this. I would remember dragging a body to the Severn River.*

Still the feeling of impending doom loomed. 'Do you have the ME's report?'

'No. I just pulled the police report. You'll need to go to the ME's office for the pathologist's report. Sam, are you all right?'

He nodded. 'Just fine. Thanks for running this, Dina.'

'You're welcome.' She studied him. 'You know who left the gun for you, don't you?'

'No, I don't. Only that it had to be someone who knew where I lived.' Which was true. They'd sent the envelope to his mother's address and he'd once lived there.

'I have to report my findings, you know. I can't just forget about this.'

'I wouldn't expect you to. But can you give me a few days? I need to get a feel for who left it for me. I have a good relationship with the folks in the neighborhood.'

'I can give you forty-eight. I'll submit my report at the end of my shift Tuesday.'

Sam took the police report she'd retrieved. 'Got it. Thank you.'

He waited until he was out of the building before letting his knees give way. Lowering himself to a bench, he read the report. The body had been found half-submerged, entangled in a beaver dam in the state park. The victim was a Caucasian male, approximately forty-five years old. Height, approximately six feet. Weight, approximately 185 pounds.

Sam made himself breathe. His father had been forty-five years old when he disappeared. He'd been six-one and roughly 180 pounds. *No. It can't be. It can't.* But what if it was?

There was a gunshot entrance wound at the base of the unidentified man's skull. Whoever this man had been, he'd been executed. *I couldn't have done that. I would've remembered.*

But he didn't remember. He'd lost a day and a half. Just . . . gone.

*Holy God, what have I done?*


*Sunday, March 16, 2.15 P.M.*


Parked behind an old gas station at the end of Maynard's street, Robinette watched the ME's van pass by, the dead cops' bodies presumably inside. Hopefully Maynard had shown up already. Hopefully he had Mazzetti with him. So far only two vehicles had left – the ME van and the pickup truck belonging to Maynard's partner, Paige Holden. The latter he knew because he'd used the minutes he'd been waiting to do a little reconnaissance, keeping it old-school.

Leaving the Tahoe behind the gas station, he'd slipped through the trees on foot, venturing only close enough to Maynard's house to see the license plates of every vehicle parked outside through his binoculars. Back at the Tahoe, he'd run all the license plates. As expected, most were registered to city or federal agencies. A few were privately owned, none by Maynard. But if the way the guy had hidden his house under layers of shell corporations was any indication, the PI wouldn't have registered a car in his own name to begin with.

Robinette crossed his fingers that Maynard was in one of the vehicles. If he wasn't, it was only a matter of time before he returned to his home to survey the damage.

A moment later, a sedan passed by – a large, bald white man at the wheel. Robinette recognized him from a city function they'd both attended – Lieutenant Peter Hyatt, Mazzetti's boss. Hyatt carried no passengers, so Robinette stayed put.

Following Hyatt was a black Escalade, windows so heavily tinted that he couldn't see who was inside. Robinette sat up straighter. Because he'd had done his homework on Stevie Mazzetti, Robinette knew two of her friends drove Escalades – Agent Carter of the FBI and Grayson Smith of the prosecutor's office. Both had visited her in hospital and at home.

Agent Carter was the primary investigator on Henderson's restaurant job. He must also be primary on these homicides because parked in front of Maynard's house had been a Chevy Suburban, registered to Ford Elkhart, the son of ASA Montgomery. Who, according to Robinette's sources, was Carter's new girlfriend.

It was unlikely that Carter was in the black Escalade.

Didn't mean that Maynard definitely *was*, but chances were better than good. Following his instinct, Robinette put the Tahoe in gear and pulled out a discreet distance behind them.

*Sunday, March 16, 2.15 P.M.*

'I'm sorry,' Stevie said softly.

Clay looked to the passenger seat where she sat staring out the window. They were driving from his house to Culp's. He'd been surprised when she'd climbed into the Escalade, but Hyatt had solved the mystery.

'Detective Mazzetti has asked to come with me,' he'd said, 'but I think she'll be safer in Agent Carter's vehicle. Don't you agree, Mr Maynard?'

Clay did, but hadn't wanted her to ride with him. It would have looked bad to refuse, however, especially as she was already buckling herself in – while scowling at her boss.

Wasn't it wonderful to be loved, Clay thought bitterly. She'd been silent through the drive, *I'm sorry* the first words she'd spoken.

'Don't be,' he said. 'It's just stuff.' He thought of the vase, shattered into a hundred pieces on his bedroom carpet. *Irreplaceable stuff.*

'Irreplaceable stuff,' she said, echoing his thoughts. Still staring out the window. 'But that's not why I said I was sorry, even though I'm sorry about that, too.' She drew a breath. 'I don't know what I said to you to make you so upset with me. On the boat, I mean. But I did make you upset and you didn't deserve that. So I'm sorry. Then I was frustrated and . . . embarrassed, and I lashed out at you. So, I'm sorry for that, too. You didn't deserve that either.'

'You have nothing to be sorry for,' he said quietly, even though within him a tornado screeched. 'You were honest with me from the beginning. I was the one who tried to change a leopard's spots.'

She shifted in her seat and he could feel her stare. 'What does that mean?'

'You don't want a relationship. You were very clear on that point. I don't know if that means with anyone or just with me. Forever or just for now. But that doesn't matter. I tried to change your mind. I was wrong to try.'

'You weren't wrong to try. You just picked the wrong girl.' Her voice was rough and she abruptly turned back to the window. 'You . . . you won't try again, will you.'

It was a statement, not a question, uttered with a desolate certainty that broke his heart one more time. 'No. You have my word.'

'I won't—' Her voice shattered. She'd hidden her face from him, but he could hear her tears. 'I won't cut you off from Cordelia. She'll be at Daphne's as often as I can get her there. Just so you know.'

It was the crayon drawing, he understood. She'd been so stunned to see it on his refrigerator. He wasn't certain that even now it had sunk in with her that the first intruder had torn it as a message. She was a target and they'd keep coming until they brought her down.

*Over my dead body.* That hadn't changed.

'Thank you,' he said evenly. 'She's a sweet kid. I appreciate it.' Yet he didn't think he'd be seeing Cordelia anymore after this. It would eventually break him into bits.

They lapsed back into silence, the hum of the tires on the road and Stevie's quiet weeping overpowered by the relentless pounding in his own head. It had started as a dull throb when he'd walked through his ruined house, but now he could barely think over the pain.

When he saw a CVS, he pulled the Escalade into a parking place right next to the door. 'I'll be five minutes or less. Keep your head down. I mean it.' He hopped out and locked up.

But ten minutes had passed before he returned, half of which he'd spent staring at the shelf of condoms. He'd finally chosen a box, tossing it into his shopping basket grimly. He'd wasted enough time on Stevie Mazzetti. As soon as this was over, he planned to meet someone new and he was not using those disgusting chocolate flavored condoms that had somehow wound up in the boat's nightstand drawer.

Paige had friends she could set him up with and Daphne had been trying to get him to notice one of Joseph's VCET agents for weeks. Lou probably had an entire list of possibilities, too, complete with photos. He'd pick one and start over.

*Hair of the dog that bit you, after all.* But even as he paid for them, he knew he wouldn't be using them. He knew he wouldn't let any of his friends fix him up with other women. He knew he'd be throwing the box away when it hit its ex-date, probably unopened.

He slipped the plastic sack with the condoms into his gym bag, then tossed the sack with almost everything else he'd bought on the console next to the driver's seat. Settling behind the wheel, he found the pain reliever and two bottles of water. He took four of the damn pills, then passed the pill bottle along with one of the waters over to Stevie. 'For your head.'

She took the medicine gratefully. 'How did you know?'

'All that crying has to have left you with a headache.' He handed her the walking cane he'd also bought. 'Height adjustable. No sparkles. There's a can of matte finish paint in the bag so we can keep you from being a beacon. The other stuff in there is yours, too.'

She peeked inside the sack. 'Tissues and a Hershey bar.' She huffed a sad chuckle. 'And a bag of frozen veggies for my face. You thought of everything.'

He put the Escalade in gear. Yeah. He was so damn thoughtful, he made himself puke. 'They're not peas. They only had broccoli with cheese sauce in those single-serving microwave bags, but it'll have to do. Let's go to Culp's.' The sooner they plugged all the BPD leaks and caught those who wanted Stevie dead, the sooner he'd be on his way. On to the next woman.

The thought really did make him want to puke.

By the time he stopped at Culp's curb, the pounding in his head had met the churning in his stomach and were fast friends. His body ached, but he'd survived worse. Or so he told himself as he helped Stevie from the Escalade. Stevie wanted to be there when Hyatt confronted Culp, which was her right.

Clay was there because he'd promised to watch her back. He didn't intend to slough off now.

Hyatt got out of his car, the slight frown on his face deepening when he saw Stevie's face. 'Are you all right?'

'Sure, just peachy. Where's Detective Bashears?'

'Parked on the next block so that he can keep an eye on Culp's back door. I just texted him that we're going to knock and that he should be ready in case Culp tries to run.' Tugging his suit coat into place, Hyatt started up the front walk. Stevie followed and Clay brought up the rear, shielding her just in case one or both of their intruders were waiting.

Clay didn't see any obvious threats lurking, but he did see several plainclothes cops. 'How many men do you have here watching, Hyatt?' he asked when they were on the front porch.

'How many do you count?' Hyatt asked, his grip on the doorknocker a white-knuckled one.

'What, bad guys or plainclothes cops?'

'Either. Both.'

'Three plainclothes sitting in three unmarked cars. A rifle on the roof of the house across the street. And the lady with the stroller.'

'Tell the lady,' Stevie added, 'that she'd be more believable as a mother if she'd glance into the stroller with an occasional "Goo-goo, gaga".'

'I'll make sure she gets the feedback.' Hyatt knocked hard. 'You sure you don't want to work for me, Maynard?'

'Very sure.' As soon as this was over, he planned to run as far away from Baltimore Homicide as his legs would carry him.

'I thought this was all hush-hush, Hyatt,' Stevie said.

'It is. Those aren't my people. With the two dead cops on Maynard's living room floor and the death of the officer at the safe house last night, Assistant State's Attorney Yates wanted to take no chances. Those are Maryland State cops. The stroller mama is their lieutenant.'

When no one stirred inside the house, Hyatt knocked again, louder. 'Culp, it's Hyatt. Open up.' But no one came to the door and the seconds became minutes.

'The TV's on,' Stevie said. 'And I saw a car parked in the garage when we walked past.'

'There are blinds on the windows,' Clay said. 'How did you see in the garage?'

'I'm short. From my angle I could see up through the slats. It's a maroon minivan.'

'Culp drives one,' Hyatt said. 'An old Dodge Caravan.'

'Could be a decoy,' Clay murmured. 'Do you have a warrant to enter the house?'

'Not yet,' Hyatt said. 'We're waiting on the judge to sign it. That's the other reason for the State coverage. If he's guilty, we didn't want him getting wind of it and bolting.'

Clay crouched behind the azaleas so that he could squint under the window shade, then hissed a curse. 'If that's Culp, he ain't boltin' anywhere. Someone's sitting in the recliner in front of the TV. I can see the toe of a man's boot and a whole lot of blood on the carpet.'

'Shit.' Hyatt made three quick calls, the first to request EMS and the second to the woman with the stroller. She immediately set toward them at a brisk jog, her team falling in behind her. The third was to Bashears, telling him to join them.

'Didn't JD approach the house to look inside?' Stevie asked.

'No.' Hyatt clenched his jaw. 'He wanted to, but Yates didn't want to tip our hand prematurely and he wanted me to be the one to confront Culp. I was on my way over here when I got the call about Hollinsworth and Locklear. When Yates heard about them, he insisted on the State coverage before we went in. This is a neighborhood. We need to avoid collateral damage.'

'Lieutenant Hyatt?' the stroller mama asked.

'Culp's either hurt or dead.' Hyatt nodded at the door. 'Open it.'

Two State cops kicked the door in and the stroller mama led the way, her weapon at her side. Her team fanned out and a few seconds later she gave the all clear to Hyatt. 'He's dead.' She pulled on a glove and touched Culp's arm. 'Close to full rigor. He's likely been dead for ten to twelve hours. The ME can tell us for sure.'

Hyatt made another call, canceling the ambulance and

requesting the ME. 'Lieutenant Levine, this is Detective Mazzetti and her . . .'

'Bodyguard,' Clay supplied tersely. Beside him, Stevie flinched.

Levine gave him a speculative once-over before turning back to Stevie. 'After the recent attempts on your life by BPD officers, I can't say I blame you for outsourcing, Detective.'

Clay shifted so that he could look around Levine. Scott Culp slumped in his recliner, listing to the right, a bullet hole at the base of his skull. 'Ten to twelve hours ago was shortly after Rossi killed Officer Cleary in the safe house,' Clay said. 'This was an execution.'

'Somebody's tying up loose ends,' Stevie agreed. 'But it wasn't Rossi. He was in the hospital. Could have been Thing One or Thing Two from Clay's house. Or the drive-by shooter. Or the restaurant sniper.' She closed her eyes wearily. 'Or anybody else who wanted me dead.'

'Thing One and Thing Two?' Levine asked.

'I'll explain,' Hyatt said. 'First, let me take this call.' He answered his cell, then went still. 'Are you *sure*, JD?' His shoulders sagged. 'Then bring him in. I'll meet you in Interview.'

Slowly Hyatt hung up and pocketed his phone. He looked like he'd aged twenty years in the last twenty seconds. 'Lieutenant Levine, would you do me the favor of sending two of your team to the home of Carla Culp in Potomac and escorting her to my precinct? We need to know what she knows about her ex-husband's past activities.'

'Have your assistant send us the address and we'll get on it,' Levine said. 'Are you okay?'

'I am all right,' he said. 'I have Mrs Culp's address. I'll text it to you. Excuse me.' He stepped away from Culp's body and made another call. 'Carter, it's Hyatt. I need Brodie over here at Culp's. Yesterday. And those two agents you had canvassing Maynard's neighbors? . . . Yeah, Novak and Coppola. Have them contact JD Fitzpatrick. He needs their assistance. Fitzpatrick has the address. Thanks, Carter.'

Stevie walked to Hyatt, put her hand on his arm. 'What's happened?'

Hyatt's sigh was heavy. 'Rossi woke up, realized he'd been caught killing a cop and decided to cooperate. He told JD that he hadn't seen or heard from Scott Culp in years.'

'He's lying,' Stevie said. 'Culp tipped him off about the safe house. Culp had access to the information. And Culp *is* dead. Rossi's lying, otherwise, Culp would still be alive.'

'He had access, but Culp's not the one who tipped Rossi off. I don't know why Culp is dead, but it had nothing to do with the safe house. Lieutenant Levine, can you secure this scene until Agent Brodie from VCET's CSU arrives? We're going to have to decide who has jurisdiction over the investigation into Sergeant Culp's murder.'

'Where are you going?' Stevie asked as Hyatt started for the door.

'To notify the families of Hollinsworth and Locklear.' Hyatt looked defeated.

'Sir. What else did JD just tell you?'

Hyatt paused, his hand on the doorknob. 'Rossi said that the leak came from my assistant.'

Stevie caught her breath, growing pale herself. 'No. He's lying. There is no way—'

'Yes, there is, Detective,' Hyatt snapped. 'Now, if you'll excuse me.' He turned on his heel and left Culp's house, headed to his car.

Stevie started after him, leaning on her new black cane.

'Sir. Lieutenant.' Hyatt kept walking and she kept following. '*Peter*. Dammit, *stop. Please.*'

Hyatt halted when he got to the car he'd left parked on the curb. Stevie caught up to him, grabbing his arm and pulling him to look at her.

Clay had followed, and now hulked over her, providing the cover she'd neglected to provide for herself. 'Stevie, you can't stand out here in the open. Come on.'

Stevie let Clay pull her away, but she kept her eyes on Hyatt's face as Clay hurried her backward toward the Escalade. 'You don't believe Rossi. You can't.'

'I don't want to,' Hyatt bit out. 'But I do. I dropped breadcrumbs, giving different information to a few select individuals because I needed to know who I could trust. Rossi knew something I'd told only one other person.'

Stevie stumbled. 'You suspected your assistant? You suspected *Phil*?' She had to raise her voice, because Clay had her almost in the Escalade.

'I suspected everybody!' Hyatt shouted bitterly. 'Somebody, multiple somebodies have tried to kill you on multiple occasions. *So I suspected everybody.*' With that he got in his car, executed a sharp U-turn in the street, and took off in the opposite direction, leaving Stevie open-mouthed and breathing hard. Stunned.

Clay bodily lifted her, shoving her into the SUV. 'Get in, goddammit.' He slammed her door and ran around to the driver's side, keenly aware that every place they found a body meant someone who had Stevie in his or her sights had been there first.

*Hell of a way to draw her out into the open*. He jerked his door open. 'You have to start—'

Stevie lunged at him, grabbing the collar of his shirt, diving under the steering column and pulling him down with her – just as the passenger window pebbled. A split second later a blast of pain burned down his back. He was thrown forward, his forehead smacking the steering wheel.

He was aware of her moving, scrambling back to her side of the car.

'Get in!' she shouted.

'Get down!' he snarled, but it was too late. Stevie cried out, pressing her hand to her side. Clay hurled himself behind the wheel, flooring it as he pulled his door shut. 'Are you hit?'

'I'm okay. It hit the vest.' She showed him her hand. 'No blood. Just a bruise.'

'How did you know he was there?'

'The State sniper slid off the roof. I figure the shooter was hiding behind the house next door and shot up. That gave him a clear shot at us.'

If she hadn't pulled him down, the bullet that had transformed the passenger window into a thousand pebbles of glass would have gone into his head. *I'd be dead.*

Clay hunkered down, cursing when he saw the cul-de-sac a few houses up. 'Dead end. We can stay here or turn around and drive past Culp's house again to get out of here.'

'We're still in his range if we wait here. I guess we're about find out how bullet-resistant Joseph's ride really is.'

'I guess we will. Hold on, honey. This might not be fun.'

# Chapter Sixteen

*Baltimore, Maryland, Sunday, March 16, 3.00 P.M.*

Clay did a hard U-turn, throwing Stevie's body against the wall of the SUV.

'Are you okay?' she asked him urgently.

'I think so. Second time in two days some bastard has shot me in the damn back.'

'You're wearing a vest, too?' she asked and he nodded.

'I took it out of my bedroom closet when Brodie gave me the grand tour of the wreckage that used to be my stuff.' He crunched his body down, so that he was barely able to see over the steering wheel. He floored it. 'Here we go, past Culp's house.'

Stevie braced herself for more gunfire, yet still flinched when it came. Her side of the Escalade took the hits, two to the front window and one to the back fender.

Clay kept his foot on the gas, easing his body up to better see through the windshield. Then hunkered down again when the back window took the final hit.

'I'd say Carter's ride fared okay,' Stevie said. The glass had pebbled around the points of impact, but the windows had remained intact. 'I'd give it four and half stars out of five.'

He laughed. 'Sorry,' he said. 'It's the adrenaline. I don't know about you, but I'm tired of getting shot at.'

She straightened in her seat and buckled up. 'Me, too.' Lightly she touched Clay's back, relieved when her fingers came back clean. 'You're not bleeding, either.'

'Always good to know.'

'Did you see if the sniper was moving?'

'No, but one of the plainclothes guys was moving around the houses, toward him. They know he's down. I'm sure they've already called for help.'

'Hyatt needs to know,' she said, dialing her boss's cell phone.

'I want to know about what's going on with his assistant,' Clay said.

'Let me call him, and then I'll tell you. I gotta say, that outburst of his at the end went a long way in convincing me that he's clean.'

'Me, too,' Clay admitted.

She held up a finger. 'Wait, it's ringing.'

'What is it, Detective?' Hyatt asked, sounding unhappy that she'd called.

'Clay and I were just shot at.'

'*What*? *When*?'

'Right after you took off. Clay had shoved me into the SUV when the sniper the State cops had on the roof went down. Clay got hit in the right shoulder blade and I got one in the ribs, but we're both in Kevlar. We're not bleeding, but we need to be checked. I don't know the status on the State Police sniper.'

Clay gave her a coldly forbidding look. 'No. I don't need to be checked out.'

'Yes. You do. You could have a fractured scapula. And I tore two stitches from yesterday's fun with guns.' Actually she'd done that when they'd been in bed earlier, but she wasn't going to mention that now. 'Lieutenant, can you get us a secure entry to the ER?'

'Of course. I'll call Levine and get status on her marksman and I'll get the ER ready for you. Stevie, I'm sorry I shouted. This thing with Phil has me rattled. I didn't plan to trap him. I didn't actually suspect him, specifically.'

'Maybe it's not true, sir. Maybe Rossi did lie.'

'No. JD didn't believe Rossi at first, but Rossi said he'd prove it. Told JD to get the cell phone they'd taken off him, that he had voicemails and texts from his source. When JD called the lab and asked them to verify, he was told that they couldn't find the phone. It wasn't with the other items taken from Rossi's person and his vehicle.'

'That doesn't mean Phil took it.'

'Phil was in the lab this morning, Stevie. He told them that he was picking up a report I'd asked for. But I hadn't asked for anything. JD's on his way to Phil's now. If he finds the phone, we'll have proof.'

'What if Phil's thrown Rossi's phone away?'

'Then we'll search his house for the phone he used to make the call. I'll let you know after I notify the families of Hollinsworth and Locklear.'

Suddenly exhausted, Stevie hung up and slumped into the seat. 'I am not stupid, but I keep doing stupid things like standing in the street where people can shoot at me.'

'You were stunned,' Clay said. 'Why? Who is Hyatt's assistant?'

She hesitated, then shrugged. He'd find out sooner or later. 'Phil Skinner.'

Clay's gaze whipped around to focus on her face. 'Skinner? The Skinner who was a homicide detective two years ago? The guy who was wounded by Nicki's killer?'

'None other.'

'Holy shit,' he muttered, shaking his head. 'Goddamn. Why would he betray you?'

Stevie sighed. 'He's not the same man he was two years ago, Clay. Pain and loss can change people. But I wouldn't have expected this of him.'

'Pain and loss.' He shook his head again. 'This is my—' He cut himself off before he said *fault*. '*I* caused his pain and loss. *Me*. I can't fucking believe this.'

'You didn't shoot him two years ago, Clay. And you're not responsible for him turning.'

'I didn't pull the trigger. But it's still on me. If I'd told you who killed Nicki when you came asking . . .' He was trembling, his grip on the wheel white-knuckled. 'You could have caught that sonofabitch before he shot Skinner.'

Two years before, Phil Skinner had been guarding JD's wife, Lucy, who'd been the victim of a psycho, bent on revenge. After killing Clay's former partner, Nicki, the man had grabbed Lucy. When Skinner had pursued, the killer had fired, critically wounding him. JD had killed the shooter, but too late to help Skinner. He'd been on disability for months before returning to a desk job, never regaining his full strength.

Stevie now knew how that felt.

'I don't know that we would have caught Nicki's killer before he shot Skinner, and neither do you,' she said levelly. 'You didn't know how many people that asshole had killed.'

'I knew he'd killed one. That should have been enough. I should have come forward.'

'Shoulda, coulda,' she said sadly. 'I still play that game. You can never win it.'

He gave her a sharp sideways look. 'You had nothing to do with Skinner getting shot.'

'No. But I had everything to do with my son getting shot.'

He blinked. 'What?'

'It was my night to pick up Paulie, but I was working late, trying to get all my reports finished before I went on maternity leave. I asked Paul to pick him up from day care. That's why they were both in that convenience store that evening.'

'Stevie . . .' He sounded devastated. 'That in no way compares to what I did.'

'Yeah, well, my brain chooses to disagree. At any rate, "shoulda, coulda" is a game you can't win. You gave me the information you possessed when you realized the scope of the guy's crimes. That has to be enough.'

'It's not. I knew the night before who'd killed Nicki. I should have come forward.'

'Okay, fine. Yes, you should have. But even if you had, we probably wouldn't have gotten him right away. And truthfully, Skinner was off his game that day. He'd been up all night with a sick baby. Lucy was lured away when she was told that someone she loved was injured, but Skinner should have been able to catch her. That she ran faster than he did was telling.'

'Lucy wouldn't have run into danger to begin with if she'd known what I knew.'

'True. Okay, ace, maybe you can win "shoulda, coulda". But even if you were responsible for Skinner being shot, you are not responsible for him leaking information to Rossi.'

'Why did he?'

'I don't know. I guess we'll have to ask him that question when JD brings him in.'

'JD's going to be conflicted, too. Skinner gets shot saving JD's wife . . . This is a mess.'

'I think that's why Hyatt asked Carter to send his two agents.'

'Novak and Coppola.'

Stevie nodded. 'He knew this would rip JD apart. JD was upset enough when Skinner's wife left him and took the baby with her.'

Clay clenched his jaw. 'His wife left him, too? When? Why?'

'About eight months ago. Like I said, Phil isn't the man he was. He came back to light duty, but he just seemed angry. Surly.' She looked at her cane. 'I can understand where he was coming from. Getting hurt on the job and not being able to come back to full duty . . . It's killing me, Clay. I think it ate him up from the inside out.'

He was quiet for a long moment. 'That's the other reason you've been digging into Silas's old cases. It makes you feel like a cop again.'

'I'm not that hard to figure out, I suppose.'

'I wouldn't go that far,' he muttered. 'So what now? Where do we go?'

'The ER,' she said, then watched the corners of his mouth kick up in resigned amusement. He hadn't meant right now, she realized. He must have meant the case. *Because he didn't mean us. I got what I wanted. There is no more us.*

She cleared her throat. 'And after the ER? We have to figure out who killed Culp. Because whoever killed him somehow guessed that I'd be by to talk to him because he was there waiting. How did he know that? How did he know *I* would be there? We know Rossi didn't tell.'

'Now that's a damn good question. Nobody should have known you'd be there.' His jaw hardened. 'Only Hyatt knew. You two were whispering in the corner. Nobody else heard.'

She sighed. 'I know. Dammit. I hate wondering about him, but I have to.' She pinched the bridge of her nose. The headache from her weeping had started to fade, but now was back. 'Going back to your theory about the break-in of your house . . . If someone was waiting for me to come back, they could have followed us. So it also could have been either of the two guys who were in your house.'

Again his lips quirked. 'Thing One and Thing Two?'

'I'm a mom. Dr Seuss was a staple. Cordelia loved *The Cat in the Hat*, but her favorite was *Green Eggs and Ham*.'

'And Paulie?' he asked gently. 'What was his favorite?'

Her heart skipped a beat as she sucked in a sudden painful breath, remembering. 'Paulie was more a *Wocket in my Pocket* boy.'

'My mom read that to me, too. Let me think . . . My favorites were the "noothgrush on my toothbrush" and the "vug under the rug".'

'Sorry.' She forced her voice to be light. 'The "vug" got the rug yanked out from under him when the book was reprinted in the nineties. Some of the scarier monsters were banished.'

'Hm,' he grunted. 'Damn censors. Well, Thing One and Thing Two are better than Mr Backpack and Mr Cocksucker, which is what I've been calling them.'

She snorted, covering her mouth with her hand. 'I like yours better.' She turned to study his profile. 'Thank you for asking about Paulie. Not many people do.'

He seemed thrown by that. 'Your parents must. Your family.'

'No, not really. My folks loved Paul and Paulie, but when they were gone, I was supposed to go on. Chin up. Don't dwell in the past. That's why I love my lunches with Emma so much. For years she just let me talk about them and she'd talk about Will, the husband she lost. It was my opportunity to have them with me again, for an hour or two.'

Clay frowned a little. 'Did your parents know you met with Emma every year?'

'No. I don't think they knew we've stayed close. They wouldn't condemn me for it, but they wouldn't understand what I get from talking to her about Paul. And Paulie. My folks don't believe in "talking about your troubles". You pick up and you move on.'

'Did Izzy know about your lunch with Emma?'

'Yes. Why?'

'Who else knew? Who else knew you'd be at the restaurant yesterday?'

'JD already asked both Emma and me that question, right after the shooting.'

'That was before the drive-by, a dead cop at the safe house, two dead cops on my living room carpet, a fourth dead IA cop, a possible dead police sniper, and now this.' He pointed to the spider-webbed glass. 'So humor me and tell me what you told JD, if you don't mind.'

'It's not that I mind, it's just that there wasn't really anyone to mention. Izzy knew, but she's our parents' daughter, too. Izzy hates conflict. She wouldn't have wanted to try justifying to our parents why I needed to see Emma to begin with, so I doubt that she told anyone. Cordelia knew. Emma's husband, Christopher, knew. Her parents, too, I assume, because she left them her hotel information in case of an emergency. That's about it. I mean, I never even told JD.'

'The restaurant knew.'

Stevie had to fight the urge to squirm. 'Not really.'

'You made reservations, didn't you?'

'Yes, but . . . we never made reservations under our own names.'

'Why not?'

'Emma likes her privacy. She sometimes gets approached by someone who's read one of her books. She's always gracious, because if they're a reader of hers, they've been grieving. But our lunch was special. Off-limits, you know?'

'So under what name did you make the reservations?'

'It changed every year, depending on who made the reservation and what was in their mind at the time. One year it was Thelma and Louise. One year, Lucy and Ethel. Last year it was Buffy and Willow because Em's a fan-girl of the Vampire Slayer. This year . . .' She looked out the window, embarrassed. 'We were Lara and Sarah.'

His brows went up. 'As in?' he asked, but from his tone she knew that he'd figured it out.

'You're gonna make me say it, aren't you?' She rolled her eyes. 'Croft and Connor.'

He grinned. 'Lara Croft and Sarah Connor? You were ready to fight, girl.'

'Like I said, I understand where Phil Skinner is coming from. I left my house yesterday so damn angry. It was the anniversary to start with and my daughter's having nightmares. Then I have this damned cane, and if that isn't enough, I've got people trying to fucking kill me. So, yeah, I was in the mood for a little terminating. I was Sarah.'

'I'd have taken you more as the Lara Croft type.'

She snickered. 'You wish.' He sobered abruptly, his jaw clenching, and she sighed. Of course he wished. That was the trouble. 'Hell. I'd kick my own ass if my leg worked right.'

'Rain check,' he muttered. 'Look, you might think no one knew you were going there for lunch yesterday, but obviously someone did. They were on the roof, shooting at you.'

She went still. 'Hold on. I'd assumed they'd followed me from my house into town, but if they did, they couldn't have followed Izzy and Cordelia out to Daphne's farm. We left the house at the same time and went different directions. There must have been two different shooters.'

'We have at least three suspects. Backpack, Cocksucker, and Drive-by.'

'And the two guys today couldn't be Drive-by, because you shot Drive-by. Neither of the guys today had shoulder wounds. So, okay. Three suspects.'

'If they're working together, both you and Izzy were probably followed. Or . . .' He glanced over at her. 'You go to that restaurant every year? The same one?'

'Yes.' She frowned. 'You think someone knew that? That they've been watching me?'

'At this point I'm inclined to believe there were two different shooters. Plus Rossi. But we can't leave any avenue unexplored. This is your life we're talking about. And Cordelia's.'

'I know. There's the ER. Let's get checked out so we can get back to work.'


*Sunday, March 16, 3.20 P.M.*

Robinette turned onto a side road, stopped the Tahoe on the shoulder, and closed his eyes.

*I made it.* No cops had followed him as he'd fled Culp's neighborhood, but that was the only good news. Maynard and Mazzetti had gotten away. *Dammit.*

Robinette ground his teeth. That black Escalade was goddamn bullet-proofed. He'd thought he'd had her. *Finally.* He thought Mazzetti's luck had *finally* run out.

But no. The woman led a damn charmed life. Or she

was careful. The latter made more sense, but the former was seeming more plausible with every moment – and every near miss.

He should have finished her off at the CVS, but the drugstore had been on a major road and he hadn't been willing to risk the exposure.

He'd really thought he'd had them when they stopped at Culp's house. That they suspected Culp of being a BPD leak hadn't been a shock. Robinette had expected as much, which was why he'd given Westmoreland the order to take care of Culp that morning. The IA weasel would have sung like a damn canary to protect his own ass.

He'd waited so patiently for her to emerge from that house . . . But the sight of the police sniper on the roof had startled him. *That was my mistake.* Robinette had fired on the sniper without thinking about which way the guy would fall – and it was the guy's fall that had warned Mazzetti.

*You lost it, man. Lost your cool.* He'd been so damn angry that Maynard had gotten her away that he'd fired at the SUV when it passed by on its way out.

And then he'd been too busy running to the Tahoe and driving like a bat out of hell to escape the sniper's pals who'd emerged from Culp's house like clowns out of a Volkswagen.

Now . . . Mazzetti and Maynard were nowhere to be found. They might go to a hospital, but he couldn't risk following. Too many people knew his face.

*Dammit. If Henderson had done the job right at the beginning, I wouldn't be in this spot now.* Although Robinette had to admit to feeling a little commiseration with his former marksman. Stevie Mazzetti was proving damn hard to kill.

*You could let it go. Walk away.*

No, he couldn't. Her digging into her ex-partner's old

cases had revealed what he'd known ever since Lippman's 'tell all' list had surfaced a year ago – that the list was far from inclusive. All of the old cases would be reviewed now, Julie's included. It was only a matter of time.

Another cop wouldn't spare Julie's case a second glance because Levi had been named Julie's killer, but Mazzetti had been determined to see him fry eight years ago. He couldn't afford to allow her to sink her teeth into him again. Couldn't risk her poking around his factory like she'd done before. Every time he'd turned around she'd been there, watching him. He couldn't let her do that to him again.

Especially now that they were gearing up production of Fletcher's new formula.

No, he couldn't quit. He'd just have to get a little craftier. A little less compassionate and a lot more ruthless. It was time to focus on the daughter. If he had the daughter, Stevie Mazzetti would crawl to him on her knees.

He needed to find where Maynard had hidden the child. It would be a place the PI himself felt safe. The photos he'd taken from Maynard's bedroom were as good a place to start as any. Hell, it was the *only* place he had to start. There'd been nothing else of personal interest in Maynard's house – unless Westmoreland had gotten to it first.

He considered the notion, then rejected it. Westmoreland was solid. Robinette would trust him – until Wes gave him a reason not to.

*Sunday, March 16, 4.30 P.M.*

'You're damn hard on vehicles, Maynard,' Joseph said as he approached Clay, who stood outside Stevie's curtained-off cubicle in the ER. 'First your truck, then my Escalade.'

The Fed's expression was so drawn, Clay had to wonder what had happened now.

'I know. I'm just glad the glass held. It pebbled, but it held together.'

'I'm glad it held, too. I upgraded the glass before Christmas. The last time I was shot at, the glass shattered.'

'Then I guess we're extra lucky.' Clay looked past Joseph to the ER bay surrounded by hospital personnel. 'How's the sniper?'

'Broke a leg and ruptured his spleen. They're sending him up to surgery in the next minute or two. He stayed conscious long enough to tell his lieutenant that he hadn't seen the shooter's face. The guy had his ski mask on again. Are either you or Stevie hurt?'

'I've got a few new bruises.' He pointed behind his back to the curtain. 'She's getting restitched. 'Why are you looking so grim? What else happened?' Panic gripped him. 'Cordelia?'

'No, she's fine.' The entry doors slid open and two EMTs pushed a stretcher into the ER. The stretcher was so completely surrounded by doctors and nurses that only the patient's legs were visible. 'That's Phil Skinner, Hyatt's assistant.'

New dread washed through Clay. 'I thought JD and two of your guys went to pick him up.'

'They did.' Joseph watched the ER staff working on Skinner with clinical detachment. But a muscle in his jaw twitched. 'Skinner shot himself. JD tried to stop him, even managed to take the gun from his hand, but Skinner had a backup.'

*Oh my God.* 'Is he alive?'

'They brought him in here instead of calling for Quartermaine, so he has a pulse.'

Clay's lungs weren't working properly. 'Shit.'

'I know.' Joseph grabbed Clay's arm when he would have paced away. 'I was told you'd probably blame yourself. That won't do anyone any good, so don't.'

'Easy for you to say. You didn't put the guy on disability.'

'Neither did you,' Joseph said firmly.

The curtain behind them whipped back. Stevie was sliding off the bed, a fresh bandage on her arm. She leaned on a crash cart to stay upright. 'Where did he shoot himself? With what?'

'In his mouth with a .380.'

Stevie winced. 'Did you retrieve Rossi's phone that Skinner took from the evidence lab?'

'We did. There was a message on it from Skinner, just like Rossi said there would be.'

Her shoulders sagged. 'Skinner really did leak the safe house location to Rossi,' she said. 'I didn't want to believe it.' Then she frowned. 'So why is Culp dead? Who did he piss off?'

'Good question. We searched Culp's house for evidence and the lab is sorting through it now. Same with Skinner's. Both guys lived like pigs, so getting through the piles of take-out boxes will be time-consuming. But Skinner's medicine cabinets were tidy. And full.'

'No Tylenol or Tums taking up space,' Stevie said quietly.

'Nothing so tame. Skinner appeared high when they got there, so Agent Novak searched Skinner's apartment while JD did CPR after Skinner shot himself. Skinner had pills in his medicine cabinet, in his dresser drawers, pockets of his suits. Oxy, Percocet, Ritalin, Adderall.'

Clay scrubbed his palms down his face. Painkillers and uppers. Because Skinner had been shot. *Because I didn't say something two years ago.*

'The pills were in baggies,' Joseph was saying, 'not bottles from a pharmacy. He wasn't going to doctors for prescriptions anymore. Skinner was buying off the street.'

'Did Rossi find out?' Stevie asked. 'Or was he Skinner's pusher?'

'I don't know – yet. Hopefully Rossi will be inclined to enlighten us or the search of Skinner's place will turn up something to explain.'

'Has Skinner's wife been informed?' she asked.

'Hyatt's on his way there now. He's had a busy afternoon with notifications.'

She sighed. 'Maybe Skinner's wife will be able to shed some light on this.'

'What did he say before he pulled the trigger?' Clay asked.

Joseph shrugged. 'Like I said, he appeared to be high. He ranted about how everyone had ruined his life – Lucy for getting him shot, Hyatt for giving him a "charity job", JD for turning on him, and even you, Stevie, for whipping everyone into a frenzy after Silas was found out.'

'Anything else?' Clay asked, not wanting to hear the answer.

Joseph met Clay's eyes. 'He didn't mention you.'

'That's hard to believe, since I'm the one who got him shot in the first place.'

'Believe what you want, but JD specifically said Skinner didn't mention you.'

Clay nodded, still not sure he believed them. 'All right, then. What about the Tahoe? Did we get any hits from the license plate we got from my security cameras?'

'Stolen earlier this afternoon from a car parked at the train station.' Joseph lifted his brows. 'But someone two streets away from Culp's house described a sand-colored Tahoe speeding away after the gunfire.'

'Mr Backpack,' Stevie said with satisfaction. 'We know he killed the two cops this afternoon. Rossi got Officer Cleary. That leaves the restaurant sniper and whoever killed Culp still unaccounted for.'

'And the shooters who've tried to get you and missed,' Joseph said. 'Don't forget them.'

'The drive-by in my front yard and the white Camry who shot at me after I left the IA meeting on Friday.' She pressed her fingers to her temples. 'God, this gives me a headache.'

'Me, too,' Clay said grimly. 'We need to consider that the restaurant sniper and Drive-by could be the same person – one who happened to know you'd be at that location with Emma.'

Stevie grimaced. 'I don't like thinking that someone's been following me since last year.'

'Or longer,' Clay said quietly.

'You're not helping,' she muttered.

Joseph cleared his throat. 'As much as I love the monikers you've given our shooters, I've always been partial to actual *names*. Tom, Fred, even Penelope. You know. *Names*.'

Stevie frowned at him. 'You're the Fed. You've got the resources. He's a PI and I'm just a cop on disability who doesn't even have her badge.'

'You don't need a badge,' Joseph fired back, giving her no pity. 'You're a cop whether you're carrying the hardware or not.' He turned to Clay. 'Brodie said you have a stingray.'

'Yes. I mentioned it when she and I were examining the debris in my bedroom.'

'Stingray?' Stevie's eyes narrowed.

'I told you about it. It detects any cell phones that aren't mine and activates the alarm.'

'You didn't tell me it was a stingray. That's the same gadget that had the Feds' panties in such a twist last year when they got caught using it in a tax fraud sting, right?'

'More like the ACLU's panties twisted,' Joseph grumbled. 'The Bureau had a warrant.'

On another day Clay might have smiled at Joseph's irritation. 'It's the same technology,' he told Stevie, 'but I'm not listening to conversations or tracking individual cellular devices.'

'But you *can*,' she pressed. 'You said you could on the drive to your house.'

'I said I *might*. It depends on if the person's phone pings while he's in the vicinity of my device. Things One and Two weren't there that long. One was there about seven minutes and Two was there only five minutes. Their phones may not have sent any signals during that time.'

'Brodie took it back with her to the lab,' Joseph said. 'One of the IT guys is working on it.'

'I gave her the access code. If she has any trouble, have her call me.'

'What will it give us?' Stevie persisted. 'Cell phone numbers?'

'Yes,' Clay said, 'but only *if* their—'

'Phones pinged,' she said, waving her hand. 'Yeah, yeah. I get that. What else? Location?'

'Not location. My system is passive – it only receives information that's released around it.'

'But the FBI used it to locate a suspect a year or so ago. I remember the hubbub afterward.'

Clay glanced at Joseph. The Fed was rolling his eyes. 'Damn judges,' Joseph muttered.

'The Feds got into hot water,' Clay explained, 'because

they had their suspect's wireless carrier alter the guy's Internet card on the phone company's end. The Feds pinged the phone with their stingrays and were able to triangulate the wireless card's location when the card pinged back. That's how they caught him. They got a court order for the wireless carrier's involvement, but they went a little light on the info they gave the judge who signed it. He didn't know the capabilities of the FBI's system. They went hunting. I'm just gathering.'

Her lips twitched minutely, then stilled. 'How long before we know if they got pinged?'

'As soon as Brodie runs the report,' Clay said.

'What are you looking to find?' Joseph asked her.

'You have Rossi's phone, Culp's, and now Skinner's cell phone. You'll get cell numbers picked up by Clay's stingray. We can get LUDs on all the numbers, and see if any of the cops called the shooters or if any of the shooters called each other. I've assumed that Restaurant, Drive-by, Backpack, and Cocksucker are connected. If they called each other we'll know for sure.'

Joseph coughed, covering a laugh. 'Stevie.'

'Hey, he named them Backpack and Cocksucker. I was calling them Things One and Two.'

Joseph shook his head. 'I guess we gotta laugh.' He tossed a set of keys to Clay. 'Grayson's Escalade is parked out front. I'll take mine in to be repaired ASAP. After this, I'm out of bullet-resistant vehicles, so don't get shot up in this one, okay?'

'We'll do our best,' Clay said wryly, but his brows bunched in frustration. 'Although they seem to be anticipating our movements damn well.'

'How did the shooter know you'd go to Culp's house?' Joseph asked.

Stevie shrugged. 'Clay and I worked through this.

Assuming the guy who drove away from Culp's neighborhood in a Tahoe after shooting at us was the same guy who killed those two cops, he hadn't been at Culp's the whole time, waiting for someone to show up. He came back to Culp's, either because someone told him we'd be there or because he followed us. My money's on the second one.'

She didn't want to believe Hyatt was dirty, Clay understood. But he'd promised to keep her safe, so he'd make sure the possibility of Hyatt's involvement didn't get brushed under the rug.

'Who could have told him?' Joseph asked. 'Who knew you were going there?'

'Only Hyatt,' Clay said. 'Other people knew we were interested in Culp, but Hyatt's the only one who knew we were going there at that moment.'

'If someone knew you were interested,' Joseph said rationally, 'it wouldn't be a huge leap to predict you'd wind up there at some point. Who knew Culp was a suspect?'

'JD,' Stevie said. 'Hyatt, and Detective Bashears, who took over watching Culp's house when JD went to the hospital to question Rossi. Hyatt told Grayson's boss, ASA Yates, who then informed the lieutenant from the State Police. She told her team.'

'You forgot about Kersey and his wife down in Arizona,' Clay said. 'I know you don't want to think he's dirty, but we have to put his name in the pot.'

'You're right,' she said. 'But I think it's more likely that Tahoe tailed us from your house. If he and his friend broke into your house to lure me into the open, that would make sense.'

Clay shook his head. 'I buy that was the first guy's motivation, but based on the way he ran up to check after the Tahoe drove away, I don't think he knew the second guy was coming.'

'I agree,' she said. 'So the first guy was waiting for me to appear—'

'Or for Clay to appear,' Joseph said, 'anticipating following him to you.'

She nodded. 'Also agreed. But the first guy got spooked when he saw the two dead cops and took off. If the second guy did follow us to Culp's, he either left and came back to Clay's, or never left and just hid from all the law enforcement. I don't think he followed Hyatt.'

'It wouldn't make sense for him to do so, if he was waiting for you and Clay,' Joseph said. 'Which means he followed you the whole way. Even when you stopped at CVS.'

Clay frowned. 'How did you know we stopped?'

Joseph shrugged. 'I found the drugstore bag in my Escalade and checked the receipt before I entered it all into evidence. I had to take your gym bag, too.' The look he gave Clay was apologetic. 'So I stopped by another CVS on my way here and bought you new stuff. It's in Grayson's Escalade.'

Clay felt his cheeks heat, knowing Joseph had found the condoms he'd bought when the Fed checked Clay's gym bag. But this wasn't the time for personal embarrassment.

Stevie had looked up, her cheeks pale but her eyes grimly steady. 'He waited while you went into the store, Clay. He could've shot me then. Joseph, can you look at the store's security tapes? See if the Tahoe was nearby?'

Joseph took out his phone and sent a text. 'I put one of my team on it. I'll let you—'

Abruptly the ER went quiet. The sniper from the State Police had been taken up to surgery minutes before and the remaining activity had been clustered around Skinner, but now the medical staff turned from Skinner's stretcher, shoulders sagging, feet dragging.

Clay's heart skipped a beat. *Oh no. Oh God, no.*

'Damn,' Stevie whispered. 'Just . . . damn.'

Joseph bowed his head wearily. 'I need to go. You two, just stay alive. Please.'

From the corner of his eye, Clay saw Joseph walk away, but his gaze was fixed on the body on the other side of the ER.

'Clay?' Stevie murmured.

He didn't look at her. 'He was a husband and a father. And a good cop until he got shot two years ago. Now he's dead. How can I not feel responsible, Stevie?'

She tugged at his arm. When he didn't move, she put her hip into the effort, surprising him enough so that she was able to turn him around, so that he faced her and not the dead cop's body. She reached up, cupped his face in her hands, and pulled until he looked down and met her eyes.

'He was a junkie, Clay, and that had nothing to do with you. He made that choice. He might have been a good husband and father once, but he ceased to be when the drugs became more important than his family. And he stopped being a good cop the instant he told Rossi where to find me and Cordelia. If you hadn't hidden us . . . If we'd actually been in that safe house, we'd be dead. If that made Skinner feel guilty enough to take his own life, then so be it. Call me harsh and unfeeling, but I'm not going to cry a single tear for him.'

Clay's jaw hardened even as he drank in the feel of her hands on his face. 'You're absolutely right.' Skinner wasn't the victim here. He'd willfully disclosed the 'safe' location of a fellow police officer. Another human being. And a child. 'I didn't think.'

Her eyes softened. 'You're tired. So am I. It's been an intense two days for both of us. Let's go rest. Recharge for a few hours. Then we'll figure out what to do next.'

He leaned closer, resting his forehead against hers, and she didn't back away. 'Okay.'

# Chapter Seventeen

*Baltimore, Maryland, Sunday, March 16, 6.15 P.M.*

Sam Hudson hated the morgue on a good day. This was not a good day – for him, for the department, or for the MEs. Especially not for the cops lying inside with tags on their toes.

He'd been aware that cops had been shot. It was all over the news, but he'd been in a fog all day. The deaths of his fellow cops hadn't seemed real, but that changed the moment he stepped into the morgue. There was a level of tension he hadn't felt on any of his prior visits.

He stopped at the front desk, manned by a security guard. 'I'm Officer Hudson,' he said, showing his badge as he was dressed in street clothes. 'Can I speak with Dr Trask?'

The guard looked mildly surprised. 'She's on maternity leave. Won't be back 'til next year.'

Sam frowned. 'I knew she'd gone out, but I thought maternity leave was only eight weeks.'

'She's taking unpaid leave so she can be home with the baby until his first birthday. She's brought him in a time or two.' The guard smiled. 'He's a cute one.'

'I'm sure he is,' Sam said, trying to sound . . . normal. 'Is Dr Mulhauser here, then?'

'He's retired. New chief's named Quartermaine. He's in the back with all the assistant MEs.' The smile faded to a sad kind of fury. 'They're all doing exams. We got a full house.'

'I heard,' Sam murmured. 'I need to pull an autopsy report. It's really important. Is there anyone here who can help me?'

'I'm sorry, but the person who pulls reports has gone home for the evening. If you leave the information, someone can pull it for you when the hubbub goes down.'

'I can help him.'

Sam turned to find a dark-haired, very curvy Latina beauty in her late twenties walking down the hall from the back. She was zipping her jacket, a gym bag slung over one shoulder.

The security guard's smile returned. 'Ruby, you're off the clock aren't you?'

'Yeah. And it's about time,' she said with grim relief. 'This has been one of the longest days we've had in months. What can I do for you, sir?'

'This is Officer Hudson,' the guard said.

'It's okay,' Sam said quietly. 'You've put in a full day. I can wait.'

He didn't mind waiting. He'd waited for over an hour in the parking lot outside, trying to convince himself to come in. He could wait a little longer to read what was sure to be very bad.

'I've retrieved the bodies of four cops today,' she said, 'and I feel like shit. Helping a live cop will make me feel better. Come with me.' She led him back to one of the offices, pointed to a chair while she dropped into the one behind the desk. 'ID number?'

Sam slid his badge across the desk. 'My ID.'

357

She studied it for a moment. 'Who do you need to look up, Sam?'

'I don't have a name. He's a John Doe. But I have the police report number.'

'That'll work.' She typed like a pro, her long, red nails flying over the keys. She was going to give him the report. It would tell him the truth.

Sam didn't want to think about the truth. Knowing the truth was coming was making him sick to his stomach. He focused on her red nails instead. 'May I ask you a question?' he said.

'Unless it's my weight, knock yourself out.'

A small smile tugged at his lips. 'How do you handle the bodies with those long nails?'

She paused, wiggling her fingertips as she admired her hand. 'They're fake. Press-ons. I put them on when I leave, take them off when I come in.' She sobered, still staring at the nails that had little rhinestones imbedded randomly, making them sparkle. 'I guess it's my way of distancing myself from what I've seen during the day.'

'And maybe keeps people from asking you about it once you've left here.'

She nodded. 'Exactly. People can be weird about those of us who work here.' She hit another key on the keyboard with a flourish, then reached for the printer. 'Here it is.' She read the page she'd printed. 'Not much here. If you have any questions, call tomorrow. We've got five cops back there – one from last night and the four we brought in today. Plus two civilians from that restaurant sniper yesterday afternoon. Nobody's in a chatty mood.'

'You are,' he said quietly.

She looked a little ashamed. 'I guess I am.'

'I didn't mean anything bad. It's how you cope.'

She shrugged. 'Maybe. This exam was done by Dr

Fremont. He retired about three years ago. He's still local and loves to help out. Keeps him off the street and out of the bingo parlors.' She handed him the report. 'Hope this helps your case.'

'It will, thank you.'

'Why did you want to look it up?' she asked.

'The gun that killed this man was recently found. I just wanted to see what was what.'

She nodded. 'Well, you got what you came for.' She turned off the computer and gathered her bag. 'I'll walk you out.'

She was quiet until they came to where they'd go their separate ways. 'Who is this John Doe to you?' she asked. 'He means something to you. I can tell.'

'I'm not sure,' he answered truthfully. 'Thanks.' He got in his car, waited for her to get into hers. When she drove away, he went the other direction, stopping at a Starbucks. He went in for a cup, just to take off the chill. Because he was colder than he'd been in a very long time.

Once he'd added cream and sugar and done everything possible to put off the inevitable, he sat down to read. Part of it he knew. Mid-forties, Caucasian. Bullet hole to the back of the head. Time of death estimated at mid-March, eight years before.

The timing was right, dammit. He'd hoped it wouldn't be. He'd hoped the death had occurred in January or April or even the previous Halloween. Any time that was *not* mid-March. But it was. Still, just the timing was right didn't mean it was his father.

*So how's the weather in Egypt?* With contempt for his near desperate denial, he searched the text for unique features, tattoos, anything to tell him that this man was *not* his father.

*Shit*. The victim was missing his appendix. So was his

359

father. But then, so were millions of people. *Doesn't mean a thing*. The victim's femur had evidence of a very bad break that had probably occurred when he was a child.

Sam's father had taken a bad fall sledding as a boy. He'd walked with a limp until the day he disappeared. Same leg. *Just a coincidence*.

There were autopsy photos attached. He didn't want to look. Didn't think he could.

Knew he had to.

Steeling his spine, he flipped the page. And forgot to breathe. The first photo was a close-up of the victim's forearm. It was the remnant of a tattoo. Suddenly Sam was ten years old, cowering on the floor as that forearm came down, the leather belt the man gripped cutting into his skin. The tattoo was a bald eagle, one wing the stars, the other the stripes on the flag.

He'd focus on that eagle whenever his father would bring out the belt. He focused on it now. Only about a third of the tat remained – the eagle's head, a little of the stars, a little more of the stripes.

John Hudson was dead. *I killed him. I killed my father.*

Slowly Sam rose, pushed his chair under the table, threw his untouched coffee in the trash. He folded the report, slid it into his coat pocket, got into his car and drove about five blocks.

Then he pulled into the deserted parking lot of a high school, staggered from his car, and fell to his knees, throwing his guts up.

*I killed him. I killed my father.* How could he tell his mother? He couldn't. It would kill her.

*I'm finished. I'm done.* No more police department. *I'm going to prison.*

The retching finally eased and he hung there on his hands and knees, drawing deep, shuddering breaths.

'Do you know now?'

He was surprised to hear the woman's voice behind him. He recognized it right away. It was the Latina ME tech who'd pulled the report.

A tissue appeared in front of his face, held by long red nails.

He remembered that her name was Ruby. He took the tissue, wiped his mouth. 'What?'

'You didn't know who the victim was when I gave you the report. Do you know now?'

'What are you doing here? Did you follow me?'

'I did. My date canceled.'

'So you *followed* me? Please. Just leave me alone. Go home.'

'I considered that, but I have a sink full of dirty dishes and four-day-old pizza in the fridge. I didn't want to go home. Plus, you looked green around the gills when you left the morgue.' She sighed, her voice going from light to very serious. 'I was worried about you, Sam.'

'Thank you. Truly, I . . . appreciate it. But I really need to be alone right now.'

'Why? Because you just threw up? Honey, I pick up dead people for a living. I have seen a helluva lot worse, trust me.'

Unbelievably, a chuckle rose in his throat. 'Your date canceled on you, really?'

'Yeah. Imagine that.'

'It's hard to.'

Her hand came into his field of vision, those long red nails sparkling in the lamplight. 'Come on. You can't stay here. This is a bad neighborhood. You could get mugged.'

Again he chuckled. 'I'm a cop, Ruby.' But he took her hand and let her pull him up. 'You need to get home. So do I.'

She shook her head. 'Who's the John Doe, Sam?'

He closed his eyes. 'God. I can't say. I can't.'

'All right. Come on, let's get some fluids in you. You puked up half your water weight.'

Feeling like he was walking across a surreal landscape, he let her lead him to her car. She popped the trunk. A moment later she was handing him a bottle of mouthwash. 'Rinse first.'

'You keep mouthwash in your trunk?'

She plunked a hand on her hip, those red nails extending like claws. 'Were you not listening, *papi*? I pick up *dead people* for a living. That's a taste that gets in your mouth and will not go away. And nobody wants to kiss me after that.'

He found himself smiling as he spit the mouthwash onto the grass next to her car. He took the bottle of water she offered and chugged half of it down at once, wiping his mouth with the back of his hand. 'Thank you. Really. You've been kind when you didn't have to be.'

'That's kind of the definition of "kind", isn't it? If you *have* to be kind, then it's coercion and therefore not truly kind.'

He blinked. 'Yeah. Okay. I think.'

She studied him in the lamplight. 'You got someplace to be tonight, Sam?'

'No.' He couldn't face his mother and he didn't want to go back to his place. 'I don't.'

'Then come with me. We can listen to some music and you can figure out what you're going to do with what you just found out.'

'What about my car?'

'Lock it up. It'll probably be here when you get back. The drug dealers in this neighborhood have much nicer cars than this. They'll likely leave yours alone.'

Somehow he ended up in the passenger seat of her car, buckling himself in. 'Ruby, how do you know I'm safe? I could be an evil person, planning all kinds of terrible things.'

She started her engine. 'Are you?'

'No.' He frowned. 'At least I don't think so.'

'Good. If that changes, be sure to let me know.'

He was shaking his head when she pulled into traffic, a small smile on his face. A small smile that quickly faded when reality set back in.

*I killed my father.* He'd dreamed of doing it so many times. Every time the bastard hurt his mother. *But I never would have done it. Never* could *have done it.* Except it looked like he had.

*Wight's Landing, Maryland, Sunday, March 16, 7.00 P.M.*

Tanner St James's kitchen was full of chatter and wonderful aromas when Stevie and Clay walked in. The aromas lingered, but the chatter abruptly quieted, six pairs of eyes staring at her.

Tanner stood at the stove, wearing an apron that said 'Kiss The Cook'. At the table were Cordelia, Paige and Grayson, and Emma and her husband, Christopher. Below the table were two dogs – Peabody lying at Paige's feet and Tanner's dog Columbo at Cordelia's.

They'd just finished dinner, and based on the clean plates in front of each one of them, it had been tasty. Stevie's stomach grumbled, reminding her that she hadn't eaten since breakfast.

Emma was the first to speak. 'You trashed my cashmere sweater, didn't you?'

Stevie wore a BPD T-shirt for the second day in a row,

the turtleneck she'd borrowed from Emma having been taken with the evidence of the shooting. Luckily, the ER doctor who'd restitched her arm had noticed the hickey and loaned her some makeup to cover it up.

Stevie shrugged, keeping her voice light. 'Yep. I'd feel bad, but I told you I'd ruin it. You loaned it to me with full disclosure.'

'Mama,' Cordelia asked in a small voice, 'why are you wearing that thing over your shirt?'

Stevie pulled at the Velcro tabs that held the flak jacket in place. Joseph had left the vests on their seats in the SUV. Given the events of the day and that her thin Kevlar armor had been taken along with the turtleneck, she'd been grateful for the gift. 'It's just a precaution, honey. I promised you I'd be very careful and this is me, keeping my promise. So, looks like you guys are having a party. I hope there's ice cream. I could really use some chocolate.'

Grayson jumped up and pulled out a chair. 'Sit. It's time to rest for a while, Stevie.'

'I slept in the car,' Stevie said, taking the seat he offered, putting her next to Cordelia. She kissed the top of her daughter's head, acutely aware that Cordelia hadn't been soothed by her explanation of the flak jacket. *Should've taken it off in the garage. Stupid mistake.*

'No, she didn't.' Clay took the seat on Cordelia's other side. 'Your mom was pretending to sleep, just like you do.' He reached over the table, hand extended to Christopher. 'You're Emma's husband. I'm Clay.'

Christopher shook his hand. 'Thank you for looking after her.'

Clay shot Emma a look. 'I tried to send her home, but she wouldn't go.'

'I know.' Christopher sighed. 'I gave up trying to order her around back in high school.'

Stevie smiled. 'You're a wise man, then. Tanner, I'm so hungry that I could eat my own cooking. If there's anything left, I'd love to have some. Christopher, it's good to see you again.'

'It's always a pleasure to see you, Stevie. Wish the circumstances were different.'

'Me, too,' Stevie said ruefully. 'Paige, how did you guys get here? I didn't see your truck outside and we have Grayson's SUV. Thank you, by the way. I appreciate you loaning it to us.'

'You're welcome,' Grayson said. 'I hope you don't need the . . . special features.'

Meaning the bullet-resistant glass. 'You and me both.'

'We picked up Christopher from the airport and drove to Lou Moore's place,' Paige said. 'We didn't want to risk being followed. Lou brought us over in the boat. It worked as a trial run for when we move Cor—' Paige pursed her lips hard, stopping herself from saying anymore.

But it was too late for that. Cordelia had heard, evidenced by her sharp indrawn breath. She tugged on Stevie's shirt. 'Mama,' she said, her voice still small.

Stevie found her daughter's eyes full of fear. 'Yes, Cordelia?'

'I heard about today. That you got shot, again.'

Stevie quickly glanced at the adults, her eyes narrowed.

Emma sighed. 'It came on the TV, Stevie. We were watching cartoons and they broke for a special news announcement. I changed the channel, but she'd heard enough to be scared. Grayson got the details from Joseph. We told her so she'd know you were unhurt.'

Stevie dropped her gaze back to her daughter's pinched face. 'Someone shot at me. He didn't hit me.' Not exactly. He hit Kevlar. 'I'm not hurt. Neither is Mr Maynard.'

'They keep shooting at you,' Cordelia said, almost

tonelessly. 'They want to kill you. Who, Mama? Why?'

'I'm not sure who or why, but I'm going to find out and make them stop.'

Cordelia gave her a look that was far too old. 'You want to move me so I won't be in the way. I heard Sheriff Moore talking to Miss Paige. They said I was in the way.' She lifted her chin. 'But I won't go. I'm not leaving you.'

Stevie was aware that all eyes were on her. 'Cordelia . . . First of all, we haven't decided to move you. We're getting ready in case we have to. Like having a "Plan B". And second, it has nothing to do with you being in the way, because you are never in the way.'

Paige had flinched, distressed. '"*Harm's way*", Cordy. You heard us say you were in "*harm's way*". That's very different than being "in the way".'

Cordelia still looked unconvinced. 'I'm not leaving you.'

Stevie blew out a breath. 'Honey, if this house is no longer safe, you will leave.' She said it firmly, but as lovingly as she knew how. 'I have to know you're safe. I don't know what I'd do if anything happened to you.' Cordelia looked away and Stevie felt the bite of helpless frustration. 'And not because you're all I have left,' she added more sharply than she'd intended.

Cordelia's gaze flew to Clay's face, her expression even more stricken. '*You told*.'

'No,' Stevie said. 'I listened in. Like he said, I can pretend to be asleep as well as you can.' She gripped Cordelia's chin gently, making her daughter meet her eyes. 'Now you listen to me and you *hear* me. You *believe* me. You are my heart. You have been since the moment I first felt you move in my tummy. If your daddy and brother had lived, you'd still be my heart. I love you the same as I would have if we were all still a family. And we *are* still a family. You and me and . . .' *Clay*. She'd almost said *Clay*.

'Izzy,' she said firmly, steeling her voice so that it didn't tremble. 'We are a family. Do you believe me?'

Cordelia nodded silently.

'Good,' Stevie said, but she wasn't sure she believed her daughter. 'Cordelia, there has not been a single moment that I have not treasured you. It's true that you're all I have left – but of your father. You are not some kind of consolation prize and if you ever thought so, you were wrong. If anything, you are more precious to me because . . . Because you and I survived *together*. We've made it through *together*.'

Cordelia's expression was weary, like she knew Stevie believed her own words, even if they weren't really true. 'I know, Mama. It'll be fine.'

*It'll be fine*. Tears rose in Stevie's throat. No wonder Cordelia didn't believe her. She'd spouted that *It'll be fine* for far too long, using it to ignore her child's hurt and fear.

No, it wouldn't be fine, not unless she could make her daughter understand.

'What I feel for you is exactly the same thing I felt for your brother and if I have ever made you think otherwise, I am sorry.' Her voice broke and she bowed her head, trying to keep the tears from starting. Because once she started, she didn't think she'd stop. 'I am so sorry.'

What seemed like a lifetime passed, and then she felt a small hand smooth her hair again and again. 'Don't cry, Mama. Please don't cry.'

'I'm trying not to,' Stevie said hoarsely, leaning into her daughter's caress. 'But I still don't think you believe me.' She looked Cordelia squarely in the eye. 'In your shoes, I wouldn't believe me, either, and you're more like me every day.' Her lips curved. 'You poor kid.'

Cordelia's lips trembled into a small smile, but it was genuine. 'Aunt Izzy says Grandma used to say that some day you'd have a little girl just like you and then she'd have her revenge.'

Stevie could feel the tension in the room begin to recede as the adults sitting around the table chuckled. 'Yeah, Grandma did say that, at least once a day. I was kind of a handful. Didn't like to take anyone's word for anything. I liked to have proof. Just like you do. So I guess I'll have to prove how I feel about you and that will simply take time. I'm going to make sure we have that time, Cordelia. I'm going to find whoever's been shooting at me and I will make them stop. But I need to know you're safe while I do. If that means moving you, that's what will happen.'

Cordelia nodded soberly. 'Where will I go?'

Stevie let herself breathe. 'Alec has been working at Miss Daphne's farm all day, adding a lot more security. The plan we grownups have talked about is for you to go there if things get too dangerous here. You'll be safe there. You can see the horses all you want. Miss Paige will be there to watch over you and Alec, too. Mr Maynard trusts them. So do I.'

Cordelia squared her shoulders. 'But who will watch over you, Mama?'

Stevie's throat thickened again. 'I can watch over myself. But if Mr Maynard is still willing, I'd like him to watch over me, too. Would that make you feel better?'

Cordelia nodded. Then shook her head. 'No,' she whispered.

'Why not, honey?' Clay asked softly. 'I'm not mad, but why not?'

She looked up at him, distress in her eyes. 'Who will watch over you?'

Stevie watched as Clay swallowed hard, trying to think of something to say.

*At least I can help with that.* 'I will,' Stevie said firmly.

'Mr Maynard and I will watch over each other. And Uncle JD and Joseph are helping, too. So what do you think? Will you go if it's necessary – without any fuss?'

'If I said no, would you be mad?'

'Yes. But more like I got mad when you touched the stove even after I said it was hot.'

Cordelia's eyes widened. 'I did that?'

'Oh yeah. And you fractured your arm when you jumped off the swing, trying to fly even though Grandma kept telling you the butterfly costume for Halloween didn't really turn you into a butterfly. You nearly turned my hair gray with that one. And then there was the time you tried to eat soap because it was pink and smelled like cotton candy.'

Her nose wrinkled. 'I remember that one. I thought it would taste so good, but it was bad.' Her lighter attitude faltered. 'You're not coming to Miss Daphne's with me?'

'Not right now. But when this is all over, I will. I promise. I'll even try to ride a horse.'

Cordelia nodded once. 'Okay, then. I'll go.'

Stevie pressed a kiss to Cordelia's forehead. 'Thank you, baby.'

'But you have to try to ride. All these people heard you say so.'

'It doesn't matter what they heard. You heard me say so and that's what's most important to me.' Stevie glanced down when plates of lasagna were placed in front of her and Clay and smiled when Tanner silently patted her back. 'Now I have to eat and talk to the grownups. Can you go play with the puppies or something? Just for a few minutes.'

Paige stood up, held out her hand. 'Let's go, Cordy. We need to practice your *kata* so that you're ready to test for your blue belt with your class when all this craziness is

369

over.' She clicked her tongue and the Rottweiler fell into position beside her. 'Peabody, with me.'

When the kitchen door swung closed behind them, Stevie rubbed her forehead hard, suddenly feeling embarrassed at having had that conversation with Cordelia in front of so many people. 'Sorry. Didn't mean to make you all feel uncomfortable.'

'No one's complaining, Stevie,' Emma said, sniffling.

Stevie chanced looking up and found Emma dabbing at her eyes with a tissue. Clay gave her a single hard nod of approval that nearly had her crying herself.

She cleared her throat, then closed her eyes in bliss when she tasted her dinner. 'This lasagna is so good.'

'It *is* good,' Clay said, sounding a little surprised. 'What did you do to it? Not that your lasagna is usually bad, but this is as good as Mom used to make.'

'New recipe,' Tanner said brusquely. 'And there's chocolate ice cream in the freezer.'

'My hero.' Stevie dug in, starving. 'Chocolate ice cream and then a nap sounds heavenly.'

'You need more than a nap,' Grayson said. 'You two need to get a full night's rest. That's why Paige and I are still here. She's going to stand watch inside the house tonight while Joseph's people guard outside. And if you had decided to send Cordelia to the farm, Paige wanted to be the one to make sure she got there safely. She thought that would put your mind at ease. As much as you can be eased right now.'

She did feel eased, Stevie realized. Not entirely, but enough that she could draw a pain-free breath. She reached across the table and squeezed Grayson's hand. 'Thank you. Both of you.'

'You'd do the same for us,' Grayson said.

'I hope to God I never have to,' she murmured, then

looked at Clay. 'If we do have to move her, I'd like to know more about the setup. You told me about the gates and the fence, but what about the house and the barn? One of the benefits of the farm is that Cordelia wouldn't be trapped in a house, that she plays with the horses. Gets fresh air. How will you protect her then?'

'The main barn is accessible from the house by an enclosed walkway,' Clay said. 'Daphne had it put in for wheelchairs. It's got glass walls, hurricane approved glass, like in my house. All the kids have to wear helmets when they ride. They aren't "bullet-proof", but the composite materials are very strong. If she goes riding, she can wear a vest.'

'You mean body armor? You have body armor in her size?'

'Unfortunately, they have to make vests in kids' sizes too. She might not realize it's bullet-proof. It looks like a normal ski vest.'

'She'll know,' Stevie said grimly. 'She's far too smart for her own good. Until this is over, I would like her to wear one. Will there be a secure line that we can use to call each other?'

Clay nodded. 'Of course.'

'And if this goes on longer than a few days, can Izzy or my parents be taken to the farm?'

'Of course,' he repeated. 'We aren't trying to keep Cordelia isolated. Just safe.'

'Thank you. And to you, too,' she said to Tanner when he put a bowl of ice cream in front of her. 'Then the destination is settled. If we do decide this place has been compromised, how fast can Sheriff Moore get here with the boat?'

'She got us from her dock to Clay's in ten minutes,' Grayson said. 'That was full-throttle.'

'Okay. It sounds like a viable "Plan B". Let's focus on finding this guy so that we don't need it. Did Forensics get anything from Clay's house?'

'We did,' Grayson said, satisfaction in his eyes. 'I got a call from Joseph, right before you two got here. Clay's stingray gave up phone numbers from the second intruder's cell phone call log. Culp called the second intruder – the one who drove the Tahoe – last night, about an hour before Officer Cleary was killed in the safe house. There were no calls from Rossi to either Culp or the Tahoe driver.'

'We call the Tahoe driver "Mr Backpack",' Stevie said. 'The other we can call "Mr Sucker", just to keep things rated G for Cordelia. There's also "Drive-by" and "Restaurant".'

'Fine,' Grayson said with a smile, then sobered. 'We're assuming that Culp gave Backpack the safe house location when he called him. We don't know if Backpack got to the safe house, saw what Rossi had done and ran, or didn't go at all. But he knew where to find you last night.'

Stevie's chest went tight. 'So if Rossi hadn't, someone else would have tried to kill Cordelia and me there.'

'It's likely,' Grayson said grimly. 'Joseph also had just received the video surveillance from the CVS you two stopped at. The Tahoe was there, in the parking lot. The driver kept his head down so the surveillance cameras couldn't pick up his features.'

'Shit,' she breathed. 'So close.'

'I'm getting tired of playing catch up to this guy.' Clay's voice was harsh. Rattled. 'We need to bring him out in the open.'

'I was thinking that, too,' Stevie said. 'I've got an idea you're not going to like.'

'If you're the bait, you're damn right I won't like it,'

Clay said. 'But we might not have a choice. Sooner or later your luck's going to run out.'

Stevie grimaced. 'I've already run out of Kevlar. Part one of my plan requires a very public declaration that Emma is going home to Florida. Maybe a news story.'

Emma and Christopher shared a look. 'We don't think that's a good idea,' Emma said.

'Why not?' Stevie asked.

'Someone's already tried to break into our house,' Christopher said. 'Today my office at the university was broken into. Emma doesn't have family pictures on her website, but I have pictures on my desk. Whoever broke into my office now has photos of the boys and Megan.'

Stevie closed her eyes. 'Oh God. I'm sorry.'

'Hush, Stevie,' Emma said mildly. 'So far, the security we've hired to protect our parents and our kids haven't reported any issues, but we're going to lay low. Christopher is flying to Florida tomorrow on a private plane. Instead of going to our house, he's going straight to Disney World. Our security people will pick him up and take him to the boys.'

'What about you?' Stevie asked.

'I'm staying with Cordelia. And when the time comes, I'll go with her to the farm.'

Stevie leaned back in her chair, blinking. 'You are?'

Emma nodded. 'I am. It allows me to lay low and not get shot at.'

'Which makes me happy,' Christopher said, his jaw tight.

Emma shrugged. 'I'm no celebrity, but my face is on the back of enough books that I get recognized in public from time to time. They don't know the boys are in Orlando, but all it takes is one person seeing me there with my kids to put the boys in danger.'

'Emma, are you sure?'

'Yes. I can watch over Cordelia and if we go to the farm, I can learn about equine therapy. I see potential for a new book. And there are, of course, the clothes. Equestrian is all the rage.'

'Should have known clothes would factor in somehow,' Stevie said with a smile. 'Has the hotel where you were staying had any more trouble with people trying to get into your room?'

'Paige checked with the hotel manager before we came here,' Grayson said. 'There have been some inquiries, mostly from reporters. Why?'

'I'm thinking that maybe "Emma" should check back into the hotel tomorrow night. If anyone was watching for her last night, Paige wouldn't have fooled them. She's almost six feet tall and Emma's only five feet in her stilettos.'

Emma looked at her shrewdly. 'If you're thinking of posing as me, don't. You can't walk like me. Even before the cane.'

'I can learn,' Stevie said stubbornly. 'I did some undercover, back in the day.'

'And your hair?' Grayson asked.

'A wig. Daphne's got plenty. I'm sure she has a short blonde one. Look, maybe nobody comes and I just end up sleeping in a hotel bed for the night. But maybe someone will think Emma knows where I am and will break in again.'

'They might open fire,' Grayson cautioned, 'like Rossi did at the safe house last night.'

Stevie winced. 'Fine. I won't sleep in the bed. But I want to draw whoever is looking for me into an enclosed environment. There's too much space to control if I'm out and about. If I can get them to come to me, I'll have the advantage.'

'Why not just check in as yourself?' Emma asked.

'A, because it would stink of a trap,' Stevie answered. 'B, because they'd shoot me before I got to the front desk. You, they'd want to keep alive so that they could make you tell them where to find me.'

'I don't like it,' Clay said quietly. 'But I can't think of anything better. We have to put a stop to whoever wants you dead. You and Cordelia can't go on like this forever.'

*You and Cordelia.* Stevie winced again, this time in her own mind. Before their interlude on the boat, he'd said 'we', again and again. She missed the comfort of being part of a 'we'.

'Can you take care of security?' Stevie asked him.

He nodded once. 'Of course.'

'Then we have a plan.' Stevie looked around the table. 'Thank you. All of you.'

'You were never alone in this, Stevie,' Grayson said.

'I know,' she murmured. 'I get that now.'

# Chapter Eighteen

Robinette leaned back in his desk chair, staring at the enlarged photo on his computer screen. He was close to finding Maynard's hiding place. He could feel it.

Robinette had scanned in the photo he'd found in the debris on Maynard's bedroom floor. The photo was of the PI with his arm around an older man's shoulders, the two of them standing on the deck of a boat. Robinette now enlarged the image until the name of the boat was clear. Only three letters had been visible – F-I-J.

*Fiji?* Maybe. A Google of 'search boats by name' brought back the recreational vessel database. And what do you know? It was searchable by vessel name. F-I-J, he typed.

Then grinned. Less than a dozen boats had F-I-J in the name. Less than half of those were currently located on the East Coast. Robinette searched the vessels' owners and his grin got wider. 'Like taking candy from a baby,' he murmured.

Captain Tanner St James owned the *Fiji* from which he chartered fishing trips. His website was extremely helpful, showing both a photo of the captain and the address of his business. St James was, without a doubt, the man in Maynard's photo.

The address – Main Street, Wight's Landing, Maryland – was a marina on the Chesapeake Bay. Google maps showed it to be an hour and ten minutes from Robinette's current location.

Robinette did a final search, just to be certain. Tanner St James was married to Nancy St James, nee Maynard. The boat captain was the PI's stepfather.

*Priceless*. This would be a place Maynard would feel safe. But it was premature to cackle. Maynard may not have hidden them on the boat itself. His father might have a house in Wight's Landing. Another Google search yielded more than Robinette had hoped for.

Tanner St James had an unlisted number, but the property records served up his address in a few seconds flat. Robinette loved the property records database. Anyone who'd ever owned a home was in there. Maynard had been smart enough to hide his own house under layers of corporations, all linked to other corporations.

But Maynard's stepfather hadn't been so careful, so his home address was viewable by any and all, and some of the people who'd viewed it hadn't been wound so tight. St James had pressed charges on a group of fruitcakes who'd tried to storm his home on an annual basis.

The old guy was no wuss. St James had chased them off with a semi-automatic rifle.

Robinette Googled one of the people listed in St James's complaint. The fruitcake had a Facebook page, of course, and turned out to be a devotee of a serial killer, kind of like those crazies who kept trying to smuggle cell phones into prison for Charles Manson. This serial killer, though, was a woman who'd committed some of her crimes in the house where St James now lived. Her photo thoroughly creeped Robinette out. That didn't happen very often.

There had been a cluster of posts around the killer's birthday, many of which criticized Tanner St James for denying them access to what 'should be a national monument', but most of the annual pilgrimages to St James's property had apparently stopped five years before.

When St James had *completely fortified his home*. The man had added a ten-foot electrified fence, a steel gate, motion detectors, cameras. Bank vault doors and bullet-proof windows, even.

'Bingo,' Robinette crowed. 'This is most definitely the place.'

The only problem was – how was he going to get in?

'I'll figure that out when I get there.' He shot the Rubik's cube on his desk a look of contempt. 'Now who's dumb?' he murmured. His oldest pal would be eating his words at the moment, if Rene were still alive. Which he was not.

Robinette cleared his Internet browser and shut down his computer. He shoved the photos into the pocket of his coat and locked his office door behind him, ready to catch himself a cop.

'Todd?' A female sigh of exasperation had him tensing. 'You forgot, didn't you?'

*Shit. Lisa.* Robinette drew a breath as he pulled the key from the lock. Ensured none of the euphoria he felt over finding Mazzetti's hiding place showed on his face. He turned to find Lisa wearing a conservative cocktail dress, diamonds dripping from her ears, and a frown on her face.

'Forgot what?' he asked, his confusion genuine. 'Brenda Lee said I had the night off.'

Annoyance flickered in Lisa's eyes. 'Brenda Lee didn't plan this. I did.'

Robinette bit his tongue and swallowed his scowl.

Made himself smile instead. 'Well, darlin', you'll have to give them my regrets. I've got someplace else to be.'

Lisa grabbed his arm. 'Don't you dare,' she said quietly. 'I have a living room full of wealthy men and women who want to donate to your rehab centers. I told you this several times. I emailed you to remind you an hour ago, but I knew you'd be here. You're *always* here.'

'They can write a check even if I'm not there,' he said coolly.

She didn't budge. 'Two of them are interested in having you run for office, Todd.'

That got his attention. 'Me? Run for office?'

'Yes, you. I wasn't supposed to tell you. They wanted to gauge your reaction, so look surprised when they ask you. Surprised and humble.'

'Lisa. I'm . . . I don't know what to say.'

'Say "Thank you, Lisa." Then get your ass into a decent suit. This one is filthy. What have you been doing? Cleaning sewers?' She dropped her hand, giving him a disgusted look.

His jaw tightened. That he'd once cleaned sewers was not well known. It had been a summer job when he'd been a dirt-poor teenager trying to save for college. Lisa's daddy had turned up that little factoid when he'd done a background check on his son-in-law-to-be.

'It was honest work,' he murmured. Keeping the malice from his voice was difficult.

'That's what Congressman Rickman says. You met him last night at your awards dinner. He admires you.' She sighed. 'I'm sorry, Todd. But I told you about this dinner. It makes me crazy that you only listen to Brenda Lee. I'm your wife. You're supposed to listen to *me*.'

'You're right.' He hated to give the information about Maynard's stepfather to Westmoreland, but he couldn't afford to lose Mazzetti if she truly was hiding at Maynard's stepfather's house. At the same time, running for office . . . *Me*. This was the opportunity he'd been waiting for. That he deserved. *And I didn't even have to kill anyone to get it.*

Plus, after getting shot at today, Mazzetti would probably be hiding out, trembling in her boots. She wasn't going anywhere for a few hours. 'I'll go change now.'

'Can you use the back stairs?' she asked. 'I don't want everyone to know that you forgot.'

'Of course.' He kissed her cheek, noting the way she stiffened, pulling away from his touch. *It's just dirt, bitch. Not poison.* He had the sudden mental image of his hands around her throat, twisting her neck like he'd done to the cops earlier that day. *Back, boy. You can't kill any more wives.* 'I'll hurry as fast as I can.'

He took off at a jog, dialing Westmoreland as he ran, then frowned. No answer. Wes was supposed to be at a coffee shop trying to hack into Maynard's office server. He'd try again later.

But a shower, a tux, and three calls to Westmoreland later, his man still hadn't answered.

'Put the phone away, Todd,' Lisa murmured as she tied his bow tie. She'd been waiting impatiently outside his bathroom door when he emerged from his shower, making that mental image of his hands around her neck refresh with vivid clarity. She brushed non-existent lint from his lapels, then flashed him a brilliant smile. 'It's show time.'

*Sunday, March 16, 8.15 P.M.*

'What is this place?' Sam looked around the nightclub Ruby had all but dragged him into.

'I told you,' Ruby shouted over the music. 'It's called Sheidalin. It's owned by some friends of mine.'

'Hell. If there are drugs going through this place and it gets raided . . . Shit.' Although he wasn't sure why he was worried. A drug charge was nothing compared to murder.

'We're not going to get raided. *Dios*, you're a fraidy-cat.' But she smiled as she said it. 'Thorne runs a clean house. Anyone caught with drugs gets kicked out and isn't allowed back. Relax. Listen to the music and let your brain rest.'

The band was pretty good, he had to admit, and the clientele . . . diverse. Goths and hipsters, aging Deadheads, and a group of bikers. Men and women dressed like bankers and . . .

And other cops. 'Hey. I know him.' Sam pointed to a man sitting at a table alone, nursing a beer and looking like he'd lost his best friend. 'Where do I know him from?'

'That's JD Fitzpatrick,' Ruby said sadly. 'He's Homicide. You heard about the cop that ate his gun this afternoon? JD was there. Tried to stop him. He saw it up close and personal.'

Sam sighed. 'This day has sucked all around, hasn't it?'

Fitzpatrick's posture abruptly changed. He sat up, leaned forward and stared at the stage where a leggy blonde wearing a miniskirt was getting ready to play the strangest-looking violin Sam had ever seen. The crowd had noticed her, too, and conversation stilled for a moment before the place erupted in applause.

And then she started to play. He'd thought it would be wild and rowdy like the number the band had played before, but instead it was sweet. Haunting.

Fitzpatrick had closed his eyes and was listening. Sam did the same, embarrassed when tears pricked at his eyelids. But the music quieted him. He felt less frenzied. Even peaceful.

Sam's eyes flew open at the sound of a chair scraping against the floor. A huge man in a snappy suit sat beside him, eyes focused on the violinist. 'She's good, isn't she?' the guy asked.

Sam looked left, but Ruby was gone. 'Look, I'm here with a friend. I'd better go find her.'

'Ruby will be back,' the man said. 'She went to the office to see the baby.'

'What baby?'

'Her baby.' He pointed at the stage. 'She had a little boy a few months ago. This is her first night back. That's why everyone went so crazy when they realized it was her.'

The violinist finished her piece and blew a kiss into the crowd. The homicide detective blew one back. 'Fitzpatrick's . . . ?' Sam let the question trail. Not his girlfriend, he hoped. Sam hated when men cheated. And he knew the guy's wife. She was the ME who was on maternity leave.

'She's JD's wife.'

'No way. He married the ME. She told me so, the last time I was in the morgue.'

The man next to him said nothing and Sam squinted at the violinist, who'd launched into the next song, this one so full of energy that the dance floor was filled to capacity in a minute. Her hair color might be similar to the ME's and both women were tall, but . . . 'That is *not* Dr Trask.'

'If you say so. Except that she is.' The man extended his hand. 'I'm Thomas Thorne. I own the place with Lucy and Gwyn, one of our friends. Gwyn's in the office, watching Lucy's baby.'

Sam had heard rumors that the ME had a wilder side,

but he'd thought it was just that – rumors. But they were true. He studied Thorne. 'I've heard of you. You're a defense attorney.'

Thorne smiled. 'Guilty as charged. Ruby seemed to think you might need my services.'

Sam closed his eyes, his stomach launching straight into his throat. 'I don't think so.'

'Okay, that's fine. I checked out your record before I came out here. You've got a good one. Ruby thinks you're a nice guy. If you need to ask any legal questions, I'm happy to help.'

'I couldn't afford you. Your shoes cost more than my car.'

Thorne chuckled. 'Ruby's a pal, so for now you can retain me for a dollar. If we go to court, we'll renegotiate. If you can't afford me, I'll find you good representation you can afford.'

'A dollar.' He'd heard Thomas Thorne was a fierce opponent in the courtroom, but Sam had never heard the guy was dirty. 'Hell, what can I lose? Is there a quieter place we can talk?'

'Yeah, come on.'

Sam followed Thorne through the crowd to a small dressing room that at first glance seemed normal enough with clothing hanging from hooks and a changing screen in the corner. But then he blinked. Bullwhips lined the walls, coiled and displayed like trophies. *What the hell?*

Thorne closed the door behind them and it was suddenly, blissfully quiet. Sam exhaled in relief. 'No offense, but that music is not my style. I really liked Dr Trask's first song, though.'

Thorne unfolded two chairs and gestured for him to sit. 'It gets a little loud for me sometimes, too.' He held out a hand, palm up. 'A dollar.'

Sam gave it to him. 'Now what?'

'Now everything you say to me is protected by attorney/client privilege. So tell me a story, Officer.'

*Wight's Landing, Maryland, Sunday, March 16, 8.30 P.M.*

Clay locked the boathouse door and set its alarm. He'd finished his check of the security system, above water and below. Everything was functioning properly as he'd known it would be.

He'd used the systems check as an excuse to get out of his father's house, to clear his mind. To catch his breath. Sitting at that table with Stevie, calmly discussing murderers and plans to catch them – using her as fucking *bait*, for God's sake . . . He would rather be in a combat zone with bullets whizzing past his ears than go through that again.

He headed back to his father's house, his step slow. *I'm tired.* He was simply worn down and couldn't afford to be. Not right now. Not when so much hung in the balance.

He let himself in the gate and was almost at the back door when he heard her voice.

'Clay?'

He stopped, not looking over at the swing where Stevie sat alone. 'Where is Cordelia?'

'She's asleep. I . . . I needed to talk to you.'

'Later. I'm going to sleep, too. Good night.' But he didn't move. Just stood staring at his father's back door. Finally, he sighed. 'What do you want?'

'There's something I need to know. What did I say that made you so angry?'

He hung his head, weary. 'Does it matter?'

'Yes,' she whispered fiercely. 'It matters to me.'

The breath seemed to seep out of him. 'You said you needed to fill your tank.'

'Yes. Because it's been a long time for me. You knew that. Why did it hurt you?'

'Because . . . Hell.' He shoved his fingers through his hair, wishing he could shove the pounding sledge-hammer out of his head. 'Someone advised me that I deserved more than someone just topping off her tank.' *That I deserved forever.*

'Oh.' The little syllable carried almost soundlessly in the night.

'I won't be a scratch for your itch,' he said, the hurt rising up to choke him. 'I don't want you that much. I don't want anyone that much. I'll protect you and Cordelia until this is over. Then I won't bother either of you anymore.'

He went into the kitchen, leaving her sitting there in the dark. He wasn't sure what he would have done had she called him back. Was grateful he didn't find out.

Paige and Grayson sat at the table with Emma and her husband. All four looked up when he came in alone, and he knew they were aware of the ongoing drama between him and Stevie.

No. No longer ongoing. Because it was past. Done. *Yeah, right. You keep telling yourself that if it makes you feel like less of a pathetic loser.*

Paige patted the empty chair next to her. 'Sit. We had another idea for Operation Bait.'

The thought of Stevie as bait made him sick to his stomach, but as he'd told her, he couldn't think of anything better. 'Okay.' He sat down. 'I'm listening.'

'We want the shooter to come for Stevie sooner versus later,' she said. 'Having Stevie simply check into Emma's room won't be enough. We need to be sure whoever broke in once will know to come back.'

'Sooner versus later,' Clay murmured. Because he wanted this done. 'And so?'

'We'll have Emma do a TV interview in "her" hotel room,' Paige said. 'Emma leaves and you and Stevie wait. Shooters come, badda bing, badda boom, you catch them.'

Clay frowned, too many questions swirling in his mind. 'I thought we were keeping Emma and Christopher low key.'

'We are,' Christopher said. 'About our returning to our kids. This would be Emma telling TV land that she'll be a guest lecturer at the university here in Baltimore next week.'

Clay's frown deepened. 'But she's not planning to lecture. Is she?'

'If you catch these shooters before then, then yes,' Emma said. 'I have a colleague who's been asking me to lecture to his psychology class for years. He'll jump at the offer.'

Clay hesitated, unsure how to put what he was thinking into words that wouldn't offend her. Then decided that hurting her feelings was better than risking her life – or Stevie's – on a plan that wouldn't work. 'But . . . I mean, I know you're a big author and all, but would this really be news? Enough to attract enough media exposure to make a difference?'

One corner of Emma's mouth lifted. 'Ordinarily, no. Haven't you seen the news?'

'No. I've been a little busy.'

'Well, your local star reporter, Phin Radcliffe, has dubbed me the "Florence Nightingale of the Harbor House Shooting Spree".'

'You're joking,' Clay said, but could see that she was not. 'Really?'

'Unfortunately, really,' Emma said grimly. '"She's tended wounded hearts for years,"' she quoted, '"but the author of *Bite-Sized* morphed from Dr Phil to Florence Nightingale as she tended wounds of a much bloodier variety."'

'Somebody got video on their phone of Emma giving that dying woman first aid,' Grayson said with disgust, 'and sold it to the media. It went viral in minutes. That video, along with interviews with the restaurant customers and staff, have been top of the news on every channel.'

'The video helped keep me sane,' Christopher confessed. 'I kept playing the video on YouTube, watching her. Reminding myself she wasn't hurt.'

Emma patted his hand, then looked at Clay. 'So, to answer your question, Emma Townsend, the author, wouldn't be enough to grab media attention. But the "Florence Nightingale of the Harbor House Shooting Spree" just might. We won't know until we try.'

'When would you do this interview?' Clay asked.

'Tomorrow, we hope,' Paige said. 'I've got Phin Radcliffe's cell phone number. He's always looking for a scoop.'

'So, assuming you get the media coverage, then what?' Clay asked. 'Details, please.'

'Emma does the interview from her suite at the Peabody Hotel,' Paige said. 'The Peabody's elevator goes straight from the rooms down to the parking garage. When she's done, we smuggle her out, smuggle Stevie in, then Stevie waits for whoever wants to make her into Swiss cheese.'

'I'm staying with Emma until the interview is done,' Christopher stated firmly.

'That's fine,' Paige said. 'We'll take you to the private plane you've chartered afterward.'

Clay nodded. 'I like this plan better than having Stevie check in as Emma wearing a blond wig. She never could have walked through a hotel lobby without her cane and it would have been a dead giveaway.' He winced at his choice of words. 'How will you smuggle Emma out?'

Paige smiled. 'Leave that to me. I have an idea.'

Grayson pushed away from the table. 'You're in trouble now, Emma. I'm going to get some fresh air, then some sleep. Clay, get some rest. You look exhausted.'

Emma and Christopher got to their feet as well. 'I've got to get my beauty sleep,' Emma said, 'if I'm going in front of the camera tomorrow.'

'Sweet dreams.' But Paige didn't look at the couple leaving to go upstairs. She was watching Grayson out on the back porch. 'He's going to talk to Stevie. He's worried about her,' she said softly, then turned to Clay. 'And I'm worried about you.'

'Save it,' he said, more abruptly than he'd planned to, but saw that Paige understood. 'I'm sorry. I'm . . . tired.' *So damn tired.*

'Then, go to sleep, Clay,' she said gently. 'I'll keep watch tonight.'

'Thanks. I'll try.'


*Baltimore, Maryland, Sunday, March 16, 8.55 P.M.*

Thorne leaned back in his chair as Sam finished his story. 'This is quite a mess.'

'I know. I should have come forward then. I didn't think anyone would believe me.'

'Why not?'

'Because my dad had been arrested a lot of times for drug use. Mostly misdemeanors. He had two felonies. One for dealing and one for beating up my mom.'

Thorne's eyes flickered and Sam had the feeling the attorney knew what it had felt like to watch his mother being beaten. 'That was your dad. Were *you* ever in trouble?'

'No. Not really. But the night the cops came, the night they arrested him for beating her up, they had to pull me off him. I came home and he'd almost knocked her unconscious, trying to make her tell him where she'd hidden her grocery money.'

'Anything for a fix,' Thorne murmured. 'The cops saw you restraining your father. So?'

'No. They saw me hitting him. Heard me threatening to kill him if he ever put his hands on her again. A neighbor had called the cops that night. I didn't.'

'Why not?' Thorne asked again.

'Because I'd called before, too many times. Mom always said we'd handle it ourselves. She always told the cops to go away. Some of them knew my dad. He'd been a high school teacher, had taught some of their kids. Hell, he'd even taught a few of the younger cops when they'd been in high school. Nobody wanted to arrest him. They tried to get him to go to rehab.'

'But it didn't work.'

'No.'

'How old were you when the cops caught you hitting him?'

'Fifteen.'

'Old enough to know better, but young enough not to think,' Thorne said quietly. 'Were you written up? Was this officially documented in any way?'

'Not that I know of. Nobody said anything to me about it then, anyway. But cops have long memories. And even if I hadn't done anything that night that I can't remember, the gun I found had been fired and I'd been witnessed to be a hothead.'

'Once. Did you ever beat up anyone else?'

'No, never. But if I got brought up on charges or even investigated by IA, all it would have taken was one cop with a long memory to come forward and my career would have been toast.'

'Possibly. Did your father go to jail the time you beat him after he'd beaten your mom?'

'Only for six months. She was too unconscious to tell the cops to go away,' Sam said bitterly. 'The prosecutor charged him with felony assault. Mom was in the hospital for days.'

'When you woke up in that hotel room, did you consider that you'd shot your father?'

Sam frowned. Tried to be honest. 'Maybe. Maybe that's why I was so scared.'

'You could have had yourself tested for gunshot residue.'

'I'd been to the firing range right before I went to the party. I'd have tested positive.'

Thorne was quiet for a moment. 'How often do you go to the firing range?'

'Once a week at a minimum. Twice if I can work it in.'

'And back then?'

'The same.' Sam lifted his brows. 'You think someone knew I'd been to the range?'

'Possibly.' Thorne studied him carefully. 'You said you checked for crimes committed with a gun that hadn't been found.'

'Over the day and a half I lost, yes,' Sam said. 'And I kept checking for several months afterward. But this body was found in the Severn, a half-mile before it dumps into the bay. That's Anne Arundel County's jurisdiction and their county cops processed it. Nobody claimed the body and there were no markings other than the tattoo. No fingerprints.'

Thorne grimaced. 'Damn fish.'

Sam's stomach went queasy at the thought. 'I didn't think to check other county records.'

'Why would you?' Thorne asked kindly. 'So, Sam, what do you want from me?'

'What should I do? If I turn myself in, I could be charged. But maybe I should be charged.' He shook his head, suddenly weary once more. 'Maybe I did do it.'

Thorne shook his head. 'You will *not* turn yourself in unless I tell you to do so. Are we clear? Good,' he said when Sam nodded. 'What about your friend's wedding? Did you go?'

'No. I woke up Friday morning and the wedding was the next day. I was too rattled to show. But like I told you, he wasn't that close of a friend. I was surprised he'd even invited me.' Sam went still as a memory bubbled up. 'Except, he didn't actually invite me. Not to the wedding. Or, technically, to the party.'

'Who did?'

'His best man, the brother of the bride. He said he was calling Dion's high school friends and teammates. Dion and I were on the wrestling team for a few years. I'd liked him well enough back then, and I thought I should go. But when I heard where it was, I didn't want to. The Rabbit Hole was not a place I would have chosen to go on my own.'

'Did Dion or his best man contact you afterward to find out why you didn't show up?'

'No. I wasn't sure what I'd done that night. I didn't remember the bachelor party, but assumed I'd gotten drunk with *someone*. I figured the guys had eventually shown up. I guess I didn't want to know what I'd done. So I let it go. I haven't seen any of them since.'

Thorne's brows lifted. 'And none of them called to see if you were all right? No one?'

Understanding dawned and Sam let out an unsteady breath. 'No. At the time, I thought that was another nail in my coffin, another indication that I'd done something horrible, that I'd been . . . I don't know, shunned somehow by the group. Now, I'm seeing it differently. What if they never showed up at all? What if there was no party? If not, then the whole thing was a setup and I didn't get drunk. I was drugged. But then I have to ask . . . *why*?'

'*Now* you're asking the right question. You've paid me a retainer, so I'll give you my advice. You can take it or leave it. It's up to you. One more time, because I want to be sure you're listening to me, do *not* turn yourself in. Do not say to *anyone* that "maybe you did it". Once you let that genie out of the bottle, it's a hell of a chore to shove it back in.'

Hope and confidence began to push away Sam's fear and doubt. He got a flash of who he was again. *I'm a cop. Not a killer*. 'You sound like you know this from experience.'

'I've been doing this job a long time. I've seen a lot of innocent men fuck up their lives by being too earnest. Don't be earnest, Sam. Be smart.'

'I will. What do you recommend I do?'

'Start with Dion. Tell him your friend's getting married and that you remembered that he'd gone to the Rabbit Hole for his bachelor party. Ask him what he thought of it.'

'You don't think he'll admit to having a party there.'

'Nope, because I don't think there was a party. After you talk to Dion, go to the Rabbit Hole. Ask who was serving during that period eight years ago. You could get lucky and find a few of the staff have been there for eight years. Maybe they'll remember if there was a party. Maybe they'll even remember you, if something happened that night.'

'I should have done it eight years ago.'

'Yeah, you should have, but you didn't, so now you're

behind the eight ball. Do you know the name of your father's dealer?'

'I never heard him mention his dealer's name. One of his friends might know, but I'd have to ask around and I'm not hopeful. As far as I know, my father didn't have any real friends. Not after the drugs, anyway.' Sam stood up, shook Thorne's hand. 'I'll call Dion tomorrow and then hit the Rabbit Hole before it opens tomorrow night.'

'Good luck. Contact me if you need my help. And, Sam? You can trust Ruby.'

'You think I should ask her to help me?'

'I think she'll get farther at the Rabbit Hole than you will. You look like a cop, even in street clothes. The sight of you will have the people you want to talk to running for cover. Ruby has a way of putting strangers at ease.'

'Good point. Thank you.' Sam found Ruby waiting at their table, drumming those long red nails of hers on the dark wood. She met his eyes uncertainly.

'I hope I did the right thing,' she said. 'In telling Thorne to talk to you, I mean.'

'You did. Thank you. Thorne says I can trust you. Are you up for some adventure?'

Her dark eyes sparkled. 'Always. Lead the way.'

# Chapter Nineteen

*Wight's Landing, Maryland, Monday, March 17, 2.30 A.M.*

Robinette hunkered down among the pines at the edge of Maynard's stepfather's property. His intel had been solid. It was amazing the things people would tell a stranger on Facebook.

There were several Facebook and webpages devoted to Sue Conroy, the mass-murdering woman who'd started her killing spree in Maynard's stepfather's beach house. The owners of those pages, the 'Sue-bees' as they'd dubbed themselves, were a talkative bunch.

They were also truly bat-shit crazy.

But helpful. Posing as a 'Newbie Sue-bee', Robinette had asked the more dedicated souls about the security measures St James had put in place. One of the devotees had gotten too close and tripped the motion sensor at the property's edge. The young man had gladly shared the exact location of the line over which Robinette should not cross. Which, of course, Robinette had not.

The house was dark now. A study through his binoculars revealed no movement in the upper bedrooms. There was an SUV parked diagonally in the gravel drive leading to the house and he could make out a man sitting in the passenger seat and a woman patrolling the house's perimeter. She was well-armed, holding an M-16 as comfortably as most women would a baby, and wore both a flak jacket and a helmet. She'd be hard to kill. *Good to know.*

There were no other vehicles visible around the house. Maynard must have parked whatever he was now driving in his garage. The PI wasn't going to be able to drive that black Escalade anytime soon. The bullet-resistant windows had performed their duty, keeping his bullets away from Mazzetti's and Maynard's heads, but the vehicle had been trashed, nonetheless.

He set up his rifle, balancing it on its tripod, before wriggling to his stomach and testing the sight. He wasn't the marksman Henderson was, but he could make a shot from this distance.

He checked his cell phone again, being careful to cover the screen to keep it from becoming a beacon to anyone who might be watching from the beach house.

He scowled. Still no calls, texts, or emails from Westmoreland. But his scowl turned to a smug smile when he saw the email from the man Lisa had arranged for him to meet at dinner. Dinner conversation had been banal, but the after-dinner chat behind the closed doors of Robinette's study had been decidedly more interesting.

His dinner guest represented a group eyeing a congressional seat that would be opening soon, due to the impending 'retirement' of the sitting congressman whose alleged kickbacks would soon be exposed. The group had wanted to know if Robinette had any skeletons in his closet, other than the suspected murder of his wife, eight years before. They thought they could spin that to their advantage as long as no further allegations would be leveled.

He'd had a damn good reason to kill Mazzetti before,

but he had even more reason now. Before, she might have inadvertently discovered evidence of his crimes while digging into all of those old police reports. If she saw him as a future political power, she'd go digging with the express purpose of ruining his chances for office, and ruining his life.

*Monday, March 17, 4.00 A.M.*

Clay crept down the stairs, trying not to wake anyone, especially his father. He hadn't wanted to answer the questions that had been in his dad's eyes. He definitely hadn't wanted to repeat the words he'd said to Stevie as she'd sat on the swing. *I won't bother you anymore.*

'You're supposed to be sleeping,' Grayson murmured from the sofa, startling him.

Clay shrugged. 'I can't sleep. It was too noisy.'

Grayson's brows went up. 'I don't hear a thing.'

'Emma and Christopher were . . . busy.' The rhythmic creaking of the headboard had been hard to ignore. And made him yearn even more for what he couldn't have.

'I guess I can't blame them. When Christopher finally got here, saw Emma was all right with his own eyes? He cried. So did Emma. Even Paige got all sniffly. Almost put a tear in *my* eye.'

'Almost,' Clay said dryly.

Grayson grinned. 'I only cry at replays of the Ravens winning the Super Bowl. *That* was a beautiful thing. Chris and Emma should finish being busy soon. Go back to sleep. You need it.'

Christopher and Emma had actually stopped rocking their bed over an hour before, but Clay didn't want to admit that to Grayson.

'I can't sleep.' Clay went into the kitchen, heard Grayson follow. 'You want some coffee?'

Grayson slapped a hand on the cabinet door, keeping Clay from the coffee canister. 'No and neither do you. What part of "You are sleep deprived" are you missing, Clay?'

Clay gritted his teeth. 'I'm telling you it's too noisy up there.'

'And *I'm* telling *you* that I don't hear anything. I swear to God I'm ready to knock you out myself, if that's what it'll take to make you rest. Your job is to guard Stevie.' Grayson's jaw was tight. 'I don't want to know what is or is not going on between you. It's not my business. She is my business, though.'

Clay held his temper. 'I know she's your friend. But you need to back off.'

Grayson's hand, still on the cabinet, clenched into a fist. 'Paul was my friend.'

Clay let out a breath, thrown by the sudden change in topic. 'I know. You worked together.'

'We didn't just work together. He was one of my best friends. I was a pallbearer at his funeral. And . . .' He cleared his throat. 'And at Paulie's. I promised Paul I'd take care of Stevie and the kids if anything happened to him. So even if she weren't my friend, which she is, I'd still have a responsibility. If you can't handle this job, I'll hire someone who can. But you're going on two days with no sleep and that's going to dull your reflexes. *So go the fuck to sleep.*'

Clay massaged his neck. 'She's humming, okay? And it was making me crazy.'

Grayson's fist dropped to the countertop, his face creased in a frown. 'What?'

'Cordelia must have had a bad dream, because she's up there humming to her.'

'Humming what?'

'Hell if I know.' Embarrassed, he turned on his heel and went into his father's office.

Grayson didn't take the hint and followed him again. 'Clay, I'm sorry. I know whatever is or isn't happening between you two is hard for you both. If it's too much, there's no shame in backing away. I'll find someone who can be—'

'If you say "be more objective", you'll wish to God you hadn't,' Clay interrupted quietly.

'I was going to say "less affected". But "more objective" works, too. And if you hit me, I'll hit you back. Then Paige will hit us both and we'll really hurt.'

Clay chuckled, his anger dissipating. 'Fine. Make sense, see if I care.' He leaned his head on the shelf over his father's desk, his head throbbing. 'I'll try to sleep. I promise.'

Grayson clapped a hand on Clay's shoulder, briefly squeezed. 'Okay. I'll leave you alone.'

'Wait.' Clay turned, a thought emerging from the fog in his brain. 'Why did Paul Mazzetti ask you to take care of Stevie if something happened to him? Was he expecting trouble?'

'No, nothing specific. I'd had a rough day – trouble outside the courthouse. Nothing like the day in December,' he said quickly. 'No shots were fired. But I'd been un-successful in getting a conviction in a rape case. I was upset and not paying attention. The victim's father was outside, waiting for the defendant to emerge and talk to the reporters. The father had a gun, waved it around. Pointed it at the defendant, pointed it at me, then at himself.'

'Tense.'

'Yeah. One of the cops outside the courthouse came up behind the father and took the gun. The father didn't struggle. He didn't really want to shoot anyone, but that he'd pointed the gun at me left me rattled. Paul was older than I was, had been a prosecutor longer. He and I went out for drinks and he got me calmed down. He admitted he was also scared of retribution. He'd started wearing Kevlar and carrying a gun in his car.'

'Was he wearing Kevlar the day he was killed?'

'Yes. He took the first shot to the chest. Got back up after the shooter killed the cashier. The bastard shot Paul in the head.'

'Was he being threatened?'

'No. He didn't have anything on his plate that had his spidey senses tingling.' Grayson said the words sadly, bitterly. 'We still investigated the possibility. Every case he'd tried, was in the middle of, or was about to try. The most likely suspects had alibis. Then the cops caught the guy who did it. It was some punk with no tie to Paul. Just a guy robbing a convenience store.'

'Did they find the gun?'

'In the guy's sock drawer. He had no alibi. Claimed he'd gotten drunk and woke up in a strange hotel. Nobody could corroborate. Claimed he was innocent, but they all do. After he was in custody, we focused on Stevie. She was pregnant and grieving. Silas Dandridge was a fucking bastard, but he was there for her in a way none of us could be. He was her partner and he kept her going, kept her eating, kept after her to take care of her baby. Then her brother Sorin read Emma's book, met her at a book signing, and introduced them. It was Emma who pulled her out of the depression, gave her the tools to go on.'

'Did you know they'd remained friends?'

'No, not like they have. Stevie's extremely private about a lot of things. So was I, before Paige. There were things in my past I never told my friends or family. Not even Joseph and Stevie. So if she wants to keep parts of her life private, I'm the last person to criticize.'

Clay nodded, considered everything he knew about Stevie and all that he didn't. He focused his attention on the wall where his father had hung pictures of his boat, of the groups he'd taken out on chartered fishing trips. So many smiles.

'Did she ever have another . . . ? Did she go out with . . . ? Never mind. It's not my business.'

'You're asking if she ever had another man in her life. If she did, she kept it secret. But I'm not sure how she would have. Between her job and Cordelia, there wasn't time for a relationship. You're the first one who's gotten under her skin. If that makes you feel any better.'

It didn't. Not really. 'Thanks.' Clay didn't move, didn't turn. Kept his eyes on his father's photos until he heard the sound of Grayson's footsteps fade away. Then he moved to follow. Maybe he'd try to sleep again. Maybe Stevie would have stopped that damn humming. He sighed. Maybe he should let Grayson find someone else to—

Clay froze, his eyes on one of his father's photos. It was the two of them together, on the deck of his boat. His mind whipped back to the video his home security cameras had taken of the second intruder. Mr Backpack. The man had knelt on Clay's bedroom floor, picked up a photo from the debris and stared at it. Then he'd lifted his gaze to . . . what?

To the boat. The model he, Tanner, and Tanner's father had made together, years before. Tanner had bought the *Fiji* with that old boat in mind.

Cocksucker had smashed it into smithereens. But Backpack had recognized the significance. Clay leaned forward until he was inches from his father's photo. *Fuck.*

The name of the boat was partially visible. He thought

he'd gotten rid of everything that could link him to his parents in the event anyone ever broke into his house, like Cocksucker and Backpack had done. But he'd missed this. *Dammit*. How had he missed this?

Could his lapse lead them here?

'Highly unlikely,' Clay said, as if saying it aloud would make it so. But whoever was after Stevie had killed too many people for him to take the chance.

Stevie and Cordelia had to be moved. Now.


*Monday, March 17, 4.35 A.M.*

Stevie lay awake, her head aching. She hadn't slept at all. She'd simply held her sleeping daughter as close as she could without smothering her. Listening to each breath, each murmur as Cordelia dreamed. Stroking her hair and kissing her forehead the one time Cordelia had awoken with a start, her little body going ramrod stiff as she trembled from the terrors of her nightmares.

*I'm here*, Stevie had whispered, now knowing her daughter dreamed of Stevie's death in addition to being held herself at gunpoint by Silas Dandridge the year before.

Then she'd hummed a lullaby she hadn't had the courage to hum when Cordelia was small. She hadn't allowed herself to remember the tune for eight years, not since the last time she tucked Paulie in, kissed him goodnight and turned off the lights.

Never dreaming she'd never have the opportunity to do so again.

The tune had been sung to Stevie by her grandmother in Romania, soothing her when she had bad dreams. It had soothed Paulie as well, sending him into sleep faster than anything else.

401

Tonight . . . the tune had not come easily, the memory of holding her little boy so fresh it might have been yesterday instead of eight years ago. At first she'd had to force the notes from her throat, but it soothed Cordelia just as it had Paulie, so she'd kept humming. Soon her little girl had drifted back into sleep, leaving Stevie far too much time to think.

Of course, her thoughts had turned to Clay who lay asleep on the other side of the wall. *I won't bother you anymore.* His words left her empty. Lonely. Confused.

*Stop thinking about him.* Easier said than done. He'd insinuated himself into her life and now she couldn't imagine him not in it, which was exactly what she'd feared would happen.

*You fraud. This hasn't been about worrying that Cordelia would get attached.* Her daughter already thought Clay hung the moon. *This was about you worrying that* you *would get attached.*

*I'm not just a fraud. I'm a coward.* And her cowardice had broken a good man's heart.

The bedroom door creaked open and Stevie stiffened, going from brooding to instantly alert, gauging how quickly she could get to her weapon and flick off the safety.

'Stevie?' Emma whispered. She was dressed. And wearing body armor. 'Wake up.'

Stevie leaped from the bed and reached for her gun and her cane. 'What is it?'

'We need to go.'

'What's happened? Who's out there?'

'Nobody that we know of, yet. Clay thinks we may have been compromised, so he's making a precautionary move. Sheriff Moore will be here in a minute or two with her boat.'

'We'll be downstairs in a minute or two then.'

'Hurry. I'll meet you in the boat.' Emma clicked her tongue. 'Columbo, come.'

Tanner's big brown dog uncurled itself from the floor next to where Cordelia slept and followed Emma out of the room. The dog hadn't left its post all night long. When Cordelia had woken from her nightmare with a start, Columbo had come to his feet, teeth bared, looking around for something to bite. A stroke of Cordelia's hand over the brown head had calmed the animal and it had returned to the floor to guard them. The animal had calmed Cordelia as well.

Maybe a dog wouldn't be such a bad idea, after all.

Stevie gently shook Cordelia's shoulder. 'Cordelia, wake up.'

'I'm awake, Mama,' Cordelia said tremulously. 'Are you coming with me?'

'I am.' Stevie made herself smile. 'Come on, let's get you dressed.'

Having slept in her sweats, Stevie was ready to go. She helped Cordelia change from her flannel PJs into warm clothes. Hand in hand, they hurried down the stairs to where Clay, Paige, and Grayson waited by the back door. All three wore body armor and helmets.

Stevie wanted to demand to know exactly how compromised they were, because by the look on their faces, the threat was more imminent than Emma had thought – or was willing to let on in front of Cordelia.

Paige wordlessly handed Stevie the flak jacket she'd worn in from the city earlier. Stevie fastened the Velcro tabs, aware of Clay's careful scrutiny. *He's checking for fear. To see if I'm about to lose it.* That told her more than anything else that he believed the threat was very real. Whatever he saw must have pleased him, because he gave her a hard nod.

403

'Emma and Christopher are already in the boat,' Clay told her, then knelt on one knee. 'Cordy, I need you to pay attention.' He guided her arms into a pink vest and zipped it up.

'It's heavy,' she said.

'It's bullet-proof,' he told her. 'Just like mine. Sheriff Moore called all over the state until she found one just your size. Now, Cordelia, you're going to put your arms around my neck and hold tight. I'm going to wrap this belt around us both.'

'Like a baby in a snuggly,' Cordelia said, making Clay smile.

His smile made Stevie's heart stumble. She'd hurt him when they'd been in that bed on his father's boat. Now that she understood what he'd thought, she also understood his reaction.

He'd been wrong, though. She hadn't considered sex with him a mere topping off of her tank. It wouldn't have been a onetime thing. It couldn't have been. She wasn't wired that way. Had she been, there would have been plenty of takers over the past eight years. No, she would have stayed with him, come to depend on him more and more.

But it wouldn't have been the 'forever' that he deserved, so it was probably better to let him stay hurt. Then he'd stay away. Better a little hurt now than a broken heart later.

'Exactly like a baby in a snuggly,' he said. He put a small helmet on Cordelia's head and tightened the strap. 'I don't expect any trouble, but I'm taking no chances.'

'I understand,' Cordelia said solemnly. She looked up at Paige. 'Are you coming, too?'

'Absolutely. I am sticking to you like glue. Your own personal bodyguard.'

'And Peabody? Can he come, too?' Cordelia asked.

'Of course,' Paige said, giving the Rottweiler at her side an affectionate scratch behind his ears. 'He'll stay at the farm.' She gave Stevie a wry smile. 'Because even though the hotel where Emma will do her interview shares his name, it's not so willing to let my Peabody through its doors again. The last time we stayed there, he shed up a storm.'

'I'm glad he's going with us.' Stevie had seen the dog stop grown men in their tracks.

'We're going to take Cordelia out to the boat,' Clay said, 'then I'm coming back for you, Stevie. Be ready at the back gate.'

'And Grayson?' Stevie asked.

'I'm going out with you and Clay,' Grayson said. 'I'll get you into the boat, then join you.'

'And I'll stay here,' Clay said, making Stevie's eyes abruptly widen.

'What?' she demanded. 'You're not coming with us? What if he comes? What if he takes another shot at you?'

Clay's smile was a mere baring of teeth. 'I hope he does. I'll be ready.' His smile gentled into something genuine. 'Are you ready, Cordelia?'

Cordelia straightened her spine, reminding Stevie of herself. 'I'm ready.' She raised her arms to Clay's neck and he strapped her to him. He checked the pistol in his holster, slung a rifle over one shoulder, then jogged from the house without looking back.

Paige gave Stevie an encouraging smile before setting out after them, her own rifle comfortably cradled in her arms.

Stevie and Grayson followed them as far as the back gate, where Tanner stood in the open doorway, jaw tense. Stevie stood next to him, holding her breath as she watched Clay and Paige run across the beach to the dock.

Clay was holding her daughter against him as if she was his own child. The sight was bittersweet – and keenly brought to mind the conversation she'd overheard the morning before.

'Clay has a daughter, too,' she murmured to Tanner, needing to speak because her nerves had her about ready to jump out of her skin.

From the corner of his eye she saw his surprise. 'He told you about her?'

'He told Cordelia. I overheard. Why hasn't he been able to see her?'

Tanner hesitated. 'Ask Clay. I will tell you, though, that it was no fault of his own. All he ever wanted was a family, to be a father to Sienna. But his ex-wife was a . . . difficult woman.'

'You mean she was crazy?'

Tanner's reply was half-cough, half-grunt. 'Ask him yourself.'

'Okay, I will.' But she didn't think she would. She wasn't sure Clay would answer her, for one. But mostly because she didn't want to cause him any more pain than she already had.

*Monday, March 17, 4.40 A.M.*

*Finally.* Robinette's heart was beating hard. Hours of lying in the sand on his belly was finally going to pay off. Two people had already gotten in the boat – the psychologist friend of Mazzetti's and a man he didn't recognize. Mazzetti wouldn't be far behind.

*How clandestine.* Had he been watching from the road, he would have missed them.

Had Westmoreland returned his phone calls, he might

have been able to cover both the road and the house, but it had been over twelve hours since he'd heard from his right-hand man.

Wes was either dead or he'd defected. If it was the first, Robinette would see that his ashes were scattered off the coast of Virginia, where Westmoreland had grown up. If it was the latter, well, Westmoreland's parents still lived in the same house. If they somehow had an accident, Westmoreland would show up. *And then I'll kill him and spread his ashes off the coast of Virginia*. Either way, the outcome would be the same.

Robinette tensed. The gate at the rear of the beach house had opened. Through his rifle scope he could see a big figure running toward the dock. It was Clay Maynard, wearing a helmet and a flak jacket. He was being covered by a tall woman with dark hair, carrying a semi-automatic rifle, a big dog running at her side. Mazzetti was nowhere in sight.

Maynard looked different. Bulkier. Robinette blinked hard to clear his vision and peered through the scope again. Maynard was carrying something.

No, he was carrying some*one*. A small someone. A child. *Stevie Mazzetti's child*.

*Dammit*. Her arms were tight around Maynard's neck, most of her torso enveloped in a pink thermal vest. Maynard was moving *fast*, the woman beside him shielding his body with her own.

Mazzetti would be appearing through the beach house gate any moment. She had to be in the house. She wouldn't let her daughter be separated from her. Would she?

Yeah, he decided quickly. She might. If she worried that her luck could never hold, she might just send her daughter away, to safety. Another second passed. Then another.

*She's not coming.* And Robinette's best leverage was about to be taken away in that boat.

*I can end this, right here, right now. Take down Maynard and he'll fall with the child in his arms. She's swaddled up like a papoose. He won't be able to cut her loose.*

Then Mazzetti would come running.

Maynard's leg was unprotected, so that's where he'd aim. But first he'd have to take out the woman with the dog. She was shielding him too well.

He lined up the sight, aimed at her leg. Squeezed the trigger.

And smiled when she went down.

*Monday, March 17, 4.41 A.M.*

Stevie's heart stopped. 'Oh God,' she whispered. 'Paige is hit. He's out there. Shooting.' *Shooting at Cordelia. And Clay.* '*Cordelia!*' She shoved past Tanner and, ignoring his shouts to stop, barreled through the back.

She was stopped by Grayson who grabbed her around the waist and yanked her off her feet, dragging her back into the shadows within the fence. 'Stevie, *no*.'

'Let me go!' She fought wildly against him, her heart thundering like a herd of stampeding buffalo. A far-away splash made her struggle more desperately and she smacked him with her cane. 'Dammit, Grayson, *let me go*.'

He grabbed her cane and tossed it to the sand, still holding her in place. 'No. That's what he wants. He's trying to make you come out into the open.'

'I don't care.' Stevie was crying, huge sobs that robbed her of breath. 'He wants *me*. Let him have *me*. Not Cordelia or Clay or Paige. Please, let me go.'

Grayson shook her so hard her teeth rattled. 'Stop this

now. Paige was hit. Don't you think I want to go running out there, too? Look. Stop being stupid for a damn second and look.'

He spun her around, still holding her as she struggled to break free. Paige had crawled to the boathouse at the end of the dock where she held her leg with one hand.

She was okay. Hit, but alive. Clay – and Cordelia – were nowhere to be seen.

'Where are they?' Stevie demanded, her heart in her throat. 'I heard a splash.'

'Paige pushed Peabody off the dock to protect him. Don't worry. He can swim.'

She renewed her struggle and he renewed his hold. 'I'm not worried about your damn dog,' she hissed. 'Where are Clay and Cordelia?'

'Clay rolled himself and Cordelia off the dock. Watch.' He handed her the pair of night-vision goggles he wore around his neck. 'Under the dock.'

Squinting, Stevie's mouth fell open in shock. 'Oh my God.'

Clay hung from the dock, holding on to the edge by his fingertips. He moved sideways as if playing on a jungle gym, Cordelia's arms tight around his neck. He was agile, fluid. *Beautiful.* He released his hold on the wood, effortlessly swinging onto the deck of Sheriff Moore's boat where he placed Cordelia into Emma's arms.

Christopher had leaned over the side and was dragging Peabody into the boat.

Then Clay grabbed on to the dock ladder, hoisted himself back up to the dock, and crawled to Paige. He checked her leg, then he pointed to the boat.

Paige half-crawled, half-dragged herself to the end of the dock, gingerly swung over the edge and dropped into the boat. She positioned herself close to the rear, the rifle she'd cradled in her arms now aimed in the direction from which the shots had come.

The boat sped away with a roar of fully throttled engines. Clay rolled to his stomach, the rifle he'd slung over his shoulder aimed at the heavily treed area beyond the beach.

*I should be out there with him*, Stevie thought. *I should be covering Clay.* But here she stood, helpless, escaping hysterics only because Grayson had kept his shit together.

Stevie let out a harsh breath as she took in the damage. The windows of Tanner's boat were shattered and hunks of the dock were gone, mostly at the edges. He'd aimed for Clay's hands as he'd taken her daughter to safety. Still, Clay had maintained his calm. *While I fell apart.*

'I'm sorry,' she murmured to Grayson, ashamed of herself. 'I lost it.'

'I almost did, too,' he admitted. 'When I saw Paige go down . . .'

'Yeah.' Swallowing hard, Stevie turned the night-vision goggles in the direction from which the shots had come. 'I'd shoot at the fucker myself, but my pistol doesn't have the range.'

'Joseph's agents that were out in the front are already in pursuit of the shooter,' Grayson said. 'As soon as Paige got to the boathouse, she radioed them with the shooter's approximate location. I imagine whoever it is will be too busy running for cover to shoot at us anymore.'

'How do you know all that?'

He tapped his ear. 'She was miked. I have an earpiece.'

'You were listening the whole time?'

'Yeah. The first thing out of Paige's mouth was that she was okay, that it was only a graze, and that if I came after her, she'd kick my ass.' His smile was unsteady. 'I was about to risk it when you came running out. It was

410

easier to be brave when I was yelling at you.'

'Glad to be of service.' She retrieved her cane from the sand. 'Sorry I hit you.'

'You should be. That hurt.'

'Paige will kiss it and make it better,' she said wryly and started for the house. She stopped inside the door and gave a very pale Tanner a nod. 'He's all right,' she said and watched the older man's shoulders sag. 'He was pretty amazing, actually.'

'That he is.' Tanner tilted his head. 'What's that sound?'

'My cell phone.' It was vibrating in her pocket. Her heart started to race again when she saw the 727 area code on her caller ID. 'That's Emma.'


*Monday, March 17, 4.45 A.M.*

'Cordelia!' In the claustrophobically small hold of the sheriff's boat, Emma struggled to hold the little girl who thrashed to be free, screaming for her mother. 'It's okay. You're okay. The dog is okay. Your mother is in the house. She's okay, too.'

But Cordelia wasn't to be calmed. She was convinced she'd seen her mother trying to run through the gate. Only one thing would calm her fears.

'Christopher, get my phone out of my pocket. Dial Stevie. Fast.'

'It's ringing.'

'Hold it up to Cordelia's ear.' Emma leaned in so that she could hear, too.

'Emma.' Stevie sounded panicked. 'Is she okay?'

'Mama!' Cordelia wailed.

'Cordelia? Are you all right?'

411

'She's fine,' Emma said firmly. 'You're fine, Cordelia,' she reiterated. 'She's just shaken up, just like the rest of us. Tell her that you're okay, Stevie. She's worried about you.'

'I'm fine, honey. I promise you. I didn't leave the gate. I don't have a scratch on me.'

'You promise?' Cordelia asked, her voice thick with tears.

'I promise. You can ask Tanner if you want to. He's here with me.'

'Mr Maynard. He's not hurt?'

'He's okay. I'll have him call you when he comes in if it'll make you feel safer.'

'It will. Tell him . . . tell him thank you. Tell him I'm sorry I screamed in his ear.'

Stevie chuckled. 'I'm sure he understands, baby.'

'Tell Uncle Grayson that Miss Paige got shot.' Cordelia's lip trembled. 'But she's okay.'

'I'll tell him.'

'We're fine. We're all fine,' Cordelia said firmly, but Emma could see her eyes. There was no conviction. Only a fierce desperation, as if saying it enough times would make it so.

'We are,' Stevie said, just as firmly, but Emma suspected she'd see Cordelia's desperation in Stevie's eyes as well. 'I love you, Cordelia. Call me when you get to Miss Daphne's farm.'

'Love you, too, Mama. Bye.'

'Bye, Stevie,' Emma added. 'I'll see you later if I manage to arrange that interview with the TV news.' She hung up and looked at Christopher who was staring at her oddly. 'What?'

'You like all this excitement. Your cheeks are flushed, your eyes bright. You like danger.'

'"Like" is a strong word.' Emma lifted a brow, remembering how, a few hours earlier, he'd made love to her like it was their first time. 'But it does have certain . . . invigorating aspects.'

Her husband's lips twitched. 'That it does.'

*Monday, March 17, 4.45 A.M.*

Clay ran across the sand, into the back gate where Grayson was anxiously waiting. No more bullets had been fired after the boat sped away and Clay took that to be a good sign.

'Paige's leg is more than a graze,' Clay told him. 'But not life-threatening. Lou's going to have an ambulance waiting at her dock. When we get the all-clear from Joseph's men, I'll drive you to Lou's so you can get your truck and go to the hospital to be with her.'

'And Cordelia?' Stevie asked from the kitchen doorway. 'When do I meet up with her?'

'You don't. Not right now at least. We don't want anyone tailing Cordelia to the farm.'

'But how will she get to the farm?'

'Lou's going to drive them. You might not like Lou, Stevie. But I trust her.'

'All right,' she said quietly. 'That's good enough for me. And after they get there?'

'I'll have coverage. Don't worry.'

'I don't think anything you can say will make me not worry.' Stevie motioned Clay to follow her into the kitchen. 'Where's my dad?'

'Out front, talking to Joseph's agents. Agent Coppola is out there now.'

'I'm going to talk to them, too,' Grayson said tensely, 'to

find out how long they estimate it'll take to give the all-clear. I need to get to the hospital to sit with Paige. She can look a killer in the eye, but hospitals make her panic. You need to stay here, Clay. The adrenaline rush from that acrobat number you did on the dock will crash soon. Like I said before – you need to sleep.' He left through the front door, leaving them alone in the kitchen.

Stevie sat down at the table, held out her hands. 'Let me see.'

Clay frowned down at her. 'See what?'

'Your hands. Let me see.' She grasped his wrists gently, raising his hands and turning them palms up. She winced. 'I thought so. Sit.' She pointed at the table. 'Please.'

Tentatively, Clay obeyed. His hands burned like fire, but it wasn't anything he hadn't experienced before. 'I'm fine, Stevie.'

'Your hands are all chewed up from the dock.' She put a bowl of water and a first aid kit on the table and took the chair next to him. 'This is going to sting a little.'

It stung a lot, but he didn't flinch. Didn't say a word. Because her hands were on his, gentle and efficient as she cleaned the dirt and splinters from his skin. He almost forgot to breathe.

She looked up, her eyes soft. In them, he saw concern and a little gratitude. But there was something more. A cautious . . . acceptance. Or maybe he was just seeing what he wanted to see.

'You knew they'd be out there,' she said quietly. 'How were we compromised?'

'I suspected,' he said, grateful his voice didn't tremble. 'Do you remember when the second intruder picked up my photographs from my bedroom floor?'

'Yes. What did he take?'

'A picture of me and Tanner, on the *Fiji*.'

'He tracked the boat?'

'I realized he'd be able to if he tried.'

She bandaged his fingers, caring for the worst of the cuts. 'Are you hurt anywhere else?'

'No.' He sat still as stone, his hands on the table, palms up. Waiting. Watching as she stared at his hands. Holding his breath as she lightly turned them over, lifted them to her face. She pressed her cheek to his left hand, her lips to the knuckles of his right. His heart pounded mercilessly while he waited for the 'thank you' that would spoil everything.

'I almost folded,' she whispered. 'Almost ran out of the gate and gave myself up.'

His pounding heart skipped a beat. He was able to visualize only too well what would have happened next. 'What stopped you?'

Her lips curved, but there was no mirth in the smile. 'Grayson at first. The man is a tank.'

'And then?'

'You,' she said quietly. 'I watched you, hanging on to the dock. You took care of yourself and my child. And you weren't afraid. So I wasn't, either. Not as much, anyway.'

He wasn't sure if he should admit he'd been terrified, too. Then the decision was taken out of his hands when the front door opened and his dad walked in with Special Agent Deacon Novak. Stevie jumped back like a guilty teenager, but lowered his hands to the table carefully. Maybe even tenderly.

*Don't get your hopes up. She's rattled.* When she saw the light of day, when she and her daughter were finally safe . . . it was likely she'd back away, again.

His father sat next to him, giving Clay's bandaged hands a hard look, as if assuring himself Clay was unhurt in any other way.

415

Deacon Novak turned a kitchen chair around and straddled it, sweeping his leather trenchcoat out of his way with a flair. He wasn't trying to be theatrical, Clay now knew. Deacon was just being Deacon. Clay figured the Fed's blood was equal parts plasma and drama.

'You want the good news or the bad news?' Deacon asked.

'Bad,' Stevie said, studying the Fed with open curiosity. Which was no surprise. Everyone looked twice at Deacon Novak. Although he was barely thirty, his hair was snow white. But it was his eyes that always drew the second look. They were bi-colored, half brown, half blue, split down the middle. Clay still wondered if the man wore contacts.

'Okay, Detective Mazzetti,' Deacon said. 'Bad news is, he got away. By the time I got there, he was gone, but I found several fresh tire prints in the sand. I also found three casings.'

'He shot at least ten times,' Clay said. 'I guess he only had time to pick up so many casings before he ran.'

'You can thank the sheriff's deputy for that. Deputy Pearson pulled over on the shoulder of the main road, just inside your dad's property line, and got to the scene before I did. Seems like your sheriff had you covered by land and sea.'

'I'm not surprised,' Clay said. 'Lou's a good cop.'

'So is Deputy Pearson,' his father added. 'Is she still on the scene?'

'Yep. She'll secure the area until Brodie and CSU get here. You should turn off your motion detectors. Your property is going to be crawling with law enforcement in forty minutes or so.'

'Did you find anything else?' Stevie asked.

'I did. I saved the best for last.' He held up an evidence

416

bag that contained a hair. 'It was snagged on a twig. I caught it with my flashlight beam. The CSU lights may turn up more.'

'Excellent,' Stevie said. 'You'll rush the DNA analysis, right?'

'We've got four dead cops and two dead civilians,' Deacon said grimly. 'We'll rush it.'

'There is another thing,' Tanner said. 'From what Agent Novak told me, the shooter was lying inches away from the motion detector. He knew exactly how far he could come before setting off your alarms, Clay.'

'How would he know that?' Stevie asked.

'Easy.' Tanner shrugged. 'He could have contacted any of the people who've set off the alarm before, trying to get into the house where "Sue got her start". If your shooter knew the location of this property, he knew I owned it. A quick Internet search on my name will bring up the history of this house and the charges I've pressed against trespassers. I'm not well-loved by the followers of the woman who kidnapped Alec Vaughn from this house six years ago.'

'Do you have their names?' Deacon asked.

'Names, addresses, Facebook and Twitter IDs. I created a fake identity for myself so I could watch them online. There are three that are particularly active – and talkative – in the killer's fan club. They're especially active in August. That's when the crimes occurred here. I'll get at least one person every August who tries to find a way in.' Tanner took the notepad Deacon slid across the table, and wrote the three names. 'I don't know how you'd track it, but if you catch the guy and find his computer, you could check it for communication with these three crazy clowns. You might be able to use it as additional evidence against him.'

'Thanks,' Deacon said, his odd eyes filled with respect. 'This is good stuff.'

Stevie was studying Tanner. 'Why do you stay here?' she asked. 'If they try to trespass so often, why don't you move somewhere where you don't have to live so locked down?'

Clay watched his father hesitate, felt his reluctance to answer. Then saw his shoulders sag.

'Because so much of my Nancy is here,' Tanner said quietly. 'She only lived here a few years, but it's all I have left of her. Surely you can understand that.'

Stevie's face became instantly, carefully blank. 'Yes,' she murmured. 'I of all people should be able to understand that.' She stood up, grabbed her cane. 'Now that the excitement has died down, I think I'm going to try to get some sleep. Clay, Cordelia asked that you call her to tell her you're all right. She was worried about you. Call Emma's phone.'

'I'll do that,' Clay said, his heart sinking. She'd already pulled away. She hadn't even needed the light of day. Just a reminder of her dead husband. Who'd always be between them.

*You'd always be second best. You'd come to hate me.* Clay started to wonder if she hadn't been right about that all along.

'I'll meet CSU and show them where to search,' Deacon said. 'We'll keep you informed.'

When everyone left, it was just Clay and his dad. Tanner opened his mouth to say something, then closed it, looking like he felt guilty.

Clay shook his head. 'It's all right, Dad. It wasn't anything you said. Stevie's made it plain that she's not over her husband. I've just got to figure out . . . how to walk away.'

418

How could he, when it killed him just to say the words? He'd have to find a way.

Tanner blew out a breath. 'It's harder than you think, son. You lost your mother and I know you miss her every day. But I lost . . . part of me. The best part. It's hard to come to grips with that.' He stood up, squeezed the back of Clay's neck affectionately. 'Harder than you think,' he repeated softly. He cleared his throat. 'I'm going to check on the pups. Stevie doesn't know it, but I promised one of them to Cordelia.'

Clay's lips curved, in spite of his heavy heart. 'Which one?'

'Mannix. The first one she picked up. He licked her face and that was it. He picked her.'

'That'll stir Stevie up,' Clay warned.

'Good. Get some rest yourself, son. I could drive an SUV into those bags under your eyes.'

It was hard to argue with that. He went up the stairs, pausing at the door to his room, where Stevie slept. He was tempted to knock. Tempted to walk right in and . . .

*And what? Take what she doesn't want to give?* Or what she'd give just to scratch her itch?

Maybe he'd accept, which didn't make him proud. Resolutely he continued to his room, closed the door behind him, and fell into bed. Alone. With Stevie on the other side of the wall.

She wasn't asleep, either. He could hear her moving around. It didn't look like either of them would get any sleep again tonight.

# Chapter Twenty

*Wight's Landing, Maryland, Monday, March 17, 5.20 A.M.*

Stevie heard the squeak of Clay's bedsprings and slowly exhaled, disappointment hitting her like a brick. She'd heard the creak of the floorboards as he'd paused outside her room and she'd hoped . . . What? That he'd burst through the door and carry her to his bed?

She got up and started to pace, not liking her own answer. Because, yeah. That's exactly what she'd hoped. But he really was done with her. She'd seen it in his eyes when his father had not-so-subtly reminded her that she'd also stayed in a dangerous house because it was all she had left of Paul. But Tanner's decision had affected only himself. Stevie's inability to move on had cost her daughter her peace of mind. Had given her nightmares.

She stilled mid-pace. Clay was speaking quietly. She focused, listening. Then smiled sadly. He was talking to Cordelia, telling her that he was 'A-okay', just as he'd promised he'd do.

Clay might have cared about Stevie on some level, but there was no question that he championed Cordelia. Defended her. Protected her. Like Paul would have, had he lived.

If their roles were reversed, what would Paul have done? *If I'd died, would he have gone on?* She didn't know. She rather hoped he would have, hoped her children wouldn't grow up motherless. Hoped Paul wouldn't have been as lonely as she had been over the past eight years.

She knew he wouldn't have forced Cordelia to live in a house that gave her nightmares.

Clay had finished his call. She no longer heard the deep rumble of his voice. She should sleep now. But although she was worn out physically, her mind didn't seem to care.

She pulled her laptop from her backpack. She could work on any number of Silas's cases that she'd hadn't yet re-investigated. But that wasn't at the top of her priority list at the moment.

Instead, she brought up a search engine and typed: 3 BR houses for sale. Izzy would live with them until she married and started a family of her own. *And then I'll be on my own. Alone.*

Stevie looked at the wall separating her from Clay, the yearning in her so strong she could almost taste it. She missed him already.

*So go to him. Tell him how you feel*. But she wasn't sure what she felt, except fear. She felt a lot of that. And lust. She felt a lot of that, too. But lust wasn't enough for him.

It wasn't enough for her either. She'd known that all the times she'd pushed him away.

She'd known it on his father's boat. When she'd told him 'Yes,' she hadn't been agreeing to a onetime thing. She'd been agreeing to far more, which had terrified her. And as usual, her fear had come out as anger. *So go to him, girl. Tell him how you feel.*

She started to rise from the bed, then checked the urge. Clay was important. *Deal with him when your mind is clearer.*

For now, she had a task that she didn't need as clear a mind to tackle.

Her Internet search had brought up hundreds of houses. Methodically she sorted by price, by location. By the kind of place a little girl would want to call home.

*Largo, Maryland, Monday, March 17, 8.10 A.M.*

Dr Sean, the doctor Fletcher had recommended, had finally finished bandaging Henderson's shoulder. 'Looks better already.'

Henderson gave the shoulder a mild roll. 'Feels better, too. I feel better.'

'Amazing what antibiotics and a good night's sleep can accomplish.' Dr Sean dropped the old bandages in a plastic bag and tied the top tightly. 'I assume you'll dispose of these yourself.'

'Yes, thanks. It's better for you not to have proof I was here.' Henderson worried about the bandages left behind at the Key Hotel yesterday morning, but it was too risky to retrieve them. *Besides, Westmoreland probably took them, once he realized I'd escaped by the skin of my teeth.*

The bastard had slashed the tires of the white rental Camry, forcing Henderson to hotwire another car and steal a delivery van. *Fleeing for my life. Betrayed by the very people I trusted.*

There had been no trouble at Sean's clinic at which Fletcher apparently volunteered with frequency. Its main clientele were girls who'd been beaten by either their pimps or johns, followed by drug addicts, and middle class girls who were pregnant and desperate. There had been no sign of Westmoreland, which meant Fletcher hadn't disclosed this hiding place.

Dr Sean sat on a stool, folded his arms across his chest. He was about thirty and still looked like he gave a rat's ass. 'I guess you know that your lifestyle is going to get you killed.'

Henderson focused on pulling on a shirt and buttoning it without straining the new stitches. 'I promise not to leap in front of any more bullets. Cross my heart and hope to die.'

Dr Sean wasn't amused. 'I'm not talking about your occupational hazards. I'm talking about your liver. It's enlarged. You have cirrhosis.'

'Old news, Doc. Started when I was on my first tour. It's flared up because I drank some vodka before I got here. I didn't have any other painkillers and I couldn't stand it any longer.'

'Uh-huh. You and I both know the truth. You've been drinking heavily for some time.'

It was true, but that didn't mean Henderson liked hearing it any better. 'I can stop. I know you hear that all the time, but I really can. I'll just get through this latest injury and I'll stop.'

The doctor rolled his eyes. 'Don't mix alcohol with the pain pills I gave you or you'll do your last tour in the morgue.'

'Yeah, yeah. I've heard it before. Thanks. And if you see Fletch again, pass on my regards.'

Henderson paid the bill with cash from a rapidly dwindling reserve and walked through the waiting room, where the TV was switched to the local morning show. It didn't matter which one. They were all the same. Too much banter and too little of the news that really mattered.

Like which countries weren't in the middle of revolutions. *I need a place to relocate.*

Hand on the waiting room doorknob, Henderson froze.

The announcer had just spoken a name that *mattered*. Henderson's eyes jerked up to the TV set mounted in the corner.

'Join us at five for a special interview as part of our ongoing coverage of this weekend's shootings. Dr Emma Townsend, who's become an internet sensation as the "Florence Nightingale of the Harbor House Shooting Spree", will sit down with our own Phin Radcliffe in an exclusive, live interview. Don't miss it. You'll only catch it here. And now, today's weather.'

*Emma Townsend*. For a brief moment, she'd been dead center in Henderson's scope. *Should've shot her first. Mazzetti would have rushed to her aid, then I could have shot her, too.*

But it hadn't turned out that way. Still, Townsend would know where Mazzetti was. And Mazzetti was the one bargaining chip that could get Robinette to rescind his kill order.

Henderson jogged outside. There were no cameras on the clinic's exterior walls. *I wouldn't have gone inside yesterday if there had been.* A quick look over the cars parked outside revealed the easiest, fastest vehicle to steal – a rusted out pickup truck literally held together with wire.

A minute later Henderson had the engine started and was backing out of the space.

*Shit*. The name stenciled on the concrete was 'Dr Sean'. *I'm stealing the poor guy's wheels.* Well, it was necessary. *I'll contact the doctor's office when I'm through with it so they'll know where to find it. Hell, I'll even fill it up with gas.*

Which was necessary anyway. The doctor's gas gauge was on E. Henderson filled the tank at an out-of-the-way station, then did a quick Internet search for the TV station's address.

*Newport News, Virginia, Monday, March 17, 10.15 A.M.*

Robinette parked a block away from his final destination, already having changed into a pair of painter's coveralls that he'd purchased at a home improvement store. Nobody gave him a second thought as he walked up to the ranch-style home with its wheelchair accessible ramp.

Both of the family cars were in the driveway, a late model Ford and a minivan equipped with a wheelchair lift device. It was exactly like the one Brenda Lee had driven for years, which made sense. Brenda Lee had helped Westmoreland pick it out.

Robinette made one final call to Westmoreland's cell phone. It went straight to voicemail, as had the last ten calls he'd made while driving the length of the Delmarva Peninsula. So it was time to get tough with his former head of security. His former right hand.

Robinette didn't think that Westmoreland had left the country. Robinette wasn't the computer wiz that Wes was, but he did know how to run a check on Wes's credit cards. Neither Michael Westmoreland nor Robert Jones – the name on the passport Westmoreland used when he was distributing Fletcher's special formulas – had purchased an airline ticket.

And if Wes had left the country? *He'll be back soon enough, if only to get his revenge on me.* Once he finished what he'd come here to do, Westmoreland would respond. Robinette was sure of it. *And then I'll deal with him.* Pragmatically, he hesitated to destroy someone who might still be of use to him, but Westmoreland no longer was. In the end Robinette had found Maynard's hiding place on his own. He hadn't needed Westmoreland at all.

What Robinette needed was a damn voodoo priest. He was half tempted to hire one, just to put some curses on Maynard and Mazzetti. Their luck was uncanny. But Maynard's skill . . .

*I wish he worked for me instead of Westmoreland. Where are you hiding, Wes?*

Robinette strolled up to the modest house, toolbox in hand. He did a casual review of the house's perimeter, emptying a bottle of accelerant as he walked. Then he stopped at the meter, and, pretending to read it, attached to the gas line the small explosive device that he'd built from items he'd purchased from the home improvement store and a Radio Shack.

He drove away, waiting until he got several blocks from the house to place a call on his cell to detonate the device. A great boom cracked the air, the resulting fireball a beautiful thing.

*Game over, Wes. It's time to come home.*

Now he needed to get home himself. According to his calendar he had dinner with a city planner at six. If he was late, Brenda Lee would have his hide.

*Wight's Landing, Maryland, Monday, March 17, 11.45 A.M.*

The smell of bacon startled Clay out of sleep. Rolling over, he reached for her – and patted nothing but empty sheets. He'd been dreaming again, of Stevie in his arms, looking up at him like he was the only man on her mind. In her heart. In her body. But it was only a dream.

His back no longer ached, but his cock more than made up for it. It was so hard it hurt. The sweats he'd slept in did nothing to camouflage the fact. That he found the bathroom at the end of the hall steamy, the scent of Stevie's shampoo heavy in the air, made it even worse.

He emerged pissed off and surly. Ready to find whoever had shot at him the night before as fast as possible because he wanted to get away from her. As far as his feet could carry him.

He stopped at his bedroom door, briefly considered changing his sweats for jeans, then decided against it. Let Stevie see what she was giving up. Except his father would be downstairs, too. Muttering curses, Clay yanked on a pair of jeans.

Shirtless and shoeless he went down the stairs, his mind wound way too tight. He didn't like himself this way. Didn't like the tight, about-to-lash-out feeling. He needed to let off some steam. Maybe he'd repair the *Fiji*, take some time off and go fishing with his dad. Or maybe he'd head out west to find his own daughter. To try one more time to get Sienna to listen to him.

Stevie was standing in the living room, staring out of the picture window at the bay, her arms crossed over her chest. She looked perplexed. He must have made a sound on the stairs because her head whipped around and her eyes went wide.

He said nothing, aware that her gaze had dropped. Aware that the jeans were only slightly better than the sweats at hiding his erection. *So what? Let her see what she's kicking to the curb.*

She licked her lips and he felt savagely satisfied. He passed her on his way to the kitchen, still saying nothing.

'Clay,' she whispered behind him. 'Wait. I need to tell you . . . You need to stop. *Clay.*'

He ignored her, hearing her cane thumping as she followed. She grabbed his arm and pulled him back, but it was too late. He pushed open the swinging kitchen door and froze.

His father was in the kitchen with a woman, the two

kissing like teenagers. Tanner gripped a spatula in one hand and the woman's breast in the other. The woman's hand had strayed a good bit lower. For a moment Clay could only stare.

He jerked his eyes up to the woman's face and realized he'd seen her before. Recently. But she'd been dressed differently. She'd been wearing a goddamn scuba diver's dry suit.

*Deputy Nell Pearson*. Who currently had her hand on his father's crotch.

*Nell's okay*, his father had said as they'd stood on the dock the day before. *I checked her out myself*. Clay guessed his father had at that.

Behind him, Stevie sighed. 'I tried to stop you,' she whispered.

There had been no need to change his clothes because he now had absolutely nothing to conceal. Catching his father with another woman was definitely a deflating experience.

And infuriating. The sound that emerged from his throat wasn't close to speech, but it served to get his father's attention. Tanner and the deputy leaped apart, breathing hard.

Tanner closed his eyes. 'Clay. I . . . I didn't know you were there.'

'Obviously,' Clay said tightly. He narrowed his eyes at the woman. 'Deputy.'

In her late forties, Nell was slender and toned where his mother had been plump. Her face unwrinkled and young-looking, unlike his mother's. She was a vibrant blonde, where his mother had embraced her gray. His beautiful mother hadn't minded looking her age. Pearson didn't have to worry about it. *Because she's barely older than I am.*

'What is this?' Clay asked icily when Pearson stared at him, wide-eyed.

Tanner shot him a warning glare. 'Watch your tone, boy,' he snapped. He slid his arm around the deputy protectively, pulling her close to his side. 'It's exactly what it looks like. Nell and I . . .' He looked down at the deputy with a rueful smile. 'What are you, honey?'

'His companion,' she said. 'I've heard so much about you, Clay. I didn't want you to find out about me like this. Your dad and I have gotten close.'

'I can see that,' Clay said coldly.

'Clay,' Stevie murmured. She gave his upper arm a squeeze. 'Take a minute. Please.'

Clay shook her off. He needed to get out. Needed to explode. He headed for the back door, but he could hear the damn thumping of her cane behind him. 'Back off, Stevie,' he growled.

He flew out the back door, needing to run. Needing to burn off this *mad*.

'You're not wearing any shoes,' she called after him. 'You'll get sick or cut your feet.'

He whipped around, saw Stevie standing in the door-way and his temper detonated. 'You are *not* my mother,' he hissed. 'And I don't want you to just be my "friend". You don't want anything more from me than protection and an occasional topping off of your tank, so you do *not* get to pretend you care. Get ready to leave. When I come back, I'm taking you back to the city.'

She opened her mouth to speak, then wisely closed it.

'Good choice,' he said harshly. He got to the back gate when something hit the fence beside him. His shoe. His other shoe hit in the exact same place.

She had a good arm. With that kind of control she could have beaned him, but had chosen to hit the fence instead.

Point taken, he looked over his shoulder.

Stevie held a flak jacket in one hand, a helmet in the other. 'Do what you want,' she said quietly. 'Just don't get shot.' She dropped the jacket and helmet and closed the door behind her.

*Monday, March 17, 12.00 P.M.*

Stevie returned to the kitchen to find Tanner and Deputy Pearson standing arm in arm, looking both shell-shocked and forlorn. For a moment the three of them regarded each other warily.

'Well,' Stevie murmured. 'This is awkward.'

Deputy Pearson looked like she was holding Tanner up. 'Sit down, Tanner,' she said.

'I'm not infirm, Nell. I don't need to sit down,' Tanner snapped, then sighed. 'I'm sorry, honey. I knew he'd be upset. I never guessed he would be like this.'

Pearson ran her hand down his arm. 'Give him time. He'll come around. It was a shock.'

*I'll say*, Stevie muttered in her mind.

Tanner poured himself a cup of coffee. 'I'll sit outside and wait for him to come back.'

The door closed, leaving Stevie alone with the deputy, who turned to the stove and began cooking. 'Are you hungry, Detective?'

'Call me Stevie. And yeah, I'm famished. But you don't have to cook for me. I can microzap something.'

'I cook when I'm nervous or upset,' she said. 'I've cooked a lot the last few days, ever since Tanner told me on Saturday that Clay was on his way with you and your daughter. It worked out, though. Tanner had a houseful of people, so none of what I cooked went to waste.'

'Ah. You made the lasagna we ate last night. And the beef stew we ate the night before. You're a very good cook.'

'Thank you.'

Stevie watched as Nell whisked a bowl full of eggs and poured them in a pan, reminded of Izzy, who honestly enjoyed being in the kitchen. 'Cooking makes me stressed out. Luckily my sister does all the cooking in our house. She lives with us.'

'You're lucky to have someone to take care of your daughter when you're on duty.'

'My sister Izzy is good that way. She makes pancakes with smiley faces to make me less "scowly". She seems to make them more frequently as the years pass,' Stevie added ruefully. 'Do you not have anyone to watch your child when you work?'

'My son is fifteen. He can look after himself now, but Tanner checks on him if I'm going to be really late. I keep a fairly regular schedule in any case. One of the perks of being a small-town deputy. When I worked Special Victims in Boston, my hours were all over the clock.'

'So . . . does Sheriff Moore know about you and Tanner?'

Nell slid a plate of fluffy eggs in front of her. 'No. We've been pretty discreet. Until today. God, what was I thinking?'

'No offense, Deputy, but I ain't touchin' that with a ten foot pole.'

Nell chuckled. 'I don't blame you. And please call me Nell.'

'I will.' Stevie took a bite of the eggs and sighed. 'You really are a damn good cook, Nell.'

'I took lessons, actually.' She brought a large mixing bowl down from one of the upper cabinets. 'My husband was the cook, may he rest in peace. When I lost him, I had to learn to cook or Ben and I would have starved. Ben's old enough to cook for himself now, but he was only four then.' She poured cream in the bowl and set it on the Kitchenaid stand. 'This'll be loud for a minute or two. It's a little more trouble but fresh whipped cream is so much better.'

'On eggs?'

Nell smiled ruefully. 'No. I'm super nervous right now. You're getting pancakes, too.'

Stevie watched her move around the kitchen efficiently, while the cream was whipping. When the mixer stopped, Stevie asked the question that had popped into her head a minute before, not worrying that it might not be appropriate. She felt a camaraderie with the deputy that was unexpected.

Maybe because they'd both lost husbands. Maybe because they were both cops. Maybe because Nell had stood up for Stevie against both her boss and her lover yesterday. 'How did your husband die, Nell?'

'Drunk driver. He went to pick up Ben from soccer practice but never made it. I'd never been on the receiving end of a notification before.'

Stevie thought of the moment she'd looked up, seen Hyatt staring down at her with dread. 'Been there, done that.'

'I know.' Nell measured dry ingredients in another bowl and mixed them by hand. 'When I met Tanner, I was not ready to start dating.' She shot Stevie a self-deprecating grin. 'He kept chipping away at my "No, Tanner", until it became an "Ohhh, Tanner".'

Stevie laughed at Nell's quick and bawdy wit. 'I like you, Deputy. Nell.'

'I like you, too.' Nell looked out the window in the back door and sighed. 'My family doesn't know about him yet. My son suspects of course, but he's not going to ask. At fifteen you don't want to think about your parents having sex lives.'

'At forty-one, either,' Stevie said gently. 'That you're close to Clay's age has to sting.'

'I figured that. I can't help how old I am any more than Tanner can.'

'You love him.'

'I do. He's proposed. I said yes.' Nell laughed a little breathlessly. 'You're the first person I've told.'

'It's an honor. And I won't betray your trust. Can I ask you another question?'

'Of course.' Nell poured the batter she'd mixed onto a griddle.

'Were you scared?'

'Of Tanner? Of intimacy? Of getting hurt again? Yes, to all. I think, though, the thing that scared me the most was screwing it up. My husband and I had been together for a long time. We'd made a child together. He was a good man. Very patient with his cop wife who went off "to the Crusades", as he used to call it. I'd get a victim under my skin and I'd go after justice. I used to think about how blessed I was that I had a man who loved me despite all my failings.'

'I can relate.'

'I thought you might. I finally realized that it wasn't the fear of losing a man again that was making me tell Tanner no. It was the belief that it could never be as good again.'

*Second best*, Stevie thought. 'I can relate to that, too. Your husband had been your soul mate. How can you find that again?'

'That wasn't it, exactly. I kept thinking, when's Tanner gonna figure it out? When's he gonna know what a problem I am, how hard I am to live with? When's he gonna realize that I'm not worth the trouble?'

'Why would he?' Stevie asked with a frown. 'You'd had a good marriage before. Your first husband thought you were worth it.'

Nell turned, holding a plate in her hand. 'But he was a saint. He loved me even though I clearly did not deserve him. You know, all the things you think after they're gone.'

'It's safer to remember the good,' Stevie murmured. 'Especially when it really was good.'

'Exactly. I was going crazy waiting for the shoe to drop. And then I realized that Tanner loved me not in spite of what I was and not despite all the things that needed fixing. But *because* of who I was.'

Stevie stared at her. A piece of the jigsaw puzzle in her mind came crashing down, filling a major hole with a pivotal realization. 'You were afraid you'd fail at a relationship the second time because your husband carried you the first time. He'd done all the work.'

'Yes,' she said quietly. 'But I was wrong. And you are, too.' She put the plate on the table and Stevie let out a ragged breath, her eyes stinging with tears.

It was a smiley-face pancake, just like Izzy liked to make, except it had a cloud of whipped cream for hair. 'Thank you,' she whispered.

Nell shrugged. 'Pancakes are easy.'

But that wasn't what Stevie had meant. 'For the pancake, too. Izzy will love the hair idea.'

Nell squeezed her shoulder. 'I have to go now. I'm on duty soon. Tell Clay I'll catch up with him later.' She took the coffee pot out to refill Tanner's mug and when she returned, her mouth was noticeably plumper, her eyes dreamier. Apparently Tanner could kiss.

Like father, like son.

Stevie waved goodbye and dug into the pancake, torn between the need to go find Clay to make things right between them, and the need to call her sister to do the same.

Looking at the smiley-faced pancake, she thought of the things Izzy did without complaint. Izzy had made them a home. *And I've never really thanked her*. Izzy had helped Stevie raise Cordelia. Her sister had more than earned the right to have a say in Cordelia's welfare.

Stevie had been harsh on Saturday, even as she'd accepted Izzy's apologies. *She shouldn't have deceived me about Cordelia and the horses, but . . .* Izzy had been right.

Stevie needed to apologize for the words she'd said, but she also needed to thank her for all she'd done in the last eight years. Izzy had done what was right for Cordelia, when Stevie hadn't been able to see the problem, much less a solution.

As had Clay. Stevie had different things to make right with him, but identical goals. She'd talk to Clay when he returned. Hopefully he'd be less angry than when he'd left.

For now, she found Tanner's secure home phone and called her sister. 'Hi, Izzy. It's me.'

*Monday, March 17, 1.05 P.M.*

Clay jogged up to the beach house, ignoring the jibes he got from Joseph's agents and CSU teams who were still processing both the patch of sand where the shooter had lain in wait and the dock area where most of the shots had landed. He guessed it wasn't every day they saw a shirtless man running on the beach wearing a flak jacket and a helmet.

And shoes, thanks to Stevie. He'd run some of the sexual frustration out of his system and now felt thoroughly ashamed of himself. He'd lashed out at his father for the very thing he'd been pushing Stevie to do – move past the death of a spouse.

He pushed open the gate and stopped. His father sat on the porch swing alone, sipping from a cup of coffee and looking tired.

'I'm sorry, Dad.' Clay let the gate close with a clang, pulled off the helmet and the jacket and settled on the swing next to Tanner. 'I had no right and I'm so sorry.'

'No problem. I've been trying to tell you all weekend, but every time I had a chance, something seemed to happen to distract me. Or maybe I was looking for excuses.'

'I'm glad you're not lonely. I really am. I've worried about you out here all by yourself. It was just . . . a shock. And I was in a shitty mood to start with. I hope I haven't ruined anything for you and Deputy Pearson.'

'You should call her Nell.'

Clay felt his heart settle. When his father said her name, it was with near reverence. 'I will. Where did you meet her, and when?'

'At a diner. Seems like I am destined to meet women at diners.'

Clay smiled. Tanner had met his mother at the diner at which she'd waited tables.

'Nell was having coffee and so was I. We started to talk and then one thing led to another.' Tanner shrugged. 'There will never be another woman like your mother. But Nell's a good woman. She makes me happy to wake up in the morning again. I hope you'll give her a chance.'

'I will. I promise.' Clay hunched forward, elbows on his knees. 'So, are you going to marry her or something?'

'Hell yeah, I'm going to marry her. She hasn't told her son. We were going to tell you first.'

'Thanks. Now that conversation at the dock makes sense. She wanted you to tell me that their dive was a drill but you and Lou didn't want to. She seemed pretty steamed.'

'She was. But I sweetened her up,' Tanner added smugly.

Clay choked. 'God. I don't want to think about that.' He lifted his gaze to his father's boat and a detail fell into place. 'Well, at least the chocolate condoms make sense now.'

It was Tanner's turn to choke and coffee spewed everywhere. Laughing, Clay pounded his father's back. 'Serves you right, old man.'

'God, Clay.' Tanner wiped his mouth with his sleeve. 'Those were a joke,' he sputtered. 'For Valentine's Day.'

'I'm glad we cleared that up,' Clay said mildly, returning to his hunched position. 'I was going crazy trying to imagine which woman could have left them there.'

'Like you have so many,' Tanner grunted.

'True enough. Right now, you're one up on me.'

Tanner sighed. 'I told you last night, son. It's harder than it seems.'

'I get that. I also feel like a giant hypocrite, mad at you for doing what I tried to get her to do. Except it's been eight years since Paul Mazzetti died.'

'In many ways, for her it's yesterday. She broke your heart once and I'm still mad at her for that. But I can't be too mad. I had to convince Nell, and her husband had been dead for eleven years. I also had to find a neutral place. Somewhere your mother hadn't been. The boat was the perfect place. A little wine, a good meal . . . You gotta charm the ladies, son.'

'I'm not gonna push her, Dad.'

Tanner sighed again. 'That was a long time ago, Clay. And for what it's worth, you didn't push Donna, either. She was mentally disturbed, that girl. *She lied*. Plain and simple. She lied to her parents and she lied to your daughter.'

'I know. But I *was* eighteen and there *was* beer involved.'

'Even so, I know you. You wouldn't push a woman. You just wouldn't. So put that out of your mind. Besides, Stevie's no Donna. Stevie's a little controlling and more than a little terrifying, but she's got a good heart. She'll see you for the good man you are. I know it.'

Clay blew out a breath. 'I have to take Stevie to the city, but I'll be back as soon as I can. I want to take you and Nell out to dinner sometime soon, to start over with her, if she'll let me.'

'She will. She already told me so. Like I said, she's a kind woman.'

Clay turned his head to give his father a sideways look. 'You wouldn't be attracted to any other kind.' He pushed to his feet, picked up the flak jacket and helmet. 'I'm freezing. I'm going inside to warm up and get the SUV packed. I'd prefer it if you didn't stay here. Whoever shot at us last night could come back. Can you stay at Nell's?'

'She already insisted. Even said I could bring Columbo, Lacey, and the puppies. Except I have to sleep on the couch. She wants to keep things G-rated for her son.'

Clay grimaced. 'I can do without the mental images. But I am happy for you, Dad. Really.' But Clay grimaced again when he went into the kitchen, the memory still a bit too vivid. Seeing his father with a woman who wasn't his mother would take some getting used to.

Stevie was sitting at the table, talking on the phone. Her gaze snapped up, searching his face, her shoulders relaxing slightly. 'I have to go,' she said into the phone. 'I'll arrange it and call you back. I love you.' She smiled at the answer, then hung up the phone.

'Who was that?' he asked when she said no more. He'd

felt no jealousy at the three little words she'd uttered, only a familiar yearning. Because there had been no lust or passion in her voice. Simply the warmth of family.

'Izzy. She wants to take my parents up to the farm to be with Cordelia, but doesn't want to risk being followed. I was going to call Grayson and ask him to drive them there.'

'Grayson's already at the farm. He texted me that he took Paige straight there from the ER. Figured it would be safer for her to recuperate there than at their town house.'

Her brow furrowed in a slight frown. 'How bad is Paige's leg?'

'More than a graze, but not enough for in-patient surgery. They had to remove the bullet and did that as out-patient. She's not going to be fully functioning for a few days at the least.'

Mild alarm skittered through Stevie's eyes. 'Then who's guarding Cordelia?'

'Joseph's got two of his agents on the road leading to the farm's private drive. Lou's inside, with Cordelia, Emma, and Christopher. Of course Maggie VanDorn and Alec are there, too. Maggie's pretty handy with a rifle and Alec can hold his own.'

She visibly relaxed. 'How long can Sheriff Moore stay?'

'Not much longer, but don't worry. As soon as I saw Paige's leg, I knew I'd need another guard to take her place. I contacted my friend Ethan Buchanan in Chicago before I went to sleep, asked him to fly out and take over.' He glanced at the clock on the wall. 'He should be landing at BWI in an hour. Tell Izzy that he'll pick her and your parents up on his way to the farm.'

'I'll call her back, thank you.' She held up her cell phone. 'I got a message from Emma. Phin Radcliffe jumped at the chance for an exclusive interview. He'll be at the Peabody

Hotel at four fifteen to check lighting and get things set up. Grayson reserved adjoining rooms on the penthouse level under Emma's name. He'll be waiting to let us in.'

'Then let's get back to the city. The sooner we lay the trap, the sooner we can catch these bastards and get you your life back.' He turned away before he broke down and begged her to share it with him. He was done. Really, truly done. 'Be ready to leave in fifteen minutes,' he said over his shoulder.

*Baltimore, Monday, March 17, 4.00 P.M.*

Sam Hudson sat on a bench outside the police department, staring at the number he'd dialed on his cell phone, and hit send before he could chicken out.

'Charm City Insurance. This is Dion Raines. Can I help you?'

*I sure hope so.* 'Dion, this is Sam Hudson. We went to high school together.'

There was a short pause then, 'Sam, sure. Wrestling team. We went to the state finals.'

'Those were the days,' Sam said with a weak smile. 'I hope this isn't a bad time. I need to ask you a few questions about your bachelor party.'

'My bachelor party? Why would you want to ask about that?'

'It's a long story and I don't want to bore you with it.' He'd almost told the lie that Thomas Thorne had suggested – that he was throwing a party for a friend and wanted info on the Rabbit Hole – but he decided he'd had enough lies and half-truths to last him a lifetime. 'Mainly, can you tell me where you had it?'

'Sure,' Dion said uncertainly. 'We went to a Caps game,

then to a bar near the stadium. Seriously, Sam, why do you want to know?'

Sam shuddered in relief. A Caps game. Not the Rabbit Hole. 'Because I got a phone call a few days before your party from a guy said he was your bride's brother, inviting everyone who'd been on the wrestling team to your party.'

A very long pause. 'My wife doesn't have a brother. Are you in some kind of trouble?'

Another rush of relief, this one followed by a bigger rush of rage. 'No, but someone else might be.' Whoever it was who'd set him up. 'I went to the bar this guy told me to go to, just to give you my best. Something was stolen from me that night.' A day of his life and his peace of mind. *And my father.* Sam had hated the bastard and wasn't sorry he was dead, but he also hated that his mother was grieving. 'It was returned to me recently, anonymously, and I'm trying to track its whereabouts for the last eight years.'

'Wow. That's . . . incredible. I can honestly tell you that I knew nothing about that call. Nobody else told me that they'd gotten a similar call. It's weird that somebody used my bachelor party to steal from you. But, hey, thanks for being willing to come, man. I appreciate it. Makes me wish I had invited you, but I hadn't seen you since high school graduation.'

'It's okay. Congratulations on your marriage. And thanks. At least I know where to start tracking this thief. Take care.' Sam hung up and felt the trembles hit.

Why use Dion Raines, of all people? It was a crazy risk to take, luring him to the Rabbit Hole that way. He could just as easily have called Dion to confirm it back then.

*No*, he remembered. *I wouldn't have.* The party was to have been a surprise. The caller had asked him not to call, not to ruin Dion's surprise.

*I was set up.* But why? And by whom? His father was dead. *Somebody either wanted me to take the blame or . . . what?* There were probably lots of drug dealers who his father owed money to. But they wouldn't have killed him, necessarily. They wouldn't have gotten their money. *And even if they did kill him, why involve me?*

That was the key.

'Hey, Hudson, you okay?'

Sam looked up to find Ruby Gomez standing in front of him, her red nails nowhere to be seen. She was still on the clock. 'Yeah. I think so,' he said. 'What are you doing here?'

'I had to drop off a report to Lieutenant Hyatt. I saw you sitting here, looking about as pale as the bodies I bring into the morgue. Did you call your pal Dion?'

He'd trusted her with the details last night and when he'd asked her to go with him to the Rabbit Hole, she'd instantly agreed. 'Yeah. There was no party there that night and his wife doesn't even have a brother.'

'That's good then. My shift is over in an hour. Where do you want me to meet you?'

'How about my place? I'll text you the address.'

'Fine. I'll meet you there, change into appropriate attire for a visit to the Rabbit Hole.'

Sam winced at the thought of what that attire might be. 'You don't have to do that.'

She grinned. 'I already packed a bag. And yes, I do have to do that if I want them to give me answers they wouldn't give a cop. You'll stay in the car. You're giving off that Jim Friday vibe.' She walked a few paces with a cardboard gait. '"Just the facts, ma'am,"' she mimicked gruffly.

'That's *Joe* Friday,' he said with a chuckle and her grin softened. He suspected she'd known that, but wanted to make him smile. 'Hey, Ruby, why did you hand-deliver the report to Lieutenant Hyatt? Why not email it?'

'It was the autopsy report on Phil Skinner. The one who committed suicide yesterday. Hyatt's out of the loop along with all of BPD. The State cops are running the investigation because an IA cop might be involved. But I've known Hyatt a long time. He's kicking himself that he didn't see that Skinner was an addict. JD is rattled, too – he watched Skinner eat his gun. I wanted to give them a little closure. Skinner's addiction had been going on for a couple years. There wasn't anything they could have done differently.'

'Can't you get into trouble for going around the State investigation?'

'If anyone finds out, probably. Thus the personal touch.'

'You're a nice woman, Ruby,' Sam said quietly.

She smiled at him. 'Thanks. Like I said yesterday, after bringing in dead cops all day, I wanted to help a few live ones. I'll meet you at your place in an hour.'

# Chapter Twenty-One

*Baltimore, Maryland, Monday, March 17, 4.05* P.M.

Henderson sat up straighter in Dr Sean's pickup. Radcliffe, golden boy of the local news, was leaving the TV station and walking with his cameraman to a news van. It was highly unlikely that Radcliffe was going to cover another story. He wouldn't cut it so close.

That meant the interview with Dr Townsend was elsewhere.

Henderson started the truck and followed at a discreet distance. Fifteen minutes later the van pulled into the parking garage under the Peabody Hotel. Snazzy. But lots of cameras.

Pulling an Orioles cap brim low, Henderson lazily drove the perimeter of the garage while the van parked and Radcliffe and his cameraman hauled their equipment to the elevator. When the doors closed, Henderson stopped the truck close enough to see the number display.

*Damn.* They only went to the lobby. The Peabody was favored among celebrities because of their privacy. Guests could use their key to go directly from the garage to their rooms, bypassing the lobby. The TV reporter and his cameraman would need to be escorted to Townsend's room.

Henderson parked the truck, snugged the cap brim lower and took another elevator to the lobby just in time to see Radcliffe and his cameraman escorted into another elevator – by none other than Clay Maynard, Mazzetti's bodyguard.

*Hot damn*. Maybe Mazzetti was here, too. Henderson watched the elevator go all the way up until the display read 'PH'. That made sense. The penthouse offered the tightest security.

Getting into the room would be difficult. Getting Mazzetti out, even harder. *But I don't have a choice*. As long as Robinette was calling the shots, Henderson didn't have a prayer of making it out of the country alive.

*I'll wait until the interview is completed. Then I'll make my move.*

Henderson went to the bar, relieved to find the TV set to the local news. The bartender looked up when Henderson slid onto a barstool.

'Seltzer water, please.' It was time for another one of Dr Sean's painkillers and as much as Henderson wanted a drink, it was true that mixing booze with pills was a very bad plan.

The bartender served the water, while checking the screen. 'I don't normally have it on the news,' he said, 'but with all the craziness this weekend, it's a good idea to stay informed.'

'A very good idea,' Henderson murmured.

A teaser for the interview came on and the bartender perked up. He turned around to look up at the set over the bar. 'Dr Townsend's a guest here in the hotel,' he said. 'Real nice lady. She got here earlier with her husband. The restaurant was closed, but they were starving, so I fed them in here. She was still shaken up, poor thing. She was there at Harbor House on Saturday when the sniper hit, you know. She did CPR on one of the victims.'

'She must be a good person.' Too bad she'd probably have to die. If Henderson went in to get Mazzetti out, there could be no survivors left to talk to the cops.

The bartender leaned close. 'Rumor has it that the woman she was sitting with was the real target. The lady detective.'

'I heard about it. A terrible ordeal for both women. And for the victims, of course.'

'You got that right,' the bartender said. ''Scuse me. I have another customer.'

Henderson got comfortable, planning to stay a while. The bartender was chatty, which was nice. Chatty people tended to give up security details without even realizing it.

The vibration of the cell phone in Henderson's pocket was unexpected and unwelcome. Only Fletcher had the number to the new disposable cell, but the caller ID didn't belong to Robinette's chemist. 'Hello?'

'It's Westmoreland.'

'How did you get this number?' *Fletcher, I'm going to eviscerate you.*

'From Fletch. Listen to me. You're in danger.'

'Duh.' Henderson looked around, expecting to see a gun. 'Where are you?'

'Somewhere over the Pacific.'

Henderson blinked. 'Excuse me?'

'I'm done. I'm out. I'm gone. I wanted you to know you don't have to worry about me. You deserve better than what he did to you.'

'And what do I owe for this treasure trove of information?' Henderson asked sarcastically.

'An IOU, to be collected later.'

Henderson scoffed. 'No way. I know you too well.'

'You don't know shit,' he said tightly. 'My parents' house in Newport News was torched this morning. *He* did it.'

'Oh my God. Were they hurt?'

'No. They were out of town on vacation.'

'That's good. What does it have to do with me?'

'Nothing. Everything. My mother's in a wheelchair. If they'd been home, my dad couldn't have gotten her out.'

'Why did he do that? Did he know you were out, done, gone?'

'Yeah. That's why he did it. I'm texting you an address. There you'll find a "care package".'

'Containing what?' Henderson asked suspiciously.

'Everything you need to . . . eliminate his threats.'

*Ah*. Eliminating Robinette was the IOU. 'Weapons? Cash? Passport?'

'Yes to the first two. Enough of the second to buy the third.'

'Why?' Henderson asked, even more suspiciously.

'Because we want the same thing.'

They might now. They hadn't yesterday when Westmoreland had come to the Key Hotel with an execution in mind. *Mine.*

Henderson moved to a secluded corner. 'Forgive me if I don't believe you, considering you tried to kill me yesterday.'

'I wasn't going to . . . you know. I told Robinette I was worried that you were running around pissed off, and that was true. I also told him that if you'd had intel about the bodyguard, you probably would have chosen a different approach. I was going to help you get away.'

'Then why did you slash my tires?'

'Because I knew you'd run before I had a chance to talk to you.'

447

'And the desk clerk at the Key Hotel? I hear he's significantly less healthy now.' He was, in fact, dead, shot to death during the 'commission of a robbery'.

That tidbit had come from Fletcher, who had completely freaked out over the murder, which was bizarre considering Fletcher's special formula had the potential to kill a lot more than just one pimply-faced hotel clerk.

'You gave the clerk my picture,' Wes said, 'paid him to warn you if I came close. He could ID me. You, too. What else did you expect would happen to him?'

*That, I can buy.* Considering Henderson hadn't intended to leave the young man alive either. 'Fine, whatever. Even if I believed you, which I don't, don't expect me to thank you.'

'I don't want your thanks. I want your skill. My folks are safe for now, but . . . Hold on.' There was a pause. 'I had to move away from a flight attendant. You want blunt, Henderson, fine. He's lost his fucking mind. He doesn't trust any of us and he's doing risky things.'

'Like?'

'Like, did you see that report on the two cops they found dead in Maynard's house?'

'Yeah. I saw it on the news.' The men's necks had been broken. 'I figured it was Robbie. That's his signature move.'

'He wasn't supposed to be there. He'd sent me to Maynard's looking for where he'd stashed Mazzetti, told me to check in with him every hour. I missed a check-in and he came to find me. I'd tripped the alarm in Maynard's on purpose, intending to wait until the PI came home.'

'Following him to the cop,' Henderson murmured. 'Smart.'

'But it didn't work. Robbie showed up after I left, then two cops showed up. He . . .' He trailed off. 'I want to avoid the word. You know what he did. Then he called me, pretending like he knew nothing about it. I told him I hadn't found anything in the PI's house so I'd try accessing his business servers. I didn't, though. I went straight to my folks, sent them on vacation. Did you hear about the incident outside the IA cops' house?'

Henderson had heard about Scott Culp's murder on the radio. 'Maynard and Mazzetti were shot at and a police sniper was wounded. That was him, too? He really has lost it.'

'I know. You may not have family, but he'll find a way to hurt you. We have to stop him.'

'Easy for you to say. You're halfway over the Pacific.' Henderson huffed a frustrated sigh. 'I'll think about it. You'll hear from me if I decide to accept.'

'No need to contact me. I'll know.'

Henderson lowered the phone slowly, stared at the incoming text. It was an address for the 'care package', in Towson, about thirty minutes away. Westmoreland was a clever bastard. *This could be a trap, meant to lure me out.* A quick double-check was in order. Henderson pulled up the phone's browser, typed *Newport News home fire* and waited.

Sure enough, the Westmoreland home had been burned to the ground. Neighbors were stunned, but grateful. The couple had left the night before, bags packed for a long trip. 'And thank God for that,' a neighbor was quoted as saying. 'Mrs Westmoreland was wheelchair-bound. She wouldn't have made it out alive.'

A second text came through. Again from Westmoreland. *Hope you've checked about the fire. Now you know I'm not lying. He's got men watching the airports for you. Wherever you run, he'll find you. You can't get out. You need to take care of him.*

So, no pressure. No pressure at all.

The television set above the bar was suddenly filled

449

with the face of Phin Radcliffe doing a teaser for his five o'clock interview with Emma Townsend.

Mazzetti was close by. *Probably right here in the hotel's penthouse suite.* Henderson could feel it. *So stick with the plan. Mazzetti is the ticket out.* But Westmoreland's 'care package' might help with the plan's execution.

*Monday, March 17, 4.55 P.M.*

Brenda Lee closed Robinette's office door behind her. 'Robbie, are you fucking insane?'

Robinette picked up the Rubik's cube from his desk and gave Brenda Lee a mild look as she wheeled her chair toward him. 'No. I'm perfectly sane. Why?'

'You had dinner with a political star maker last night. You told him you were considering running for office. Why didn't you ask me first? I had to read about it in this morning's paper. And then today you just disappeared. All day. Where were you? I called you repeatedly.'

He decided to ignore her demands regarding his whereabouts. Brenda Lee wasn't the kind to approve of what he'd done to the Westmoreland family home. To the political office question he would reply.

'Lisa set it up. It was a spur-of-the-moment thing.' He tilted his head. 'I don't have to ask your permission. I don't work for you, Brenda Lee. You work for me. Please remember that. Now if there's nothing else . . .'

She blinked at him. 'Don't let the door hit my ass on the way out? That's it?'

'I didn't say it that way, but yes.' He had work to do. His morning adventure hadn't ended as well as he'd hoped. The elder Westmorelands hadn't been home, having left for a last minute vacation, and the scene was being investigated as an arson. Robinette hadn't been going for finesse. He'd been aiming to teach Wes a lesson. But Wes had been a step ahead. Still, it served a purpose. Robinette had known Westmoreland long enough to know that he wouldn't be able to let such an insult to his family stand. He'd come after Robinette for revenge. *I can be patient.*

Now he had to figure out what to do about Stevie Mazzetti. His path to the Westmorelands had also served the purpose of getting him out of Dodge in the way the cops surrounding Tanner St James's house had least suspected. They had searched for him on the Bay Bridge going west back into the city.

Instead, Robinette had gone south, crossing over the Chesapeake through the tunnel in Virginia, avoiding detection. There had been the toll camera, true, but he'd hidden his face as he'd gone through. There would be no recognizable photo.

Still, he had to get to Mazzetti soon. If she was still at that beach house, she'd be on high alert. Not to mention that the place was surrounded by cops – Baltimore, island local, and Fed.

Brenda Lee's voice cut in on his thoughts. She was blinking at him like he'd lost his mind. 'You realize that when you put in your bid for office that your finances are open for review?'

*What?* Oh. She was still upset about his bid for office. 'I considered that. We're clean.'

'Your pharma books are clean. Your little contract manufacturing operation is far from it.'

Robinette frowned at her. 'Fletcher's work is entirely separate. Separate crews, separate storage, and separate accounting.'

'Same production facility. Your other shift managers

451

know the equipment was used during the night. Now they assume it's a legitimate contract manufacturing operation – that you're renting unused capacity to another company that's using it to make medicine. Vaccines, for God's sake. If people start snooping around, they're going to want to see your records. They're going to want to meet this so-called other company. And then what will you do?'

'You'll get rid of them.'

'Me? *Me?*'

'Yes, you, *you*,' he said calmly. 'That's your job, right? To redirect unwanted attention.'

'Yes, of the social elite so they see you as a benefactor. Not of government officials.'

'They're just as malleable as everyone else. More so. They see what they want to see.'

'And what if someone wants to see that you're guilty?' she whispered fiercely.

*Guilty.* The word was like a sledgehammer to his head. 'I'm not guilty,' he said. 'I did not kill my wife.' The words came so easily. He almost believed himself.

She blinked again. 'I never said you did. I never thought you did. I wasn't even talking about that. I'm talking about those little bundles of "peace" you sell to the highest bidder so they can intimidate their neighbors into submission.'

'That's peace, of a fashion,' Robinette said, smoothly.

'That's treason,' she whispered. 'If you get caught, you will be imprisoned. They can give you the death penalty, Robbie. And you'll take the rest of us down with you.'

With Henderson on the run, Westmoreland AWOL, and Fletcher caught in multiple lies, the 'rest of us' constituted only Brenda Lee, and she was clearly getting seriously cold feet. This was not good. A less than confident PR person signaled trouble in the ranks. That would be a bigger beacon for scrutiny than his business affairs could ever be.

Maybe it was time to completely clean house.

But who would he get to replace Brenda Lee? *Calm down and stop thinking crazy. Brenda Lee is still loyal. She's just trying to keep you out of jail.*

'Think about this logically,' he said, still projecting a calm he now did *not* feel. 'As a congressman I'll have access to information that will help us direct our shipments to the most stable of the tribes and will redirect unwanted attention.'

'You're justifying.' She shook her head. 'They will want tax records and employment records. They'll want information you fought to keep out of police hands eight years ago. They will make that information public. It won't take long before some smart nerd figures that you're living a champagne lifestyle on an imported beer budget. They'll know you've got extra income and they'll dig until they find it. You'll ruin us all. What's wrong with the way things are?'

He shrugged. 'I don't know. Maybe I'm bored.'

'*Bored?* You're willing to risk our way of life because you're *bored*?' She closed her eyes, calming herself. 'You don't run for office because you're *bored*.'

'No, you run for office to establish connections that will make you even richer.'

'*No.* You run for office to serve the public.'

She sounded like she really believed that. This was worse than he thought. 'We served the public,' he said bitterly. 'Look where it got us. You're in a chair. You'll never walk again. Where were you when I called you to represent me eight years ago, Brenda Lee?'

She paled at his blunt assessment. 'Unemployed. On food stamps.'

'And your son had to take free lunch at school. You served your country, but you couldn't even buy peanut butter to make a sandwich for your son. And me? I came back without a penny to my name, without a skill I could legally use. We served and we got screwed. It's time for us to get a little payback, don't you think?'

She nodded, firmly. 'Yes. You're right. I've always agreed with you about this.' She lifted her chin. 'What do you want me to do?'

This was the Brenda Lee he trusted. 'I want you to check every aspect of my business and personal life. I want you to make sure there are no loose ends. No skeletons hanging in closets.'

'What about that cop? The one who accused you of killing your wife? The one who killed your son? She might resurrect her lies if she sees you running for office.'

'She won't be a problem.'

Brenda Lee's eyes narrowed. 'What are you going to do?'

He smiled. 'Absolutely nothing. Haven't you been watching the news? She's got dirty cops on her tail because she ratted them out. I won't have to do anything about her. Her own kind are taking care of the problem for me.'

'I've been watching the news. I know she's getting what's coming to her.' Brenda Lee looked at Levi's photo. 'She harassed you over the murder of your wife when you were innocent and then robbed you of your son. I don't care if her hands were lily white on every other case she ever worked, she deserves what's happening to her for what she did to you alone.'

That Mazzetti had robbed him of his son was the true part of the partial truth he'd fed Brenda Lee, that he'd fed the others as well. Levi never would have actually shot anyone. If he'd lived, Levi would have served a reduced sentence or maybe even been put into court-ordered rehab. But Mazzetti killed him in cold blood.

That Mazzetti had harassed him was also true. That Robinette was innocent of the murder of his wife was the lie part of the partial truth. Levi hadn't killed Julie. *I did that.*

None of that Brenda Lee could ever know. He needed her hating the cops. Hating Mazzetti in particular. 'That's my girl,' Robinette said with a smile.

Brenda Lee raised her forefinger. 'But what if I find things in your finances that I can't redirect? If I can show you that it's too dangerous, will you abandon this bid for office?'

'For now. I'll take a pass, tell them I need more time for my charitable affairs. We'll fix whatever loose end you couldn't manage to hide. Then I'll run again the next opportunity I get.'

'That sounds fair.' She put her chair in reverse. 'But do me a favor. Next time Lisa has an idea like that, please tell me first. I can't protect you if you keep me in the dark. And don't forget. You have dinner with—'

'The city planner at six,' he finished. He straightened the tie. He'd come home and gone straight to the shower, washing away any lingering evidence that he'd lain in the sand, shot at a child, and burned down a house, and still had had time for a power nap before dressing for his dinner meeting. 'See? I'm all ready to go. Don't worry. It'll go just great.'

When she'd gone, he opened his laptop to check on the latest Mazzetti news. Listening to a feed from the BPD all the way from Wight's Landing to Virginia and back to Baltimore, he'd heard the details of the massive manhunt in progress. The Bay Bridge at the northern end of the peninsula had been at a standstill all day, the result of a roadblock and car searches. They'd been especially checking black Toyota Sequoias and sand-colored Chevy Tahoes.

They had seen him and Westmoreland, probably via cameras at the PI's house. *But they haven't seen my face.* There had been no physical description other than his height and weight.

Robinette hadn't freaked out, but had been smart enough to take back roads home, returning the Tahoe to his storage facility where it wouldn't be spotted by some nosy security guard. He'd have to find alternate transportation from here on out. A vehicle at least as old as the Tahoe had been. He still didn't want to risk being tracked through GPS.

But other than that, the news was good. The sniper who fired on a Wight's Landing dock – and who was likely responsible for the restaurant shooting – was still at large.

They got that mostly right. Robinette was still at large and he'd directed the restaurant shooting, although he hadn't fired the shots. He wondered where Henderson was. Maybe the bullet Maynard had fired as Henderson had fled the scene had done the job.

Maybe Henderson was dead. The thought cheered him as he scrolled down to read more news, then his finger froze on his track pad. *Well, that's interesting.* Emma Townsend was giving an interview with Phin Radcliffe. Right now.

He switched on the TV and sat back to watch.

*Monday, March 17, 5.05 P.M.*

Sam opened the door to his apartment to Ruby. 'Thanks for coming.'

'Stop thanking me,' she said. 'I told you that this is for me as much as it is for you.' Her eyes settled on the TV. 'Is that the interview with Dr Townsend? I wanted to see that.'

Sam nodded. 'They just got started. The woman's been through a lot the past few days, but she seems to have it together.' He sat down on his sofa and awkwardly motioned her to join him, surprised when she sat on the middle cushion, close to him, instead of taking the other end.

But she didn't seem to be flirting and Sam couldn't figure her out.

'She's classy,' Ruby said, thoughtfully tapping one of those long red nails on her equally red lips, 'or so I was told. One of my colleagues retrieved the waitress who was killed in the restaurant and he heard Dr Townsend talking to the cops and was really impressed.'

Sam found himself watching Ruby as she watched the interview. Her face was relaxed, expressive, engaged. He could simply watch her for hours.

Then the interview was over and Ruby rose. 'Now, where can I change my clothes? We have a skeevy strip joint to crash.'

Sam laughed. Her quicksilver mood changes kept him on his toes. 'End of the hall, on your left.' He watched her walk the length of his hall and bells started ringing in his ears.

Just watching her walk got him hard and overheated. *She is way out of your league, Hudson.* Ruby was a Lamborghini whereas his previous relationships had been with good, solid Chevys. *You'd never make it out of second gear with a woman like that.* He was already about to pop his clutch. He laughed, at himself this time. *Do yourself a favor and stick to what you know.*

He turned back to the news where the anchors were discussing Phin Radcliffe's interview.

'That Mazzetti was the target has been widely accepted,' one of them said. 'According to a source who wishes to remain anonymous, Mazzetti and Dr Townsend have met at that restaurant every year, on the same day. Saturday was a tragic anniversary for the detective.'

'Indeed,' the other anchor said. 'It was the eighth anniversary of the day that her husband, Prosecutor Paul Mazzetti, and her son were murdered in a convenience store robbery.'

Sam slowly came to his feet, staring at the screen. A horrible dread blanketed him and he had to force himself to breathe. *Saturday*. He'd been a cop too long to believe in coincidences.

*Eight years ago, Saturday*. The day he'd lost was most likely the same day his father had been murdered. Definitely it was the same day that Mazzetti's husband had been murdered.

Her husband, the prosecutor. Sam's father, the ex-con junkie.

*And me, out like a light for a day and a half, potentially framed for a crime I didn't commit. The murder of my own father.*

His stomach, already dicey, began to churn. Sam began to pace. Could they be connected?

Had Mazzetti's husband prosecuted Sam's father? No. Sam remembered those trials. Mazzetti was not the name of either prosecutor.

Paul Mazzetti's murderer had been convicted and was serving time. Sam could see the man's mug shot being displayed on the TV screen this very moment.

Then why was John Hudson killed? *Why drug me?* Why leave the gun next to his hand? Why send his father's effects? And why send the matchbook from the Rabbit Hole?

It was as if someone was leaving breadcrumbs for him. Wanting him to discover who really had killed John Hudson.

'Well?' Ruby asked. 'What do you think?'

Sam glanced at her, then did a distracted double take. Her scarlet dress was barely a Band-Aid, her shoes, five inch-stilettos. Her face, sensually exotic. Her black hair was tied back with a filmy red scarf, the ends of which she'd arranged artfully over breasts that were one deep breath from escaping the 'dress'.

'Oh my God,' he whispered. 'You're . . .'

'Sluttily amazing?' she supplied with a grin.

'No.' On any other woman the outfit would be slutty. But on Ruby, it was . . . 'Beautiful.'

She approached, managing to walk smoothly in those skyscraper heels. 'So why do you look like you want to throw up again, *papi*?'

'Ruby, I need to get my hands on the video from a convenience store robbery.'

She blinked. 'Okay. *That* I didn't expect. Which one?'

'The one eight years ago that killed Paul Mazzetti. Eight years ago this past Saturday.'

Her eyes widened. 'The same day you lost? We should go to the police station. Ask them to pull the tape from the evidence storage room.'

'I'd prefer that no one know that it's me who's asking. Not until I know what's what. Let me think.' He frowned when Ruby stepped out on his balcony to make a call on her cell phone.

She returned, pulling his sliding glass door closed. 'I talked to one of my contacts at the newsroom. They have a huge video archive. I asked for videos of every convenience store robbery for the past ten years in which there was a fatality. I told him we're trying to ID a John Doe. It'll take us more time, but no one will know specifically what you're asking for.'

'Thank you.'

'You're welcome. You do realize that they caught the guy that did that robbery, right? He's serving a life sentence.'

'I know, but I also know we've got a string of coincidences and I don't believe in those.'

'Neither do I,' she admitted. 'It'll take the news studio a few hours to pull all of the tapes. Now, are you ready for a little pole dancing?'

Sam shook his head. 'No. But let's go anyway.'

She took his arm. 'You want me to drive?'

'Absolutely no. I'm still a little dizzy from last night. You drive too fast, Ruby.'

She laughed. 'You drive too slow, Sam. You gotta live a little.' Her smile faded. 'You never know when I'll roll you into my morgue.'

He lifted her chin, studied her eyes. In that moment she wasn't a Lamborghini way out of his league, but a woman who saw too much death every single day. 'What if I promise to run the yellow lights? Would that help?'

Her smile returned, but sadder now. 'Yeah. It would.'

*Monday, March 17, 5.25 P.M.*

The interview had gone well, Clay thought from his post at the hotel suite's door. Emma was a natural at this. Probably because she was being herself.

He caught Christopher's eye and gave him a quick nod. Emma's husband was solid. He'd kept calm as they'd carried out their plan. It wasn't easy knowing that your woman was going to be bait. Stevie wasn't even Clay's woman and it was killing him to know she was in the next room, quietly waiting for a gunman to try to kill her.

But Stevie was no sitting duck. Armed to the hilt, she cradled a semi-automatic rifle that he should have given her that morning at his father's beach house. Clay had worried about her ability to walk quickly across the sand while holding an M-16, but if he'd given her a rifle, she might have been able to cover him and Paige on the dock. Which is what she'd quietly told him when he'd unpacked the weapons on their arrival at the hotel.

They'd been the first words she'd spoken to him since they'd left his father's house. On the trip into the city she'd busied herself making phone calls – to her family to tell them to expect Ethan to pick them up, and to Cordelia, to assure herself that her child was all right. From her frequent chuckles at whatever Cordelia said, the child was either fine or making a damn good show of it. Probably a bit of both.

Neither of them had mentioned the incident on the back porch or the words Clay had flung at her. The words he'd flung at his father and Nell. He and his dad were okay. Clay had made things right. But he and Stevie . . .

There was nothing to make right because there was nothing there. Not anymore. There couldn't be. It didn't matter that on the drive into the city, even as she'd made her calls, she'd watched him with a disconcertingly level gaze. She wanted him. That was no secret.

Just not enough. He kept telling himself that so he didn't blurt out a pathetic plea for whatever scraps she was willing to throw him. It was just not enough.

Still Clay worried, because she sat in the adjoining suite waiting for a killer. But at least she wasn't alone. Joseph had agents in the other two suites on this floor and Grayson sat with her, having left Paige at the farm to recuperate when he brought Emma and Christopher into the city.

Ethan was at the farm now and Clay breathed a lot easier. He trusted Grayson and Paige, just as he trusted Joseph Carter. But he knew Ethan Buchanan, had served alongside him in Somalia. They'd risked their lives for each other many times. Ethan would keep Cordelia safe.

'And . . . we're done.' Phin Radcliffe gave his cameraman the signal to stop taping, then turned to Emma with a high-wattage smile. 'That wasn't so painful, was it?'

As they'd expected, Radcliffe had thrown Emma a few curve balls, trying to trick her into revealing Stevie's location. Emma played it perfectly, redirecting him with a nervous smile. Once she even darted her eyes toward the suite's bedroom door, before hastily looking away.

Radcliffe wrapped up the interview, but kept looking at the bedroom door curiously as he and his cameraman packed up their things.

'No, it wasn't painful at all.' Emma rose unsteadily, looking exhausted. 'But if you don't need me anymore, Mr Radcliffe, I'll excuse myself. I haven't slept well the past few nights.'

'Understandable,' Radcliffe said. 'Thank you for your time.'

'Thank you for providing the phone numbers for local grief counselors. You never know who's watching. If one person at the end of their rope reaches out for help, it's worth it.'

She went into the bedroom, opening the door only wide enough to squeeze through – as if hiding the room's existing occupants.

Clay bit back a smile. Emma was very good. He turned to Radcliffe. 'I'll walk you down.'

Radcliffe glanced at Clay before returning his gaze to the bedroom door. 'So you're Dr Townsend's bodyguard now?' he asked casually.

Clay just looked at him, confirming or denying nothing.

Radcliffe half-shrugged. 'I was under the impression that you were Mazzetti's bodyguard. I understand you were with Mazzetti on Saturday when she was shot at in front of her house and again this morning when shots were fired at the house owned by your father.'

Clay opened the suite's door. 'I'll walk you down,' he repeated.

Radcliffe's lips twitched as he shouldered a bag of equipment. 'And of course, I can't help but recall your presence on the courthouse stairs in December,' he said as he walked through the door into the hall. 'I was there, covering the trial. You saved her life then, too.'

'Her surgeon gets the credit for that,' Clay said, punching the down button for the elevator.

Radcliffe kept his eyes on Clay's face. 'I guess I'm surprised you've let Mazzetti out of your sight, under the circumstances. Or maybe you haven't.'

It was exactly what they'd wanted him to assume, but that the man continued to push made Clay mad. He said nothing, allowing his annoyance to break through. Radcliffe's eyes gleamed triumphantly as the elevator doors slid open.

The reporter was still smiling when Clay walked them out of the elevator into the parking garage. 'Thank you, Mr Maynard. I really do appreciate the opportunity to interview Dr Townsend. Please give her and Detective Mazzetti my best when you go back upstairs.'

Clay kept his expression blank, but let anger drip into his tone. 'I advised Dr Townsend not to speak with you,' he lied. 'But she wanted to be sure that people knew about the counseling resources open to them after the events of the weekend. That's important to her.' Which was a hundred percent true – and had enabled her to come off as so damn sincere. That part of her interview had been no act. 'You do realize that your speculations as to Detective Mazzetti's whereabouts could compromise the safety of both women? Their very lives?'

Another half-shrug. 'But that's your job, isn't it? To guarantee their safety? Mine is to report the news, and like it or not, Townsend is news. Mazzetti is even bigger news. So you do your job, Mr Maynard, and I'll do mine. Have a great day.'

Clay felt a twinge of guilt. They'd used Radcliffe and his cameraman to set a trap. It was conceivable that the two could get hurt.

'Radcliffe, be careful. Someone wants to kill Detective Mazzetti. That they'd try to use you to get to her isn't impossible. The police would give you protection if you'd accept it.'

Actually Clay wasn't sure that last part was true. But he needed the men to understand the severity of the threat. He wanted them to be careful.

Radcliffe laughed. 'You want us to allow the cops to tail us? I know you don't like me, Maynard, but do I look stupid to you?'

'Just be careful,' Clay repeated. 'Please.'

# Chapter Twenty-Two

*Baltimore, Maryland, Monday, March 17, 5.25 P.M.*

Robinette switched off his TV with a frown of disgust. That was no interview. That was the baiting of a trap. The cops wanted him to believe Stevie Mazzetti was hiding at the Peabody.

Did they think he was stupid? Stevie was unlikely to be there and the Peabody Hotel would be the *last* place he'd find Cordelia Mazzetti.

The child was the key. Get the child and the mother would follow. He knew the kid wasn't at the Peabody or at that beach house, but he didn't know where she was at the moment. He did, however, know where Cordelia had once been. Or rather Henderson had known.

Scott Culp, his IA mole, had told him that the shooter who'd attempted the drive-by in Stevie's yard had followed Maynard when he'd been driving the kid home.

*I should have let Henderson debrief before I gave Westmoreland the kill order.* Henderson had gone under. Which was good in terms of not leading the cops to Robinette's doorstep, but bad in that it also cut him off from everything that Henderson knew.

Robinette couldn't even track the path Henderson had driven that day. Instead of taking a company car, Henderson had rented a white Camry to throw the cops off the trail because Mazzetti had been shot at the day before by a man in a white Camry. Which Robinette had considered very smart – then. Now, not so much.

But . . . Henderson *had* carried one of the disposable phones that Robinette made available to all his people.

'And that I *can* track,' he said aloud, pleased. Tracking the path that Henderson's phone had taken on Saturday was even better than tracking the path of Henderson's car. Cars could be changed, as Henderson had demonstrated, but people kept cell phones on their persons.

But that would have to wait until after his dinner with the city planner. He had, after all, given Brenda Lee his word that he wouldn't be late.

He wasn't worried. Mazzetti would be waiting for the trap at the Peabody to be sprung, from wherever she hid. Since he had no plans to be mouse to her cheese, she'd wait for a long time.

After all, he thought grimly, no one else seemed to be after her anymore. Since that cop, Tony Rossi, had fallen for the safe house trap, no one else had shot at her. *Nobody but me.*

If Robinette wanted Mazzetti gone – which he definitely did – he'd have to do it himself.


*Monday, March 17, 5.35 P.M.*

'Maynard thought we'd let the cops "protect" us?' the cameraman asked incredulously.

'He's desperate,' Radcliffe said. 'But he might be right. Be careful and we'll be fine.'

Henderson frowned, listening to their conversation from the doctor's truck a row of cars away from the elevator. Chances were they knew which suite was Mazzetti's. They'd tell, one way or another.

'Fine, I'll be careful, but I gotta unwind. You want to go to Milo's?'

Radcliffe shook his head. 'Man, you know how I hate that place.'

'But willing women love it. You've got a pretty face. I need all the help I can get.'

Radcliffe laughed. 'I think I'll pass.'

Henderson rolled up the doctor's truck window, watching the reporter and his cameraman head toward their van. According to her interview, Emma Townsend would be staying at the Peabody through the end of the week and, reading between the lines of that snippet of conversation between Maynard and Radcliffe, Mazzetti was indeed here, in the hotel.

Getting to her would be difficult. Getting her out alive . . . even more so.

A room key was required to access any of the floors above the lobby. That wasn't an issue for any of the floors below the penthouse level. Following a fellow guest into an elevator, then 'searching' one's pockets for the room key usually prompted the other guest to produce theirs to start the elevator. But the penthouse required a special keycard.

The maids would have one. So would a room-service employee. Getting them to give up their keycard wouldn't be too hard. A gun to the head was a reliable incentive to force their compliance. *But I don't have a gun.*

Westmoreland claimed to have left one in his 'care package' which was handy. Getting Mazzetti out alive would require killing anyone with her. Rendering them

467

unconscious was too risky. Unconscious people had a tendency to come to at inconvenient times.

Henderson started the truck's engine, hoping Westmoreland's 'care package' was everything he'd said it would be.

*Monday, March 17, 5.50 P.M.*

Clay let himself back into Emma's hotel room and started to laugh. Emma had been transformed into a ten-year-old boy who glared at him from beneath the brim of a cap bearing the logo of the Washington Capitals hockey team. She wore a jersey over a pair of loose-fitting jeans and the hair peeking out from under the cap was a dirty brown.

'Paige has a mean sense of humor,' she muttered. 'I hope my kids don't hear about this. We're Tampa Bay Lightning Fans.'

'How did you get your hair brown?' Clay asked.

Christopher held up a spray can of temporary dye. 'Paige's getaway disguise.'

'Paige's good, you gotta admit,' Clay said. 'I'd take you for a kid at a glance. If anyone got a close look they might guess, but the luggage cart will keep people from getting in the elevator with us.' They'd loaded up a cart with empty suitcases. 'I'll take you downstairs.'

'No, you stay with Stevie,' Grayson said from the adjoining doorway, now open. 'I'll take them. We've got all of the suites on this floor booked, so no one will bother us on the way to the elevator. Joseph is waiting in the parking garage to take Emma and me to the farm. One of his agents will drive Christopher to meet his plane, then Joseph will come back to this room tonight. He's placed agents in the third and fourth suites, so you'll have backup. You ready, Em?'

'Yes,' Emma grumbled. 'I look stupid. But it is an admittedly effective disguise.'

'Smile,' Christopher said, then took a photo with his phone. 'Blackmail for future favors.'

'You'll pay for that.' She gave Stevie a hard hug. 'I'll look after Cordelia. You stay alive.'

'It's a deal.' Stevie remained in the doorway as Grayson, Emma, and Christopher left, then it was just the two of them. Alone in a hotel room.

And she was watching him in that disconcertingly level way.

Clay cleared his throat, breaking the silence. 'So far, so good.'

'I agree.' Stepping into the adjoining room, she turned off the TV before sitting at the desk where she'd set up her laptop next to the M-16 he'd given her. 'Emma was amazing, as usual.'

He followed her, closing the door behind them and ensuring the door to the hallway was deadbolted. Which it was, because Stevie was a careful woman.

She set her cane against the desk and touched her laptop track pad, bringing up a page full of houses. He crossed the room to look over her shoulder. 'What's this?'

'I'm house-hunting,' she said quietly, not looking at him. 'I didn't understand how living in our house was affecting Cordelia. Now I do. So we're going to move.'

'To where?'

'Don't know yet. But, if you wouldn't mind, I would like you to evaluate whichever house we choose for security. I never want my daughter to feel afraid again.'

*My house is secure.* The words popped into his mind before he could block them. *You could live there. With me.*

*Both of you. We could be a family. And I'm pathetic.*

Except that she'd bandaged his hands early that morning, kissed his skinned knuckles. Pressed his hand against her cheek. And she'd watched him. For an excruciating hour in the SUV between Wight's Landing and Baltimore, she'd watched him.

'Of course I will,' he said. 'What kind of house are you looking at?'

'Single-story houses with big back yards. That way I don't have to fight with the stairs and Cordelia can run and play like a kid should. I'll need a fence around the property. A tall one. Otherwise I won't feel safe letting Cordelia play. I won't be able to get to her fast enough, like I couldn't this morning when she was in danger. Even if Grayson hadn't stopped me, I couldn't have run fast enough.' She closed her eyes briefly. 'And that scares the hell out of me, Clay,' she admitted quietly. 'What if I'm never able to run again?'

A mad Stevie he could handle, but a vulnerable Stevie . . . He sighed, feeling himself getting sucked back in and hating himself for it. 'I know the fear. I was shot when I was in the Marines. Took me a long time to come back.'

'Your Purple Heart?'

'Yes. The bullet hit me right above the knee.'

She turned in the chair to look up at him, her gaze curious. 'You never answered Hyatt yesterday. How did you kill the seven other enemy soldiers that day to save your platoon?'

'Half my platoon,' he corrected. Then shrugged. 'I broke the first guy's neck, stole his knife, gutted the second guy and took back the rifle he'd stolen from me. Then the rest of the enemy went down like dominoes. Any of the others would have done the same.'

'Perhaps. But you did it.' Curiosity became approval and Clay straightened abruptly, needing to take a deep breath before he did something really stupid, like rush her again.

She closed her laptop. 'How did you do come back from being shot?'

'A lot of physical therapy. You've been going, haven't you?'

'Mostly. I've been busy dodging bullets lately. Before that I was diligent, even though it hurt like hell. I wanted to get back to work. Now I just want to be able to protect Cordy.'

'What did your doctor and therapist say?'

'That I should regain most of my strength and range of motion. I haven't, though.'

'It takes months, Stevie. How long since you did your exercises?'

'Almost two weeks. I know what to do, but like I said, I've been a little busy.'

'Two weeks? Your muscles are probably tight as a drum.'

'They are.'

He saw the pain behind her eyes now that he was looking for it. A vulnerable Stevie weakened him. Stevie in pain . . . He sighed again. 'Do you have a pair of shorts with you?'

She gave him a wary look. 'Yes.'

'Put them on. I'll help you with your stretches.' He pointed to her suitcase. 'Go change. We have hours to kill. Might as well do something productive.'

*Monday, March 17, 6.40 P.M.*

Sam straightened in the driver's seat when Ruby emerged from the Rabbit Hole. Several men on their way into the bar stopped in their tracks, their eyes bulging and tongues rolling out like carpets as she walked by. He wanted to gouge their eyes out and cut those slobbering tongues out of their heads, but he sat, outwardly calm as Ruby opened his passenger door and slid in.

'What's wrong?' she asked. 'You look mad.'

'It's nothing. It's fine. What did you find out?'

She arched a brow. 'If you want to know, you have to tell me what "nothing" is.'

He rolled his eyes. 'Just that . . . those men. Watching you like you're steak on a plate.'

'You're right.' She twisted to buckle her seat belt, her breasts threatening to escape. '*They* are nothing.'

'You could have worn a turtleneck,' he grumbled.

She chuckled. 'But then I wouldn't have found out about Kayla.'

He turned to face her, realized her mascara had run, smearing her eyes. 'Were you crying?'

'Oh, yes.'

He started to get out of the car. 'Who touched you? Give me a description. They won't be able to touch anyone for a long time with casts on their hands.'

She grabbed his arm. 'Whoa, there. I cried on purpose. It was part of the act.'

Grudgingly he relaxed, embarrassed by his caveman outburst. 'Sorry.'

'Don't be. It's kind of cute.' She smiled at him. 'And so are you.'

His cheeks heated. He felt twelve years old. 'Fine. So, who is Kayla?'

'If we're lucky, she was the one who was working here that night eight years ago. I went in, told them I wanted to apply for a job.'

'They believed you?'

'No. But they weren't supposed to.' She grinned, delighted. 'They accused me of being a cop. Can you believe it?'

'No,' he said flatly and her grin widened.

'Me either! That's when I turned on the waterworks. I told them I was really trying to find my sister, that she'd disappeared ten years ago. Our mother was dying, and I needed to find her.' She fluttered her hand to her forehead, laying it on thick. 'So that Mama could say goodbye.'

Sam found himself grinning as well. 'And? What did they say?'

'That no woman matching her description worked there, and how could we be sisters if the woman I was searching for was blonde and blue-eyed? I told them we'd all been adopted, that we'd all come from abusive homes.' She sobered abruptly. 'That convinced them. I guess not many of the women they hire to strip come from Beaver Cleaver homes.'

He sobered as well. 'I guess not. So how did you find Kayla?'

'I asked if they kept employment records back eight years. They did and they were all on the computer. They let me check until I found a woman that matched the description of the waitress who'd taken your drink order that night and who'd worked in the club eight years ago.'

'They just let you use their computer?'

'No, not exactly. I showed them a picture of Mother.' She pulled the photo from her cleavage, handed it to Sam.

It was warm from her skin and Sam thought if he'd been

behind the desk in the club, he'd have given her anything she wanted. He forced himself to focus on the photo. The woman was Caucasian, somewhere in her sixties. Thin and sickly. 'Who is she?' he asked curiously.

'My mother,' Ruby said quietly. 'She died last year.'

Sam's gaze flew to hers. *Oh no. Not Ruby.* 'She adopted you,' he murmured.

*We'd all come from abusive homes.* His imagination conjured a dizzying array of scenarios, but he had the feeling that Ruby's truth was worse than anything he imagined.

'She did. So I guess I wasn't acting so much as projecting. Kayla could have been one of my sisters. More of us went right than went wrong, but the ones who fell into the life broke my mother's heart.' She took the photo from his numb fingers. 'It's all right, *papi*. I turned out just fine. My mama went to her grave proud of me.' She cleared her throat. 'And that's huge.'

'Yes, it is.' He studied Ruby from a new perspective. 'Tell me about Kayla.'

'She'd only been working there a month when you came in that night. She lasted a year.'

He sighed. 'So she's dead.'

'No, she quit. When he saw her photo in the personnel file, the owner remembered her. He got real sad. Told me she'd gotten sick. Got "the HIV".'

'Oh God.' Sam clenched his eyes closed for a brief moment. 'I remember thinking I should force her to leave with me. Call her parents and make her go home. Wherever that was.'

'Home's not always the answer. Sometimes home can be worse than this life.' She gestured to the bar. 'And that's a hard truth to swallow.'

'My dad used to beat me,' Sam said softly, 'and he beat my mother. But before he got into the drugs and then later, when he was finally, really gone, it got better. Home was a place I wanted to go. But I was grown by then.'

She grasped his hand tight. 'Then you understand.'

'A bit. I wish I could have done something for that girl, though. She broke my heart.'

'You're a good man, Sam Hudson.' She tilted her head, watching him. 'I checked you out, you know. While I sat outside Starbucks last night, waiting for you to read the autopsy report. You've volunteered with foster kids. Big Brother, Boys' Club. Coaching baseball and soccer. That's why I followed you and why I took you to Thorne. You could have become selfish and mean, but you didn't. I respect what you've made of yourself. I knew Thorne would, too.'

Sam didn't realize how tight his chest was until it began to loosen. 'Thank you, Ruby.'

'You're welcome. I have a last known address on Kayla Richards, on North Patterson Park. Let's see if she still lives there.'

'Wait.' Sam did a quick search on his phone. 'There's a Kayla Richards, who lived on Patterson Park five years ago, but now lives in Bladensburg.'

'Outside DC,' Ruby said. 'You did a background that fast?'

He started the car. 'No, that's just the white pages of the online phone book.'

'Then I'll do a background check while you drive.'

'That'd be good.' He glanced over at her. 'Ruby, do me a favor, would you?' He reached into the back seat and grabbed his jacket. 'Put this on, please. You have to be freezing.'

'I'm quite comfortable, actually.'

He blew out a breath. 'Fine. The truth is, I can't concentrate on driving with you . . . bursting out of that dress. I'm going to wreck my car and we'll never get to Bladensburg.'

She shrugged into his jacket, then turned to him with a sweet smile. 'That's the nicest compliment I've had in a very long time, Sam.'

*Monday, March 17, 6.40 P.M.*

*Oh. My. God.* Stevie lay face down on the bed, unable to move. Clay had been a far worse slave driver than her physical therapist had ever been. She'd taken a hot shower, but her leg still ached. If someone came into her hotel room right now with a gun, she'd have to let them shoot her because she couldn't move.

But she didn't have to worry about that. Clay was armed and had been the entire time he'd pushed her to do her exercises. And the entire time she'd been in the shower.

She'd have been lying if she'd denied wishing he'd barged in and kissed her senseless. But he hadn't. But they had hours yet. *Might as well do something productive.*

'Shit!' Her torso jerked up off the bed when a bag of ice fell on the back of her thigh.

'You gotta ice it down,' he said quietly. He'd said little during the session, touched her even less. She'd hoped he would. Wondered how she would respond. But it was moot. He'd kept his hands to himself.

'Hate ice,' she muttered into the pillow. 'Ice hurts.'

'You want to run again? Then you have to pay the piper.'

'I already did. Too many times.'

'Stop feeling sorry for yourself.' He said it without reproach, instead as a simple truth.

Groaning, she forced herself to sit up. Keeping the ice

on the back of her thigh, she massaged the front. 'If I can't feel sorry for myself, can I hate the little bitch who shot me?'

'Sure. Although you got the final word.'

Because she'd shot the teenaged girl who'd sprayed bullets into the crowd on the courthouse steps. Shot her and killed her. 'I'm not sorry. I'd do it again in a heartbeat.'

'You have a good eye and a steady hand. And you kept your cool.' He sat in a chair, as far from her as he could get and still be in the room. 'You saved Daphne's life, Joseph's, and who knows how many others that day because you took the shot.' Clay looked down at his feet. 'I was proud of you that day. Terrified as hell, but proud.'

Her hands stilled on her thigh. 'Why didn't you tell me?'

'I figured you had to know how I felt.'

'I guess I did. But it's nice to hear.' She resumed massaging her sore thigh muscles. 'I wish Paige was here. She dropped by my house once when I'd just come home from PT and did this thing with pressure points. It was the only time I didn't hurt after a session.'

Clay hadn't moved. She wasn't sure he even breathed, he sat so still. Then his shoulders sagged minutely. 'Lie back and close your eyes.'

She narrowed her eyes at him. 'Why?'

'Paige showed me a few of the acupressure points. I can at least make it so you don't hurt.'

She complied, closing her eyes and holding her breath as she waited.

'Breathe,' he commanded softly as he knelt on the edge of the bed. 'You have to breathe.'

But then his hands were on her left thigh and she forgot to. Keeping her knee straight, he slid his thumbs upward a few inches. She tensed when he applied pressure, breathing only when he'd reminded her to do so once again. He released the pressure, then massaged her quads with strong, confident strokes. She let out a low moan of relief.

'Feels good,' she whispered, her eyes still closed. 'Much better. Thank you.'

Then she tensed in a far different way when his hand swept up her thigh, his touch gentle but firm. His fingertips brushed over the puckered scar left by the teenager's bullet.

'It's not pretty, I know,' she said, wishing her skin was flawless, her muscles whole.

'It's part of you,' he said roughly. 'It means you survived.' His other hand swept up her right leg, up her thigh, then both hands were stroking. His touch changed, no longer firm and clinical, but soft and almost reverential. Almost . . . foreplay.

He lifted her left leg over his shoulder and that fast, he was between her legs. He pushed his shoulder into the back of her thigh, his hand gripping her calf, stretching the muscle with little rocking movements.

'You need to keep the leg straight when you do this,' he said softly and a shiver raced across her heated skin as he pushed harder, his face coming closer to her core each time his shoulder pressed against her thigh. She lifted on her elbows, the sight of his dark head between her thighs intensely intimate. Erotic.

She wanted him. Wanted him closer. Wanted his mouth on her. Her hips shifted, lifting off the bed of their own volition and he froze, his mouth still six inches from where she needed it. It might as well have been six feet.

She heard him draw a deep breath as she held hers. As close as he was, he had to smell her arousal. After a long, long moment, he shuddered and dipped his head closer, until she could feel the moistness of his breath on her skin.

*God, please let this be foreplay.*

She could hear his ragged breathing as his hands moved up, then down her thigh, his thumbs teasing closer and closer with every stroke. Finally she could stand it no longer and her hips arched, bringing her body into contact with those clever thumbs of his – and her nerves exploded. Her head dropped back on a low moan and she shivered again, violently this time.

It was good, but not nearly enough. A water pistol against a forest fire. She burned. Wanted more. Needed more. Needed all of him. Inside her. *Now.*

She lifted her head to look down at him again. His head was still between her legs, his mouth hovering a breath away from where she burned. He looked up, his gaze locking on her face, hot and needy.

*Say yes,* he'd demanded before. She'd obeyed. Now she opened her mouth to say it again.

But he jerked away, leaping to his feet as if she'd electrocuted him. His phone was in his hand a moment later. A second after that, her own phone buzzed, skittering across the nightstand.

Cursing silently, she sat up, reached for her phone. It was a text from Joseph, sent to them both. *We're back. I'm next door. Agents Novak and Coppola are in the other suites.*

She lifted her narrowed eyes from the message to find Clay hightailing it to the bathroom.

'I didn't get to take a shower this morning,' he called over his shoulder, his voice like a rusty hinge. 'I'll take one now that Joseph is back to keep watch.'

Stevie glared at the adjoining door. She knew Joseph was oblivious to what he'd interrupted, but she was glad he was on the other side of the door. Otherwise she would have smacked him with her cane. *Thx*, she texted back. *All quiet here.*

*U up for a game of cards?*

Stevie scowled at the bathroom door. Clay had turned the shower on. He was probably naked by now. *No*, she typed back to Joseph. *Will try to sleep.*

*Like hell I will*, she thought. Grabbing her cane, she pushed herself to her feet. The bathroom door was slightly ajar, so with one finger she pushed it open. Peeking in, her eyes went wide.

Clay stood in the shower, his body visible through the etched glass. He was hunched over, hands flat against the tile, his head up to let the spray hit his body full force.

She crept closer, saw that his eyes were squeezed shut, his jaw clenched. He was fully and gorgeously aroused. She wanted him. *Now.*

She flatted her hand on the shower door, then pulled back abruptly. The glass was ice cold. Belatedly she realized there was no steam in the bathroom.

*Oh, for God's sake. He's taking a cold shower? Really?* Annoyed with the both of them, she pushed the glass door aside and turned off the water. He remained in the same position, turning only his head to look at her, eyes black and piercing.

She drew a deep breath, her body going deliciously liquid. Her eyes slid down his torso, greedily taking in all of him. And there was a lot to take in.

With an effort, she forced her gaze upward to meet his. He looked like he wanted to . . . devour. Her heart was racing, her blood pumping.

'I know what you want,' she said, her voice raspy and guttural. Like a stranger's. 'You want forever. You want a family. I can't promise you forever. I can't promise you tomorrow, because I could be dead.' His eyes flared dangerously and she almost took a step back. But she didn't because she wasn't finished yet. 'I'm sorry that I hurt your feelings yesterday, but you misunderstood. I didn't mean that I was "topping off my tank". To top off a tank, it has to have something in it to start with. My tank is *dry*, Clay. *Bone dry*. I'm as close to being able to top it off as I am to the damn South Pole.'

'What did you mean, then?' he asked, his voice as guttural as her own.

'I meant that I would need a long time before I was full again. Before I felt remotely "normal", whatever the hell that is. I'm like a dried-out sponge. You told me I was scared. Hell, yeah, I was scared. I still am. I'm more scared than I would be if you pointed a gun in my face.'

'Why?'

'Because the gun I know how to handle. This, I don't. What if I can't do this again?'

He eased back from the wall, turning to face her fully, water dripping down every honed muscle of his amazing body. 'Do what, exactly?'

She bit her lower lip, fighting the urge to touch. Clenching her hands at her sides to keep from reaching out to squeeze the erection that strained toward her. *'This*. Us. Sex. A relationship after the sex. I don't know what I'd do if . . .'

'If?'

She swallowed hard. 'If you decided you didn't want me after all. You've put me on this pedestal for two years and it terrifies me. What if I can't live up to that?'

His eyes flickered wildly, as if shocked at the very notion. 'God, Stevie. I—'

She held up a hand, stopping him. 'Let me get this out while I have the courage. I *never* intended to have a one-night stand, to use you and discard you. That you even thought I could do such a thing . . . Well, you don't know me as well as you believe you do.'

'I'm . . . I'm sorry.'

'It's all right. I don't know myself very well lately, either. That's why I was so angry, in the boat. I think I always knew that once I admitted I wanted you, that would be it. I was making a commitment and that scared the shit out of me. When I get scared, my go-to emotion is anger. I know I hurt you. And I'm sorry for that.'

'A commitment,' he repeated, his murmur barely audible. 'But for how long?'

Her shoulders sagged. 'I don't know. I told you, I can't promise you forever. Life happens. Death happens, too. But I would promise to give you everything that I am, for as long as we were together. If that's enough for you, great. If not, I'm just wasting your time.'

He stood there studying her, still as a statue, his face expressionless. And then she knew for sure. She'd waited too long. Hurt him too deeply. Even though his body was still clearly on board, his mind and heart were not. And that was something Stevie understood far too well.

She let out a breath, endeavoring to be as stoic as he. She had no right to temper. No right to tears, although she could feel them rising in her chest. 'I can see you've already come to that conclusion,' she said quietly. She took a towel from the warming rod, placed it in his hands. 'Dry off or you'll catch a cold.'

She turned away, needing space. She wanted to be alone but didn't dare leave the suite. She'd ruin everything they'd planned and maybe even get herself killed. But her throat was burning, her control quickly slipping away. *Just . . . move. Get your ass out of here before you break down and cry.* Because then he'd feel sorry for her and she couldn't bear his pity.

She'd reached the bathroom door when his hand shot over her shoulder, slamming it closed. Trapping her between the door and a very wet, very naked, very aroused man.

Caged in from behind, she closed her eyes on a shiver when his lips skimmed the line of her neck, hovering over her ear. 'It's enough,' he whispered hoarsely. 'If you mean it, it's enough.'

The shiver became a shudder of relief. 'I do. I mean—'

He spun her around, his mouth taking hers, the kiss instantly wild, darkly possessive. Her cane hit the tile with a clatter as she hooked her good arm around his neck and pulled herself higher, trying to situate that erection where it could do some good.

Without breaking the kiss he shoved her shorts down her legs, cupped her butt in the palms of his hands and lifted her off the ground. Supporting her weight with one hand, he plunged two fingers deep inside her.

She bit back a shocked cry as the pleasure ripped through her. 'God.'

'You're wet.' He growled the words. 'I want to eat you alive. But not yet. I need to be inside you. Say—'

'Yes,' she interrupted, her hips desperately seeking. He withdrew his fingers, wrapped her legs around his hips. 'For God's sake, Clay, ye—'

He slammed up into her, entering her with one savage thrust. Then he froze and they stared at each other, lips parted, breath sawing in and out of their lungs.

'Mine.' He ground the word out. 'Tell me you're mine.'

She nodded breathlessly. She felt stretched, filled. Utterly possessed. 'Yours.'

It was like an explosion. She wasn't aware of the fragile

hold he'd had on his control until it snapped. His fingers bit into her thighs as he set a hard, fast, wild rhythm, plunging deeper with every stroke. God, so deep. *So good.* He felt so good.

*This was right.*

Her hands found his shoulders and hung on as she met him thrust for thrust, her eyes focused on his. Until her vision began to blur, her body beginning to tremble.

*Now. Do it now.* 'Clay. Please. Faster.'

With a groan he let go, jackhammering into her, impossibly harder. Impossibly faster. Winding her tighter until she felt like a coiled spring ready to break free.

She heard a low, strangled cry. Knew it was her own. Then heard his feral growl as the first wave hit her, the orgasm riding the line between pleasure and pain. Still he plunged, dragging it out. Dragging her under.

'Again,' he rasped against her ear. 'Come for me again, Stevie. Right now. Let me feel you come again. *Now.*'

She had no choice but to obey, and when the second one hit, her scream was totally silent. She fell back against the door, sated, drained, her hands still clutching his shoulders when his powerful body arched. She forced her eyes to open and could only stare, enthralled.

He was beautiful. His teeth clenched, every muscle strained. And then he began to shake, his body jerking as he found his own release. He stumbled and she felt the full brunt of his weight as he fell against her, smashing her into the door, a deep, primal, desperate groan rattling up from within him. His head rested on her shoulder, his chest heaving as he fought to catch his breath. She held him close, stroking his back, his hair, anything she could reach.

Gradually his breathing evened out and he straightened his legs, supporting his own weight again. Allowing her to draw a full breath. Her heart still pounded and her limbs felt like jelly.

But that barely registered, because within her was this amazing peace.

He lifted his head, met her eyes, and her pounding heart skipped a beat.

He felt it, too. She could see it. But in his dark eyes she also saw awe. Adoration, even. Respect. Everything she'd hoped to see. Everything she'd feared she wouldn't.

He brushed his lips over hers. 'Stefania,' he whispered. 'Finally mine.'

Her eyes stung, filled. Spilled, wetting her cheeks. Some of it was the crash after the adrenaline rush, more intense than she'd had in years. Maybe ever.

But mostly it was relief. It was hearing her given name in his velvet voice. It was feeling cherished again. The sex had been mind-blowing. The look on his face . . . made it perfect.

He let her legs slide down his until her feet touched the floor. One arm around her waist, he wiped at her tears with his free hand, his forehead creased by a panicked frown. 'I was too rough. I hurt you. God, Stevie, I'm sorry.'

She pressed her fingers to his lips. 'No. I'm fine. Nothing's wrong. Everything's right.'

He blew out a breath. 'Good.' He studied her for a moment, his eyes narrowing. 'Wait. You thought I'd be disappointed?' he asked incredulously. 'Really?'

He'd understood. Why did this continue to surprise her? She nodded. 'I guess I did.'

'But now you know I'm not.'

She nodded again, her lips turning up in a small smile. 'I think that was pretty clear.'

'I should hope so,' he said mildly. He eased her arms from the sleeves of her T-shirt, pulling it over her head as if she were a child. He peeled back the edge of her bandage, checked her stitches, nodding when he found them intact. Then he startled her by scooping her up into his arms and stepping into the shower. He wrapped a hand towel around her bandage. 'Keep your arm out of the spray,' he said and turned the water back on. 'Warm, this time.'

'I should hope so,' she echoed, then lifted her brows. 'But I already had a shower.'

'One can never be too clean. Especially for what I have in mind.'

Another delicious shiver pebbled her skin. 'You mean we're not done?' she teased.

His eyes glittered. 'Not even close.'

*Towson, Maryland, Monday, March 17, 8.50 P.M.*

This wasn't a 'care package', Henderson thought, turning in a slow circle. This was a goddamn bunker. Westmoreland had food supplies for months. Medicine, bandages.

Fletcher didn't know about this, of that Henderson was certain. *Otherwise, the doc would have had the supplies to treat me at the Key Hotel on Saturday night.* There would have been no need to risk exposure at Dr Sean's free clinic.

Westmoreland had always been the most private member of their group. Still. *Wow.* This place had everything.

Knives, nun chucks, and boxes of ammo of at least three different calibers, but oddly, only one gun. The nine mil Sig had been cleaned recently, the serial number filed off long ago. That it had a silencer was a plus.

There was a tub on one of the shelves that said 'Ether'. It proved to have not only ether, but also fentanyl and ketamine. All very useful knock-out drugs. Another tub held syringes. Another, stacks of cash in small bills.

*Westmoreland, you have got to be the most organized hoarder I've ever known.* Henderson searched every shelf, marveling at this treasure trove.

And then the tub of a different color caught Henderson's eye. It was bright blue where the rest of the tubs were all the same basic green. Inside . . . Henderson's throat caught. *My stuff.* It wasn't a lot of stuff, but it was better than nothing.

Westmoreland had set the fire that burned down Henderson's entire apartment building. *He must have retrieved my stuff first. At least he knew I wasn't home.* Unlike Robinette's attempt to kill Wes's parents.

Henderson's eyes stung at the sight of the family photo that had hung on the apartment's living room wall. Everyone in the photo was gone now. *Except me.*

Wes had set the fire, but had saved a few treasures. *Sweet.*

At the bottom of the tub was an item that made Henderson's heart beat faster. A silver flask, a gift given three years ago by Westmoreland, Fletcher, and Brenda Lee – on the day of Henderson's fifth anniversary with the company.

Henderson twisted off the top and sniffed. Then smiled. It was still filled with the brandy it had come with. Well, technically not the exact brandy. That was gone long ago. Henderson just kept refilling it and nobody would have been the wiser, if anyone had thought to check.

*Just a taste.* The first swallow brought a relieved sigh. *So good.* The next swallow was as good as the first. It was four swallows later before realization set in. *You're going to get drunk.*

*Stop drinking and get to work.* Filling a bag with Westmoreland's supplies didn't take long at all. *Now I'm ready to take Mazzetti down.*

*No, not yet.* There was still the matter of getting Mazzetti's exact room number. If Henderson hit the wrong room, a victim could send up an alarm. At a minimum it meant killing any witnesses. And that tended to get messy if there were too many.

*Milo's Venus, here I come.* At the bar waited a cameraman whose sole goal was to get laid. *Buddy, it's your lucky night. Or at least it will be until I kill you.*

# Chapter Twenty-Three

*Baltimore, Maryland, Monday, March 17, 8.55 P.M.*

Clay stared up at the hotel bedroom's ceiling, sated. Completely blissed out.

He should sleep so that he'd be alert to stand watch, but he didn't want to. A piece of him worried that he'd wake to find none of this had really happened. That he hadn't just had the best sex of his life. Twice. Or that he didn't hold Stevie Mazzetti in his arms. But he had. And he did.

The second time they'd actually made it to the bed, and, though he'd wanted to conveniently 'forget', they'd remembered to use protection. He'd honestly forgotten the first time, but who could blame him? To his credit, it was he who'd remembered the second time, watching her eyes widen as she'd counted the days, murmuring that they were probably okay.

But her words hadn't been accompanied by relief. Instead her eyes had filled with a dark yearning that rekindled his hopes for the family he wanted – with her.

Then she'd taken the condom out of his hand, rolling it

down his cock with an agonizing deliberation that made him forget his plans to go slow. He hadn't scraped the surface of what he wanted to do to her. With her. For her. Warm and fragrant, she curled into him now, her head on his chest, her legs intertwined with his. Her fingers gently toying with the hair on his chest.

He was happy. And he couldn't remember when he'd ever felt this way. He kissed the top of her head. 'What changed your mind?' he murmured. 'About me?'

Her fingers paused in their petting. 'I don't think I changed my mind as much as I saw things more clearly. I think I always knew. I was just too scared to admit it.'

'Then what made you un-scared?'

He felt her smile against his skin. 'Your daddy's new girlfriend. She's a very nice woman, Clay. You should get to know her better.'

'I already told my dad I would. I was wrong. He deserves to be happy.'

'I know. So does she. Apparently Tanner had to do some serious wooing because Nell wanted them to be just friends.'

'He said as much. The wooing part. Said he charmed her into changing her mind.'

She laughed softly. 'Charm, manipulation. Potato, po-tah-to.' She sobered. 'What made her change her mind was that she finally realized she was afraid to fail.'

'Fail who? My dad?'

'More like a fail *what*. She was married to a good man. She said she was afraid she'd fail in any other relationship.'

He frowned. 'Because he'd been the best and no one else would be as good as he'd been?'

'No. Because he'd been better than she. The better partner. The better person.'

Clarity hit him like a brick. 'Oh. And she was just a

hanger-on, lucky to have had the ride.'

'Sounds silly when you hear it said out loud,' she murmured. 'But it's true. I thought I was afraid I'd mess it up with you, because I was afraid to open myself up again.'

'That's what I thought the problem was.'

'And it was, partially, because loving and losing might be better than never loving at all, but it totally sucks ass.' She squared her shoulders. 'I told myself I was afraid of hurting you, because you'd never be good enough.'

'Second best,' he said quietly and she cringed.

'I was trying to scare you away.'

He cupped her jaw, fanning his thumb across her cheek. 'I figured that out myself.'

'I know, but I hate that I hurt you. Now I realize the real issue was that I was afraid *I'd* never be good enough. That *I'd* be second best. And I hate to fail.'

'Really?' he deadpanned. 'That comes as a total shock.'

'I'm serious.'

'So am I. More serious than I've ever been in my life. Because *this*, Stevie, whatever it is we have, is the most important thing in my life.'

'I know,' she said again. 'And, with the exception of Cordelia, mine, too. Thank you for giving me so many chances, even though it hurt you. You've been more than patient.'

'It was worth it. *You're* worth it. I always knew that. I just stopped believing it would ever happen for us. I kept telling myself to forget about you, to find somebody else. But I couldn't. There is no one else for me. There hasn't been since the day I met you.'

Her eyes warmed and she smiled almost shyly before kissing him, long and lush. 'If I could move,' she murmured against his lips, 'I'd be jumping your bones right now.'

He snorted a surprised laugh, watched her eyes sparkle. 'If I could move, I'd beat you to it.'

She returned her head to his chest and sighed, content. 'We can vie for position later.'

He smiled up at the ceiling. Trust Stevie to turn sex into a contest. He couldn't wait.

For a long while they lay there, saying nothing, but gradually contentment gave way to something that had been bothering Clay for a while. He wondered if this was a good time to bring it up, then realized there would be no good time. Just a less bad time.

Might as well get it all out in the open. For better or for worse. 'Stevie? You said that nobody in your family talks about your husband and son. Why don't they?'

She stiffened. 'Why do you ask?'

'Because I'd like to know.'

She was quiet for so long he thought she wouldn't answer. Then she blew out a breath. 'I love my parents, Clay. They're good people and they sacrificed a lot for us.'

'I know they're good people. But all families have issues. If I'm going to be a part of your life, I'll be spending time with your parents. I'd like to know. Did they . . . like Paul?'

'They loved Paul like a son,' she said defensively. 'And Paulie . . . He was the only grandson.' She drew a breath and held it for long seconds before slowly exhaling.

*She's calming herself.* This wasn't going to be easy. He stroked her hair, saying nothing. If she told him, fine. If not, he wouldn't force her.

'Paulie was treated like a prince. But after . . . no one mentioned his name.'

'Why, honey?'

Her swallow was audible in the quiet of the room. 'My parents came from Romania. I guess you figured that

492

out. Their accents are still strong. What you don't know is that Sorin and I were born there. We left when we were six.'

'Why?'

'Because it was the eighties and people were being murdered,' she snapped bitterly. 'All kinds of people. Just because the government could.'

'You defected?'

'Yes. My father became a high school science teacher after we moved here, but there he worked for the government. He was a physicist. Working on nuclear fuel extractors.'

And it had been the tail end of the Cold War. 'He developed weapons.'

'Not according to the government then, but I think so. He still doesn't discuss it. He was watched, all the time. So was my mother. And my aunt. My father's sister.'

'She died?'

'She was murdered. Hit and run as she was crossing the street. But we knew it was deliberate. We saw it happen, my father and I. She tried to run, but the car swerved so that it could hit her. She died there, in the street, in my father's arms.'

And little Stefania had witnessed the grisly event. Clay kept his voice level even though he wanted to curse. 'Why did they kill her?'

'She was also a scientist and had been vocal about her disagreement with the fuel research program. I picked up that much from the arguments she and my father had after Sorin and I were supposed to be asleep.' She shrugged slightly. 'Cordelia comes by it honestly.'

'And then?'

'They never mentioned it. Never mentioned her, ever again. Except when we'd gotten out and come to America, my mother was pregnant again. My aunt's name was Izabela.'

'They named Izzy after her.'

'Yes, but they never said so. I asked about my aunt once. My father clammed up, said the dead were dead. Light a candle for them at Mass if you so desire, but talking about them solves nothing. So when Paul and Paulie died, I knew better than to bring them up.'

'Does Izzy know about your aunt?'

'Only what I've told you, because that's all I know.'

'But you *saw* it. Your dad's six-year-old witnessed a murder. Did he get you counseling?'

'No. There wasn't such a thing in Romania at that time. But even if there had been that's not Dad's style. You suck it up. Be strong. Don't air the family laundry in front of strangers.'

Now so much more made sense. 'Did he think you'd just forget?' he asked quietly.

'I guess so.' She let out another sigh, this one sad. 'Just like I thought Cordelia would forget. That she could go on sleeping in her bed. Eating at the kitchen table where Silas held a gun to her side. Sitting on the floor in front of the TV on the new carpet I had put down because I couldn't get Silas's blood out of the old one.'

'But you did try to get her help, Stevie. You took her to therapists.'

'But it wasn't helping and I didn't try anything different.'

'Now you are.'

'Only because Izzy forced the issue.'

'Do you talk about your husband and son to Emma, during your lunches?'

'Yes. At first, I'd phone her a few times a week. Then every few months. Then I went back to work and we started our yearly lunch. And over time . . . it got better. I healed enough to get through the day.'

Clay knew her healing wasn't done, but he was glad to hear her say it. 'You talk a lot about Paul. But not your son.'

She stiffened again. 'So?'

'Would you tell me about him? About Paulie?'

She swallowed hard. 'Would you tell me about Sienna?'

It was Clay's turn to stiffen. How the hell had she known? Then he remembered the conversation with Cordelia as she'd stood on the stairs at his father's house. 'You weren't asleep Sunday morning. You were listening.'

'I didn't mean to spy on you. I meant to spy on Cordelia. She tells you more than she tells me. So? Will you?'

'I tell you about Sienna and you tell me about Paulie?'

'Seems like a fair trade.'

Maybe not. There was so much about how he handled his situation that left him ashamed.

'There's not much to tell,' he said. 'I married Sienna's mother right after high school. She'd just broken up with a guy she'd been going steady with for three years. I was the classic rebound date. We drank too much beer and did it in the backseat. I was two weeks from leaving for basic training at Parris Island when she told me that she was pregnant and I was the father.'

'So you married her.'

'Yep. She wanted me to "quit the Marines". I told her I couldn't, that I'd signed a contract. She pouted, told me if I loved her, I'd find a way. You don't get out of a military contract, so I did the only thing I could. Risked her father's wrath and manned up. He was a scary sonofabitch, her father. He did not approve of the marriage, but approved of having an unwed mother for a daughter even less, so he allowed it. I went to boot camp, sent her letters every week and most of every paycheck. She cashed the checks, never sent a letter to me. This went on for five months.'

'And then?'

'She finally sent me a letter. Told me she'd lost the baby. I'd finished boot camp and was in training school. I tried to get leave, but a miscarriage wasn't a good enough reason in those days. I had a 72-hour leave between training and deployment so I went home, tried to find her. My dad helped me search, but she was gone. Her family said she'd moved and wouldn't give me a forwarding address. I couldn't stay to find her. I was shipping out. I got to Africa and seven months later got another letter, this one from her attorney.'

'Requesting a divorce?'

'Yeah, and me halfway around the world. I granted it. I mean, it wasn't like she was the love of my life at that point. She clearly didn't even want to talk to me. I figured the emotional trauma of the miscarriage made dealing with me too painful.'

'Did you want the baby?'

'At first? No. I wasn't even nineteen years old and potentially going into a combat zone. But the more I thought about it, yeah, I wanted it. She never told me what it was, a girl or a boy.'

'Since Sienna is alive, she obviously lied about the miscarriage.'

'She did indeed. I came home on leave between tours, met up with some old buddies. Heard she'd gotten married again – to the guy she'd gone steady with through high school. That he'd been willing to take her, even though she had a six-month-old baby at the time.'

She propped her forearms on his chest. 'What'd you do?'

'Went to find her. That was my child. She didn't want

me to know about the baby, because she knew I wanted it. She didn't want to share custody with me. But it turned out that her old high school flame beat her senseless and dumped her for another woman with no kid.'

'A real winner.'

'Word in the neighborhood was that she'd gone out West to live with an aunt. I went to see her father because I wanted answers, but I got a black eye instead.'

'He hit you?'

'Pretty hard. I wanted to hit him back, but my parents had taught me better. Her father said I'd broken her spirit and I had no idea what he was talking about. Finally her mother told me that because I'd divorced Donna, she'd been forced to take up with that "no-good old boyfriend".'

'She told them that *you'd* divorced *her*?'

'Yeah. I told them I could prove she'd divorced me, but they said I'd just faked whatever papers I'd bring them and not to bother.' His gaze skittered away and he looked at the ceiling, the walls, anywhere but Stevie's eyes. 'They said they knew what kind of man I was.'

'What did that mean?'

'They'd told her to sue me for child support after the second husband dumped her. She told them she wanted nothing more to do with me. That . . .' He trailed off, afraid to say the words in front of her. Unwilling to see the doubt cloud her eyes. She thought him a hero.

'Clay? What had she told them?' She gripped his chin, held him so that he had to look at her. He closed his eyes, remembering the shock and shame of that day like it was yesterday.

'She told them that I'd forced her,' he said, so quietly he almost didn't hear himself.

'Excuse me? She told them that you forced her to have sex?'

His face heated. 'Yeah.'

'Well, she lied. Plain and simple. What did you tell them?'

'That she'd lied. That she told me she'd lost the baby and they said, of course she had. What else did I expect her to do? Because I'd got her drunk and forced her, she was so terrified of me that she waited until I was halfway around the world before cutting me out of her life. And out of "her baby's" life. That if I didn't leave, they'd press charges and ruin my career.'

Her mouth bent sadly. 'How could she do that to you? How could she lie like that?'

'You're sure she lied,' he murmured.

'Of course. She lied about everything else. But more importantly, I know that's not you.' She tilted her head, eyes sharp. 'Oh my God. That's why you kept asking me to say yes. After all this time, you still worry that she was telling the truth.'

'No, it's not that, although for a long time I did worry about that. I didn't remember forcing her. In fact, I remember the opposite. I remember her climbing all over me. She couldn't wait to do it. But alcohol screws with your perceptions.'

'I don't believe it,' Stevie stated flatly. 'I think that she told her parents you'd divorced her when they pushed her to demand child support. When they didn't stop pushing, she made up the story about what happened in that back-seat, just to cover her tracks. Her parents were inclined to believe the worst about you anyway.'

'My parents always believed it happened exactly as you just said.'

'Because they know you.'

That she was so sure warmed him. He kissed her forehead. 'Thank you.'

'So, if it wasn't worry about what happened that night, why did you want me to say yes?'

'Because for a long time I did worry that it was true. It changed me. I never wanted to feel that kind of doubt again.'

'I suppose I can understand that. Where is Donna now?'

'She died right before Christmas. Cancer. I saw her a few times over the years, out in California. Found my daughter, too. Sienna. She was six years old. She looked like me. Dark hair, taller than the other kids. She was at school, on the playground at recess. I watched her through the fence until she saw me and ran away screaming. Donna must have shown her pictures of me. Told her that I was dangerous.'

It still haunted him, the memory of his child running from him like he was a monster.

'She turned the child against you. Oh, Clay. What did you do?'

'I didn't have time to do anything at that moment. I was between deployments and being shipped out the next day. I applied for a leave to find Donna again, but it was weeks later that I got the time off. She'd moved, but I finally found her. She'd hidden Sienna away and wouldn't let me see her. I sent cards, letters, every birthday, every Christmas. I tried to see her a dozen more times over the next five years, but Donna threatened a restraining order. I was a cop by then. I knew how it would work. She'd get her TRO and I'd lose my job.'

'But why did she hate you so much?'

'I begged her to tell me. She would close the door in my face. But one time, the door opened again and it was Donna's aunt, the one who'd taken her in. Her aunt apparently knew the truth. She whispered that Donna could never let her father know, that he'd "die of a broken heart".'

'Drama runs wild in that family,' she said. 'You could have demanded a paternity test.'

'I considered that, but the lawyer I hired talked me out of it. If I won, so what? I'd get partial custody of a child on the other side of the country. At the time I was stationed in DC and was about to be deployed again. How could I ever see her often enough to make her see I wasn't the person Donna made me out to be? I hired a PI, ironically enough, to make sure that Sienna was healthy and that Donna wasn't abusive. Sienna was happy and by all accounts Donna was a good mother. She married a third time to a guy with kids of his own. According to my PI, they made a nice family – home in the suburbs, white picket fence. I decided Sienna should have that. My PI and I parted ways. And then I changed my mind two days later. She was my child. I couldn't just walk away. I rehired him.'

'And then? What happened?'

'My PI got arrested. Donna saw him taking pictures of Sienna and reported him to the cops as a pedophile. By the time he and I got that sorted out and the charges against him dropped, Donna had disappeared with my daughter. For a while, all I was able to find was a post office box. I kept sending Sienna letters, but she never answered. I kept looking and found Donna a few years later, but Sienna was "never home" when I tried to visit. Three years ago she turned eighteen. I tried one more time.'

'She still "wasn't home"?'

'She was home. She just refused to come to the door, so I let it go. Until this past January.'

'What happened in January?'

'You almost died in December.'

'I don't understand.'

'My mother made me promise, on her deathbed, that I'd try again to see Sienna, to forge some kind of relationship

500

with my daughter. But years had gone by and I hadn't gone out to California. Dad kept reminding me that a broken deathbed promise is worse than a lie and therefore a really serious sin. Which didn't bother me that much, until I needed to pray.'

'When I got shot,' she whispered. 'Clay.'

He shrugged. 'So, when you were bleeding on the courthouse stairs, I promised God that I'd keep my promise to my mother. In January I went to find Donna, discovered she was dead. The neighbors said that Sienna had gone back to school. The university said she'd taken the year off to care for her mother and stated no plans to come back. I've tried to find her, but she doesn't want to be found. If Donna told her what she told her parents, I can't say that I blame her.'

Stevie pursed her lips. 'When all this is over, you and I are going to California and we're going to find that girl. I'll talk to her myself. This can't be allowed to continue. You're a good man, Clay Maynard, and your daughter needs to know that.'

Warmed from his head to his toes by her faith, he kissed the tip of her nose. 'We'll talk when this is over. But thanks. Now, you made a promise to me. A little quid pro quo, please.'

The determination in her eyes disappeared like mist, replaced by dread. He kissed her mouth gently. 'Talk to me, Stevie. Tell me about your son.'

*Bladensburg, Maryland, Monday, March 17, 9.15 P.M.*

Ruby closed the car door behind her, then shivered. 'It's getting really cold out there.'

'Imagine if you were still in that dress,' Sam said dryly.

501

She'd changed into black slacks and a soft lavender sweater. Unfortunately his blood hadn't stopped rushing through his veins. She no longer threatened to spill out of her top, but the sweater draped so nicely over her breasts that he had to shove his hands in his pockets so that they wouldn't reach out and touch.

'I'd have frostbite. Kayla's not home. The landlady said she'd be back any minute.'

'What kind of place is it?' Sam asked, looking at the large old house that was Kayla Richards's current address. They'd sat outside for over two hours because no one had answered the door and Sam was beginning to wonder if they were wasting their time.

Finally a car had pulled into the garage and Ruby had once again worked her magic. Sam had watched her talking to the landlady, who'd been suspicious initially. Ruby had won her over in less than a minute, leaving the woman to close her front door wearing a smile on her face.

'Your basic boarding house. The landlady said that Kayla worked as a secretary at a law firm, but on Monday nights she takes a class at the university. She's getting her degree.'

'That's good. Is she healthy?'

'Didn't ask. She's alive and that's all that matters to our investigation at the moment. But the landlady didn't look sad when she spoke of her.'

'I'm glad to hear that.' The background check Ruby had run revealed that Kayla had a record for possession of crack, enough for her personal use. She'd taken a plea, done a stint in rehab, then had no other issues with the law.

'I was, too. I was glad to hear she was getting a degree,' she added wistfully.

'Have you ever considered going back to school?'

'Only every day,' Ruby said with a shrug. 'I haven't gone back, though.'

'What would you major in?'

She glanced at him sideways, almost like she expected him to laugh at her. 'There's a forensic science program at UMBC.'

'I've heard about it.' The University of Maryland's Baltimore campus offered a number of law enforcement related majors. 'I considered the police science program a while back, but I decided against it.'

'Why?' she asked seriously.

'I'm happy where I am. And going to school would mean a huge time commitment, which would take time away from other things.'

'Like the volunteering and coaching.'

'Yeah. And taking care of my mom. You're not happy where you are, are you, Ruby?'

'I'm not *un*happy. But I've been considering a change for a long time.' Again she gave him a sideways glance. 'I've been considering becoming a death investigator.'

'You'd make a good one. You've been around death scenes for what, ten years now? You know your way around the corpses, but you have a way with the living. What's stopping you?'

Her eyes had warmed. 'Thanks, Sam. But unless I want to get my investigator's certification at the same time as my AARP card, I'd have to go to school full-time.'

'Which means quitting your job with the ME. You'd have no income.'

'Oh, I'd have some income. I've being doing freelance work for Thorne, consulting work when he needs a death scene analyzed. He's already told me he'd hire me.'

'Then I repeat – what's stopping you?'

'I've worked as an ME tech for so long. I know people

503

are comfortable with how I do that job but some people think I'm flighty. Maybe they wouldn't respect me on a crime scene.'

'Then they'd be wrong. When all this is over, I'm taking you to the UMBC registration office and you're going to get enrolled. But right now, we have company.' He pointed to an older model VW coming toward them. It parked on the curb and out climbed a woman.

'Is that her?'

Sam nodded. 'I think so. You ready to roll?'

'Sure. Just try not to do the Joe Friday routine. Let me do the talking.'

But that wasn't to be. Kayla Richards took one look at the two of them approaching and came to a halt on the sidewalk. She searched Sam's face carefully, her own growing shadowed. She appeared healthy and strong. But her eyes filled with dread, her face registering a resignation that Sam understood far too well.

Somehow he knew that Kayla Richards had known this day would come.

'I wondered what happened to you,' she said quietly.

'You remember me, then?' Sam asked and she nodded. 'My name is Sam Hudson. This is Ruby Gomez. We'd like to ask a few questions about that night, eight years ago.'

Kayla closed her eyes. 'Are you going to call the cops?'

Ruby put her hand over his. 'Should we, Miss Richards?' she asked softly.

'I'm not sure. I had nightmares that maybe you'd died. I am so glad to see you didn't.'

'What happened that night?' Ruby asked still gently, but with an authority that had Kayla straightening her spine.

Kayla checked her watch. 'Can you give me ten minutes? I have a child to tuck in.'

'How old is your child?' Sam asked.

Kayla met his eyes squarely. 'She's eight and a half.'

So her child had been six months old that night. 'Can we wait inside? It's cold out here.'

'Of course. My landlady has a parlor she lets us use. You can wait there.'

*Baltimore, Monday, March 17, 9.25 P.M.*

Stevie was trembling. Clay tightened his arms around her. 'It's all right,' he whispered. 'You don't have to talk about Paulie. You don't have to remember anything you don't want to.'

'I don't need to remember. He's always there, in my mind. I don't know where to start.'

'What was his favorite color?'

'Yellow,' she whispered. 'Paulie loved yellow. He'd use the yellow crayon down to a nub and the other colors would still be brand new. Suns and cars and dogs . . . all ended up yellow.'

He smiled against her hair. 'Favorite food?'

'Lasagna. He liked Paul's better than mine, which wasn't really fair. Italians make lasagna better than Romanians. But he did like my macaroni and cheese.'

'Right out of the box?'

'Best kind. He was beautiful. His hair was golden like Paul's, but his eyes were brown like mine.' She drew a deep breath, held it. 'He loved to play rugby with my dad and he was a major Orioles fan. He could remember all the players' statistics. My dad used to say he'd be a mathematician like him and Paulie would cry. He kept thinking Dad meant magician and those guys scared him. Especially when they pulled the scarves out of their mouths.'

Clay's chest was becoming wet. She was crying and it broke his heart. Still he kept his voice crisp. 'That is pretty creepy. I can see his point.'

'He wanted to be a lawyer and a cop. Said he'd catch the bad guys, lock 'em up and throw away the key.' Her laugh was watery. 'I guess he overheard Paul and me say that a time or two. He really wanted a baby brother, but when I told him Cordelia was a girl he put both hands on my stomach and said he'd teach her sports anyway.' She laughed again but it was more of a sob. 'He'd already made a pile of all of his toys that he planned to give her. He was a good boy. He was a good boy who tried to save his father from a bad guy. And he got shot, Clay.' Her body shook now, the sobs stealing her breath. 'That bastard shot my baby in the chest and he died.'

Clay swallowed hard. 'You can stop now, Stevie.'

She shook her head hard. 'I was supposed to pick him up from day care, but I'd stayed late to finish a report. I can't even remember the subject's name now. I lost my baby over some guy who probably killed his wife and framed his son and I was going to prove it if it was the last thing I did. So I stayed late. I didn't pick him up.'

He rubbed her back, trying to calm the spasms that twisted her body as she cried her heart out. 'It wasn't your fault, Stevie. You know that.'

'I *know* I didn't pick up my son,' she said, her teeth clenched. 'I *know* if he'd been with me that night that he'd still be alive. But he wasn't. He was with Paul who went into a convenience store to buy a lottery ticket for his mother, just like he did every damn day.'

Clay's radar went off, but he said nothing. Grayson had assured him that Paul Mazzetti's murder was an accident. That the defendants on his caseload had been investigated then cleared of involvement in his murder.

Her tears tapered, and her arms now wound around his neck, holding on for dear life. Her sigh was ragged. 'The guy was a junkie. The gun shook in his hand.'

Clay frowned. 'How do you know the gun shook in his hand?'

'I saw the tape. Over and over again.'

'Why?' he asked, horrified.

'I kept thinking I'd see something the cops had missed. But all I saw was a guy in a ski mask shooting my husband and my son and the cashier. Finally Silas stepped in, took my copy of the tape away. Yelled at whichever cop had given it to me.'

'How could anyone kill a child?' Clay whispered.

'I don't think he'd planned to. He shot Paul first, in the chest. The cashier went for her gun and he shot her in the head. But Paul was wearing a vest, so he got up. Paulie was in the car, or so Paul thought. The look on his face when Paulie rushed into the store . . . My son had the heart of a lion and no fear.'

*Sounds like someone else I know*, he thought, but would never voice the words. Stevie carried enough guilt for a hundred people. No way would Clay add even a drop to it.

'Paul was fighting the robber for his gun when the guy pulled the trigger. The bullet passed through Paul's arm and hit Paulie in the chest. Paul . . . he went down on the floor with Paulie, tried to do CPR. Tried to stop the bleeding, all while he protected him with his own body. With his last breath. The robber could have run. Could have left them alone, but he didn't. He shot Paul again, in the head. And then he ran.'

'Your husband was the best kind of father.'

Stevie nodded. 'He was. I thought about him early this morning when you were under the dock, Cordelia strapped to your chest. I thought that regardless of how you and I ended up, you protected my child like Paul would have. Like her own father would have.'

Clay's throat closed. 'Thank you,' he whispered hoarsely.

'It's a fact. But you're welcome anyway.' She pressed her cheek against his chest. 'God, my head hurts.'

'I know, honey.' He cradled her head in his hands, pressing his thumbs into her temples. He released the pressure and was gratified to hear her sigh. 'Better?'

'A little.' She was quiet then for several minutes. Then she finally said, 'You asked me why I don't talk about my son. I . . . can't. It still hurts too much. It's been eight years and it might as well have been yesterday.' She brushed at the puddle her tears had formed on his chest. 'I gave away some of his clothes, but left his room the way it was. I knew I should have turned it into an office or something, but every time I started to, I'd get these panic attacks.'

'You don't have to do anything with it. You grieve on your own schedule. I'm sure Emma told you that.'

'She did. But I was still . . . ashamed, I guess. Here I was, running grief groups with the cops and I couldn't manage to deal with my own loss. I'm a hypocrite.'

'No, honey, just human. Maybe running the groups helped keep the grief at arm's length.'

'It did. We mostly talked about the loss of fellow cops. Of spouses. Kids, not so often.'

'Because it was as hard for them as it was for you.'

'You make it sound so sensible.'

'It is. You're no hypocrite, Stevie. You're just a woman who was dealt a really shitty hand. You get to cope with it however you choose. If you decide to talk about him again, I'm here.'

'Thank you.'

He held her then, saying no more, just stroking her back, her hair. Massaging her scalp until he felt some of the tension leave her body. Finally, she slept.

Clay slid out from under her carefully, covering her with the blanket. Standing next to the bed, watching her breathe. She looked so young, he thought. He wondered what she would have been like before her world had been shattered. But then their paths wouldn't have crossed and they wouldn't have ended up here. He could never be grateful that her family had been so cruelly stolen. But he could spend the rest of his life making her happy.

In the end, that was all anyone could do.

He checked his phone for the time. It was getting late. If Stevie's shooter was going to take the bait, it would either be when there were lots of people around in the hotel, or nearly none. They were past the time for lots. In another hour or two, there would be nearly none.

He pulled on jeans and a shirt, making sure he was buttoned and zipped, his hair combed, before lightly knocking on the adjoining door.

Joseph appeared, his brows lifting. 'You okay? Where's Stevie?'

'Asleep,' he said quietly.

Joseph frowned, studying him. 'Just asleep?'

'Yeah. What more should there be?'

Joseph shrugged and stepped aside, gesturing Clay into the other room. The aroma of pizza hit him hard and his stomach growled.

'Damn. I forgot to eat dinner.'

'I bought extra. Help yourself.' Joseph sat down at the table, his laptop open. 'I'm hooked into the hotel's security system. I can see the elevators, the hallways, and the stairwells of every floor. Novak and Coppola are also watching. If somebody comes close to Stevie, we'll see him. Keep your phone on and with you. We'll text you.'

Clay loaded a plate with half of Joseph's pizza, inhaled it, then leaned back in his chair. 'I hope at least one of these guys shows. Do you have agents in the laundry area? If I planned to sneak in, getting a uniform would be my first priority.'

'We have undercover agents in the laundry, house-keeping, and room service. If our targets try to steal uniforms, we'll let them. If they get violent, my agents have orders to take them down. Above all else, we have to keep the employees and guests safe but our base plan is to let them get into your room. If we stop them downstairs and we find no hard evidence connecting them to the murders, they could claim they simply planned to burgle. We want to get them for six homicides and five attempts on Stevie's life.'

'Damn straight,' Clay growled. 'What about the Sequoia and the Tahoe? Have they been spotted anywhere else?'

'The Sequoia the first intruder drove away from your place is in the wind. Same with the Tahoe. We've had BOLOs out on both of them since yesterday. Since the shooting at the dock this morning, we've been searching the toll plaza cameras on the interstate, at the border crossings, and at airport lots. Nothing so far. Descriptions of the cars and general physical characteristics of the intruders have been posted to state, local, and federal law enforcement Facebook and Twitter accounts. We've got the phones staffed in case a citizen recognizes them. Now we have to wait for one or both of them to make another move.'

'I hope they make it soon. I really want this to be over.' Clay frowned because Joseph was studying him again. '*What?* Do I have pizza sauce on my shirt?'

Joseph looked a little uncomfortable. 'No.'

'Then why are you staring at me?'

The Fed lifted both hands, palms out. 'Hey, I'm just following orders.'

'From?'

'Daphne, Paige, Emma, and Maggie VanDorn.'

Clay's eyes narrowed. 'What orders?'

'To see if anything's happened between you and Stevie. The women figure that with the two of you trapped in a hotel room, something's gonna give. So can I tell them something happened so they get off my back?'

Clay felt his neck heat and knew the blush was crawling up his face. 'You're kidding me.'

Joseph grinned. 'Afraid not. But at least now I can give a positive report.' His smile faded, his eyes growing serious. 'It's all good. Right?'

'Yeah,' Clay mumbled. 'Very good.' He dragged his hands down his face. 'At least there was no betting pool.'

'Of course there was.' Joseph checked his phone again. 'Based on the latest email, it looks like it's a three-way photo finish between Ethan, Paige, and . . . oh.' He smiled. 'My sister Holly, too. You and Stevie will have to tell them who got closest to the actual time.'

Clay wanted to be annoyed, but found himself laughing. 'You guys are crazy.'

'Nah. Just tired of watching the two of you dancing around each other. I sent you the link and password to the hotel's camera system. You can watch it from your own room if you want to. And take what's left of the pizza. I'm sure Stevie's worked up an appetite.'

Clay thought about her crying in his arms. 'Maybe not. She told me about her son. About the day he and Paul were killed. It ripped her up.'

Joseph's eyes filled with sympathy. 'I didn't know her

then, but Grayson tells me it was one of the worst things
he's ever been through. That their killer is behind bars
doesn't bring the satisfaction everyone thinks it does.'

'No. It doesn't.'

*Monday, March 17, 9.30 P.M.*

Robinette stared at his computer screen on his desk in
satisfaction. He'd been tired after not having slept in more
than a day, his brain temporarily numbed by the dinner
with the city planner Brenda Lee had scheduled him to
schmooze, but he'd been re-energized, his blood humming.

He thought at first he'd misread the path Henderson's
phone had taken Saturday afternoon, but after checking
the address and the property owner, Robinette knew he'd
just hit pay dirt.

Having started at Mazzetti's home on Saturday,
Henderson had driven to Hunt Valley, to a farm owned by
Daphne Montgomery, assistant state's attorney and friend
to Mazzetti.

Montgomery's fiancé was FBI Special Agent Joseph
Carter. Before taking up with Carter, Daphne Montgomery
had often been seen on the arm of none other than Clay
Maynard.

So all the pieces pointed to this being a perfect hiding
place for Mazzetti's child.

After driving to Hunt Valley, Henderson had driven
back to the city, to Harbor House. Then, after the botched
restaurant job, back to Hunt Valley. Several hours later,
Henderson took a circuitous route that ended with the
botched drive-by job in front of Mazzetti's house.

So . . . If the child had been at Daphne Montgomery's
farm on Saturday, it was possible they'd stashed her there

again. He needed to be careful. If she was there, she'd be well guarded. If Mazzetti had joined her there, there would be even higher security.

The good news was, the cops were looking for either a Sequoia or a Tahoe and he'd be driving neither. Henderson wasn't the only one with hot-wiring skills.

On his way to dinner, Robinette had spotted a Jeep even older than the Tahoe parked in a supermarket's parking lot. On his way back, the Jeep had still been there, so he'd parked his own car several blocks away, walking to the supermarket. The Jeep was now parked far enough from the factory that it wouldn't be obvious, but close enough that he could walk to it.

Which he'd do, now that he knew where he was going.

What he wasn't so sure of was what he'd do when he got there. He wasn't planning to get caught and no longer had any employees he could trust enough to be his canary in the coal mine.

Excepting Brenda Lee, of course, but he couldn't send her into hostile territory.

Then he smiled. He knew exactly how he'd test security around the farm and occupancy therein. If he was right, he'd gain valuable intel. If he was wrong, he'd have a midnight snack.

# Chapter Twenty-Four

Kayla Richards's hands trembled as she poured Sam and Ruby cups of coffee. 'I was twenty-one years old that night, a single mom, drug addict, and terrified. It doesn't excuse what I did. I've been clean for five years. It took having social services take my daughter away to wake me up. I went to NA, did the twelve steps. Made amends to everyone I'd hurt with my addiction. But I didn't know who you were, so I couldn't make amends to you. I'll start tonight and then you can decide what my consequence will be.'

'I think I should tell you,' Sam said quietly, ignoring Ruby's warning frown. 'I am a police officer. I'm not here in an official capacity, but I or another cop could be later.'

Kayla gasped. Her hands shaking violently, she set her cup on the table, grabbing a napkin to clean up the coffee she'd spilled. 'Were you a cop then?'

'Yes.'

She gave a little moan, then appeared to pull herself together. 'All right,' she said, folding her hands in her lap. 'You ordered a beer that night, and I served it. I didn't

514

know when I gave it to you that it was spiked. But I did know after you passed out, which wasn't more than fifteen minutes later. I started to call 911, but the bartender grabbed my arm. He said if I made the call, I'd lose my job. I had a hard time getting that job, because I had a previous record. But I started to call again anyway. And then he threatened my daughter.'

'What did he say?' Sam asked, steel in his tone. Threats against the innocent pissed him off.

'He said that crib death was "so sad". That mothers put their babies in their cribs and . . . poof! They wake to find their babies dead. Wouldn't it be sad if that happened to my little girl?'

*Poor thing*, Sam thought. She'd been between a rock and a hard place and she'd protected her child. 'So you knew I'd been drugged, but you didn't drug me. You just didn't get me help.'

'Yes. I'm sorry. Um, if you have to arrest me, will you give me a few hours to find someone to take care of my daughter? I have friends now who I can trust. I can call them. That way social services won't take her again. I couldn't stand not knowing where she was.'

'Social services will place your daughter in foster care,' Ruby said, more sharply than Sam thought she needed to. 'Unless you have family in the area.'

The color drained from Kayla's face. 'I don't have family, but I have appointed legal guardians for my daughter should I become ill.' Her chin lifted slightly. 'I have HIV. Right now I'm stable, but that could change. My daughter's care is the most important thing to me. So if you'll allow me to make some arrangements first, I'll turn myself in.'

'You don't have to do that,' Sam said. 'Technically, you didn't break a law.'

Her eyes widened. 'I didn't?'

'No. If the police had contacted you and you'd lied about it, then you would have broken the law. If I'd been a child and you a teacher or health care professional, you would have broken the law. Not reporting this crime wasn't a crime.'

Kayla's head fell back as she caught her breath. 'Oh my God.'

'Not a statutory crime. Just a moral one,' Ruby muttered.

'Ruby,' Sam murmured.

'Sam,' she murmured back. 'You're too tenderhearted for your own good.'

'You believe her, too.'

Kayla looked at Sam, then at Ruby, hope evident on her face.

'I know,' Ruby said, rolling her eyes. 'Damn my heart, too.'

Sam squeezed Ruby's hand. 'It's a good heart.'

She made a grumbling sound, but looked pleased. 'Will you let me do the talking now?'

'Knock yourself out, honey.'

Ruby cleared her throat. 'Miss Richards, are you all right now?' she asked crisply.

Kayla's color was better, her eyes less wide and frightened. 'Yes, thank you. I've felt so guilty for so long. I watched the news for days after that, looking to see if you got reported missing or were found dead. If that had happened, I would have called the police anonymously. But I never saw your face again, until tonight.'

*And doesn't that story sound familiar?* Sam thought ironically.

Ruby must have been thinking the same because the edge in her voice softened. 'What happened after Officer Hudson was drugged?' she asked.

'The bartender told me to take the rest of the night off. So I did. But I was driving out of the lot when I saw you being dragged out. You looked drunk, but I knew you'd only had one beer and you were sober as a judge when you'd arrived.'

'Who dragged Officer Hudson out?'

'A big guy. He was about fifty, maybe mid-forties. Bulky, like he'd played football. Dark hair, but really short, like a military buzz cut. He had an ordinary face. He was maybe six-two and two hundred pounds or so. I can describe him to a police artist if that will help.'

'It will,' Ruby said. 'Sam, can you line that up?'

'Yes. I have a friend who's a sketch artist. Would you be able to come in tomorrow?'

'Yes, my boss will be okay with that. He's a good guy. How long do you think it will take?'

'A few hours,' Sam said. 'Give me your phone number and I'll call you when I have it set up. There's usually a waiting list for artists.'

Kayla quickly wrote down several phone numbers, then added a name. 'This is the name of the bartender. Ricky Trenovi. He helped the big guy carry you out. Ricky's in prison now, for assault on someone else.'

Sam took the paper she offered. 'Consider your amends to me as having been made.'

'Thank you.' Kayla squeezed his hand hard. 'Thank you so much.'

Sam waited until he and Ruby were alone in his car to speak. 'I'm going to the prison to talk to the bartender. I've got some vacation time coming, so I'll just take a day off. Hopefully my artist friend has some time in his schedule tomorrow and I can juggle the two.'

'Make it three,' she said, checking her phone. 'My contact in the news studio has pulled all of the footage we

517

asked for. He can meet us at the studio in the morning. Nine A.M.'

'Us?'

She nodded, one brow lifted. 'I have some vacation time coming, too. If you think I'm going to bail now, just when this puzzle's getting interesting, you've got another think coming.'

She might say she was in it for the puzzle, but Sam thought she just might be in it for him, too. 'I can pick you up early, take you to breakfast.'

She smiled. 'I'd like that.'

*Hunt Valley, Maryland, Monday, March 17,*
*10.45 P.M.*

Yawning, Emma walked into Maggie VanDorn's kitchen to find Maggie, Alec, Paige, and Daphne sitting at the table with Ethan Buchanan.

Ethan and Alec were focused on their laptop screens. The women were cleaning guns. The table was full of weapons – rifles, shotguns, pistols, revolvers. On one end of the table was a stack of bullet-proof vests – six adult-sized and one child-sized. Many of the guns came from Clay's extensive collection of personal weapons, which hadn't surprised her in the least. She had, however, been surprised to find that Maggie had a collection almost as extensive. It had belonged to her late husband, but she was a crack shot. Maybe even better than Paige.

This Emma knew because the first thing Ethan had done on his arrival that afternoon was take all of them out to an unoccupied pasture to fire test shots. Of all of them, Daphne was the least skilled, a fact that had annoyed the prosecutor. By dinner time, she hit the target every time.

Emma had been impressed with Daphne's determination as well as Ethan's patience.

Clay had good friends and they were completely loyal to him. Emma wished Stevie would wise up before Clay became so discouraged that he gave up.

'Cordelia's finally asleep,' Emma announced to the group.

All eyes glanced up, then lips began to twitch.

'Looks like you dozed off, too,' Paige said. She pointed to her own head. 'Bed head.'

Emma went to the mirror and scowled. She'd repeatedly washed her hair, trying to get rid of the brown spray dye they'd used. After several shampoos, she'd dozed off with her hair wet. Now the color of dirty dishwater, it stood in spikes all over her head.

'This is your fault, Paige,' she called around the open door, then winced, hoping she hadn't woken Cordelia. The child had fought sleep for a long time, begging to stay up until her aunt Izzy and grandparents had been driven home by Grayson Smith, who'd continue to watch over them through the night.

Emma wet her hair down and attempted to finger-comb the spikes into submission before returning to the kitchen. 'Just remember,' she whispered with a glare, 'that payback's a bitch.'

'Oh, I'm so scared,' Paige deadpanned, but still she grinned.

Emma patted her head. 'What?'

'Not you,' Daphne said, her own smile a mile wide. She held up her cell phone. 'News.'

'What news?' Emma asked suspiciously. 'We caught the shooters?'

Daphne's smile dimmed. 'Not yet.' She lifted her brows. 'But Operation CAS is a success.'

'CAS?' Emma asked, confused. Then she understood and her own grin broke free. 'Clay-And-Stevie.' She clapped her hands. 'Who won the pool?'

'Three-way tie between me, Ethan, and Holly,' Paige said.

Maggie frowned. 'I thought it would be earlier, dammit.'

Emma sighed happily. 'This is really good. And about time, too.'

'I feel sorry for Clay,' Alec said, shaking his head. 'I mean, I'm glad he and Stevie are finally together but I never want to have my love life watched like that.'

Ethan tousled the young man's hair with paternal affection. 'You're just mad you didn't win the pool.'

Alec's scowl was purely for show. 'It's true.'

'One of these days, you'll—' Ethan's phone rang and they grew quiet, waiting expectantly. 'Buchanan.' His brows rose abruptly. 'No, we didn't . . . That sounds like a plan.' He hung up. 'That was one of the FBI agents assigned to watch the entrance from the main road. Someone ordered pizza delivery to this address. The Feds let him pass without stopping him, but they're following him to the gate.' He slid his phone into his pocket. 'They want us to stay put.'

Emma looked at the ceiling. Cordelia's safety was why they were all there. 'We're going to sit here on our hands and let a killer corner us? I'm not okay with that, Ethan.'

'I said it was "*a* plan". Alec, Maggie, grab your weapons like we practiced, suit up, and come with me. Daphne, stay here. You might not pick off a gunman, but you can spray anyone coming through the front door with bullets. Just keep the sight lined up like I showed you.'

Daphne nodded. 'I will,' she said as Ethan, Alec, and Maggie buckled into their vests. 'Paige, where are you, mobility-wise?' Ethan asked.

'Can't run yet, but I can still shoot. I'll go up to Cordelia's room. Anybody who wants to get to her, goes through me first.'

Emma already had a rifle in her hands and a pistol in her belt. 'And me.' But she was thinking of her own family as well. *Please, God, don't let it come down to that*.


*Monday, March 17, 11.05 P.M.*

Paige had set Alec's laptop on the dresser in the room where Cordelia was sleeping so that they could watch the front gate via the camera feed. Paige sat at the foot of the bed and Emma sat on the floor, her back up against it. Her gun was pointed at the door, the safety off, her trigger finger ready to shoot any nasties who were foolish enough to try to get in the room.

Not that Emma thought it would come to that. Joseph's people were already close by and Ethan wasn't letting anyone come through the gate. Still her heart pounded in her chest.

'They're coming for me, aren't they?' Cordelia whispered, making Emma jump.

She turned to find the child's eyes wide open. 'You're supposed to be asleep.'

'I woke up when you went downstairs and I listened outside the kitchen. When Mr Ethan started giving out guns, I ran back up. I didn't want to get into trouble.'

'Then why did you even tell me?' Emma said, amused despite the tension of the moment.

'Because I have questions.'

'What questions?' Emma asked.

'Well, first, are they coming for me?' she asked calmly, but her lip quivered.

521

'No,' Emma said firmly. 'They might try, but they're not getting you. Next question?'

'What did it mean when Miss Daphne said that CAS was a success? You said it meant "Clay and Stevie". What happened to my mom?'

Emma coughed. 'Well. First off, your mom is fine and probably happier than she's been in a very long time because you're safe – and you are safe. But she's also happy because . . . well, hmm. Mr Clay has liked your mother for a long time.'

'I know. But Mama hasn't liked him back. Aunt Izzy says my mama is insane because Mr Maynard is yummy.'

Emma laughed. 'She said that to you?'

'No. She said it to Miss Daphne last week when I came for my riding lesson. I listened.'

Paige tapped Cordelia's nose. 'We need to put you under the "cone of silence" so we grown-ups can talk without being spied on. All you need to know is that Mr Clay and your mom are happy together tonight. We'll have to see what happens when all of this craziness is over.'

'My friend's mom's boyfriend moved in with them. Will Mr Maynard move in with us?'

'Probably not right away,' Emma said. 'Your mama is careful, especially with you. Now I want you to at least close your eyes and pretend to sleep.'

'What are you watching on the computer?'

'This is not your business,' Paige said, her tone changing to one that demanded obedience. 'Go to sleep, Cordelia. That's not a request.'

'Yes, Sensei Holden.' Immediately Cordelia's eyes closed and Emma was impressed.

'That's my girl', Paige smoothed a hand down Cordelia's back, then turned the laptop screen so that Cordelia couldn't see it. Together they watched as Maggie came into view, looking like Barbara Walters channeling Rambo.

Alec and Ethan were nowhere to be seen.

A young man in the uniform of a pizza service alternated pacing and staring up into the camera, having rung the bell at the gate several times. Now he stared at Maggie, horrified.

Maggie was pointing back at the road and the pizza guy took a step backward, then another.

'He doesn't look like an assassin,' Emma whispered.

'No, he doesn't, does he? But Bundy didn't look like a serial killer either.'

Paige had a point, Emma thought, then blinked. Ethan had come out of nowhere and was now on the outside of the fence, creeping up behind the pizza guy. Ethan grabbed the boy's hands, pulling them behind his back. And unless the kid was the best actor around, he'd just been scared nearly to death. Had there been audio, Emma was certain they'd have heard a piercing scream.

'How did Ethan get out of the fence?' Emma asked, stunned.

'Bolt hole. A portion of fence that's separately controlled. He could turn off the voltage just there and climb over.'

'What about the barbed wire?'

'He knows how to avoid it. At least I hope so if he and his wife want more kids someday.'

Another car pulled up to the gate, parking diagonally behind the pizza delivery car, blocking his escape. Two men in suits got out, weapons drawn as they approached the gate.

In the same moment, Ethan tensed on the screen and Paige tensed beside Emma.

'What the hell?' Paige checked her cell. 'One of the motion detectors just got tripped.'

'The alarms go to your phone?' Emma asked.

'Yeah, along with the location. This one is on camera six.' Paige typed furiously, splitting the screen so that both the camera at the gate and one that pointed into the woods were shown. A figure dressed in black was partially visible, keeping behind the trees, advancing toward the gate.

'We need to tell Ethan,' Emma hissed.

'He knows. The alarm went to his phone, too. He's telling the Feds now.'

Ethan was saying something to one of the agents when the man in the suit dropped like a rock. 'Oh my God,' Emma whispered. 'What just—'

But she didn't get a chance to finish the question because seconds later the other agent followed. Ethan threw himself forward, taking the pizza delivery boy with him.

In shock Emma watched blood pool on the driveway. It belonged to the Federal agents.

It flowed from what was left of their heads.

Emma was grateful there was no audio. She glanced over at Cordelia. The child's eyes were open wide once more, her little face pale. But she hadn't moved.

'Cordelia, put on your helmet and your vest and get under the bed,' Paige ordered. The child soundlessly, instantly obeyed.

Paige dialed her cell phone, cursed. 'Joseph's goes right to voicemail. I'll try Novak.' This call went through and the conversation was brief. 'Novak says they heard the whole thing. The agents were miked. Reinforcements are on the way.'

'Paige, *look*.' Emma pointed to the camera in the woods. Alec was coming up behind the intruder, his rifle aimed. He'd followed Ethan over the fence.

The man in black was running toward the gate, toward Ethan and the pizza guy, when Alec fired, a bright flame bursting from the barrel of his rifle. The man did a half-spin mid-stride and slammed his back into a tree trunk, his weapon tumbling from his hands. He gripped his left arm with his right hand, then started to run again, this time toward the main road.

'Alec got him!' Emma cried.

Paige typed again, adding the camera at the end of the driveway to the first two on her screen. 'What the hell?'

Emma frowned. It was a Jeep, not a Tahoe or a Sequoia or a red Chevy or a white Camry. 'Either the guys who broke into Clay's house ditched their vehicles or we have a new shooter.'

Ethan had jumped to his feet and gun drawn, took off after the shooter, firing as he ran. But the man in black jumped into the Jeep and raced away.

Ethan stopped running, aimed at the Jeep, and took a final shot. The Jeep was out of camera range by this point, but by the disgusted set of Ethan's shoulders, it was clear he'd missed.

'Goddammit,' Paige whispered. 'He got away. Again.'

Ethan turned back, running toward Alec, who was looking pretty disgusted himself.

There were footsteps on the steps and Daphne appeared in the doorway. She was pale, her hands trembling. 'I called Joseph. He's put out a BOLO on the Jeep. Alec's not hurt.'

Emma stared at the delivery guy, still on the ground, now shaking wildly. 'And him?'

'He appears to be legit. His manager confirmed they got a call for delivery to this address. He'll allow Joseph's team access to his phone records. Backup's on the way.'

'Aunt Emma? What's happening?'

Emma jolted at Cordelia's tearful voice from under the bed. She slid to her knees and opened her arms to Stevie's little girl, helping her take off the helmet and vest. 'You're okay. I'm here and I'm not leaving you.'

'I want my mom.' Cordelia was shaking, crying. 'I want my mama, please.'

'I know. I think it's best, though, if your mom stays where she is until we get this sorted out. We're all safe where we are, your mom included. But I don't know if it's safe to move between places yet and if we call your mom, she'll try to get to you.'

A small breath shuddered out of the child. 'Then don't tell her I said I wanted her to come.'

'We won't tell her,' Paige promised. 'Not just yet.'

'I'll ask Joseph not to tell her yet, either,' Daphne added. 'We'll keep both of you safe.'


*Baltimore, Maryland, Tuesday, March 18, 1.45 A.M.*

'Stevie,' Clay whispered. 'Wake up.'

Stevie blinked her eyes open, but the room was dark except for the glow of a computer screen. *This is the Peabody Hotel*, she thought, orienting herself. The events of the past few hours flew through her mind. Clay and sex. Cuddling, sharing secrets, mourning their children. Tears. Lots of tears. She took stock of her body. Aches in unusual places.

*And I'm still naked*. Whereas Clay was fully clothed. She sat up, tucking the sheet under her arms. 'What?' she whispered back.

'Look.' He pointed at the screen of the laptop on the nightstand. 'Hotel security system.'

A man had stepped out of the elevator, dressed in the tux-like uniform worn by room service personnel. His head stayed down so there was no view of his face.

Stevie slipped out of bed and pulled on the sweatpants

and T-shirt that Clay had draped over a chair while she slept. He arranged the pillows to make it look like a body slept in the bed, then took position next to the bedroom door.

She shoved her feet into her shoes, flicked the safety off her gun, then joined Clay at the door. He'd taken the left side, so she took the right, setting her cane against the wall.

'Which do you think? Drive-by, Mr Backpack, or Mr Cocksucker?' she whispered.

'Doesn't matter. I have bones to pick with all three.'

'The adjoining door?'

'Closed, not locked. Joseph's waiting for our signal.'

'Which will be?'

'Yelling his name,' Clay whispered dryly, then pressed his finger to his lips.

The front door opened almost inaudibly, then closed with a quiet snick. If the man was coming, he had a very light tread. Stevie could hear nothing. But then the bedroom door opened and he slipped in, gun raised.

Clay moved, throwing the man on the floor in a movement so quick that Stevie almost missed it. The gun flew out of the man's hand and slid across the carpet, out of his reach.

Clay shoved his knee into the intruder's back, holding his wrists together, but the man continued to kick, so Stevie dropped to her knees, digging her kneecaps into his calves. She shoved her gun into the intruder's back with one hand and with the other grabbed her cane and whacked the bastard's head with the curved end, hard. 'Stop struggling.'

But the man's struggles increased, so Stevie hit his head again with her cane, harder this time. 'Joseph! Now would be good!'

'I'm here,' Joseph said from two feet behind her. He'd

been there watching, Stevie realized. *Letting me get a few licks in.* Crouching opposite Clay, Joseph cuffed the man's wrists, giving them a far harder yank than necessary to test their security, then from his coat pocket he pulled a set of shackles and handed them to Stevie.

Stevie applied the shackles with even less care. The man grunted in pain, which was far more satisfying than Stevie had expected. 'Let's see his face.'

Clay rolled him over, and there was a second of total silence as she, Clay, and Joseph stared, shocked.

'No fucking way,' Stevie breathed. 'He's a she.'

Their intruder was a woman in her mid to late thirties. She was slender but broad-shouldered. Built like a man. Her dark hair appeared to be a wig and her slouched walk had hidden the existence of her breasts from the camera.

Stevie leaned in close. 'Who the hell are you?'

The woman made a show of pursing her lips tight.

Joseph tossed Clay and Stevie latex gloves before pulling on his own. 'Let's have a look at your hardware.' Joseph picked up the Sig the woman had been carrying and frowned. 'No serial number.'

The woman rolled her eyes, saying nothing.

'Joseph?' Agent Novak entered the room. 'Coppola's still on watch in case any of her friends decide to join the party. Everybody okay?'

'We're fine,' Stevie told Novak. '*She's* not having the best day, though.'

Novak blinked. 'Who is she?'

'So far she hasn't introduced herself,' Joseph said.

'I'd like to know which killer she is,' Stevie said coldly. 'We can simplify things quickly. Drive-by has a bullet wound right *here*.' She jabbed the end of her cane into the woman's left shoulder, watching her flinch, agony rolling over her face.

528

'Fucking bitch,' the woman moaned between clenched teeth. 'You fucking *bitch*.'

'Nikita has a boo-boo,' Stevie said even more coldly. 'I am *so* sorry. I'm sometimes clumsy with my cane, especially around people who try to kill my child in my own front yard.'

'And you,' Clay added calmly, but his eyes snapped with fury. 'She shot at you, too.'

'Oh, yeah.' Stevie pushed herself to her feet, allowing the cane to slip on the carpet, driving it into Drive-by's shoulder again.

The woman moaned. 'I'll sue you for police brutality.'

Stevie laughed bitterly. 'I'm not a cop anymore. I'm on disability. You broke into the hotel room of an ordinary citizen. You're lucky I didn't shoot your ass.'

'Stevie, we do want her conscious to talk,' Joseph reminded her mildly. 'Evidence bags, please, Agent Novak.'

Novak produced them. 'Ready when you are, boss.'

Joseph dropped the woman's Sig into the first bag, then recited her Miranda rights and removed her wig, revealing a short cap of blonde hair. 'Nothing in the wig's lining.' He began patting down her pockets. 'Silencer for the Sig. A switchblade. A set of car keys.' They went into evidence bags. 'And a syringe. Looks like she planned to drug someone.'

'Why?' Stevie asked. 'She tried to kill us on Saturday. Why not just shoot us all now?'

'She'll tell us sooner or later,' Clay said quietly. 'She's got booze on her breath. My bet is she had to take a drink to calm her nerves. Shaky hands are an occupational hazard for an assassin. Given time, she'll sell her soul for a drink.'

The woman looked at him with eyes filled with hate, but said nothing.

Joseph nodded. 'Looks like you're right. That's it for her pockets.' He unhooked the small waist pack that had been hidden by her uniform jacket. 'A second clip filled with hollow-point bullets.' He pulled out a small, unlabeled amber bottle, twisted off the top and took a whiff and blinked rapidly. 'Whoa. Ether. I guess this is Plan B if the syringe didn't work.'

'Or to keep whoever she'd drugged sedated,' Clay said.

'Possibly.' Joseph removed a silver flask. 'It's probably booze, but I'm not gonna sniff it. Let the lab test it.'

Stevie caught a glimpse of writing on the back of the flask. 'Can I see that?' Ignoring the woman's glare, Stevie aimed her phone's flashlight at the words engraved in the silver. '"To JH from the team. Happy Five. Many more." Isn't that special? She's part of a team.' She started to put the flask in the bag Novak held, then stopped. 'There's something stamped in the base.'

The woman went still, her eyes becoming abruptly calm.

'It's probably the hallmark of the flask's manufacturer,' Novak said.

Stevie upended the flask. 'Maybe, but I think Miss Drive-by here just got really scared. Anybody got a magnifying glass?'

Novak produced a loupe from the pocket of his black leather trenchcoat. 'Use mine.'

Stevie squinted at the little mark next to the depression in the base. 'There are two marks. One is a letter "B" in a diamond. The second is a picture, a tree with an acorn in front of it. The text below it is "FPL" with one of those R-in-circle marks.'

'Registered trademark.' Clay got his laptop from the night table, tapped the keys. 'I searched "FPL logo acorn silver". No silver makers show up.'

Stevie stared at the magnified image, something about it

tugging at her memory. 'I'm going to take a picture of it, if that's okay with you, Joseph.'

'Fine,' he said, watching their captive, who lay statue-still with her eyes closed. 'You're right, Stevie. She doesn't like that we saw that mark. I'll get the lab working on it, ASAP.'

He patted down her legs and arms for additional weapons, pressing harder than necessary on her left shoulder. She shrank back, sweat beading on her upper lip.

'I wonder who treated her?' Stevie said.

'Whoever it was will be charged with harboring a fugitive when we find him. Agent Novak, let's get her out of here, then I want you to find the vehicle that goes with those keys.'

'What about us?' Clay asked quietly.

'Stay here and get some sleep,' Joseph said. 'Room's paid for all night. I'll send one of my agents to occupy the adjoining room, just in case JH's "team" decides to mount a second offensive. We'll put Miss JH in an interview room and let time be our friend. If she's got a flask in her pack, it shouldn't be too long before she gets very cooperative.'

'Don't count on it,' the woman spat as Joseph and Novak hauled her to her feet.

'Wait,' Stevie said. She stood in front of the woman and studied her face carefully.

The bitch narrowed her eyes. 'What?'

'You could have killed my child and not lost a minute's sleep, couldn't you?'

The woman laughed bitterly. 'Like you did? You're a murdering hypocrite.' Shaking her head, she lifted her gaze above Stevie's head, effectively dismissing her.

Stevie watched as the woman was dragged away. 'What the hell did that mean?'

'I wonder whose child you killed,' Clay said thoughtfully, locking their door.

'I never killed a child,' Stevie said defensively. 'Never.'

'I don't think you did. But maybe you killed someone she loved. It could explain this single-minded focus on eliminating you. It might have nothing to do with fear of discovery because of Silas's crimes. It might be good old-fashioned revenge.' He pulled Stevie to the bed and held up the blanket. 'Get in.'

She obeyed, her churning mind coming to a screeching halt when he pulled off her sweats and T-shirt. 'Wait. What is this?'

'You heard the Fed. We're going to go back to sleep.' Shucking off his jeans and shirt, he joined her under the covers. 'Eventually, anyway. I don't imagine you'll sleep until we figure out what she meant.' He settled his laptop on his knees, giving her an openly appreciative once-over. 'But that doesn't mean I can't enjoy the view while we do.'

Stevie did some looking of her own, liking what she saw. 'I like the way you think.'

*Tuesday, March 18, 2.30 A.M.*

'What took you so long?' Robinette snarled. He'd called Fletcher to come to his office hours before. He'd been lying on the sofa, trying not to think about how badly it hurt. He'd made it through the entire fucking Gulf War without sustaining a single gunshot wound only to be shot in the woods by some nerdy kid with fear in his eyes.

Fletcher winced at the sight of his wound. 'I didn't have the phone in my room so I didn't get your message until I got up to go to the bathroom. Then I had to get the right supplies. I don't usually carry lidocaine in my pocket. What happened to you?'

'I got shot,' he snapped. 'What the fuck does it look like happened to me?'

Fletcher held a filled syringe to the light. 'Who shot you? Watch out, this is going to sting.'

Robinette clenched his jaw, riding through the wave of discomfort from the injection. 'None of your business,' he said roughly.

'You come to me for first aid and for occasional sex. It's my business when someone puts a bullet in your arm.'

'Just get it out.'

Fletcher poured four fingers of Robinette's best whiskey. 'Drink this.'

Robinette gulped it down. It sloshed in his stomach and he had to fight to keep it from coming back up, especially when Fletcher gave him a second injection. 'Shit.'

Fletcher grabbed a wastebasket, set it next to him. 'Tell me if you're gonna vomit. I don't want to cut you up worse than you are. You need to get an X-ray. Your ulna could be fractured.'

'I'm not going to a hospital.'

'Of course you're not,' Fletcher said with an eye roll.

Robinette closed his eyes, gritting his teeth now against the nausea. That damn kid at the farm had come out of nowhere. Carrying a goddamn assault rifle. What the hell?

'Just be quiet and sew me up.'

Fletcher worked for several minutes in blissful silence, then ruined it by talking. 'Have you been watching the news?'

'No.' Because he *was* the news. He didn't want to hear about his fucked up attempt to breach the Assistant State's Attorney's compound.

'I heard the story while I was getting my stuff to come

meet you. I think Henderson got caught tonight. Hey! Hold still.'

Robinette blinked hard, trying to focus on Fletcher's face. The whiskey was finally taking effect. 'Whaddya mean, Henderson got caught? Where?'

'At the Peabody. There were news reports of an arrest on the penthouse level and that a woman wearing men's clothes was dragged out by police. That friend of Detective Mazzetti's, you know, Dr Townsend, was staying there. She did an interview with that Radcliffe fellow.'

'I saw it. What makes you think it was Henderson? Could have been a fan of the doctor's wanting an autograph.'

'There was a short statement by the guy in charge of the operation. Here, bite down on this.' Fletcher slipped a strap of leather in his mouth that tasted sweet. 'Sorry, it's my watchband. I didn't have anything else for you to bite down on. I have to extract the bullet now. Anyway, this Fed, name was Carter, said that VCET, the task force between BPD and the FBI, had been in complete control the entire time and at no point were any staff or guests at the hotel in danger. It was a trap. For a minute, I thought you'd been shot there, but the Fed said they'd apprehended their suspect without a single shot fired.'

'I figured it was a trap,' Robinette said, his words muffled by the strap between his teeth. Then a wave of intense pain hit him and he felt himself going under. *No.* He fought the sensation. Fought to stay awake. But the world grew wavy and strange.

*More than whiskey*, he thought dully. 'You drugged me.'

'I knew you wouldn't cooperate otherwise. If you flinch, I could slice a nerve and leave you unable to use this arm for the rest of your life. Stop fighting it. Go to sleep.'

'Can't go to sleep.'

'Yes, you can,' Fletcher said in a singsong voice that echoed. 'And you will.'

'Going to . . . kill you.' He struggled but the world was growing dark. 'Drugged me.'

'You'll have to catch me first.'

'Tell Brenda Lee . . . bail Henderson out. Can't have . . . talk.' Then he heard Fletcher's words. *You'll have to catch me first.* Fletcher was leaving. *Leaving me.* 'No. *Don't go.*'

Warm lips pressed against his brow. 'Goodbye, Robbie.'

# Chapter Twenty-Five

Stevie rested her head on Clay's shoulder, but he could feel the tension in her body. 'I remember every shot I ever fired on the job, Clay. Every wound and every fatality. I don't remember "JH" or Miss Drive-by, or whoever the hell she is. And I *never* shot a little child.'

'You're seeing Paulie and Cordelia when you think "child". My mother called me her child until the day she died,' Clay said quietly.

'Drive-by didn't look old enough to have an adult child.'

'Neither does Daphne, but Ford is twenty. Maybe we're talking about a teenager.'

Stevie closed her eyes. 'There have been only two teens during my whole career.'

'Marina Craig was one,' he supplied. 'The girl on the courthouse steps.'

'Yes. She wasn't going to stop shooting until someone stopped her.'

'And the other?' he prompted when she didn't continue.

'His name was Levi Robinette.' Her body suddenly tensed. 'Oh my God.'

He tilted her chin so that he could see her eyes. They

were filled with a horror that chilled his blood. 'What? What is it?'

'Levi Robinette. He was the son of . . . oh, God, what was his father's name? Todd. Todd Robinette.' She started to breathe faster. 'This was the case. The one I told you about last night – the case I was working the night Paul and Paulie were killed. I was trying to get it reopened.'

'Reopened? Then it had been closed?'

'It had been closed twice already. It was supposed to look like the wife and her employee died in a car accident and that's what the ME called it, but I got him to take another look at the victims' head wounds. He agreed the wounds were made with a blunt instrument and not a result of the accident. The accident had been set up to make it look like Julie and her head chemist had been having an affair and were running away together. I made Todd for the murderer, but could never pin it on him. He had an alibi, but I still had this gut feeling that he did it. I knew I'd missed something.'

'Like what?'

'I didn't know, but it didn't fit. The pieces didn't fit. I kept asking questions of the other employees and there was hardly anyone who respected Todd or even liked him for that matter. They all loved the woman's first husband, but he'd died a few years before.'

'So what happened with Levi?'

'We brought Todd in for questioning and he brought his attorney. I can't recall her name off the top of my head, but she was in a wheelchair – a war injury, I think. She urged Todd to tell us what he knew and he did. I remember he cried and I kept thinking, crocodile tears. He said his son was an addict. That Levi had been acting strangely since the death of his stepmother.'

'Not his biological mother, then.'

'No, she'd died, years before. Julie, the victim, was Todd's second wife. The first wife died of an overdose when Todd was deployed. Julie and her first husband had taken Levi in. By all accounts, the boy loved her dearly.'

'Why would Levi kill her then?'

'Levi was an addict. Todd told us that Levi and Julie had argued about money, that she'd cut him off and he couldn't get his drugs anymore. Todd allowed us to search Levi's room, and we found the murder weapon – a bat – in his closet.'

'And then?'

'Silas and I found him at a friend's house. The friend had loaned him his car and Levi had escaped through the back door and was driving away. I shot out one of his tires and Levi jumped out of the car, started to run. I tried to talk to him, but he was high and scared. And armed. He started shooting. It was a neighborhood. It was a spring day and children were playing outside. Levi wasn't specifically aiming, but kids were everywhere.'

'What happened when he started shooting?'

'I . . . shot back. First in the arm. I tried to debilitate him, but it just made him wild. He ran to a group of kids, grabbed one and was trying to use him as a shield. I had to stop him.'

'Where was Silas?'

'He'd gone to get the car, hoping to cut Levi off. He caught up with me after I'd already shot Levi a second time. He was sixteen. I was . . . devastated. The boy was dead.'

'You saved other potential victims.'

'I know, but . . .' She pressed her lips together. Regained her composure. 'I got put on desk duty pending the investigation of the shooting. Silas closed the case. Levi

Robinette was listed as the probable killer of his stepmother, Julie.'

'But you didn't believe it.'

'No. Levi was skinny and someone with some strength was responsible for killing Julie and her employee. Even if he'd been high at the time . . . I couldn't see him being lucid enough to plan putting them in a car and crashing it. I didn't agree with the ruling.'

'But you found the murder weapon in the boy's room.'

'I know. And it had his fingerprints on it. I can't explain it other than a feeling in my gut.'

'I trust your gut.' *And my own.* Clay's gut was telling him that this was very bad even before he Googled Todd Robinette. He stared at the results. 'Stevie, does the name "Filbert Pharmaceutical Labs" ring a bell?'

'"FPL",' she whispered. 'That was Julie's company. Filbert was her maiden name. Her father had started the drug business when she was a small child.'

'Todd Robinette is now the president and CEO. Apparently they've grown considerably in the last eight years. Now they ship vaccines all over the world.'

She slid the computer to her own lap and Googled images for 'filbert'. 'The nut on the silver flask isn't an acorn. It's a filbert, their logo. Unless she stole the flask, Drive-by worked for Filbert Labs.' She looked up at Clay. 'I don't think she stole it.'

'Neither do I, but we have to keep that option open. If it was hers, then Todd Robinette was her boss. Did he hate you for the death of his son?'

'Oh yes. He did.'

'What happened after you shot Levi?'

'IA investigated me, which was procedure. Todd made a big stink about how he'd begged us not to hurt his son, that he'd cooperated only because he wanted help for Levi, but there were enough witnesses to vouch that I had no other choice than to shoot Levi. IA cleared me, but by then it was time for me to go on desk duty anyway because of my pregnancy.'

'But you didn't let it go.'

She closed her eyes. 'No, I didn't. I never seem to be able to let things go.'

He brought her hand to his lips. Kissed her fingers. 'I don't consider that a failing, Stevie.'

'Then that makes one of us, I guess.'

'Why didn't you let it go? What was bothering you?'

'The whole thing. Robinette was slick, you know? He had all the answers before I asked the questions. Cried in all the right places. Told us about his son at exactly the right moment. There were other things, too. Really specific issues with his story. I can't remember all of them now, but I know they'll be in my notes.'

'Did your boss agree to reopen the case?'

'I don't know. I never submitted my report. I was working on it when Hyatt came to tell me about Paul. After that . . . nothing made sense, not for months after. Now Todd's getting his revenge. But why did he wait *eight years*?'

'Because other people weren't shooting at you eight years ago. But then cops like Tony Rossi started shooting at you, trying to keep you from exposing the investigations they fixed. Perpetrators and their families tried attacking you to keep you from discovering that they'd bought their innocence and let someone else go to jail for their crimes. What better way for Robinette to camouflage his vendetta?'

'He would have taken my child because I took his,' she whispered.

'You didn't "take his". You removed a clear and present danger to a neighborhood.'

'I know. But Levi was only sixteen. I'd talked to him about Julie when Silas and I started to investigate. He was distraught and I thought it genuine. He cried in my arms, Clay.'

'Did you think back then that Levi's father set him up to take the fall?'

'I did. That made me so . . . angry. That a father could do that to his son. When I think about that and then I think about Paul . . . He protected our son with his dying breath.' She shuddered, her body growing still. He could almost hear her brain click, re-engaging.

'But the past doesn't matter now,' she said practically. 'That he's trying to kill Cordelia and me *today* is the issue. His hate has had eight years to fester. I doubt he's going to just stop.'

'We'll make him stop. For now, we'll tell Joseph. He can keep Robinette under surveillance. He'll also want to use this information when he questions JH, whoever she is.'

'All right. But I want to witness her interrogation.'

'So do I. I'll ask Joseph to call us when he thinks she's about to break.'

Clay made the call, leaving a message summarizing what they'd discovered about Todd Robinette on Joseph's voicemail when the Fed didn't pick up. 'There. That's done.'

'Thank you.' Stevie became quiet, but he wasn't fooled into thinking she'd gone to sleep.

'What's happening in your brain?' he asked.

'Just . . . playing with the puzzle pieces. Seeing how they all fit together.' She tried to slide off his lap, but he held her firm.

'Stay here. Let me hold you.'

'I wasn't leaving. I just want to look at your laptop again.'

He guided her so that she sat between his legs, her back to his chest. He gave her the laptop, then locked his arms around her stomach and propped his chin on her shoulder so that he could see the screen, too. 'What do you want to see?'

'The security video from your house. Mr Cocksucker and Mr Backpack.'

He found the file for her. 'Why?'

'Because Drive-by works or at least worked for Filbert Pharmaceutical Labs. FPL is run by Todd Robinette. That Drive-by was acting on his orders to kill me isn't a huge leap.' She ran through the video, freezing the frame at the moment the second intruder's face was directly facing the camera. 'There was something about Backpack's eyes. Creeped me out but I didn't know why. Now that I know what I'm looking for, it's obvious to me.' She toggled the screen, bringing up Filbert Pharmaceutical's website, clicking on the CEO's bio page. 'Do you see it?'

Clay saw a man in his early forties with curly dark hair, a thin mustache, and clear blue eyes that crinkled at the corners when he smiled. The same clear blue eyes that were visible through the ski mask worn by Mr Backpack. The man who'd killed two cops. The man who'd followed them in his Tahoe, shooting at them in front of dead IA cop Scott Culp's house.

'Yeah,' he said quietly. 'The eyes are the same.'

She went back to Robinette's bio page. 'He served in the first Gulf War. Was decorated for saving the lives of several of the soldiers under his command.'

'My medals. He picked them up, out of the debris on my bedroom floor. Respectfully.'

She scrolled through the pictures of the staff. 'Drive-by isn't here anywhere. Damn.'

'It was unlikely he'd post photos of his assassin on his

corporate website.' He gave in to temptation and nuzzled her neck, her shiver doing wonders for his ego. 'It's bad PR.'

'Yeah, well, a girl can hope.' She went on clicking through the photos on the website. Then she paused, went back to an earlier picture. 'Huh. Her, I know.'

The woman in the photo was about the same age as Robinette, her short blonde hair giving her a competent air, her easy smile making her seem inviting. Genuine. Trustworthy, even. The wheelchair in which she sat gave her additional credibility.

'Brenda Lee Miller,' Clay said. 'She's his "Director of Community Affairs". And a veteran. She was paralyzed in an attack on an armored personnel carrier outside of Baghdad.'

'She's also the attorney who accompanied him when I hauled him in for questioning on the murder of his wife eight years ago. What do you want to bet that Brenda Lee served with him?'

'Easy enough to check. And if she did, maybe Drive-by did, too.'

'And Mr Cocksucker as well,' she added dryly.

'We'll get his real name. We'll get all their names. But he'll still be a cocksucker to me.'

'I'm with you on that.' She clicked back to Robinette's bio. 'Brenda Lee Miller may not have the title, but she's his PR guru, too. Look at these pictures – Robinette receiving award after award for his *humanitarian* work. Brenda Lee is quoted praising him, she's photographed with him, and she's the contact for appearances and requests for donations. She spun shit into gold.'

'We'll need hard evidence to get close to him,' Clay said. 'He's coated himself in Teflon. It'll be rough getting a charge to stick on what we have now.'

'Then we'll just have to hit him with the pan, won't we,' she said grimly.

God, he loved this woman. That she was here, with him in bed, was more than he'd hoped for. But still he wanted more. He wanted to tell her he loved her. And he wanted to hear her say the words back. For now, he'd be content with what he had.

'Is your brain about done?' he asked.

She nodded, setting his laptop back on the nightstand. 'For now. Let's get some sleep.'

*Tuesday, March 18, 7.45 A.M.*

For the first time in eight years, Stevie woke up with a man.

And what a man Clay was. He instantly dominated any room he entered. The bed they'd shared was no different. He took up two-thirds of it with his big body, but Stevie had never felt uncomfortable or cold. How could she, when he'd cuddled her close all night?

She'd missed this, the cuddling. Paul had always held her spooned against him, one arm possessively hooked around her waist. How many times had she woken to the feel of his aroused body pressing against her? So many that she'd taken it for granted that he'd always be there.

She wouldn't make the same mistake again. Not with Clay. Not for as long as she had him in her life. It was impossible not to make comparisons. Both men were handsome. Paul had had the body of a track star, lean. Honed. Clay was built like a bulldozer. Hard and strong.

Both men were honorable. Stubborn in their own way. And manipulative, also in their own way. Paul had charmed her into acquiescence. Clay simply rearranged the world around her so that his way became the path of least resistance. Paul would have respected that.

And that's as far as she'd allow the comparisons to go. She'd had a satisfying love life with her husband. She now had the opportunity to enjoy sex again, with a man she equally respected.

And enjoy it, she had. Clay was as powerful, as single-minded in his lovemaking as he was with everything else.

She lifted her head, studying his face in the light that filtered through the drapes. She had never seen him sleep, she realized. The effect was startling. He looked so young. Carefree, even. The sharp angles of his face seemed softer, the ever-present line down the middle of his forehead nowhere in sight. His mouth seemed fuller, the fine lines at the corners almost invisible.

She hadn't known how much worry he carried. It made her want to carry some of it for him.

For now, though, she'd woken to a man in her bed for the first time in eight years and she intended to make the most of it. Leaning in, she kissed his mouth with the barest of touches. Little brushes, gentle nibbles, she explored. She knew the moment he woke because the kiss came to life, becoming lush and full of movement. His hands skimmed up her sides to capture her breasts as a low growl of approval vibrated in his chest.

He rolled, settling between her thighs as fluidly as if he'd done it a thousand times. He slid down her body to draw one nipple into the warmth of his mouth, alternating between hard pulls and gentle suckling that had her hips seeking, reaching while his hands roamed, touching, enticing, making her want so much more.

She closed her eyes and let herself go, let herself enjoy the way he handled her body, the way he made her feel beautiful. Confident that whatever she craved, he'd more than satisfy.

He switched to her other breast and she threaded her fingers through his hair, pulling him closer as the seeking of her hips grew more urgent. Until she was twisting under him, grinding her core into the hard bone of his sternum. She needed more. She needed him.

'Clay, now. *Please*.'

In the blink of an eye he was looming over her, bracing his hands on either side of her head. He was breathing hard, his dark eyes focused ... *on me. Only on me*. She reached above her head, entwining her fingers with his, one hand, then the other.

'Say my name,' she said, her whisper so soft she couldn't hear herself.

But he'd heard. His eyes grew darker as he shifted his hips, entering her. She sucked in a breath, needing to grow accustomed to the thickness of him all over again.

'Stefania,' he said quietly. Reverently. 'My Stefania.' And then he began to move, slowly at first, then surging faster, harder. Held her suspended as his body went wild, driving into her with an intensity that propelled her closer, so close she could almost touch it ...

And then she did, shattering into a million pieces, hearing her own shocked cry. In a daze she drifted back down, conscious that his body had grown taut, his eyes clenched shut. With a low groan, he came, his erection kicking within her, his body spasming until he finally went still.

His head dropped forward as if he hadn't the energy to hold it up any longer and he fought to catch his breath. He carefully rolled to his side, bringing her with him so that they lay face to face. 'I want,' he murmured, 'to wake up like this every morning for the rest of my life.'

*Just like this*, she thought. *Exactly like this*. Suddenly she needed him to know it. 'So do I.'

His eyes opened, searching hers for truth and evidently liking what he found. He pulled her close, burying his face in her neck, and she felt his lips move against her skin as he spoke, his words utterly soundless.

Still, she knew what he'd said and yearned to give the words back to him. But it wasn't the right time. So she held him. The seconds became minutes and Stevie found herself wishing they were simply two normal people, able to lie in bed and hide from the world.

But at this moment they were far from normal. A knock at the door intruded on the quiet, drawing a mild snarl from Clay. 'Go away,' he muttered.

'Our coach just turned back into a pumpkin.' She pressed a kiss to his shoulder. 'It's time to go to work.'

The knock was repeated, louder and longer this time. 'Open up. It's Joseph.'

Stevie got out of bed, slid into her clothes, and found her cane. 'Just a second,' she called.

But Clay got dressed and got to the adjoining door first. He opened it to a weary Joseph. 'What's wrong?' Clay demanded. 'You look like shit.'

While she and Clay had slept and indulged in some quality morning sex, it was clear that Joseph had enjoyed neither. His eyes were haggard, his tie tugged loose, his posture worn.

'Let's sit down,' Joseph said and panic speared straight into Stevie's heart.

'What's happened to Cordelia?' she demanded, grabbing his arm.

'She's fine,' Joseph assured her. 'Totally fine. I didn't mean to worry you. I've just had a long night.' He sat at the table, shrugging when neither she nor Clay sat with him.

Stevie was holding herself rigidly, waiting for the bad news she could feel coming. Clay stood behind her, keeping her upright. 'Is it Robinette?' she asked. 'Did you bring him in?'

'Not yet. I have his home and office under surveillance, but I don't have cause to bring him in for questioning yet.'

'What about Drive-by?' she pressed. 'Do we have an ID?'

'Not yet,' Joseph said again. 'Her prints aren't in the system – neither AFIS or the military's. If she served, she must have requested her prints be removed from the database.'

'Which means she had an honorable discharge,' Clay said. 'If she served.'

Stevie nodded. 'Makes sense for an assassin to get her prints wiped. What about the gun?'

'Good news there,' Joseph said. 'Ballistics ties it to two other – recent – homicides. Scott Culp from IA and the clerk of the Key Hotel who was killed in what had been assumed to be a robbery. So we can get her for the attempt on your life and two other murders at a minimum.'

This was getting better every moment.

'Deacon Novak found her vehicle,' Joseph continued, 'an old rusted-out pickup truck. She'd stolen it from a doctor who runs a free clinic.'

'He must have patched her up after I shot her,' Clay said.

'He's denying it, although I didn't expect him to admit to it. He's compelled by law to report any gunshot wounds but he didn't. Novak's working on getting a court order so we can search the clinic for evidence that she'd been there. While we wait, I've got agents going through the clinic's trash. It's slow going, since it's a biohazard.'

'Did they find anything of hers in the truck?'

Joseph's eyes grew hard. 'A cell phone. When we matched it up with the phone we took from Culp's body and the LUDs from the phone picked up by your stingray system, Clay, we got connections. The second intruder into your house, the one who killed the two cops—'

'Robinette,' Stevie interrupted coldly.

'Probably,' Joseph allowed. 'He was called by Culp a few hours before he was killed.'

'Culp was telling Robinette where to find the safe house,' Stevie said. *Where he would have killed my daughter and me without blinking an eye.*

Joseph nodded. 'Right. But he called a *different* number several times that afternoon before arriving at your house, Clay.'

'Were you able to track that phone?' Clay asked.

'Not right away. We tried, but it had gone off-line. But then, that phone called the disposable we found in Drive-by's stolen truck yesterday, right before Emma's interview. Drive-by received the call while sitting at the bar downstairs, in this hotel. The call came through a satellite service provided by one of the trans-Pacific airlines.'

'Somebody left the country,' Stevie said angrily. 'Shit. Well, what did Drive-by say when you confronted her with all of this?'

'I haven't yet. I wanted her to stew in her juices a little longer and I thought you'd like to be there when I did confront her. Plus, I've been a little busy.'

'Your long night,' Clay said. 'What happened, Joseph?'

'There was an attempt to breach the gate at the farm last night,' Joseph said, rubbing his hands down his face. 'It was unsuccessful, but we are not without casualties.'

'Who?' Stevie asked hoarsely. 'Emma? Daphne?'

Clay's swallow was audible. 'Alec?'

'No to all the above. I lost two men. Everyone else was unharmed.'

Stevie dropped into a chair, her knees gone rubbery. 'Oh my God. Joseph, I'm sorry.'

He nodded, his jaw taut. 'Thanks.'

Clay moved behind her chair, his hands on her shoulders. 'When did this happen?'

Joseph looked down at the table, his jaw growing tighter. 'About eleven thirty last night.'

It took a second to sink in, but when it did, Stevie saw red. *'What?'* She came out of her chair, both hands on the table as she leaned into Joseph's space. 'You knew last night when we caught Drive-by in our room. You knew and you didn't tell us?'

Joseph looked up and Stevie sucked in a shocked breath. His eyes were dead. Dark and dead. He'd lost two men, she reminded herself.

Slowly she backed away until she was in her own chair. 'Okay. I'll try that again, more calmly this time. Why didn't you tell us? I had a right to know.'

'And what would you have done, Stevie?' Joseph asked wearily. 'Jumped in your car and raced to Cordelia to make sure I wasn't lying and that she was really all right?'

Her chin lifted. 'Yes.'

Joseph shook his head. 'Allowing you to race out there, maybe right into his sights if he was still waiting somewhere along the road? No. It wasn't going to happen. Cordelia was safe inside the gate. You were safe here. Given the same situation, I'd do it again.'

'I could have at least called my daughter on the phone,' Stevie whispered. 'She must have been so scared.'

'She was. But Emma was there and once it was all over, Cordelia was all right. She doesn't know about the lost men.'

'Of course she does,' Clay murmured. 'Her listening skills are the envy of NSA.' He squeezed Stevie's shoulders lightly. 'She's okay, honey. You sent her there to keep her safe and she is. What happened exactly, Joseph?'

'Somebody ordered a pizza delivered to the farm, but my agents knew it was a hoax and so did Ethan. Ethan had set up a plan and drilled the troops.' One side of Joseph's mouth lifted wryly. 'He must have been one hell of a Marine.'

'He was.' The pride in Clay's voice was unmistakable.

'He had Maggie and Alec with him. Paige and Emma stayed with Cordelia. Daphne guarded the downstairs. Ethan deactivated the bolt hole section of fence, went over, reactivated, approached the pizza guy at the gate from behind while Maggie confronted him head-on. Ethan believed he had the situation under control and had subdued the intruder – who turned out to be a real pizza delivery guy, poor kid. Ethan was about to hand him over to my agents, but at that point the alarm detected a second intruder, one who proved to have a rifle and a far steadier hand than Miss Drive-by. Both my agents went down in less than five seconds.' Joseph swallowed. 'He shot them in the head.' Another pointed look at Stevie. 'The bullets that killed them matched the bullet the ER doc took out of Paige.'

'I'm not an idiot, Joseph,' Stevie said levelly. 'That the shooter was the same man is not a shock. It was probably Robinette, too. I realize he might have been waiting to kill me when I ran to Cordelia. But you have to understand. I'm a mother who put her child into the care of others. You should have told me. I could have at least called her. Let her know I love her even if I couldn't be with her at that moment.'

Joseph sighed. 'I'm sorry, Stevie. You're right. But I just

had to do three notifications to next of kin. I'm . . . I'm running on empty.'

Stevie reached across the table, gripping his hand. Then she blinked. 'Wait. Three notifications? I thought you lost two agents.'

Joseph sighed again. 'I wondered how Drive-by knew to come straight to this suite last night. Phin Radcliffe found his cameraman's body this morning. He went to check on him when the guy didn't answer his phone or show up to work. Found him dead in his car.'

Stevie closed her eyes. 'Hell. We laid a trap and used those two men to do it. We're responsible for that man's death.'

'No,' Clay said, sliding his hands up her shoulders to the curve of her neck. 'I told them the cops would give them protection and they said no.'

'I had agents on protective detail,' Joseph added. 'Both Radcliffe and his cameraman eluded them. This morning, Radcliffe told us that his cameraman had gone to a bar to unwind. We got video from the bar showing him sitting with Drive-by.'

Clay sat in the chair beside Stevie, his expression guilty despite his assertion that they were not to blame. 'Are we any closer to having a real name on her?'

'No. But she's really shaky now. Needs that morning belt to get her going. That's one of the reasons I came. To tell you that she's about ready to give us some answers.'

'How did Radcliffe find his cameraman?' Stevie asked.

'Tracked his phone. They had a buddy system set up because Radcliffe's life is "routinely threatened", in his words. He's pretty rattled, as you might expect.'

Stevie sighed. Joseph had endured a long night. And her daughter was safe. Still she had to fight the urge to run to the phone and call her. *You will call her. Get the information you need and then call your daughter and tell her you love her.*

'The shooter was most likely Robinette or one of his men. He took out two of your agents,' she said. 'What happened then?'

'The shooter started running toward Ethan and the poor pizza delivery guy. I think he planned to use one or both to get Maggie to let him through the gate.' Joseph looked over her head at Clay, his mouth curved in a true smile. 'But Alec stopped him.'

Clay stared at him. 'How?'

'Alec got the same motion detector alarm that Ethan had, about the shooter. He deactivated the bolt hole, went over, and reactivated, just like Ethan had shown him. He followed the shooter and got him in the arm.'

'Was Alec hit?' Clay asked hoarsely.

'Not a scratch. Well, a few scratches from twigs. None from bullets.'

'But the shooter got away?' Stevie hoped the answer would be no. Knew it would not.

'Yeah, unfortunately, in a Jeep, which probably means he knows about the BOLO on the Tahoe. But Alec kept his cool. Kept himself safe and gave us some evidence.' Joseph looked grimly satisfied. 'Bastard left some blood behind.'

'Then we'll be able to tie him to the shooting at the dock,' Stevie said with a hard nod. 'He left a hair behind, there in the trees where he waited to take his shots.' She took Clay's hand. He looked a little gray. 'Alec is okay.'

'I know, but . . . my God. He's . . . he's like a son to me.'

Stevie squeezed the hand she held. 'You can call and talk to him just like I'll talk to Cordelia. Satisfy yourself that he's unharmed. Joseph, when will you interview Drive-by?'

'After I shower and change. Give me thirty minutes.'

Joseph walked to the door, then paused and checked his phone with a frown.

'What is it?' Stevie asked. 'Please, not more bad news.'

'No,' Joseph said. 'But puzzling. We've had techs checking toll cameras for that Chevy Tahoe since the dock shooting yesterday morning. We found it coming over the Bay Bridge late Sunday night from Baltimore, but the camera didn't get his face. He wore a mask and covered most of it with the brim of a baseball cap. He used the E-Z pass lanes, so no booth operators interacted with him.'

'So you got a registration on the E-Z pass?' Clay asked eagerly.

'Yes, but it didn't match the Tahoe. The E-Z pass sticker was probably stolen from another car. That's not the puzzling part. It's the route he took.'

'Why?' Stevie asked. 'The Bay Bridge is the route everyone takes to the beach.'

'But it's not the way he went back,' Joseph said. 'We tried to find him coming back over the bridge, but got nothing – because he drove south to Virginia first. We got him going through the Bay Bridge Tunnel towards Newport News at nine thirty A.M.'

'Why would he do that?' Stevie wondered. 'Could he live down there?'

'Maybe. There have been no confirmed sightings of the Tahoe since then.'

'And last night's shooter drove a Jeep,' Clay said. 'My gut tells me they're the same guys, but I could have sworn Drive-by was male, too. Has the Jeep been found?'

'Kind of. He pulled a page out of Drive-by's notebook and torched it. So far we've found no viable blood samples. Right now, our best bet is to break Drive-by. I'll meet you in thirty.'

'That gives me time to call Cordelia,' Stevie said. 'And Clay to call Alec.' She hesitated. 'Joseph? Thank you for keeping my daughter safe.'

Joseph's smile was tired. 'Always, Stevie. Like I said, you've put your life on the line for so many of us, so many times. It's time for us to give back.'

'Two men did,' she murmured. 'Now that I've had a chance to calm down and think . . . I'm so sorry for those men and their families. I'd like the names of the agents you lost so that I can write letters to their next of kin, thanking them for their sacrifice.'

Joseph nodded. 'That would be nice. They were good men. They'll be missed.'


*Tuesday, March 18, 9.03 A.M.*

'I wish I could let you take the videos with you, but you have to watch them here.' Ruby's news studio contact pointed to a computer monitor on a desk in an otherwise empty room. 'Rules,' he added with a shrug. 'Buzz me when you're done. I'll walk you two out.'

Sam frowned as two station employees passed by the room's open door, weeping quietly. They were not the first people he'd seen crying in the newsroom. 'What's happened here?'

The man sighed. 'We lost a cameraman last night. He went out for a drink and left the bar with the wrong woman. She shot him then stole his wallet and all his gear. We're in . . . shock.'

'I'm sorry,' Ruby said softly. 'I usually hear about these things, but I took a day off.'

The man shook his head. 'Pascal was always picking up women in bars. I worried that he'd pick the wrong one. I'm supposed to be in the control booth. Call if you need anything.'

'We will,' Ruby said. 'Pull up a chair, Sam.'

Sam did, and watched Ruby's long red nails clatter on the keyboard as she ran a search on the rows and rows of titles and dates. 'We want March 15, eight years ago. Here it is.' She glanced over at him soberly. 'You ready?'

He nodded. 'Play it.' When she did, Sam forgot to breathe.

The man who walked into the convenience store that March day eight years ago moved like his father. His hands were his father's. His face was hidden from the camera by the Orioles cap on his head. 'That's my cap. Oh my God. He wore it that day.'

And it had been returned to Sam three days ago.

Ruby looked doubtful. 'How can you be sure?'

'Stop the video, on that frame. Can you enlarge?' She did and he pointed to the screen. 'There's a chunk missing from the plastic band in the back. See it? I had a dog then. It was before my father got addicted. The dog was chewing on my cap and when I yanked it away, part of the plastic band got notched out by the dog's teeth. The cap was in the package that got delivered to my mother's house on Saturday.'

'Oh,' Ruby murmured. 'Should I go on? The rest of this is hard to watch. I remember seeing it over and over during the trial.'

'You went to the trial?'

'I retrieved Mr Mazzetti's body.' She swallowed hard. 'And the body of his son. I always go to the trials, if I can. At least for a day. I figure it's the least I can do.'

Sam's heart turned over. 'I've been to a few autopsies for just that reason. I figured someone should.'

'You don't need to watch the rest of this, Sam.'

'I do. I need to know, Ruby. Please play the rest.'

'All right.' She hit play and the video continued. Sam's father reached up under the cap and pulled a ski mask over his face. Then he walked to the counter, pulled out a gun and shot Paul Mazzetti in the chest and Mazzetti went down. *Oh God.*

The cashier made a sudden move – a gun. She'd pulled a gun from beneath the counter. Sam watched his father shoot the woman in the head and she collapsed onto the counter, the blood rushing from the wound. And then . . . Sam blinked as Paul Mazzetti got up.

The prosecutor had worn a bullet-proof vest. His father's back went ramrod stiff – shocked that Mazzetti wasn't dead. His father hesitated, then pointed his gun at the man's head.

Just as a little boy ran into the store, his young face contorted with fury.

Sam's racing heart pounded faster, harder until all he could hear was his pulse thundering in his ears. *No*, he wanted to shout. *Stop.* But there was no stopping it. It had been done.

His father pulled the trigger.

'The bullet passed through Paul Mazzetti's arm,' Ruby said quietly. 'And . . . hit the boy.'

The little boy crumpled to the floor, Paul Mazzetti hovering over him as he twisted around to grab Hudson's gun. Another shot – this one to Mazzetti's head – and Mazzetti fell on top of his son. A full ten seconds passed as Sam's father stared at the two bodies on the floor.

'The boy wasn't dead yet,' Ruby murmured. 'The paramedics told me that he died right after they got there.' Her fingers brushed his cheeks and Sam realized he was crying.

He watched, numbly now, as his father ran from the store.

Sam pressed his fist against his lips, the tears flowing freely down his face. Ruby tucked some tissues into his free hand. As he used them on his cheeks, it registered in his mind that the tissues smelled like her. Spicy. Sweet. He drew a breath as she rubbed his back.

'Why?' he whispered. 'Why would he do such a thing? He didn't even take the money.'

'Maybe he got scared and just ran, Sam.'

'Then why drag me into it?' He took the mouse and rewound the film, freezing it so that he could look at his father's gun. 'This isn't the gun I found next to me. Why drug me and leave me in a hotel room with a different gun next to my head? The gun that killed my father? Why?'

She said nothing. Just rubbed his back with big, sweeping circles.

'He wore my hat. My hat, Ruby. Why?'

'Maybe it made him feel close to you.'

'While he was murdering three innocent people?' Sam cried. '*No.* I don't want him to have felt close to me. I don't want him to have even been my father, but that's out of my hands.'

'My father died when I was five, Sam. He was a drug dealer and was killed in a deal gone very bad. He sold poison to children. Yet every night he'd tuck me into bed and sing to me. You can't choose your parents and you can't choose how they feel about you.'

'You're right. I know you are. What are you doing?' he asked when she took the mouse.

'Checking something. I didn't pay attention to it before and I don't think it came up in the trial.' She rewound the tape again, hit play, then froze it. 'Look. He's standing at the oil can display and he takes out his phone. Looks at something. What's he looking at?'

It was an old-fashioned flip phone with a small screen. 'Can you enlarge it?'

'I can try.' She enlarged, re-centered, enlarged again. 'It's a person,' she finally said, and he could see it, although the picture was now hopelessly pixelated. 'Tied to a chair.'

And then Sam knew. 'It's me,' he whispered. 'Oh my God, *that's me*. There was a cushion on the floor next to me when I woke up. I remember it was this hideous orange color.' His finger trembling, he pointed to an unfocused blob of orange. 'It's the chair cushion.'

'That's why you were taken,' Ruby whispered. 'So that your father could be forced to do this terrible thing.'

Sam closed his eyes. 'And he did it. For me. I can't believe this. He killed a man . . . killed a *child*. Dammit, Ruby, what am I supposed to think? What am I supposed to feel?'

She was quiet, her hand back on his back, rubbing big circles again. 'That he loved you? That he was very flawed, but at the end . . . he loved you.'

'No. If he'd really loved me he couldn't have killed for me. How can I live with this? How can I live knowing three innocent people died? How do I make amends for this?'

'You did nothing wrong, Sam. You did nothing wrong.'

'I hear your words,' he said, his throat gone too thick to breathe. 'But I can't accept them.'

She rested her head on his shoulder. 'Then for now I'll accept them for you.' She exhaled slowly. 'Last night you forgave Kayla Richards for allowing you to be drugged and dragged away. You didn't blink an eye, even though she actually *did* do something wrong. But you forgave her. Eventually you'll find that forgiveness for yourself. Even though you have done nothing that demands forgiveness or amends. You are a victim, Sam.'

'Not like the Mazzettis. Or that cashier.'

She sighed. 'I see so many families come into the morgue, grieving. I can't tell you how many times they raise their faces to God and demand to know why. Why the deceased was taken and not them? It's survivor guilt you're feeling, *cariño*.'

He nodded, not wanting to deny her words because she clearly believed them.

Ruby smiled sadly, as if reading his mind. 'If you ask me – and you did – I think you'd be better served throwing all this upset . . . this energy into figuring out who did this to you.'

On that he could wholeheartedly agree. 'You're right. I need to find out who Kayla Richards saw dragging me out of the Rabbit Hole that night.'

'When will that police artist be available?'

'I still haven't heard from him. I need to report this but Thorne made me promise I'd come to him before I talked to the cops.'

'Then call him and ask him to meet us.'

Sam made the call, looked at Ruby with relief when he'd hung up. 'He wants me to talk to JD Fitzpatrick. Thorne will come with me. He says Fitzpatrick can be trusted to handle this.'

'Thorne is right. I can personally vouch for JD. His wife, Lucy, was my boss before she went on family leave. JD's a good man.'

Sam nodded. 'I've heard that from a lot of people. Will you come with me, too?'

'I'd like to see anyone try to stop me.'

# Chapter Twenty-Six

Henderson hurt. The cravings had become bad a few hours before and now the need for a drink was nearly unbearable. *Just a little. Just a taste. Just enough to take off the edge.*

*I need to be able to think. I can't think.*

They'd dumped her in an interview room, shackling her leg to a ring in the floor, taking her out once to use the bathroom. She had no concept of time, had no idea of how long she'd waited.

Henderson supposed on some level she'd known the setup at the Peabody would be a trap. Unfortunately, wherever that level was, it hadn't been front and center of her mind last night when she'd made her decision to go in and get Mazzetti. *And now I'm fucked. Busted.*

Except they couldn't prove anything. They could get her for B&E and carrying a concealed weapon, but they couldn't pin anything else on her.

*So what if they had her flask? She'd swear she stole it. They couldn't prove shit.*

The door opened and a woman in her mid-forties walked in. She wore a charcoal suit, a fuchsia blouse and

561

three-hundred-dollar shoes. 'Miss Smith, I'm your attorney, Cecilia Wright.'

*Miss Smith.* The Feds still didn't have her ID'd, Henderson thought. 'Who sent you?'

'I've been retained by a friend. I'm trying to get you out on bail.'

Henderson frowned. 'Which friend?'

Wright looked pointedly at the two-way mirror. 'I'll share that information in a more private place. Say nothing. Let me do the talking and I'll get you out of here in no time at all.'

*Robinette*, Henderson thought. He'd hired the Wright woman to get her out. *Then I'll be where he wants me.* Out in the open and vulnerable. *Bye-bye me.*

The door opened again, admitting the Fed who'd cuffed her the night before. His smile was caustically brittle. 'I'm Special Agent Carter. I trust you remember me from last night.'

Cecilia Wright closed a hand over her wrist. 'I've advised my client to say nothing.'

'I'm sure you have,' the Fed said. 'But I think I can change her mind.'

*Tuesday, March 18, 10.30 A.M.*

'Sit down, Sam,' Ruby said, patting the chair beside her. 'You're making *me* nervous.'

Sam halted his pacing and forced himself to sit along with Ruby, Thomas Thorne, and Kayla Richards in the small meeting room on the homicide floor of BPD.

'I'm sorry,' Sam said. 'How much longer will Fitzpatrick make us wait? My sketch artist friend said he might be able to squeeze us in before noon. Kayla has to get back to work.'

'I can stay as long as you need me,' Kayla said. 'My boss was very supportive of me coming down here. Like I said last night, he's a good guy.'

'So's Fitzpatrick,' Thorne said. 'Try to relax, Sam.'

Sam nodded, aware that his nerves had nothing to do with Kayla's timetable and everything to do with the fact that he was about to spill his story to a fellow cop. Most of his story anyway.

Thorne had advised Sam to begin by filing a complaint for the assault against him at the Rabbit Hole. That would allow any evidence they gathered, including Kayla's description of his attacker to the sketch artist, to be admissible should his case come to court.

'JD just texted me,' Ruby said. 'He's on his way.'

A minute later the door opened and JD Fitzpatrick entered the small room. Thorne took up most of the space, but Fitzpatrick and Sam, both about the same size, took their share.

Fitzpatrick quickly scanned their faces before taking his seat. 'Ruby. Thorne.'

'This is Officer Hudson,' Thorne said. 'The cop I called you about.'

Fitzpatrick gave Sam a quick once-over. 'You were at Sheidalin on Sunday night.'

'Yes, I was. I enjoyed your wife's music, very much.'

'I'll tell Lucy you said so.' Fitzpatrick turned to Kayla. 'You, ma'am, I don't know.'

Kayla's hands trembled but her voice was clear. 'My name is Kayla Richards.'

'She's a witness to a crime, JD,' Thorne said.

'An assault.' JD gave Thorne a hard stare. 'Why me? Why did you want me for this?'

'Because we want the best,' Thorne said and Fitzpatrick snorted.

'You sweet-talker you,' he said sarcastically. 'Okay, Hudson, let's hear it.'

Sam told him about the phone call from his old classmate's non-existent brother-in-law luring him to the Rabbit Hole and waking up a day and a half later. He said nothing about the gun, on Thorne's advice. He also said nothing about his father's involvement in the convenience store robbery, or the murder of Paul Mazzetti and his son.

But he wanted to. It was all Sam could do not to confess it all.

Kayla filled in the gaps, repeating the story she'd told them the night before.

Fitzpatrick looked up from his notepad. 'So we're filing the assault complaint against an unknown suspect and the bartender, who's currently in prison for a separate assault.'

'That's right,' Sam said.

Fitzpatrick studied him shrewdly. 'Why now, Officer?'

Sam opened his mouth to answer, but Thorne broke in. 'Officer Hudson received a package on Saturday, the eighth anniversary of his assault. In it was a matchbook from the Rabbit Hole. Being a police officer, he began to investigate.'

Fitzpatrick frowned. 'That would have been March 15, eight years ago?' He held Thorne's gaze for so long that Sam started to worry. 'That was an eventful day, Counselor.'

Fitzpatrick knew. Or suspected. It wasn't a huge stretch, Sam supposed. The detective was Stevie Mazzetti's former partner. He'd know her personal history.

Thorne didn't blink. 'Like I said. We want the best.'

Fitzpatrick shook his head, then looked at Kayla with a gentle smile. 'Miss Richards, would you mind waiting outside in the hall for a moment?'

'Of course not.' Uncertainly, Kayla gathered her purse and left the room, closing the door.

Fitzpatrick turned to Ruby. 'Ruby, what the hell is this about?' Thorne started to speak again and Fitzpatrick shot him an annoyed look. 'I asked Ruby, not you.'

Ruby sighed. 'Can you just file the report for now, JD? Please? Know that if this becomes bigger, you'll have been in on it from the beginning. We'll want your help. For now, it's better to leave the story where it is.'

'Better for who?' Fitzpatrick asked stubbornly.

'Better for me,' Sam said honestly. 'Maybe better for a lot of people. Please, Detective. I need your help.'

Fitzpatrick blew out a breath. 'Fine. I'll file the report.' He fired up the computer on the desk and logged into the system. A few minutes later, the printer on the desk spit out a single page. 'Here you go. You're officially a crime victim, Officer Hudson.'

'Thank you. I promise that I'll tell you everything as soon as I can. You have my word.'

'I appreciate that, Officer. You're lucky I know these two through my wife. I even like Ruby.' He glared at Thorne. 'The counselor here is a different story.'

'You're just jealous,' Thorne said scornfully, 'because I always win at poker.'

'Because you cheat.' Fitzpatrick's words were mild, however.

'Don't let those two fool you,' Ruby said, taking Sam's hand in hers. 'Thorne is godfather to JD and Lucy's baby.'

'I didn't know that,' Sam said.

Fitzpatrick returned his attention to Sam. 'And Stevie Mazzetti is my son's godmother.'

'I didn't know that either.' Some of the tension in his shoulders loosened.

'It'll be okay,' Ruby murmured. 'You're in the best of hands, Sam.'

Sam looked at her hand, still holding his. 'I know.'

Fitzpatrick stood up. 'I'll pay a visit to the bartender at the prison as soon as I can.'

'I'll do that,' Sam said but Fitzpatrick shook his head.

'On this case you are no longer a cop, Hudson. Stay away from the witnesses. I'll work with your sketch artist, but only because he's a department resource and they're damn hard to get. Don't set up any more interviews or any more sessions with artists or anyone else. I'll interview the bartender as soon as I can, but now I have to be somewhere else. We've been a little busy the last few days. If you'll excuse me.' He hurried out, checking his phone.

Thorne rose as well. 'I have to be in court after lunch, so I won't be reachable by phone. Text or email me when the sketch artist has finished with Miss Richards. Ruby, Sam, be careful. I don't like the way this case is going. Too many damn coincidences.'

Sam followed Thorne out, found Kayla leaning against a wall, her eyes wide.

'What?' Sam asked. 'What happened?'

'A group of people just took the elevator down. One of them was that detective that's been on the news. Mazzetti, I think her name is. That poor woman.'

*You have no idea.* Sam's phone buzzed in his pocket, allowing him to focus on something other than the image of his father killing Detective Mazzetti's family. 'It's a text from Damon, the sketch artist.' Sam frowned. 'His morning session went long and now he has no time before lunch to squeeze us in. He wants to know if you can come back at four o'clock?'

'Of course,' she said. 'I'll see you then.' With a little wave she got into the elevator.

Sam looked behind him to where Ruby stood in the doorway. 'Nothing's going to happen until later. You might as well go home or at least enjoy your day off.'

'What about you?'

'I'm going to check out the convenience store clerk. Find out about her next of kin.'

'Still planning to make amends for your father, Sam?' she asked, so gently.

'I have to try.' Three lives lost. Four, counting his father. Families left behind to grieve. *Including mine.* 'I haven't told my mother. I don't know how to even start. She has a heart condition. I'm afraid this is going to kill her.'

Ruby came to him, wrapped her arms around his waist, leaned her forehead against his chest. 'Would you like me to come with you when you tell her? For moral support?'

He held her to him, resting his cheek on the top of her head. 'Yeah. I think so. Thank you.'

'All part of the service,' she said.

He hesitated, then decided it was better to know than to wonder. 'How many people get this service?' He'd meant to keep his voice light, but that wasn't going to happen. Not today.

'You,' she said simply. 'Just you.'

He shuddered out a relieved sigh. 'Thank God for that. Listen, you don't have to stay here with me. I'll be fine. You should spend your afternoon off doing something for yourself. Maybe go to the university and apply to the forensic science program.'

She flashed him a smile. 'Maybe I will. Would you like me to come back for the artist session?'

'Yes. And then maybe we can go to dinner?'

'Sounds good.' Her smile faded. 'Don't do anything crazy, please. I agree with Thorne. I don't like the way any of this is headed.'

'I promise.' Sam started to go down to the precinct library where he could research the convenience store clerk's next-of-kin but changed his mind, parking his ass on a bench with a view of the elevator. Hopefully, Mazzetti would return from wherever she'd gone.

He didn't know what to say, but he needed to say something. His father had ruined her life.

*Tuesday, March 18, 10.35 A.M.*

'She doesn't look like the woman we subdued last night,' Stevie murmured, standing on the observation side of the interview-room glass while Drive-by sat on the other.

'I figured a few hours without a bottle would make her twitchy,' Clay said.

And twitchy she was. The woman was constant, jerking motion. A foot bobbing, her fingers drumming, even pulling her own hair. In contrast, her attorney sat calmly beside her.

Joseph sat at the table across from her, watching her curiously.

'What are we waiting for?' Drive-by demanded.

Her attorney frowned. 'Miss Smith. I asked you to let me do the talking.'

'Miss *Smith*?' Stevie asked. 'She couldn't come up with anything more original than that?'

'She doesn't know that we know her real name,' Hyatt said, shutting the observation room door behind himself and Grayson as they entered.

Stevie's brows lifted. 'What is it?'

Hyatt came to stand beside her. 'Jean Henderson. She and Robinette served together as MPs and she's a marksman, so she could be our restaurant shooter. So far she's the only suspect with a gunshot wound to the shoulder consistent with the driver who fired on you in your yard.'

'Jean Henderson.' Stevie stared through the glass, clearly remembering the sounds of the glass shattering behind her, the screams of the restaurant patrons. The sightless eyes of the waitress who'd been standing behind her chair. The hopelessness of Elissa Selmon's husband as Emma tried to save his wife's life.

And in her own front yard, she remembered the terror in Cordelia's eyes when Clay picked her up off the ground and carried her into the house. *Jean Henderson, I hope you fry*.

'I expected her attorney to be Brenda Lee Miller,' she said aloud. 'Who is this woman?'

'Cecilia Wright,' Grayson said. 'She's doing this pro bono.'

Clay frowned. 'How was she assigned or hired or whatever?'

'Good question.' Grayson dropped his chin, murmuring into his lapel. 'Go ahead, Joseph.'

Joseph stretched, making himself comfortable. 'We know who you are, Miss Henderson.'

Her attorney didn't blink an eye. Henderson gave the woman a long, hard, suspicious stare before returning her attention to Joseph. 'That's not my name. You are mistaken, Agent Carter.'

'No, I'm not.' Joseph tossed photos of Henderson onto the table, all provided by the military. 'We know who you work for.' He tossed another photo on the table – that of Todd Robinette, standing behind a podium. That got a reaction – out of both women.

Henderson went abruptly still, like a plug was pulled on all her nervous motion.

Her attorney laughed. 'Agent Carter, really. That's Todd

Robinette. He's a successful businessman and a philanthropist. Surely you're joking.'

Joseph gave the attorney a sharp look. 'I've got eleven bodies in the morgue. I'm not in a joking mood.' He turned back to Henderson. 'We know where you lived.' A photo of a burned-out apartment hit the table's surface. 'And we know what you've done.'

Carefully he lined up crime scene photos – the restaurant, Stevie's front yard, Scott Culp's house, the hotel where the clerk had been found, and the news cameraman's car which had blood splattered all over the inside of the windows.

Henderson scanned them all, her eyes returning to Scott Culp's house with a puzzled frown.

'And we know who you've killed,' Joseph added. Beneath the crime scene photos, he lined up photos of faces – Elissa Selmon and Angie Thurman from the restaurant, Phin Radcliffe's cameraman, IA detective Scott Culp, and the young clerk from the hotel.

Again her eyes narrowed slightly at the last two photos.

'She didn't do Scott Culp or the hotel clerk,' Stevie said. 'I wonder who did?'

On the other side of the glass, Henderson was shaking her head. 'Who are they?' she asked, gesturing widely at all the photographs.

'You mean who are *they*?' Joseph countered, pulling Culp and the clerk away from the others. 'This is Scott Culp. He was a cop. Worked Internal Affairs. Sergeant Culp called this number a few hours before he was killed.' He slid a sheet of paper across the table to Henderson.

Her eyes flickered for an instant. But it was enough.

'That's the number they picked up from your stingray,' Stevie murmured. 'Mr Backpack, aka Todd Robinette.'

'*That* number called *this* number.' Joseph slid another

sheet of paper across the table. 'Who later called you. So, you're connected to Sergeant Culp.'

Again her attorney laughed. 'And I'm connected to every person on the planet according to Kevin Bacon. You've got nothing, Agent Carter. Charge her with B&E and let her go.'

Joseph ignored the attorney. 'This young man,' he said, tapping the photo of the clerk, 'was found dead behind the desk of the hotel where he worked.'

'Tragic,' the attorney said, 'but he, like Sergeant Culp, has nothing to do with my client.'

'Your gun killed them, Miss Henderson,' Joseph said. 'The gun you carried last night.'

Henderson's eyes snapped up to stare at Joseph's face, her cheeks becoming a dull, mottled red. 'Sonofa*bitch*,' she snarled.

'Somebody set her up,' Clay murmured. 'My money's on that trans-Pacific caller.'

'Miss Smith,' the attorney reprimanded, her voice like a whip. 'Say nothing.'

Joseph shrugged. 'She doesn't have to. Ballistics said it all.'

Henderson's jaw clenched. 'I want a deal.'

Her attorney stayed calm. 'Miss Smith, if you do what I say, I can get you out of here.'

Henderson's mouth curved in an ugly smile. 'I'd last a whole thirty seconds after walking out of here with you. You may consider your ass fired.' She crossed her arms over her chest. 'I want a new lawyer. Somebody that I pick out of the damn phone book. And I want a deal.'

'No deal, Joseph,' Grayson said into the microphone on his lapel.

'Depends on what you have to say,' Joseph said to Henderson, ignoring him.

'You want Robinette?' Henderson asked silkily.

'Maybe,' Joseph replied. 'Depends on the price.'

'I want out of here. I want immunity. I want a seat on the next flight to Sao Paulo.'

'Gotta hand it to the bitch,' Stevie said. 'She's bold.'

'More like desperate.' Clay glanced down at Stevie, considering. 'She didn't hire her own lawyer and she doesn't trust whoever did, probably Robinette. Joseph put Robinette's home and office under surveillance, but has anyone actually seen him? Could he have been the one who called Henderson from over the Pacific yesterday afternoon?'

'No,' Grayson said. 'Robinette couldn't have called her because he had dinner with the city manager last night, here in Baltimore. Joseph's aide has created a timeline of Robinette's movements over the last few weeks. His PR person is very prompt with his Facebook updates.'

'Well, whoever called her from the plane probably gave her the gun,' Stevie said. 'He must have killed Culp and the clerk with it. I'm betting it was Thing One. Remember how he looked when he came back to find Robinette had broken the necks of those two cops? He knew his boss had lost it. I'd leave the country, too. We don't need her for Robinette. We've got blood and hair to nail him. We want Cocksucker.'

On the other side of the glass, Joseph coughed, then roughly cleared his throat. 'I was thinking more along the lines of a ply upgrade on the toilet paper in your cell,' he said, responding to Henderson's blatant request for safe passage out to Brazil.

Henderson's eyes flashed rage. 'I'm not going to prison,' she stated flatly.

Joseph stood, gathered the photos from the table. 'I have five victims that say you are. How you live while you're there is up to you.' He walked to the door, leaving Henderson fuming.

'Carter,' Henderson barked before he got out of the room.

Joseph paused, his hand on the doorknob, brows arched. 'Yes?'

'Where did he call from?'

He looked over his shoulder. 'Who?'

'Miss Smith, please—'

Henderson pivoted in her chair to face the attorney. 'You shut the fuck up!' She turned back to Joseph. 'You have my phone. I'm no fool. I know you know where the call came from, the one I got yesterday afternoon.'

Joseph studied her for a long moment. Then shrugged. 'Somewhere over the Pacific.'

Henderson's lips firmed. 'He's your killer and he's left the country. I can give him to you.'

'We can still figure him out,' Stevie murmured into Grayson's lapel. 'If he served with her and Robinette, we can cross-reference his name to flight manifests of trans-Pacific flights yesterday. Assuming he flew under his own name.'

'I don't need your help that badly,' Joseph said to Henderson. 'I have you for three murders – Culp, the clerk, and the cameraman. CSU will find something to tie you to the restaurant. Even if they don't, you'll go to prison for the rest of your life.'

Henderson shook her head. 'Don't think so. See, Robinette wants your cop. Bad. He doesn't care who he wastes to get her. She's gonna live her life on the run, because he's never gonna stop hunting her.'

Her attorney smacked the table. 'Miss Smith. Stop this. You're admitting guilt.'

Henderson didn't flick the woman a glance. 'And

Mazzetti's little girl? Todd Robinette would kill the kid and not lose a second's sleep. He'd laugh, in fact. It would make his day.'

If looks could kill, Henderson would be on the floor, gasping her last. *I want to see you fry*, Stevie thought. But she controlled herself because she wanted to see Robinette fry even more.

Joseph leaned against the door, a relaxed smile on his face. 'Now who's going to believe that? A man like Mr Robinette, so kind, so generous with his fortune. He funds rehab centers for teens. Receives awards from the city for his good deeds. He'd never kill a child.'

Henderson's eyes narrowed. 'Don't mock me, Carter.' Then she smiled.

A chill ran down Stevie's spine. 'She's like a fucking cobra.'

'This is the real Henderson,' Clay murmured. 'She's muscled her way through her cravings for booze.'

'You think you know Todd Robinette?' Henderson asked, laughter in her voice. 'You don't know jack shit.'

'This interview is over,' the attorney said, coming to her feet.

'Why is she still here?' Henderson asked mildly.

Joseph was ignoring the attorney, his eyes on Henderson's smiling face. 'What do you mean, we don't know jack shit?' he asked quietly.

Henderson shrugged, stared at her fingernails. Looked up with a smugness that, if it was an act, was a damn good one. 'Sao Paulo is beautiful this time of year.'

'Sao Paulo is beautiful any time of year.' Joseph opened the door and looked over his shoulder. 'Too bad for you because you'll never see it again.'

*Tuesday, March 18, 10.55 A.M.*

Joseph closed the observation room door behind him. 'Impressions?'

'I don't think she's bluffing,' Clay said slowly. 'She knows something big. She was saving it for last, in case you didn't rise to the Cordelia bait.'

'I agree,' Joseph said. 'She's—'

'Excuse me!' They turned to see Henderson on her feet, as close to the glass as her chain would allow, the smug smile still on her face. 'If I get snuffed while in holding, it was Robinette. And as for what he has planned? Let's just say that the bodies you have piling up in your morgue will be like drops in the ocean. That is all.' With a little wave, she went back to her chair.

Stevie shook her head. 'She's something, all right. She's afraid to leave with the attorney. I'm of half a mind to make her. Only half,' she rushed to add when Grayson opened his mouth to protest. 'Can we get a search warrant for Robinette's house and business? Maybe we can find out what she's talking about.'

'On Henderson's say so?' Grayson shook his head. 'No. We don't have anything of Robinette's to compare with the hair and blood we found. He was never arrested for the murder of his wife and his prints and DNA are no longer in the military's database, either. He and Henderson submitted "proper requests through channels" to have their personal data deleted.'

'It was their right,' Joseph said. 'That, in and of itself, isn't damning.'

'But it is damn convenient for them,' Hyatt grumbled.

'True,' Joseph allowed. 'Simple association with Henderson isn't enough for a warrant either. It's her word against his. All we know is that they knew each other in the past. Let's come back to Robinette later and talk about the third shooter now, the one who probably set Henderson up before fleeing the country.' He turned to Stevie, amused censure on his face. 'You have to stop calling the guy "Cocksucker". I nearly swallowed my tongue.'

But Stevie barely heard him. She was still back on Grayson's comment, a scene from eight years ago playing in her head with startling clarity. 'We have Robinette's DNA.'

'Where?' Grayson demanded.

'In the evidence room.' She turned to Hyatt. 'Remember when I was trying to get his case reopened? Silas had closed it, declaring Levi Robinette to have been his stepmother's killer.'

'You never believed the boy did it,' Hyatt murmured.

'No, I didn't, but the evidence said otherwise. Robinette must have planted the murder weapon in Levi's room before leading us there to find it. Todd had a bad smoking habit then, two packs a day. He was always careful not to leave any butts behind or leftover cups of coffee for that matter, but I kept following him until I caught him at a careless moment. One of his employees grabbed him when he stepped outside to smoke – there was a fire in the warehouse.'

'Lucky,' Grayson said, a gleam in his eye.

Stevie snorted. 'Lucky nothing. That employee hated Robinette's guts. His name was Frank Locke and he worked in the lab. He directly reported to the head chemist who was killed along with Robinette's wife, Julie. Locke cared for both of them, was grieving them. And he did not believe they'd been having an affair – like whoever killed them wanted it to appear.'

'He helped you obtain evidence,' Clay said.

'He did. I was standing outside, waiting for Robinette to

come out. I'd stopped going into the plant to talk to him because he was always "unavailable".'

Clay's lips turned up. 'So you stalked him.'

'Basically. Anyway, Todd lights up. I'm hiding in the shadows, praying he gets careless when Locke runs up, grabs Robinette's arm. They have a quick conversation I can't hear, then Robinette yells, "What the *fuck* have you done?" He throws the cigarette to the ground, puts it out with his shoe, and starts running. Then, when they get to the door, Locke looks right at me. Gives me this look like, "Make this count." So I bagged the butt, and hightailed it out of there.'

'So the lab ran it?' Grayson asked, all but rubbing his hands together with glee.

'No. Turnarounds were longer then, and he was way back in the queue because it wasn't a high priority case. Two days later Todd comes in with his attorney, telling us the sad story about Levi. We found the bat that was used to kill Robinette's wife and her alleged "lover" in Levi's closet, we confront him, he starts shooting. And then . . .' She faltered. 'Then I killed him.'

Clay rubbed her back. 'He gave you no choice.'

'Levi was set up. I bought into it. I let Robinette manipulate me, even though I knew in my gut, in my heart, that he'd done it. Now that boy is dead and nothing will change that.'

'That made you angry,' Clay said quietly.

'It sure as hell did.' Stevie's voice wobbled and she didn't care. 'That's why I kept pushing to reopen the case. Robinette got away with it. That he's crawled out from under his rock *now*, that he's started this vendetta against me for killing Levi? It's outrageous. The man is insane.'

'Nobody's arguing with you,' Clay said. 'The good thing is that the cigarette butt you bagged should still be testable, right? We just have to locate it and resubmit it.'

'I'll go down to the evidence room myself,' Hyatt said. 'I'll walk it to the lab, make sure they know it's a priority. We'll get him this time, Stevie,' he promised on his way out the door.

Stevie nodded, too raw to say another word. She hadn't thought about this case in eight years, pushing it into the recesses of her mind along with all the pain of losing Paul. And Paulie.

'I know how hard all this must be for you,' Joseph told her, 'but I need to circle back to the third shooter. I think it makes sense to assume he served with Robinette and Henderson. I think it's less likely he's traveling under his own passport, but we'll check it out.'

'Unfortunately he has the build of half the men in the military,' Clay said. 'Matching a body type won't narrow it down. We can get an eye color, but his goggles distorted his features.'

Stevie returned to the glass, leaning against her cane, watching as Henderson was escorted out of the interview room. The woman turned her gaze to the glass as she walked by, as if knowing people were watching. The amused confidence she exuded pissed Stevie off, cutting through the numbness into which she'd briefly retreated.

Her brain, beginning to function again, grabbed another detail that leaped from the mist of her memory and jumped onto center stage. 'Why did Robinette drive to Virginia?'

'Excuse me?' Joseph asked with a frown.

'You told us that he crossed the Chesapeake Bay at the northern end, driving from Baltimore to Annapolis and across the Bay Bridge to get to Wight's Landing and Tanner's beach house. That's on the Maryland end of the Eastern Shore.'

'I get the geography, Stevie,' Joseph said dryly. 'Where

are you going with this?'

'I don't know. Yet. But we do know that, after the shooting at the dock, Robinette escaped by driving south, *four hours* out of his way to the Virginia end of the Eastern Shore. Then he came back across the Bay through the Bay Bridge Tunnel, which would have put him down by Newport News. That meant he had to drive another four hours back up to Baltimore. He went eight hours out of his way. Why?'

'He was afraid he'd be caught going back over the Bay Bridge,' Joseph said with a shrug. 'He barely got away from Tanner's property before Sheriff Moore's deputy arrived at the scene, followed closely by Deacon Novak. He didn't want to risk it. That makes sense to me.'

'What about it doesn't make sense to you, Stevie?' Grayson asked.

Frowning, Stevie walked to the whiteboard on the observation room wall and picked up a red marker, tapping it against her chin. And then she knew what bothered her.

Quickly she sketched a map of the area. 'You've got the Delmarva Peninsula here. It's separated from Baltimore and Annapolis on the mainland by the Chesapeake Bay, crossable by the Bay Bridge at the top. Delaware and Philly are north, then you've got all these little roads going south, cutting through the Maryland part . . .' she squiggled some lines '. . . ending up at the tip of the Virginia part and then back to the mainland via the Bay Bridge Tunnel.'

'Thus the Del-Mar-Va name,' Joseph said, shaking his head. 'What gives, Stevie?'

'Oh, I see,' Clay murmured, giving Stevie a nod of approval. 'Robinette didn't need to go eight hours out of his way to run from the law yesterday morning.'

'Exactly,' Stevie said. 'He could have gone east across the peninsula, toward the ocean, then north to Delaware. If

579

he took side roads, he could have bypassed the Delaware Turnpike, the Bay Bridge, *and* the Bay Bridge Tunnel. And *all* of their toll cameras. He would have been back in Baltimore by breakfast.'

'Instead he drives eight hours and risks exposure on another toll camera,' Joseph said. 'Okay, I'm with you now. Why would he do that?'

Stevie shrugged. 'I don't know. I have to assume he had some reason to go to Virginia. Now, we do know the first intruder into Clay's house yesterday was shocked to see that Robinette had murdered those two cops. He hightailed it out of there, remember?'

'And then left the country a few hours later,' Grayson said. 'Most of the flights or combinations of flights that would have put him over the Pacific when he called Henderson would have left the East Coast around six P.M. Sunday evening.'

Stevie nodded. 'We also know that Robinette made a lot of phone calls to his phone number on Sunday morning before he arrived at Clay's and killed the cops.'

'Like Robinette was getting twitchy about something, maybe,' Clay said. 'It sounded like Henderson believed Robinette was out to kill her. Maybe he was twitchy about Intruder One, too. Not crazy about that moniker, though. Just doesn't have the same ring as Cocksucker.'

Joseph's lips twitched, then he sobered. 'That man probably killed Culp and the clerk. Killing Scott Culp, I get. Culp leaked the whereabouts of the safe house to Robinette and once it became clear Hyatt had rigged it to flush the leak out, Culp became a loose end. However, the clerk's still a mystery.'

Stevie sat down, her leg having begun to ache. 'Why would Robinette try to kill Henderson? Just because she missed?'

'Maybe he was afraid she'd get caught,' Clay said. 'And then do what she just did – offer to give him up in return for a deal. She became a loose end, like Scott Culp. He had police informants. If he found out I'd shot her, he might have been afraid she'd left blood evidence behind that could ID her. Again, giving her the opportunity to betray him.'

Another detail jumped to the middle of her brain. 'Joseph, you showed Henderson a photo of her apartment, all burned up. Can I see it?'

'She never blinked when I showed it to her,' Joseph said, handing Stevie the picture. 'She already knew he'd burned down her place.'

'When did this happen?' she asked.

'Saturday night, about two hours after she shot at you.'

Stevie nodded. 'That makes sense. She probably tried to go home Saturday night. If I'd been shot doing a drive-by shooting, I'd try to crawl home, patch myself up. But she couldn't go home because Robinette already burned it down.'

'No,' Joseph said, 'he had to have had someone do it for him. He was accepting a Humanitarian of the Year award from a civic group when the fire occurred.'

'May have been Intruder One that did the fire,' Grayson said. 'He took care of killing Culp. Sounds like he's Robinette's muscle.'

'What if Henderson went to that hotel, the one where the clerk was found dead?' Stevie pointed to the photo of the burned-out apartment. 'She couldn't go home because it was burned up. She had to go somewhere to get patched up.'

'And if Intruder One had been sent to follow her . . .' Clay shrugged. 'It makes sense.'

She rubbed the back of her neck, then relaxed when

Clay took up the task for her. The man had amazing hands. 'Assuming all that, then at some point Henderson left the Key Hotel and ended up at the free clinic,' she said, 'because she stole the doctor's truck. Between leaving the free clinic and murdering Radcliffe's cameraman, she gets a call from Intruder One, from somewhere over the Pacific. Fast forward a few hours and she breaks into Clay's and my room at the Peabody Hotel, armed with a weapon that she is later very surprised to learn had been used in two murders. She felt betrayed. Betrayed enough to give Intruder One up, too.'

'They were friends,' Clay said. 'He calls her, knows she's in trouble, tells her where to find some weapons. She doesn't expect him to set her up for the two murders. But why would he do it? He's on his way to Asia. Why would he call her from the air to give her weapons?'

Clay's hands had moved from her neck to her shoulders and Stevie had to bite back a moan. 'She thought Robinette was out to kill her. Maybe Intruder One expected her to go after Robinette and not come after us in the hotel room.'

Joseph shook his head. 'All of that might be true, but none of it addresses why Robinette went to Virginia, if he did, indeed, go there on purpose.'

Stevie looked at her crudely drawn map again. 'We know the time at which he crossed the Bay Bridge, here,' she pointed, 'from the toll booth records. And we know when he left Tanner's property – seconds after he finished shooting at the dock. And when he hit the Bay Bridge Tunnel, down here, again, from the toll records. So we can track his path that far. Can you have your agents check for any unusual occurrences along his path during this time period?'

'The timeline developed by my aide,' Joseph said, 'shows that Robinette couldn't have started for Wight's

Landing until late Sunday night. A news article said that he hosted a dinner party that night at his home at which he agreed to consider a run for public office.'

Stevie's mouth fell open. 'You have got to be kidding! That makes me sick.'

'Agreed,' Joseph said, 'but that he's doing so many events and appearances gives us the ability to track his past movements. My team will know what time to begin and end their search, plus the points in between.'

Clay's hands stilled on Stevie's shoulders. 'You might have just narrowed down the list of soldiers who served with Robinette. We already knew we could search based on his eye color from the security video from my house, shoe size, too. But now we can also filter our search by anyone who has a Virginia address, now or in the past.'

'Or family in that area,' Stevie added, grimly following the direction his mind had taken. 'Robinette was willing to kill Cordelia to draw me out. He was willing to set up his own son for a murder he committed. Maybe he figured he could flush Intruder One out the same way.' She stood up, having made a decision in that moment. 'Are we done for now?'

'You are,' Joseph said. 'I have a ton of work to do. Why?'

'Because my child needs me, and I need her. I'm taking a break for a few hours to spend time with Cordelia.'

# Chapter Twenty-Seven

*Baltimore, Maryland, Tuesday, March 18, 1.45 A.M.*

*I'm dead*, Robinette thought, curling into as tight a ball as he could. He knew he wasn't really dead, but at this point he sure wanted to be.

*Fletch poisoned m*e. There was no other explanation. This was no mild sedative wearing off. *And then Fletch left and took the formula. I'm ruined. There's nothing left.*

'Todd?' Lisa pushed his office door open because Fletch had left it unlocked. 'Are you all right?' she demanded. Then, abruptly, concern became contempt. 'You're drunk.'

'No. Not drunk.'

'Then what's this?' From the corner of his eye he could see she held an empty liquor bottle.

'Not mine.' Fletch had left it. *To get me in trouble with Lisa*. It was a final slap in the face.

'Don't lie to me, Todd. What scandal's about to hit the paper and ruin your political career before you even have one? I barely fixed that last bar fight. Goddammit, I'm sick of you.'

She hadn't fixed anything. Brenda Lee had made that lawsuit go away. 'Same goes.'

She grabbed his injured arm and yanked, trying to pull

him to feet. He groaned and vomited. All over her new Manolos. So there was some justice in the world.

'You did that on purpose,' she hissed. 'If you're so sick of me, why did you call me?'

'No one left,' he said, his mind roiling. On some level he knew he should stop talking but he couldn't stop himself. 'All gone except for Brenda Lee. She can't carry me.'

There was a long moment of silence. 'I hate you,' Lisa said, her voice breaking.

He'd made her cry. Good. He'd do worse when he woke up. If he lived.

'Just get me home.' The cavalry would be there soon enough. He'd called Brenda Lee before he'd called Lisa. She'd meet him at his house and would take him someplace he could sleep this off in safety. Brenda Lee was the last one he trusted.

*Hunt Valley, Maryland, Tuesday, March 18, 11.45 A.M.*

'Do you want the good news or the bad?' Stevie asked as she hung up her cell phone and reached across the console to hold his hand. They'd been halfway to Daphne's farm when the call had come in from Lieutenant Hyatt. From the sound of the call it was mostly bad news.

Although it was hard to be truly upset at the moment. Stevie sat next to him, inviting his touch. They were finally on their path together when he'd almost given up hope.

'Good news first,' he murmured.

'Joseph's agents connected Robinette's travel path through Virginia to his past. A Newport News home burned down mid-morning on Monday. It belonged to a Michael and Winnifred Westmoreland. They weren't home, but had they been, firefighters were doubtful they would have made it out alive. Mrs Westmoreland is disabled and uses a wheelchair.'

'Cold. But not a surprise. What's the connection?'

'Michael Westmoreland, Jr. He wasn't an MP with Robinette, but was stationed in the same camp at the same time. He's a computer guru, apparently, and the head of security at Filbert Pharmaceutical Lab. His eye color matches Intruder One's. So now he has a name.'

'Have they matched Westmoreland to a flight itinerary yet?'

'They're still working on it. But that Robinette tried to kill his parents would be motive for helping Henderson take him down.'

'True enough. What's the bad news?'

'Robinette's cigarette butt is missing.'

Clay shot her a quick, surprised glance. 'What? How?'

'Nobody knows. It's just not there. I suppose it could have just been lost, especially since I went on leave at that time and the case had been closed. I doubt the lab would have pitched it. Either it was deliberately removed from the evidence-room or it got mislaid.'

'Shit.'

'I know. But I'm sure Robinette has plenty of DNA left for us to procure with less-than-honorable methods.'

'And if that requires tooth extraction by blunt force?'

'I said I'd hit him with the frying pan, didn't I?'

Clay chuckled. 'You did. Although your cane seems to work pretty well, too.' Never complacent, he glanced into the rearview mirror, pausing when something else caught his eye.

Somebody was following them. Somebody in addition to the person that was supposed to be. Joseph had sent Deacon Novak to watch their backs until Clay got Stevie safely within the farm's gates. Deacon's red SUV was clearly noticeable two cars behind them.

This new car was a small sedan. Hyundai, silver four-door, at least seven or eight years old.

'What is it?' Stevie asked, picking up on his changed mood.

'We have a visitor. Do me a favor and stay down. Please?'

She glared at him, but slunk down in her seat – while she drew her gun. 'Far enough?'

'No. Sao Paulo isn't far enough, but it'll have to do. Call Novak. Tell him to fall back a quarter-mile or so. We're going to get off at this next exit in a hurry. Hopefully the Hyundai won't be able to follow, but I want Deacon with us either way.'

She did as he asked and he gauged the distance to the next exit. Waiting until the last moment, Clay yanked the car onto the exit ramp, earning him some blaring horns – and a look at the Hyundai's back license plate as it zipped past, missing the exit. Novak's red SUV took the exit at a more normal pace.

'We lost him,' Clay said, satisfied. 'You can sit up now.'

With a little wince she did so. 'Did you get the license plate?'

If he told her, she'd feel obligated to track down the driver and Clay wanted her out of the game. *Safe*. At least until she was a hundred percent healed. And he wanted her to have this time with Cordelia, unconflicted by all the things she 'should be doing'.

So he lied. 'Not enough of it to be useful. You winced a second ago. Are you all right?'

Stevie shot him a sharp look that said his abrupt topic change hadn't fooled her. 'My shoulder hit the car door when we took the exit. I'll be fine. How far are we from the farm?'

'Twenty minutes. Put your seat back and rest.'

Another sharp look. 'I'm not a flower, Clay. I don't need you to protect me.'

'I know,' he said quietly. 'But *I* need to protect you. I hate seeing you hurt.'

'I hate seeing you hurt, too. But what if I manage to get this leg working again so that I get my old job back? What if I'm on active duty? Will you be able to deal with that?'

'I've dealt with it for the last two years.' He glanced at her, found her eyes narrowed in concern. 'I would never ask you not to be a cop, Stevie. It's who you are.'

Her face relaxed and he returned his gaze to the road.

'Why aren't you?' she asked, genuine curiosity in her voice. 'I mean, why isn't it who you are anymore? What changed? Why did you leave DCPD?'

He shrugged. 'I'd served for years with Marines who would've died for me and I for them. I came back and immediately applied for the police academy. I'd been raised by a good, decent cop. Dad's friends were good, decent cops. I knew there were bad apples out there, but never expected to work for one. Not right away.'

'Your boss was corrupt?'

He nodded once. 'A real bastard. I couldn't look the other way.'

'So you left?'

The words *just like that* didn't leave her mouth, but he heard them anyway. 'Not exactly.'

'Then you went to IA?'

'Not at first, but later I had to. Conversations with IA have a way of getting out and my dad was still on the force, coming up on retirement. My boss had made friends in high places and I didn't want to ruin anything for my father. I put it off until I had proof.'

'What did you do?'

'I followed my boss, got photographic proof that he was accepting bribes from businesses who were on the shady side. That wasn't a surprise, because that's what I knew he was doing. I was surprised to find him working with a local drug dealer. The pictures, in addition to the time and place for a major drug deal, got IA's attention. My boss got caught. Did a little time.'

'And then you quit?'

'Not at first. No clean cop wants dirty cops around, but nobody really trusts you after you've been talking to IA.'

'I know about that,' she murmured and he sighed.

'I know you do. But I stuck it out – until another dirty cop stepped in to fill the void my boss had left. As a patrol cop, I couldn't do anything to stop the corruption and I didn't know who was trustworthy. And nobody trusted me. At that point I didn't have anyone to watch my back and it got dicey a few times. So I quit and went into the private sector. I've got rich clients, but I take on a helluva lot of ones that can't pay, too.' He heard the defensiveness in his voice. 'That's all.'

'You chose your battles,' she said quietly. 'You're able to achieve a similar goal now as you did wearing a uniform. To serve and protect. There's nothing wrong with that.'

He exhaled, unaware he'd been so tense until that moment. Unaware he'd been so afraid of her response. 'Thank you,' he said and from the corner of his eye, saw her smile sadly.

'You might even have chosen the wiser path,' she murmured.

He frowned. 'I never said that.'

'I know. But we are going to see my daughter who I've

hidden away for her own safety and we did just have to exit the highway in a less than safe fashion because I'm being followed. Again. So whether you said it or not, doesn't change the facts.'

He opened his mouth to reply, but she shifted her body so that she stared out the window, deep in thought. He let her think in peace, saying no more until they arrived at Daphne's farm.

Stopping to check in with the agents Joseph had stationed at the property entrance, Clay drove up the private drive, briefly veering off the paved road to get around the area marked off with crime scene tape, a grim reminder of the two agents who'd lost their lives the night before. There was more crime scene tape in the trees bordering the fence where Alec had fired on the shooter, most likely Robinette.

'Two agents,' Stevie murmured. 'Gone.'

'I know,' Clay murmured back. 'Alec and Ethan would have been next.'

And then Robinette would have tried to get through the gate. To Cordelia. He didn't say it out loud. He didn't have to. It was written all over Stevie's face.

She straightened in her seat, lifting her chin. 'But they weren't and neither was Cordelia. She's fine because everyone did their jobs and because you planned this security very well.'

Warmth spread in his chest, dispelling the ice that had started to form at the thought of what might have happened. Reaching through the window, he punched a code into a keypad, then drove through the gate when it opened for him. Agent Novak remained outside, parking diagonally across the drive as he had at the beach house.

Clay stopped in front of the barn and turned off the engine, taking in the grounds, the new cameras. The splashes of yellow from the daffodils that still bloomed. It seemed like they should have died long ago, that it had been weeks since he'd seen them.

That it had been only three days seemed impossible. 'This is it.'

Stevie looked around, nodding. 'Gates, fence, cameras, private drive. It's as well-protected as you said it would be.' She got out of the vehicle and drew a deep breath. And listened.

'What do you hear?' Clay asked her.

'Nothing.' She turned to smile at him. 'It's quiet and peaceful.'

And then a shriek shattered the quiet. 'Mama!' Cordelia came running out of the barn as fast as her legs would carry her and threw her arms around Stevie's waist, nearly knocking her over. 'I told them to tell you that you didn't need to come, but I was wrong. I wanted you here.'

Stevie lifted her chin. 'What's this? Uncle Joseph never told me you said that.'

'I told him that I was *fine*.' Her lip quivered. 'But I wasn't, really,' she confessed.

Stevie's eyes shattered and the breath she drew was ragged. 'Oh, baby. I didn't know.'

'I know, Mama.' Cordelia hugged her. 'Then Aunt Emma told Uncle Grayson to bring Grandpa and Grandma and Aunt Izzy back here. He did, early this morning before he went to court, but I still wished you were here.' Cordelia's face broke into a sunny smile. 'Now you are!'

Stevie smiled back at her, smoothing Cordelia's disheveled hair off her forehead. 'I'm here. Not all night, because I have to work later, but we have several hours, okay?'

'Okay. Come on.' She tugged Stevie's hand. 'I want to show you Gracie. She's mine.'

591

'Yours? Really?' Stevie allowed herself to be led toward the barn.

'Really. Miss Maggie said if you said it was okay, I could have her. For my own.'

'That's something we'll need to talk about, honey. A horse is a big responsibility.'

'That means no.'

'No, it means we'll talk. Show me this horse. I can't wait to meet her.'

Clay watched them walk away, then turned toward the house to talk to Alec and Ethan, only to find them coming down the hill to meet him.

Ethan looked calm. Unrushed. It was a good sign.

But Alec . . . Clay had expected the boy who'd become like his own son to have his head high, his shoulders back. Last night he'd done what none of them had managed to do – he'd actually hit Robinette with a bullet. Alec had stopped him. Momentarily, yes, but he had stopped him. But Alec didn't look proud. He looked angry.

Angry, but unharmed. Breathing a quiet prayer of thanks, Clay wrapped his arms around Alec's shoulders and squeezed hard. 'You're okay,' he said quietly, as he stepped back, searching Alec's face.

'Yeah,' Alec muttered. 'I'm fine.'

'He's been playing Monday morning quarterback with himself all day,' Ethan said mildly.

Clay met Alec's eyes. 'Which part are you replaying?'

'All of it.' Alec rolled his eyes. 'But mostly the part where I was aiming for the bastard's heart and hit his arm.'

'The bastard *was* moving,' Clay pointed out. 'We've only practiced with stationary targets. We'll train with moving targets in the future. You'll figure it out.'

'I hope I never have to again,' Alec whispered. He closed his eyes. 'God. That was . . .'

'Terrifying?' Clay supplied, as kindly as he could. 'The first time I went out on patrol, my hands were shaking. After the bullets stopped flying, I was sick. A bunch of us were.'

'I would have puked,' Ethan said, 'if I'd had anything in my gut to throw up. I was so nervous, knowing we were going out to actually fight, that I hadn't been able to eat.'

Alec's eyes flew open and he looked from Clay to Ethan and from the look on the boy's face, Clay thought Alec might have been sick, too. 'You're serious?' he asked.

'Never more,' Clay said. 'There's nothing heroic about the act of shooting someone, Alec. What was heroic is the consequence of your action. Cordelia is safe.'

'And I'm standing here, breathing,' Ethan added. 'When I said thanks, I meant it.'

Alec's cheeks darkened as embarrassed pride finally crept into his eyes. 'You're welcome.'

Ethan's mouth curved sympathetically. 'And when that poor pizza delivery guy stops hyperventilating, he'll thank you, too.'

'I want all the details about last night,' Clay said. 'I want to know how the security systems functioned down to the nth degree. But later. First I have a plate for you to run.' He gave Alec the license plate from the Hyundai. 'He was following us on the highway. I think he'd been there from the time we'd left the city.'

'Did your Fed tail get this info?' Ethan asked with a frown.

Clay was certain the Fed had, mainly because Novak hadn't called him to ask for it. 'Probably. Novak's got a sharp eye. I didn't want to discuss it with him in front of Stevie, because she doesn't know I have the plate, but I'll make sure he knows.'

'I'll get on it right now,' Alec said, running back up the hill to the house.

When the boy was gone, Ethan turned to Clay with raised brows. 'So, where is she? I'm supposed to meet her and take notes or Dana says I can't come home. She says she's been waiting too many years to meet the woman who drags you out of your rut.'

'I'm not in a rut,' Clay protested. 'Not anymore.'

'And we're glad.' Ethan clapped his hands once. 'So, she's in the barn with her daughter? Cute kid, by the way. Thinks you're Superman.'

Clay felt his cheeks heat much like Alec's had. 'It doesn't take much to impress her.'

'Uh-huh. What do you plan to do with that plate information, once Alec digs it up?'

Clay started for the barn, Ethan falling into step beside him. 'Exactly what you think.'

Ethan frowned. 'Alone?'

'Definitely not with you. I need you here. Protecting them. So, yes. I'm going alone.'

'Fine. But I'm slapping a tracker under that SUV you're driving. I want to know where you are, in case you get into trouble.'

'That's fair.' Clay opened the barn door, found Izzy standing outside one of the stall doors, her eyes closed, her lips pursed hard. 'Izzy?'

Izzy looked up, startled at first. Then she smiled and walked to meet them and he could see that her eyes were shiny with unshed tears. 'Clay.' She reached up on tiptoe and kissed him on the cheek. 'Thank you,' she whispered. 'For keeping her safe. For making this happen.' She swallowed hard. 'This is more than I hoped for.'

'Me, too,' he whispered back, then cleared his throat. 'Where are your folks?'

'Up at the house with Maggie and Emma, helping move storage boxes out of Maggie's spare bedroom so that we can all stay here tonight. With Ethan, Alec, Paige, and Emma here, she didn't have beds for everyone last night, which is why Mom and Dad and I went home and ended up missing all the excitement here.'

'I offered to give them my bed,' Ethan said, 'but they said no, that nobody would sleep in "bags on the floor" on their account. I couldn't make them stay.'

Izzy gave Ethan a commiserating look. 'It's the way they are. You can't argue with them.'

Clay chuckled. 'Stevie comes by her stubbornness honestly, then.'

'That she does,' Izzy said with a longsuffering sigh, then she smiled again, pointing to the stall where she'd been standing. 'They're in there. Go see.'

Clay found Stevie and Cordelia together, brushing the horse called Gracie. Stevie was intense in her focus, just as she was with anything that mattered. Cordelia's face was as bright with happiness as a star.

*They're mine*, he thought, his heart ready to burst. His to take care of. Protect. To love.

Cordelia looked up at him. 'Gracie likes Mama. See?'

Clay smiled down at her. 'I can see that. Stevie, I need to talk to you for a minute.'

She gave the brush to Cordelia and stepped out of the stall and into his arms. 'Be careful,' she said, kissing his mouth hard, and above the sound of his pounding heart, he heard Cordelia giggle. 'At least take Novak with you,' Stevie added.

The kiss had distracted him. 'What?'

'You're going to check out the car whose license plate you "didn't see".'

Beside him, Ethan snorted. 'Busted, Slick.'

Stevie pulled away to offer her hand to Ethan. 'You must be Ethan. Thank you for coming to help. I appreciate it more than you'll know.'

'I think I know,' Ethan said, shaking her hand. 'Clay's been there for me enough times. It was my turn. Plus, Alec did most of the work.'

Stevie smiled. 'So I heard.' She turned back to Clay. 'The license plate?'

Clay sighed. 'I didn't think you'd believe me, but it was worth a try.'

'I would've done the same thing. How long will you be gone?'

'A few hours probably.'

She kissed him again, to Cordelia's delight. 'I'll be here when you get back. Don't get yourself shot and I'll try not to get stepped on or squashed.'

'Mama,' Cordelia chided when Stevie returned to the stall. 'Gracie is gentle.'

'I hear you and I believe you, Cordy, but she is really big.'

Cordelia's small voice wafted over the stall's wall. 'A dog isn't nearly so big, Mama.'

'No,' came Stevie's wry reply, 'even one of Mr Tanner's puppies, fully grown.'

Outside the stall, Izzy beamed and Ethan gave Clay a single nod.

Clay walked away with a smile on his face.

*Baltimore, Maryland, Tuesday, March 18, 3.15 P.M.*

Sam shut down his computer. The convenience store clerk killed by his father eight years ago left behind a daughter and a grandson. Their neighborhood wasn't close to middle class, but it wasn't the projects, either.

The boy's mother had a misdemeanor record for shoplifting – she'd stolen food from the very convenience store in which her mother had been murdered. The judge gave her community service in a food pantry. After that, her life and her son's life had improved. Someone had given the woman a job. She, like Kayla Richards, had gone back to school. Now the boy's mother was a dental hygienist and they seemed to be doing all right financially.

When the dust settled and he knew who had motivated his father's actions that day and why, he'd approach the woman and her son to find out how he could make restitution.

He had no idea what he'd say to her. Or to Stevie Mazzetti.

It looked like whatever he'd say, it wouldn't be today. He put on a jacket and grabbed his keys before locking his apartment door behind him. He was meeting Ruby and Kayla and his sketch artist friend at the precinct at four. And then he'd see the face of the man who'd dragged him from the Rabbit Hole that night.

The man who was responsible for him waking up a day and a half later. Who'd probably killed his father. And who had somehow forced his father to kill three innocent people.

He walked out of his apartment building and – froze when a hand clamped on his shoulder.

'We need to talk, Officer Hudson.'

*Shit*. All these questions they'd been asking . . . He'd worried about the dust they were kicking up. *Fine. Bring it on. Just stay away from Ruby and Kayla*.

Twisting his body into a spin, Sam jabbed his elbow into the man's gut, satisfied at the surprised grunt. Sam followed with a right cross, but the guy was ready, blocking him and sending him staggering back with a punch to the jaw that momentarily had him seeing stars.

*Enough of this.* Sam ran up the steps, spun, and landed a kick solidly to the guy's chest that had him staggering back. Sam drew his gun, unsurprised to see the man had done the same.

'Drop your weapon,' Sam said levelly.

The man smiled and it wasn't friendly. 'You first.'

Sam found his phone, blindly dialed 911, pausing before he hit send. 'You can tell me what this is about, or I can call for backup. Either way, you're not walking away without some kind of damage because I'll shoot you where you stand.'

Malice glittered in the man's dark eyes. He was maybe an inch taller than Sam, broad as a doorway, and held himself like a fighter. Or a soldier. He needed a shave but his dark hair was precisely combed, despite their scuffling. He also had a chest like a steel wall and a fist like a wrecking ball. Sam's elbow was just getting feeling back in it and his foot was still numb. He had to fight the urge to check for missing teeth.

'Well?' Sam prodded. 'Who sent you?' He threw off some malice of his own as he came down the stairs, closing the gap between them. 'And I swear to God, if you've touched either of the women, I'll aim for something you're really gonna miss.'

Confusion furrowed the man's forehead, but his gun didn't waver. 'What women? I'm not after any women. I want to know why you were following Stevie Mazzetti this afternoon.'

Sam realized where he'd seen the guy. 'You were with her at the police station today.'

The malice returned. 'I'm with her just about everywhere she goes. Why the tail, Hudson?'

*He's Mazzetti's bodyguard.* Sam remembered the black SUV's quick exit off the highway. The driver had made his plates. Sam lifted his free hand, palm up. 'I'm standing down. Please do the same.' He lowered his gun until it was parallel with his leg.

The man did the same, but produced his own phone. 'You haven't called the cops yet. I'll give you five seconds to tell me why you were following Stevie Mazzetti and then I'll call.'

'Go ahead. Have them contact Detective Fitzpatrick.'

The man's eyes narrowed abruptly. 'Have to admit I wasn't expecting that.'

Before Sam could respond, another voice came from the shadows, dryly smug. 'I could have told you that.'

Both Sam and the man twisted to look, then Sam's eyes widened. It was like a scene from a comic book. From the shadows came a tall guy with white hair, wraparound shades, wearing a black trenchcoat that flapped in the wind.

The first guy's eyes rolled. 'Novak.'

Novak grinned. 'Maynard.'

So Maynard was the guy with the iron fist. Sam frowned, trying to place where he'd heard the name, then remembered – Maynard's home had been the one broken into on Sunday, the place where the bodies of the two cops had been found, their necks broken.

'Took you long enough to get here,' Maynard grumbled.

Novak shrugged. 'I've been here for over an hour. You walked right by me.'

Maynard frowned. 'Where?'

'Hiding behind the dumpster. The trenchcoat is more than a fashion statement, you know. I blend into the dark.'

Sam shook his head. 'Who *are* you?'

Novak approached, one hand holding his badge, the other holding his coat back enough to show he'd kept his weapon holstered. 'Special Agent Deacon Novak, FBI and VCET. This is Clay Maynard, a private investigator working for Detective Mazzetti.' He turned to Maynard. 'Officer Hudson here filed a complaint this morning – for an assault on his person that occurred eight years ago. On March 14. He was drugged in a bar and woke up a day and half later in a strange hotel room with no recollection of the time he'd lost.'

Maynard frowned at Novak. 'He lost March 15? What the hell?'

'That's what I thought,' Novak said. 'And so did JD Fitzpatrick when he took Officer Hudson's statement. JD said they specifically requested him.'

'They?' Maynard asked.

'My attorney, Thomas Thorne,' Sam said, 'and my . . . friend, Ruby Gomez from the ME's office, went with me when I filed the complaint.'

'He was also accompanied by a witness to the assault,' Novak said. 'A Kayla Richards.'

'Ruby and Kayla are the women you didn't want me to touch, I suppose,' Maynard said and Sam nodded. Maynard rubbed his neck. 'The three of us should go somewhere quiet to talk.'

Sam looked from one man to the other. 'Okay.'


*Tuesday, March 18, 3.30 P.M.*


Clay flexed his fingers as he sat on the sofa in Hudson's living room. Hudson disappeared into the kitchen, reappearing with two ice bags. He tossed one to Clay before slapping the other on his own jaw.

Clay put the ice bag on his hand, wincing. 'You got a jaw like a rock, Hudson.'

Hudson's smile was not amused. 'My mother always said I was hard-headed. Agent Novak, would you mind taking off your glasses? I like to be able to see a man's eyes.'

With a shrug, Novak complied. Hudson's eyes narrowed thoughtfully as he studied Novak's odd irises, then he, too, shrugged. 'This day just gets stranger,' he murmured. 'Mr Maynard, to answer your original question, I was following Detective Mazzetti because I wanted to talk to her. Only to talk.'

'How did you find her to follow her?' Novak asked.

'I was at the station this morning, giving Fitzpatrick my statement, and I saw her with him,' Hudson pointed to Clay, 'and a few other people. I knew I needed to talk to her, so I waited until those two left the station and followed.'

'What did you want to talk to her about?' Clay asked.

'March 15, eight years ago. The day her husband and son were murdered. And the day I lost.' Hudson paced his small living room, then stopped, turning to meet their stares head-on. 'What I didn't put in my complaint was that I woke up in that hotel room with a gun by my hand. It had recently been fired. I didn't know what I'd done. I checked all reported crimes, checked hospitals for gunshot wounds, but nothing turned up.'

'Where's the gun?' Novak asked.

'I turned it in to Ballistics. They got a hit. A John Doe pulled out of the Severn River a few months later. I went to the ME's office to request the autopsy report. That's where I met Ruby Gomez. The man who'd been killed by the gun in my possession was my father, John Hudson.'

Clay exchanged a wary look with Novak. 'You think,' Clay said, 'you killed your father?'

'At first I did. My father was an addict. He beat my

mother. I hated him, but I didn't think I could've killed him. I didn't remember doing so. But I lost more than a day and I didn't know.'

'So you consulted an attorney?' Novak asked. 'When? Why?'

'I didn't. Ruby set it up for me on Sunday, and I went with it. Thorne's given me good advice. He'd be shitting a ring right now if he knew I was talking to the FBI without him here.'

'We can wait for him,' Novak offered.

'No. I'm done with this. I've got the witness who saw me drugged and a sketch artist waiting at the station. I want to know who it was that drugged me. Because that person probably killed my father.'

'What does this have to do with Stevie Mazzetti?' Clay asked.

Hudson started pacing again. 'It didn't make sense that I'd be left with the gun. If one of my father's dealers had killed him, there was no need to bring me into it. I knew it had to be something bigger. And the one thing that happened that same day was big.'

'The murder of Paul Mazzetti and his son,' Clay murmured.

'And a convenience store clerk,' Hudson said bitterly. 'I can't forget about her, either. Ruby and I viewed the footage of the robbery. I'm convinced the man who shot three people that day was my father.'

Clay's chest seized up. 'They caught the man who did those murders. He's serving life.'

'They caught someone, but I don't think it was the right guy. The man in the store surveillance video walked like my father. And he wore my hat. Which, along with his things and a matchbook from the bar where I was drugged, was returned to me this past Saturday. The same day

Mazzetti gets attacked – twice. Coincidence? Hell no.'

Clay shook his head, the ramifications too many to parse. 'You're kidding me.'

'I wish I were. This is a nightmare. When my father disappeared from our lives, I figured he'd OD'd somewhere or made the wrong person mad. This . . . this is worse than I ever imagined. This is going to break my mother's heart. It's already broken the hearts of Stevie Mazzetti and the family of the store's cashier.'

'Why didn't you tell this to JD Fitzpatrick?' Novak asked.

'Because until I got an ID on the guy who drugged me, it was all conjecture and I had the weapon. I'm a cop, Novak. I know how this works. And with all the dirty cops we've had popping up all over the place lately, I figured people would assume I was guilty before asking any questions. Thorne advised me to file the complaint so that whatever evidence I gathered from here on out would have an evidentiary chain.'

'Why do you think your father robbed the store and killed three people?' Novak asked.

'When Ruby and I studied the store's video, we noticed my father looking at a photo on his phone. It was me, tied to a chair in the hotel room where I woke up the next morning.'

'You think he was coerced into robbing the store,' Novak said.

Hudson swallowed hard and when he spoke, his voice trembled. 'I think he was coerced into murder. He didn't take any money. But he did make sure that Paul Mazzetti was dead.'

'Did your father have a connection to Paul Mazzetti?' Novak asked. 'Did he prosecute him on any drug charges, maybe?'

'No. My father had gone to jail twice already, once for assaulting my mother and once for possession. But neither time was Paul Mazzetti involved. It doesn't make sense.'

*Oh God.* Pieces of conversation filtered through Clay's mind. It suddenly made sense to him. His stomach pitched, bile rising to burn his throat. It made perfect, hideous sense.

He heard Stevie's voice, choked up and furious. *I bought into it. I let Robinette manipulate me, even though I knew in my gut, in my heart, that he'd done it.*

*That made you angry*, Clay had said and Stevie's voice had broken.

*It sure as hell did. That's why I kept pushing to reopen the case. Robinette got away with it. That he's crawled out from under his rock now, that he's started this vendetta against me for killing Levi? It's outrageous. The man is insane.*

No, not insane. And not a retaliation against the death of the son Robinette had served up as a sacrificial scapegoat.

'Dear God,' Clay whispered as it all became crystal clear.

'What?' Novak demanded. 'Clay, you're white as a sheet. Are you all right?'

Clay shook his head slowly. 'No.' He might never be all right again.

Stevie had retreated into herself for *eight years* believing her husband and son had been victims of a random act of violence. For *eight years* she'd carried the guilt of putting her son in the wrong place at the wrong time because she'd been too busy to pick him up at day care.

Too busy trying to put Todd Robinette away for murder.

An effort she'd abruptly abandoned to the shock and unparalleled grief of losing her family.

What would happen when she found out the truth? That they'd been murdered on purpose. To throw her off

Robinette's trail. Because she wouldn't let Robinette get away with it?

It would destroy her.

Clay slowly came to his feet. 'We need to get Hudson to the station. We need his witness to tell the artist exactly who she saw.'

The artist would draw a picture of Robinette. Of that Clay had no doubt. *And then I'll kill the SOB. I'll rip his head off with my bare hands.* And god*damn* the consequences.

*Tuesday, March 18, 4.30 P.M.*

Sam found Ruby waiting with Thorne outside the conference room the sketch artist had been summoned to that morning. 'Where's Kayla?' Sam demanded.

'In there with Officer Damon, the artist,' Ruby said. 'He had only a few minutes to spare between appointments so I told them to go ahead.'

Thorne took one look at him, and the two men with him, and frowned. 'You told them everything,' Thorne said flatly. 'Without waiting for me.'

'I did,' Sam confirmed. 'I appreciate all your support. I really do. But it was time to tell. And these two think they know who Kayla saw that night.'

Thorne looked at Maynard, then Novak, seeming unsurprised to see them both. 'I figured we'd meet up sooner or later. You want to dish? Who do you think Kayla saw?'

Maynard shook his head, his expression grim. 'Not yet.'

At least Maynard looked almost normal, physically anyway. When he'd grown so pale earlier, Sam had first thought he'd kicked him too hard and done some permanent damage. That wasn't the case, although whatever

605

this was about, it was damn bad. Sam had seen a lot of men get bad news and none had ever looked like Maynard had.

'You were smart to have your client report his assault,' Novak said to Thorne. 'Gave him just enough credibility to defuse a tense situation.'

Sam winced when Ruby feathered her fingers over his jaw. She gave Novak an angry look. 'You hit him?'

'*I* hit him,' Maynard said. 'But he hit me first.'

'You men are worse than children,' she said. 'Did you at least put ice on your jaw?'

'I did,' Sam said, smiling because she sounded like his mom. 'I'm fine, Ruby.'

'He was more worried that I was coming after you and Miss Richards,' Maynard added. His voice was tinny, like he forced it from his chest, but the words were the perfect ones to say.

Ruby's eyes softened in the way Sam had so quickly come to anticipate. 'That's sweet.'

Cheeks heating, Sam had no idea how to answer, but was saved from having that fact known by the opening of the conference room door.

Sam's artist friend, Damon, had an odd, wary look on his face, blinking when he saw the crowd that had assembled. 'You're all going to want to see this,' he said.

Kayla's eyes widened as the group filed in. Sam patted her shoulder. 'You okay?'

She nodded. 'I hope I did all right. The artist seemed . . . surprised.'

'Let's have it,' Maynard said tightly. Everything about the PI was tight, like he was ready to explode. Novak must have sensed it too, because he put a steadying hand on Maynard's arm.

Damon flipped back the cover of his sketchpad and held up the picture he'd drawn.

It was like someone had tossed a bomb in the room.

Thorne's jaw dropped. Novak swore. Ruby's hand flew up to cover her mouth in horror.

And Maynard crumpled, only managing to hit a chair on the way down because Novak and Thorne grabbed him.

Sam leaned in, stared at the picture. *Oh . . . Oh no.* As recognition dawned, Sam understood both the significance of the face that Kayla had described and the horror that filled the room.

Ruby turned her face into his chest, silently weeping. Sam stroked her hair, unable to give any comfort. *I keep thinking it can't get worse.* But it kept seeming to.


*Tuesday, March 18, 6.45 P.M.*

Stevie paused, her keycard poised over the door to her room at the Peabody Hotel. She looked over her shoulder at Joseph, who seemed normal. Totally, unflappably normal.

Except that he wasn't. She didn't know what was wrong. But something definitely was.

*It can't be Clay.* If he were hurt, Joseph would have taken her to him at the ER.

'What is it?' she demanded. 'I swear to God, Joseph . . .'

He held up his hands in surrender. 'I was told to bring you here, so I did. You go in your room, I'll go next door. Novak and Coppola are in position, same as last night. Just in case.'

'Fine. Thanks for the ride.' Stevie ran the key through the reader and stepped through the door, thinking she had time for a quick shower before getting back to work. She'd been thinking about the witnesses she'd interviewed while investigating the murder of Robinette's wife the first time around. She had time to see at least one tonight. She'd start with—

She stopped, the heady aroma of flowers filling her head. Clay had filled the room with roses. Dozens and dozens of roses in every imaginable color. The table in the front room was set 'fancy', as Cordelia would call it – a white linen tablecloth with china and silver and crystal wine goblets. A bottle of champagne chilled in a silver ice bucket.

A single rose lay across her plate.

She picked it up carefully, then realized there were no thorns. He'd stripped them away. She sniffed the rose, then looked up to find him in the doorway to the bedroom, watching her.

'I missed you,' she said quietly.

He smiled. 'I ran you a hot tub. I figured after riding a horse today, you'd need one.'

She laughed. 'It'll probably be worse tomorrow.'

His eyes flickered, the emotion gone so quickly she almost missed it. 'I'll give you another massage. You won't feel a single thing tomorrow.'

She crossed the room to him, walking into arms that came around her so tightly that she had to suck in a quick breath. 'What is all this? The flowers and the table?'

'I realized that I wanted to take you on a date,' he said lightly. 'But I can't right now, so I thought you could use a little romance. First a bath, then I'll have dinner sent up.'

She pulled back, searched his face. Saw nothing amiss. Still, she felt a knot of dread form in her gut. Something was very wrong. 'Okay,' she said.

The tub in the bathroom was enormous, big enough for two. Which was apparently exactly what he had in mind because he stripped them both to the skin, scooped her into his arms, and lowered her into the steaming water before joining her there.

He positioned her between his legs, her back to his chest. 'So,' he said, 'tell me about this afternoon. How did it go?'

She told him about her inept attempt at riding and that she and Cordelia had looked at real estate listings online and that her little girl seemed to have started believing that she was more than Stevie's consolation prize.

All the while he touched her, long sweeping strokes, soaping up her legs, her arms, taking care to avoid the stitches from Saturday, which were finally starting to heal. She decided that she'd been looking for trouble earlier because things had been calm all afternoon, that nothing was wrong. And when he began to wash her breasts, she decided that Clay was just fine.

She stopped thinking when his hands stroked up her inner thighs, his thumbs teasing her most intimately. She leaned back, tilting her head to the side, giving him access to her neck. He took full advantage, running his lips up over her skin, murmuring praises that made her sigh.

His hands were gentle, as was the first orgasm he coaxed from her body, like riding the swell of a wave. She stretched, arching her back as she pressed the back of her head into his shoulder, then relaxed. 'Mmm.'

His arms tightened around her when she started to slide into the water. 'You liked that?'

'I did.' Then she surprised him by turning in his arms and straddling him. She kissed him as sumptuously as he'd just made her feel. 'I thought of you, all afternoon.'

His hands found her buttocks, began to knead, his lips curving. 'Did you now?'

'I did. Especially when I was riding. I kept thinking of you.' She tilted her hips, finding his erection, sliding down on him until she'd taken all of him in. It was his turn to arch and she ran her hands over his chest, delighting in the feel of him, inside and out.

She began to move, and he groaned, both arms reaching back so that he could grip the sides of the tub, defining the muscles in his pecs and arms. His head fell back, his eyes closed, as she rode him, slowly at first, then harder and faster. He came on a shout, his hips punching up, sending water sloshing over the sides of the tub. She dug her nails into his shoulders to hold on until his body stilled, watching him as he fought to fill his lungs.

He lifted his head, blinked his eyes open. 'You didn't . . .'

'Not yet. I was enjoying watching you. But I'm sure you can rectify the situation.'

He released his hold on the tub to touch her face, his fingers trembling. 'I'm sure I can.' He helped her from the tub, wrapped her in a towel, scooped her up in his arms once again and carried her to the bed. 'But first I'll take care of those sore muscles.'

'They're not sore yet,' she protested.

'Exactly.' He laid her down, knelt between her legs and began to massage her just as he had the night before. 'I was imagining you this way last night,' he said smoothly, sending shivers across her damp skin. He lifted her leg over his shoulder and leaned his weight into the stretch. 'But tonight I plan to go through with everything I imagined.'

She closed her eyes as his fingers hit every pressure point, anticipation building as her bent knee brushed her breast. He'd spread her so wide . . . 'Which is what?' she asked hoarsely.

She had her answer a second later when his tongue slid up into her. She bit back a moan, conscious of Joseph next door and his agents patrolling the halls.

'Don't hold back,' Clay whispered. 'I want to hear you. Please let me hear you.'

She forgot to be self-conscious as he licked and tasted, dragging sounds from her throat she was certain she'd never made before. And where the orgasm in the tub had been a slow ride on a wave, the second hit her with the force of an avalanche. Clay wouldn't let up, sucking and biting, not allowing her to pull away when her over-whelmed body mindlessly tried to do so. He didn't stop until the last shudder had stilled, until she lay limp and unmoving beneath him.

'Oh my God,' she breathed. 'What was that?'

'Did you like it?' he asked, his voice low, gravelly.

'Yes. But you nearly killed me.'

He said nothing to that, rising to loom over her, hands planted on either side of her head. She stared up into his dark eyes, unable to look away. 'Can you take me again?' he whispered.

'Yes. Always.'

# Chapter Twenty-Eight

*Baltimore, Maryland, Tuesday, March 18, 7.25 P.M.*

He'd do this. He'd make it good for her. He'd make it good for the both of them, even if it killed him. And if the pain in his chest was any indication, it just might.

*Always*, she said.

He'd hoard every touch, every taste, every sensation, because he knew when he told her the truth . . . *No.* He wouldn't think about that now. There'd be time later. *Too much time.*

He slid inside her, feeling her muscles contract around him.

Perfect. She was perfect. This . . . was perfect.

*Keep it together, Clay. For her.* He swallowed, feeling like acid burned its way down his throat. His arms trembled and he locked his elbows to keep himself from crushing her.

He'd do that soon enough. When he told her that she was the reason her family had been destroyed. That she'd been the target. She'd pull away from him, retreat into herself. Maybe not all at once. She might cling to him in shock. But it wouldn't last. She'd punished herself for eight years when it wasn't her fault. It wasn't now, but she wouldn't see it that way.

She wouldn't blame him for being the messenger. He knew that. She'd blame herself. Punish herself. Happiness? *She won't accept it. Won't think she deserves it.*

*She'll pull away. Leaving us both alone.*

*But you're not alone now.* At this moment, for as long as it lasted, he had the world in his arms. *So enjoy it. Make her enjoy it. Give the two of you something good to remember.*

He rocked into her, his body gathering speed and force, and he gritted his teeth when she came a third time, the contractions milking him to the point of breaking. But he didn't allow himself to follow. *Not yet.*

'Again,' he rasped in her ear. He swiveled his hips and she caught her breath. 'Again.'

'How can you do this?' she said, panting. Her eyes were closed, her head thrown back, her pulse pounding at the hollow of her throat.

'Do what?'

Her eyes opened, filled with lust and need. 'Make me crazy for you again.'

'God. Stevie.' His orgasm threatened to overpower him, but he held it back long enough to withdraw, flip her to her stomach and plunge into her from behind.

Her shocked cry was muted by the pillow. Roughly she arched her back, shoving her body back into him, driving him deeper inside her. 'Now. Do it, Clay.'

He let go, pummeling her hard, so hard she had to brace a hand on the headboard to keep her head from banging into the wood. When her body went rigid he let himself fly.

It was over far too soon and his mind begged for one more time even as his body struggled to recover. He rolled them both to their sides, keeping them joined.

When he could draw a breath to speak, he whispered in her ear, 'I love you, Stefania. I need to say it out loud.' *Just once.* But he kept those last two words to himself.

She said nothing for what seemed like a long time and he was afraid she'd fallen asleep without hearing him. Which would be just as well.

When she spoke, the gravity of her tone startled him. 'Why did that sound like a goodbye?'

*My Stefania.* Too damn smart for her own good.

He was fighting for the courage to respond when she pulled away from him. Sliding out of the bed, she limped into the bathroom. A minute later she emerged, wearing one of the hotel's robes and leaning on the cane she'd left by the tub. She tossed him the other robe.

'What happened today, Clay?'

He forced himself to sit and put on the robe. He patted the bed next to him. 'Sit down, Stevie. It's going to take me a few minutes to explain.'

She sat down on the chair four feet away, waiting.

He'd known she'd pull away. But God, it hurt.

'I, uh, ran down the name of the guy who followed us this afternoon. He's a cop.'

'Another dirty cop?' she asked, dismayed.

'No. Seems to be a good guy.' He told her about Sam Hudson's assault and his lost day.

The color drained from her face. 'March 15? Eight years ago?'

'Yes.' He told her about the gun Hudson had found and the package he'd received, eight years to the day later. The day she'd been shot at twice. He told her about the cop's search to find answers. 'The man killed with the gun was his father, John Hudson.'

She flinched. 'He killed his father? Why? And what does this have to do with me?'

Clay braced himself. 'No, he didn't kill his father.' He explained how Hudson checked out the video from the convenience store. She didn't have to be told which one.

She became even paler. 'They caught the man in the video, Clay. They caught the man who killed my husband and my son.'

Clay was quiet a long moment, trying to find the inner strength to finish. 'No, honey. Whoever's sitting in prison right now didn't kill your family. He resembles the real killer. Very closely resembles him. But the man in prison now didn't do it. John Hudson did.'

She shook her head. 'Why?'

He told her about John Hudson checking his phone, about him looking at the picture of his son. 'We think he'd been threatened, coerced, whatever.'

'That's why he never took the cash,' she murmured. 'But why?'

He left that question alone for a moment, wishing he could leave it for eternity. Knowing he couldn't. 'We identified the man who drugged Sam. A witness saw a man drag him away from the bar that night. We assume that was who left the gun on the hotel room floor next to Sam.'

'That man would also have killed Sam's father.' She swallowed. 'After John Hudson finished killing Paul. And Paulie. It was one of Paul's cases then. I've always wondered.'

Clay shook his head. 'No. Not Paul's case.'

'Then who . . .' Her mouth fell open slightly, her eyes growing wide and horrified as understanding broke through. 'No. No. It's not true.' She pushed to her feet and began to pace, her cane thumping against the carpet. 'It can't be true. It was *my* case? *Mine?*'

Clay said nothing, letting her mind do what it did best.

She stopped pacing abruptly, her shoulders bowing, her free arm flat against her stomach. 'It was Robinette. Robinette killed my son. My husband. To make me leave him alone.'

She spun around, her eyes dark against her dangerously pale face. 'I'll kill him.' She was breathing faster, her words tumbling over each other. 'I'll rip his skin off his body. I swear it.'

She marched to her suitcase, pulled out a pair of jeans. 'I'm going to make him bleed.' Her voice broke. 'I'll make him beg me to let him die.'

'Stevie.' Clay jumped off the bed, ran to her, holding her shoulders, pulling her back against his chest. 'Stevie, wait.'

'You can't stop me.' She was crying now, huge sobs that broke his heart. She struggled, trying to break free of his hold. 'You cannot stop me.'

He held on tighter. 'It wasn't Robinette. Are you listening to me?' He gave her the gentlest of shakes. 'It wasn't Robinette.'

'What?' She stopped struggling. 'Then . . . who?'

Clay closed his eyes, forced himself to speak the name. 'Silas Dandridge.'

Her former partner. The man she'd trusted to watch her back. The man who'd betrayed so many. He'd ruined so many lives. Including hers.

Stevie went completely still, not even breathing. 'What?' she asked in barely a whisper.

'Silas dragged Sam out of the bar that night. We think he sent a photo of Sam unconscious to his father, threatening him if John didn't obey. We think he was hired by Robinette to throw you off the trail. Because you knew he'd killed his wife and set up his son to take the fall.'

She said nothing, not a word.

'And then after Christmas, you started digging into all

the old cases, finding the ones that Stuart Lippman never recorded on his list. People started attacking you, shooting at you. Either Robinette figured his attempts would be camouflaged by all the others or he was afraid you'd uncover his crime. Or both.'

'I didn't even remember his name,' she whispered.

'I know, baby. I know.'

'Silas?' she asked, her voice so small. 'Are you sure?'

'Yes. It was him.'

'He kept trying to get me to back off. To accept that Levi had done it. Now I know why.' She threaded her fingers through her hair and yanked. 'I can't think.'

'I know.'

She pulled away from him, hugging herself with her free arm. 'I need to think.'

Clay dropped his hands to his sides. 'I know.'

She backed away a step. Out of his reach. 'Who knows about this?'

'Joseph, Hyatt, JD. Grayson. Thorne. Ruby Gomez.'

She frowned. 'Why Thorne and Ruby?'

'Hudson's hooked up with Ruby Gomez. She took him to Thorne and Sam hired him.'

'Oh.' That was all she said before she walked into the front room, closing the bedroom door behind her.

Clay sat on the edge of the bed, dropped his head into his hands. She'd already shut herself away. Already put distance between them. It was exactly what he'd expected she'd do. But he didn't feel like he'd expected to feel.

He was numb. It would wear off sooner or later, but for now, he was blessedly numb.

*Tuesday, March 18, 9.55 P.M.*

Stevie looked up at the clock over the TV. Two hours. She'd been sitting at this linen-covered table with its china and silver and crystal, surrounded by five dozen roses, for two hours.

She'd cried the first hour, sobbing into the linen napkins until they were so soaked that she could wring out her tears. But the second hour she'd spent thinking, sorting, analyzing. Planning.

Clay had given her the time and space she'd needed and for that she was grateful. She was done thinking, though, and ready to act.

She pushed herself to her feet with a wince, grabbed her cane. Draped the damp napkins over the chairs to dry. Then opened the bedroom door to find Clay sitting at the desk, working on his laptop. He was fully clothed, his long-sleeved shirt buttoned up to the collar, his cuffs also buttoned. He even wore a tie, knotted with military precision.

'Hi,' she said, closing the door behind her.

He didn't look up. 'Are you all right?'

She leaned back against the door. 'Not really. But I will be.'

He'd made the bed and straightened her clothes. A peek in the bathroom confirmed he'd mopped up all the water they'd sloshed out of the tub and hung the towels to dry. Keeping himself busy while giving her time to think.

'What are you doing?' she asked, when he didn't turn around.

'Catching up on some business. I was behind before. Now I'm more behind and Paige is going to be out for a few weeks with her leg.'

She'd never considered that he'd simply dropped his

business to help her. *I should have*. She'd been selfish. More than once in their relationship, she realized. He'd given all. She'd given . . . what? Her body? Her 'everything' for as long as it lasted between them?

Suddenly that didn't seem like nearly enough.

'Is there anything I can do to help you?' she asked.

He rubbed the back of his neck. 'No. But thank you.'

He was being distant. And way too formal. 'Clay, you're scaring me, and after what we've been through over the last few days, that's saying something. Would you look at me? Please?'

She watched, as his broad shoulders squared. He swiveled the chair so that he faced her, a pleasant smile on his face. But his eyes were vacant. 'What can I do for you, Stevie?' he asked, his voice impossibly kind. But not loving. Not like it had been.

'I've been thinking.'

'That's what I figured you were doing.'

'And some crying.'

'I know. I heard you.' He swallowed. 'I'm sorry. I hated to tell you.'

*Yes, he would have hated it*. It was another realization that hit her hard. He would have hated to give her that news, knowing it would hurt. But he had. After giving her 'a little romance'.

She crossed the room, sat on the side of the bed closest to him. 'Why did you?' she asked softly. 'Whose idea was it for you to tell me?'

'Mine, with Joseph's agreement. Grayson and JD wanted to bring you into the station and tell you there. I wouldn't let them. You needed time to process. Time to think. Privacy to react.'

Which was what Clay had given her. She studied his face, another moment coming to mind. 'You were there that day, too,' she murmured. 'The day I confronted Silas face to face, a year ago. I knew that he'd done those terrible things, but didn't really believe it until I saw his face.'

'And the gun he was pointing at you,' Clay said tightly.

'That, too.' Silas had been willing to kill her that day so that he could escape to save his own child. It was a few hours later that she'd found him holding Cordelia, his gun pressed to her daughter's side in order to force Stevie to help him.

*You'd sacrifice my child,* she'd asked, *to save your own?*

*In a heartbeat,* had been his answer.

She'd considered that while doing her thinking surrounded by five dozen roses. Silas had proven already that he'd had no loyalties, had proven he'd murder to further his own agenda. That Silas Dandridge had forced the murder of her husband hadn't been all that hard to accept.

'I remember watching Silas drive away that day and it was in that moment that I finally realized that I'd trusted, at times even unwittingly aided, a monster. I was in tears. Then I turned around and there you were.' She swallowed hard. 'Every time I need you, you're there.'

He closed his eyes. 'Please don't thank me. Do not.'

'All right, I won't. Can I ask why you filled the front room with flowers?'

He lifted a shoulder. 'I told you. I thought you deserved a little romance before—' He cut himself off, pressing his lips together to keep from saying more.

'Before? Before what? Before you told me about Silas? Why—?' She stopped because she knew the answer. *I love you. I need to say it out loud.*

She thought she'd heard a goodbye in his words. She'd been right.

He believed she would, in her heartbreak, walk away from him.

*And why wouldn't he? It's what I've done before. I shut myself away for eight years.* She'd pushed her friends away for months, trying to fix the world all by herself. *Stevie, you're an idiot.*

'You were going to give me a perfect night before you had to break my heart, weren't you?'

He surged up out of his chair, walking to the closet where he needlessly straightened the shirts he'd hung there. 'That was the idea. I thought you deserved it. That we deserved it.'

Her throat closed and she cleared it roughly. She knew how long he'd waited for her to come around. Hell, half of Baltimore knew how long he'd waited. *Two years.* But he'd told her a most painful truth, all the while believing she'd retreat, that she'd pull back into herself again. And even believing she'd already done so, here he was. Protecting her still.

*What are you waiting for, Mazzetti? A neon arrow to fall from the sky?*

'Clay, I'm not . . . broken. I'm still in shock and I don't know what I'll be like tomorrow or the day after. But I do know that at some point, the reality of this is going to hit me hard and I'll need someone to hold me up. I'd really like that person to be you.'

He turned slowly, his expression one of total relief. 'Good. Because I want it to be me, too.'

'Lucky for me, then, that you're so damn good at it,' she said soberly. Because this was important. 'You hold me up, Clay. You have for a long time, even when I didn't think I wanted you to. You've always been right there for me.'

'Because I love you,' he said quietly. 'I'm sorry if you're not ready to hear it, but it doesn't change how I feel.'

She walked over to him, gripped his tie in her fist and yanked his head down for a hard and fast kiss. When they drew back for air, she kept her grip on the tie, keeping his face close to hers. 'I'm ready to hear it.' She watched him draw a breath. Watched him hold it as he waited, his dark eyes vulnerable. Expectant. 'Because I love you, too.'

His eyes closed. 'Could I hear that again, please?' he whispered.

Releasing his tie, she traced the hard angles of his face with her fingertips, then kissed him again, more softly this time. 'I love you. I think I have for a long time. But I wasn't ready to accept it. I know you don't want me to thank you, but I'm going to anyway. Thank you for letting me have the time and space I needed, tonight and for the last two years.'

He pulled her to him and she willingly, eagerly went, wrapping her arms around his waist. 'I thought you'd blame yourself,' he said unsteadily. 'I was afraid you'd punish yourself. That you'd build a wall around yourself again. That you wouldn't let me in.'

'I don't want to build any more walls around myself. I missed so much because I did that before. But I do blame myself. How can I not?'

He sighed. 'Stevie, what Robinette did . . . what Silas did . . . you didn't cause any of that.'

'No, not directly. But my actions caused Robinette to react and my family paid the price. Paul, Paulie . . . they're gone. And Cordelia's been paying the price her whole life because I built a wall around my heart. That's why this time has to be different.'

He rested his cheek on top of her head, his sigh weary. 'Stevie, saying it *has* to be different won't make it so. As long as you blame yourself, it won't be different. It can't be.'

She pulled back far enough to see his face. 'But it is. The blame is different. And what I'll do with it is different, too. That's what I was thinking about when I was in the other room.'

'I don't understand.'

'See, when it was random, losing Paul wasn't my fault. He stopped at that store every night to buy a lottery ticket for his mother. Paul was going to be there at the same time the robber was, regardless of anything I did or didn't do. But Paulie *was* my fault. If I hadn't been so focused on my work, I would have saved my son. That's always been the hardest part for me.'

'And now?'

'Losing Paulie isn't any easier to accept now than before. Nothing about that part has changed.' Her little boy's face was in her mind, the way he smelled. Like cookies. Tears filled her eyes and she blinked them away. 'If I'd picked him up like I was supposed to, he'd be alive. I own that. But Silas knew he'd be with Paul. He knew, and he let the hit happen anyway.'

Clay frowned. 'Silas knew? How?'

'While I was in there thinking, I made myself remember the last hours of that day, before Hyatt came to tell me about the shooting. Silas left on time that night, but he stopped by my desk on the way out. Saw me working on the request to get Robinette's case reopened. He gave a big sigh and reminded me that it was my night to pick up Paulie.'

'Had he ever done that before?'

'No. I thought it a little odd at the moment, but after Hyatt notified me . . . Everything just folded up and disappeared. I didn't forget anything. It was just too painful to remember.'

'I can relate to that. Tell me what you're remembering now.'

'Paul and I planned day care pickup, put it on our calendars at the start of each week, but some nights we'd switch off at the last minute if something came up, just like most couples do. Silas had to have checked my calendar to know it was my night, but when he reminded me, I told him I'd asked Paul to get him. Silas knew Paulie would be with Paul.'

'Sonofabitch.'

'Yeah. Well, he proved other times that he didn't care who he hurt to get his way. I don't know why I thought I should have been exempt. That I wasn't is what makes this scenario different from a random killing. I mean, Robinette reacted because I couldn't leave well enough alone. But I *shouldn't* have left it alone. You can't let the bad guys win. The moment you do, you're part of the problem. Does that make sense?'

He rested his forehead on hers. 'Yes. It does.'

She drew a breath. 'I have to live with the fact that Paul and Paulie are dead because of a choice *I made*. Paul . . . He would have understood. I think he would have made the same choice. But Paulie . . .' She closed her eyes against the pain stabbing her chest. 'He never had the chance to choose. So do I blame myself for that? Yes. I will every day forever. Would I make the same choice again, knowing what I know now? Probably not and I have to live with that, too. But now I know it was orchestrated. For eight years I believed it was bad luck. Karma. Circumstance. Whatever. But other than killing myself, there wasn't anything I could really do to punish myself. I've felt so damn helpless.'

'But now you have someone real to blame,' he said softly.

She nodded. 'Now I have someone to make pay. And to do that I need your help. Silas is dead, but Robinette is alive and kickin'. Help me nail him to the wall.'

His smile was harsh. 'I'd like to see anyone try to stop me. What do you need?'

'A connection. Somehow, somewhere, Robinette and Silas crossed paths. Silas worked for Stuart Lippman, the defense attorney, and all of Lippman's dirty work we've uncovered to date originated within the justice system. Lippman would note the arrest of anyone from a rich family, call them and say, "I can make your troubles go away – for a price."'

'But Robinette was never actually arrested,' Clay said, 'so there would have been no reason for Stuart Lippman to contact him with an offer to make his troubles go away. Yet Silas was involved and to your knowledge he only did dirty work for Lippman, and only because Lippman had threatened Silas with harming his child. If Robinette had approached Silas on his own, Silas might have turned him in.'

'Exactly. Which means Robinette and Lippman connect some other way.'

Clay thought a minute. 'I think I know where to start. Why don't you call for room service? I'm going to call Alec.'


*Wednesday, March 19, 8.00 A.M.*


All eyes were on them as Clay and Stevie walked into the conference room on the homicide floor. *Very tired eyes*, Clay thought. He and Stevie appeared to be the only ones who'd gotten any sleep the night before. After a late dinner, she'd fallen asleep in his arms. Before she did so, she told him once again that she loved him. Clay had the best night's sleep of his life.

The faces around the table . . . not so much. Hyatt, Grayson, and JD looked shattered. Joseph, weary. His team – Novak, Coppola, and CSU's Dr Brodie – were sympathetically grave. To have dirty cops in the department was bad enough, but Silas's act was one of ultimate betrayal.

'I'm okay,' Stevie said without preamble as she and Clay sat on either side of Joseph, who sat at the head of the table. 'I take it that we're all assuming that Silas didn't wake up that morning and decide to have my husband and son killed. He was hired to do so, and at the time, the person who had the most to gain was Todd Robinette. He wanted me off his tail eight years ago, because I believed he'd killed his wife. Killing my family distracted me so that his case was dropped. Given that Robinette's the one shooting at me now, it makes sense that he hired Silas and he doesn't want me to expose him for all of his past acts.'

'That's where we are,' Joseph confirmed.

'Good,' she said with a hard nod. 'Because I'm pissed off and ready to take Robinette down.' Murmurs of agreement rippled around the room. 'Do we have a warrant for his home and business yet?'

Grayson scowled. 'I couldn't get a judge to sign one based on the ramblings of a "clearly deranged woman" who broke into a hotel room. Everything else we have is circumstantial. We'll need physical evidence to bring him in. I told the judge we had blood and hair, tried to get a court order forcing Robinette to provide a DNA sample, but I got shut down. I underestimated Robinette's PR machine. He's made a lot of friends in high places over the last eight years.'

'Pretty much what I figured,' Stevie said. 'Do we even know if he's still in the country?'

'He is,' Joseph said. 'I've had agents outside his home

and his factory since you told me his name last night. Told my people to stay out of sight. We don't want to spook him into running. He left his factory at about noon yesterday afternoon and went straight home. My agent said Robinette "didn't look so good". His wife picked him up and drove him.'

'He was shot in the arm,' Clay said. 'But it wasn't serious. He didn't bleed that much.'

'I don't know how badly he's hurt. The word from my agents was that he looked like he was about to throw up. His wife appeared most displeased.'

'Have we talked to her?' Clay asked.

Joseph nodded. 'I did, personally, an hour after she brought him home. A maid answered the door, wouldn't let me in. Neither would Lisa Robinette. I told her that I was pursuing an allegation made by Jean Henderson, who'd served with Robinette in the Gulf War.'

'And she said what?' JD asked.

'What you'd expect. That Henderson was delusional. And that if I had any other questions, to contact their attorney. Then she shut the door in my face. But she had been taken by surprise. And she was pissed, although she tried to hide it. About thirty minutes after I left, the PR person arrived – Brenda Lee Miller – and left a few minutes later. One of my agents followed her, too. Other than that, there hasn't been any movement outside their house. Hopefully Lisa hasn't killed him. She was pretty mad.'

'Trouble in paradise?' Clay had run a background check the night before when Stevie had been doing her thinking. 'They haven't been married that long. Robinette married Lisa Laffley, wife number three, about two years ago. The Laffleys are prominent fixtures on the political scene. Very rich. Lisa was considered a top catch when she chose Robinette after her debut.'

'Her debut what?' Hyatt asked.

'Her debut *ball*,' Stevie said. 'The wealthy elite apparently still do this.'

'You're joking,' Agent Kate Coppola accused, eyes narrowed.

Stevie shook her head. 'I was surprised too, but it's true. Lisa had her debut ball right after she graduated from Bryn Mawr. She seems smart enough.'

'Why did she choose Robinette, then?' Coppola asked.

'The man can be charming,' Stevie said grimly. 'If she believes herself in love, she could be a hard sell. But if the bloom is wearing off the rose, we might get to him through her.'

'We'll try,' Joseph said. 'But not until we can figure the best way to do it.'

Dr Brodie spread lab reports on the table. 'If we can somehow get her to supply us with a hairbrush or toothbrush, that would be great. We have the DNA profiles from the hair found at the beach house and the blood found at Daphne's farm. They're an exact match. Now if we only had something to match them to.'

Stevie's head came up, her eyes finding Clay's. 'We do, actually. What about Levi?'

'You're right,' he murmured. 'That would connect Robinette to the crime scene.'

'Levi? Robinette's son?' Joseph leaned back in his chair, nodding. 'We can show a familial relationship. Did you run DNA on Levi eight years ago?'

'No,' Stevie said, 'because he was never formally charged and booked, but we can. The ME's office keeps blood samples, right? They autopsied him.'

'I'm on it,' Brodie said, typing on her phone. 'Just texted the lab with the request.'

'I just hope the kid's blood didn't disappear like his

dad's cigarette butt,' Hyatt said darkly.

'If it has, we can dig him up. Levi is buried next to his biological mother in a little parish cemetery, south of Baton Rouge.'

'How did the boy's mother die?' Joseph asked.

'Overdose,' she said. 'That Levi had followed in his mother's footsteps was one of the things Robinette lamented when he brought us the boy on a silver platter. She died while he was stationed in Iraq and he couldn't get leave to come home. He arranged with his friend, Rene Broussard, to take Levi in. Rene was married to Julie, who cared for Levi like he was her own.'

'Hold on.' Agent Coppola frowned. 'Robinette married his friend's wife? How?'

'Rene had died a few years before,' Stevie said. 'He was found half-naked and dead in a known hangout for prostitutes. Julie was devastated according to her employees, and nobody thought she married Robinette for love. Remember the employee that created the distraction so that I could get Robinette's cigarette butt? He told me that Julie was afraid that Robinette would take Levi away, after Rene died. The employee believed that Robinette had leveraged Julie's affection for Levi to get her to marry him and give him a "cushy VP job".'

'So Julie married Robinette,' Coppola said, 'and gave him the job he wanted. But then Julie was killed. Why?'

'I don't know.' Stevie swallowed hard. 'I never had the opportunity to find out for sure. Julie was found in a car with her head chemist, made to look like they were running away together. I figured then that Robinette had gotten power hungry and killed Julie to gain control of the pharmaceutical company. I guessed that the head chemist was too loyal to Julie to cooperate after she was dead so Robinette killed him, too, or there was something else going on – like maybe the two knew something about Robinette they shouldn't know. What that was, I don't know. But one thing that everyone in the factory was sure of was that Julie loved Levi and that Levi loved her, too. I agreed. I didn't believe Levi killed her. But after Levi was dead, Robinette apparently didn't want him buried near Julie, so he shipped the body south.'

Hyatt turned to her with a frown. 'Wait. How do you know where the boy's buried?'

Her chin lifted slightly. 'Because I went to the funeral.'

JD's brows shot up. 'You really were on Robinette, weren't you? Did he see you there?'

'I didn't think so at the time. Now, I'm not so sure.'

Hyatt looked stunned. 'You went all the way to Louisiana? How? I never approved it.'

'I flew,' she admitted. 'I was on admin leave after I shot Levi and I had time. I believed his father had set him up. I wanted to watch Robinette's behavior at the funeral.'

'What did Paul say about this?' Grayson asked, looking as stunned as Hyatt.

Stevie smiled sadly. 'He bought my plane ticket. He didn't want me driving to Louisiana because I was pregnant and tiring more easily. We didn't have a lot of money and I felt guilty that my stubbornness had cost us some of our savings.' Then she met Clay's gaze. 'He said I wasn't stubborn, that I was tenacious and he didn't consider that a failing.'

Clay squeezed her hand. 'Because it's not.'

Her smile was small and sad. 'But I tugged the tiger's tail a little too hard, didn't I? I think now that Robinette must have seen me there, because a week later, Paul was gone.'

'Not your fault, Stevie,' Clay said. 'What happened at the funeral? What did you see?'

'Not much. Robinette had friends standing around him at the graveside, but I didn't see anyone there for Levi. I remember thinking that. No grandparents, teachers, relatives. Nobody. There was no fuss, no excitement. Nothing to see.'

'How did you know the people there were Robinette's friends?' JD asked.

'One of them was Brenda Lee in her wheelchair. The others stood around her and Robinette like they'd known each other for years. All straight and tall . . . like they were all military. Wait a minute.' She drummed her fingers on the table, her eyes unfocused as she searched her memory. 'One of them might have been Henderson. And a big guy who might have been Westmoreland. Joseph, do you have his photo?'

Joseph found it in his folder and gave it to her. 'Is this him?'

'I think so, yeah. I need to go home. To my house.'

'Why?' Clay asked, surprised.

'Because I took pictures of the people with Robinette that day. They're on the camera I was using before Paul was killed.' She faltered for a moment but then her chin came up. 'I assume it got packed away. I never saw it again, but Izzy might know where it is. I need to find it.'

'Wait.' Joseph pulled her back into her chair when she started to rise. 'Why is the camera so important? We know about Brenda Lee Miller, Henderson and Westmoreland.'

'But there were others there,' she said. 'Let's assume that Robinette killed Julie to get control of the company. The employees said he was a figurehead who spent more time golfing than working. They said the real brains had been Julie and her first husband, Rene.'

'That Robinette killed his wife for power I can buy,'

Joseph said. 'What does that have to do with the funeral pictures you took with your camera?'

'Brenda Lee became his PR person when Julie died,' Stevie said. 'You told me on the phone yesterday that Westmoreland is the head of security for Filbert Pharmaceutical Labs. Robinette got control of the company and brought in his cronies from the old days. If we can find some of those other people, maybe one of them can lead us to Westmoreland.' She hesitated, then shrugged. 'Or shed more light on Henderson's assertion that we don't know "jack shit" about Robinette. That's been worrying at me.'

Joseph grew quiet. 'Me, too. I don't think she was bluffing. Okay, we'll get the camera. Novak, that's yours. Izzy's at the farm. Ask her about Stevie's old camera.'

'And when I find the funeral photographs?' Novak asked.

'Check their faces against FPL's website,' Joseph said, 'and send a copy of the photos to my Army contact, the one who found Westmoreland for us yesterday.' He looked at Stevie. 'I can see you thinking. What else do you have?'

'I was thinking about the roles that Robinette would need to fill when he took over Julie's company. Julie was the face of the company and Robinette took that role, supported by his PR person. But Robinette would also need a new chemist, for example. The old chemist was found dead with Julie. They both had the same blunt force wounds on the backs of their heads.'

'Sloppy when you think about it,' JD said with a frown. 'Robinette seems too smart to stage an accident that was so obviously a murder.'

'It wasn't all that obvious,' Hyatt said, giving Stevie a look that was equal parts regret and approval. 'Stevie diagrammed the accident scene, showed how the crash couldn't have caused the head injuries and got the ME to change his cause of death determination to homicide.'

'Because a few of the employees had reached out to me, told me it smelled fishy to them,' Stevie said. 'I figured Julie's murder was not premeditated. If Robinette had had time to plan, he wouldn't have been so sloppy. Control of the company was the only motive that made sense, unless he really did discover them having an affair.'

'Even if it was a crime of passion,' Agent Coppola said, 'he set up his son to take the blame.'

Stevie exhaled quietly. 'And then hired Silas Dandridge to shut me up, one way or the other. It made me wonder how Robinette and Silas crossed paths. Silas worked for Stuart Lippman, the defense attorney. The cases we've seen so far have been connected at their source by court cases. The real guilty parties were contacted by Lippman or one of his underlings and sold the opportunity to make their crimes disappear *after* they were either arrested or charged.'

'By framing innocent people,' Grayson said. 'But Robinette was never charged with Julie's murder. Never even arrested. And he isn't named on the list of cases Lippman left behind.'

'Robinette must have had a few bad moments after Lippman died,' JD added, 'worrying that his name would be on the list. He must have thought he was home free when nobody came after him. Until you started digging, Stevie. You started turning up cases that weren't on Lippman's list. Robinette must have been worried you'd expose him. So he tried to kill you.'

'That's where I came out last night,' Stevie agreed.

'But how Robinette connected with Lippman and Silas is still the question,' Hyatt said.

'We might have the answer,' Stevie said. 'Clay's assistant Alec has a program that takes persons of interest in an investigation and finds connections.'

'It's how we connected Tony Rossi to Danny Kersey, the retired cop in Arizona, who gave us Scott Culp in IA,' Clay said. 'We asked Alec to run Robinette against the participants in Lippman's cases – the names had come from Stevie's personal notes and all the police reports she'd been re-investigating. He worked all night and got one name – Virgil Barry.'

'Virgil Barry's son is on Lippman's master list,' Stevie said. 'Virgil Junior was arrested for assault and battery, but the weapon used on the victim was found under the bed of another young man, who was later charged and convicted. Virgil Junior's arrest was dropped.'

'How does Virgil Senior connect to Robinette?' Joseph asked.

'They golfed together,' Clay said. 'The article Alec found was about an annual team scramble for charity. Robinette and Virgil Senior played on the same team for years.'

'So we talk to Virgil Senior,' Joseph said with a satisfied nod, but Stevie shook her head.

'We can't,' she said. 'He and his wife were shot to death in a home invasion and robbery a few days after Levi Robinette's funeral.'

'And a few days before Paul and Paulie were killed,' Clay added quietly.

'Of course they were,' Joseph said, disgusted. 'Were their killers caught?'

'No,' Stevie said. 'Virgil Senior and his wife were killed next to the locked safe in his home office. The investigator concluded that they were killed because they wouldn't open the safe. But if Robinette got Senior to tell him how Junior's charges disappeared, Robinette wouldn't have let him live. I can't imagine Virgil Senior voluntarily gave him Lippman's name. In the cases we've reopened to date, Lippman's clients said that they were told if they shared

Lippman's identity, they'd die, and so would the children they'd paid to protect. My theory is that Robinette threatened Mrs Barry to make Virgil Senior cooperate. When Virgil gave Robinette Lippman's name, Robinette killed them both. Of course, we can't confirm any of this with Virgil Senior, but the timing is too perfect to be coincidental.'

'I agree,' Joseph said. 'Since we can't talk to the father, what about the son? If Virgil Junior's case was on Lippman's master list, he would have been re-investigated this past year.'

Stevie shook her head again. 'He would have been, but Virgil Junior committed suicide shortly after his parents' murder. OD'd on pills.'

Grayson frowned. 'Then that's a dead end. That Robinette and Virgil Senior golfed together is circumstantial. Unless we can show how Robinette hired Lippman, we can't connect him to Paul's murder. We can still get him on the murders and attempted murders over the past few days through the DNA he left behind at the beach and at the farm, but not on conspiring to kill Paul and Paulie. I'm sorry, Stevie.'

'It's okay. I figured as much.' Stevie glanced at Hyatt. 'But there is one other possibility. According to Lippman's master list, the cop who covered up Virgil Junior's crime was Elizabeth Morton. She was also the cop that investigated the murder of Virgil Senior and his wife.'

Hyatt sighed wearily. His expression was matched by the others in the room except for Kate Coppola, who looked confused.

'Elizabeth Morton was Homicide, wasn't she?' Agent Coppola asked.

'She was one of mine,' Hyatt said, 'but Lippman had coerced her into working for him by breaking her son's leg. He still walks with crutches.'

'Elizabeth was Phil Skinner's partner,' JD added, the tightness in his voice a clear indication that he hadn't begun to get over witnessing the man's suicide, just a few days before.

'She also killed both Silas and Lippman,' Stevie said. 'She killed Silas in my living room to keep him from giving us Lippman's name.'

'And she killed Lippman because she'd finally planned to take her son and run and wanted to make sure he wouldn't follow her,' Grayson finished.

Stevie nodded. 'Elizabeth may be able to confirm that Robinette connected with Lippman. She's doing her time at Jessup. We could be there in less than an hour.'

'The question,' Joseph said, 'is which one of us will she talk to. We know she hates Clay and me. We helped catch her last year when she was trying to escape after killing Lippman.'

'And I testified against her,' Grayson said. 'As did Paige. She hates us, too.'

'I'll go,' Hyatt said. 'Stevie, you'll be with me. You and she are part of the same club – both of you have had your children threatened. Lippman broke her son's leg and Silas held your daughter at gunpoint.'

Stevie had paled. 'And killed my son.'

Hyatt flinched as if she'd struck him. 'I know. I'm so sorry.'

The fight seemed to drain out of her. 'Me too. When do we leave for Jessup?'

'As soon as we're done here,' Hyatt said. 'We'll need to inform the investigation team from the state. This isn't related to Scott Culp and the IA scandal, but a conversation with any dirty cop skirts the boundaries we were given by the State's Attorney's office.'

'Let's just recap,' Joseph said. 'Novak's working on

getting Stevie's photos from Levi Robinette's funeral so that we can hopefully identify more of Robinette's employees. Brodie is getting a sample of the boy's DNA, either via autopsy samples or exhumation. JD?'

'I'm going to prison, too, but not the same one as Stevie and Hyatt,' JD said. 'I want to get the statement from the bartender who drugged Sam Hudson. If he'll confirm Kayla Richards's ID of Silas, then that'll be one more "I" dotted when Grayson brings this case to court. I'm hoping he knows more of the story, like how John Hudson met up with Silas in the first place.'

'Good luck. Grayson?'

'I have to go to court, but Daphne's got the draft of my warrant. If you get anything physical linking Robinette and Silas, call her and she'll revise the warrant and get it in front of the judge.'

'I have a question,' Stevie said. 'If Elizabeth Morton isn't willing to talk, do we have any leeway in making her an offer? Reduced sentence? Anything?'

Grayson looked skeptical. 'Maybe. I'll call my boss on my way to court and will let you know your parameters. Don't count on any big concessions, though.'

'I don't want to offer her anything,' Joseph said coldly. 'But we may have no choice. Clay, I assume you're going with Stevie.'

'You assume correctly.' There was no way in hell Clay was leaving her side.

'Just . . . stay out of Morton's view. I'd like to avoid making her contrary from the get-go. Kate, I have two things for you,' Joseph said to Agent Coppola. 'I want to know more about that lawyer who showed up to represent Henderson yesterday, Cecilia Wright. Henderson didn't want her, seemed to think Wright was in cahoots with Robinette.'

'Cahoots?' Coppola teased. 'You've been hanging around Daphne too much.'

Joseph's mouth curved briefly, but then the weariness moved right back in to claim him. 'Find out who hired Wright or how she connects to Robinette's organization. Does Wright work for him? Did he coerce her? Bribe her? Did she serve with Robinette? I want the connections.'

'Got it,' Coppola said. 'And the second thing?'

'This second thing is your higher priority. Get close to Lisa Robinette. I want her husband's DNA *today*. Check with me before you execute anything. I'll make sure you have backup. Let's meet back here at one. We're done here.' He sighed. 'Now I have to go to a meeting to plan two department funerals.'

'I know,' Hyatt said. 'I just planned three.'

On that grim note, they dispersed.

# Chapter Twenty-Nine

Elizabeth Morton had changed, Stevie thought when the woman was brought into the interview room in handcuffs. Her eyes were like empty holes, lifeless. Soulless.

Stevie glanced up at Hyatt from the corner of her eye. His face was pained.

'Elizabeth,' he said, his deep voice rusty.

Stevie could find no sympathy for the woman who'd sold her soul many times over.

'Why are you here?' Morton asked, her voice as dead as her eyes.

'We got new information yesterday,' Stevie said. 'About Silas.'

Elizabeth rolled her eyes to stare at the ceiling. 'So?'

'My husband and son were murdered, eight years ago, on March 15.'

A slight hitch in Elizabeth's breathing was the only indication she'd heard.

'For eight years I've believed it was a random crime. Yesterday I found out that Silas set it up, coerced a man I never met to murder my husband. And my five-year-old son.'

'I'm sorry for your loss,' Elizabeth said bitterly, not meeting her eyes.

'I hope you're willing to prove it. We know that Todd Robinette hired the murderer of my family.' Stevie caught Elizabeth's slight wince. 'Robinette hooked up with Lippman, we believe through Virgil Barry. Covering up Barry's son's crime was one of your cases.'

'Go talk to Barry, then,' Elizabeth said coldly.

'You know I can't. You know he's dead.'

'Is there a question in there anywhere?' Her tone dripped acid, but beneath was hesitation.

'Yes,' Stevie said, 'there is. Several, in fact. Did Virgil Barry give Lippman's name to Robinette? Did Robinette hire Lippman? Did Lippman assign Silas to kill my family?'

Elizabeth's eyes filled with sly calculation. 'Why should I help you? What's in it for me?'

'The opportunity to do the right thing,' Stevie said. 'The opportunity to make amends.'

'The only right thing is anything that gets me out of here a day sooner.' She stood. 'Talk to your friend, Grayson Smith. Come back when he's ready to make a deal. Guard! Take me back.'

'No,' Hyatt said, his deep voice cracking like a whip. 'Sit down, Elizabeth.'

A twisted smile. 'No offense, Lieutenant, but you're no longer my boss.'

'Maybe not,' Hyatt said, his jaw clenched hard, 'but if you don't start talking right now, I will personally ensure you are moved as far away from your son as possible.'

Elizabeth's step faltered, her cheeks growing pale. 'You sonofabitch.'

'Maybe,' he said. 'You got sympathy during your trial, because Lippman hurt your child to ensure your compliance. But Stevie's son is *dead*. *Murdered*. Because you were too *weak* to stand up and do the right thing. It's time to do the right thing now, Elizabeth. So sit down.'

Elizabeth sat, visibly vibrating with fury. 'I want a deal.'

For a moment, no one spoke. Then Stevie let out a quiet breath. 'I'll give you a deal.'

Elizabeth's eyes narrowed suspiciously. 'You're not authorized to make me any deals.'

'Stevie,' Hyatt began, but Stevie lifted her hand.

'Listen to me, Elizabeth. Robinette targeted my surviving child to ferret me out of hiding. Not once. Not twice. But three times. Do you think your son is safe because Lippman is dead? Do you think Robinette won't find out that we were talking to you? Do you think your son's life will have any value when Robinette finds out you can turn evidence against him?'

'I have no evidence,' Elizabeth said, her chin lifting slightly. But her lips trembled.

'You were willing to make a deal a few minutes ago. I'd make sure he knew that.'

'You're bluffing,' Elizabeth said, her face grown even more pale. 'You wouldn't tell him.'

'Are you willing to risk your son's life on that?' Stevie asked, holding Elizabeth's gaze.

Elizabeth laughed bitterly. 'Didn't think you had it in you, Stevie. What's your deal?'

'You do the right thing by my Paulie and I'll keep your son safe from Robinette. Tell me the truth, with details that we can corroborate, so that Grayson can nail Robinette's ass to the wall.'

Elizabeth closed her eyes. 'Yes,' she finally said. 'Robinette tried to hire Lippman to get the cops off his back, said that he'd come recommended by Virgil Barry. Lippman was furious. Sent me to deal with Barry, since he'd been mine, but Barry and his wife were dead. I closed their murder investigation and thought I was home free, but then Lippman accepted Robinette's job.'

'Why didn't Lippman just kill Robinette?' Hyatt asked.

'Robinette had a recording of Barry telling him everything. Robinette gave it to his attorney to be mailed to the prosecutor if he died suddenly. Lippman had been beaten at his own game.'

'But why Silas?' Stevie asked, pained. 'Why didn't Lippman assign you?'

'Because he had a sick sense of humor. And because Silas still fought him when he got a job he didn't like. He figured he could break Silas and get Robinette off his back, all at once.'

Stevie remembered then. Remembered how Silas had grieved with her, almost as if it had been his own family that had died. That hadn't been grief, she understood now, but guilt.

'Do you have any proof of this, Elizabeth?' Hyatt asked.

'No. But there's always the recording Robinette made of Virgil Barry's confession. He may have thrown it away after he heard Lippman was dead, but you might get lucky and find where his attorney hid it.' Elizabeth's eyes sharpened. 'You will protect my son?'

Hyatt nodded. 'We will. You won't have to worry about him.'

Then he hesitated, as if unsure he wanted the answer to his next question. 'Elizabeth, did you know Stevie's husband and son would be killed?'

'No,' Elizabeth said. 'When I heard Robinette had approached Lippman, I figured she'd be the one killed. Not her husband and son. Lippman was very unhappy with Silas that day. But Robinette was happy. Stevie was off his case. If Lippman punished Silas, I never heard about it.'

'How did you know Lippman was unhappy?' Hyatt asked with a frown.

'Pillow talk.' Stevie must have shown her disgust because Elizabeth laughed again. 'I'll do anything to keep my son safe, Stevie. If I'd been assigned, you'd be dead. But Silas was weak.'

Stevie wondered how she could have worked with this woman for years and never have really known her. *Same way you worked with Silas all those years.* 'Why didn't Silas kill me?'

'He liked you. Respected you because you never took the easy way. That was his mistake. If he'd just killed you, it would have made it easier for all of us in the long run.'

Stevie blinked. 'O-kay. You realize I hold your son's safety in my hands, right?'

Elizabeth's laugh was now hollow. 'You talk big, Stevie, but at the end of the day you won't abandon him. That's not who you are.'

Unexpected warmth uncurled in Stevie's chest. 'Thank you.'

'It wasn't a compliment,' Elizabeth snapped. 'If you'd left well enough alone, my son wouldn't need your damn help. He'd be fine. So do not thank me.'

'That's okay. I don't consider doing the right thing to be a failing.'

*Baltimore, Maryland, Wednesday, March 19, 1.00 P.M.*

After a phone call to assure Cordelia she was all right and a quick stop at a local deli, Stevie and Clay returned to the conference room to find the group already there and waiting. 'We brought lunch,' Stevie said, holding up the bag of sandwiches they'd bought.

Eyes lit up, followed by murmured 'thank yous' as the sandwiches were passed around.

'What did you find?' Joseph asked her as he unwrapped his.

Stevie filled them in as the group ate. 'Apparently Silas couldn't bring himself to kill me.'

JD glowered. 'So he had Paul and Paulie killed instead. Sonofabitch.'

Joseph nodded, his expression dark. 'And there isn't anything we can do to him, but we can get Robinette. We have to. JD, any luck with the bartender?'

JD shook his head. 'Never made it to the prison. Turns out the bartender's dead. Shiv in the gut in the shower by another inmate. Guess who'd arrested that inmate?'

'Silas,' Stevie said grimly.

Hyatt's shoulders sagged. 'I wonder which of *that* man's family members Silas used to threaten him into committing murder.'

'I thought the same thing,' JD said. 'The guy was serving life without parole for three murders. He didn't have anything else to lose on the inside. But he's dead, too. Heart failure. I did make some headway though. I had another talk with Sam Hudson who'd been talking to some of his father's old friends. One of them knew John Hudson's dealer, who I actually knew, too. I arrested him when I was in Vice. He told me that John had started selling for this dealer, but came back empty handed after being fronted a significant supply. He'd been stopped by a cop, carrying enough to qualify for a felony, which would have been his third strike.'

'Guaranteed prison time,' Clay said.

'Yep. But the cop "had a heart". Confiscated his stash in his "greedy ham-sized hands" and let him go with a warning.'

'Silas,' Stevie said grimly. 'Well, that explains some more about "how" Silas got to him.'

'I've got something,' Agent Coppola said. 'The attorney Henderson fired yesterday, Cecilia Wright, went to school with Brenda Lee Miller. They were sorority sisters.'

'I'm sure lots of people went to school with Brenda Lee,' Joseph said with a disappointed frown. 'Doesn't imply a connection.'

'Because you didn't let me finish. Wright's daughter attends one of Robinette's rehab clinics. There was a long waiting list but Wright's kid magically went to the head of the line. Miller couldn't have represented Henderson, or we'd have a connection to Robinette.'

Joseph nodded. 'Good. What about Lisa?'

Coppola's eyes gleamed. 'She was *very* pissed off at her husband after picking up his drunk ass at the factory the other day. Apparently she's one of those vindictive sorts that tosses out her husband's belongings when he's been naughty.'

Clay's face broke into a grin. 'She threw his stuff in the garbage?'

Coppola grinned back. 'She did. So I took out the trash.'

Joseph wasn't smiling. 'I thought we agreed you'd have backup before approaching Lisa.'

'I didn't approach her. I approached her house. Specifically her trash cans.'

Joseph closed his eyes. 'Dammit, Kate. I don't want to bury any more agents.'

Coppola's face fell. 'I'm sorry, Joseph. You were in a meeting and I didn't want the trash truck to come and take our evidence. I had the surveillance guys backing me up.'

'Okay. Fine. But next time, I'd like my instructions followed. What did you find?'

Coppola retrieved a box from the corner. 'We got clothes, shoes, and toys.'

Stevie grimaced. 'Sex toys?'

Coppola laughed. 'You've got a dirty mind, Stevie. I like that. No, not sex toys. Golf clubs and tennis rackets. His Xbox. And this.' From the box she pulled out an evidence bag that held an old Rubik's cube that had been solved.

Stevie went still. 'That was on Robinette's desk eight years ago. That one, or one just like it. I thought it was weird, because Robinette didn't seem like the geeky type. I asked Levi about it, when I questioned him about Julie's death. He said it had belonged to Julie's husband, Rene, which made sense as Rene *was* a geek. He was the head chemist at the factory before he died.'

'Why did Robinette have it on his desk?' Dr Brodie asked.

'Levi said that his father and Rene had gone to high school together and were best friends. That was why Rene and Julie had taken him in when his own mother died. The cube was the one thing of Rene's that his father had wanted after Rene died, because Rene had played with it back when they were kids. Levi said his father kept it for sentimental reasons.'

'Robinette, sentimental?' Clay shook his head. 'Doesn't play for me.'

'Me either,' Stevie said. 'Can I see it?'

'It doesn't work,' Novak said. 'Seems to be glued together.'

Stevie frowned. 'Someone ripped some of the stickers off. Did Lisa do this?'

'I'd say it's a good possibility.' Lying behind the box was a bag of golf clubs. Coppola drew one of the clubs from the bag – it was severely bent. 'I wouldn't want to get on her bad side. The tennis rackets look worse. And it looks like she ran over his Xbox with her car.'

'Yikes. Seems a little extreme for him just getting drunk. I wonder what really happened between them.' Stevie turned the cube over, inspecting all sides. 'Why would this be glued?'

Clay held out his hand for the cube. 'I had one when I was a kid. Took me weeks to solve it. My old partner, Ethan, can do it in less than a minute.' Then he frowned. 'This feels weird.'

''Cause it's glued,' Stevie said.

'No, it's not balanced.' Clay held it to his ear, gave it a shake. 'There's something in here.'

Dr Brodie tested the cube's weight. 'You're right. Should we see what's inside?'

'Do you need to photograph it first?' Joseph asked.

'We did that,' Coppola said. 'I had the lab photograph everything right away. I left the clothes with CSU so they could check for hair or skin samples. I just brought the toys with me to show you the wrath of Lisa.'

'Then open it,' Joseph said.

Brodie opened her tool kit and selected a thin blade, a white cloth, and a pair of gloves. 'It's harder to pry because the top layer doesn't twist.' She scraped at the glue that held the cubes immobile, then made a triumphant noise when the first cube popped off. 'The center's been cut away, along with one of the interior arms that holds the cube in place. It's a deliberate cut that would have required the right tools to do.' She pried away a few more tiles, shook something metallic into her hand. 'And here we go.'

Stevie leaned over the table, staring. 'A bullet. Is that . . . blood?'

'Appears to be,' Brodie said.

*Hell*, Stevie thought. 'Rene Broussard was murdered during a mugging.'

'He'd been with a prostitute,' Joseph said. 'How did they know that?'

Stevie grimaced. 'Because his pants were down around his ankles and he had a lipstick smudge, and not on his collar. The autopsy report said that the bullet had been removed. Cut right out of him. His killer was never found.'

'Looks like we just found him,' Hyatt said grimly.

'Sonofabitch,' Stevie said, incredulous. 'Robinette kills Rene, marries his widow, then kills her too? And then keeps the bullet on his desk, hidden in his pal's childhood toy as a trophy?'

'All for control of the company,' JD added with a shake of his head. 'How much net worth are we talking about?'

'Hard to say,' Stevie said. 'They're privately held. That made it hard to get information on Robinette's business dealings eight years ago. If the blood on this bullet matches Rene's, that *has* to be enough for a warrant.'

'I agree,' Joseph said. 'Given Elizabeth Morton's testimony, we might already have enough.' He called Daphne, gave her the information. 'She's revising Grayson's warrant as we speak, but says we still need physical evidence. She's going to ask the judge to be on standby and rush him the warrant once we have the physical evidence in hand. Novak, you look like you're about to spew. Do you have something to share with the class?'

'I do indeed,' Novak said. 'I have several things. First, Robinette's posse. Stevie, your sister knew where your camera was, but we didn't need it. She'd downloaded the photos to a CD years ago and put them in her safe deposit box for the day you were ready to look at them.'

*Oh.* Stevie's heart melted at her sister's thoughtfulness. 'That sounds like Izzy.'

'She also kept copies on her hard drive so she emailed me the pictures you took at Levi's funeral. There were four people around Robinette. Brenda Lee Miller, Jean Henderson, Michael Westmoreland, and this man.' Novak turned his laptop around, showing them the photo.

The man was very handsome, Stevie thought, his dark blond hair carefully combed, his black suit fitting him well. 'Now that I see the picture, I have a vague recollection of him back then. But I've seen him more recently – on Filbert Labs's website. He's the head chemist. James something.' The piece fell into place in her mind. 'Fletcher. James Fletcher.'

'We read his profile,' Clay said. 'There's no mention of military service.'

'You're right,' Novak said. 'But he did serve in Iraq during the time Henderson and Robinette served together. He was a doctor, but he got a dishonorable discharge.'

Clay's brows went up. 'Oh. Do we know why?'

'Not yet. But . . .'

Stevie narrowed her eyes. Novak clearly had something bigger to spill. 'But what?'

'He's currently in custody, a guest of the German BKA. They grabbed him as he walked off the plane in Frankfurt, about ninety minutes ago.'

The questions came flying from around the table. 'Why?' 'How?'

Stevie leaned close to Clay. 'What's the BKA?' she whispered.

'Their FBI,' Clay said. 'The *Bundeskriminalamt*.'

Novak's odd eyes were sparkling with excitement. 'Stevie, I heard you say as I was leaving that Robinette would have needed a new head chemist because he killed the last one along with Julie. I called the factory and asked to speak to Fletcher, but he wasn't there. I went by his

649

apartment and his neighbor said he'd seen him leave yesterday morning with a large suitcase so I started a check on the airports, to see if he'd left town. While I was waiting, I got the photo files from Izzy, so I knew I was on the right track. A few minutes later I found he'd flown out of Reagan National to Toronto, transferring to DeGaulle, then to Frankfurt. Luckily for us, he's traveling on his own passport. Anyway, I put out a BOLO with Interpol.'

'You've been busy,' Stevie said.

'Which was why I was so happy you brought lunch. I didn't have time to eat.'

'Poor baby,' Joseph said dryly. 'So the Germans grabbed him after seeing your BOLO?'

'They did and they're holding him and have seized his luggage. They can keep him for a few hours while we figure out what we need to do.'

'Well done, Deacon,' Joseph said and Novak gave a single hard, pleased nod.

'What about me?' Coppola said with a frown. 'I went through the garbage.'

'Rich people's garbage,' Novak pointed out.

'Still garbage.' Coppola grimaced. 'Still nasty.'

'Well, I went to prison,' Stevie chimed in. 'Do I get an attaboy, too?'

'You all get gold stars,' Joseph said. 'We have Brenda Lee under surveillance and the BOLO we filed for Westmoreland yesterday is still in effect. Now we need Robinette.'

'We have the blood samples from Levi Robinette's autopsy,' Brodie said, 'and I've already started the lab on the DNA analysis, but it'll be tomorrow before we have results. Now that I have Robinette's suits from the garbage, I can search for hairs on the fabric. Hopefully we'll get a match to the hair we found at the beach.'

'Do it,' Joseph said. 'As soon as you have that, we'll get our warrant. I'll assign teams to search Robinette's home and factory.'

Stevie had opened her mouth to say she was accompanying them when Novak gasped.

'Oh my God. Joseph, wait.' Novak looked up from his laptop, his eyes no longer sparkling. 'The Germans just arrested Fletcher. He was carrying enough sarin to kill everyone in the airport if the seal on the bottle had broken.'

Stevie heard the shocked gasps, her own included. 'Whoa,' she said. 'I didn't expect that.'

Clay sat back in his chair, his jaw lax. 'That sonofabitch,' he hissed. 'Robinette's making chemical weapons. That's why he wanted control of the pharmaceutical company so badly. How did the Germans find the sarin?'

'The BKA was searching Fletcher's luggage,' Novak said, 'and were about to open what he'd labeled a perfume bottle when he stopped them, all pale and panicked. They were suspicious because of how well it was packed, but they really hadn't planned to open it. They were just bluffing to give us some time. But then Fletcher blurted out what it was.'

'Can't say that I blame Fletcher for panicking,' Brodie said, shuddering. 'Good God.'

'What was Fletcher's final destination?' Joseph asked.

'Lagos. From there he could have hooked up with any number of terrorist cells.'

'Which would have been *just* what we needed,' Joseph said sardonically. 'I'll let Daphne know so she can amend our warrant.' He dialed Daphne again then began mobilizing SWAT units and HazMat teams.

Clay drummed his fingers lightly on the table. 'We didn't find Henderson's passport, did we?' he murmured, quietly enough so that he didn't interrupt Joseph's calls.

'No,' Novak said. 'She has one, but it wasn't on her. It may have been destroyed along with her apartment in that fire.'

'Westmoreland has a passport in a different name,' Clay said. 'I'll bet Henderson does, too.'

'Where are you going with this?' Stevie asked.

'I can't imagine Fletcher was the primary deliveryman,' he said, 'not traveling on his own passport and carrying it in his checked luggage.'

'It is amateurish,' Brodie agreed. 'Robinette seems too smart for that.'

'Fletcher was running away and probably needed money to live on the run,' Clay said, 'so he took the sarin, planning to sell it. He wouldn't have had to look hard for customers.'

'What if they've done this before?' Stevie asked quietly. 'What if Robinette's been using his factory to make weapons of chemical warfare for the last eight years? He'd need deliverymen with passports that couldn't be traced back to him. Like Westmoreland.'

'We'll get the facial recognition software going,' Novak said, 'to see if we can find Westmoreland and Henderson in the crowds at the major world airports.'

'For the past eight years?' Brodie protested.

'If we have to,' Novak said grimly. 'But I'm betting we'll get a hit at Lagos sometime in the last year. If Fletcher is an amateur, if he hasn't been involved in previous deliveries, and if they have done this before, Fletcher may have picked a previous customer he knew of.'

'That's a lot of ifs,' Brodie said doubtfully. 'But I guess it's a place to start.'

Novak shrugged. 'Plus Fletcher might give the Germans some information once it sinks in that he's been caught. Anybody traveling on their own passport with a chemical weapon in their checked luggage is probably not going to hold up under interrogation too long. I'd give up Robinette in a heartbeat if it were me.'

'This is why Robinette needed you dead, Stevie. It was never about his son,' Clay said.

'I know.' It made more sense now. 'I was looking into all the old cases. If I'd opened his again, I might have caught on to his sideline business. He had the perfect opportunity when people started shooting at me.'

'He took advantage of the fact that other people wanted you dead, too,' JD said. 'Bastard.'

Joseph came to his feet, holding his phone. 'Daphne just got our warrant for his house and the factory. SWAT teams are on their way to both places. JD, Deacon, Kate, you're with me.'

'I'll get back to the lab,' Brodie said, 'and prepare it for any sarin samples you find.'

Stevie stood up. 'I'm going, too, Joseph. I'll stay out of your way, but I deserve to see Robinette brought to his knees.'

Joseph looked at Clay. 'You, too, I take it?'

'If she goes, so do I. And she does deserve to be there.'

'If I tell you no, you'll just do it anyway,' Joseph finally said. 'I'd rather know where you are. Just wear body armor, get a gas mask, and stay behind the line.'

*Wednesday, March 19, 2.55 P.M.*

He wasn't dead, but Robinette felt like his gut had been pulled out through his navel. He'd spent nearly twenty-four hours lying on Brenda Lee's garage floor vomiting his insides up. When he got his hands on Fletcher . . . *I will fucking kill the bitch.*

But first, he thought, staring at the screen of the ATM in his bank's drive-thru lane, he was going to kill Lisa. And by God, he'd make it hurt.

'What's wrong?'

He turned to look at Cecilia Wright, who sat in the passenger seat of her minivan, watching him as though he was a striking rattlesnake. Brenda Lee's best friend was a smart woman.

He'd hidden under a blanket in the back of Brenda Lee's minivan to get out of his house and into her garage, thinking he'd put distance between himself and the Feds. They'd been outside his factory and his home – but then they'd also been outside Brenda Lee's home. The Feds knew.

He knew he'd left blood at that farm – and he'd never left DNA behind before. His only saving grace was that he had no DNA profile on file anywhere that the Feds could compare the blood to. They'd ask him to voluntarily submit a sample, but he'd refuse and they'd never get a warrant to take his DNA, not on the circumstantial evidence they possessed. But knowing that the FBI congregated outside his property and outside Brenda Lee's had left them both shaken.

He and Brenda Lee agreed that he needed to get out of town for a while. Somewhere that he could rest without being recognized. So he'd dragged himself into Brenda Lee's bathroom and cleaned himself up, the razor she used to buzz cut her son's hair aiding his disguise. His mustache and most of his hair filled a trash bag he'd taken away with him.

He'd leave no DNA behind that the cops could use against him.

Brenda Lee had smuggled him out of her garage under the same blanket, letting him out behind her son's school.

The private gate kept the Fed tail from following them onto school property where Cecilia Wright waited, having just picked up her own six-year-old daughter.

Edgy and pale, Cecilia had buckled her daughter into the backseat of Brenda Lee's minivan, then had driven Robinette – hidden under another damn blanket in yet another damn minivan – past the Fed waiting outside. They'd stopped on a side street where he'd taken the wheel, tired of hiding under blankets.

His plan had been to first hit the ATM and then to drive to the airport where Cecilia was going to rent a car for him in her name. But step one had stalled out.

'My bank account seems to be empty,' he said mildly.

'I . . . I can loan you some money,' Cecilia said with a terrified stutter.

Idly he wondered what this woman owed Brenda Lee that she was willing to aid him. Then he remembered they'd taken her teenager into one of their programs when no one else would. If they hadn't, the teen would have gone to juvie. Which was where the kid had belonged, in Robinette's opinion. But Brenda Lee had begged and Robinette had allowed it.

He was damn glad that he had. 'I might take you up on that. Give me a moment.'

Robinette dialed his home phone, intending to lure Lisa out. So he could fucking kill her.

'Todd?' Lisa answered, a relieved sigh whooshing out of her. 'You've had me so scared. Where are you?'

'Why do you want to know?'

'Why do I want to know?' she echoed, sounding bewildered. Lisa did bewildered very well. 'I suppose I understand why you'd ask. I was terrible to you yesterday. I was hurt that you only called me because there was no one else. I . . . was wrong.'

He liked the words. Didn't trust the sentiment.

'I seem to have a problem with our bank account,' he said. He had other accounts but he couldn't access them from here. He also had cash in his safes at home and at work. Had he not been puking his guts up the day before, he'd have cleaned those out. Of course he didn't plan to tell Lisa about his cash reserves. She'd steal him blind. 'There's nothing in it.'

'That's because I moved the money, because I got visited by the FBI. Henderson is making outrageous claims. I figured if the FBI came looking for your assets, they'd freeze them.'

'Where did you move them?'

'To my account, the one I had from before we got married. But I took a large amount in cash in case you need to pay someone to deal with this Henderson mess for you.'

'That's what I pay Brenda Lee for.'

A long pause. 'Then I suppose you don't need the money,' she said sweetly, and he knew he'd pissed her off again.

He gritted his teeth, kept his tone civil. 'No, but I'd like to have it.'

'Then I'll give it to you. I think we should lie low for a few days,' Lisa said. 'Let all this hubbub die down. You might still have a political career if we play this right.'

In a third-world nation he'd never heard of, Robinette thought bitterly. 'I need a car.'

'I'll pick you up. The police are still out there, but it's just one car that's parked way down the street where they think I won't notice them. I can slip out the back and cut through the woods to the neighbor's house. Dad said he'd send a car for me. Are you at the bank now?'

'Yes,' he said warily.

'Then I'll pick you up and we can go away for the

weekend. I know a great spa where we can relax and let whatever craziness Henderson is spouting blow over. You'll come back rejuvenated and ready to talk campaign strategies. I'll be there in thirty minutes.'

She thought this would blow over in a weekend? *Is she that stupid?* 'Don't be late.'

'I won't,' she said warmly. 'We'll have a wonderful time. Just the two of us.'

Robinette hung up, stared at his phone for a long moment. Lisa might be clueless, but she wasn't stupid. It was likely that she was luring *him* into a trap instead of the other way around. So . . . should he stay or run?

*Stay*, he thought. *But be ready to run.* Decision made, he put Cecilia's car into gear.

'Where are we going?' Cecilia asked, still watching him carefully.

Robinette parked in the corner of the nearly empty lot. 'You're going to call a cab to take you home. I'm going to stay here and meet my wife. When I've finished with your van, I'll let Brenda Lee know and she can bring you back to pick it up. I'll also accept the loan you offered as well as the use of your credit card. Don't worry. Brenda Lee will reimburse you.'

Wright got out her purse. 'All right. Whatever you say, Mr Robinette.'

*Whatever you say, Mr Robinette.* Forced out of Lisa's throat, those words would sound like music. He stared at his hands. Imagining them wrapped around Lisa's slender neck. Then imagined them around Mazzetti's. The words would sound even better forced out of Mazzetti's throat, he thought. He'd make the bitch say them – and more – before he was done with her.

But first things first. Money, rental car, plane ticket, deal with Lisa. Then he would deal with Mazzetti.

*Wednesday, March 19, 5.45 P.M.*

'This isn't good,' Stevie muttered for what had to have been the hundredth time as she paced behind the long line of law enforcement vehicles parked in front of Robinette's home, a mansion on a secluded lot at the end of a very long, private driveway blocked by an ornamental gate. She and Clay were inside the gate, but so far away from the house that they could barely see Robinette's front door without binoculars.

Outside the gate, news station vans and twice as many cars lined the street. The reporters had been waiting all afternoon, as soon as the word had gotten out that SWAT teams had converged on Robinette's house and factory.

The officer guarding the gate had allowed them to pass, but only on foot. No unauthorized vehicles were permitted on the premises so they'd had to park the SUV outside the gate. Once inside, the officer had informed her that he had 'orders from Special Agent Carter' to keep her as far from the house as possible. For her own safety of course.

Which left Stevie cursing Joseph in ways that became increasingly more creative as the afternoon passed. She finally stopped cursing and pacing to peer through her binoculars.

'What are they doing in there?' she demanded. 'It's not like they don't have enough cops. What is taking them so long?'

Clay knew she was venting her frustration, so he'd wisely said little as she'd raged. It was far better that she expend her wrath on Joseph than on him. But she was right. The alphabet soup of coverage included the FBI, ATF, BPD, SWAT, and even the CIA. With so many cops from so many agencies in there, the lack of news couldn't be positive.

'They've been in there for hours,' she said. 'Why haven't they found him? How many places can a man hide?'

She sounded calmer now, so Clay ventured a response. 'In a house that big? I'd say a fair number.'

She sighed, her voice growing small. 'What if he's not there, Clay?'

He gently squeezed the back of her neck, her only accessible skin. They both wore body armor from the waist up – Joseph's condition for them being allowed here at all. 'You heard Joseph. Nobody's left the property since Brenda Lee Miller left yesterday and one of Joseph's people followed her.'

'I know. I just hate not being in there. I hate having to wait way back here, twiddling my thumbs. I hate not knowing what's happening.'

'I'm not too crazy about it myself,' he admitted, then checked his binoculars when Robinette's front door opened. 'It's Joseph. Here he comes.'

Joseph stopped four times to talk with various staff before getting to them. That his expression was closed didn't bode well. That the long line of law enforcement cars had begun to move, exiting the property in a single file line, was even more telling.

'I'm sorry, Stevie,' Joseph said. 'I'd meant to brief you, but time got away from me.'

'*Did you find him?*' she demanded in a low voice.

'No.' Joseph's jaw was tight. 'He's not in there. Somehow he got away.'

Stevie stared at him. 'How?'

'My agents assure me that no one entered or left the property after Brenda Lee left yesterday. We just got a warrant to search her house. It appears that she smuggled him out. She has a van because of her wheelchair. He could have hidden in the back. The agent also lost sight of her for a few minutes when she picked her son up from school. It's a private school with a gate and he didn't want to risk detection at the time. Robinette might have gotten out there.'

Stevie paled. 'He could be going back to the farm. After Cordelia.'

Joseph shook his head. 'We've got people lined up along the farm's driveway and at all access points in the woods. We've got the cameras and infrared sensors. They can't approach by car, foot, or even on horseback.'

'What's Robinette's wife saying?' Clay asked.

'Absolutely nothing. She's planted herself on a sofa and hasn't said one word, except to demand her attorney. Luckily they have staff that can tell a sinking ship when they're on one. The live-in cook says she heard Lisa screaming yesterday afternoon. First at Brenda Lee, then even more after she left, mostly calling Robinette unprintable names. That's when Lisa cleaned out his closet and dumped his toys. And she did drive over his Xbox. There are still pieces of it on the garage floor. Then the cook heard nothing and got worried. She went to Lisa's room, found her crying on the phone with her mother, saying she was getting a divorce.'

'Did the cook see him?' Clay put his arm around Stevie's shoulders. She was trembling.

'No. She said she hadn't seen him since Brenda Lee left.'

Stevie took a deep breath. 'Why did Lisa want a divorce?'

'She told her mother that Robinette was having an affair.'

Stevie frowned. 'With Brenda Lee?'

'No, with James Fletcher.'

Stevie straightened abruptly. 'Oh. That would explain some of her rage. No woman wants to be upstaged, especially a twenty-three-year-old debutante.'

'If she didn't know that Robinette was bisexual, that must have been a shock,' Clay said.

'It wasn't Fletcher's gender,' Joseph said. 'It was his relationship with Robinette from before Lisa's time. She was apparently jealous of all the time Robinette spent with his team. The cook said Lisa particularly dislikes Brenda Lee because Robinette listens to everything she says. That Brenda Lee came over when Lisa brought him home from his office was the lighted match in the tinderbox.'

'He'd called her, too?' Stevie asked.

'I guess that's what Lisa assumed. Lisa lit into her, accusing her of trying to steal her husband. Brenda Lee took offense and started yelling too. Cook said she tried not to listen.' Joseph rolled his eyes. 'But then Brenda Lee screamed that *she* wasn't the one having an affair with Robinette. That everyone knew it had been Fletcher. "*For years.*" Since long before Lisa was in the picture. Long before she was "even in high school".'

Clay winced. 'Oh. Low blow.'

'I know. The cook said it got really quiet and Brenda Lee apologized for telling Lisa that way. That it was best if she just "got used to it". That "Fletcher wasn't going anywhere".'

'Except,' Stevie said, 'he was. He would have been halfway to Paris by then. Almost makes me feel sorry for Lisa.'

'Don't reach for the tissues yet. Lisa accused Brenda Lee of stirring this up to thwart Robinette's bid for office. Brenda Lee told her that if she really wanted to be a political wife, she needed to dump Robinette and find another man. That Robinette's relationship with Fletcher was the least of her worries. Then the cook said Brenda Lee left.'

'Wait.' Stevie frowned. 'She left without even talking to

Robinette? He must have gone straight to her van to hide. She knew his plan and aided him.'

'We'll charge her with it,' Joseph promised. 'I'm going to Brenda Lee's right now. I'll update you when I have news.' He hailed a young agent who came running. 'Get a car, please.'

Joseph started to walk away, but Stevie grabbed his arm. 'What about the factory? Could he have gone there?'

'No, but we did end up using the HazMat guys. We found gallons of sarin stored in aluminum bottles.'

'Keeps it fresh and deadly even longer,' Clay said grimly.

Joseph frowned at him. 'I don't even want to know how you know this stuff. The lab techs swear they knew nothing about it and the day shift logs support that. They make vaccines during the day, but said Fletcher worked a lot of nights contract manufacturing for other companies. There were no records for those batches and the companies don't exist, except on paper. Oh, and you're gonna love this part. The sarin Coppola and Novak found was boxed up and ready for shipment. Guess how it was labeled?'

'Not as perfume, I take it,' Clay said.

'No. As vaccines. That's how they were getting it to their customers. All of Robinette's philanthropy, all that providing vaccines to third-world nations at a fraction of their cost was nothing but a smokescreen. My car's here. I'm going to have a chat with Brenda Lee. I'm leaving a crew to guard the house, in case— Hold on.' Joseph took his cell phone from his pocket. 'It's Coppola. Kate,' he answered. 'What do you have?'

They watched as Joseph's body straightened, his eyes growing sharp. 'Which one? When?' Then, 'You've alerted airport security? Excellent. I'll meet you there in thirty.' He hung up, gave Clay and Stevie a hard nod. 'Cecilia Wright's credit card was used to buy a plane ticket to Mexico City, and not for herself.'

'For Robinette?' Clay asked with a frown. 'He wouldn't be that foolish, would he?'

'No. He knows we're looking for him. The ticket is for Eric Johnson. I figured Robinette would have a secondary passport, just like Westmoreland did.'

'Which airport?' Stevie asked. 'BWI, Reagan, or Dulles?'

'I'll have one of my agents escort you to the farm,' Joseph said, ignoring her question. 'Stay there until I call you. Please, Stevie. I need to know you're safe. I have to go now.'

Clay watched him go, followed by several more law enforcement vehicles and the last of the news vans, who had correctly sensed a break in the story. When all the taillights disappeared, he said quietly, 'To the farm like he asked you? Or to the airport?'

She let out a breath. 'I'm not convinced he's going to Mexico City. He had to know we'd check out Cecilia Wright. Had to know we'd find out she was Brenda Lee's friend.'

'I thought the same thing.'

She looked up at him with a rueful smile. 'I figured you did. I want to see Robinette dragged away in cuffs more than just about anything, but if he's still out there . . .' She shrugged. 'He might be trying to get to Mexico, but if he isn't, I don't want Cordelia alone.'

They slipped through the fence. With most of the other cars already gone, their black SUV looked a little lonely as they approached it. 'Careful,' Clay cautioned, grabbing her arm when she stumbled over a tree root. 'Don't f—'

His leg abruptly crumpled, dropping him face first into the dirt. *Don't fall*, he thought as white-hot pain shot through his leg, the sound of the shot registering a split second later.

He'd been hit. *Stevie*.

'Clay? Clay?' Her voice was close at first, then further away. Then nothing at all.

Fighting his panic, he struggled up on one knee to look for her. The panic won, twisting him from the inside out when he saw her cane abandoned on the grass.

Stevie was being dragged toward the SUV, a hand over her mouth and a gun at her forehead. Her holster was empty. Robinette had her and he'd taken her gun. Clay glanced around wildly, looking for backup, but everyone had gone. *Robinette had Stevie*.

'If you call for help, I'll kill her,' Robinette said softly. 'I swear it.'

# Chapter Thirty

*Perfect*, Robinette thought. *Better than perfect.* He'd come back planning to sneak past the one cop Lisa claimed was waiting outside, so that he could grab his backup passport and run.

But now he had the grand prize. *Stevie Mazzetti finally belongs to me.*

She was, however, a lot stronger than she looked and fought like a wildcat. He shoved the barrel of her own gun harder against her temple. 'Settle down,' he whispered in her ear. 'Or my next shot takes out Loverboy.' Who was still on the ground, but starting to stir. 'You don't want to watch him die, now do you?'

She shook her head, breathing through her nose in short pants. She stopped thrashing, but her body was still tense. She was waiting for an opportunity to get away.

He didn't intend to allow that to happen. 'You're going to walk with me to your SUV, nice and easy.' The SUV was an exact duplicate of the one he'd shot up in front of Culp's house, but when he ran the plates, it made sense.

The new SUV belonged to Grayson Smith, Joseph Carter's brother. With any luck, the window glass would also be a duplicate – bullet-proof.

He started moving, but she wasn't cooperating, so he dragged her. Not only was she stronger than she looked, she was heavier, too. But he *was* weak, thanks to goddamn Fletcher.

He'd find the bastard and Fletcher would wish he'd never been born. The thought made Robinette tired. The list of people who'd be wishing they'd never been born had mushroomed.

He still had to deal with Lisa, but he'd get to her later.

He'd expected his wife had been lying about meeting him at the bank, but he'd waited – until Brenda Lee called to tell him it was a setup. Cecilia had told her that he was waiting for Lisa, but now that his wife had discovered the truth about his long-term affair with Fletcher, Brenda Lee had worried that Lisa was giving him over to the police out of spite.

Robinette hadn't worried – until he'd driven by the factory to see the news vans and the horde of cops. And the guys in HazMat suits. And then Lisa was his last concern.

The Feds knew what Fletcher had been making during the night. He'd been stunned. To hell with worrying about Mazzetti reopening Julie's murder investigation. He had Homeland Security on his ass now. He needed to get out of the country. He needed his fake passport, in the safe in his home office. The fact that he drove Wright's mini-van, and that he'd so drastically altered his appearance, added to the fact that he was desperate . . . He'd decided to chance it.

But his heart had sunk as he'd driven Wright's minivan past the line of news vans. There were more cops at his house than there had been at the factory. There was no way he was getting to his fake passport now. The cops were probably combing his office and if they hadn't blown his safe open already, they soon would.

His mind had been racing, searching for another solution, when he saw the key to his escape – Stevie Mazzetti and Clay Maynard walking through his front gate. Joseph Carter would make a trade for Mazzetti's life. One trouble-making cop for a one-way ticket to anywhere.

*How I'll kill her later will have to be a question left for another day.*

The tons of cops searching for him suddenly didn't worry him – they annoyed him. They wouldn't find him in the house – because he wasn't there. Eventually they'd give up, go elsewhere and then he'd make his move. Mazzetti would leave with them and he'd follow her. But they hadn't gone fast enough, so he'd given them a little nudge.

One ticket to Mexico City bought online for the non-existent Eric Johnson using Wright's credit card, six hundred bucks. Watching the Feds scatter on a wild goose chase – priceless.

A few steps more and he'd be out of here.

*Wednesday, March 19, 6.07 P.M.*

Above Robinette's hand, Stevie's dark eyes were wide with fear. Until she saw Clay moving. Then her eyes narrowed, snapping with fury. She was pissed off, not terrified.

*That's my girl.* A pissed-off Stevie was a force to be reckoned with.

Clay looked up, found Robinette staring him down.

'I want to see your hands,' Robinette demanded. 'Good,' he added when Clay complied. 'Now your gun. Two fingers. You know the drill. Make one wrong move and I'll splatter her brains. Goddammit,' Robinette barked. Stevie had begun thrashing like a wild animal, taking all of Robinette's strength just to keep her overpowered.

*Giving me time to get my shit together.*

Robinette tightened his grip, lifting her off the ground so that her feet dangled. She kicked, twisting to position her feet where they'd do the worst damage. Robinette shook her hard and Clay could see her blinking rapidly.

The bastard had shaken her so hard she'd seen stars. Her kicks slowed until her feet went still. 'Good. Now, Maynard, take your gun by the barrel and toss it over here, slow and easy.'

Gritting his teeth, Clay again obeyed, tossing the gun so that it hit the grass and slid, coming to rest a few inches from the SUV.

Stevie grabbed for Robinette's arm, pulling her body up so that she could breathe. Then her wild fighting began again.

'Tell her to stop struggling and she can live.'

'Save your strength, Stevie.'

Robinette's lips curved. 'Not what I had in mind, but it will do for now.'

'Glad . . . you approve.' *God.* It hurt. Clay hadn't hurt this badly since . . . well, since the last time he'd been shot in the leg. An unexpected jolt of humor shocked him, shook him loose from the grip of pain.

It was the adrenaline, he knew. But it had served its purpose. Now he could think.

The barrel of Robinette's gun was at an awkward angle to Stevie's forehead, thanks to the helmets they both wore

That they wore flak jackets, too, was the only reason he wasn't dead. The only reason Robinette had aimed for his leg, the only part of his body left unprotected.

Clay looked over his shoulder. A few agents remained, but they were in the house with Lisa Robinette. No one was close enough to see. He could only hope someone had heard the shot.

His pants were already wet with blood from the knee up. He was lucky – the bullet had missed his femoral artery, hitting his thigh a few inches below his groin.

*Thank God for that, too,* he thought grimly. He'd be needing that part of his body when they got out of here. Because they would. Clay would entertain no other outcome.

'Throw me your car keys,' Robinette demanded. 'Now.'

No fucking way that was going to happen. There was no way Robinette would let her live.

Clay made a quick, calculated move, letting Robinette believe that he was going for the gun that he'd tossed away, grunting when a second bullet hit his right arm. He wore Kevlar under his shirt, but Robinette couldn't see it. Clay moaned, grabbing his arm and rolling as if he'd been hit, curling up in the fetal position.

Robinette's growl of fury was Clay's reward. During the seconds Robinette had fired, his gun had no longer pointed at Stevie's head and she'd used those seconds the best way possible.

Throwing herself into him like a tornado, she punched and kicked. Robinette checked her a moment before she kneed him in the nuts, slapping her so hard that she flew against the SUV.

*You are so gonna die.*

Still hunched in a fetal position, Clay went first for his backup revolver, concealed in his left pants pocket. He shifted then, grimacing as he went for his phone in his right pocket which was too damn close to the bullet in his leg. He silently cursed when his phone failed to turn on. It was soaked with his own blood. Useless.

He straightened, coming up on one knee just as Robinette grabbed Stevie by the fasteners on her flak jacket with one hand, lifting her in the air again, his gun shoved under her chin as he pulled her against him. She still looked dazed.

'Keys, Maynard. I want your damn keys!'

'Okay, okay,' Clay panted, leaving his arm against his side, hoping Robinette wouldn't see his revolver. He didn't dare shoot now – the bastard was using Stevie as a shield. 'Just don't hurt her. Please don't hurt her.' Holding on to his sanity by a thread, he dug his keys from his pocket and hesitated, trying to think of something to do. Anything to do.

Then he realized that Robinette held his gun awkwardly, like he'd never held one before. With his left hand.

Was Robinette right handed? Why didn't he just switch hands? Why was . . .

*Oh*. Understanding came in a rush. Robinette only had one arm powerful enough to hold Stevie – his right. Because a certain kid had shot him in the left arm. *Alec, I love you*. The kid must have injured Robinette worse than they'd assumed.

Clay tossed the keys, letting them fall so that they were inches out of Robinette's reach.

'Fuck you, Maynard,' Robinette snarled.

'My right hand's all bloody.' Which was true. The hole in his leg was bleeding faster after his theatric roll across the ground. 'I can't throw left-handed. The keys slipped.' Which was a complete lie. He wanted Stevie to pay attention to Robinette's left hand.

He wanted Robinette to come closer. The bastard would

either have to release Stevie or force her to move. He wouldn't do the first. *The second buys me time.*

Robinette shot Clay a killing glare. 'You're a fucking liar. I should shoot her right now.'

'But you won't, because you need her to get away,' Clay said, forcing steel into his tone. Robinette spun Stevie so that she faced him, marching her backward until he could cover the keys with his shoe. 'Kneel.'

Stevie was still blinking rapidly. 'I'll fall.'

Robinette shoved the gun into her windpipe, making her choke. 'Then you'll die. Kneel.'


*Wednesday, March 19, 6.10 P.M.*


Stevie put all her weight on her right leg, lifting the left as she knelt. *This is just yoga,* she thought. She'd seen Izzy do this hundreds of times. *Too bad I never actually attended class.*

*Tomorrow,* she thought. *Tomorrow I'll start yoga.*

Today she had better things to do. Like get her goddamn gun back. She'd heard the shot, seen Clay go down and immediately had drawn her weapon. But Robinette had grabbed her from behind, taking her gun and her phone. He'd thrown her phone into the trees, dammit.

He'd kept her gun. Robinette knelt with her, keeping pace. Keeping her own gun shoved against her throat. *Dammit.*

Robinette slid his foot off the keys Clay had thrown . . . thrown with his *left* hand. *Oh.*

It was then that Stevie realized how awkwardly Robinette held the gun - with his left hand. Alec had shot him in his left arm. He'd been holding her against him with his right hand.

*Got it. Right arm strong, left arm weak.* Robinette's left arm was his vulnerable area.

Still holding the gun at her throat, Robinette reached down to scoop up the keys in his right hand. Deliberately she listed slightly to his left. His gun followed her movement, throwing him off-balance and distracting him. Just for a moment. But that's all she needed.

Simultaneously, she jabbed one fist into his upper left arm and used the heel of her other hand to knock the gun away from her throat.

Robinette pulled the trigger, but he was a moment too late. The shot was six inches wide, missing her and landing somewhere in the nearby trees.

Immediately, another gun fired and Robinette howled, his left hand flexing on reflex, the gun dropping to the ground. Clay had shot the bastard in the same place Alec had. Robinette fell to his knees reaching for the gun he'd dropped – the gun he'd ripped from her hand when he'd first grabbed her – but Stevie was a little bit faster.

Taking her gun back, she shoved the barrel under his chin.

She had Robinette where she wanted him. *At my mercy.* Her hand was steady as she stared into his eyes. His eyes were deadly as he stared back into hers.

'If you expect me to beg you not to kill me, you'll die waiting,' he said.

It wasn't what she *expected.* It was what she *needed.* She needed to kill this parasitic, sociopathic sonofabitch. He deserved it. He deserved far worse. *He killed Paul. He killed my son.* To save his own miserable ass.

She was no longer filled with rage. Her mind was clear. She could do this. With a single bullet she could end it all. Today. She would never have to be afraid of Robinette again.

She owed it to Cordelia. Owed her daughter a life without fear.

Paul had died protecting their son. Stevie had seen the video more times than she could count. She'd seen the flash of certainty in her husband's eyes. The despair. He'd known he was about to die. *He had to have been thinking of me. Of our child he'd never see. Of our son he hadn't been able to save.*

She owed it to Paul to protect Cordelia.

'I should kill you,' she said, her voice still a bit hoarse.

'But you won't,' Robinette said with a smile, smug in his conviction.

She didn't rise to the bait. She simply looked at him. *Paul. Paulie.* An eye for an eye, right? She was just sorry she could only kill him once.

'Are you sure?' she murmured. 'Are you very sure?'

His eyes flickered, the first hint of fear. His eyes skittered away, focusing on a point behind her head, and Stevie knew without looking that Clay had his backup piece trained on Robinette.

He'd said nothing, but she knew if she killed Robinette right here, right now, that Clay would have her back. He'd tell the cops it had been an accident. He'd swear she'd killed Robinette in self-defense.

He'd protected her with his life, offered her his soul. He would lie for her, of this she had no doubt. *But I would never ask him to.* Because it would taint him. Taint them.

It was no way to start a life together.

Nor was this the way to protect Cordelia. Because if her daughter ever asked for the truth about Robinette's death, Stevie couldn't lie any more than she'd ask Clay to.

*Are you sure?* she asked again, this time to herself. *Be very sure. You'll never have this moment, this opportunity again.*

'Clay, are you all right?' she called behind her, her decision made.

'Jim Dandy. You?'

The words came out tight. Agonized. *He's been bleeding all this time. Hell. I am the worst girlfriend ever.* 'I'm okay.'

Quickly she took the cuffs hanging from her belt. 'I'm going to back up,' she said to Robinette. 'You're going to roll onto your stomach and put your hands out to your sides where I can see them.' She eased back on one knee, pulling the gun out from under his chin, keeping it trained on his heart. 'Roll over. Now.'

With a hateful glare, Robinette started to roll, but kept rolling and too late Stevie saw the gun tucked at his back in his waistband. Then it was in his hand, pointing squarely at her face.

She didn't stop to think. Just did what she was trained to do, adjusting her aim, squeezing the trigger and watching as he jerked backward, his eyes gone wide with shock as her bullet connected with his forehead. Before she could suck in her next breath, two more shots shattered the air, both kill shots.

Robinette's head had suddenly become well ventilated. He wasn't getting back up again. Ever. Stevie crawled backward to get to Clay. He was lowering his gun, his face deathly white.

*Oh God. Not Jim Dandy. This is much worse than I thought.*

Memories of December swirling in her head, Stevie gave a quick, frantic look for her phone while she ripped off her flak jacket. 'He took my phone and threw it, the bastard. Let me stop this bleeding and then I'll get help.' She pulled her long-sleeved T-shirt over her head, revealing the Kevlar she wore under it. 'How much blood have you lost?'

Clay had rolled to his back and was struggling to sit up. 'Who fired the other gun?'

Stevie stared at him. 'I thought you fired both shots.'

'No, just one. Who fired the other one?'

'I did.' Hyatt pushed open the gate and stepped through. 'I also contacted 911. The EMTs will be here any minute.'

'How long were you there?' Clay asked, grimacing as Stevie tied her T-shirt around his leg exactly as he'd done for her that day on the courthouse steps.

'Most of the time. I heard the shots, but couldn't get a clean bead on Robinette until Stevie stuck her gun up under his chin.'

'Why didn't you tell me you were there?' Stevie stared, then understood. 'You would have let me kill him too, wouldn't you?'

Hyatt shrugged. 'You deserved justice. I brought Silas and Elizabeth into my department. Never saw them for who they were. I let them run unchecked for years.'

Stevie focused on Clay's leg, putting pressure on the wound. 'It wasn't your fault, sir.'

'I disagree. If I'd listened to you eight years ago about Robinette, you'd still have your husband. And your son. Standing down today, it was the least I could do.'

Not sure what to say to that, she bent closer to Clay, checking his wound. The bleeding seemed to be slowing, but he'd lost an awful lot of blood. His pants were soaked with it.

'I couldn't do it,' she admitted in a low voice. 'Couldn't kill him in cold blood. I'll probably regret it later, because I had my chance and didn't take it, but . . . I just couldn't.'

Clay gripped her arm, getting blood all over her Kevlar. 'If you'd been sure, I would have supported you, no matter what. But if you weren't sure, you did the right thing. There are some things you can't undo.'

She leaned in, brushed a kiss over his mouth. 'Thank

you. Once again you gave me the time and space I needed to think.'

'Always.'

Tears sprang to her eyes. 'I love you.'

'I love you too, but don't cry. I'm not dying. I just got you. I'm not going anywhere.'

'Damn straight you're not.' She could hear the sirens now. 'Except into an ambulance.'

He closed his eyes wearily. 'Stay with me, Stefania.'

'Always.'

*Thursday, March 20, 9.15 A.M.*

Sam froze, his hand poised an inch from the knob on his mother's front door. 'I don't think I can do this, Ruby.'

'You can. And I'm going to help you.' She twisted the knob, let them inside. 'Hello!'

His mother came around the corner, stopping short when she saw Ruby with him. 'Sam. I didn't expect you until tonight. Why aren't you at work? And who have you brought to see me?'

'This is Ruby Gomez, Mom. She and I ... well, we are ...' He stuttered to a helpless stop.

'I'm his friend,' Ruby said. 'It's so nice to meet you, Mrs Hudson.'

His mother smiled. 'Well, this is a lovely surprise. Come in, sit down. Can I get you some coffee? Tea?'

'No, thank you. I'm fine. You have a beautiful home.'

'Thank you, Ruby. It seems awful big and quiet these days, though. Now that Sam's off on his own. He grew up here, you know.'

'I know. He told me.'

Sam felt awkward in his childhood home as he followed

Ruby and his mother into the living room. His mother sat in her favorite chair and Ruby sat on the sofa, patting the cushion. 'Have a seat, *papi*,' she said, quiet encouragement in her voice.

Sam sat beside her, gathered his courage. 'Mom, I . . . I need to talk to you.'

'Oh dear,' his mother said, distressed. 'Are you pregnant, Ruby?'

A surprised laugh burst from Ruby's throat, one she quickly turned into a cough. 'Oh no, ma'am. I've only known Sam a few days.'

'Oh, well, good. Not that I'd mind, you understand.' His mother gave him a meaningful look. 'I'd like to be a grandmother.'

'Mom,' Sam groaned softly. 'Please.'

'I'm just sayin'.' His mother's eyes suddenly widened, her mouth rounding in horror. 'You're sick. Oh my God, you're sick.'

'No, Mom, it's not that. Let me talk. This isn't easy. I met Ruby a few days ago. I was at the ME's office. The medical examiner,' he clarified.

'I watched *Quincy*,' his mother said, her voice trembling. 'I know what an ME is.'

'Ruby was helping me get some information. She's stuck with me from the beginning. She's a good person, Mom.'

'Sam,' Ruby murmured. 'You're making this worse for her. Just tell her.'

Ruby was right. His mother's skin had gone an alarming gray. 'This is about Dad.'

His mother took a long look at Ruby before returning her gaze to his face. 'He's dead then. We knew that, Sam. If that's what you're afraid to tell me, I already knew.'

He shook his head. 'There was something in that

package we got on Saturday, something that didn't belong to Dad.' He told her about the matchbook, about the time he'd lost, about his search for the truth. And then he told her the truth.

His mother's breathing had become shallow, but when he told her about Paul Mazzetti and his son, she began to cry. 'Oh my Lord. Sam. How can this be true? How could he do this thing? This horrible, evil thing?'

'Someone threatened to hurt me if Dad didn't kill Mr Mazzetti. He was protecting me.'

She covered her mouth with her hand, tears rolling down her cheeks like rain. 'He wouldn't have needed to if he'd never done the drugs to begin with. Poor Mrs Mazzetti. Does she know?'

'Yes, she does.'

His mother's tears continued to fall. 'My husband took her husband. Her child. How can I ever make amends for this?'

'She doesn't expect us to, either of us. She called me this morning to tell me so.' And Sam had been so impressed. With all the woman had been through in the past few days, she'd taken the time to call him. She had been so incredibly kind and concerned for his mother. 'She told me to tell you that you aren't responsible. That she doesn't want you to feel any shame over this. She was concerned this news would be bad for your heart.'

Sam's mother blinked, wiping her cheeks with hands that shook. 'Mazzetti? I've heard that name, very recently. She's been on the news. She's the one people have been trying to kill.'

'Yes,' Sam said.

His mother's eyes sharpened. 'Why her? Why did someone threaten John to make him kill her husband?'

Not only had Stevie Mazzetti consoled him, she'd given

Sam permission to tell his mother what she needed to know. The news media would have it soon enough, she'd said.

So Sam told his mother, watched her eyes grow wide again, then heartbreakingly sad.

'It's so hard for me to understand how people can be so bad,' she said quietly. Then she frowned. 'How did she know about my heart?'

*That's a good question.* Sam glanced at Ruby. 'I suspect you had something to do with it?'

'I stopped by the hospital this morning to see her.' Ruby shrugged. 'I was there anyway, to transport a body. I've known Stevie Mazzetti for years and she's one of the good ones. And I knew Sam was dreading telling you about your husband, Mrs Hudson. He was afraid it would trigger another heart attack. I knew Stevie would want to help. I hope you aren't upset that I told her about your heart.'

'No, of course not.' His mother patted Ruby's hand. 'It was very sweet of you to care.'

'Mom, this is going to be all over the news. There was a shootout last night and the man who orchestrated the murder of Paul Mazzetti was killed. Dad's name will come up. You need to be prepared.'

'The media may paint him as a victim of sorts,' Ruby said. 'It might not be so bad.'

'However the media paints it, I'll handle it,' his mother said firmly. 'You stop worrying about me, Sam. I will be fine. I mean it. You deserve a life of your own. A family of your own. Of course, a grandchild to hold would be an immense source of solace.'

'Mom,' he groaned.

Ruby laughed. 'I don't mind, Sam. Why don't you go get your mother some tea? She can ask me all the questions that I know she's wanting to ask.'

'I'd love some tea,' his mother said with a smile. 'And I have lots of questions.'

Sam dropped a kiss on the top of his mother's head as he got up. 'I'm sure you do, Mom.'

'So, Ruby,' he heard his mother say as he went into the kitchen. 'Who does your nails? They're incredible.'

'They're press-ons. I can get you some.'

His mother laughed. 'I'd poke my eye out.'

Sam found himself smiling. It really was going to be all right.

*Thursday, March 20, 12.30 P.M.*

Clay's eyelids weighed five hundred pounds. He struggled to lift them, but it was worth the effort because Stevie was the first thing he saw. She'd fallen asleep in the chair next to his hospital bed. He took a long moment, just to look.

She seemed carefree in a way he'd never seen her. In a way he'd always wished for her. Finally it looked like things were going to be all right.

He took a brief check under his sheet. Everything was intact, which was a big relief.

'Find what you're looking for?' Stevie asked, her voice sexy and rusty with sleep.

Clay grinned weakly. 'Just checking.'

'It's all there,' she said, holding a cup to his lips. 'Sip. Don't gulp, or you'll throw up.'

'Yes, Mom.'

She pretended to scowl, but didn't quite pull it off. 'The doctor said you came through the surgery just fine,' she said, sitting on the edge of the bed. 'They were able to repair all the damage and you should be out of here tomorrow at the latest.'

He searched her face. She had some bruises and a cut on her temple that someone had treated with a butterfly bandage. But everything else seemed . . . 'Perfect,' he said huskily. 'You look perfect.'

'I'm a little banged up, but all in all, damn lucky. You were, too. The doc said that if the bullet had been a little to the left, you would have had the same injury I did. We'd have to get matching canes. "His and her" physical therapists. We could drag each other up the steps.'

She said the latter lightly, but he could hear her worry. 'I know you want to run again,' he said, 'and we'll work on that once I'm out of here. But understand that if you never do, if this is as good as your leg ever gets, it doesn't matter to me. I take you, gladly, just as you are.'

Stevie swallowed. 'That's . . . wow. You really do know how to say the right things to me.'

'Of course I do. I love you.'

Her smile set his heart at ease. 'I love you too.' She caressed his face, stroking her fingertips along his jaw. 'So. You want the scoop after all the dust settled?'

He leaned back against the pillow. 'Hit me.'

'Robinette had escaped with Brenda Lee Miller. He got out at her son's school when she went to pick him up, just like Joseph thought. She may have been able to spin Robinette into a "respectable philanthropist", but she folded quick when she heard Fletcher had been caught by the Germans with the sarin. She didn't think Robinette had killed his wife, though. She really believed that Levi had done it. When we told her about the bullet we found in that Rubik's cube – and that DNA from the blood on it matched Rene Broussard's – well, she broke down.'

'She realized that Robinette had been using her from day one.'

'Yeah. She seems to have a smidge of conscience left,

but just a smidge. She knew about the sarin. Joseph got her to tell him where to find the accounting ledgers for the "other side of the business" by promising he'd do what he could to get her imprisoned close to her son.'

'Kids are the biggest vulnerability to the parents who love them,' Clay murmured. 'Did she accept that Robinette set Levi up?'

'Yes. She took that hard, too. She also had believed he loved his son.'

'I'm not sure Todd Robinette loved anyone other than Todd Robinette.'

'That's the truth. She said that each one of the four of them – herself, Fletcher, Henderson, and Westmoreland – owed a personal debt to Robinette. He'd pulled her out of a burning personnel transport vehicle. He'd fixed a crime for Henderson. Apparently her drinking was nothing new. She was suspected of killing a former lover after a drunken brawl, but the MPs could never find the body and Robinette was her alibi.'

'And Fletcher?'

'Serious PTSD. Just imploded one day and was hospitalized, but not before he was accused of sexually assaulting another soldier and dishonorably discharged. He couldn't get a job after that, so when Robinette hired him as his head chemist, he was grateful. Brenda Lee said they all knew that Fletcher and Robinette had a relationship, but it wasn't discussed. Fletcher was jealous of Lisa, but he knew Robinette would never take them public. Brenda Lee felt sorry for him.'

'Even though he's a terrorist?'

'She saw him as a tortured soul. I think Robinette had an uncanny eye for picking people who weren't completely plugged into reality. Westmoreland is an enigma. None of them knew what Robinette had done for him, but Brenda

Lee thought it was something financial. Robinette used his position as an MP to accrue lots of favors, personal debts, and extortion victims.'

'Like Silas did, just as a cop.'

'Very much so. Of the four Westmoreland was the least emotionally connected. That he was the first to fly the coop when Robinette started to unravel wasn't a surprise to Brenda Lee.'

'She saw Robinette unraveling?'

'They all did. They all thought he was starting to believe his own spin. Brenda Lee said that she nearly had a coronary when she heard Robinette was interested in public office. Some of that was Lisa's doing. Robinette grew up dirt poor in the bayou of Louisiana and being accepted and respected was important to him. Lisa understood that and figured she could give him respect and put distance between him and his four friends she felt so threatened by.'

'That makes a lot of sense. Have we found Westmoreland?'

'No. It looks like he's gone under. He has contacts in terrorist cells all over the world. He'll have friends to hide him.'

Clay ground his teeth over that. 'That sucks.'

'Some loose ends can't be snipped,' she said with a shrug. 'Interpol has him on a most wanted list. They found that both Henderson and Westmoreland had traveled extensively to war-torn areas on phony passports. Robinette had created identities for employees that never existed. They delivered his vaccines to third world nations, then took a side trip to deliver the real goods. Apparently Fletcher is a genius. He developed a way to manufacture and package the sarin that increased its shelf life by two to three times. That's what he was carrying with him. He's cooperating with the German authorities. That's all Joseph would tell us.'

'What was Robinette doing at his house last night? If he'd escaped with Brenda Lee, why did he come back?'

'Ah. That would have been because Lisa moved all of his money from his bank accounts and canceled his credit cards. He had a phony passport in his home office safe and came back to get it so he could get away.'

'Why did Lisa take his money and cancel his cards?'

'Because of the affair with Fletcher. That cook that "tried not to listen" in on her employer's personal business told us that she "accidentally" overheard Lisa telling her mother that she'd "fixed him", that no man was going to get away with cheating on her.'

'Did the cook actually do any cooking?' Clay asked wryly. 'Sounds like she spent all her time listening behind doors.'

'She had her eye on a bigger prize – payment for a tell-all article. She'd overheard the after-dinner conversation between Robinette and the political guys who wanted him to run. Figured she'd scoop up tidbits she could sell to the tabloids.'

'Good old-fashioned capitalism. Gotta love it.' He squeezed her hand and changed the subject. 'Did you go back to the farm last night?'

She shook her head. 'The farm came here. Everyone but the horses. The whole gang is here. It's SRO in the waiting room. Emma and Ethan and Maggie, Paige, Izzy, my parents. Grayson and Daphne came in early, but they had court this morning. They'll be back later. Same with Joseph and his crew. They've got a mountain of reports to file. Hyatt's here. He's getting along famously with your father, by the way.'

'Somehow that doesn't surprise me. Did Dad bring Nell?'

'He did. She and my mother,' she rolled her eyes, 'are picking out china patterns and Izzy's been egging them on.'

'Does that bother you?' he asked carefully. Because he could already see them living as a family, in a big house with the puppy. And more children. Definitely more children.

She smiled and he relaxed. 'Not at all. Although I am a little nervous about the growing menagerie. Maggie gave Cordelia a horse and your father gave us a puppy.'

*Us.* 'I like the sound of that.'

'A drooling, shoe-chewing puppy?' she asked but he could see she knew what he meant.

'No. "Us".'

'Me, too. On the "us". The jury's still out on the puppy.'

He traced her mouth with his fingertip. 'You know you're gonna say yes. You might as well do it now and get it over with.'

'I know,' she said glumly. 'I'm a sap who's going to clean drool and buy new shoes.'

'No. You're a mother who loves her child . . . A child who, by the way, has run the most effective campaign for getting a dog of any kid I've ever seen.'

'I know. She's earned it.' But then she frowned, something clearly still on her mind.

'If you're that against the dog, I can try to talk her out of it.'

'No, it's not that. It's about Sam Hudson. I called him to tell him what happened last night and to tell him that he shouldn't feel responsible, but something bothered me about his story. He said he got a package in the mail with his father's things.'

685

'Along with the matchbook that led him back to the Rabbit Hole. You're wondering who sent the package?'

'I know who did it. I figured the only one who could have was Silas's wife, Rose, or his attorney. I called Rose after I got done talking to Sam, and I asked her point-blank. She admitted it. She said that their personal attorney had given her letters from Silas, along with instructions to mail the package to arrive on Saturday – the eighth anniversary of John Hudson's death.'

Clay frowned too. 'Shouldn't that attorney have turned them in as evidence?'

'I asked Grayson and he said not if they were personal communication between husband and wife. Now that we know what was in it, they damn well should become evidence and in Sam's case, they have.'

'But?'

'What if there are more letters? What if there's a letter for me? When Rose admitted she'd sent it, I asked if there were more. She hung up on me without answering.'

'So what do you want to do, Stevie?'

'I want to go see her. In person. I want her to look into my face and tell me that Silas left nothing for me.'

'What more are you looking to learn, honey?' he asked gently. 'I mean, as soon as they let me out, we'll go. I promise. But what are you hoping to hear? An apology? Would you even listen to it? Would you *want* to?'

'I don't know. Maybe I do want an apology. But it wouldn't be worth much, would it? He could have sent that package to Sam at any time if he really was sorry. He could have stopped working for Stuart Lippman if he'd really been sorry. He could have not hired someone to kill my family to begin with.'

'Kind of what I'm thinking,' he said.

'Silas sending the package after he was dead was

cowardly. No, you're right. I don't want to know. I don't want to hear an empty apology. I do believe I'll let this one go.'

'We should mark the calendar,' he said with a smile.

'Smart ass,' she said, but she smiled back. 'Are you ready to entertain the masses?'

'The sooner I do, the sooner we'll be alone again, right?'

'Kind of what I'm thinking,' she said lightly.

'Then I'm more than ready.'


*Thursday, March 20, 1.00* P.M.


Everyone stopped talking when Stevie walked into the waiting room. 'He's awake,' she said. The chatter restarted, everyone coming to their feet and hitting her with a barrage of questions. 'He's fine. He's alert. He wants to see Cordelia and Alec, first. Alec, will you take Cordelia with you? I'll be back in a few minutes. I have to get some food.' Now that Clay was awake, she finally had an appetite again.

'We'll go with you,' Emma said. She and Izzy and Maggie VanDorn started gathering papers from the table where they'd been sitting.

Stevie narrowed her eyes. 'What are you guys planning?'

'Not your wedding, if that's what you're thinking,' Izzy said tartly. 'That's Mom's arena.'

Maggie shook her head. 'You poor dear.'

Emma snickered. 'We're writing my next book,' she said, taking pity on Stevie, 'on equine therapy. Maggie and I are co-authoring it and Izzy's going to do the photos.'

'It keeps me off the street,' Izzy said wryly.

'I think it's a great idea,' Stevie said. 'Izzy, you'll do the photos justice. You've got a good eye and a beautiful heart.'

Stevie had asked Izzy to show her the photos she'd downloaded from her old camera, needing something to occupy her mind while Clay had been in surgery. With Cordelia on her lap and Izzy by her side, she'd looked at hundreds of pictures of Paul and Paulie. Some she'd taken herself, but most had been Izzy's. She had always been the photographer in the family. Her sister had taken all those shots and had created a beautiful memorial to the family they never discussed. They'd smiled and laughed and cried and when they were done Stevie felt . . . not healed, but healing. It was progress.

'Thank you, Stevie.' The startled gratitude in Izzy's eyes told Stevie she'd been selfish with her sister, too. Izzy, like Clay, had always been there for her, never asking for anything back. Stevie had known that Izzy liked to play with cameras, but had never seen her sister's gift. She did now. She slid her arm around Izzy's waist, hugging her casually, and the minute hesitation before Izzy hugged her back was another revelation. 'Does this mean we'll see you here more often, Emma?'

'Yes, but there are equine facilities in Florida, too. All over the country, actually.'

'We're thinking about a fact-finding trip,' Maggie said.

'Just be honest and call it a road trip,' Stevie said, making them all grin. 'I can see the three of you in a convertible with the top down, driving across America. I wish I could go.'

'What's stopping you?' Emma asked. 'We'll do it in pieces and over the course of six months. You can come on some of the trips. Come summer, you can bring Cordelia and I'll bring Christopher and the boys and we'll have fun.'

'Fun.' She frowned, considering it. 'I could do fun.'

Izzy squeezed her playfully. 'I'll give you a tutorial on fun first.'

Stevie met her sister's eyes. 'I'd like that.' She shrugged off the emotion. 'Besides, I'm not sure what kind of job I'm going to be fit for. I may never go back to active duty.'

'Don't say that,' Izzy protested. 'Of course you will.'

'You know, I'm okay if I don't go back.'

Emma blinked. 'What planet are you from and what have you done with our friend?'

Stevie smiled. 'A year ago, hell, a week ago, those words never would have occurred to me. Now I'm reassessing my priorities. Cordelia is number one. My career has put her through more in two years than anyone should suffer over a lifetime. I can change that. I *will* change that.'

'What about all of Silas's cases?' Emma asked. 'There may be more to uncover.'

'There probably are more,' Stevie agreed. 'But I won't be the one to uncover them. I told Hyatt to spread the word that I'm not digging anymore. I'm not the only cop who can spot a fixed case. Especially since the State Police are now running the Lippman investigations while IA sorts out their shit. I want people to stop shooting at me and my family. We've had enough.'

'I couldn't agree with you more,' Emma said softly, pride in her eyes. 'But what will you do? I can't see you living the life of leisure.'

'I can't see my bills paying themselves yet, either,' Stevie said dryly. 'I'll find something to do. Something amazing. I'm just not sure what it is yet.'

But that wasn't true. She had the germ of an idea. But she had to think it through before telling anyone. Keeping the notion close to her vest, she pointed to the door. 'Ladies, I'm starving. Let's go eat.'

They'd made it to the elevator when she heard a man call her name.

'Detective? Detective Mazzetti?'

Stevie turned to see a couple tentatively approaching. The woman was a stranger, but the man's face was familiar. The last time she'd seen him, he'd been hustling Todd Robinette back into FPL's factory so that she could retrieve Robinette's used cigarette butt.

'Frank Locke,' she said, meeting them halfway. 'It's good to see you.'

'And you as well,' he said. 'This is my wife, Amy.'

Amy's expression was grave. 'Detective.'

Stevie looked from Locke's face to his wife's. 'What can I do for you?'

'It's what I can do for you,' Locke said, sliding a backpack off his shoulder. He handed it to her. 'These are Harvey's lab notebooks, transferred to DVD.'

She took the backpack with a frown. 'Harvey? You mean Harvey Ballantine, Julie's head chemist, the one who was killed with her?'

Locke nodded. 'Harvey's wife gave these to me a few weeks after his funeral. It was some time before I looked at them. Losing Harvey was such a shock.'

'I know it was,' Stevie said gently. 'I barely made B's in chemistry, so I won't understand these notebooks if I try to read them. Why are you giving them to me?'

Locke drew a breath. 'They tell why Harvey and Julie were murdered.'

Stevie stared at the backpack, then back up at Locke's face. 'Then tell me why.'

'Robinette came to work for Rene and Julie when he got out of the Army,' Locke said. 'He started out in the warehouse, an entry level job that everybody did at some point in their career, even the PhDs. Rene made sure of it. He wanted people to understand how the company worked and to appreciate every worker's task. But Robinette had a bad attitude. He hated the warehouse, hated that he had to work with people he considered beneath him.'

'Why didn't Rene fire him?' Stevie asked.

'He wanted to, but Robinette was his friend. And every time Rene tried to give Robinette feedback, Robinette would threaten to leave and take Levi with him.'

'Which would have broken Julie's heart,' Stevie murmured.

'Rene's too,' Amy said. 'They both loved Levi like he was their own.'

Locke sighed. 'They did. Robinette didn't care about the boy, except to use him as a pawn. Then as a weapon. Then later a scapegoat. Robinette did the shipping in the warehouse. Harvey found out he was stealing.'

'How?' Stevie asked.

'Right before he died Harvey noticed an increase in the number of batches that didn't meet quality standards. He was trying to figure out why, you know, what was going wrong with the equipment. He found out there was nothing wrong. Good batches had been marked as bad so that they'd be rejected. Those batches went to the same area that the expired vaccines went. Harvey got suspicious – partly because he'd never liked Robinette. None of us did. Rene had died and Robinette had forced Julie to marry him so that she could keep Levi. Robinette was strutting like a peacock.'

'Frank,' Amy said softly. 'Stick to the story.'

'Sorry, Detective. Anyway, Harvey hid a camera in the warehouse.'

'And found Robinette shipping to his own customers?'

'Exactly. But not just the good stuff Robinette had diverted. Harvey saw that he was shipping the expired stuff, too. The expired vaccines should have been destroyed. They wouldn't have hurt anyone, but they wouldn't work either. Diverting the good stuff was stealing. Shipping expired vaccines as good ones? That's . . . criminal. More criminal anyway.'

'Did Harvey confront Robinette?'

'Not that he wrote about. One of his last entries was that he was taking his findings to Julie. If she confronted him . . .' He shrugged. 'Julie was like Rene. She wouldn't have stood for stealing, but putting the health of children at risk? Because these were vaccines that kids got, to keep them from getting sick. Julie wouldn't have tolerated that. But she probably wouldn't have reported him right away, either. She was one to try to settle things with the individual. And she walked on eggshells with Robinette anyway, because of Levi.'

'So if she told Robinette what she knew, he'd have to get rid of her. If he figured out that Harvey knew, too, he'd have to get rid of them both.' Stevie sighed. 'Hell.'

'There's one more thing,' Locke said. 'Harvey noticed that the good vaccines being diverted to the reject area began to accelerate after Rene died. I don't know if that has anything to do with anything, but before that, Harvey believed that Rene also knew.'

Stevie thought of the bullet in the Rubik's cube. 'It means something,' she said quietly. 'What happened to you? I always worried that helping me get that cigarette butt would get you into trouble.'

'I think I would have been in trouble anyway. After Julie was gone, Robinette cleaned house. Fired everyone who'd been vocally opposed to him. I was one of the first to go. Amy and I moved away, near our grandchildren. I didn't look at the books for a long time. Then one day, I was cleaning out my desk and found them. I started reading and found the truth.' He looked away. 'I should have come forward.'

'You were afraid to come forward.'

'There was that,' he agreed. 'That Harvey had been killed was a warning to all of us. That Robinette sacrificed Levi . . . his own son . . . It made me afraid for my family. I didn't read Harvey's notebooks for years. When I did, I figured it was too late. Nobody believed Robinette was a killer then. Nobody but you anyway. By the time I knew the truth, he'd cleaned up his image. I didn't think anyone would believe me. I should have known you would. I'm sorry.'

She nodded. Made her lips curve. Tried not to think about how much misery could have been avoided if he'd come forward. Locke did come forward before, she told herself. Helped her get evidence, and lost his job in the process. 'Why bring these to me now?'

'We saw the news. Heard what Robinette was doing now, with the sarin. Heard what he did to you and your family. It really is too late now, but I thought you'd want to know the truth.'

Stevie drew a breath. 'Thank you. The truth is always good to know.'

Locke lifted his hand, weakly. 'Take care, Detective.'

'You, too.' She watched them go, waiting until the elevator doors closed to close her eyes.

'You okay, Stevie?'

She turned to see JD standing behind her. 'Where did you come from?'

'The other bank of elevators. I always get lost in this hospital. I came to see Clay, but saw you talking to that couple. I'll take the DVDs to the station for you, unless you want to do it.'

She handed the backpack to him without hesitation. 'You can have them. I'm done.'

JD's brows went up. 'Done with this case or really done?'

693

'Haven't decided yet. But I promise you'll be one of the first to know. But you should probably start breaking in a new partner. If I do ever come back, it'll be a while.'

JD looked sad, but unsurprised. 'My next partner has some big shoes to fill. I'm going to see Clay now. You call me if either of you need anything.'

He walked away and Stevie sighed, then frowned. 'What was I going to do?'

'Eat,' Emma said. 'You were going to eat.'

Stevie gave her a sideways glance. Emma stood with Izzy and Maggie off to the side where they'd been quietly watching. 'Oh yeah. I'm still starving.'

Izzy put her arm around her. 'Come on, let us take care of you for a little while.'

Stevie swallowed hard. 'I think I like the sound of that.'

*Hunt Valley, Maryland, Friday, April 4, 1.30 P.M.*

It was a beautiful house. It took Stevie's breath away, thinking about the possibilities, about how much Cordelia would love it. The house was Victorian style but new construction, which Clay said would make installing security systems easier.

It sat on three acres of rolling farmland, close to Daphne's farm. It meant that Cordelia could go riding more often and that Stevie could *try* more often.

She still hadn't gotten comfortable with the idea of sitting on top of a twelve-hundred pound animal with big teeth. Even though one of the horses at the farm did seem to like her. At least she could brush him and not hyperventilate. She even kind of liked him back.

Her daughter was proud of her for being brave. So . . . progress.

'Well,' Clay said quietly from behind her, 'what do you think?'

She tore her gaze from the beautiful view and turned to face him ruefully. 'I love it. But there's no way I can afford it.'

'I can,' he said.

She was incredibly touched and a little scared. 'Have I told you today that I love you?'

'Three times, not that I'm counting,' he said, but his dark eyes were carefully mild, which meant he was very emotional behind his mask.

'I don't want you to take this wrong. I plan to spend a lifetime with you. But I have a seven-year-old daughter.' His frown was quick and dark and she knew he'd misunderstood. 'Stop right there,' she ordered. 'This isn't me being afraid she'll get too attached to you. That train left the station a long time ago. This is about me wanting to set a good example.'

His frown relaxed a hair. 'Explain, please.'

'Simply put, I don't want her to think it's okay to jump into a permanent relationship with the first man she dates. To Cordelia, you are the first man she's ever seen me with. After three weeks, it's too soon for me to be accepting houses from you. That's not a good example.'

His frown disappeared. 'I agree. That's one of the reasons I didn't suggest you move in with me, even though I really want you to.'

'One of the reasons?'

'The other is that two men died in my house. I want Cordelia to have a place that is safe. Where no one has died violently. Plus I want space, enough that our friends can come stay whenever they want. There's even enough room in this house so that Izzy can live with us. She could have her own suite and a private entrance.'

She was even more touched now. 'You're okay with Izzy living with us?'

'As long as she wants. I want acreage where a big dog can run. And there are no deed restrictions. I could build a stable for Gracie and Cordelia could ride every day. This place fits the bill for everything I want.'

'But the bill is *huge*. I can't afford the mortgage, even if a bank was crazy enough to give me a loan. Which none would consider doing with my job situation up in the air. Which brings me to something else I wanted to talk to you about.'

'I'm not ready to end the conversation about this house,' Clay said, calling her on her ploy. 'But I'll put it aside for now. What else did you want to talk about?'

'My job. Hyatt called me yesterday.'

His expression shuttered. 'Why?'

'He wants me to come back, just not to the detective squad. They created a position, a liaison to work with the State cops as they investigate IA. Scott Culp was on Robinette's payroll. They want to make sure the rest of IA is clean. They want me for the liaison job. It's a promotion and a pay raise.'

'What did you decide to do?'

'I haven't yet. I wanted to talk to you first.' She knew it was the right thing to say by the look of relief on his face. He hadn't wanted her to go back to the force, in any capacity. She hadn't realized that before. 'Because I had another idea. The night you told me about Silas you said you were behind, that you'd be more behind because Paige was out. She's back now, so are you still behind?'

He shrugged, his eyes now considering. 'It's not so much a question of behind as of lost potential. The security side of the business is going well. Alec is handling a lot of things for me and Alyssa keeps the office running smoothly. I could take more personal security jobs if I had more people I could trust to be bodyguards. After we lost Tuzak . . . Well, I haven't had the heart to find someone else.'

'What about Paige?'

'I need her on the PI side. She would be a natural for bodyguard work, though.'

'What if I took over the PI side?' Stevie asked, rushing the words out of her throat before she lost her nerve. 'I'm walking better. I might never run, but I'm a damn good investigator. I'd have to get a license, but that shouldn't—' She scowled. 'Why are you laughing?'

He crossed the room, kissed her soundly. 'I was wondering how to bring it up. I kept hoping Hyatt would tell you that you'd be on permanent disability so that you'd have to consider other options. But are you sure? You'd leave the force?'

'Clay, I became a cop to help people, to do the right thing. I did help people and I like to think I've done the right thing as consistently as I could. The Baltimore PD isn't the only place I can do that. I can still help people, working for you. Paige says she pulls some all-nighters, but most of the time she's home for dinner. I want to be home for Cordelia. And I want to be home for you. And if I can help you help other people along the way, why not? What do you say?'

'I say you're hired.'

She smiled, leaning up on her toes to seal the deal with a kiss, but he stopped her.

'Not so fast. We need to agree on the terms. I never planned to buy this house in my own name,' he said, swinging the topic back to the beginning.

She rolled her eyes. 'We're back to the house?'

'We are. I buy all my property through corporations and

bury them in other corporations. If someone finds me it's because they really want to and they're really good.'

'They found your dad,' she pointed out.

'Because he bought his house in his name. For the majority of people, that's not a problem, but you and I aren't the majority, Stevie. We make enemies. I protect what's mine, and the first rule is to not let them find you in the first place. So I'll buy this house through the business.'

'So technically, I'd be renting office space,' she said. 'Not letting you buy me a house.'

'I think that would keep you from being a fallen woman in Cordelia's eyes. So, partners?'

She blinked. 'I'm not a partner. I'm just starting.'

'You bring street cred. As does Paige. You're a nationally known detective. She's a nationally known martial artist. I can't think of better partners to run my PI and bodyguard businesses. I've already had my attorney draw up the papers listing the three of us as full partners. I haven't told Paige yet. I was waiting to tell you first.'

Her chest was tight with emotion – gratitude, love, and excitement. It was the perfect solution, which came as no surprise. Perfect solutions were what Clay did best. 'I'd get special partner benefits, right?'

'Like what?'

'Like exclusive access to the senior partner, any time of the day or night.'

His eyes lit up. 'Of course.'

'Then I guess the only question is when can I move in?'

'As soon as you choose paint colors for the walls. I bought the house yesterday.'

Her mouth fell open. 'You sneak. You manipulated me again.'

He slid his arms around her waist, holding her loosely. 'Are you mad?'

'Not really. Nothing you can't make up to me anyway. We have two hours before Cordelia needs to be picked up from school. I suggest you use it wisely.'

He nuzzled her neck. 'I think I have some idea of how to start.'

'Somehow I thought you might.'

If you enjoyed

# WATCH YOUR
# BACK

by

Look out for her new hardback, coming Autumn 2014

Go to www.headline.co.uk to find out more

<u>headline</u>

# You Belong to Me

## Karen Rose

### DISTURBING

When forensic pathologist Lucy Trask stumbles across a mutilated body in her local Baltimore park, its face unrecognisable, her sole concern is that it might be her old school teacher Mr Pugh.

### DESTRUCTIVE

But the victim is actually another man from her past. Who killed him and why he was left for Lucy to find is unclear but what appears to be a number '1' burned into his back proclaims that this corpse won't be the last.

### DEADLY

The discovery of a second branded body raises worrying questions: how many more lives are at risk? And can Lucy solve the killer's gruesome puzzle before his thirst for revenge is complete?

Acclaim for Karen Rose:

'Intense, complex, and unforgettable' James Patterson

'Page-turning' *Sunday Express*

'An engrossing read which fans of crime thrillers will love' *News of the World*

978 0 7553 7392 5

**headline**

# No One Left to Tell

### Karen Rose

#### GUILTY

Ramon Muñoz has spent five years in prison, convicted of a murder his family is convinced he didn't commit. In desperation they turn to private investigator Paige Holden for help.

#### UNTIL PROVEN

Paige cannot resist the family's pleas, but when Ramon's wife is brutally executed she is thrown headlong into a case which will place her job, her friends and her life in jeopardy.

#### INNOCENT

As Paige risks everything to prove Ramon was set up, she comes to realise that there is more at stake if Ramon is freed than she could have ever guessed. Can Paige stay alive long enough to unmask an unstoppable killer who will not rest until there's no one left to tell?

Praise for Karen Rose:

'More shockingly detailed than anything in Karin Slaughter or Patricia Cornwell's thrillers . . . engaging' *Irish Independent*

'Intense, complex, and unforgettable' James Patterson

978 0 7553 7396 3

**headline**

# Did You Miss Me?

## Karen Rose

### LEFT

The last thing Ford Elkhart remembers is taking his girlfriend back to her car. Now he's lying tied and gagged on a cold, dark floor, with only one chance to escape before he ends up like the bones surrounding him . . .

### ALONE

Assistant State's Attorney Daphne Montgomery is devastated by her son's disappearance, and is immediately convinced that his kidnapping is connected to the white supremacist she's just had jailed for murder.

### IN THE DARK . . .

FBI Special Agent Joseph Carter isn't so sure – especially when he learns that Ford's girlfriend is also missing. Is Ford's abduction payback for Daphne's courtroom victory? Or is he a pawn in an even more dangerous game?

Praise for Karen Rose:

'Rose juggles a large cast, a huge body count and a complex plot with terrifying ease' *Publishers Weekly*

978 0 7553 7400 7

**headline**

# Don't Tell

## Karen Rose

### DON'T LOOK

Desperate Mary Grace Winters knew the only way to save herself and her child from her abusive husband was to stage their deaths. Now all that remains of her former life is at the bottom of a lake.

### DON'T TRUST

As Caroline Stewart, Mary Grace has almost forgotten the nightmare she left behind nine years ago. Slowly she has learned to believe that her new life, and new identity, is here to stay.

### DON'T TELL

Then her husband uncovers her hidden trail. Step by step, he's closing in on her and everyone she loves. Now Caroline must decide whether to flee again or whether the time has come to stay and fight . . .

Disturbing and scary, Karen Rose's brilliant new thriller proves that you never know what goes on behind closed doors . . .

Acclaim for Karen Rose:

'*Count To Ten* takes off like a house afire. There's action and chills galore in this non-stop thriller' Tess Gerritsen

'*Scream For Me* is intense, complex, and unforgettable ' James Patterson

978 0 7553 7115 0

## headline

# Have You Seen Her?

## Karen Rose

### MISSING

One by one, young girls disappear from their beds at night. Each one is pretty with long dark hair. And each one is found brutally murdered.

### SEARCHING

As each girl is discovered it becomes clearer to Special Agent Steven Thatcher that there is a serial killer at work. Finding the person responsible is Steven's over-riding objective and it doesn't help that his teenage son, Brad, is suddenly behaving strangely.

### PREYING

Brad's teacher, Jenna Marshall, is determined to meet Steven and find out why her star pupil has gone off the rails. But when she does, the watching murderer sets his sights on beautiful, long-dark-haired Jenna. He will not stop until he has the treasure he craves – can Steven find the killer before he finds Jenna?

Acclaim for Karen Rose:

'Intense, complex, and unforgettable' James Patterson

'The new girl on the block in terms of exhilarating, full-throttle writers' *News of the World*

978 0 7553 7118 1

**headline**

# I'm Watching You

## Karen Rose

### ADMIRATION

As a star prosecutor for the Chicago Public Defender's office, Kristen Mayhew is no stranger to success, but even she cannot always secure a conviction. It's therefore only a matter of time before she herself becomes the victim.

### OBSESSION

Kristen has a secret admirer who follows her every move and seems to know her every thought. He kills the criminals she herself is powerless to stop, then sends her letters offering the murders as tokens of his respect.

### MURDER

Kristen's life is out of control. As the body count rises, the killer's obsessive need for retribution will make Kristen a target, along with everyone she holds dear . . .

Following *Count to Ten*, the riveting *I'm Watching You* will confirm Karen Rose's status as the new queen of the thriller.

Acclaim for Karen Rose and *Count to Ten*:

'Rose delivers the kind of high-wire suspense that keeps you riveted to the edge of your seat' Lisa Gardner

'Karen Rose's *Count to Ten* takes off like a house afire. There's action and chills galore in this non-stop thriller' Tess Gerritsen

978 0 7553 8520 1

## headline

# You Can't Hide

## Karen Rose

### YOU DON'T KNOW WHO I AM

Someone is tormenting psychiatrist Tess Ciccotelli's patients, pushing them to commit suicide, and setting her up to take the blame. But even police pressure won't make her break her oath to protect their secrets.

### YOU CAN'T STOP WHAT I AM DOING

Detective Aidan Reagan understands Tess's need to safeguard her clients but all the clues suggest that a nameless, faceless enemy is set on destroying her career, her family and, finally, Tess herself.

### YOU CAN'T HIDE

As Reagan and Tess race to stop the killer, one thing becomes clear – the noose is tightening around Tess's neck and there is nowhere for her to go . . .

Tense, taut, terrifying – *You Can't Hide* is Karen Rose at her very best. Be prepared for anything.

Acclaim for Karen Rose:

'Intense, complex and unforgettable' James Patterson

'Rose delivers the kind of high-wire suspense that keeps you riveted to the edge of your seat' Lisa Gardner

978 0 7553 8483 9

## headline

# Nothing to Fear

## Karen Rose

### A kidnapping

Sue Conway is out for revenge. Recently released from prison, she is determined to find everyone who helped put her there. So when Sue abducts an eleven-year-old deaf boy, it's only the first stage in an elaborate plan . . .

### A secret

Running to Chicago, Sue heads to Hanover House, an inner-city women's shelter, run by Dana Dupinsky. Dana safeguards many secrets in the lives of those around her but she would never harbour a kidnapper. That is, if she knew one was living at the shelter . . .

### A killer

Dana only realises the true extent of the danger that awaits her when she is thrust into the middle of Sue's evil game and those around her start to die in increasingly violent ways . . .

Ready or not, here Sue comes . . .

With nail-biting thrills, *Nothing to Fear* introduces you to Karen Rose's most chilling killer ever.

Acclaim for Karen Rose and *Nothing to Fear*:

'Rose delivers the kind of high-wire suspense that keeps you riveted to the edge of your seat' Lisa Gardner

'A pulse-pounding tale that has it all' *Cosmopolitan*

978 0 7553 8521 8

## headline

# Count to Ten

## Karen Rose

### AN ARSONIST
Abandoned to the foster-care system, two young brothers end up in an unimaginable hell. When one dies, the other vows revenge on those responsible.

### A FIRE INVESTIGATOR
Chicago Fire Department veteran Reed Solliday is sickened. An autopsy has revealed that a young girl found in the wreckage of an explosion was raped and murdered before fire ripped through the house. Solliday must now join forces with the police if they are to find the killer . . .

### A DETECTIVE
Determined to bury herself in work after her partner is shot, Mia Mitchell is immediately confronted by her most challenging case – an arsonist who has escalated from fire to rape and murder.

*Count to Ten* is the incendiary novel from the brilliant Karen Rose.

Acclaim for Karen Rose and *Count to Ten*:

'Rose delivers the kind of high-wire suspense that keeps you riveted to the edge of your seat' Lisa Gardner

'Karen Rose's *Count to Ten* takes off like a house afire. There's action and chills galore in this non-stop thriller' Tess Gerritsen

978 0 7553 8519 5

### headline

If you can't get enough of

# KAREN ROSE

Go to www.headline.co.uk to discover
more of her pulse-pounding books

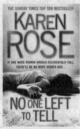